ROMA
Amor

ROMA Amor

A NOVEL OF CALIGULA'S ROME

SHERRY CHRISTIE

BEXLEY HOUSE BOOKS

ROMA AMOR. Copyright © 2016 by Sherry Christie. All rights reserved.

The BHB colophon is a trademark of Bexley House Books.

For information, write to Bexley House Books, 117 Kelley Point Road, Jonesport, ME 04649.

www.roma-amor.com

ISBN-13: 9780692596326
ISBN-10: 0692596321
Library of Congress Control Number: 2015960610
Bexley House Books, Jonesport, ME

Map and family tree by Still Point Press, LLC
Cover design by BespokeBookCovers.com
Printed in the United States of America

To all those who struggle with a story they want to tell, and those who help make it possible. Especially Harry.

The poetry of history lies in the quasi-miraculous fact that once, on this earth, once on this familiar spot of ground, walked other men and women, as actual as we are today, thinking their own thoughts, swayed by their own passions, but now all gone, one generation vanishing into another, gone as utterly as we ourselves shall shortly be gone, like ghosts at cock-crow.

G.M. Trevelyan

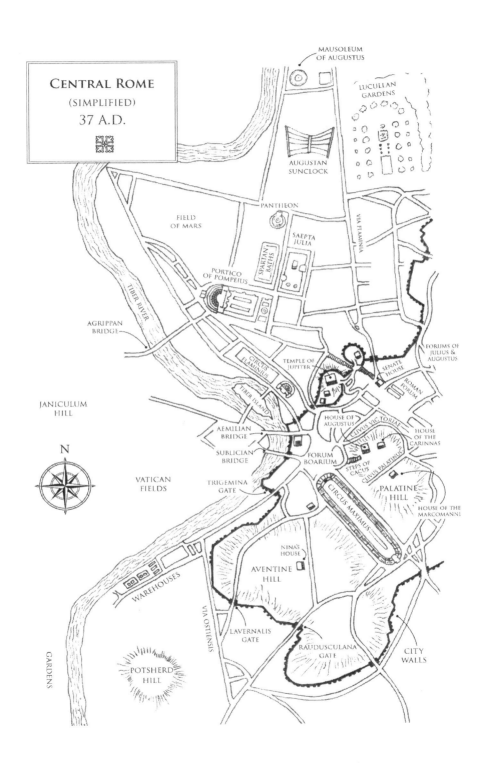

CENTRAL ROME

(SIMPLIFIED)

37 A.D.

MAUSOLEUM
OF AUGUSTUS

LUCULLAN
GARDENS

AUGUSTAN
SUNCLOCK

PANTHEON

FIELD
OF MARS

VIA FLAMINIA

SAEPTA
JULIA

SPARTAN
BATHS

PORTICO
OF POMPEIUS

TIBER RIVER

AGRIPPAN
BRIDGE

FORUMS OF
JULIUS &
AUGUSTUS

CIRCUS
FLAMINIUS

TEMPLE OF
JUPITER

SENATE
HOUSE

ROMAN
FORUM

TIBER ISLAND

JANICULUM
HILL

HOUSE OF
AUGUSTUS

CLIVUS VICTORIAE

HOUSE
OF THE
CARINNAS

AEMILIAN
BRIDGE

N

SUBLICIAN
BRIDGE

FORUM
BOARIUM

STEPS OF
CACUS

CLIVUS PALATINUS

VATICAN
FIELDS

TRIGEMINA
GATE

CIRCUS MAXIMUS

PALATINE
HILL

HOUSE OF THE
MARCOMANNI

NINA'S
HOUSE

WAREHOUSES

AVENTINE
HILL

VIA OSTIENSIS

LAVERNALIS
GATE

RAUDUSCULANA
GATE

CITY
WALLS

GARDENS

POTSHERD
HILL

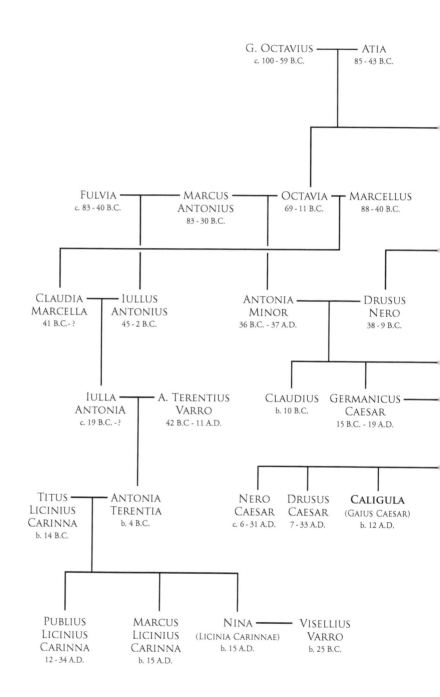

G. OCTAVIUS
c. 100 - 59 B.C.
ATIA
85 - 43 B.C.

FULVIA
c. 83 - 40 B.C.
MARCUS
ANTONIUS
83 - 30 B.C.
OCTAVIA
69 - 11 B.C.
MARCELLUS
88 - 40 B.C.

CLAUDIA
MARCELLA
41 B.C.- ?
IULLUS
ANTONIUS
45 - 2 B.C.
ANTONIA
MINOR
36 B.C. - 37 A.D.
DRUSUS
NERO
38 - 9 B.C.

IULLA
ANTONIA
c. 19 B.C. - ?
A. TERENTIUS
VARRO
42 B.C - 11 A.D.
CLAUDIUS
b. 10 B.C.
GERMANICUS
CAESAR
15 B.C. - 19 A.D.

TITUS
LICINIUS
CARINNA
b. 14 B.C.
ANTONIA
TERENTIA
b. 4 B.C.
NERO
CAESAR
c. 6 - 31 A.D.
DRUSUS
CAESAR
7 - 33 A.D.
CALIGULA
(GAIUS CAESAR)
b. 12 A.D.

PUBLIUS
LICINIUS
CARINNA
12 - 34 A.D.
MARCUS
LICINIUS
CARINNA
b. 15 A.D.
NINA
(LICINIA CARINNAE)
b. 15 A.D.
VISELLIUS
VARRO
b. 25 B.C.

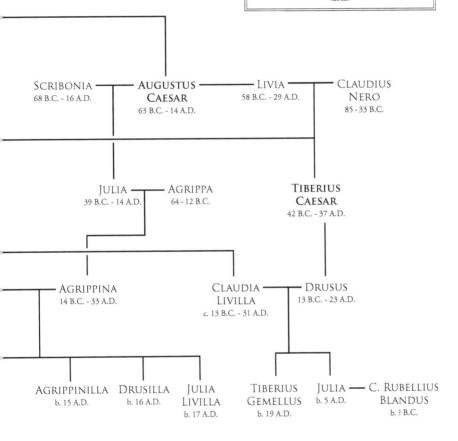

SCRIBONIA
68 B.C. - 16 A.D.

AUGUSTUS
CAESAR
63 B.C. - 14 A.D.

LIVIA
58 B.C. - 29 A.D.

CLAUDIUS
NERO
85 - 33 B.C.

JULIA
39 B.C. - 14 A.D.

AGRIPPA
64 - 12 B.C.

TIBERIUS
CAESAR
42 B.C. - 37 A.D.

AGRIPPINA
14 B.C. - 33 A.D.

CLAUDIA
LIVILLA
c. 13 B.C. - 31 A.D.

DRUSUS
13 B.C. - 23 A.D.

AGRIPPINILLA
b. 15 A.D.

DRUSILLA
b. 16 A.D.

JULIA
LIVILLA
b. 17 A.D.

TIBERIUS
GEMELLUS
b. 19 A.D.

JULIA
b. 5 A.D.

C. RUBELLIUS
BLANDUS
b. ? B.C.

ROMA
Amor

HOSTAGE

At first the girl was less trouble than I expected.

A glance back along the column showed me her coppery hair flashing now and then amid the mouse-colored cloaks of her warriors. At night she vanished silently into a tent with her women. Of course I posted a watch, even amid the placid fields and vineyards of Umbria, but she seemed resigned to captivity. The most bother I had was obtaining fresh meat every day for her and her little band of carnivores.

It was something of a letdown. After spitting murder on the battlefield, to have grown so tame! But such is the nature of barbarians: quick to violent emotion, lacking the self-control in which we Romans are trained.

"You look pleased with yourself, Tribune," said the centurion riding beside me. "A triumphal return, eh? Hostage and all."

He had put on his medals today, seven of them gleaming on the harness strapped across his chain mail. The legionaries had taken the covers off their wing-blazoned shields, and the cavalry horses sported amulets, ribbons, and gaudy tufts of wool on their manes and bridles. I wore my crested helmet and embossed breastplate, polished mirror-bright.

"Ready to parade before Caligula himself," I agreed.

"Gods grant him long life." The centurion slapped at a mosquito.

After days of rain the sun shone wanly, a luminous coin in a hazy sky. Crows jeered at the troops striding by, trailed by pack mules and baggage wagons. Muddy-legged slaves looked up from hoeing a field. Boys chased along, shrilling for a view of the soldiers' swords. The October air smelled of wet pines and trampled leaves, turned earth and wood smoke.

My horse broke into a trot, sensing the journey's end. It was little more than a mile now to the Villa Publica, where I would relinquish my hostage and escort, hand in the dispatches I carried, strip off arms and armor, and reenter the sacred precinct of Rome as a private citizen.

I turned, splashing through puddles in the wheel-worn slabs of stone, and rode back past soldiers and troopers to the Germanic ponies. As usual, the six Marcomanni warriors gathered protectively around their young priestess. As usual, I tried to ignore her immodesty. Although her long skirts were decorous enough, seeing a girl astride a horse was still unsettling.

"We will reach the Field of Mars soon," I told her uncle Maelo, head of the tribespeople escorting her. He was a big hard-muscled man, with a thornbush of a beard and long tangled hair that a topknot kept out of his eyes. "Someone from the Palace will take charge of you there."

He was glowering at tombs under the trees. "In little houses of stone, how can spirits go to the gods?"

The girl spoke up. "That is why Romans keep them there," she said in more fluent Latin. "To scare away enemies like us." She stared haughtily at me.

"Aurima." Maelo switched into their own language, which sounds like a dog growling. My own knowledge of Germanic was too scanty to be sure, but I guessed he was telling her to stay quiet.

I said, "We Romans honor the spirits of our dead, priestess, and pray they will watch over the family."

Her uncle translated for the others. They shifted in their saddles, averting their eyes from the sepulchers on either side of the road.

I looked down at her from the back of my roan stallion, which stood a good two hands taller than her pony. Aurima wore her best for our arrival in Rome: silver banded her brow and swirled up her wrist. Her eyes were the pale green of *aminea* grapes, her sunburned nose as straight as a blade, her mouth wide but wintry. With her chin raised, the strong cheekbones and bold jaw betrayed her savage breeding. It was far too willful a face to ever be thought comely.

She turned away, her braid brushing the fallen hood of her blue cloak. I imagined for a moment that thick plait undone, her hair cascading in gleaming copper ripples down her bare shoulders. . . .

Forget it, Carinna; she is not for you. In an hour—possibly two, allowing for administrative delays—I would be riding up to the doors of my family's house. No, I would stop first at the Spartan Baths for a sweat and a good scraping. And a girl, some agreeable wench who did not smell like a wet horse.

I was turning back toward the head of the column when Maelo said, "What is it?"

Aurima sat up stiffly on her pony, her eyes fixed on a pilastered rotunda half hidden in a grove of cypress. She drew an amber pendant from under her tunic and called out a long phrase in a loud strained voice: an incantation against wayward spirits.

Dead leaves plastered the bronze doors of the tomb behind the cypresses, doors so black with age that they seemed to stand open on darkness. I had shut and locked them myself three years earlier, after a last prayer in front of a shiny new urn. Among the epitaphs of our distinguished ancestors, the inscription above its alcove had been pitifully short: *Publius Licinius Carinna, son of Titus, grandson of Titus, whose life fell short of the honors to which his valor would have entitled him. Died at the age of twenty-two years.* The same age I was now.

The girl could not possibly know that. Until now, she had never been more than a few days' ride from the Danube. So the reason for her nervousness must be simpler: something in my demeanor, a gesture or glance of which I was unaware, had drawn her attention to my family's mausoleum on the Hill of Small Gardens.

A crow screeched from the tomb's conical roof. And a voice in my ear whispered: *Your turn, little brother.*

I whipped my head around so quickly that my helmet crest tugged at its lashings. No one was near enough to have spoken so softly to me.

Little brother . . . ?

By Mithras's Dog! What made me imagine ghostly whispers from a dead man? The Lord of Light had long since judged whether the good my brother had done in life outweighed the evil. His spirit was in paradise or hell, not here.

The Marcomanni rode past. Aurima turned and eyed me, clutching her amber talisman. "Mithras guard me," I muttered, and leaning over my horse's shoulder spat on the ground.

As I moved along the ranks, soldiers who had never seen any place larger than a legion camp yelled out, half joking: Would there really be black-skinned Pygmies? Camelopards as tall as a house? Sea battles in a giant pool? Hermaphrodites?

I laughed. They would find it all, I assured them, everything they could imagine, in Rome.

———✣ ✣———

The Field of Mars had changed.

The firetrap tenements and ramshackle hovels were gone that had infested this great expanse, clasped in the looping Tiber. The pigs and dogs and fowl scratching in scabby patches of grass, the rags of women's and babies' wash drooping over dusty rows of turnip and cabbage, the scutter and clamor and stink of an impoverished, flea-bitten rabble: all vanished. Now graveled promenades bordered with surprisingly large new trees linked monuments that had once been all but hidden. Beyond the tall Egyptian obelisk that shows the time on sunny days, the gilded statue of Augustus atop his huge round mausoleum pointed to temples and theaters and shopping arcades nearer the city walls. A hedge of dark glossy laurels ringed the massive altar where his successor Tiberius would have been cremated in April.

In spite of my feelings about Caligula, I was impressed. In just six months, he had done more to ennoble Rome than Tiberius had in twenty years. There was new construction, too; near the arcade of the Saepta Julia I could see the boom of a crane and the arc of its circular treadmill. My heart lifted with excitement, and the memory of the whisper I might have heard slipped away.

We topped a rise. And before us, at last, was the great city.

The centurion drew in his breath. "So this is Rome," he said.

Though he tried to sound unmoved, his mouth went slack as he stared at the hillocky jumble of brown-tiled roofs and treetops that sprawled into the far distance. Threads of smoke meandered upward from all over the city, mingling in a dun smudge. Behind the tall arches of the Aqua Virgo that bestrode the highway, the red columns of the Temple of Jupiter loomed over the city wall.

I could barely keep my smile from broadening into a grin. The stallion caught my mood and pranced a few paces.

Then the rhythm of the moving column changed. Not the cavalry, who were still in formation with tassels tossing, nor the legionaries, craning for a sight of the metropolis. The cursed Marcomanni had stopped dead in the road.

The centurion's whistle shrilled over the rumble of wheels, hooves, and nailed boots. The cavalry commander raised his hand. Wagon drivers hooted to their mules and hauled on the reins.

"Bowels of Tiwaz," Maelo exploded. "There my sister's daughter must live?"

Spittle streaked his russet beard, reminding me unpleasantly of slugs in bracken. "Keep going," I said. "We are nearly there."

Maelo's half-grown son gabbled something in Germanic. His voice broke into a boyish squeak, and soldiers snickered. Maelo interrupted the youth's rant: "She must live far away." He pointed north. "With many trees."

"Impossible," I said. "Hostages may not leave the sacred boundary of Rome."

The other Marcomanni grumbled when he relayed this. Hands went to knife hilts. From behind me came an answering rustle of hooves and clink of troopers' sword belts. Blast it! In a few more minutes I would have brought in an orderly, smart-looking vexillation to the Villa Publica.

I lifted a hand for calm. "Caesar will give Aurima a pleasant place to live." Since she was officially his ward, this was probably true.

The girl blurted out, "I refuse."

"You have no choice," I snapped. Coming from a land of dangerous beasts, trackless forests, and impassable bogs aswarm with biting insects, how could she object to living in a civilized place?

I tried for more tact. "Once you learn our ways, you and your people will appreciate the peace Rome offers." It sounded pompous, but I believed it.

Her eyes flared. She shook her head so vehemently that her braid twitched like a cat's tail.

Could this be the same girl who had dared to charge a Roman cohort with an ax? Possibly it was the time of the month when a woman's uterus wanders. Hysteria, the quacks call it.

In any case, if this journey was to finish with credit to me, I had to put an end to her balking. I reached for her reins. "You promised to obey. Come along."

Aurima wrenched her pony's head around. But there was no escape the way we had come; the wagons and their dismounted occupants blocked the width of the Via Flaminia.

SHERRY CHRISTIE

Maelo's son jumped his mount over the roadside ditch toward the gardens of Sallustius, yelling to her to follow. Mithras knew where he meant to go, but in the event he went nowhere. His pony's forefeet sank into rain-softened earth and it pitched rump over nose. Hurled free, the boy floundered in the mud. Too bad he had not broken his fool neck.

Aurima swung her mount the other way, onto the Field of Mars. After a moment of shock Maelo and the four other warriors kicked their own ponies and scrambled off the road on her heels, yipping wildly.

I shouted to the cavalry commander. His squadron thundered after the fugitives, ribbons and banners flying.

Why had I thought a barbarian would keep her word? Treachery was in her blood. If her god-cursed father had had any honor to begin with, he would not have had to secure a truce with his daughter's life.

Spray billowed from the sodden turf as Aurima and her band raced toward the tree-edged Tiber behind Augustus's grand mausoleum. Finding no bridge, they would be caught and forced to surrender . . . if Fortuna was kind.

The Marcomanni women shrieked like Harpies. Legionaries bellowed madly, as if watching teams race in the Circus. They would be betting on the outcome. Betting on or against my disgrace.

My fingers tightened on the reins as I sat watching from the road embankment, but I tried to look unperturbed. Tribunes do not chase after runaways.

The fugitives galloped past the southern curve of the mausoleum and disappeared behind it. Gulls flurried up, squealing, over the statue on the dome.

With horror I watched Scapula's troopers veer around the north side of the tomb to intercept them. "No," I said under my breath. Fishermen commonly spread out their nets to dry on the shrubs between river and mausoleum. The treacherous meshes would be as impassable as quicksand. I pushed myself up in the saddle for a better view.

Serpent take it! Back came the cavalry in a spatter of wet grass and gravel, forced to circle the long way around Augustus's tomb.

The nets had also barred the fugitives' escape northward. They burst out from behind the mausoleum, dashing south along the Tiber. If they followed the riverbank all the way to the Agrippan Bridge and escaped across the Tiber into the countryside, it would take a vast and humiliating effort to catch them.

6

I unlaced the chinstrap of my helmet and slung it to a mule driver. My eager stallion hardly needed a signal to bound off the causeway. Mud geysered up as he stretched into a gallop.

There was no hope of dignity; I strove only to keep from falling off. My bronze breastplate rubbed up and down with the horse's strides, digging into my armpits, gouging my throat. Jolting in the four-horned saddle, I cursed the Marcomanni, then Scapula, then my own thoughtlessness. Parade armor is designed for formal displays, not cross-country chases.

Birds racketed out of the trees. Home-going workmen yelped and leaped aside. Paths became pavement; groves gave way to colonnades and shrines and the partly rebuilt arches of the Theater of Pompeius. Blinking away wind-tears, I reined in by the flooded foundation pit of a construction site. My shortcut should have put me ahead of the fugitives, but instead of hoofbeats I heard the growl of the Tiber, swollen with rain, rushing down to Ostia and the sea.

I had to stop them before they arrived at the bridgehead. Or else . . .

The consequences swarmed around me. Bringing more shame on our already disgraced family. Betraying the man I had made of myself during three years on the frontier. And once more justifying my father's contempt.

I halted again at the Agrippan Bridge. Empty carts rattled over the span, bound for the Vatican fields. Hucksters touted nearby food shops. A wine-seller joked with grimy laborers, swilling hot water into their drinks from a rickety grill. They turned and stared at the horse huffing clouds of vapor, at me wild-haired and red-faced, sweating in the padded waistcoat beneath my armor.

Daylight was fading. The arcades, warehouses, and stables lining the street looked as flat as frescoes. Above the long wall of the Circus Flaminius, the crimson pillars of Jupiter's temple on the Capitoline had faded to the color of old brick.

The whisper I thought I had heard drifted back to me: *Your turn, little brother.* A warning? Was it my turn to dishonor our family?

A litter jinked past, flanked by bodyguards and trailing the expensive scent of cassia. I heard something else then, hardly louder than the grumble of fast-moving water: the pelting of many hooves.

I turned my horse crosswise on the bridge ramp and drew my sword, straining to see past the bronze foliage of an oak. My heart thudded in my throat.

The six riders burst into sight. Dogs barked. People scattered. Steadying the horse, I lifted my sword and shouted, "Halt, in Caesar's name!"

The Marcomanni ponies collided with each other, neighing in fright. A rider tumbled to the pavement. Over the commotion I heard the cavalry squadron pounding down the street. "Drop your weapons," I bellowed.

Aurima let out a defiant yell and kicked her pony into a passage leading back to Pompeius's theater. Did the cursed wildcat not know when to give up?

I chased her through muck and runnels of rainwater, past scarred walls, stable gates and shop fronts, under vine-clad balconies that darkened the passage. Boys playing ball scrambled out of the way. A shrieking woman snatched up a child. Filth spat into my horse's face, into my own eyes and hair.

But I had two advantages: long-legged Spider, my roan, was faster than her undersized nag, and I knew this neighborhood. When the theater loomed up over heaps of construction rubble, I swerved the stallion into her pony's side. The runty beast tumbled onto its haunch, hooves scrabbling on the pavement. I turned back to see it lurch up again with the girl still clinging to its back. She booted it into the nearest alley, her cloak hood bellying behind her in the wind of her haste.

When she tried to turn onto the Via Tarentina, I crowded her with my sword raised. Her only escape was through an archway flanked by smiling sea nymphs, which took her into the main courtyard of the Spartan Baths.

A dead end.

By now most of the bathers had departed for their dinner, and only a few litters and sedan chairs remained there. But scores of slaves still waited: bearers and bodyguards, messengers and linkboys. Some who were warming themselves at a brazier turned to gape; others rose from the curbing of the Neptune basin.

Aurima came to a halt. She looked around at the pillars of the arcade, the statues of Tritons and Nereids, the broad steps to the entrance hall of the baths. Her hands fell from the reins.

The cavalry crowded in behind us. Scapula said, "We have all the others, Tribune."

I sheathed my sword. "Good," I said. I dismounted and went over to the basin to wash my face and arms.

Maelo shouted something in Germanic. Aurima gave no sign that she heard. She sat straight, bright-cheeked and breathless, staring at nothing.

"Get down," I said.

She seemed not to hear that, either. Her mount was still blowing. It had no heart for further resistance, even if she did.

"Get down," I said again, between my teeth this time.

She swung a leg slowly over the pony's rump. When she slid to the ground, I put my foot next to the toe of her boot. She tripped over it and I pulled her against me. She was outlandishly tall for a woman, nearly my own height. The thick mass of her hair, frayed out of its plait, smothered my face. My hands found the dampness of sweat beneath her breasts.

The girl struggled to free herself. I turned her around, meaning to mock her for trying to escape, but the rage and desperation in her eyes silenced me.

Then her gaze flickered for a moment, and I saw through to her spirit. Or perhaps even further, for I saw the home she had lost, the forest and marshes and rivers, and felt the anguish of her captivity. I do not believe in magic, but there was no other explanation for this blaze of insight; for I considered the Mark to be a harsh and unlovely wasteland, and would not have guessed it meant more to her than life.

But it was too late for pity. Her fate was to seal an alliance with a foreign king or lord. Mine was to carry out whatever duty my father would ask of me. I reached under her cloak and took the curved silver knife from her belt. "Bind her wrists," I said to Scapula. "The others', too. They will walk the rest of the way." The Villa Publica was scarcely a bowshot distant, so this was no great ordeal. The real punishment would be the humiliation of being brought in like prisoners instead of free men.

As the order was carried out, I looked down at the small knife I held. Had she used it to cut healing herbs? Or Romans' throats?

The silver crescent caught the ruddy light of the sky, and its shine seemed to dull with a skim of blood. In its place I saw, all of a sudden, the longer and straighter blade that had fallen from my brother's hand.

I thrust the knife into my sash, immaculately tied that morning, now mud-stained and half undone. "So, priestess," I said, and wrenched the sash knot tight, "welcome to Rome."

CHAPTER 2

HOMECOMING

Nina laughed, tucking up a strand of dark hair that had escaped the knot at her nape. "Trust you to capture the rebel's daughter instead of his son."

"You misjudge me," I said, feigning indignation. "I am a new man, sober and god-fearing."

"Oh, you are as sober as a flea," she said. "And twice as irritating."

I stifled a grin in a sip of *mulsum*. "The girl makes a better hostage, actually. Germans have great respect for women. Some tribes even trace their families through the mother's side."

She arched her brows. "Then perhaps we are the barbarians?"

"Stop provoking your brother, Nina," Mother said. "May I not see my twins at peace with each other?" She glanced at me, and a smile deepened the creases around her eyes. "Gods be praised for your safe return, Marcus."

"And yours, Mother," I said, hoping she was finally home for good. It must have been lonely at her great-aunt's seaside villa since the old lady's death.

Her graying hair was rolled back in the old-fashioned style she had always favored, and the lily scent of her embrace had lightened my heart. But it stunned me to find I could lift her like a child, so frail had she become.

She kissed her fingers and touched them to an amulet Nina wore at her neck. "Juno Savior, Mother, Queen, accept the humble thanks of this mother for protecting her children."

With the sole of my sandal I pushed the brazier closer to their couch. Had I not been listening for Father's arrival, I could have sunk into a contented daze. The room had the familiar acrid smell of winter at home: sour plaster, wet wool, smoldering charcoal. Light from the three-tongued floor lamp glowed on the frescoes, the polished desktop, the statue in the corner. I thought briefly of my promise that Aurima would be well quartered. To a girl accustomed to a hut of sticks and thatch, a patrician house like this would be luxury beyond imagining.

"Now the question that has all of Rome abuzz," Nina announced. "What lucky female will marry Marcus Carinna?"

I made a face. The best sort of wife, to my mind, was someone else's.

Mother took a date from the server's dish. "Spare us the grimaces, Marcus. It has been shamefully long since your betrothal was annulled."

"No loss," I muttered. My *sponsa*'s father had decided not to marry his daughter into the family of a man charged with treason.

"Scores of noble papas have been hinting to Father about their little girls," Nina added with relish.

How fortunate for me that our family's star, all but extinguished during Tiberius's reign, had risen high after the inauguration of his successor. "I drink to Caligula's good health," I proclaimed sardonically, and drained my cup of hot honeyed wine.

None of us had spoken of my brother. To my mother and sister, his loss would long ago have become part of the past. But to me, who had left home so soon after his death, memories of him darted from room to room like a lost bird.

Draperies shivered; the front doors had opened. Muted orders came from the atrium, and the shuffle of many feet. Father had returned.

Not wanting to rush out like an eager boy, I rose deliberately, shrugged my wool mantle higher on one shoulder, and brushed a crease out of my tunic. As he conversed with the litter bearers, his body slave, and the house steward, my nerves stretched like bowstrings. Now that he had summoned me back to Rome, what would he demand of me?

He stood waiting for me in the atrium, swathed in a heavy striped mantle, as dignified as a statue on a plinth. The fair hair combed forward on his brow had silvered while I was gone, but I saw no change in his flinty gaze or the firm set of his mouth.

"At last, Marcus," he said. His voice was gravelly, as if it pained him to speak. I touched my lips to his cheek, and he clasped me against him in a gust of cold air and balsam scent.

Then he coughed. As I ought to have known, it was the grippe that had roughened his voice, not sentiment. "Come, sit down and wet your throat," he urged, as if I were a guest who had just arrived. "You should have sent word ahead. I would have brought our friends and clients to welcome you."

He had evidently notified Mother to come from Antium, so he must have known I was near Rome. But I held my tongue; after so long, I did not want to quarrel with him.

I followed him into the small dining room, aware of Mother's and Nina's gaze. "Perhaps it is just as well," he went on, "since you nearly lost the hostage you were bringing back. That would have been a calamity, and no mistake."

Serpent take it! Which of his swarm of informers could have brought him the news so soon? I managed a shrug. "She did not get far."

Nina tried to change the subject. "By Juno's girdle, brother, you swagger like a cavalryman who has mislaid his horse." Her eyes shifted from me to Father. "One would hardly recognize our weedy Marcus, eh, Papa?"

He was too preoccupied with stirring the brazier to respond. "Well, my boy," he said at last, settling into his chair, "we have waited a long time for your return."

"Well, Father," I said, mimicking his tone, "you might as well not have sent for me. Since Caligula has recovered."

"I feared we would lose him. It was a near thing." He coughed again, stretching his legs for his old body slave to unlace his boots.

"People even vowed to die in his place," Nina put in. "Did you hear—"

Father raised a finger to silence her. "At any rate, three years in a one-year post is long enough. What appealed to you in that god-forgotten place?"

I shrugged. "Border patrols. Battle drills. Road-building."

No doubt he understood that I obscured my most notable accomplishment on purpose. But instead of asking about it, he said, "And now you are here without a household. You sold them all?"

"All but Phormio. I had debts to settle. And I reckoned on using some of Publius's slaves." But I had already discovered from Nina that they were gone: my brother's body slave, his secretary, scribe, accountant, dresser, bed girl, clothes-mender, and guards. All those who had attended him here and accompanied him to the villas of his friends, and to Tiberius's court on Capri, had been sold.

"We had no need of them," Father said. He reached for a folded writing tablet on his desk. "Tell me about this ill-conceived jaunt into a Marcomanni uprising this summer. Why did the legion commander not lead the expedition himself?"

I groped my way back from puzzling about the missing servants. "Well, he . . . It was . . ." Curse it, as many times as I had rehearsed the tale on the journey south, he still made me stammer like a schoolboy! I tried to untwist my tongue. "It was to remind the, uh, the rebels that we supported their lawful king. A show of force."

"And Poppaeus considered you showier than himself?"

"He trusted me to—"

"Apparently the rebels were not impressed." He opened the tablet's leaves.

I was waylaid by a familiar impulse to escape to the nearest wineshop and drink until his derision no longer mattered. I managed to say, "The war leader, Ingiomar, spread a rumor that we were coming to drive them from their lands." I looked over at Mother and Nina. "Men joined him from all over the Mark."

Mother frowned. "The king allowed this?"

"He could not stop them. The Marcomanni have the most primitive kind of democracy; every man can do as he wants."

Nina waved away the server's flagon of *mulsum*. "So he just ran rampant, this rebel chief?"

"Ingiomar. They call him Ironhand." I half hoped she would ask how he had earned the epithet, allowing me to show off what a formidable foe I had defeated, but she had become distracted by a nicked fingernail.

Father was studying a message scribed in the dark wax of the tablet, his lips moving in a murmur. More loudly I announced, "When he ambushed my vexillation, he meant to start a war. Like Harman."

I said the Great Traitor's Germanic name in a properly throaty growl—another bit of boastfulness, I admit. If asked, I could even have explained that it means "weasel," which is fitting. His name in Latin, Arminius, is much tamer.

I went on, "Ingiomar expected retaliation after he massacred my men, which would stir up the whole Marcomanni nation against us. Then he would rouse the neighboring tribes, surge across the Danube, and sack the provinces."

Nina's eyes widened. The swing of Mother's earrings stilled. And Father at last raised his head.

"With Caesar so deathly ill . . ." Mother bit her lip.

Nina said, "But it never happened, Mama. Marcus defeated him—this Ironfist, or whatever he calls himself."

I barely noticed her loyal support, for I was waiting for my father to speak. I had seen the scars he earned fighting barbarians in the Great Rebellion when he was my age. He knew how easily Ingiomar's revolt could have led to another massive uprising. With so many generals struck down by Tiberius's mistrust, our legions grown lazy, and a young Princeps near death from some unknown malady, we might have lost the northern provinces, endangering Italy and Rome.

Instead of responding, Father began to twiddle his stylus between thumb and forefinger, making it tap a crickety rhythm on the tablet's frame.

Nettled, I cut the account short: "We fought off the attack and captured his daughter, and Ingiomar sued for a truce." I met my father's gaze. "But you must know that from the governor's dispatch."

His eyes narrowed at this challenge, or perhaps he recognized the sore pride behind it. "Your exploits were not unnoticed," he said. "Caesar himself wishes to congratulate you. Lepidus will arrange it in the next few days."

Would Caligula agree that my place was on the frontier, protecting our empire from barbarism? Or had Father persuaded him to keep me here, whether or not I wished it?

It was Publius who had been bred to climb the rungs of public life, eventually to join our forebears who had been overseers of taxes, roads, and waterworks, Treasury officials, givers of games, builders of public edifices, magistrates, lawmakers, governors, and generals. I, the second son, had been permitted to eavesdrop on his education until resentment and jealousy got the better of me. Oh, I understood rebellion.

I had hoped Father was glad enough to be rid of me, or perhaps proud enough of my service on the frontier, not to compel me to take my brother's place. Vain hope! He would have me in service as an acolyte, pimp, and bribe-bearer for some power-hungry praetor or Senator, who would teach me to fawn on the mighty, betray my allies, and trample my enemies.

My lack of enthusiasm must have shown. "Your old life is finished, Marcus," he said sharply. "No more drunken foolery and risking your neck on a racetrack."

"Go easy, Father dear," Nina said with startling boldness. "Our Marcus has reformed, and is as meek as a dormouse." She slid off the couch. "Excuse me; I have drunk a little too much. Mama, do not trouble . . ."

But Mother had already risen. Lamps in the atrium outlined them as they left: my tiny mother, my slender sister, the two women I loved most in the world.

Father dismissed the slaves. I got stiffly to my feet. "By your leave . . ."

"Come into my office," he said, picking up his untouched cup of wine.

I hesitated, assuming Mother and Nina would return to keep the peace. It did not occur to me then that they had left us to make peace for ourselves.

The room where my father transacted all our family business had been kept warm for his use. A draft blew aside the brazier's muzz as I entered, and in the stronger light I saw the suffering stamped in his face, in the depths of his eyes and the folds at his mouth's corners. He said, "How many times have I wished you here! And each time I would horn my fingers like a superstitious peasant." His brows tilted. "No one is more fearful than a man with a single son. I saw the worst happen to you in many ways: a fall from a horse, a miasma, an enemy spear. . . ." His voice thickened. Turning away, he lifted his cup and drank.

I tried not to show my surprise. I was unused to such emotion from him.

Head bent, he set the cup on his desk. A few heartbeats later he turned back to me. "Sabinus spoke well of you in his dispatch. The Senate has voted you a commendation."

Hope of returning to the North surged in me. "Would I not serve the family—" I began, but he interrupted me.

"Caesar needs you," he said, and my words died on my lips.

He went on, "Since his illness, he faces treachery and danger on all sides. He needs a friend whose loyalty and courage he can trust."

"I am not my brother," I said. My voice came out gruff, almost a growl.

"Allow me to decide what Rome requires."

"Rome cannot require me to befriend Caligula!"

He gripped my elbow. "Listen to me."

"Father, I am not Publius!"

"By heaven, I know it!" He let his hand fall. "But you are all I have left."

This must be a nightmare. Surely I was asleep in my fur-strewn bed at the fortress. In a moment my bed girl would elbow me awake.

My father said, "Sit down."

I dropped into a chair. He said, "Two weeks have passed since the fever left him." His voice frayed, and he coughed. "When no one knew whether he would live, many gave their allegiance to his cousin. Gemellus's supporters are not glad to have been forced back from the brink of power."

"If they are plotting treason, that is the Special Cohort's business," I retorted. "Not mine."

Father sat down. He took up the stylus again and tapped it in the palm of his hand, studying me.

"There is something more important for me to do." I tried to speak coolly. "I believe the world is a battlefield where the forces of light and darkness meet, and Mithras alone can help us."

"You worship the god of our Parthian enemies?"

"He is our god now. Transfers from the Third Gallica brought him to Carnuntum." Without thought I touched my right wrist, where the cut had been made to mingle my own blood with that of the sacrificed bull. "I am an initiate, a soldier of Mithras sworn to fight for order and truth."

"Perdition, boy, it is order I ask you to fight for! Caesar needs your help."

"The frontier is where this battle must be fought. With the barbarians who would bring darkness upon us."

He frowned and tossed down the stylus. I kept on, "You mock me for spending three years as a tribune. Augustus set the term at a single year, did he not, because he feared men of our class challenging him for control of the legions. Which means control of the State."

He opened his mouth. I said, "I beg you, let me finish! And we assist in our own castration. How many Senators let their sons bypass the tribuneship so they can appear sooner in the public eye?" I did not need to add, "As you did with Publius," but fury brought it out of me.

His face was as red as Samian ware. "Are you done slandering the Divine Augustus?"

"My quarrel is not with Augustus. It is Caligula I do not trust."

"You hardly know him. He says he has not seen you since his great-grandmother's funeral ten years ago." He glared at me. "And call him by his proper name: Gaius Julius Caesar."

Gaius Julius Caesar, indeed! He was unfit for such a distinguished name, this lickspittle who thought my father's dreams entitled him to an empire.

Father rose from his chair. "Augustus knew his heir must be a capable general. He did not choose Tiberius out of affection." He blew his nose on a server's towel. "He knew that without control of the legions, there would be chaos. Civil war first: rival armies pillaging and burning the countryside. Then the barbarians, finishing whatever is left."

He frowned again. Behind him, life-sized in bronze, Ares the Insatiable glared from beneath his tipped-back helmet as if they were comrades in arms.

"Now consider this," he went on. "Gaius Caesar has no military training. Not even a year as a tribune." He cleared his throat again. "Do you see why he needs you?"

What I saw, all too clearly, was my father's ambition. It was not out of loyalty that he had saved Caligula from old Tiberius and then schemed to hoist the ignorant fool onto Tiberius's throne. He wanted to gain the power the Old Goat would never have granted him. Now he reckoned he could seal Caligula's gratitude by delivering me to him.

"You must help me protect him. Peace in Rome depends on it." His voice husked. "I promise you all my support. You will find me in a position to—"

"How will you support me, Father?"

"With money, of course; a suitable marriage . . . And naturally, Lepidus and I have many allies. . . ."

"What will you do if a Special Cohort spy swears he heard me speak treason? Will you accept it, and hand me the knife?"

His eyes widened. I plunged on, "You ask me for obedience, as you did Publius. But you abandoned him on the word of a lying freedman. Will you do the same to me?"

In a whisper so faint I hardly heard it over the sizzle of charcoal in the brazier, he said, "Do you believe that?"

I started to say, "I know it," but my voice cracked.

"Marcus." He began to cough again. "Do not . . . accuse me. . . ." He tried to say something more, but the coughing racked him too fiercely. His eyes and nose streamed, and he groped for another rag.

Slaves drawn by his paroxysm hovered in the doorway. I beckoned them to help him. But as I turned away, his hand shot out to catch my sleeve. I said, "Let me go, Father."

A growl rumbled in his throat. His helplessness infuriated him. Even after Mother hurried in he would not ease his grip, and in the end I had to free myself.

CHAPTER 3

LORD OF THE LABYRINTH

With the night, a chill had descended on the city. Mist loomed from water running in the street gutter, and huffed from the mouths of Nina's litter bearers as they carried her homeward.

"A touch of gout," she was saying. "Governors indulge in far too many banquets."

We had begun the climb up the Aventine Hill, past silent shop arcades and blind courtyard walls. On one wall someone had written, JUPITER AND APOLLO, SAVE YOUR ROMAN PEOPLE—HEAL OUR BELOVED GAIUS CAESAR. The paint had bled during the past days of rain, so that GAIUS looked like CLAVUS, "boot nail." Appropriate, since his childhood nickname of "Caligula" came from the little boots he had worn in his father's army camp.

The walk was clearing my *mulsum*-sodden senses, as I had hoped it would. Suddenly realizing that Nina had stopped talking, I groped for something to say. "So Varro's ship reached Crete safely?"

A watchdog barked from behind a wall. "Shut up, spawn of Hades," shouted the chief bodyguard, and it barked more frenziedly.

My sister leaned closer to her drawn-back curtain. "Marcus, you offer to escort me home after completing a journey of a thousand miles, and then make inane comments about my husband, to whom you have always been indifferent. What is on your mind?"

The darting light of the linkboy's torch made my footing uncertain, but I risked a glance at her face, a pale three-quarter moon behind the curtain. "Nina, a strange thing happened today."

"You were bewitched by your runaway priestess," she guessed.

"Stranger than that." I kept my voice low so her slaves could not overhear. "I heard Publius speak to me."

"*Bona Dea!*" She clutched the silver amulet on her breast.

Her bearers, bodyguards, and personal servants tramped on in a ragged rhythm. The sounds of music and gay chatter rose from a house we passed.

"What did he say?" she whispered.

"'Your turn, little brother.' As if he knew what Father would ask of me."

She was silent for a moment. Of course she knew Father and I had argued. "Should a sober and god-fearing man not be glad to restore our family's honor?"

"I would rather restore our honor by pacifying a new province. By extending the reach of order and law. Not by prancing around Caligula Caesar's purple skirts."

"Gods grant him long life," she murmured reflexively. "But it was Father's honor I meant."

I snorted. "I thought so."

"Tiberius shamed him horribly for what Publius did. Whenever Father tried to protest his abuse of Caligula, he would say, 'Quit lecturing me about my heirs, Father Kronos; you are proof one should eat them at birth.'"

"May he rot in Tartarus, the old monster."

"Hush, brother. His is not a spirit to anger." She kissed her amulet quickly. "We should honor his generosity. After the fire last year, he gave a million sestertii to rebuild homes and apartments here on the Aventine."

"Every coin of it bloody," I muttered, unmoved by any need to appease the old Princeps' ghost.

"Stop, Marcus! Leave what is past in the past." More quietly she said, "Publius would want you to take his place with Caligula. If you heard him speak to you, that is why."

I had not expected her, my lifelong ally, to side with Father. She began to tell me about Caligula's virtues and Father's pride in him. He treated the Senate with modesty and deference. He had won over the people with gifts, races, games, plays, and banquets. He was piety itself, having personally brought the ashes of his mother and brother back to Rome and dedicated the temple to Augustus that Tiberius had neglected. He had even shown magnanimity rare in a ruler by adopting his cousin Gemellus, his rival for the throne. I wanted to ask if he also drove the sun across the sky and lit the stars at night, but bit back my sarcasm.

In the atrium of Nina's house, aglow with welcoming light, slaves swarmed to help their young mistress out of her litter. Any damage the fire had done here had been well repaired by her stepson Galerianus, who made frequent visits to substitute for his absent father as head of the household.

Nina steadied herself on my arm. "Will you do as Father wishes?"

"What choice have I?" I grumbled, brought back to my own dilemma.

She looked up at me, dark-eyed and earnest. "The gods spared Caligula because he means a new beginning for us. You will see."

Brusque with irritation, I patted her hand and lifted it toward the waiting arm of her old nurse. "Good night, *cara.*"

"Wait, Marcus." Nina caught my wrist with both hands. When I bent down, she said into my ear, "Before Varro left for Crete"—her voice sank even lower, to avoid rousing the spite of a jealous god—"I think we made a child."

I tried to hide my dismay. Justly is it said that a pregnant woman has one foot in the grave. Varro already had Galerianus as his heir; why did he have to imperil my sister again? She had already borne him one child that had not lived long enough to be named.

Nina whispered, "I am not sure yet, so tell no one."

Being full of contrariness myself I hated her submission to fate, but was not brute enough to say so. "I will sacrifice for your good fortune," I told her, and she gave me a heart-wrenching smile of gratitude.

I refused her offer of guards to escort me home. Although I carried nothing but a knife, the only weapon allowed within the city's sacred limits, I was not inclined to be timid. Perhaps I was less sober than I thought.

My footsteps echoed in the street, barren of trees that before the fire had overhung courtyards and house fronts. Where a grove sacred to Diana had stood, there was now just smoky darkness. Bracketed torches here and there wore crowns of mist.

Enough stars peeped through the haze to show it was well past midnight. I had not realized how long Nina and I had talked.

Publius would want you to take his place, she had said. To become the companion of Caligula Caesar, who had not lifted a finger to save my brother, his closest friend, from his brutal great-uncle Tiberius.

I reminded myself that I was a soldier of Mithras, a warrior of truth. No matter what my sister believed, a man's spirit could not return from the next

SHERRY CHRISTIE

world. The voice I had heard must have been that of my own guardian *genius,* counseling me to accept my father's will.

A child wailed somewhere above. A man shouted in exasperation. Shutters banged.

Where in Mithras's name was I?

No longer among the elegant gated residences on the Aventine's summit, for certain. Somehow I had taken a wrong turn in a murky landscape altered by the fire, and was now skidding down a dank alley that reeked of piss and cabbage. Balconies teetered high overhead, and the pale shapes of wet wash hovered in the darkness. A cat growled up at me from its prey. Tiberius's million had been ill-spent; this part of the Aventine was as seedy as ever.

Still, the descending alley was bound to lead somewhere familiar. In fact, it spat me out onto the Vicus Portae Trigeminae, lined with warehouses serving the Tiber wharves. Torches and lanterns bobbed and flared in the fog-blurred street. Wagons rumbled, carts creaked, men cursed, fowl squawked and honked, and four-footed beasts blatted, grunted, lowed, and brayed, on their way to the Forum Boarium. It was market day, or soon would be. Well past time for a man with any sense to take himself home.

I had barely set foot in the street, spattered with dung and feathers, when a pair of mules sprang out of the mist. "Look out, dolt," someone shouted. The mules swerved as I jumped back, and the empty wagon they pulled locked wheels with an oxcart full of pigs. The drivers bellowed. The pigs squealed.

Something brushed against me in the confusion. I turned, slipping my army knife from its sheath under my cloak. The cutpurse, a grimy boy, backed away from the foot-long blade and vanished into the dark.

Sheathing my *pugio,* I crossed the road and pushed my way onto the Sublician Bridge. Lit cressets on posts glowed on mist rising from the river. The swollen torrent, squeezed between its triple-tiered embankments, humped and hissed like an angry serpent. Uprooted saplings laced with dirty foam slewed through the wooden bridge pilings, and boats moored to the quay bounced and tugged at their lines. The wet air smelled odd: not of fish bait and sewage as it usually did, but of earth and carrion. A dead sheep swept by in the turbulence.

My thoughts turned to the Agrippan Bridge upstream, and to the covey of Marcomanni who had so nearly flown across it to freedom. At the memory of holding Aurima, damp-hot and seething, my fingers tightened on the parapet.

If Fortuna had favored me, I would have fought a different battle with Ingiomar Ironhand's daughter. But she was both a maiden and a priestess, and no sensible man would have dared despoil a hostage of such great value. My randy urges would never—could never—be consummated.

Anyway, she was the State's responsibility now, not mine. Plenty of other women would welcome a valorous tribune commended by the Senate.

I leaned over farther to watch the river sluicing over the mid-level quays. The lowest sections, seldom reached in summer, were well underwater. On the top level—

My attention was caught by a dark face looking up through the mist. A boy crouched on steps leading down to the mid-level quay, his feet in the rushing water. Probably a beggar or cast-off slave trying to fish out flotsam he could sell.

No, he was hiding. And with good reason. The five men poking at a pile of smashed fish traps and snarled line a few paces away were, or had been, gladiators. No mistaking those tree-trunk necks and scarred arms. A couple wore helmets, and all were armed. On the steps leading up to street level, a sixth man, better dressed than the others, fingered a helmet's bedraggled plume. I guessed the five were his guards. But what had brought them here at this unholy hour?

A cat leaped out of the pile of rubbish. The men shouted and jumped back, weapons raised, but it leaped to the top of the embankment so fast that a stone hurled after it clattered uselessly on the stone wall.

I moved back from the parapet. The brutes were bored and looking for trouble; no need to draw their attention.

A woman sidled up next to me. "Care for some company, lover?"

Her greasy hair draggled from its pins around a raddled face, and her stained *meretrix*'s toga stank of wine and old sweat. "Not now," I said.

She peered over the rail to see what I was watching. One of the gladiators had spotted the young lurker and was hauling him out of concealment. The dark boy shrilled in protest, flailing a crippled arm.

The sixth man had not yet turned his face to the light. Something about the cut of his fair hair, or perhaps the shape of his head, teased my memory. If he was a patrician, I would probably know him. I might even be related to him.

The whore stroked my forearm, fingering the thickness of my wrist wallet. Having marked me as someone of means, she was not easily deterred.

"Four coppers for a poke, eh? Watch the water if you want; it's the same to me."

The sixth man gestured with the helmet plume toward the river. One of his guards seized the youth's legs and upended him.

"Three coppers, then, as it's so late." The woman groped for my crotch.

The gladiator swung the boy around and hurled him like a discus. He sailed over the moored boats, arms flying, and plummeted into the misty river.

The woman shrieked. The boy surfaced in the tumbling flood, then disappeared. She gasped, "Gods above!" and ran, hiking her skirts, toward a roiling mass of sheep's backs pushing into the marketplace.

The gladiators had heard her cry. Three of them pounded up the steps onto the bridge and closed around me. Encumbered by cuirasses and cross-belts, greaves and wrist guards, they puffed billows of breath into the night. At once I regretted my lack of an escort. They knew I was a witness to murder.

A brute with a scarred nose grinned. "Look what we've found, brothers."

"A Senator's son, for sure." This came from another lummox who thought that tying back his greasy hair in a goat's-tail made him look barbaric. He felt my cloak. "Who's your papa, golden boy?"

If there is anything a young tribune learns, it is not to show fear in front of men who are used to violence. I made my voice casual, with an undertone that was not casual at all: "Take care not to make a mistake, friends."

"The mistake's yours, my honey." The third gladiator brandished iron spikes on the knuckles of a bulky mitt. "Here all by yourself, snooping on others."

The Sublician Bridge is barred to wheeled traffic when the river floods, so it was nearly deserted. The few idlers near enough to notice melted into the fog.

I turned toward the relative safety of the bustling marketplace. The *whick* of a sword leaving its scabbard made hairs rise on the nape of my neck.

The man with the scarred nose leered over the tip of his blade. "Let's teach him respect, boys."

The three of them could dispose of me without anyone else noticing. And tomorrow, perhaps, my father would be told that the body of his last son had just been hauled from the roaring Tiber.

"You there," I shouted down to the sixth man. "Call off your dogs. They annoy me." If he came from a Senatorial family, he would know me. There are not so many patricians in Rome that we can be tossed off a bridge like spoiled fish.

A voice roared from the quay below, "Bring him!"

The three men followed as I descended the stair, wary of my footing on the slippery stone. The river yanked at boats tied to the mooring rings, thumping them together, slatting yellow spray over their sides.

I looked up from my feet to see that the sixth man no longer perched on the steps. Another of the guards waited for me instead. He wore an army helmet with no crest, no doubt a veteran's castoff, and a cuirass of molded leather with crossed belts for sword and knife. He barred my way with a raised hand.

Thickening mist had shrunk the light from the high cresset into a fuzzy moon. I frowned, peering into the darkness beyond him. "Where is your master, who gives himself the right to take others' lives?"

"I am here," said a muffled voice. The sixth man loomed out of the murk, a creature with a large misshapen head. A Minotaur.

I caught my breath. But it was not a bull's head upon his shoulders. He wore the broad-brimmed helmet of a Thracian gladiator with a high crest, shaped like a leaping beast, that still sprouted a few plumes. It was the flare of the brim over his shoulders that had put me in mind of horns.

The visor covering his face showed only the glitter of eyes behind a bronze lattice. What foolery was this? "Silius?" I asked sharply. It was the sort of trick my old friend would play. But this man's hair had been light, not dark.

The helmeted man shook his heavy head slowly. He was leaner than Silius, almost gaunt. For a moment I was reminded of the skeleton painted on Lepidus's dining-room wall who counseled *Know yourself.*

"*Gnôthi sauton?*" the man echoed, and I realized I had said it aloud. "Do you reproach me?"

His voice stirred a fragment of memory. "Who are you?" I asked. He spoke the same polished Greek as I, learned from tutors and laborious study of Xenophon and Thucydides.

He laughed, a bark of amusement deadened by the visor. I repeated impatiently, "Who are you?"

"You must know who I am," he said. His Latin was educated, too.

The bodyguards sniggered. I could hardly make them out, so densely had the fog closed in.

He pointed to his head. "The horns," he said. "Surely you can see them."

I blinked stupidly at the scarred crown of the helmet. His muffled voice said, "I am the Lord of the Labyrinth."

"And I am the Queen of Crete. Take off that helmet and show yourself."

Chuckles rumbled around us. I was tired of being sported with. "I saw you order that boy cast into the river. Start thinking of what you will tell the praetor."

"A useless cripple," he said. "The Treasury has been spared the cost of his dole."

"Is it lawful now to murder anyone you please? I expected better justice, now that the Old Goat is gone."

"Tiberius was unjust to you? Yet you still live and walk free."

"Oh, his injustice was more subtle," I said. "He would invent charges of treason to make young men's fathers more obedient."

"You speak of your brother."

He did recognize me, then. But there was a strangeness in his voice that I took to be contempt for Publius's treason. "My brother was innocent."

"Was he?"

I scowled into the crossbars shielding his eyes. "The charge was preposterous. Tiberius would have dismissed it if my father had let him banish Caligula. They butted heads like two god-cursed rams."

"Your father won. Caligula was not banished."

"Tiberius won. My brother is dead. And is thought faithless by such as you." Why was I bothering to defend Publius to this jeering unknown? I would report what I had seen to the district magistrate; he could pursue it if he liked. "We will meet again without your visor to protect you. Or your guards."

The gladiators let me pass, but the man in the helmet fell into step with me. "You need an escort. This quarter can be dangerous."

I almost laughed. "Not to me. My father has destined me for greater things."

"Indeed?"

"He will ribbon me, and anoint me between the brows." I smiled without amusement. "I am his gift to Rome. His second sacrifice . . . which he hopes will be as well received as the first."

His footsteps stopped. Looking up, I saw only fog where the bridge should have been. The stone quay underfoot seemed to bob uneasily on the river surge, and I was dizzied by a sense that the world had torn free of its moorings and drifted in the infinite Aether.

"Give me his knife," the helmeted man said.

I slapped a hand over the sheath, but too late. One of the gladiators held out my *pugio*, hilt foremost, to the man in the Thracian helmet. He tilted it toward the distant light. "My father had a knife like this," he said. "From him I learned to gamble on AMOR; and on ROMA, to take oaths."

I stared at the words carved on either side of the knife guard. "But I must have them both, the Roma and the Amor," said the hollow voice. "For I cannot accept a grudging sacrifice."

The words echoed in the dripping mist, as if in some maze of mystery and death. He lifted the blade between us. I stepped back—into a guard's unyielding bulk. And my own knife, in the grip of this faceless Minotaur, touched my throat.

So near was his high-veined hand that I could see the pattern of the ring on his forefinger. The ring was a signet, and the device upon it was a rising phoenix.

He whispered, "So by your love of Rome, say if you will yield to me."

Such a moment burns itself into the senses. To this day I can recall the mist on my cheeks, the rustle of breath behind the helmet's jaws, and the glint of madness in the pale imprisoned eyes.

I swallowed. "I am already vowed to you by oath, Caesar," I said.

CHAPTER 4

ROMA AMOR

He bent his head and pulled off the gladiator's helmet, and I saw his features at last. Despite their new angularity, I recognized in this grown man of twenty-five the youth who had been my brother's friend.

His face was triangular from broad brow to narrow chin, with deep-sunk eyes, a long straight nose, and the delicate, almost feminine half smile one sees on portrait busts of Germanicus and the Divine Augustus. When he became Princeps he had added his father's and his great-grandfather's names to his own, and now none but the legions were allowed to call Gaius Julius Caesar Augustus Germanicus the nickname by which my family had always known him: Caligula.

"Be done staring," he said. "I know I have lost flesh; in my illness I ate nothing for days."

I tried to think of an intelligent comment. What came out of my mouth instead was "How did you know me?"

He pitched the helmet to one of his guards. "You have not changed so much, except to look more like your father."

The man in military uniform spoke up: "Are you alone, young Carinna? Hardly wise."

I reached for my knife, which he had taken, but he held it away. "Tut! The footing is uneven here, and we cannot allow you to hurt yourself."

It was a clumsy admonition that I, unlike these cretinous fools, was not trusted to carry a weapon in the Princeps' presence. I, whose great-grandfather had been his grandmother's half-brother!

Furious to be trifled with, I ordered, "Hand over my knife, soldier." Of course I should have known that no ordinary ranker would be escorting Caligula Caesar, but indignation and embarrassment had overmastered my wits.

"Give him his *pugio*," Caligula said. "Day will break soon, and we must see young Carinna to his bed."

I resheathed the knife. "I can look after myself."

The hand with the phoenix ring fastened upon my arm. "I insist. I could not face your fearsome sire if you came to harm."

The mist blurred his expression, but his tone made it a command. And so I climbed the steps ahead of him with the guards all around, like a prisoner under escort. We passed into the Forum Boarium, and a stinking expanse of blood and dung opened before us.

The flare of scattered torches gave the market the grisliness of a burned hamlet. Streamers of smoke floated above the tented awnings of butcher stalls. Dark forms moved among penned captives. Dogs snarled and scuffled over scraps, and pigs shrieked as they were slaughtered.

A Princeps could have anything: the most beautiful women, the wittiest companions, the most able servants, the finest food and drink. Was this why my brother had died, so Caligula Caesar could roam the foul streets with a band of louts?

Despite his rank, I could not hide my hostility. "Why are you wandering the city at this hour?"

He stopped beside me. Although he was a shade taller, we stood near enough eye to eye. "The same reason as you, perhaps," he said.

"With respect, I am not barely out of my sickbed. But if you wish, I will see *you* home."

His brows drew together. The soldier, if such he was, drawled to him, "By Dis, this must be the only fellow in Rome who wants nothing from you."

"Who asked you, oaf?" I snapped.

The man pulled off his helmet, and the light of a nearby torch shone full on his face. He had the head of a mastiff, heavy-browed and strong-jawed. Cropped brown hair clung tight to his skull, and more tendrils climbed up from his knotted neckcloth. He was shorter than I and thicker, with a muscularity that gave the impression of greater size.

He cocked his head, amused by my stare. "You know me?"

I said, "You are Lucius Furius Saxa, commander of the Special Cohort of the Praetorian Guard."

His smile widened.

"You forced my brother to kill himself."

Expression vanished from his face, like marks smoothed from a writing tablet.

"The charge of treason," I said to Caligula. "It was a fabrication, was it not, invented to discredit my father?"

Muscle bunched in his jaw. He tried to turn away. I caught his arm. "Why did you not speak out? You could have told everyone it was untrue, a pretext trumped up by this lying bastard."

"Who, how, why?" he mocked. "The point, O Theseus, is not to learn what waits at the heart of the labyrinth. The point is to escape alive."

His pale eyes were as opaque as the enameled gaze of a statue. He intended to tell me nothing.

I could be stubborn too. "Then, Caesar, I may as well return to my legion."

After a moment he said, "Wait here." Saxa joined him under a tree by the Temple of Hercules, and they bent their heads together.

Well done, Carinna. In the time it takes to boil an egg, I had managed to displease the most powerful man in the world. He could send me to count shekels in the treasury of Antioch, or to oversee slaves in a Cappadocian quartz mine.

The gladiators had been tossing offal to dogs and wagering as the animals fought, but a sudden screech announced that they had found a more agreeable sport. One of them had yanked a plump young woman away from a butcher's booth and pushed her down onto a patch of straw. Another brandished his curved *sica* at the bloody-aproned butcher, grinning at the man's outraged shouts. As the rest crowded around, the lout with the little goat's-tail hitched up his tunic.

The brutality lit off my anger like a torch in a haymow. I seized the shoulder of Goat Tail's cloak, jerked him around to face me, and smashed the pommel of my longknife into his mouth. He yowled, spraying blood and shards of teeth, and grabbed for his own blade. By then I had stepped behind him and pressed the knife's edge to his throat, not tipping his chin up as Caligula had done to me, but pressing it down so the tender vessels in his neck bulged and the merest nick would drain his life.

His fellow gladiators eyed me like wolves. "Get him," someone muttered, but none of them moved.

The man hawked and spat out more blood. It ran across my hand, startlingly warm.

I felt his shoulders tighten. He was going to take a chance that rather than cut the throat of an imperial bodyguard, I would let him pull free.

I put more pressure on the knife blade. "Be still." Despite being outnumbered, or because of it, I was giddy with exultation. My own pulse thumped in my neck. "I have not had a chance to put down a barbarian since leaving the frontier. That is what you are, eh? Certainly not a law-abiding man."

He slewed his head for a sideways glance at his comrade with the spiked gloves, who stared briefly before shifting his eyes away. Not in submission, but to better measure the distance between us.

Obligingly I pretended to watch the woman being pulled to safety. When the fellow with the *caestus* darted behind me, I spun my captive around so he took the kidney punch instead. With a squeal like a dying pig, he doubled over and collapsed in the mire.

I gestured an invitation with my knife tip. "Anyone else?" But the man with the spiked gloves held back, scowling, and the others had turned shy.

Light applause sounded behind me. "To the victor, a wreath," Caligula murmured. His smile twisted at the corners.

"I beg your pardon," I said. "I had no business disciplining your men." I was not displeased, though, to have shown him my mettle. Father's chief bodyguard had been a champion gladiator too, a *retiarius*, and I had learned a great deal while failing to outwrestle him in the *palaestra*.

Caligula glanced at the fallen guard, and his smile became genuine. "Send them off, Saxa. You and this young hero will be escort enough."

Saxa's deep voice was low: "Caesar, I beg you to heed me."

"Enough of your growling, thrice-damned Cerberus! What will happen is in my stars."

He began to walk toward Janus's four-faced temple and the Palatine Hill. Caught unaware, I hastened to follow. Saxa jogged after us, his cuirass and weapons belts creaking and jingling.

The night was beginning to pale. An official in a toga straightened from examining a butcher's weights, frowned, and looked more closely at the three of us. Caligula was right to hurry; with daybreak his anonymity would be gone.

I caught up with him. "Caesar, allow me to return to the North."

He turned his face out of torchlight into shadow, but not before I glimpsed his surprise. Without looking at me he said, "Your father told me you would be loyal. Yet I seem to have summoned not Achates but Erinys."

"I am no Fury, cousin," I said. "I just want to know why you did not denounce the Special Cohort's charge against Publius."

He stopped. "Why did I not make myself a target for Tiberius, who sought an excuse to get rid of me? Is that what you mean?"

"You could have saved him. You are Augustus's great-grandson."

"My father, my mother, my brothers already murdered . . ." A tremor ran through what he might have meant to sound like anger. "Should I have died, too?"

"An honorable man would have stood by his best friend," I insisted.

He twisted his head away, licking a trickle of blood spilling over his bitten lip. "Sweet Isis! Is it not enough that I am driven into the streets to escape him?"

Saxa interrupted, "Take heed, young Carinna. You are not immune from *laesa maiestas* yourself."

I turned on him, my sinews still quivering from the brawl. "I need not answer to you, you god-cursed carrion-eater."

The Special Cohort commander pushed himself so forcefully between us that I had to step back. "You are free with accusations, for one whose own past is hardly honorable," he sneered. "I recall a rowdy dinner party where you tried to put on the death mask of your host's grandfather and shattered it."

"An old lie. It was an actor's mask."

"Was it? Your noble family is adept at covering up your failings. And as I recall, the governor of Pannonia is related to you. Did he exaggerate your bravery, perhaps?"

Rage welled up in me, but this time I managed to control it. Insult is theater, not truth, as every hotheaded young orator learns in rhetoric class.

"Your brother was guilty," Saxa went on. "If Caesar had tried to save him, they would both have died. That is what he is trying to tell you."

Caligula glowered at me, his own wrath now real. "By all gods high and low, if you continue to insult my dignity by raking over the past" —he stabbed my chest with the finger that bore Augustus's ring—"I will exile you to a small rock in a distant sea."

I would not lower my eyes or mumble the apology he wanted. Instead I said, "When my troops heard you were dying, we were three days' march beyond the frontier. They clamored to retreat to safety." He seemed about to speak, but I went on, "I told them that if they meant to disobey my orders, they would have to kill me first."

The shock in his deep-set eyes surprised me into a humorless smile. "And for a while I thought they might," I said. Elbowing my way through the market crowd, I headed for home.

———

He would certainly send me away, no doubt to one of the more desolate spots between the Nile and the Britannic Sea. He had too much conceit to abide a Carinna who would not pander to him.

My heart sagged when I thought of relating this encounter to my father. It would disappoint him, but that was nothing new. Perhaps I would have liked to find that Caligula Caesar was, after all, the demigod Father wished him to be.

Not a coward. The one failing I could not forgive.

Heavy-legged with weariness, I climbed after a donkey heaped with firewood. Around me people were unfurling awnings and raising shutters in the dark street. Slaves unloaded amphoras from carts; shopkeepers shuffled their goods into trays and baskets. Before going to Carnuntum I had thought nothing of this massive effort of replenishment, yet somehow a million mouths were fed in this place where no one farmed or hunted.

On impulse I turned into a passage that led to the top of the Greek Steps. Below lay the old Forum, wreathed in mist. The Atrium of Vesta sent forth a thin stream of smoke into the opaline sky. Beyond the round temple of the goddess, market stalls floated in fog near the Temple of Divine Julius. The chime of voices rose from wraithy figures gliding across the shadowed plaza.

The bankers' offices were still dark in the Basilica Aemilia, but at the end of the Forum a constellation of torch flames climbed the Capitoline Hill. At the highest point, a ray of dawnlight glinted off the golden chariot atop the Temple of Jupiter Best and Greatest.

If I have a soul, as I believe I do, it was then and still remains rooted in the promise of Rome. I breathed the scent of daybreak, sweet with new bread and wood smoke, and felt my heart ease.

With care I slipped my knife from its sheath, took it in both hands by hilt and tip, and saluted the brightness in the eastern sky: "Hail Lord and God, unconquered Sun. Hail creator of Light; hail Mithras, who has divided the earth from the heavens, light from darkness, the day from night, the world from chaos, life from death, and creation from destruction."

As I lowered the knife, it turned over in my fingers. Where dark ROMA had been, now AMOR smiled up at me. And somewhere in the city I heard, like a barbaric battle cry, a distant cock's clarion welcoming the sun.

CHAPTER 5

MAIDEN'S BLOOD

"Wake up," said a voice. Was it already time to go out and stir up the sentries? "Later," I mumbled, nose in the pillow. Let them have a few more minutes out of the rain.

Over the rustle of the downpour Phormio said again, "Marcus, wake up."

I rolled over, expecting the bobbing glow of a lamp, and was surprised by gray afternoon light. On the wall opposite, instead of grimy scrawls where some predecessor had marked the days of his tribuneship, I saw a faded fresco of Endymion stretching his hand toward the Moon Goddess.

By then I was sitting up, feet braced on the cold floor. Memories flung themselves at me: My dispute with Father. The Sublician Bridge. A boy cast into the river mist. Caligula. Saxa.

I groaned. It seemed only moments ago that I had toppled into bed and winked out like a snuffed candle while Phormio was still unlacing my boots.

"I see we have resumed our old habits," he observed aridly.

"I am not drunk." I got up and shuffled to the chamber pot. My thighs ached from the hard ride across the Field of Mars.

"Good. The patron has invited you to dine."

"Serpent take it!" Chariot races and games had been decreed in thanksgiving for the Princeps' renewed health, and I had intended to spend the day assessing likely prospects at the Greens racing stable. "What does he want?" Had Caligula—Mithras save me, the Princeps, the recovered Princeps himself!—already complained about me to Lepidus, his favorite brother-in-law?

Phormio's voice sharpened. "Why do you ask?" Why, he meant, would Lepidus have any reason other than to welcome me back to Rome?

My *paedagogus*, the companion of my long exile, looked out of place now in the house where he had raised me: his face was sun-browned, and so thin that his nose had become a beak and his ears jutted like the handles of a *kantharos*. Above the mark his hat brim had left, his bald crown was as pink as a pig's snout.

"Just answer me," I said. "I know there are no secrets from slaves' ears."

He frowned. "I have no idea why he wants to see you." At his gesture, the young boy with him tipped a steaming ewer over the basin. I rinsed my hands, bent, and splashed my face.

Phormio said, "You shouted in your sleep."

My hands stilled on my cheeks, dripping water. What could I have dreamed of? Of Caligula denying me the truth about Publius? Of the presence at our family tomb that the priestess Aurima had also sensed?

"You have not done that for a long time," he said more gently.

I wiped my face with the server's towel. "My bad dreams are a weakness, Phormio. I do not want to talk about them." I threw down the towel and headed for the door. Unpleasant as it would be, I had to tell Father about meeting his cherished Princeps before he learned it from Lepidus or Caligula himself.

About to thrust the curtain aside, I happened to glance at my knuckled grip on the doorframe. My hands were larger than my brother's had been, so I wore his signet ring on my little finger.

I clenched my fist. If my bitterness had not already cost me the chance to gain Caligula's friendship, I must do my best. *For you, brother.*

Phormio picked up the towel and folded it. "The baths are ready," he said. "Better not be late for your father and the patron."

Mother frowned at my mantle, mottled from inexpert cleaning. "Are those your best clothes? Turtle, find your master's russet *chlamys* with the gold threads." She tried to pluck some slack into a silver chain she had given me long ago, which was now tight around my neck. "It will have to do until we can improve your wardrobe."

"I have had little need for finery," I muttered.

"Obviously." Her tiered earrings swayed as she looked up at me. "And your hair! Phormio, could you not barber him better?"

"My hair is thick because of the helmet, Mother. A man cannot carry so much weight on his head with only a leather cap to cushion it."

The lines etched above her lip deepened as she pursed her mouth, bright with rouge. Uneasy as I was about the coming confrontation with Father and Lepidus, I recognized anxiety in her edginess. "Is it no longer fashionable to be the last to arrive?" I jibed, but she turned away.

While Turtle and Phormio wrapped and pleated the *chlamys* on me, arguing over the length of tunic to let show, she allowed her maid to drape a *palla* over her carefully curled hair. Only when I was assisting her down the worn steps of the vestibule did she speak.

"I will not ask where you spent the night, Marcus, but you must not wander around by yourself," she said, too quietly to be overheard by the servants clopping and rasping behind us in their clogs and nailed shoes. She did not raise her eyes from her jewel-studded sandals. "The city is dangerous, and your father has enemies."

"I was not accustomed to need an escort in Carnuntum," I said.

She gave me a sharp look. "Did every cutpurse and brigand not know you for a legion officer?"

I clamped my mouth shut, accepting the rebuke. My argument with Father had clearly upset her.

The bearers outside lifted her sedan chair to the level of the step. I opened its half door and handed her in.

The rain had ceased, though trees and eaves still dripped. A rivulet flecked with pine needles jostled crookedly down the paving stones. The Tiber would be running even higher under the Sublician Bridge.

"Mother," I said over the chief bearer's pace count, "last night I happened to meet . . ." I noticed her secretary hovering on her other side, and with a jerk of my head sent him away.

"Am I to guess?" she said. "Was it Silius? I hear he has become quite a successful advocate." She smiled. "He had enough practice on your behalf."

Silius must have known I had returned to Rome, but I would sooner have been beaten with spiked sticks than seek him out. I lowered my voice. "It was Caligula I met."

Her brows rose. "At the Palace?"

"I asked him why he did not try harder to save Publius."

She made a small incoherent noise. Then, so softly that I could barely hear her over the tramp of our escort, she said, "Did he answer you?"

I glanced up from the uneven roadway to find her looking at me. I said, "They rolled over like dogs for Tiberius. He and Father."

"Your father did all he could. You must not think he gave up easily."

Of course she had to protest; the inevitability of my brother's death was all that made her grief bearable. She could not let herself believe, as I did, that a more vigorous defense might have saved him.

"Right, left. Right, left," the chief bearer chanted softly.

"Publius's slaves," I went on. "Father let that tightfisted crookback Galba buy them all and take them with him to Upper Germany. It was not right. They were part of the *familia*."

"Oh, Marcus. Let it go. I did not want them here as . . . reminders."

On impulse I said, "I understand why you went away when Publius . . . when he and I were both gone. But surely you can come home now."

"I think not, my dear." She sighed. "Since Antonia died, may her spirit rest, I have become one of those stubborn old women who does as she pleases. As long as Caesar permits me to stay at the villa, I have no need to return to Rome."

Sensing the unhappiness her answer caused me, she touched cold fingers to my elbow. "One day when there are children's voices in the house, perhaps their eccentric grandmama will return home to stay."

I grimaced at the reminder of my inevitable betrothal. She might have a grandchild soon if Nina was pregnant, but it would not belong to our family.

Mother withdrew her hand. "You are always welcome to visit me in Antium, you know. A short day's ride and you will be there."

I looked away from her at a cloud of twittering birds that flew past us and settled noisily in a tree.

The chair bearers strode on. The fountain that stood in front of Lepidus's doors came into sight, pouring water freely for a neighborhood that did not need it. Even householders without aqueduct taps had cisterns overflowing with rain.

"Marcus," my mother murmured.

She told the bearers to stop, and beckoned to me. "What is it?" I asked, leaning into the sedan chair.

The scent of lilies clung to her pale powdered cheeks, and her eyes were dark and brilliant in the autumn dusk. "I wish you had not come home," she said. "You were safer on the frontier."

━╬ ╬━

With a sigh of satisfaction I slid an oyster laden with chopped leeks and Spanish fish sauce into my mouth. Lepidus was well known for his table; even at a small dinner like this, each dish was splendid.

"Anyone would think you starved while you were gone," Father said, still hoarse but sounding more like his acerbic self. He was abstemious, even here where he need not fear being poisoned.

"Have pity on him, Titus; I doubt there is a decent cook north of the Alps," countered Marcus Aemilius Lepidus. His rings glittered in the lamplight as he waved the platter of oysters back toward me.

Drusilla giggled. Lepidus had followed convention in placing his young wife on the broad dining couch beside me, a risk he might regret. I was admiring the swelling grace of her bottom when her bashful titter plunged me into the past.

I stood amid columns of the Temple of Ops with the daughters of the hero Germanicus. The three of them lingered there after sacrificing, while a throng clamored outside to see them: blond Agrippinilla, hissing some comment to her swarthy spouse; Drusilla, nervously twining a curl of chestnut hair around her finger; and Julia Livilla, laughing at something my brother Publius had murmured to her. For a moment his dark head was next to hers, Livilla's crimped curls brushing his cheek as intimately as if they were already married, and then she repeated his remark to Drusilla, who giggled nervously.

Mother said to our patron, who reclined beside her, "Marcus Aemilius, I would wish our Princeps to set a good example for my rootless son. Can you not persuade Caesar to remarry?"

"My brother-in-law has been too busy, Terentia." Lepidus smiled, rinsing his fingers in rosewater. "Besides, he feels no urgency after adopting young Gemellus."

"Gods grant him long life," Father put in. As if he believed in gods.

It seemed I was not to be chastised for insulting Caligula Caesar, since no one had so far mentioned the encounter. Under cover of their conversation, I leaned close to Drusilla. "I am waiting for my kiss of greeting, cousin."

Her mouth quivered. "You never claimed a kiss when I was young and foolish enough to give you one, Marcus Licinius."

"You were too well guarded by your grandmama, Julia Drusilla." I smiled, mostly with my eyes—a trick that is often useful with shy women.

Color flooded into Drusilla's cheeks. I was gratified to see that the sweet, chaste girl I had known was still easy to tease. "Aunt Terentia, your son's need of a wife seems more pressing than my brother's," she said, moving from my couch to settle beside Mother. "I have a cousin of ours in mind. . . ."

I sighed and helped myself to a quail's leg from a serving dish, wondering how much longer this dinner would last. As I was about to take a bite, Lepidus said abruptly, "Well, young man, we will no longer be deceived."

The skin around his good-humored mouth was dusky with beard shadow, as it would have been since midday. His dark hair had turned to blackened silver while I was gone, and love of fine food had thickened the flesh under his chin. Wry brows like smears of ink frowned over his pouchy eyes.

"Deceived? About what?" I put down the quail's leg, looking from him to Father.

They eyed me from either side. By Mithras's Dog, had they known all along how I had offended Caligula?

I steeled myself. I might have commanded troops on the frontier, but here I was still a very junior member of the family.

Lepidus continued, "Sabinus said he has never been so impressed by a broad-stripe tribune." He glanced at Father. "Remind me of his words, Titus."

"'Tenacious,'" Father said. "'Just.' 'Resourceful.'"

"We are told that with minimal support from your legion commander, you broke up an extortion ring run by two centurions."

"How . . ." I began uncertainly.

Father interrupted, "I sent for you, it is true, in case of trouble with the succession." *In case Caligula died,* he meant, but years of circumspection kept him from speaking so frankly. "But we have been granted a new beginning, and you will be part of it." His voice grew ragged. He took a sip of wine.

Lepidus leaned closer. "We want the man who saved two legion cohorts and a cavalry wing from a barbarian ambush." He wagged a finger at me, smiling. Tiny sparkles of perspiration glittered among the beard roots on his upper lip. "No longer will we accept the hoax of Marcus Carinna the irresponsible idler."

I sat up on my couch. Before Father could object, I said quickly, "I hope that means a part in the campaign I have heard about, Marcus Aemilius."

A glance passed between the two of them. I plowed on: "Is it true? In two years we will push past the Rhine and the Danube? Invade Britain?"

"So it is planned," Lepidus agreed.

My heart leaped. To campaign in the North! Beyond the Rhine, where Germanicus had so nearly crushed the rebellious tribes. And Britain, the Divine Julius's last frontier . . .

Tossing down his napkin, Lepidus rose from the couch and excused himself.

"The legions need a war," I called after him. Then he was gone, and I had no audience but my father and the two women. "They fester with corruption—"

"Not now, Marcus." The effort to lower his voice made Father cough again.

I pretended I had not heard. "In Upper Germany, the officers of the Sixteenth are so rapacious—" Speaking loudly in hopes Lepidus would hear, I did not notice the approaching footsteps.

Flute trill and drum patter ceased abruptly. Drusilla gave a cry of gladness and scrambled up from her couch.

In the doorway stood Caligula Caesar. No longer was he the unremarkably dressed loiterer I had met hours earlier by the Tiber. Gold gleamed at his wrist and throat; his dark mantle was studded with tiny gems that winked in the lamplight. A hairdresser had combed and curled hair as fair as my own, a not unusual trait among descendants of Marcus Antonius. His forceful, querulous presence filled the room.

I clambered to my feet and joined in my parents' greeting. He embraced his sister, then moved her gently aside. "So there is something you want from me after all," he told me icily.

I had readied myself to attend him out of duty, but Lepidus's confirmation of the campaign in two years changed everything. After decades when

Tiberius had let Augustus's borders decay, at last we would push back the forces of darkness to the edge of the world!

"I want the truth to be known," I said. "In thirty years of idleness, our soldiers have come to believe that German magic is stronger than Roman steel."

"Nonsense," he retorted. "When the time comes, we will obliterate them."

Father smiled. "Spoken like a true son of our finest general."

After being on the receiving end of Marcomanni ferocity, I did not believe victory would come so easily. But who would publicly contradict a Princeps?

"But the army . . . ?" Drusilla asked doubtfully.

"All will be well with the army, my dear," Lepidus reassured her.

"What Marcus Licinius said about corruption and idleness . . ." She looked from him to Caligula, who was glaring at me.

It dawned on me that she had been raised on tales of the decades-earlier legion mutiny in which their parents had nearly died. Hastily I said, "Julia Drusilla, you need not doubt the army's loyalty. Our soldiers wept when they swore allegiance to the son of their beloved Germanicus." I gave her my most sincere smile. "They adore your brother. They would follow him to Thule and back."

She managed a smile in return. Her fingers kneaded a fold of her *stola*.

Mother sat up on her couch. "Gaius Julius, if you will permit me to steal your sister away, I would like to see the sandalwood chest Herodias sent her from Judaea."

Caligula's bark of laughter had something of affection in it. "Of course, Aunt Terentia. And you may always call me by my old name."

"You honor me, Caligula dear," Mother murmured, and I warmed toward him a little for not forgetting her kindness in his boyhood.

As the women's footsteps dwindled away I was about to resume my comments about the army, but Father silenced me with a raised forefinger. Cousin or not, evidently I was too lowly to speak to the Princeps without being spoken to.

Caligula looked up at the candelabrum hanging over our heads. "So I need not fear the legions' devotion, Marcus Licinius?" The clustered flames cast sparks in his gray eyes. "Yet I am told that troops in the Trans-Danube recently mutinied against their commander."

"Mutiny!" Father exclaimed. "Whose troops were these?"

Lepidus frowned darkly. "I have heard nothing of this."

Caligula leveled his stare at me. "Would you entrust me to such devotion, Tribune?" His voice was as brittle as weathered bone.

All three of them looked at me. I cursed the impulse that had led me to blurt out the story to him. "They did not actually mutiny," I said, trying to sound unruffled. "They were alarmed and dismayed, like men everywhere, by the rumor you were near death. When I addressed them, discipline was restored."

Horror and anger warred in my father's face. Inwardly I winced, knowing he was humiliated that the others saw I had withheld this from him.

"And you covered it up. Why?" Caligula's face was rigid, the muscles tight at the corners of his mouth. I was unpleasantly reminded that a few hours earlier, I had seen him order a boy's death.

How to enlighten a man with no experience of command? I had a felicitous thought: "Their alarm sprang from their love for you. And their return to duty, from their love for Rome."

He was not mollified. "You should have had them decimated."

"They did not actually mutiny," I repeated firmly. "And when Ingiomar ambushed us the next morning, they held fast. Because of their discipline the rebellion did not spread, the provinces were not endangered, and the Senate and people did not panic while you lay ill."

His glare was wild and suspicious. "I must think about it," he said. "Lepidus, bid my sister a good night for me." He turned to the doorway.

My spirits sank. He was rumored to form likes and dislikes quickly, and to seldom change his mind.

"One moment, Caesar," Father rasped. "How did you learn of this incident?"

Hoping to redeem myself, I said before Caligula could answer, "Last night Fortuna brought us together. We were talking of another matter, and I chanced to mention it."

"Last night?" he echoed, looking stunned.

"Yet you omitted it from your report to the governor," Lepidus persisted.

I paused to consider my words. On the wall behind Father's couch, the painted skeleton lifted an admonitory finger: *Know yourself.*

"I called my officers together after the battle," I said, "and told them the valor I had just witnessed had clouded my memory."

My father's face reddened. If the light had been better, I would probably have seen smoke issuing from his ears. "You offered to conceal insubordination?"

"You must understand," I said. "The men were mortally afraid of a barbarian attack. But when it came, they destroyed the myth of Germanic superiority themselves."

They stared as if I had spoken in Etruscan. I tried again: "Had I punished them, they would never have forgotten their fear. Now they will never forget their victory."

Another pause. Then Caligula drew in breath noisily through his nostrils. "I must speak with you alone, Marcus Licinius. Walk with me."

I was glad to leave behind the seething anger and chagrin I had roused in my father and our patron. And now I hoped most desperately that I had not burned my bridges with Caligula Caesar. For a role in the northern campaign, I would grovel as if he were the Great King of Persia.

Attendants flocked around as he entered his litter. Night had fallen, but so many lanterns and torches surrounded us in the street that it was nearly as bright as day. Self-important freedmen bumped into me; hurrying slaves brushed past; gaudily dressed courtiers tittered and called out to attract the Princeps' attention. I trailed the litter bearers, listening with growing exasperation to the chatter of these rump-kissing sycophants. Not caring to plead my case amid a gaggle of geese, I lengthened my stride to ask if I might call on him in the morning instead.

But it was too late. We had reached the Palace.

My clerk in Carnuntum, an Alexandrian raised on tales of pharaonic pomp, once asked me if one must prostrate himself before Caesar's throne. I was amused to tell him that he was far from the mark. In the first year of Caligula's reign a Princeps was still just the First Chosen of Roman citizens, in theory no better than the rest of us, and his residence was neither sumptuous nor imposing. In fact, the Palace—an agglomeration of houses acquired by Augustus and Tiberius—was so unimposing that foreign dignitaries had been known to wander past while looking for it.

Unnoticed by a crowd outside the torchlit forecourt of the House of Augustus, Caligula's bearers carried him through a guarded gate into a dark lane. In a courtyard cluttered with building materials he dismounted from the litter, and most of his retinue were dismissed. There remained only a few servants and I, so far ignored.

I followed him through a covered colonnade and into an expansive garden, silent under the night sky. The ruddy light of our attendants' torches leaped and stuttered over flagstones and flowerpots, stout cypresses and laurel hedges, statues and piles of earth. A light breeze brought the scent of still-damp pine.

I tried a little affability, at which I had no great skill: "I have always liked this garden. My *paedagogus* used to test me on the names of plants here."

"Tiberius let it fall to ruin," Caligula said. "He never had a thought for beauty, unless it walked on two legs and simpered."

I gave up on pleasantries. "You are gloomy tonight, for a man who was knocking on Hades' door."

"It was Holy Mother Isis who saved me. Just as she restored Osiris to life after evil struck him down." For the first time I heard passion in his voice. "I told the Senate that the celebration for my recovery must be dedicated to her. And I will build a temple to her—not some piddling shrine, but a beautiful Isaeum that will show the world how she is honored here."

Shock at his praise for Isis silenced me. This effeminate Egyptian cult had been banned in Rome by both Tiberius and Augustus. Was he brash enough to openly insult Jupiter, Juno, and the rest of the official pantheon?

My disapproval must have been obvious. "By the way, it is customary to answer when the Princeps speaks to you," he said waspishly.

"Why, I apologize," I said. "Of course you expect amiable chatter from a cousin so long unseen."

"Not that long unseen. I did expect your father to be aware that we met."

"I am not my father's spy, if that is what you are asking."

"Why would I ask that? I have no secrets from a man who has been a second father to me."

"What a terrible burden."

He laughed out loud, that sharp bark like a fox.

Restlessness overcame me. "What are your plans for the war in the North, Caesar?"

"That accursed business! I am sick of it already."

I was too startled to speak. "The eyes of the world are on me in my first year," he explained fretfully. "It is up to me to display the power and glory of Rome. To plan feasts, dramas, games, races more spectacular than anything ever seen. And idiots keep petitioning me for a contract to supply mules to the army, or to beg for their town to be a what-do-you-call-it, a stage."

"Staging area," I murmured.

His pale eyes flicked to me, then away. "So. I will win some victories, I will return in triumph with some barbarians in chains, and there will be no more speculation about whether I am the equal of my father."

I followed silently as a slave lit the way down a flight of steps that opened onto a terrace sheltered by evergreen oaks. Rooftops scaled the slope beneath the terrace, falling away to the valley below.

Caligula squinted across at the Capitoline Hill. "Not long ago," he said, "I watched a man leap from the Tarpeian Rock."

Nina had told me the tale. "I was surprised you made him do it."

He shrugged, eyes still on the precipice. "He had vowed to jump if I recovered my health. I do not like an oath-breaker."

"I myself believe a man's word is the earthly form of eternal Truth," I said. "Why did you bring me here, if not to talk about the campaign?"

The breeze flicked wisps of hair on his brow. As my vision sharpened, I could see a decision firming in his face. He said, "I will appoint you a Quaestor of Caesar for the coming year. You will learn how my fiscal accounts are managed: the revenue from Egypt and other imperial provinces, the income from gifts and estates."

I had not expected this. For a second time I was speechless.

"When you are familiar with the procedures, you will represent me in dealing with the officials who oversee these accounts. Later, perhaps, you may have responsibility for them."

When I said nothing, his voice took on an edge. "Do you understand? This is a position of great importance. And eventually, of great authority."

"I am too young," I protested weakly. By law, quaestors must be at least thirty years old.

He waved that aside as a triviality. "It is the appointment I would have given your brother, had he lived."

I turned to look out over the city. Wood smoke on the wind stung my eyes, blurring the lights below to twinkles.

It was a gift of huge value, a stepping-stone to wealth and influence. I knew I ought to leap upon it with eager gratitude. Yet the prospect of spending my days with bead-clicking accountants and clerks, of grappling with financial reports from across the empire, horrified me.

Caligula's voice became impatient. "Come, say you will do it. I told you I would not take you unwilling." Turning, I saw him hold out his hand to me.

How could I say, "Let me help bury the myth of German magic, and push back the boundaries of empire"? Refusal would insult him and shame my family.

When I lifted my hand from the railing, a briar came with it. I plucked out the thorn, and a pearl of blood welled up at the base of my thumb. Caligula stiffened as I clasped his wrist. "Maiden's blood," I said sardonically.

He left without looking at the dark smear my hand had printed on him. The crunch of his footsteps faded, and I was alone with the night cries of the city.

Lepidus came toward me, his sandals scuffing on the tiled floor. "Your parents have already left," he said. "Do you need an escort home?"

"There is something I must ask you first," I said.

"Very well." He rumpled his hair with both hands as if stirring up his wits. "Come into the tablinum."

I followed him into a reception room that smelled of spiced wine, leather, and old papyrus. Light from a hanging lamp picked out title tags dangling like snowflakes from scrolls in a rack.

As the heavy curtain swung shut across the doorway, I went on, "Caesar told me he will appoint me his quaestor."

Lepidus smiled and nodded. "As your father and I proposed." He waved me toward one of the chairs flanking an elegant desk. "In overseeing his accounts you will find him somewhat extravagant, but take no notice. The novelty of being Princeps will wear off soon enough."

I made no move to sit down. "He said it is the position he would have given my brother."

"To be sure. Well, Marcus, it grows late. What did you wish to ask me?"

I said, "I want to know how you could allow Publius to kill himself."

Halfway into his own chair, he caught himself and stood up again. His eyes widened beneath the thick occulting brows. "I beg your pardon?"

"You could have sent him away. Or let him stand trial. The Senate might have exonerated him."

Anger thinned his voice. "Are you questioning my judgment?"

I plunged on: "At worst, he would have been exiled. And by now Caligula would have pardoned him and brought him home."

Lepidus's breath hissed out. He turned to study a water clock that had been stilled for the night. After a moment he said evenly, "Young men are restless and eager for their day to come. They make jests; they speculate about the future." He looked back at me. "But you must understand, the choice was his."

"Was a joke about Tiberius's long life vile enough to die for?" It made no more sense today than it had three years earlier.

His face darkened. "The first of many lessons you must learn, young man, is not to reproach those to whom you owe obedience."

I tried to hold back my own temper. After being praised for tenacity and courage, it was infuriating to be treated like a boy.

"You must also learn not to keep secrets from your father and me. If I am ever again surprised the way I was tonight, you will regret it. Is that clear?"

I unclenched my teeth. "It is, Marcus Aemilius."

He came so close that I was assailed by his musky cinnamon perfume. "Your task—your one and only task—is to win Caesar's trust. You will not succeed by reminding him of the pain of losing his dearest friend. Understand?"

"I do."

"Good." He stepped back and smiled, teeth bright in the dark beard shadow. "You look fit and limber. We must have a *trigon* match soon, eh?"

I was unable to keep bitterness from my voice. "When the troops I commanded put an end to the Marcomanni rebellion, I did not expect to be rewarded with the duties of a money counter."

The warmth of Lepidus's smile cooled. "You are not listening, Marcus," he said. "I have just told you what your duty is."

CHAPTER 6

THE TWO FACES OF JANUS

Tiberius's soldiers had bricked up Drusus Caesar under my floor. I could see him down there, pounding bloody fists on the rough walls, screaming for mercy until his voice cracked.

My yells of horror brought my brother to the doorway, his dark hair briary from sleep. "Just a dream," he muttered, when I blurted out what I had seen. "You drink too much." Yet it was true: Tiberius had starved Drusus to death, leaving young Caligula, Publius's friend, as the last of Germanicus's sons.

"Shall I read to calm you?" Phormio asked. Of course I had woken him, too. "One of those gory passages you like."

He started to read aloud about the battle with Ariovistus from my tattered copy of the *Gallic Wars*. Publius sat on the end of my bed. His company surprised and pleased me, for the three years between us were still a chasm.

"Go to sleep, little brother," he said. His signet ring sparked in the lamplight as he played with a cushion's tassel. "When you wake up, I will be dead."

My eyelids sagged, and my head began to fill with Lethean darkness. I struggled not to give in. Must stay awake this time. Stay awake to stop him. . . .

And I woke.

The little room sprang up around me. On the wall, Endymion yearned for smiling Selene.

My room. My bed. And Phormio beside me murmuring, "Peace, Marcus, peace," to call my soul back from where it had been.

The thundering of my heart slowed. I untangled myself from the covers and slid shakily onto my feet.

The house slept. Out in the atrium the water in the pool was still, the sky above it starless. I took the hearth lamp to the alcove where the latticed cabinet stood. The door gave a tiny creak as I opened it, a sound that might have been a cricket's night song.

Publius's death mask glimmered in the lamplight. His eyes were closed, his expression serene, as if he had died in bed like the old men whose faces surrounded him.

I sank down in a crouch with my arm braced on my knee, holding the lamp toward him like an offering. Studying the dark curves of his face, I tried to make them into sun-gilded skin, to imagine his eyes open, his lips about to part. Careful of the brittle wax, I touched my knuckle to the cold, smooth cheek.

To love, the philosophers say, is to put the good of another before one's own. Adherence to one's ordained duty, *pietas*, exalts a greater good—honor—above all else. Is duty, then, not a higher form of love?

Until his death, I had balked at the duty expected of me. Life, passion, pleasure were the currencies I valued; honor was a worthless coin from a foreign land.

But now . . .

I looked toward the dimness of the altar where he had stood that day. A shadow took shape upon it: a ghost knife, its blade stained black.

"O Mithras," I said under my breath, "I pray you, do not ask it."

I made the Sun sign to protect myself: head, heart, shield arm, sword arm. When at last I dared to take the light nearer, the image of the knife melted away. In its place lay a stick of incense, ready for the morning sacrifice.

I replaced the lamp at the feet of the pirouetting Lar. My shadow fell across the cabinet as I latched its door, shutting away the dark faces' sightless reproach.

In the still of the night I heard a rusty cough, and turned to see my father standing in his bedroom doorway. I retreated silently, ashamed that he might have seen my fear.

"Up with the sparrows, Naso? Or have you even been to bed?"

"Oho! Visiting your little honey on the Caelian, were you?"

Even with a pillow clamped over my ear, I could hear the jabber from the vestibule. "Move your fat rump, Ulato. My feet are frozen. I've already been to sacrifice at Tiberinus's temple so he'll keep my warehouse from flooding."

"Better sacrifice to Pluvius to stop this cursed rain, then," someone said.

Another voice: "I hope the patron feels generous. My roof has started to leak like an old man's prick."

"Temper your hopes. Young Marcus may have already rubbed him raw."

"By Hercules, my friend, you are behind on the news!"

"What news? What's the rascal done now?"

"Got himself an appointment as a Quaestor of Caesar, that's what."

Voices chorused in surprise and disbelief.

"My kitchen maid heard it from Lepidus's sauce boy in the spice market. Good girl that she is, she rushed right home to tell me."

"At his age? What next: consuls who have not yet begun to shave?"

"My dear Balbus, age has nothing to do with it. Gaius Caesar knows how to repay his debts."

Some of the voices were familiar, belonging to men whose families had been our clients for generations and who had known me from the cradle. Others I did not recognize—new clients, no doubt, washed in on the rising tide of my father's fortunes.

Now they were greeting him, with felicitations on my new appointment. I sat up as Phormio came in with bread, cheese, and a cup of thin wine. "They are all agog to compliment you," he said, setting down the tray. "Eat your breakfast while I put out your clothes. There is still time for greetings before you take them to call on Marcus Lepidus."

"Not today," I said. "There is something else I must do this morning."

"More important than joining your father at the *salutatio*?" His eyes narrowed. "Marcus, you are the heir of the house now."

And one day I would have to support them all. Dole out food and money, rescue them from leaky roofs and lawsuits, and muster them whenever I needed an impressive escort. But not today. On the other side of the city, in the vaults of the Special Cohort, was a record of what had really happened three years earlier. As Caligula's quaestor-designate, I now had the authority to ask for it. To see the proof of my brother's guilt, as everyone had insisted, or of his innocence, which would mean they had lied to me.

A fingernail tapped on the doorpost. A woman called, "Are you awake, young master? Your mother wishes to see you before she leaves."

—‖—‖—

Shadowless gray daylight suffused my mother's sitting room. As I entered, her maid Olympias folded a *palla* and laid it atop other clothes in a basket. Mother's secretary placed a new ink block in his writing case before looking up, wiping his hands fastidiously with a rag.

Mother was seated in one of the wicker armchairs, frowning at herself in a mirror. She set it down to reach for my hands, congratulating me on my forthcoming appointment. "But do not count on me to return for the usual banquets, my dear. Come to Antium instead, and I will give you a fine dinner."

I slouched into one of the other chairs. The mosaic floor was like ice beneath my bare feet. Indifference to hardship built character, Father always said, so the furnace was never lit before mid-November. "Leave us, Olympias, Dio," I told them, and both slaves went out.

Mother regarded me expectantly. Uncertain how to begin, I evaded her eyes. Little cupids weaving rose garlands danced around the edges of the dusky ceiling, a doting husband's long-ago decoration to please his young wife. The cupids had fascinated me when I was little, thinking they depicted Nina and me.

"Caligula is weak," I said. "He is fearful, and trusts nothing."

Mother picked up the steel mirror again, but did not look at herself in it. "You must obey your father, of course."

"How can you defend him, Mother? Would you let him barter both your sons for a cracked pot?"

My mother laid the mirror in her lap. She said to it, "If one could only love, and love, and never hear the voice of duty . . ."

"Publius could make a difference here, but I cannot. It seems more important to me that the barbarians believe in our strength."

She did not speak. I said, "Should I not do what will serve Rome best?"

Still her eyelids, frail as moth wings, hid her gaze.

My throat tightened. "I will obey him, but . . ." I wanted to say, *It is hard.* Yet I had overcome adversity before by force of will, and I did not want her to fear for me. I wagged my head and made a smile.

She held out a hand, and I rose to take it. When I bent to kiss her cheek, she clasped my face in her hands. "My dear son," she said softly. "When I am far away, I can close my heart and pretend I have no children. But you, even more than your sister, always seem to know where I keep the key."

She looked up at me, her eyes brilliant. Then, so briskly that I might have imagined that brief weakness, she gave me a tiny nod of dismissal. "Now that you have become so distinguished, Marcus, do get your hair cut."

Her reminder of my duty shamed me. And when her sedan chair left for the city gate where her carriage waited, my resolve to visit the Praetorian Camp flagged. Why risk Caligula's anger by so blatantly doubting his word? I had old friends to call on, women to beguile, a new crop of charioteers to assess. With the festival honoring Caligula's recovery little more than ten days away, there would be rehearsals and practices, outings and dinner parties galore. If I decided later to review the records, they would still be waiting for me.

Normally I would have been content that duty so neatly aligned with pleasure. But when I examined myself more closely, as Mithraic training had taught me, it was clear that for all my bold talk of Publius's innocence, I feared discovering that he had been justly accused. I, who was meant to fight for Truth, was afraid to learn what was true.

And so I made myself call on Lucius Furius Saxa that day, setting in motion events that would change many lives.

After living for so long in a legion fortress, I expected to find familiarity in the Praetorian Camp's grid of streets, barracks, storehouses, stables, and workshops. But the Praetorians' fourteen-foot battlements are of concrete and brick, not Carnuntum's turf and timber, and the air that day smelled not of wild forests but of acrid smoke from the public pyre to the south.

Nerves made a knot in my gullet when I entered the courier post. Saxa stood with his back to me, studying a wall map of Italy, the provinces, and the outlands. A white-haired officer beside him held a pointing stick tipped back on his shoulder. The great trade routes rayed out on the map before them: the Amber Road from Carnuntum north to the Suebic Sea, the Silk Road from Damascus east to India, the Ivory Road from Alexandria south to Numidia.

The burly Special Cohort commander looked older than torchlight had painted him, with more gray than brown in his tight-cropped hair. Like me, he wore a plain tunic shortened above his knees by a knife belt. The fringed black cloak of a Praetorian cohort commander was his only insignia of rank.

Both men turned at the sound of my footsteps. Saxa's heavy-jawed face stretched in a smile. "What brings you so far from your usual haunts, young Carinna?"

A handful of dispatch riders squatting on benches looked up from game lines scratched in the floorboards. "Carinna?" the other officer echoed. "Tribune of the Fifteenth? Led the vexillation ambushed in the Trans-Danube?"

Leather squeaked and boots scuffed as the couriers shifted to see better. "The same," Saxa said, his smile now magnanimous. "He did well, for a young fellow more used to commanding house slaves than cohorts."

"Good work putting Ironhand back on the leash," the officer told me.

I was strung too tight to acknowledge the compliment. "I have private business with you, Commander. In your office."

"Let us get on with it, then." Saxa gestured for me to accompany him.

I matched him stride for stride, determined that he would not deny me my brother's file. Of course it would not say, *Special Cohort Commander Saxa fabricated a case of treason against Carinna's son in order to please Tiberius Caesar.* Yet there would be gaps in it: a lack of informer's testimony, missing investigative records. Or would he have invented them, too? Saxa had learned the trade of cobbling up indictments from an expert: Tiberius's fearsome Praetorian Prefect, Sejanus, who had caused the deaths of many good men.

We entered the headquarters courtyard. The armory's thick bronze doors stood open, showing in its dusky shadows a ghost army of stacked armor, shields, swords, sheaves of javelins, and casks of bolts and sling bullets. Whoever commanded the Praetorian Guard controlled the only armed force stationed in Italy, meant to protect the Princeps from ambitious leaders of provincial legions. Not by chance was the current Praetorian Prefect Caligula's close ally.

Saxa strode through a doorway in one wing of the *principia*. A lumpish clerk got to his feet, bumping a cluttered table. When a scroll rolled off and unwound across the floor, the clerk hastened to grab it in case I was a spy.

Saxa held out a hand for it. "Anything new?" He unfurled the scroll and glanced at its contents.

The clerk eyed me. Saxa made a dismissive gesture, as if I were a slave come to clean the floor. The clerk said, "The Princeps had a poor night."

Saxa snorted and tossed down the scroll. "When does he not?"

His smoke-grimed office, like the courier post, was dominated by a painted map of the world. In the blank expanse of Scythia, a round seal showed two-headed Janus ringed by the words ALWAYS FAITHFUL, ALWAYS PREPARED. A fitting symbol for the Special Cohort, since the god who looks both ways has two faces.

Saxa pulled out a chair behind his worktable and sat. "So Caesar will appoint you to oversee his purse. A nice reward for your father's help." Knowing that men of my class consider making and managing money to be the business of inferiors, he might as well have said that I would be wiping Caligula's rump.

I shot back, "Well, I am told the Princeps has need of men he can trust."

Saxa inhaled noisily. "I am short of time. What do you want?"

The moment had come. A fist of apprehension clutched the base of my throat. "I want to review the records of the treason charge brought against my brother," I said. "I will see them now. Immediately." Before anything could be misplaced or altered.

"I cannot oblige you. Since he was never tried, the file may not be made public." Saxa tipped his chair back on two legs and leaned against the wall.

"I am Caesar's representative. Whatever I ask, it is as if he asked it."

"I must remind you that your appointment has not been confirmed."

"It will not please him that you think the Senate may not confirm it."

Saxa's jaw muscles bunched. He stared at me, eyes hooded.

I met his glare without blinking. "I demand the file in Caesar's name."

"He hoped you would not ask." A grim smile twisted one corner of his mouth. "He thought your brother would not have wished you to see it."

My mouth was so dry that I did not try to respond.

At last he sat up, the chair creaking under him. "Very well. For your father's sake, I would have kept the truth from other eyes. Even yours."

His calm certainty stunned me. I tried not to show it, but my heart turned leaden. "Bring me the file," I said. "All of it."

There at last were the official documents of the case, pasted edge to edge in a single scroll. I laid it carefully on the table as if it might shatter. Saxa had gone out to talk to his clerk.

For a long while I did not move. The skin across my cheekbones felt cold and tight, and my belly floated queasily under my ribs.

I lifted the tag tied to the spindle. Cos. L. Vit. ac Fab. Persic. P. Lic. Carinna T. F. L.M. In the consulships of Lucius Vitellius and Fabius Persicus, Publius Licinius Carinna, son of Titus . . . What was "*l.m.*"?

Laesa maiestas, of course. Treason. So common under Tiberius that they no longer needed to write it in full.

I pressed to my lips the ring that had been my brother's. Then I stood up, opened the scroll, and flattened the yellowing papyrus against the tabletop.

The first document announced that a charge of harming the Princeps' dignity had been brought against Publius on the Ides of June. It was stamped with two dark seals. One showed two-headed Janus, the same seal embellishing the wall behind me now. The other, of a many-legged scorpion, was the signet of the Prefect of the Guard. Genuine enough, perhaps.

There was an informer's report after all. A Celtic freedman gathering birds' eggs on the cliffs near Tiberius's Caprean villa had heard two men talking on a bench above him. He had recognized the voices of Caligula Caesar and Publius Carinna, who were discussing the suicide of a governor Tiberius had accused of crimes against the State. The informer swore he heard Publius Carinna say, "He keeps Atropos so busy snipping other men's lives that she has no time to scissor his."

I let out my breath softly. This was the treason: to have wished for the death of the Old Goat, then nearing eighty but still infuriatingly hale. For a lie, it was well done—and plausible to anyone who did not know my cautious brother.

Next were notes in a clerk's hand. Saxa had gone to the Praetorian Prefect asking whether to pursue the matter. Ten days later he had talked again with the Prefect, who told him that Tiberius desired a discreet investigation.

Then—what thorough inventiveness!—the informer's questioning was included. No proof of his emancipation could be found, so he had been examined under torture like a slave. It appeared that Saxa had conducted the alleged interrogation himself, according to the record.

Cdr. Saxa: Can you be certain whose voices you heard?
I am assistant supervisor of the Princeps' dining room. I have seen and heard both men many times. It was Caligula Caesar—Gaius Caesar, that is—and Publius Carinna I heard.

Cdr. Saxa: Which one spoke the words about Atropos?
It was Publius Carinna who said those words. I swear it by my love for our Princeps Tiberius Caesar, may he live forever.

Cdr. Saxa: You accuse a Senator's son of speaking treason?
I believe he wished the Princeps' death, may the gods curse him. That is the truth. Please spare my hands so I may again serve the Princeps at his table.

Cdr. Saxa: You are lying. You were paid to make the Princeps believe young Carinna is plotting against him.
On my children's heads, I swear I do not lie. I only wanted to protect the Princeps. Please believe me.

Cdr. Saxa: I will give you one last chance to speak the truth.
Please, sir. I swear by Toutatis, by Vatvims, by Belenos that young Carinna said it. Have mercy, it is true.

The account ended with a notation: "Witness insensible. Interrogation halted. Witness died in the night."

I blinked and read the transcript again. A grinding ache started between my brows.

Saxa's subsequent report to the Praetorian Prefect was brief:

Under questioning, the witness confirmed he heard P. Carinna advocate the death of the Princeps. I have no choice but to report this.

The scroll was more slender now; just a few sheets remained. I unrolled the next section, and saw on it my own family seal.

No mistake. The impression in dark wax was a *carina,* a ship's hull—the image on my own ring. Above the seal, several lines had been written in the hand of my father's scribe. It was a letter, creased and worn from handling.

> T. Licinius Carinna to the most illustrious and honored Princeps of the State, Tiberius Julius Caesar Augustus:
>
> My son has admitted that he said the words overheard by an informer and reported to the Special Cohort in early June. He meant no harm to your *maiestas* but merely thought himself witty, as foolish young men do.
>
> I beg you to allow him to leave for Massilia. There he may undertake such studies as will not excite your displeasure, while attending to business interests of his family in Gaul. I pledge that he will return to Rome only with your permission.
>
> Be assured that in displaying your clemency, you will win the acclaim of the Senate and earn the gratitude of a father who will be deeply in your debt. I humbly pray you, noble Caesar, to grant this petition.

My son has admitted that he said the words. . . .

My father's seal, my father's words. Abasing himself to save my brother's life. Flattering the monster Tiberius with praise for his mercy and his noble character. All in vain.

I stared at the letter until the lines began to wriggle in front of me, like wounds whose blood still pulsed. Then I fumbled for the last sheet of papyrus, which bore five entries in different hues of ink:

> Warrant served IV Non. Aug.
> Senatorial court to be convened Kal. Sept.
> Accused returned to Rome VIII Kal. Sept.
> Accused died at own hand Kal. Sept.
> Case closed III Id. Sept.

I sat down, spreading my forearms to keep the scroll flat. After some moments I put a hand up to my eyes, and the papyrus rolled itself tight like a door closing on the underworld.

There was no untruth, after all. Just the last act of a tragedy that had begun when Germanicus Caesar chose Titus Carinna as one of his senior tribunes. From their friendship had sprung my father's loyalty to Germanicus—a loyalty that had encompassed Germanicus's sons, pitting Father so inflexibly against Tiberius that the old Princeps had welcomed this chance to retaliate.

Tiberius was beyond my fury now. Saxa had merely followed orders. Publius himself had chosen to spare our family the dishonor of a conviction for treason. There was no one to blame.

No one but myself.

At nineteen, I had been no longer a child. I had dedicated my first beard the year before and put on a man's toga. I could have shamed Tiberius by offering myself in my brother's place. Instead I had spent those weeks drinking and womanizing and posturing at the racing stables, unwilling to act like the man I was supposed to be.

What a joke, that Lepidus had praised my courage! Father knew better: I was not as good as Publius. I was simply all he had left.

Saxa's clerk came in with a cup. "Thought you might welcome this," he said. He glanced knowingly at the scroll.

I drank the wine without tasting it. Over the rim of the cup my gaze lit on the painted seal: Janus peering left and right, always faithful, always prepared.

The clerk picked up the scroll. "Wait," I said. This time I looked at the paper, not the words. The individual documents, written by different hands, used papyrus from different batches with varying weaves and degrees of polish.

I gave him back the scroll. He seemed about to speak, but said nothing.

CHAPTER 7

SNARES

"Where have you been?" Father demanded.

"Exercising one of my horses." I hoisted my pinned cloak over my head. Light from the atrium lamps glistened on the muddy trickle from my boots.

"You should have come with me to Seneca's, where your appointment had everyone abuzz." He must have returned only recently himself; he still wore dinner clothes, and his face was flushed with drink. "Marcus, a great deal has been sacrificed for your opportunity to become Caesar's friend and adviser. You cannot fail me."

"I do not intend to fail." I let the doorkeeper's boy take the heavy cloak.

"Then tell me why you disappeared today, instead of presenting yourself to help him with his preparations for the new festival."

I had spent the afternoon on the Field of Mars, working myself and my sorrel warhorse in cavalry exercises until the stallion was lathered white. As if it were possible to sweat out the pain I had dealt myself at the Praetorian Camp.

He waited for me to justify my discourtesy to his treasured Caligula. I was tired of disappointing and enraging him. "I ask your pardon, Father," I said.

The fierceness vanished from his manner. "I am having a brazier brought to my office," he said. "Come and talk with me."

⇥⇤

The brazier had not yet arrived, and the room was cold and gloomy. Waiting for him to change out of his finery, I dropped into a leather folding chair and watched a slave light the floor lamp. Ares emerged from the shadows, white enamel eyes glaring as the flames rippled over his body. He was ancient, four hundred years old maybe, wrought during Athens' golden age when Rome was only a hill town in a malarial swamp.

What would the Licinius who brought home this keepsake have made of us: one brother guilty of treason, and another who had not fought to save him?

I looked up as my father came in. Though clad now in plainer clothes, he had not taken off the gold torc he had worn to dinner. The open collar of thick twisted cables, a gift from Germanicus, reminded me of their exploits in the North. I felt more humbled by this barbaric trophy, my own deeds overshadowed by what he had achieved.

He sank heavily into a chair opposite mine. "Marcus, I pray you will one day have a son who tries you as grievously as you do me."

I lowered my eyes. Pride stuck in my throat like a fishbone.

He took a cup from the server and sipped from it. Other slaves set down a brazier between us.

I leaned on my elbows, hands clasped under my nose. My thighs were numb from the cold, and mud-spattered up to the grimy edge of my riding breeches.

Father put down his cup to warm his fingers over the brazier. "Speak, then."

I sighed. "I have been to the Praetorian Camp." The boy gave me a cup of hot *mulsum.* I set it down. "I saw the Special Cohort file on Publius."

The room was still. No clatters, no voices, not even the scuff of a sandal or a rustle of clothing. I looked up into my father's immobile face. Without taking his eyes from me, he aimed his thumb at the doorway. The servers departed.

I said, "You acted as you thought right, to protect the rest of the family. I beg your pardon for suggesting you knew he was falsely accused."

He said nothing.

Unnerved by his silence, I stumbled on, "He was so clever, so cautious.... I wanted to believe he was"—I fished for words—"never reckless like me."

Father stared at me, his mouth vised shut. I said, "I cannot fault you or Lepidus for not defending him more vigorously, when I myself did nothing."

"Stop," he said, his eyes gone distant.

The wheeze of his breath filled the silence. His fingers rubbed the raised figures on the redware cup over and over. At last he said, "I should not have hushed you. Do you have more to say?"

"Just to ask . . . if you will forgive me."

He exhaled, and a little cough bubbled in his chest. It sounded almost like a chuckle. "It is you who should forgive your brother."

There was a long pause. He shifted in the chair. "He was . . . what every man hopes for in a son. Brave, steadfast, dutiful . . ." His eyes glittered as he looked past me into the dark. "If I could have saved him . . ."

He would have traded my life for Publius's, had Tiberius allowed it.

I hauled myself to my feet. "That is all I had to say. Good night, Father."

"Wait," he said, stretching out a hand that did not quite touch me. "Tell me, after what you saw today . . ." His gaze traveled to the scenes on the wall, then back to my face. "Will you be loyal to Caesar?"

That was what it was all about: not my brother or me but Caligula Caesar, the doted-on, the sacrificed-for. I said, "Is that why I was bribed with a quaestorship, to make sure I will not desert to Gemellus?"

"Sit." He waved me down. "Speaking of Gemellus, he wrote today to welcome you back to Rome."

I bit back a flare of temper. While I was away, no one but Phormio had dared read my messages without permission. This was my father's way of reminding me that by law and custom, his power over me was unlimited.

Father went on, "He invites you to call on him."

"He should call on me, the presumptuous little snot. How young is he? Sixteen? Seventeen?"

"Gemellus is neither stupid nor callow." Father took another sip of *mulsum*. His throat flexed behind the gold knobs capping the ends of the torc. "And he was not raised to wait patiently for an adoptive father to die of old age."

His mother had been a ruthless woman, said to have smothered his twin brother as an infant so Gemellus would have no rival as heir to the throne. A few years later she had poisoned his father in hopes of marrying a likelier successor to Tiberius. I said, "Then Caligula should exile him."

"As Tiberius would have done? Without proof?"

The words took me back to Saxa's office, to the imprint of my own family seal on an imploring letter to Tiberius. Shame weighed in my belly. I grasped the arms of my chair to rise.

"I can think only the worst of this new liaison," Father said, paring his thumbnail with the small knife he always carried.

Curiosity halted me. "Who is it now?" I asked, supposing that Caligula's notoriously lustful eye had lit upon a new Aphrodite.

"You have not heard?" He resheathed the blade. "Gemellus has become Julia Livilla's lover."

"Livilla! Is the bitch so jaded that she must seduce her brother's adopted son?"

"You sound jealous. Were there relations between the two of you?"

"Of course not! She was Publius's *sponsa.*"

"Mind your tongue, then. Caesar is not as keen as you to condemn her."

"Then I will remind him, Father, that we Carinnas do not hesitate to address treason, even in our own family."

It caught him off guard. He was surprised at first, like a man who sees a line of blood spring up on his arm, not having felt the cut.

"Forgive me," I said at once. "I spoke without thinking."

He shook his head. "Well put, Marcus. I will be sure to correct anyone who thinks you merciful."

I felt heat in my cheeks. "Go," he said in a harder voice. "And tomorrow, make sure the Princeps knows you are grateful for his generosity."

Nearing the kitchen, I heard much joking and hooting. The house slaves were speculating whether there would be a holiday for them during the festival. They fell silent when I entered.

Phormio was toasting bread over the stove grate with Father's private secretary. He abandoned his toasting stick to follow me to my bedroom. "Out in the cold all day," he muttered. "You will be lucky not to catch this grippe. People are barking like dogs all over the Palatine Hill." He hung my knife belt on a peg and went to the clothes chest for a dry tunic.

I said to his back, "There is something I must tell you."

"About your brother?"

So he had already guessed. I said, "I was wrong."

Without turning he said, "I am sorry to hear it, Marcus." He had never been as convinced as I of Publius's innocence, saying it was not for him to question the judgments of the mighty.

"I still think he could have been saved. But he was not . . ."

". . . the blameless victim you thought." He closed the lid of the chest.

I let out a short laugh. "How could I have been so credulous?"

"Because . . ." Phormio said, and stopped. "You loved him." His bony shoulders humped as he braced himself on the chest, pressing his free hand to his heart. I was touched that he might be weeping, for I had found no tears in myself.

"Do you remember," he murmured, still turned away, "the time they raced each other from your great-aunt's barge? It must have been the end of summer; yes, was it not young Gaius's eighteenth birthday? I can see them now . . . striding up the beach at the same time, wet and laughing . . . one dark, one fair, as brown as tanned leather, like Achilles and Patroclus."

I had not moved or spoken, but he looked around at me as if I had made some comment. "The Lady Antonia told your mother how fortunate she was to have not one pair of twins but two, and everyone laughed. You must remember."

"No," I said. There were many gaps in my memory where Publius had been.

Anguish at having failed my brother struck me even harder. I glanced at the small ivory plaque of Mithras that I had placed in a wall niche, but even the god crouched with his knife at the bull's throat seemed to rebuke me.

It rained again during the night, and the sky was still dark and gravid when I set out on my penitential mission to the Palace. Phormio had slept badly; he grumbled that he would have to send a boy to fetch a public sedan chair, since Father had taken ours.

"I will walk," I said. "And you need not accompany me."

"I must remind you that your mother wishes you to have an attendant."

There had been little risk the day before when I was on horseback, but today I wore a dignified long tunic and mantle unsuitable for riding. "Very well; I will take . . ." I ran mentally through members of the *familia.* "Jason," I said at last. "Fetch him for me."

"Useless lump," Phormio muttered, but he trudged off.

I yawned and eyed my bed with longing. Father had summoned me at some infernal hour before dawn to discourse on how the Princeps' private accounts were disposed. I had trailed after him, trying hard to listen attentively through the ministrations of his *tonsor,* body slave, and *vestispica.*

Jason burst into the room with a shove from Phormio. The boy I remembered had become rawboned and gawky, with heavy brows and bunched jaw muscles that gave him a surly aspect. When full grown, he was meant to become a litter bearer like his father, a slave of Lepidus's who had sired him on one of Mother's serving women. In the meantime, no task was thought too mean for him; he was at everyone's command.

An unpromising attendant. But I had known him most of his life, and trusted him. "You will be my *servus viator* today," I said. "Phormio, find him a decent tunic and a cloak."

"Thank you, young master," Jason mumbled. The appellation startled me. Publius had always been the young master; I was only a spare, like an extra wheel carried on a long journey.

Now, excited about our destination, he could not fathom why I preferred to go on foot like a commoner instead of being carried. "Besides," he added, gesturing up at the scowling clouds, "you are daring Jupiter Pluvius to ruin your clothes."

I silenced him. The distance was short, and after Father's lecture I had no heart for flaunting my distinction as Caesar's quaestor-designate. Publius would have gloried in the position; I did not know how I would endure it.

By chance we came upon a couple of trousered Celts. For a moment I stared unthinkingly at the long red hair of one of them, then realized why it had drawn my eye. What would the fiery priestess Aurima think of me, if she knew I must beg Caesar's forgiveness for having questioned his honor?

Still thinking of her, I was surprised to be admitted quickly to the forecourt of the House of Augustus, then into the house itself. I was in the imposing reception room only long enough to be eyed by the many other favor-seekers when a slave eeled through the crowd to summon me.

Leaving behind the stares and resentful mutters, I accompanied my guide through large public rooms with floors of colored marble, splendid frescoes, and bedecked ceilings into a more private part of the house, built to a less imposing scale. The slave left me in a modest atrium.

Only then did I have the clarity of wit to appreciate that this had truly been the home of Augustus. Now he was the Divine Augustus, a near-legend who had restored civil order from chaos; but he had been a man my father knew, a living man who had walked this very floor of black-and-white hexagonal tiles, weeping for legions destroyed by the Germanic renegade Harman.

In the small atrium I was later to know so well, I recognized for the first time the fragility of the principate. It was not tradition or law that stood between us and darkness; not the Senate or even the army, but a single man: Augustus's great-grandson, Caligula Caesar. The man I had doubted and must now conciliate.

"We will speak of it no more," Caligula said. A blob of red wax dripped onto the papyrus before him. He pressed his signet into it. A secretary took it away and put another in its place. A clerk leaned down with a stick of wax and a burning taper.

"I am grateful to you," I said.

"He was your brother. Of course you wished to believe he was blameless." He stamped the document. "I do not suppose the file made pleasant reading. You should have taken my word."

His manner did not invite me to ask for a chair. There was none in this small room except the one in which he sat.

"It pains me that I do not have your trust," he went on. The secretary slid another sheet in front of him.

"I did not intend—" I began.

Caligula slammed down his ring so hard that the puddle of wax spattered crimson over the papyrus. "It pains me!"

The unexpectedness of it shifted me back a step. The freedmen and slaves around him peeped from under lowered eyelids.

"I had to know," I said.

"And now you do." He resumed work as if there had been no interruption. Documents were whisked down before him and then away by the hands of his staff, as in one of those factories where pottery lamps are turned out by the hundreds.

"Have I your leave to go?" I said at last. "Or am I simply to stand here admiring your efficiency?"

He pressed down the phoenix seal once more. "The trick," he said with a glance, "is not to read them." It might have been a joke.

Still another document was slipped under his nose. He frowned. "How many more, Etruscus?" Before the chief secretary could answer, he stood up. "I will finish later." He slid the ring back onto his finger.

I was looking at him when he swayed. I reached out a steadying hand, but a bejeweled fellow with a Pan-beard rushed forward, exclaiming in Alexandrian-accented Greek, "Etruscus, how can you let the Princeps work so hard when he is barely recovered! Lord Gaius, are you all right?" Dismissing me with a glance, he slid an arm familiarly around Caligula's shoulders. "Come now, my lord, rest for a while. I will send in my Nymphidia to please you, and that little lyre player."

Caligula let himself be drawn away by the Greek. "Who was that?" I asked Etruscus, who stood seething at the admonishment as his clerk gathered up papers.

He glanced sharply at me. Then his high brow smoothed, perhaps at the recollection that I was newly arrived in Rome. "That is Kallistos, your honor."

In Greek *kallistos* means "beautiful boy," which told me the man was either a slave or a freedman like Etruscus himself. "And Nymphidia," I said. "His wife?"

"His daughter," the chief secretary answered brusquely.

I caught Jason snickering and clipped him on the arm for his impertinence. For ambition's sake many a father, rich or poor, would gladly pander his child to a more powerful man. Was that not why I myself had been sent here?

Etruscus excused himself to finish his work, and a house slave escorted me back to the entrance. Although I was sure my foolish hopes of Publius's innocence had antagonized Caligula, I hid my low spirits from the waiting throng.

"Your honor, your honor," a voice called behind me.

It was another slave in the red-bordered tunic of the House of Augustus, this one a handsome golden-skinned youth. "A message from my master the Princeps," he said.

Conversations stilled all around. I sensed ears stretching toward me from every direction. Was it a rescinding of my promised quaestorship? A command to never again appear in his sight? I glanced around but saw no private nook in which to receive the news. "Softly," I told the boy.

He lowered his voice. "My master wishes you to attend him in the morning at the stables of the Greens faction."

I smiled with surprise and pleasure. "Very well."

The youth flicked a glance at Jason, then back to me. His eyes were much older than the rest of him. "He also said, your honor, that your slave is ugly and could you not bring one who is more comely."

I paid little heed to this criticism of my choice in attendants. So I had not spoiled my chances! Father would be delighted.

Jason lagged behind on the way home. It was a few moments before I noticed, for my mind was full of the coming joys of horses and racing. Seeing him bent over a puddle in the street, I called, "Are you sick?"

"What?" He looked up. "Oh. It's nothing, master." He scuffed a pebble into the water.

"Hurry, then," I said. After I told Father the news, there would be time to answer the invitation of a former girlfriend whose husband was visiting his vineyards in Praeneste. Perhaps my duty as Caesar's quaestor would not be so onerous after all.

CHAPTER 8

O FURIES!

The horses plunged around the turn and charged straight at us. The two charioteers were well matched, their eight horses so tightly crowded that they might have been a single team. It was the driver on the inside I watched most closely, a promising youngster from Cisalpine Gaul nicknamed Malleus, "the Hammer."

The Greens trainer signaled an end to practice. But instead of slowing, Malleus cracked his whip over his horses' backs. The second driver did the same.

Beneath my feet the earth shivered, and the thunder of hooves racketed off the wooden walls of the training track. As other spectators fled, the trainer stood scowling with hands on hips. I held my ground beside him, too proud to show fear to the man who had first challenged my courage.

At the last moment Malleus touched his lash to the shoulder of his off horse. The other driver shouted and whipped his own team. The horses dragged the low-slung chariots around the turn, so near that a shower of wet sand and bark spewed across our feet.

When they started up the straight on the other side, Malleus had gained a length on his rival. "He drives like a madman," I said.

"'E'll do wha'ever it takes t' win," said the trainer. "Ne'er knew 'f you would." Crude stitching from an old horse-kick pulled up his mouth on one side, giving him the snarl of a tusked boar.

I looked out at the track where I had once been dragged on my belly by the reins knotted around my waist, scrabbling for my knife while my terrified horses tried to escape the half-hitched chariot thrashing and bounding behind them. When I saw Silius's white face afterward, it gave me pure joy to have cheated death.

For a moment I imagined myself lashing a winning team across the line to the admiration of a copper-haired maiden. *Dream on, Carinna; sooner will pigeons roast themselves and fly into men's mouths.* Along with the whippy slimness of youth, I had lost proficiency with a racing team.

The chariots slowed when they came abreast of the rescue squad. As the two drivers wheeled around toward us, the slaves picked up their stretchers, hooks, and knives and plodded toward a side gate.

The first drops of cold rain splashed on my nose and cheeks. I followed the trainer under the gateway arch. "I hear Ferox's near-inside horse has the rheum," I said. He had been known to have a rival team's droppings smuggled out so he could paw through them.

He squinted at the approaching chariots. As slaves ran past to catch the horses' bridles, he said, "Wanta know who'll be champion nex' year?" He nodded toward Malleus. "Bet on 'im."

As he strode forward to berate the drivers for their prank, clamor erupted behind me. Caligula Caesar had arrived at last.

I headed for the noise, then realized Jason was hanging back. "Keep up with me, boy."

"You should have brought Phormio," he mumbled.

"Mind your manners," I snapped. My *paedagogus* was still too weary from the long journey to attend me. If Caligula disliked Jason's looks so much, let him give me a handsomer slave.

The harnessing barn was mobbed, with the imperial retinue crowded in among the stable attendants. I drank in the smells, Elysian to me, of horse sweat and dung, hay, leather, and axle grease. Grooms wriggled through the throng to unhitch the teams as the drivers dragged off their sand-spattered helmets. It all reminded me of Silius, but to my relief I did not see him.

The Princeps' laughter crackled above the turmoil. The two charioteers bantered with him, grinned and swaggered and let him test the sinews of their arms. Everyone hooted at his broad insults. Much was made of Gemellus's bet on the last race of the coming festival: five thousand on Ferox of the rival Blues.

"Let us give Rome a race to remember," Caligula shouted over the noise. "In honor of Isis who saved me, I will award one million sestertii to the winner."

There was a collective gasp at the magnitude of this prize, then a roar of acclaim and delight. I, too, cheered his largesse. Did it matter that this sum would have covered a thousand legionaries' wages for a pay period?

You will find him somewhat extravagant, Lepidus had warned.

Malleus's team was being unharnessed to one side: two stallions, dun and bay, and two brown mares. Smaller than saddle horses, overbred and high-strung, they stamped and rolled their eyes at the hubbub, nostrils flared as wide as wine cups. Their hides steamed in the cold. I imagined what it would be like to drive them: the eye-watering ecstasy of speed as they yanked me forward, the earthquake rumbling up my legs.

He'll do whatever it takes to win. Never knew if you would.

Had our family's *dignitas* not prevented me from racing in public, I would have proved I could rip off a rival's wheel or crowd another chariot into the *spina*. But it was obvious to me now that what I loved most about racing—the danger, strategy, and skill—had merely prefigured the exhilaration of making war.

Malleus shoved in beside me. The horses swayed up to him, ears angled toward his endearments: "Keep pulling like you did today, my Flamma. . . . Admeta, well done . . . . Celer, you handsome fellow . . ." He whispered something to the dun stallion, who shook the tickle of breath out of his ear. "Corner tighter for me, Passerinus, or you'll be a slave's dinner," he told the bay.

He was little more than a boy, short like most race drivers, but restraining headstrong horses had given him the shoulders and arms of an ape. When he turned to me, his narrow windburned face hardened into arrogance.

"To think," I said, "I am meeting a man about to become a millionaire."

Malleus grinned, baring splintered stumps. "Give Venus a golden kiss for me, sport."

He had started racing after I left Rome, so he saw me only as a moneyed enthusiast. I ran my tongue thoughtfully along my own teeth, and was grateful to have quit the Circus before it maimed me.

I caught up with Caligula as he was touring the stables with the prefect of the Greens. Even though a roofed portico kept off the rain, the chill was piercing enough to discourage all but a few followers. Slaves toiled to sweep away drifts of dirty straw ahead of the imperial boots. In front of a stall, the groom responsible for the horse inside faltered through a recitation of its record.

The prefect saw me first. He was unlikely to ever forget that Silius and I had once spirited away one of his racing chariots and left it on the high podium of the Temple of Castor. "I might have known you were too slippery to be done in by barbarians, young Carinna. Your new quaestor was so plaguesome as a boy," he confided to Caligula, "that I reckoned him secretly an agent of the Blues."

"Anyone would have turned blue after your haranguing," I said. "Hardened centurions on the frontier gaped at the curses I learned from you."

The prefect snorted. The others waited to see if the Princeps was amused.

Scarlet of nose and cheek, he was plumped out by several layers of tunics under a heavy cloak silvered with moisture. "We must talk," he said, hardly moving his pale lips. He nodded toward the stall. "This will do." To his Pan-bearded freedman he added, "Kallistos, make sure we are not overheard."

The top half of the stall door was already open. A young dapple-gray stallion, tethered crosswise, turned his head to eye us with hay wisps dribbling from his mouth.

The Greens prefect told the groom to bring out the horse. "No need," Caligula said. "Your precious beast will not be harmed."

"It is your safety that concerns me, Caesar. The horse—"

"The horse seems calm enough," I cut in. This was sheer hubris; I liked being able to display my ease with a skittish racer. Signaling Jason to wait outside, I followed the Princeps' mist-spangled cloak into the stall.

"Phew, what a stink," Caligula muttered. Shuffling through fetlock-high straw, he edged around the wary horse and tilted his offended nose toward a grate high in the brick wall.

I murmured soothing words and rubbed the horse's face. I knew this beast; I had driven him myself, when he was not too valuable to trust to an amateur.

Caligula turned to shout, "Close the doors, and do not interrupt me."

The stall dimmed as the top and bottom halves of the door swung shut. "A million sestertii," I mused. "As your quaestor, should I have something to say about that?"

"Shut up," he muttered from the other side of the horse.

"What?" Was this another blasted rule, that I might not speak to him unless addressed?

The little stallion tossed his head uneasily, and amulets braided into his tin-colored mane chinked together. I moved closer to calm him.

Caligula tucked his hands inside his mantle. "I must ask a service of you. A task you may confide to no one, even your father. I will have your oath on it."

I shook my head. Though flattered and eager to redeem myself, I could not forget the great mistake I had made in distrusting Father.

"He cannot know, Carinna. Give me your word."

"You say he has been a father to you, and you would deceive him?"

"You stubborn wretch! I have a good reason."

I slid my fingers under the horse's mane and stroked his neck. Relaxed by the touch, he began to nibble from the hay bin.

Caligula asked abruptly, "What do you want?"

The answer that sprang to my lips was *To leave you and Father to each other.* But I said instead, "To make amends for my brother," which was also true.

He stared at me as if I were a stranger. His thin face was drawn taut; shadows filled his eye sockets. "What do you mean?"

"I will try to become the Achates that you wanted him to be." I looked across the horse's nose at him. "Command me."

He swallowed visibly. But he did not speak, and for a long moment I thought he found my offer ludicrous.

All at once he blurted out, "I must know if Gemellus is loyal to me."

Alarmed, I shook my head again. "I am unsuited—"

"I have given him everything. I have adopted him as my son." He heaved out a breath that swirled in the chill. "Let him think Publius's death has made you disaffected with me. Find out if he . . . if he is plotting against me."

"So whether or not he is disloyal, everyone will believe I am?"

He drew back. "It is what I know that matters."

"And Saxa?"

"The plan is his."

How easy it would be for the commander of the Special Cohort to maneuver me into a treason charge, with Caligula—again—conveniently mute. I shook my head a third time. "With respect, Caesar, I cannot do it."

"Carinna, there is no one else of whom I can ask this."

Sensing the tension, the gray horse lifted his head. His ears flicked back and forth between us.

Caligula said gruffly, "Gemellus has corrupt advisers; I have warned him against them. Give me proof and I will punish them." His eyes held a plea. "But I must know if his heart has been turned against me."

Confused and angry, I had to look away. Watery light picked out the shine of more amulets hanging above the feed bin. A hammer handle protruded from the bin; the groom must have been interrupted while nailing up another charm.

His voice rose another notch. "You were brought back to help me. Your father promised."

Goaded past piety, I flared, "May I not be allowed to restore Rome's honor?"

"I am Rome's honor," he shouted.

The stallion shifted his hindquarters, hooves rustling in the straw. "We cannot talk here," I said. "You out there, open the doors!"

Voices babbled outside. The bolt scraped back, and the top half of the stall door swung outward. Anxious faces popped into the opening.

With a snort the horse backed away. His dappled rump hit the end of the stall, shaking the wooden partitions.

"Leave us," Caligula bellowed. "I will say when I am done."

The door crashed shut. The stallion reared in alarm, looming like an elephant in the cramped stall. I scrambled back. Hooves thudded down where I had stood, and hindquarters like a huge mottled fist slammed me against the wall. I managed to catch the headstall and brought the stallion to a halt.

The fright had jolted me out of my anger. I tried again to calm the beast, murmuring reminders of our time together. He pranced and pawed, scuffing the straw into mounds.

"Come with me, Caesar." I stretched out my free hand toward him. The stallion's name came back to me: Fulgor, so called for his lightning starts. He was Sicilian bred, when agitated as unpredictable as a crooked arrow.

Caligula was pressed against the bricks of the outer wall. Rainwater leaking from a corner of the high window made a silver rivulet down the shoulder of his cloak. "Tell me about Gemellus," he said raspily. "That is the command I give you."

Fulgor's ears swiveled toward his voice. I saw unease glinting in the horse's white-edged eyes.

"I know Tiberius raised him to hate me." Caligula's throat clenched, squeezing his voice higher. "But he is content to be my son. He is loyal." He pushed his fingertips into his eye sockets. "You will prove he is loyal."

The stallion's ears flattened, a dangerous sign. "Let us talk somewhere else," I said hastily. "I fear for your safety here."

"They say I need guards inside my house. And a food taster—with my own family!" His bloodshot eyes glared. "They tell me to put him away and starve him, as my mother and my brothers starved. To poison him, as my father was poisoned."

Rain scuttered on the roof tiles and rushed past the high vent, filling the stall with dampness and gloom. Drips splatted on floor bricks bared by the stallion's restless scuffling.

I tightened my grip on the halter. "We will talk later," I said urgently. "Leave now. I will hold the horse."

Caligula squeezed his eyes shut and clamped both hands to his temples. "They all leave me," he moaned. "They all die."

I could have slipped out and sent Fulgor's groom to remove the horse, but leaving Caligula in the stall would be the act of a coward. Holding the horse's head tightly, I slid around to the Princeps' side.

He had turned his face to the weeping bricks and was breathing in harsh keening gasps. I let go of the halter to take his arm. "Come with me, cousin."

"Has my family not suffered enough?" He slipped out of my grasp and sank to his haunches. "Gods, no more!" His hands clawed at his tawny hair. "O Furies, let me be!"

With a squeal the dappled stallion reared again, this time to his full height. Striped hooves beat the air near Caligula's bent head.

I threw myself between beast and man, snatching at the halter again. Yellow teeth as big as oyster shells snapped at my fingers. The horse thudded down stiff-legged. Tail tucked low, hindquarters bunching, he backed toward the shrieking crowd jammed in the gap of the opening door.

"Fulgor," I shouted, but the stallion was beyond heeding. Both hind hooves lashed out, and amid the cries of terror there was a *crump* like an ax blade cleaving a ripe squash. Someone hung there, mouth agape, held up by the press of others around him.

I lunged again and caught the halter. But the horse flung up his head, screaming, and I lost my grip. The poor beast was terrified, hind legs flying in frantic bursts, hooves crashing against the walls. The spotted rump jolted nearer and nearer to Caligula, huddled howling in the corner with his arms wrapped around his head.

Then all was quiet. Or perhaps the stillness was only inside me.

The little stallion staggered and lurched down on his knees. I seized his forelock with my free hand and pulled his head toward me, so that his sturdy legs kicked out on the far side of the stall. I was looking into the dark eye when it grew opaque and the horse breathed a last faint sigh. "Forgive me," I whispered, for who knows whether the beasts too may not testify when our souls are judged?

I let the hammer drop. Someone helped Caligula to his feet. Goggling at the dappled carcass, he reeled into waiting arms. He was still staring as they bore him out of the stall, slung in a cloak.

The dwindling noise of his departure was followed by the slap of running feet. Men came rushing across the stableyard, Malleus foremost. Rain streamed out of his hair, down his cheeks. "What is it?" he panted. "I heard one of the horses—"

I stumbled out of the stall, and his voice caught as if he had been choked. He lurched to the doorway. A shrill cry burst out of him, an almost womanish squall of grief.

Leaning on Jason, I made my way to a rain-slick bench under the eaves of the portico. Beside it lay a dead slave, his head awash in the gutter. Graven in the front of his tunic were the marks of the stallion's hooves.

I would have to tell Father that Caligula's brain fever had returned. All the game pieces would be set in play once more: Gemellus, Lepidus, the Senate, governors, legions . . . Enemies would mass on the frontiers while garrison commanders waited to learn who ruled in Rome.

O Furies, let me be!

They had destroyed his brothers and parents. Now, I thought, they were coming for him.

Riding home from the Greens stables, I heard shouting from the top of the Palatine Hill. My heart jerked: the people had learned their Princeps was ill once more. Again I cursed my careless arrogance in allowing him to enter the stall.

"What's that racket?" Jason asked. The noise grew louder. Whoops and yells, and clangs and bangs and booms of pots and pans being beaten.

A man came running down the street. "Good news," he cried. "A boy!"

I reined in my horse. A greengrocer's slave sweeping rubbish into the gutter paused to listen, and a couple of old women gossiping in a doorway peered into the street. "What are you talking about?"

"Agrippinilla." The man grinned like an idiot. "It will be a boy."

I blinked at him stupidly, so different was it from what I had expected to hear. Caligula's eldest sister was at her husband's villa, not even in Rome. It took me a moment to recall that she was expecting a child. But surely Nina had written that it was not due for another month or two?

"A boy, that's what the seer says!"

"Shut your stupid face!" one of the women cried, with an apprehensive glance at the sky. The other made a fig of her fist to ward off bad luck.

"Germanicus's grandson," the man shouted, oblivious, and ran on with his news.

"A boy," Caligula said. He paced the room. "Kallistos, did I say three silver tripods for Juno? Make it seven. And I will give Isis a robe in cloth of gold." He saw me and smiled broadly. "The Chaldean says Agrippinilla will have a son."

I fumbled for a smile, but he was already clasping my elbows and kissing my cheek. "Gods grant it will be so," I muttered awkwardly. An empty prayer, but it was useless to invoke Mithras; the Lord of Light did not occupy himself with childbearing. "The people are shouting the news of Germanicus's first grandson."

A shadow crossed his face. I had managed to remind him that his own son had died at birth with its mother. "The women of our family are good breeders," he said, shrugging off the melancholy. "My mother bore nine and raised six."

"When I last saw you, I feared . . . That is, you are unhurt?"

"Carinna, it will happen. It will be a boy." His eyes sparkled, edged with tears. "I know it."

"Astrologers are not infallible," I began warily.

"That is not how I know. I know because of what you did."

"What do you mean?" My head felt as if it would float off my shoulders like a dandelion puff. I could not forget the look in the stallion's dying eye, the cost of my treachery.

"Quickly, Kallistos, let him sit." As the bearded freedman placed a chair behind me, Caligula said, "The October Horse."

I stared at him dumbly. "The Ides are past. I was not here." In this ancient ritual, two-horse chariots compete in the Field of Mars. Then the off horse on the winning team is speared and beheaded—a sacrifice to thank Mars for a successful campaigning season. In the rest of the gory spectacle, gangs from the Subura and the Sacra Via fight to claim its head, and its bloody tail is mounted in the Forum.

Caligula said, "As a victor in war, you propitiated Mars for me with this sacrifice. Now Isis will be able to keep Agrippinilla safe."

Bile rose in my throat. Trying not to imagine the dappled stallion's head impaled on the Regia wall, I scarcely took in this jumble of theologies. "I will leave you, Caesar. I came only to be sure you were well." I had not sat.

"Touch my forehead," he said as I was turning away. "Let me see if I can feel the power."

I laid my hand on his brow. His lashes sank down, as blond as awns of ripe wheat. I looked at the bony curves and angles of his eye socket, his cheekbone, his jaw, the vulnerable sweep of his long muscular neck. His pulse beat strongly beneath my fingers.

Had it not occurred to him that if a male child of his sister's blood were to join the family, Gemellus would have even more reason to fear being supplanted?

I drew the Sun cross on his brow. Caligula's eyes flew open. "What are you doing?"

"I am asking Mithras to protect you, Gaius Julius Caesar Augustus Germanicus." I spoke his formal name carefully, to be sure the god could not mistake who sought his favor.

He regarded me uncertainly. Then Drusilla ran in, her face rosy from the cold, and threw herself into his arms with a yelp of joy. They embraced each other, laughing, and I withdrew.

A message came not long after I reached home, delivered by a uniformed Praetorian officer who waited while I read it. There was no sender's name, but the seal was one I recognized: two-headed Janus, looking back and ahead.

> We regret to hear that an unruly horse attacked you at the Greens stable this morning. Gods be thanked, no one else was with you. Your quick thinking and slow tongue are to be commended.

So that was to be the official story, and I was to tell no other. Fortunately, I had already ordered the awestruck Jason to silence. Nodding that I understood, I handed back the tablet.

That night Rome erupted in a frenzy of joy. The gods had restored their favor to us: Caligula the beloved had recovered his health, and a male child was to be born to a daughter of Germanicus. The streets swarmed with drinking, brawling, and fornication.

Later, the lurid glow of bonfires discolored the darkness. For a while I joined the slaves who had been sent up on the roof to watch for sparks. Embers soared like stars on that late-October night, and our eyes watered as tongues of flame streamed up all over Rome.

It is ironic that so much fire presaged the birth of Nero, who would watch from the Palatine nearly thirty years later as two-thirds of the city burned. But at the time, I hoped it meant that Caligula Caesar had succeeded in turning his luck.

CHAPTER 9

ROMULUS AND REMUS

S omeone had written on the wall across from Tiberius's old house. Sheltered by the roof overhang from a dirty mist that stank of smoke, the scrawl was blurry but readable:

GEMINUS PRIMUS
GEMELLUS PROXIMUS

A twin was first; Gemellus will be next.

His supporters were bold, to proclaim a connection with Romulus on the very site of the settlement the two brothers had founded. No wonder Caligula feared the young whelp might give him a push into the afterworld.

The doors of the House of Tiberius opened directly onto the pavement. There was no gated courtyard, no horde of visitors' slaves and conveyances, not even an outside doorman. The monotonous *tink, tink, tink* of a metal hammer came from a shop hung with cooking pots in one side of the house front. If not for an oak wreath sculpted above the doorway in honor of Tiberius's German Triumph, one would hardly know this had once been the residence of the old Princeps.

Jason stepped out of the way of a street slave sweeping up ashy debris from the night's revels. "Caesar's son lives in this old place?"

I lifted both hands to the sky, for it must be noon, but my prayer to the unseen sun brought no answering grace. How was I, sworn to Caligula Caesar, to deceive Gemellus about my loyalties?

"How pleasant to see a pious man," said a cheerful voice.

I had not heard the doors open. But there, stepping out onto the pavement with a retinue of others behind him, was Gaius Silius.

For a moment I gawked like a peasant at him, elegantly and immaculately dressed with scarcely a hair out of place. Once they had called him the handsomest boy of our generation, and men had vied for his company. Now, grown to manhood himself, he had lost none of his dark and dangerous beauty.

Others crowded around him: a few clients, his body servant, his secretary. I knew them all. And Pertinax, of course. The big Gaul glowered at me. I was glad I had dressed well to visit Caligula's adopted son.

"*Salve*, Marcus." Silius gave me his broad, charming smile.

My face warmed at his intimate use of my personal name. "*Salve*, Silius," I returned, pointedly using his family *nomen*.

Silius's smile faded. He shook his head mournfully. "Here is my old comrade Marcus Carinna back from a perilous frontier," he said to the others, "but so bigheaded after his affray with the savages that I may no longer call him by his *praenomen*."

They chuckled, all but Pertinax. I knew they were hoping for a quarrel.

I recovered my wits. "Do not let me keep you from your duties." During my absence he had been appointed magistrate of the Tenth District, that is to say of the Palatine, no doubt with substantial assistance from Pertinax's purse.

I stepped aside, but Silius did not stir. Pertinax coughed and shifted his boarish bulk. His brushy eyebrows overhung sharp eyes wrapped in squint-wrinkles; hairy knuckles clasped the folds of his mantle to his chest. "Silius, let us move on," he said in his nasal Narbonnese accent. "We all yearn for a fire and a hot drink."

"Of course," Silius said absently. His eyes flickered back to Tiberius's house, and I guessed he was curious about why I was calling on Gemellus—the very thing I wondered about him.

Then he was gone. Jason rapped on the door to announce me. I was admitted, and someone went off in search of Gemellus. I wandered about the atrium, decorated with frescoes in the style of a bygone era, and peered into a reception room full of clutter, trying to understand what it would mean if Silius was in league with a traitorous Gemellus.

A sneeze sounded from the interior of the house. A moment later its master appeared: a slightly built youth with a pale, coarse-skinned face and hair the color of dead grass. He had been plump when I last saw him, and as spotty as a poppy-seed bun.

"Gemellus," I said. "I hope you are well." His likeness to Tiberius—an arched nose, a bulbous chin—was more obvious now that the puppy fat was gone.

"Trying not to catch this blasted grippe," he said, showing me his barley-corn teeth. "It seems following the Eagles agreed with you, Carinna."

He should have greeted me with a handclasp at least, for like most off-spring of noble families we were related. Instead, an uncomfortable moment passed while he fondled a hairy amulet hanging on a chain at his throat.

"Why so aloof, cousin?" I grasped his palm, as smooth as a woman's, flung my other arm around his shoulders, and kissed his cheek. His musky perfume, as thick as incense, nearly gagged me.

After an instant of stiff surprise, he gave me a reciprocal peck and pulled away. Obviously he did not like to be touched. I said, baiting him, "But perhaps I am overly familiar, now that you are Caligula's heir."

"When he was ill, it was Drusilla he named his heir," he said. "Not me."

I feigned surprise. "I thought surely he had changed his will while I was on the road." I recognized his amulet now: it was a poison stone, one of those lumps from a beast's stomach that is supposed to counteract hemlock, deadly mushrooms, and other banes.

Gemellus's spit-colored eyes seemed to bulge, an unfortunate effect of arching his almost invisible brows. "My adoptive father seems unsure whether I deserve his trust."

"And now, it seems, he will have a nephew he may place ahead of you," I commiserated, as if resenting the malevolence of fate. "We kinsmen must help each other, eh?" This was an entirely specious argument, since I was only a distant relation while he and Caligula were first cousins.

But the lad was quick to respond. "You are right, Marcus Licinius. Come, let us share a drink on this dreary day." He snapped his fingers at a slave. "House sandals, at once, for my cousin Carinna."

It seemed I had been ingratiating enough. I chided myself for enjoying the deception, even though it was for the sake of Rome. I had to remember that I was here, a soldier of Mithras, in search of truth.

While a slave unlaced my boots, I sought a topic about which I could be sincere. "My mother told me you visited her in Antium now and then."

Gemellus shrugged, worrying at his amulet again. "I stayed with her and Grandmother Antonia when I traveled for my grandfather the Princeps. Rest his shade."

"I cannot regret his passing," I said. "But he died too soon for you, eh?"

The slave stopped washing my feet. Gemellus's face lost its expression of vacant amiability. "The gods' will," he murmured. Yet in his eyes I saw it chafed him that he had been too young to contend with Caligula for the principate.

He led me into a corridor where blistering stucco made pale patterns high on the dark-hued walls. Unlived-in while the old Princeps was on Capri, the house still smelled of mice and dry rot. It was certainly in greater neglect than the House of Augustus, which swarmed with painters and plasterers and mosaic-layers.

I stopped him where we could not be overheard. "Gemellus, rumors have reached me doubting your loyalty to Caligula."

The implied question brought anger to his pallid face. "By Castor's cap! Must I vow myself to him every day and twice on festivals?"

I said nothing. He reached out to peel a flake of old paint off the wall. "Many important men are my friends. The Senate Leader. The Prefect of Egypt. And younger men, too, who believe in my future . . . like Gaius Silius."

He caught my eye. I said without inflection, "I see."

"Silius finds it hard to forget why his parents killed themselves," Gemellus went on. "I believe their sacrifice has been shamefully ignored. As has his desire for justice." He pushed himself away from the wall. "But I am not the Princeps, of course."

I gave a noncommittal shrug.

His voice sharpened. "Do you share Silius's views?"

"At one time he and I thought much alike."

After a few more paces, he turned again. "Did the two of you really dress up as girls to enter the baths during women's hours?"

I was surprised into a half smile. He gave a bray of laughter.

A servant scurried up and whispered into his master's ear. "I must excuse myself for a moment," Gemellus said. "Make yourself at ease, my friend." He waved me toward a doorway and called out as a slave pulled the curtain aside, "*Carissima*, here is an old friend to join you."

I stepped cautiously into a dining room overheated by several braziers. Smoke hazed its bacchanalian frescoes, making the motionless attendants in red-edged tunics seemed painted too.

"Mind the draft, idiot," a woman rasped. The slave hastily dropped the curtain, and I found myself alone with Julia Livilla.

The youngest of Caligula's three sisters reclined on one of the couches set around a triangular table. "Lo, Ulysses is home from the wars," she said in a voice that could have curdled milk.

Her dark-brown hair was pulled back into a matronly knot, but a light shift of finely pleated linen, girdled under her bosom, revealed the lush curves of breast and hip with shocking intimacy. As her chin lifted, I noticed amid the loose curls spiraling against her ear the glitter of four strands of intricate golden chain tipped with tiny pearls, swinging from a trefoil earring set with two carnelians and an emerald. My eyesight was not as acute or as expert as it might seem, for I knew the earrings. I had been with Publius when he bought them for his gay-tempered *sponsa* from a jeweler in the Porticus Margaritaria.

Matching her mockery, I said, "After so long, Penelope, you must be weary of your loom."

"Did your father tell you there were favors to be claimed? Is that why you slunk back to replace your brother?"

I sat on the nearest couch and signaled for a drink. Sweat prickled on my upper lip in the heat. I said, "I am not here to claim favors."

"Then what is it you seek, Marcus? Consolation?" Livilla stirred her wine with a finger. "My nights are not spent unraveling his shroud. As you must know." Eyeing me insolently, she slipped the finger in and out between her lips.

The eroticism was wasted on me. "Indeed," I jeered, "they say you ply your shuttle diligently, night and day."

She flung her cup at me. Pale wine spewed across the table, and the glass cone fell out of its silver vine-leaf holder and shattered on the floor.

I lunged to my feet. "They joke about you in the barracks: 'Let no man call Vinicius's wife promiscuous. After all, she will not sleep with Vinicius.'"

The anger smoothed out of Livilla's oval face, erasing the lines between her plucked brows and at the corners of her encarmined mouth. Her nose was short and uptilted, which gave her the look of a saucy young girl when she smiled. "Does that amuse you?"

"Well, I am pleased it is not said of my brother's wife."

"You insinuate that I would have betrayed him?"

Her vehemence infuriated me; it was I who had the right to be offended. "Perhaps you think he would have tolerated Gemellus and your other lovers?"

She snatched up a cushion to heave at me. When I tried to grab it away, she clung to it and yanked me down on top of her.

I struggled to rise. She seized fistfuls of my hair in both hands, pulling my face down next to hers. "Are you jealous, Marcus?" She smiled again, her dark-blue eyes a handspan from my own. "Did you lie awake at night, wishing you had your brother's license with me?" She squirmed beneath me with practiced sensuality, as if it pleased her to be half crushed with my elbow jammed against her breast.

"Stop," I said hoarsely. My eyes watered from the pain of her grip. An earring inches from my nose glistened like stars swimming in a lake.

"Is that what really vexes you, my honey? That so many others have been given what you could not have?" She laughed as a drop of my sweat made a small starburst on her pale-powdered cheek. "Then take it now. Why not you too?"

"Livilla," Gemellus exclaimed behind me.

Suddenly released, I rolled away and nearly fell off the couch. When I found my footing, she was departing in a flurry of crinkled linen.

Gemellus had stepped aside to let her pass. He smiled unpleasantly. "You were gone, I think, when Grandfather made Marcus Vinicius return from Ephesus to marry her. One can only wonder how he endured the passage to Italy, for the puddle-jump to Capri turned him as green as a fresh fig." He sniggered. "Hardly a frisky bridegroom, according to the bride."

"No doubt she was glad to be wed," I said shortly. Tiberius had found one excuse after another to put off her marriage to my brother: a bad dream, misaligned stars, the birth of a five-legged heifer.

He cuffed away a redheaded slave who had knelt to mop the wine. "You did not wish to marry her yourself?"

"I hope the wife I take will not cuckold me with every other man in Rome." Although I had tried for a bantering tone, the retort came out harshly. I found my cup and sipped slowly, to seem less disturbed.

"But think: you would now be brother-in-law of—" Gemellus caught sight of Livilla's wineglass, broken into opalescent shards like an eggshell from which something exotic had escaped.

His eyes shot to the young red-haired slave. "You dolt, those cups were my mother's!" He slapped the boy's face. "Get out!"

The server fled to the doorway, then paused to glare at his master's back. "Seize that boy," I called out. Nothing is more dangerous than defiance in a slave.

Gemellus whirled. The server vanished. Sounds of a scuffle came from the corridor, and a moment later a man poked his bald head inquisitively past the curtain. "Take the boy away," Gemellus snapped. "I will deal with him later." He sank onto the end of my couch. "The little calf is no use as a server," he complained. "I may as well give him to my guards."

I had no interest in his household problems. "I asked you earlier, friend, about certain doubts voiced in my hearing. I do not feel you have answered me."

He calmed himself with a deep breath. "Do you not?" Another server put a cup into his hand. He examined the wine for a moment, then dipped the repellent amulet into it. Gravely he drew it out again and wiped it on the server's tunic.

My thirst vanished. I set down my own wineglass, still half full.

Only then did he look up at me. "It was Caligula's fault, after all, that your brother died."

"What?"

Satisfaction dawned in his eyes before he hid it behind sandy lashes. My voice rose. "What do you mean?"

He sucked at his wine carefully. At last he said, "Grandfather was left-handed, you know." He licked his lips. "When he pursued an end, he never went at it the obvious way."

"Are you saying Publius was not his target?"

Gemellus studied one of the frescoes over the rim of his cup. "He blamed your brother for filling Caligula with grandiose notions." He looked back at me. "So when he was given an excuse . . ."

The unsaid words hung between us. He arched his colorless brows. "It let him remind Caligula of his power, you see. In a left-handed way." Taking my stony stare for incomprehension, he explained, "When lightning strikes another man just a step away, even an atheist begins to believe in God." He lifted his cup. "Of course, it also gets rid of the man struck by lightning." He sipped again.

I could not speak. Was that why Tiberius had not pardoned Publius? To teach Caligula a lesson?

Gemellus said, "I was too young to ask my grandfather for clemency on your brother's behalf. But I was surprised Caligula did not." He added, "A Princeps' friendship should be more constant, should it not?"

"I must be on my way," I said abruptly. "Thank you for your welcome."

"Before you go, tell me what happened at the racing stables yesterday. You were there, I hear, when my adoptive father was nearly killed by a horse."

"A stallion killed a slave and had to be put down," I said. "The Princeps was perfectly safe."

"What a pity. For Malleus, I mean; they say the horse was in one of his teams." He rose and led me out into the clammy corridor, where servants clustered around us. "Let us dine together soon to celebrate your appointment as Caesar's quaestor. And I want your advice about the legions."

I said nothing, but Gemellus must have sensed that the bait attracted me. With all his informers, did he know that Caligula, Lepidus, and my father had ignored my opinions? "Alexander was my age when he began to conquer the world," he said. "And the Divine Augustus was little older when he set foot on the road that led to Actium."

"Is it the rest of the world you would conquer," I asked, "or Rome?"

His pale eyes darted away, then back to me. "We waste millions trying to defend an indefensible frontier. Let us draw the line at the Alps, and leave the Northerners to their own barbarity, eh?" He sniffled. "Blasted grippe . . ."

The bald man drew a stoppered vial from his mantle's pouch and gave it to him. Gemellus drank, grimacing. "You know the Germans. Bloody savages . . ." He handed back the vial. "Let them kill each other; it is none of our affair."

Though horrified by his small-mindedness, I made myself say, "You may be right." By Mithras's Dog, how would I atone for the lies I was telling him?

"I knew you were a man to rely on. One word more, Carinna." He nodded at another curtained doorway. "We will not be heard in here."

The small room stank of bad drainage. The mosaic floor was stained and dingy, the frescoes scabrous with age and neglect. In one corner, a dog's-head spigot drooled a trickle of water into a basin, whose overspill ran in a trough under the two pierced seats at the back. Though the gurgle of flowing water made it a good place for secrets, it was hardly the sort of tasteful retreat where a man might relax while listening to a reader or musician.

Gemellus signaled the *latrinarius* to leave. Apprehension mingled with my anger. Now he would ask me to pledge myself to him, and how would I reply?

"Marcus Carinna," he said, "I have need of brave men. Will you take my hand?" He held out his palm.

"What are you asking of me, Gemellus?"

"Only friendship. For now."

Had Caligula anticipated this moment? Did he and Saxa expect me to pledge myself in support of a sly and ambitious young rival?

I hesitated briefly before meeting his eyes. "I vowed allegiance to Caligula with my legion. But to the extent that duty allows, count me your friend."

"You are honest," he said. As he stepped forward to clasp my hand, the toe of his sandal caught on a crumbling edge of the floor tiles. To steady himself he grabbed something hanging on a peg beside him, a robe or a cloak. When he clutched at it, a scrap of paper the size of a man's hand slipped from behind it and sailed onto the floor.

He regained his balance. "See how Caligula shames me, housing me in this hovel!" He slammed the side of his fist against the wall, and a slab of painted plaster fell and detonated at his feet. "Six months here, and my repairs still must wait on everyone else's!" He was so absorbed in this tirade that it took him a moment to realize I was not paying attention. "What are you looking at?"

I handed him the piece of papyrus. Holding it up to the light that fell past the curtain's edge, he muttered the words written on it:

As Remus crouched with Romulus beneath the she-wolf's tit—
Not brothers, these, but kinsmen made more close by legal writ—
Romulus the elder, who loved Remus as a son,
Told him to cherish Mother Wolf in thanks for all she'd done;

For one day, grown in glory, Rome would dazzle all men's eyes,
And from its seven humble hills an empire would arise.
He fell asleep, to dream about the fame of which he spoke,
And woke to find young Remus in a handsome wolf-fur cloak.

His face darkened. He turned the paper over, as I had, to peer at the un-polished side. It was first-quality Augustan papyrus, an expensive medium for an anonymous satire. He brandished it at me. "Where did this come from?"

I nodded toward the wall where the robe still hung. He swept the garment aside, exposing only cracked plaster. The paper had been slipped behind the folds of clothing, free to fall out when they were disturbed.

"By Castor's cap! That whoreson Phoenix—how dare he slander me?" Gemellus crumpled the papyrus in his fist and hurled it toward the slotted seats. It skipped on an edge and fell in. Luckily, much of my boyhood educa-tion had involved memorizing ancient orations, so I had already learned the words.

The bald servant drew back the door curtain. Gemellus motioned him away with a furious slash of his hand. "Keep this to yourself, Carinna," he hissed. "Look, I have two Circassians, beautiful girls, sisters. When you come to dinner, I will have them both serve you."

It was agreeable to see this petulant youth squirm. "Splendid," I said. "But this was probably a copy."

"All gods curse that mudslinger!" The gristle in his neck worked up and down. "Do you know who he is? Tell me, and I will give you the Circassians."

I shrugged. Bitingly clever lampoons had been quoted to me in letters from Rome, but no one admitted knowing who wrote them.

"When I find out, I will have his balls! *Latrinarius*, come at once! Did you put that vile thing where I would find it?"

His noisy expostulations were making my head throb. I said, "Gemellus, listen to me," but could not penetrate his angry interrogation of the slave. When I interrupted him with a hand on his arm, he jumped as if it were a smith's red-hot tongs. "Gemellus," I said again, in a lower voice.

"Was it you who put it here?" he snapped.

The charge outraged me. "Of course I did not, you ass-headed dolt."

"Admit it, your father put you up to this!"

Shaking my head, I walked out on his ranting. He did not even grant me the courtesy of a farewell.

Waiting in the atrium as Jason laced my boots, I fumed silently. All I had learned from this skirmishing was that Gemellus wished to embitter me against Caligula and draw me into his own camp. I had let myself be distracted by his limp-cocked notion of abandoning the North to darkness and barbarism. He might take no pride in being a Roman, put here by the gods to bring order to the world, but that was hardly evidence of treason.

Silius probably knew whether the boy was dangerous. I had only to swallow my self-respect and ask him.

By Mithras's Dog, if Caligula suspected Gemellus of treachery, he ought not to wait for proof! In his place, I would send the boy into gilded exile in Athens or Rhodes and tell him to stay there until he was summoned. It was folly to keep a serpent in one's bed just because it had not bitten yet.

The bald factotum appeared from the interior of the house. "Master wants you," he told the atrium slaves, and they scuttled off without a word.

Except for the doorkeeper in his alcove, there were no servants about. The house was unnaturally quiet. "Where is everyone?" I said.

Jason stared blankly from beneath the unkempt bar of his brows. Then I heard the shriek.

Fear and fascination transfixed the watching slaves. Scores of them, perhaps the entire *familia*, were crammed into a courtyard in the mizzling rain. Armed guards crowded them against the walls.

I pushed through to the top of the courtyard steps. Gemellus stood in the middle of the open area, holding a knife. A guard beside him gripped the water closet attendant by the arms.

"Master, please, I know nothing," the *latrinarius* whimpered. He sagged and was hauled up onto his knees by the guard. "Someone must have come in while I was cleaning, master . . . while my back was turned. . . ."

"I will count to three." Gemellus pressed his knife against the slave's throat. "One." It was a modest blade, no longer than an index finger, but well able to take a man's life. "Tell me where that filthy libel came from."

"I— I—" The *latrinarius*'s eyes rolled wildly.

Gemellus said, "Two."

Across the yard, a horse thrust its head out of a stall. The slaves pressed against the stall door shifted aside. Among them was the redheaded server.

Something made him aware of my gaze, and he glanced at me over the heads of the throng. We were looking straight at each other when the water closet attendant cried, "Him! It was him, the Thracian boy."

"What?" Gemellus's head snapped around.

The red-haired boy looked at the pointing finger and froze. His neighbors drew away from him. The horse tossed its head and disappeared inside its stall.

The *latrinarius* babbled, "He said . . . he needed to see if you had left something there. I remember now. I thought nothing of it. . . ."

The guard sent him sprawling with a shove. Gemellus beckoned with his knife to the serving boy. "Come to me."

The young slave shook his head so violently that his wet curls slapped his cheeks. "Not true," he said. "He lies." His gaze caromed around the courtyard.

Gemellus slouched toward him. "Why should I believe you, little calf?"

The boy's fists knotted, but he held them at his sides.

"Tell me who bribed you." Gemellus flung the knife down on the bricks between them. "See, you have nothing to fear."

The server stumbled back. A stone water trough behind his knees brought him up short.

Gemellus punched him in the chest. "Tell me now, sheep-eyes, or I will give you to my gladiators."

"I speak true, master. It was not—"

Gemellus hit him again, and the boy tumbled backward. A gout of water surged over the edges of the horse trough as he vanished head and torso inside it. His legs kicked frantically in the air, sandals flying. When he clutched at the sides, trying to haul himself out, Gemellus pushed his head underwater.

With his elbows trapped inside the narrow trough, the boy could only claw uselessly at Gemellus's sleeves. From my vantage I saw his red curls thrashing. A hair ribbon whipped like a snake in waterweed.

A sigh passed through the crowd. A girl gasped, and was hushed by a woman next to her. No one moved.

Gemellus was too preoccupied to see me coming. I pried his wrist away. Then, seizing the boy's flailing arm with my other hand, I yanked him out of the trough in a deluge that doused both of us.

Disbelief contorted Gemellus's flushed face. "What . . . What . . ."

"I believe he told you the truth, cousin. It is the *latrinarius* who lied."

He found his tongue. "What affair is it of yours?"

I had not meant to humiliate the disagreeable little toad before his entire household. To help him salvage his authority, I said, "You meant simply to punish the boy for his insolence, I am sure. But looking down from the steps, I saw he might cheat you of his life."

As the Thracian boy choked and coughed at our feet, the glaze of blood-lust faded from Gemellus's colorless eyes—burned off, it seemed, by rage. He said between his teeth, "I will not forget this, Carinna."

"I did not do it to spite you," I said.

"Why, then? Do you fancy the boy?"

"Truth is important—"

His braying laugh overrode me. "You fancy him," he repeated, loudly enough for everyone else to hear. He smirked around at them, prompting nervous titters. With a grandly dismissive wave at the wretched boy, he said, "Take him, then, and welcome!"

I did not want any gift from him, certainly not an ill-behaved young beast from the wilds of Thracia, but was too angry to back down. "Very well, I accept."

I hauled the boy to his feet by the back of his tunic. Shreds of dirty straw matted with horse dropping dribbled off him. He was still coughing, but so vigorously that it was obvious he would survive.

"Wait," Gemellus said in a different voice. "Perhaps . . ."

"Have you changed your mind? I would have taken him as an apology for your insult about the lampoon, but you may have him back. If your honor allows."

Gemellus's jaw twisted. It would have been a grave insult for him to withdraw a gift. I thought he was about to answer, but instead he turned and stamped into the house. I pushed the boy toward Jason and, richer by one cast-off serving slave, left the House of Tiberius.

Phormio was blunt, as usual: "So you have made an enemy of Caesar's son over this boy?"

"You know I have sworn to uphold truth," I said. "I had no choice."

Perched on my clothes chest, Phormio crossed his arms and glared at the young slave. The Thracian boy gazed sullenly at the floor. His red hair hung in strings, and his wet tunic clung to his narrow chest.

"His name is Hesperus. He is fourteen years old, more or less. His family was sold into slavery after stoning a tax collector," I said, having gleaned this on the way home. "He will attend you. Fetch things, clean up, run errands."

Phormio gave a disparaging snort. "Hill-country yokel . . . Might make a stable boy of him. Never a house slave."

"Do what you like with him, then," I said. "And you need not fret about Gemellus. I am in Caligula's confidence."

Curiosity lit up his tired eyes. "In what respect?"

"I will tell you later." I did not reckon that my pledge of secrecy included my old *paedagogus*, from whom I had no secrets. "Along with a good lampoon. In the meantime, perhaps you will stir yourself and take him to be washed."

Phormio rose with a grunt. "You should give him back," he muttered.

The boy spoke up, startling us both. "It is no matter," he said, hoarse from the water he had spewed. "I am dead anyway. You will see."

The tablet in my hand said GIVE BACK BOY. I looked from these words to my father, who had just written them.

"I have paid for him," I objected. "He cost me two Circassians."

Father frowned. He lay propped in bed, swaddled like a pharaoh's mummy. Turtle had patted a lard-and-garlic poultice on his chest, bundled him to the ears in a scarf, and tucked a hot wineskin under his chin. This was his usual method of nursing a scratchy throat when he was to speak in public the next day.

I tried to hide my irritation. "Very well; I know you do not want to be in debt to Gemellus. Tomorrow I will send him a gift to compensate for the boy."

Father nodded emphatically. He made a grasping gesture toward the writing tablet, and I passed it back to him. With brusque slashes of the stylus, he carved in the dark wax WHY HE GAVE TO YOU.

"He did not want him any longer." It was the simplest way to avoid explaining why I had interfered in Gemellus's disposition of his own property.

My father cast his eyes skyward and sank back against his pillows. It was just as well I had been forbidden to tell him about assessing Gemellus's loyalty. He would have thought my performance ludicrous.

My stomach growled, tormented by the aroma of garlic. I stood up. "Are you finished with me, Father?"

Clutching the hot-water bag to his chest, he reached for the tablet again. I stifled a yawn. There had been far too much of the temperamental Caesars lately for my liking.

Father snapped his fingers and held up the tablet to me. He had written WHO IS PHOENIX.

I said, "He is probably well born, since he knows what people in our circle say and do. Although I suppose he might be a well-educated freedman."

He took back the tablet. Under WHO IS PHOENIX, he wrote FIND OUT.

CHAPTER 10

RUFUS

"Well, colleague," Bassus said, "I am pleased to welcome you to the best sinecure in the empire." He dabbed a dribble of wine off his first and second chins with an edge of his mantle. "Ten amphoras of this; it's very nice," he said to the wine broker, whose clerk made a note.

"I was told there is much to keep one busy in overseeing Caesar's accounts," I said. Father had told me my responsibilities in exhaustive detail.

Bassus snorted. "The freedmen and slaves do all the work. And quite well, too. After being on their own while Tiberius vegetated on Capri, they do not need oversight. Or welcome it." He gestured to the broker. "You say you have a twenty-year-old Faustian Falernian? Let me have a taste."

I said, "But you are accountable to the Princeps."

"Oh, to be sure! But Caesar needs no one to carry his messages to the Senate; he delivers them himself. As for spending, who would tell him he cannot have his little boat, or his golden couches, or a new wing to his villa in—*hic!*—Speluncae?" His eyes fixed greedily on an amphora being brought toward us.

"I see." I rose, wishing I had not bothered to track him down at this warehouse in the Field of Mars.

"One thing, Carinna." My fellow Quaestor of Caesar tipped up his head and scowled at me. "People are used to bringing their pleas and petitions to me. I will have a third part of any gifts you receive. It is my right." He reached for the cup the server held out without looking away from me.

I could barely hide my distaste. "How did you get your appointment?"

"He owed my father a favor." Bassus winked. "Same as you."

⊫⊰ ⊱⊪

A clearer picture of my future role was taking shape. I was to be rewarded with toothsome bribes for prestigious but undemanding duties, which would leave me plenty of time to solicit Caligula's friendship. Yet I did not see how I would earn his trust without successfully sounding out Gemellus's loyalty. It was a thankless task, and one to which I was completely unsuited.

I told myself again that after failing to save Publius, I could not refuse this burden. If I reminded myself often enough, I would accept it. It was only a matter of will.

I went to the Palace, reckoning that by this hour Caligula would be awake. I would tell him about calling on his adopted son the day before, and make him laugh by recounting Gemellus's reaction to the lampoon. "Sorry, Quaestor," said the centurion of the guard, who had already learned to recognize me. "Caesar left at first light for Ostia. Inspecting a boat he's having built."

The news came as a relief. His journey to the seaport, twenty miles away, meant at least another day to achieve the unlovely assignment he had given me.

On the way home, the words "wolf-fur cloak" caught my ear as I pushed past a group of men outside a hot-drink shop. They exploded in laughter. Miming donning a cloak, one of them jostled me off the sidewalk into the filthy stream that ran in the gutter. "Watch yourself, man!" I snapped.

"Beg pardon, I'm sure," he jeered. "Look, lads: a noble gent pegging along on his own two hooves!"

Jason leaped onto the sidewalk, pulling his knife. He might have skewered the fellow if I had not dragged him back toward me. "Idiot," I hissed into his ear. "When I need your help, I will tell you so."

"Something wrong?" A couple of Father's fellow Senators had witnessed the fracas. I felt obliged to explain, as the rowdy tipplers took themselves away, that it had resulted from a provocative satire.

Ah, the "Romulus and Remus"! Racing around the city like fire, they said. Did I know who had written it? The Princeps was furious about it.

"Indeed?" I said. Perhaps it was as well that he had not heard it from me.

"It ill becomes Caesar's quaestor to smile at mockery of Caesar's *dignitas*," one of them scolded. "Perhaps you are in sympathy with Gemellus?"

I sobered at once. It was too stark a reminder of the old days when a man could die for a joke.

Gemellus had written that morning asking me to return Hesperus to him. He had no wish, he said, to inflict on me a lout of a slave in whom I would discover no redeeming value. I sent back an ebony chest containing nine goblets of Judaean glass, newly bought at a price far exceeding that of an unskilled barbarian slaveboy, with a note of thanks for his generosity to me. Having taken ownership of Hesperus, I had no intention of handing him over to be murdered.

The two Senators waited for me to confirm or deny my partisanship. I said, "I am in sympathy with the Divine Augustus, who must be shaking his head with despair in the afterworld."

The first Senator huffed, "You would do better to say where you stand." The two of them swept off with their retinues.

"Where I stand? I stand on damned thin ice," I said to empty air, and Jason laughed.

Why had they reckoned I might know Phoenix's identity? Did they suspect it was Silius, my old partner in japes and pranks before he fell in with that social-climbing, money-grubbing Gaul?

I must ask Nina. My sister heard all the gossip; she would know who Phoenix was.

This thought went out of my head as soon as I came within sight of my father's house. A resplendent litter and its bearers stood outside, surrounded by attendants and guards clad in red-bordered tunics. As we approached, I heard an uproar inside: voices shrilling in demand and protest. "Run," I told Jason, who dashed ahead to pound on the door.

Julia Livilla glared as I entered. Beside her a beefy man streaked with sword scars gripped Hesperus's elbow. Holding tight to the frightened boy's other arm was Phormio, scarlet with exertion.

The contentious voices died away. I said, "Release my slave."

The gladiator glanced at Livilla, his scarred brow wrinkled in uncertainty. "Now," I barked.

Livilla nodded with an air of indifference, and the man let Hesperus go. The Thracian boy drew back toward Phormio. Finger marks burned on his arm.

Evidently Father had not yet returned from the law courts, and the house steward had been unsuccessful in handling the situation. I said coldly, "What brings you to my house, Julia Livilla?"

"For a cup of wine, I will tell you." She sneered at the servants standing around. "It seems no one here knows how to treat a noble guest properly."

I showed her to a chair in the small reception room. With a sweeter smile she said she had come to see how Gemellus's redheaded server was faring.

Why should Caligula's sister care about an unruly and unhandsome slave-boy? "Hesperus is no longer Gemellus's," I said. "He is mine."

Livilla pouted. "The gods know why, but he wants the boy back. For old times' sake, Marcus, let me take him. What would such a small kindness cost you?"

That annoyed me: the wineglasses and chest had been costly enough. I said, "I have told Gemellus I will keep him."

"What if I could persuade him to give you one of his Circassians instead?"

I smiled back. "I would not force him to separate two sisters."

"Perhaps he would give you both of them. Lovely girls—skin as white as thistledown." She slanted her eyes at me as she drank. "They bruise very easily."

She held out her cup. I twitched a finger at the young server, and he slipped forward with his ewer.

"This fellow is much prettier than that cow-faced Thracian," she said. As he bent over her to pour, she slid a hand up the inside of his thigh. The boy froze.

"Take care," I said. "My father would not want his best wine put at risk."

Livilla eyed me with lazy insolence as her fingers moved under the server's tunic. I felt myself stirring and had to shift position; Priapus has no care for a man's dignity.

She knew I was aroused. Wiping her fingers delicately on the boy's tunic, she murmured, "You were very rude to me yesterday."

"Not without reason."

The server backed away. I sent him out of the room, for she had flustered and excited him.

Livilla studied her wine. A lamp lit against the day's dimness found luster in her dark curly hair. "I know we do not think much of each other," she began, then lifted her sooty-lashed eyes to me. "But please do not tell Gemellus what I am going to say."

I said nothing. Mastering myself had not improved my temper.

"The truth is, Marcus, my head hurts terribly at times. Ever since . . . since your brother died." Her fingers sketched furrows on her brow. "I have found only one remedy." She dropped her hand to her lap. "You will laugh at me."

"Go on."

"The Thracian boy . . . He has a way of kneading my neck that helps the pain go away." Her dark-blue eyes beseeched me. "You cannot imagine the distress I will be in without him."

"Poor Livilla," I exclaimed. "You should have told me immediately."

"Then you understand?"

"Of course. You must come over whenever your head hurts, and I will tell him to rub your neck for as long as you like."

Livilla's girlish face screwed up in rage. It had been a nasty trick to play on her, but no less nasty than her blaming imaginary headaches on Publius's death. Fortunately our best drinking set was silver, not glass, so her cup did not break when she dashed it to the floor.

She flung herself out of her chair. "Very well, if you must know. I want the boy because Gemellus and I like him in bed."

Hearing the sister of the Princeps of Rome boast of intimacy with a slave struck me aghast. I stood up. "Leave my house at once."

"What pious wrath! Never fear, I will not cross this threshold again."

"And when you pass the altar where my brother died, you would do well to ask pardon from his shade."

"Ask pardon?" Livilla retorted. "After what he let them do to him? I spit on your god-cursed altar!"

The possibility of it made my own head buzz like a beehive. Had Julia Livilla, who would have borne my family's heir, really allowed a slave to put his seed in her? Was she capable of so befouling her family name and discrediting her brother's *maiestas*?

Someone told me Hesperus was in my sleeping cubicle. I flung aside the curtain and strode in to demand the truth from him.

Instead I found Phormio lying on his own pallet by my bed. "What is the matter with you?" I demanded.

"Nothing serious. A sausage last night, perhaps." His voice was subdued. "I did not expect . . . to regret the Spartan fare of Carnuntum." He gave me an unconvincing smile. "I will be fine."

I chose to believe him. "What possessed you to wrestle with that ruffian of Livilla's? You should have insisted that they wait for me."

Phormio gestured at Hesperus, who squatted against the opposite wall. "She was about to take him." He drew a shallow breath. "So different now . . . I hardly knew her."

I tipped my chin toward the boy. "Have you questioned him yet?"

"Pardon, Marcus. I will do it soon."

"I will see to it." I beckoned to Hesperus. In the doorway I turned back. "Phormio, why did you risk angering Livilla for a slave of so little value?"

"Because of . . . what you paid for him."

That puzzled me. I had only been joking about the Circassians.

"Gemellus's enmity," Phormio said. "Everyone knows."

I looked at the Thracian boy waiting to follow me, and thought I might wish Gemellus had drowned him after all.

I took him into Father's office. "Close the door," I said, and sat down with the floor lamp behind my shoulder so its light fell upon his face.

Hesperus stared at the floor. Thracians breed red hair and blue eyes, but not the delicacy most men prefer in bed boys. He was broad-browed and broad-cheeked, and would soon outgrow his youthful slimness. Phormio had shorn his long curly lovelocks, and instead of the obscenely short *chiton* worn to please tipsy diners, he now was clad from neck to knees in a coarse-woven tunic.

Cautious relief swept me. He did not look old enough to play a man's part with a woman. If Livilla had felt the touch of his young hands, no great harm was done. Even some respectable women enjoy a male slave's massage.

"I want answers from you," I said. "If I do not believe you, I will send you back to Gemellus."

"No use," he told the floor. "I die soon. No one lives if Gemellus say die."

"Gemellus has given you to me. It does not matter what he says."

He shook his head. "Gemellus is the son of Caesar. What he want, you must do, like or not."

"I am the son of a Senator of Rome," I said. "No one commands me against my will, not even Caesar himself. Do you understand?"

"Yes, master." I could tell he did not believe it.

He had been Gemellus's slave for almost a year, ever since his former owner had made a present of him for New Year's Day. He told me the name of the man, a vain old coxcomb with more money than sense.

"Why have you not learned better Latin?"

"My old master teach me Greek. I learn Latin now, master."

I picked up a horse statuette that Father used as a scroll-weight. "Tell me how you served Gemellus," I said in Greek, running my thumb along its neck.

He said in the same language, "After he came to Rome with the new Caesar, I mixed wine. I served at dinner." Lamplight gleamed in his red-gold hair. He would have been an exotic ornament for a patrician dining room.

I put down the statuette. "Did he take you to bed?"

His fair skin flushed. "He did, *kyrios*."

"Were there others with you?" I held my breath, hoping Livilla had lied.

"Sometimes." It was a mumble.

The little brute knew something he did not want to admit. "Who?"

"Slavewomen."

"And the Lady Julia Livilla? Look at me, boy!"

He took a deep breath that swelled his narrow chest, but did not raise his eyes.

I shot out of the chair and clouted him. "You touched her? You pleasured my brother's intended wife?"

He heard the fury and disgust in my voice, and his cheeks paled around the white mark of my blow. "I did not know about your b-brother, *kyrios*."

But Gemellus knew. The little serpent must have thought it a great joke to give me this accursed slave.

"Does Gemellus want to kill Caesar?" I rasped.

The question took him by surprise. His face worked. I thought he was about to weep, but what escaped was a twisted smile.

"Is that amusing? Will you laugh when I let the Praetorians question you?"

"But . . . such things are not said in bed, *kyrios.*"

"You served at his table, sheep-wit. What did you hear?"

"I do not listen, unless they speak to me."

I glared from an arm's length away. Close enough to hurt him. "Why should I believe you?"

He ought to have cringed. Instead he said, "My Latin is not enough good to understand them, *kyrios.*"

"If I thought you had lain with Caesar's sister," I said, "I would send you back to Gemellus with your balls in your mouth."

His strained face went even whiter. The mark of my slap bloomed scarlet. "I did not do the forbidden thing with her, *kyrios.*"

"Even so, I cannot let it be known that she pleased herself with you."

From his expression I guessed that he was about to promise me silence, but he stopped himself. What meaning has a slave's word?

My anger had turned from hot to cold. Because Livilla had been Publius's *sponsa,* her unspeakable behavior soiled his memory and our family's honor. Whether Hesperus remained here or was sold, sooner or later he would talk. Her depravity would become known throughout the small village that was patrician Rome, and Father's enemies would turn the scandal against us and Caligula.

Which left only one choice: to silence him.

To emulate Mithras, the great Judge of Souls, I strive always for fairness and honesty, but none of the scores of miscreants I sentenced as a tribune had posed a dilemma like this. Since the boy was a slave, whether or not he had intended to do wrong did not matter.

And that, in the end, tipped the scales: his life was worth less than the good name of our family and Livilla's. I would have it done as soon as Father's chief guard returned. Cleon had made a hundred kills in the arena; it would be easy for him to dispose of a young slave who knew too much.

I dropped back into the chair. The boy's shoulders had tensed, and the expression in his blue eyes was guarded. I said, "That will be all, Hesperus."

What fabulist had named him for the evening star: the auctioneer who sold him, or the old peacock who bought him? "What is your real name?" I asked.

"All those who knew it are gone," the boy said. "Father. Mother. Sisters."

"Tell it to me," I said.

He knew then what I intended. In Latin, as if it mattered to explain it in my own language, he answered slowly, "That one is free. This one"—he touched his chest—"is a slave. The gods do not know this one. When I die, I say my real name so the gods know me."

With dignity he added, "When Gemellus try to killing me, I say my name. But in water I think they do not hear." He stood unflinching, no taller than my shoulder, a half-grown cub who but for a mishap with a far-off tax collector might one day have become a lion.

"Look at me," I said. Slaves are not supposed to look in their masters' faces, but I would not judge boy or man without seeing his eyes.

His gaze met mine with a sort of cynical resignation, as though I had lived up to his expectations after all.

Fortuna had treated him badly, but it was not up to me to repair his luck. Yet disquiet stirred in me, a strange reluctance to condemn him to death.

"Wait here," I said abruptly, and went into the atrium. I meant to look for a sign from Mithras, but the sky was thick with cloud. On impulse I laid a hand on the fire-stained altar.

It was as if I had finally come within hearing of someone who was trying to speak to me. I heard a voice say, "Spare him."

After so long, I had persuaded myself that the warning on the Via Flaminia had been nothing but a mule's wheeze or a sigh of wind. Here in the house of my father, whose Stoic beliefs left no room for fantasy, I was unready for this shock.

"Why?" I asked aloud, to hear the voice again as much as to know the answer, but there was no reply. I looked around. Looked up. Nothing.

Hesperus kept his eyes down when I returned. Still rattled by what I had heard, I studied him. What made this illiterate Thracian goat-boy worth sparing?

In my memory Livilla snarled, *Gemellus and I like him in bed.*

I cleared my throat. "Boy," I said heavily.

He did not look up. "Boy," I said again, "swear to me, on your gods who know your true name, that you will never speak to anyone about the Lady Julia Livilla."

Hope blossomed in his face. He said at once, "I swear it, master."

"No one, ever. Or I will see you dead. Do you understand?"

"I understand, master."

"Swear it in your own language, then. And say, 'If I break this vow to my master Marcus Carinna, may my gods abandon me forever.'"

Watching him stumble through an incomprehensible declaration with both hands held up to heaven, I found no complacency or slyness in his expression. He might, of course, have been reciting the names of the goats he used to tend.

Doubt swept over me again. Had I not reminded myself that a slave's oath had no value? When he ended his barbaric jabber, I growled, "Come along, then."

He stiffened at the roughness in my voice. "As you wish, master," he said in a monotone, and opened the door for me.

"By the way," I said, looking down at him, "you are no longer Hesperus. From now on you will be called Rufus."

The name was hardly distinctive, but his eyes widened in astonishment. "Thank you, master," he said, finally understanding that he would live.

"'Red'? How original," Father said, when I told him I had renamed Hesperus. He gestured for his plate to be taken away. "And will you start calling Phormio 'Beaky'?" He was in a good mood; the trial of a client he was defending had ended in acquittal.

I had told him that Livilla was angered by my refusal to surrender Rufus, but not her scandalous revelation. He would have demanded to know why I had not immediately had the boy put to death, and I was still unsure of the reason.

"Anyway, Phormio will teach him what is expected of him," I concluded, signaling for more roast fowl. I had left Rufus with my *paedagogus*, who still felt unwell this evening. Bad food can take the iron out of a man.

Father grunted. We both fell silent over our small dinner. I would have relayed the two Senators' comments about the "Romulus and Remus" lampoon, but he would only have questioned me again about Phoenix; and recounting my dispiriting conversation with Bassus would have made him think I was complaining about the position he had obtained for me. Instead, I told him I had been to see Caligula that morning but found him gone to inspect a ship in Ostia.

Father twitched a finger in denial. When he had swallowed a bite of stewed apple, he corrected me: "He is impatient to speak with Agrippinilla about the prophecy. The Ostia story was given out to reduce the size of his retinue, but he has gone to see his sister at her husband's villa."

I felt reprieved. Traveling to and from Pyrgi would take a slow-moving imperial entourage a couple of days each way. I was contemplating how to spend five or six days of freedom when my father spoke again. "This morning Lepidus told me"—he wiped his lips with his napkin—"that you may have saved Caesar's life. Can that be true?"

"At the racing stable? I told you about that." I gnawed off a last shred of meat and tossed the bone onto the floor.

"You said you put down the horse. You did not say Caesar was in its stall when it killed a slave."

"He should not have been in there. The fault was mine." I met his eyes. "So I remedied it."

I was glad he did not ask why Caligula and I had been alone with a high-strung stallion. Perhaps the fact that we both loved racing seemed reason enough.

I wanted to confess, "I thought he had gone mad," to tell him of Caligula's dread that Gemellus had turned against him. But having promised to keep the secret, I could only ask, "If Gemellus has a rival in Agrippinilla's son, what do you think he will do?"

"Do not sell the vintage before the vines are planted," Father said. "Infants often fail to survive." He sneezed as we rose from our couches.

I said reflexively, "Gods save you," and wondered if I should ask for Gemellus's preventative for grippe.

He waved away the apotropaism. "You are well, I hope? Sosander tells me you have not had a woman since your arrival."

I had to smile. "I am well."

"Good. You must nourish the male principle in yourself, my son." He clapped my shoulder. Apparently I was in his good graces for having protected Caligula Caesar. Perhaps that, not the successful jury verdict, was even the cause of his contentment. In any case, it was the most amicable encounter we had had since my return.

Phormio was snoring on his pallet. Rufus got up from the floor, ready to be of use. I undressed for bed, once or twice slanting a glance at him.

The ropes squeaked as I cast myself onto my sleeping couch. With a deep breath I pulled the quilts up over my crossed legs. Phormio's snores went on. I stared at Rufus, whose hair gleamed like old gold in the lamplight.

After a few minutes I slid onto my feet and went to Father's office. The drone of his voice stopped when I pushed the door fully open, and he looked up.

"Father," I said, "has a ghost ever spoken to you?"

CHAPTER 11

RIVER OF BONES

"A ghost?" he repeated. He was sitting at his worktable; one hand rested on an open scroll. His private secretary perched on a stool with a writing tablet propped on his knee.

I stood in the doorway, feeling foolish. He would tell me that I knew better; there was no such thing as ghosts. Perhaps that was what I wanted to hear.

He clicked his tongue softly, as if closing a door on his previous thoughts. "None has ever spoken to me," he said, moving the little horse weight to hold down the scroll. "But I have heard one."

"Whose ghost was it?"

"No more tonight, Nicander," Father murmured. The secretary quietly gathered his materials and left.

"I have interrupted you," I said, trying to sound matter-of-fact.

"My memoirs will wait. Do you really wish to know?"

"I do."

"Sit down." He half rose, tightened the heavy wool robe over his loose sleeping tunic, and lowered himself into his chair again.

I picked up a quilt from the couch and dragged it around my shoulders. As I sank uneasily onto the stool, he said, "It was a mule."

"A *mule?*"

He shifted his gaze to the wall behind my head. When the silence stretched on, I started to explain, "The first time I heard—"

My father held up a hand. "You must deal with your own ghosts, Marcus."

After a moment I said, "How have you dealt with yours?"

He toyed with the scroll-weight, turning it around in his fingers. Finally he said, "I have been writing my recollections of the years with Germanicus."

A pang struck me. Despite my resolve, it was hard to be reminded that he had spent his young manhood campaigning with the great general, when I was doomed to an administrative job of chasing denarii.

He began to unroll the scroll toward its beginning. I saw it was marked with many strikeouts and insertions. "Of this part Germanicus said little in his own memoirs, since it would have called into question Tiberius's decision to end the German War."

I knew he must mean the aftermath of the Varian disaster, which he had never related to me. Carefully, as if the wrong question might cause him to fall mute, I asked, "What should he have said, Father?"

He found the place he wanted and began to read: "'That night we made camp two miles away. Germanicus could not sleep, and I walked with him through the encampment. He looked up at the stars, which in the northern sky are many, and said, "May they forgive us, that we have been so slow to avenge them."'"

His finger kept its place on the scroll, but he was no longer reading. "In the morning we rode out ahead of the army, and we found the pass where they died." His voice became hoarse. "Slaughtered like sheep in a pen."

I knew the numbers; what boy does not? Three legions, three squadrons of cavalry, six auxiliary cohorts: fifteen thousand men. The entire command of Quinctilius Varus, governor of Germania, all lost.

"Arminius took their Eagles, arms, and armor and left them where they fell." He coughed and sipped from his cup. "Those he captured, he mutilated and killed. The officers he burned alive."

He took a deep breath. "When I looked on their remains six years later, men and horses and mules jumbled together, I thought that to the gods on high it must resemble a river of bones."

Having survived Ingiomar's ambush, I knew what Varus had done wrong. He should have deployed trustworthy scouts. He should have held back the main body of troops and sent a vanguard through the pass.

"Varus was incompetent," I said. "As I told you, we need better generals."

"Which you are not," he snapped, roused from his memories. "You are a tribune with barely three years of garrison command."

I frowned, confused by the abrupt shift in subject.

"One day you may have the judgment and experience to be a general. You are not one now." He shook his head at me. "You had good fortune, that is all."

My cheeks warmed. "I rallied my men! The attack—"

"You condoned mutinous behavior in your troops. A commander must be harsh. Pitiless. Nothing is more important than duty. Nothing."

I would have argued that I had stopped the mutiny before it began, but he cut me off. "Be still. You asked about this, and I will finish it." He turned away, and lamplight cast the side of his face against the dark like the portrait on a gold aureus: the brow furrows, the long belligerent nose, the deep crease that curbed the muscles of his stubborn mouth.

I could not remain here in his shadow. Within a year, he would make me Caligula's eunuch.

He was silent for a long while. "We dug great burial pits, five of them," he said at last. "Our men wept as they gathered what was left, and cursed through their weeping as they fought the rooted grass for ribs and arm bones. . . . Of course an officer cannot show weakness, so I went on ahead until the sound of the work parties became faint. When I knew they could not hear me, I dismounted." His eyes fixed on a frescoed panel behind me, a window into a different place.

"The mist was dense there, which hid much of the . . . the appalling wreckage. Thinking myself alone, I shed my own tears." He coughed again. "And made vows to avenge them."

He cleared his throat. "Then, close by, I heard the clanking of a bell on a pack mule's collar. My horse laid back his ears and jibbed.

"I thought . . ." He sighed. "I am not sure what I thought. There was too much horror all around to think." His fingers closed over the scroll-weight. "I calmed the horse and led him toward where I had heard the sound."

He rubbed his thumb across the bronze figurine. "In the mist I came upon the bones of a mule. From its collar hung a bell engraved *First Cohort, Fabricius's century*. It had been silenced, stuffed full of grass so they could steal away after dark." His fist clenched on the little horse. "Of course, they did not escape."

He looked me square in the face. "So when you are making a decision that may cost men's lives, Tribune, think hard before you choose. Remember the mule's bell." He set down the scroll-weight and reached once more for his cup.

The pathos of it would have made a sphinx weep, but his account had lit a fire in me that burned too hot for tears. "Yet in the end," I said, "you did not capture Harman. Arminius."

"His own kinfolk killed him."

"And you recovered only two of the three Eagles."

He sensed my agitation, and his eyes narrowed. "Marcus, do not confuse rashness with bravery. The new campaign is necessary to defend the provinces. Caesar does not need you persuading him to take chances for glory."

"You mistake me, Father," I said. "I know the campaign is not to bring him glory, although he may think so. It is to make sure the Germans remember until the end of the fucking world why they must fear us."

My father let the scroll furl up. "How you pull against the bit!" he said. "Go to bed; you weary me."

I flung off the quilt and crossed to my own cubicle. It had begun to rain again, slashing golden in the torchlight, roiling the surface of the atrium pool.

Phormio was trimming the wick of the little night lamp. The yellow glow as he looked up stretched his face into the mask of a tragic actor, lips and brows contorted in concern.

I sat heavily on my bed. Phormio stepped over the sleeping Thracian boy, who lay rolled in a shabby blanket, and closed the curtain across the doorway. I said, "It was not just good fortune."

With his usual perception he knew at once what I meant. "What else was it, then?" He stooped to pick up his own covers and shook them out. "Courage?"

"Force of will," I said after a moment.

"You will not lay claim to courage?"

Instead of answering I leaned over and smothered the lamp flame with my bare palm. Darkness fell, and I held fast to the pain until I could sleep.

I do not remember that I dreamed, but when I awoke, the idea was fully formed in my mind. I said, "Phormio, I want my best tunic. And I will borrow Father's green mantle, the one he wore to Lepidus's dinner." I rolled out of bed. The rain had quit. "Are you better, by the way?"

Phormio sent Rufus off for hot water. "Oh, I will live." He stumped to the clothes chest. "Are you going to call on the patron?"

"Lepidus? No need." My breakfast already waited on the bedside table. I stuffed cheese into my mouth, wincing at the soreness of my burned palm.

"Then may I ask what you intend?" My high spirits often made him huffy, as though he distrusted what might follow.

"Make haste with that tunic. I am freezing." I washed down the food with watered wine. "I will bring Maelo and the priestess to talk with my father."

My old *paedagogus* turned to me. "For what purpose?"

"I will have Maelo explain Ingiomar's plan. And why the ambush failed."

Rufus poured me water, vaporous in the cold. I splashed my face and neck, and felt my jaw to see if it warranted being razored twice in two days.

"Maelo had no part in the attack," Phormio reminded me. "Else he would not have been allowed to escort the hostage here."

"Well, then he can relay what she says." It made no difference, as long as Father heard about the battle from a source that meant more to him than I did. "Or I will question her myself."

"Humph. She would not tell you if your hair was on fire. Sit down and let me shave you."

As he barbered me, my mind drifted to a trampled marshfield beside a brown river. The morning smelled of men's blood and shit, of choked campfires and battered grass. Churned mud sucked at my feet. A centurion's stick cracked on the backs of exhausted men rebuilding the palisades. Voices shouted for stretchers. A young clerk retched as he counted casualties. Every detail was crisp, heightened by the passion of battle, survival, victory.

I saw her first as a body bundled in a stained cloak, slung over a soldier's shoulder. The centurion stopped him and his comrade. "What's that?"

"A girl," the soldier said loudly, so I would overhear. "We thought the tribune might like to, ah, interrogate her, since he knows the lingo."

They set her on her feet and unwrapped her. Her long braid of copper-colored hair was tied up so as not to hinder her in battle, and her bare arms and pale slack face were smeared with dirt and blood bleached pink by the rain.

The soldiers saw my interest and grinned, teeth as bright as bone in their muddy faces. After so long, they had finally found a bribe I would accept.

I grinned too, remembering. Aurima of the Marcomanni and her bushy-bearded uncle would certainly sway my father.

"Hold still," Phormio grumbled. "You know this is unnecessary, Marcus."

At first I thought he was referring to the shave, which, having straw-colored hair, I did not need every day. Only when leaving the house did I realize he might have meant my determination to earn my father's respect. But that made no sense to me, and so I did not heed it.

CHAPTER 12

INGIOMAR'S DAUGHTER

Three of the Marcomanni heaved themselves to their feet in the atrium of the guesthouse. Dice lay tumbled on the floor between them, atop a fine cloth mottled with footprints and water stains. The household shrine held a bust of Caligula beaming regally upon the fly-infested head of a calf.

The three warriors scowled as I climbed the vestibule steps. I had grown used to their long hair and magpie's-nest beards during the journey south, but here in a proper house they looked as obscene as rats in a granary. Their rank odor, beery and bloody, coiled around me. Even a blind man would have known them for barbarians.

They stood so close to the top of the steps that I could not take the last stride without being jostled. "Greetings, Maelo," I said. "Cotto. Segomo." Although I loathed and distrusted the lot of them, I was determined to be polite.

Aurima's uncle eyed my fine mantle of sea-green wool bordered with silver embroidery. He had never before seen me dressed as a man of wealthy family. "Tribune? Why are you here?"

"I wish to be sure your sister's daughter is being well treated," I said. "And then I would speak with you both."

Maelo pondered, stroking his roan mustache with thumb and forefinger. Segomo muttered and shook his head. Cotto offered something lugubrious in Germanic. The flies buzzed.

"Well, where is she?" I tried to hide my impatience. A hostile confrontation now would spoil the honeyed approach I had meant to use.

Maelo barked something peremptory at his son, who stood by the door trading glares with Jason. The command, according to my rudimentary understanding of Germanic, was "Fetch it," which made no sense. He would have hardly have ordered his niece to be fetched like a cloak.

Skirts flurried at the edge of my vision, but it was Aurima's elderly maid-servant disappearing into the back of the house, not the priestess herself. I was turning back to Maelo when a man came into the atrium through another doorway. Or rather, a eunuch—presumably the "it" the boy had been told to fetch.

"By Euterpe's flute!" the creature said, dabbing a napkin to his lips. His face was as round as a loaf of bread, and two men of normal size could have fit inside his gilt-crusted blue tunic. As he waddled toward me, he touched two fingers to his golden curls—a gesture that might have seemed a salute, had he not clearly feared that the Marcomanni would snatch the wig off his head.

They watched, grinning, to see how I would deal with him. "I am Caesar's quaestor, and wish to see Aurima," I said, allowing my irritation to show.

My soon-to-be-official title produced the expected flinch of respect, but then something else: Relief? Unease? The eunuch said, "I am the house steward, your honor: Paris of Apollonia."

The name was familiar. Could this great creature possibly be the famous erotic dancer of Augustus's day? "As passionate as Paris"—I had used the phrase myself, with only a vague idea of its origin.

How Fortuna delights in raising us, only to cast us down! Despite the many gifts he must have received from admirers, the onetime idol of bawdy dinner parties now served in a guesthouse to earn his pension from the State.

Avoiding my eyes, he said, "I fear she will not talk to you, your honor."

"I am sure she will. Bring her to me."

Still he hesitated. I glanced from him to the Marcomanni. They were murmuring to one another, their derision turned to discomfort. "Is she ill?" I demanded, but did not wait for an answer.

The passage into which the maid had disappeared led to a pleasant garden—or the remains of one. It was now a desolation of hacked-off stumps and muddy flower beds. At one end, a fountain splashed water into a half-moon basin where a woman was scrubbing clothes. Charred debris from a drenched campfire blackened one of the paths. More flies hovered around an open pit.

The gray-haired maid squatted by a small bay tree, the only vegetation left standing. A long body lay in a puddle of rainwater at its base, half hidden by a drift of sodden leaves. Unbound hair flowed like dark wine across an enshrouding bearskin. No tremor of breath stirred the mounded leaves, from which one hide-wrapped foot forlornly protruded.

She was dead.

My heart lurched. What would happen on the frontier when her father learned she had died in Rome?

The little maid saw me standing in the shade of the portico. Glaring, she rose with fists clenched.

"Aurima waits for the Goddess to take her," Maelo growled behind me.

By Mithras's Dog, was she still alive? I slogged through the wet leaves to her side. The maid backed warily away with a hand on her slave collar.

Aurima's eyes were as flat and lifeless as a stagnant pond. Bits of twig and leaf had caught in her matted hair, and grime was gray around her ear. A fly lit on one unplucked eyebrow and crawled down the freckled mosaic of her cheek.

I crouched, heedless of my mantle trailing in the rotten leaves, and touched my fingertips to her throat. A pulse beat there, faint and fast.

She looked at me. For an instant she was the fiery girl of the battlefield; but the ember died as quickly as it had flared to life. Her eyes dulled, unseeing.

I heard the eunuch's fluting voice: "She will not eat, your honor. . . . Sleeps under the tree, like an animal . . . These brutes will not allow—"

"Be still," I snapped. The bearskin was slick with rain. She must have lain here all night in the downpour. In Germanic I said, "Stand up."

Aurima lay still, her gaze unblinking. Her parched lips did not move.

I gripped the icy hand curled against her breast and hauled her to her feet. The bearskin slithered off. Her tunic, muddy and wet, was the same she had worn when I brought her to the Villa Publica eight days earlier. The amber pendant swung from her neck.

She would not stand, or could not. I let her slide down onto her rump and crouched in front of her folded legs, steadying her shoulders with my hands. She stared emptily at me. Hunger had hollowed her cheeks.

Too softly for the others to hear, I said in Latin, "Do not give up."

Her exhalation felt like a feather on my cheek. She turned her head away.

I locked her chin between my thumbs, forcing her to look at me. She closed her eyes. "You have people here," I said. "You live in a fine house, and may come and go in the greatest city in the world. Soon you will marry a king or a prince. Who would not envy you?"

No response.

"Then I see Rome has nothing to fear from the Marcomanni, whose women are so weak." Exasperation edged my voice.

Her gilded eyelashes twitched. Color began to stain her face.

"When I want something, I fight until I get it." I put my head next to hers and whispered, "I do not surrender."

Her eyes opened. They were like birch leaves in the wind, sometimes green, sometimes flaring silver. "Go away."

"Leave you to lie in this flea-ridden fur until you go to your gods? Is that how your father's daughter should die?"

I thought the fire within her had caught at last. But as she looked at the pillars on every side, her shoulders sagged. "No gods here . . ."

One of the warriors muttered, "She must do what wishes the Goddess."

Goddess be damned. I scooped her into my arms and stood up.

A commotion erupted behind me. Maelo snapped a few peremptory words that quelled it.

I willed Aurima to open her eyes, to squirm and shout to be released. But she lay limp against me, long wet ribbons of her hair cascading over the folds of my green mantle. Her downy lashes lay still on cheeks smudged with tears and dirt, her cracked lips parted as if she had given up the effort of keeping them closed.

Taking a deep breath—for all her fasting, she weighed as much as a man—I carried her to the fountain basin and dropped her in.

Her shriek rang over the others' cries of shock and fury as water exploded up around her. And then water was the only sound, slopping back and forth in the shallow pool, spilling over the curbing into puddles on the walkway.

She struggled to sit up, and leaning against the curb wiped in a daze at hair streaming down her face. The maid rushed to her side. I discovered then why her furious countrymen had not immediately assaulted me: young Jason was fending them off with his knife.

Instead of joining them to avenge the indignity to his niece, Maelo shouted a command that made them fall back. They scowled murderously as I addressed them in simple Latin: "This girl is no longer the daughter of Ingiomar

Ironhand. Here in Rome she is the daughter of Caesar. Hear me now! I speak for Caesar." I put contempt in my voice. "How can the proud Marcomanni allow their priestess to die in the dirt—a maiden whom Caesar would make the wife of a king? Are you not ashamed?"

Maelo stared at me, his expression hidden by his unkempt beard. Perhaps waiting to see if I succeeded in saving her where he had failed. Or inspecting me for the best spot to sink his own knife.

His impulsive young son started to speak, but I overrode him: "If Aurima dies, it will be sacrilege, a crime against the gods of Rome. And by the gods of Rome, I swear that if she dies, so will you all, in darkness and dishonor."

I turned to the eunuch, who was enjoying the discomfiture of his barbarous guests. "You, Paris, make sure the priestess has whatever she cares to eat and drink, even if you must scour the seven hills to find it. I want her clothed according to her station as Caesar's ward. Have a bed made ready for her wherever she wishes. And by Mithras's Dog, see that these savages learn how to live in a proper house! Do you understand?"

"But I—" the eunuch began. Then his face smoothed, and he went on, "Of course, your honor."

I turned at last to Aurima, hunched shivering on the fountain rim in a spreading puddle of water. Her slave had hurried away to retrieve the bearskin.

She looked up hastily as I loomed over her. Her nose was running, her eyelashes stuck together in starbursts, her sodden hair poured over her skull and shoulders like molten copper, and the ruinous tunic clung to her like a cast shadow. A streamer of pondweed had garlanded itself around the mound of one tender breast, the nipple taut with cold, as visible as if she were naked.

I bundled my woolen mantle around her and crouched at her level. I did not wish to humble her any further in front of her people. Softly I said, "You must eat and wash yourself, and sleep beneath a roof."

Aurima's lips twisted. "You cannot make me eat."

"I want you to live."

"Not here. Never."

"If you eat," I said, "I will take you out of the city one day."

It was a promise I had no right to make. As I had told her, hostages are supposed to stay within Rome's religious boundaries. My own recklessness startled me—and, I cannot deny, sparked a thrill I ought to have suppressed.

Aurima shut her eyes. "When?" she whispered without looking at me.

"When you are well again."

"Tomorrow."

"You will not be strong enough."

"So I eat," she said, and fixed on me eyes that had become purest green.

I felt lightheaded, and had to steady myself with a hand on the fountain curb. "We will go when you have regained your strength. No sooner."

She put out an imperious hand. I took it in both of mine and raised her to her feet. Clasping the sea-green mantle around her, she swayed away from me until she could lean on her slavewoman. "The Goddess wills me not to die here," she said to the others, speaking Latin for my benefit. "Bring food and drink."

Perhaps that was the moment when the seed her green gaze had sowed took root in me. A dry heat suffused my face and eyes as though I were fevered, and her voice floated in my ears.

The front door was unattended. I let myself out and nearly shut it on Jason, whom I had forgotten.

Before we had gone ten paces, he burst out, "Held off all those wild men, didn't I? You wouldn't be fit for sausage if I hadn't."

"Well done," I agreed.

"Why did you leave the master's mantle? His best one, Turtle told me."

I shook my head and kept walking. After a moment he said, "Curse it all, here," and took off his own cloak. I put it around myself, unaware of the cold.

Bewitched. I was bewitched.

Why else would I have promised to break one of the most ancient of laws for her? If I was caught, my appointment as Caesar's quaestor would go up in smoke. As for my family name, I dared not imagine how that would be blackened.

Yet I longed to restore the fire to her eyes and the pride to her bearing. Longed to tumble that girl, sacred hostage or not. But as a soldier of Mithras, I could not commit that crime.

"Jason," I said. When he shambled up beside me, I ordered, "Tell Cook to prepare a stew for Aurima, with plenty of meat. Then see with your own eyes that she receives it."

"I will take it to her? By myself?"

I frowned at his astonishment. "Be polite to the Marcomanni. Do not scratch yourself, and do not allow that fat eunuch to get his paws on the food."

Jason squared his shoulders. "You can depend on me, young master."

The term jarred on me again. "In private I am 'Marcus' to you."

"Can I say you will throw her into the fountain if she does not eat?"

"Imbecile, she is a priestess! You will treat her with respect."

His face colored. I ought not to have assumed that his indifferent up-bringing had taught him manners. "Tell her the food is a gesture of esteem, signifying Caesar's care for her well-being."

He mumbled the phrases to himself all the way home. While I, spell-bound, thought only of a green-eyed girl for whose sake I was willing to disgrace myself.

Phormio roused himself from a nap to ask what had happened with Aurima and what had become of my father's expensive mantle. I was describing the encounter to him when a dinner invitation arrived for me, too last-minute to be much of a compliment but still a chance to impress influential men.

"Tell me again what you have promised this girl," Phormio said, writing my acceptance at the foot of the invitation. He handed back the tablet to be returned to its sender.

"Do you think I should let her die, and ruin the truce her father made?"

I might have known that would not be the end of it. While I readied myself to dine, my old *paedagogus* gave me his counsel: "This is a great opportunity, the appointment Caesar has offered you." He signaled Rufus to hand me a frayed twig dipped in salt. "If you take the girl out of Rome, no matter if all six Vestal Virgins escort you . . ." He shook his head. "Too many people know your reputation."

I scrubbed my teeth. Memories flooded me of Aurima's breast against my arm, her long bare legs, the curves of belly and thigh limned by her wet tunic.

Phormio tried again: "Your father's enemies will seek to discredit you."

I rinsed out my mouth and spat. "I gave her my word."

"Perhaps, Marcus, you gave her Caesar's word? Could Caesar not find someone else to grant her wish?"

He was right, of course. I was a young man of promise, soon to be promised to a yet unknown female of equally illustrious birth, and must not risk my future with a hostage under the Princeps' protection. I should make some official at the Palace aware of her need to escape the city.

"Better for her, too. After all, you embarrassed her greatly."

"You need not belabor it," I grumbled.

"I suppose we must buy you a bed girl," he began, but stopped at the sound of a voice in the vestibule.

Jason was clearly pleased with himself. "Here is your mantle, Marcus," he said. "I made the priestess get up from her bed, and I gave her the stew and said what you told me."

So Aurima had been in a bed; that was an improvement. Phormio hung Father's mantle on a peg. "What did she say?" I prompted.

"She asked when she can leave the city."

"I hope you told her she must be patient." I rubbed scented oil over my jaw with both hands and reached for a towel to blot the excess.

Jason looked less happy. "She said it must be tomorrow."

Phormio's hand with the clothes brush stopped in midair. I said, "Absolutely not. She will not have recovered her strength."

Jason's face wrinkled in apprehension. "She said she never knew a Roman to keep his word. And her curse will be upon you if you do not keep yours."

I threw down the towel. "Fetch my cloak. I will settle this now."

"I apologize for my clerk," said Homilos. "He should have known of your new appointment, Quaestor." He burped a discreet zephyr of spiced wine.

The Princeps' secretary for alliances and embassies was a neat-featured freedman with a gossamer beard framing rosy lips. Extricated from a banquet, he looked more annoyed than apologetic, but he was astute enough to direct his scowl at his swarthy clerk instead of at me. "To have inconvenienced the son of Senator Carinna"—he had evidently forgotten my own name—"when you could have assisted him yourself. You donkey!"

The clerk obligingly hung his head. I said, "This must be seen to at once. The girl is not in good health."

Homilos became aware of an errant flower petal on his sleeve and flicked it off. "Something can no doubt be arranged in ten days or so." The clerk coughed. "Though it may take rather longer because of the

Plebeian Games. Let us say in early December, to be safe. Assuming Caesar, as Pontifex Maximus, will allow it. Hmm, Syrus, would the Senate also have to approve?"

"It must be sooner," I told him. "In two or three days; no more."

"Out of the question, I fear. Such an excursion is no easy matter to organize." His cheeks bulged with a suppressed yawn. "In truth, one would try for December only as a favor to yourself and your esteemed father."

How long did it take a stubborn girl to starve herself? I said, "By then she may be dead."

"I beg to doubt it." He gave me a superior smile. "These barbarians exaggerate everything. Quite like children, you know."

A bribe might have worked, but I would have had to beg the money from my father. Instead, I was politely urged to submit my request to the Princeps when he returned to Rome.

The doorkeeper bowed me out into the street. It seemed everyone on the Palatine Hill was at dinner, as I should have been. Melodies and laughter chimed from the interiors of nearby houses, and torchlight flickered on litter bearers waiting outside for their owners.

I had no desire to continue on to my host's dinner party. I sent my litter home and walked away from the houses, down a lane bordered on one side by the back of the Temple of Victory and on the other by a crumbling wall. Jason followed me on the grassy track, silent but for an occasional foot-scuff on a stone. In the unseen distance, the swollen Tiber rustled like rain.

Just past a rough stone well, the lane ended in a scrubby pasture that fell away toward the rooftops along the Clivus Victoriae. I bent down for some rocks and flung them hard, one after another, into the darkness of the slope.

In the morning I would send Jason to her with a message saying she could not leave the city for a month. Another promise broken by another perfidious Roman, just as she had expected. She could hardly despair over that.

But perhaps she would. Perhaps the crushing of hope would sharpen the edge of her misery, so that death would seem a pleasure. There were faster ways to take one's life than to refuse food.

I dropped another stone through the rust-swollen grating of the well. It belched back a juicy and sonorous *plunk.*

A change in weather had blown away the clouds and smoke. The moon had set, and the sky over the Janiculum Hill was laden with stars.

. . . The stars, which in the northern sky are many . . .

I sat down on the well's edge. "You will not let her curse you, Marcus?" asked Jason, hunkered on his haunches.

"She has cursed me already," I said.

The guides had vanished. "Captured," said one of the junior tribunes. "Bellona be my witness, we'll find them flayed and hung in an oak tree as an offering to Wodun."

We were standing on the earthen rampart, looking over the palisade at the forest that loomed beyond our encampment. Smoke from cooking fires hung in the still afternoon. Horses and mules champed the beaten grass, tails switching, and mosquito-plagued men slapped at themselves. Their oaths and the clatter of mess tins roused in me the mingled pride and anxiety of a commander who had never before led troops into a war zone.

The missing guides, loyal tribesmen provided by the Marcomanni king, failed to trot out of the trees. "More likely they deserted," I said.

The head scout nodded. "Scared by that witch-girl's curse."

No one scoffed at this. Discipline and duty are no shield against the threat of a cold hearth, cold loins, and a cold death.

On a paved road, we would have reached the king's stronghold in two more days. On the Amber Road with its wheel ruts and boggy sloughs, it would take five or six, all within the borders of Ingiomar Ironhand's lands.

The rebel leader did not wait long. At first light two days later, he struck.

Thirty-seven legionaries and auxiliaries dead or dying, sixty-seven badly disabled. Ingiomar's priestess daughter, to whom this toll was owed, fell stunned by a blow from a javelin butt. The only woman taken alive, she would have met a brutal death had the two soldiers who seized her not decided to make a gift of her to their tribune.

And I, who had called her my enemy, realized I could not abandon her.

CHAPTER 13

CROSSROADS

The women might have been carved in a frieze, their clothing bright against the ocher procession of the peristyle's far columns. Nina sat on a bench with her back to me, wrapped in a saffron-colored *palla*. Hearing my footsteps, she twisted around, bracing herself on her arm.

Behind her, as straight as a caryatid in an Athenian temple porch, stood Aurima. She faced me with great composure, hands clasped at her waist. Her coppery hair waved back from her fair brow into its braid. Over her shoulders cascaded her long blue cloak, the hood thrown back. Beneath it I glimpsed a red overtunic that fell to her shins, and the skirt of an unbleached tunic that touched the lacings of her leather boots.

Her face seemed to lose what color the cold had given it. I was aware of her slavewoman, Nina's attendants, and Jason nearby, but I had become part of the frieze, transfixed by the sight of her.

Nina broke the spell. "Pray explain, Marcus, what you intend to do."

I began to breathe again, displeased with myself. Had I not prayed to Mithras that morning for help in withstanding this fascination? I kissed my sister's cold cheek. "Has she been here long?"

"I am well, thank you. Think nothing of the inconvenience; I am glad to make my husband's house available to my brother for his assignations."

She spoke with a low clipped rage, her dark eyes afire. I said, "It is not what you think."

"Indeed? Then why did you have Jason bring her here?"

I slid onto the bench and put my finger to her lips. "Hush, Nina. She is a wild creature trapped in a city. I promised her a forest."

"Are you mad? This is your hostage, is she not—that awful Ironfist's daughter?"

"I swear by Mithras my intentions are pure."

"You must think I was born in a cabbage patch," she retorted, but with less heat. "What happened to your hand?"

I had bound a rag around it; lifting Aurima the day before had chafed my scorched palm. "Nothing important," I said. I looked at her for a moment longer, wondering if it was pregnancy or the discovery of its absence that made her so irritable; but it was her choice whether or not to tell me.

I rose and turned to Aurima. "The journey will be long and cold. Do you still wish to come?"

She nodded slowly. "What did he say?" the gray-haired slavewoman cried in Germanic.

Aurima lifted her head higher, conscious of my scrutiny. Though her skin stretched tight across the bone, it had been scrubbed clean. The sun glinted in the plait of her hair, and glowed in the amber pendant on her breast. But her eyes were guarded: today I was again the Roman officer she loathed.

Well, that would make my vow of discipline easier to keep. "What will happen today is not to be spoken of," I said. "It must be thought you remained here with my sister. Do you understand?"

Disbelief came into her face, transforming to contempt. "Do not tell me what must be thought. I am a priestess of Ostera," or so I thought the name to be. In Germanic she added another phrase whose meaning I guessed: her fisted left hand, palm down, sprang open with fingers splayed. She had cast her fortune.

Wonderful. Perhaps she had learned that she would make the trip without falling out of the chariot. "Come with me," I said. "Your woman must stay here."

The slave understood this without need of translation. She fell to her knees and seized Aurima's skirts, shrieking, "Take me with you."

Aurima slapped her. The woman collapsed in sobs at her feet.

Nina smiled brightly at me. "Gods bless your journey," she said.

Harnessing the second mare to the yoke, the hostler at the Winged Feet livery swore as the other one nipped him. "These two ain't the pair I'd take for an outing with a lady. Especially not with this light chariot."

The lady in question stood hooded in her cloak, looking at nothing. Since she had refused to enter a hired litter and I could not make her walk all the way to this stable at the Capena gate, I had been forced to let her ride behind me. Not astride, of course; I would have danced on the Senate floor in a bridal veil sooner than let a woman hold my stallion between her legs.

While Jason yanked tight the laces of my wide driver's belt, I checked my knife in its sheath. A man is mad to set foot in a chariot without the means to cut himself free.

Aurima glanced at me. At the knife. Why was I so sure she no longer wanted to murder Romans?

I flipped a coin to Jason, and another to the hostler who handed me the whip. "Enjoy yourself, sir," the man said with a sly grin. I nodded, as one does, but whatever was being contemplated in that coppery head certainly did not include erotic dalliance.

My heart lifted as the team trotted onto the Via Appia. Sunlight burnished the paving stones and laid crisp shadows beside tombs lining the road. Blue sky dazzled clean and clear as far as the crouching hills to east and south, sowing strips of itself in ditches choked with rainwater. The cold breeze that had swept away the clouds and smoke bounced the limbs of pine trees and streamed the mares' tails. I could not have asked for a handsomer day to commit sacrilege.

Aurima crouched beside me on a little shelf of a seat, clinging with one white-knuckled hand to the craven's bar in front of me. I bent down and shouted into her ear, "Lean against my leg and put your arm around my waist."

She looked away, and I laughed. This northern frost-maiden was unlikely to ever lay a willing hand on me.

The mares' manes rippled as they surged against the harness, ears cocked for a signal to gallop. But the roadside turf was ridged with frozen ruts, and I would not risk their unshod hooves on the pavement at any gait faster than a trot. The miles rattled by, other traffic edging aside, while I tried to reclaim skills seldom used on the frontier.

At a crossroads where there was a basin fed by a spring, an urchin ran out from a shrine to Hecate, offering to hold the horses while they drank. I clambered stiff-kneed out of the chariot. Turning away to give Aurima privacy for her needs, I pulled off the leather helmet and stretched my shoulders. I was joking with the boy who clutched the reins when she said behind me, "What is this place?"

"It is sacred to the goddess of crossroads," I explained. "She and her dogs and wolves are said to prowl the night with spirits from the underworld."

I meant to tease her, but her face paled. More gently I said, "Our journey is half done." I nodded toward the graveled road we would take through the honey-colored fields into the hills. "Can you endure it? Or shall we give up?"

Aurima tightened her lips: answer enough. Another woman might have complained of the cold, of aches from the jolting, but I doubted that Ingiomar's daughter would ever admit frailty to a Roman who had called her weak-willed.

While I talked, a heap of rags beside the shrine had lurched upright. "Lady Hecate's blessing on your travel, sir," it panted, limping toward us on a crutch.

Sparse white hair flew about a March-apple face, all spots and wrinkles. I tossed the sexless old creature a copper for good fortune, and was digging for another to give the urchin when I heard Aurima say, "For the goddess."

Cupidity gleamed in the beggar's eyes, as black and shiny as apple seeds. I bent open his knobbly claw. She had handed him the golden drop of amber on its cord.

What ailed the girl, giving a beggar a gem worth more than a good cloak? As I snatched it, the old wretch squawked, "She's offering it to the Lady. For luck on the journey."

Aurima glared at me. "Give back my fire-stone."

"This creature will trade it for a bellyful of wine."

"Obey me!" She pointed toward the shrine. "Put it there. On the top."

I had let her have her way about the litter, not wanting to cause a scene that would attract unwanted attention, but this was too much. Girls in civilized societies do not give orders to men.

Reading my thoughts, she said more temperately, "In the name of the Goddess I ask it."

"Is it for his goddess or yours?" I asked. It is not wise to leave offerings for unnamed deities.

"Mine. My goddess, Austro."

I tried to repeat it, but "Ostera" was the closest my tongue could manage. "Is she the goddess of killing Romans?"

"She is the goddess of light," Aurima said.

It was as if the moon had spun around in the sky to show its other side, the one we cannot see. I could not imagine Mithras, who is wholly a man's god, having a female counterpart.

"Put it there," she repeated, pointing to the top of the shrine.

It was as tall as a man, a squat obelisk of lichened stone with a crude figure of a dog carved on the side facing the highway. Unnerved, I made the Sun sign for protection.

Aurima watched me reach up behind the obelisk to place her offering on the small shelf that rimmed its shoulder. "Now," she said, "I ask the Goddess to guard it." She lifted her right hand high. As her face tipped toward the heavens, her hood fell back and her hair turned to flame in the sunlight.

I felt the breath leave me. So must she have looked when she cursed those who aided Rome. O God, why did it stir my desire and not my anger?

The old beggar began to back away. Without opening her eyes Aurima let her arm sink down, wrist arched, until her forefinger pointed directly at him.

She spoke the curse in her own language, where she had power. The few phrases I grasped sparked in me an impious twinge of lust and awe: "Night for ever . . . Fires be cold . . ."

Shrieking a charm to turn away her magic, the old man scuttled off on his stick. When he screwed up his courage later to investigate, perhaps he would suppose it was Hecate who had transformed the amber into a silver denarius.

I was not sure why I had slipped the pendant beneath the bandage on my hand. It seemed strange to me that Aurima wished to abandon her talisman. I told myself it was too valuable to leave behind, but most likely I wanted it just because it was hers.

When she insisted on continuing, I said I would lash her into the chariot. Otherwise, if she lost her grip, I might not be able to catch her before she fell.

"Do not tie me," she said.

"We have some distance yet to go."

"Then go faster."

"Very well," I said, and wheeled the horses onto the graveled road. A shout to the team, a flick of the whip, and they lunged forward, kicking up stones and pebbles that rattled on the front of the chariot like a volley of sling bullets.

I coaxed the pair into rhythm together and urged them on even faster. They broke into a gallop, all madness and joy as horses are when set free to run. I forgot everything: Father, Caligula, Gemellus, gods, and laws. By Mithras's Dog, how I had missed this!

The road skirted a clump of skeletal poplars, then ran between stubbled fields with ditches on each side reflecting blue in their depths. Two men chopping up a fallen tree paused to stare. The chariot lifted over a culvert and slammed to earth again, and I would have lost my footing if I had not grabbed the craven's bar. My fingers clenched hard over Aurima's, so tightly it must have hurt her; then I found my balance again and sang out to the horses.

Far off on a hill, orchards and gardens spread down from an elegant villa. A plume of smoke rose from a brush fire. Beside a cottage, a woman stopped digging in a vegetable patch to watch. Her dog put chase to us, barking. Pheasants flushed from the roadside scrub took flight with a clatter.

I was grinning like a fool, the horses flowing out of my fingers, taking in everything at once. I saw pebbles on the track and a hawk in the sky, a scar on the brown mare's rump and a streamer of Aurima's coppery hair flying in the wind. Braced hard against the craven's bar, I felt her hand pressed like a fiery knot into my belly, and that was pleasure, too.

Once past the turning for the villa, the road dwindled to two tracks in the matted grass and curved up a slope clad in scarlet grapevines. I slowed the team. Snorting and chewing on their foamy bits, they trudged up past the hip-high rows of twisted vines. The fields of Latium slid away beneath us, the great south road marked in the distance by its dark border of trees.

When we were nearly to the hilltop, I said to Aurima, "Stand up, priestess."

She tried to rise but could not. I switched the whip to my left hand so I could lift her to her feet. Her hands flew out to clutch my cloak, then the rail; the loose strand of her hair blew against my cheek.

I prayed, *O Mithras, do not let me weaken*, even as I tightened my embrace to keep her from falling. But by then the horses were trotting over the brow of the hill, and below us lay what I had brought her such a long way to find.

TEMPLE OF APOLLO

The temple stood on an outcrop below the hill crest, overlooking a grove of pine trees that lapped at its foot. Built round with a conical roof where doves nested among the tiles, it had been there for so long that no one remembered who had dedicated it, or when. Few visited it, for it was neither convenient nor grand in the Hellenic style.

"The Temple of Apollo Latiaris," I said. "The grove is sacred to Apollo's twin, Diana the Huntress." I had remembered the trees covering a vast expanse. Now, educated by the endless forests of the Mark, I saw they formed little more than a small wood.

Aurima gazed at the grove. A tremor ran through her, and she slumped onto the chariot's tiny seat.

I leaned down, thinking she had fainted. She lifted to my face eyes that were purest silver.

When I could speak, I said, "We cannot stay long. Two hours, no more." Still she looked at me and I at her, and I felt she was seeing into me as I had seen into her in the courtyard of the Spartan Baths. When I made myself turn away and start up the team again, it seemed my bringing her to Diana's grove had been at her command all along.

As the horses stepped into the woods, their hooves sank into piney duff. Sunlight broke into shafts slicing between tall trees, then shrank to new-minted coins glinting on wet moss, then vanished. I halted the team to let my eyes adjust.

"I want to be with the Goddess," Aurima said.

"If you promise not to hide from me."

She smiled bitterly. "Where can I go?"

I told her I would return after watering the horses. When she stepped down from the chariot, I tugged the hilt of her little curved knife out of her belt. She snatched at it, but I had already moved away, tucking the blade into my wrist cuff. I would not take the chance of her attacking me when I came back.

Instead of protesting she looked off into the woods, stony-faced. I studied her in vague unease. But she was no longer armed; what need had I to worry?

While the horses drank from the spring beside the temple, I unlaced the broad belt and crouched to wash myself. As I was drying my face with my cloak, a voice said, "May Apollo smile upon you, traveler."

The little priest who tended the temple shuffled down the steps toward me. Bald and bearded, gnarly as a mandrake root, he remembered me at once: "Carinna the Younger! So Apollo has drawn you back again." With a toothless leer he added, "Or is it Eros you worship today?"

So he had seen us arrive. "Not today, alas," I said. "Have you any food to spare?" The drive had given me a gnawing hunger.

"I do, and will gladly share it. But first I must remind you that you may not go armed into Diana's wood."

He struggled up the steps again, and I followed. It was colder inside the temple, despite an opening at the peak through which peered the blue eye of heaven. Doves fluttered in and out, littering the floor with their droppings.

But the worn stone altar was unsullied, as was the tall statue of Apollo beyond it. After so many years his paint was faded, and in places worn down to the milk-white marble. Yet the god still stood on his plinth as he stood in my memory, naked with bow in one hand and quiver slung over his shoulder, his head lifted to gaze into the distance.

This was how I imagined Mithras: this Far-Shooter with his implacable stare. So much had he seen: the Carthaginians, perhaps, tramping across the fields of Latium. Roman slaughtering Roman in bloody civil war. And the young man who would become Augustus, marching on Rome to avenge the Divine Julius's murder and secure his power against the Senate.

I laid both knives on Apollo's altar and put my hands together in the shape of Mithras's flame. "O Lord of Light, Slayer of the Bull, hear your soldier Marcus Carinna. You who know all my faults, grant me the discipline to overcome my bodily desires. Help me remember my duty to defend Rome's law and those who are under its protection. In such a way will I bring you honor, O Mithras."

A useless prayer, perhaps. A man prey to carnal lust cannot expect much help from a god born of rock.

The priest's sandals slapped behind me. Laden with a half-moon of dark bread and a jug stoppered with a cheese wedge, he said, "Your noble father, Senator Carinna: is he well?"

I gave a nod. He placed the food in a niche by the door, where the bust of a benefactor might once have stood. "And your brother . . ." His faded eyes lifted to Apollo. "I pray he is at peace in the Sun."

"I hope it is so," I said.

The little priest nodded. "He told me you would find a god one day."

"He came here?"

He scratched his beard. "A young man not as tall as you, with dark curly hair? And"—he gestured toward his own forehead—"an arch to his eyebrows, as though he had just heard a clever joke?"

"When did you see him?"

A dove fluttered down onto the priest's shoulder and peered at the food with shiny-eyed greed. He stroked its head. "Let me see. The amphitheater had just burned in Tusculum, for he told me Caesar would be paying to re-build it."

Lightning had struck Tusculum's old wooden amphitheater only a few days before Publius's death. "Why did he come here?" I said. "How long did he stay? What else did he tell you?"

Flustered, he kneaded his lips. A second dove sailed down to perch on his other shoulder.

"I— I cannot be sure now," he stammered at last. "But perhaps he stayed the night in the temple. It was summer then, not an odd request." He waved away a bird that had landed on his head, and it glided down to join the others flocking on the pavement between us. "A matter on which he needed Apollo's guidance, he said . . ."

"What matter?"

He shook his head. "Great men do not confide in me. I am not a *pontifex* or a *flamen*, just an old schoolmaster who tries to care for Apollo's altar."

I grimaced in frustration. He reached for a broom propped against the statue's plinth and began to sweep pine needles that had blown in around the altar. After a few strokes he stopped. "Your father can tell you more, surely."

"My father?"

"Did I not say? They were here together, your father and your brother. My slave looked after their horses, for they brought no one with them."

Father had never told me about coming here with Publius. They would have been gone from home for most of two days and a night. How could I not have known it?

Obviously, I had not been at home myself. Carousing with someone, sleeping with someone, idling with someone at the baths. "You spoke with them; there must be more you can recall," I persisted.

"They walked in Diana's wood. At times they talked." The old priest lifted a bony shoulder in a shrug. "Only once did I speak with your brother. Night was just descending, I remember. He asked me if there were more stars in the sky than there had been in my youth. Of course there are, I said, since many people have perished since I was a boy."

His eyes softened. "He told me it must be consoling to believe souls are eternal. And I remember now, he spoke of courage."

A piercing sorrow swelled in my throat. So he had known even then what awaited him.

"Perhaps this will please you: his very words were *I wish I were as brave as my brother.*"

I groaned aloud. The startled doves exploded up and streamed like smoke through the roof opening.

The old priest resumed his sweeping. Recalling why I was here, I strove to swallow my grief. "When they departed, was he . . . Did he seem . . ."

The priest shook his head. "My slave told me they left at dawn, but I did not see them myself." He claimed to know no more, and there was no one else to ask, for the slave had since died.

Not daring to leave Aurima on her own any longer, I started reluctantly down the steps of the temple. The grove of pines spread out before me, hiding its dark secrets from the autumn sun.

Had Father convinced Publius that there was no chance of acquittal by the Senate? Had they argued about whether the shame of a single indiscretion was worth his life?

"Young Carinna." It was the priest, with the milk jug and bread I had forgotten. I promised an offering for the temple when I retrieved the knives later. As I stowed the food in the chariot, he said, "There is something else. . . . Perhaps you should know it."

I paused, about to untie the reins from the hitching post.

"With age, I am less at ease with the night. Often I do not sleep until the light of Apollo's Chariot brightens the sky." His bony fingers fumbled in his beard again, as if searching for a memory in the tangle.

"Go on," I said impatiently.

"That night it was very hot. My water pitcher was empty, so I left my hut and came to the spring to fill it. At the top of the steps I saw someone asleep in the starlight, sitting against that pillar"—he gestured—"with his chin on his chest. The doors of the temple stood open, and inside I heard noises. Quiet noises, but sharp. A fox, I thought, and I tiptoed past to get my broom and drive it out.

"But it was not an animal." He worked his lips over his gums.

It was Publius, I thought. Anguished, sleepless, looking his death in the face. My dutiful brother had had no hope of defying Father's wishes.

"It was your father," said the priest, dropping his voice to a whisper although there was no one else to hear. "I saw him in the light of the vigil lamp, standing with his hands pressed to the wall. In front of him was a darkness, something more than shadow." He sighed. "Then I heard the sound again, and I realized the darkness was his cloak. He was biting on a fold of it, so his weeping would not wake your brother."

I thought of the river of bones. Of the ghost Father had heard in the mist as he mourned the death of legions. *When you are making a decision that will cost men's lives,* he had told me, *think hard before you choose.* As he wept over his decision not to fight for Publius's life, did he remember the mule's bell?

Lost in sorrow, I was slow to realize that Aurima was gone. The deadfall where I had left her lay propped on the stubs of its branches, deserted.

I vaulted over the fallen tree and stopped. In the gloom of the woods I could make out no footprints, nor was there any undergrowth to show her path by its disarray. A countryman might have tracked her passage, but I was city-bred, a man of streets and roads.

Why had I asked for her promise not to hide? Everyone knew truth had no meaning to barbarians. She had probably laughed to herself, for her gods would consider it praiseworthy to deceive a Roman; and as soon as I was gone, she had slipped off among the trees, knowing it would soon be dark and I would never find her. Or worse: perhaps she had stolen away to kill herself with a knife hidden in her boot.

The extent of the catastrophe staggered me. I would have to explain to that pretty-boy freedman Homilos, to my father and Lepidus, and eventually to Caligula Caesar how I had lost a hostage outside the city.

If she was dead, the Marcomanni would assume I had murdered her. That meant the Danube frontier at risk, the northern campaign tainted before it began. How could I have been such a fool?

Then the trees sang out. Just one note, high and bold, like the peal of silver *cymbala*, but it cracked and broke off.

An instant's terror shot through me. It seemed to be the voice of the goddess Diana, warning that I was unwelcome in this shadowy wood.

The song began again. It was a woman's voice: at first hoarse, then stronger and surer, in a language that was not mine.

I plunged through the grove.

She sang to the trees with her back to me, as if she had not heard my blundering arrival. It was no pretty girlish melody but a call, a challenge, and a paean all at once. I would not have been surprised to see a god-sent stag come, summoned, into the clearing.

Then the song ended. She turned and faced me just as she had stood in Nina's peristyle: her chin high, her clasped hands almost hidden by the dark cloak. Her eyes were half closed, her face without expression.

It was I she had summoned. But for what?

Behind her rose an old pine, scabbed with lichen. Resin bled, bright and pungent, from fresh scars in the rough bark. With the end of her cloak pin, she had scored a crescent with its horns up. Inside the crescent, crude but unmistakable, was the long-skirted figure of a woman.

I looked from the scratched image to Ingiomar's daughter. Neither breeze nor birdsong disturbed the stillness. I could hear only my own heart, thudding in my ears like danger battering at a barricaded gate.

"Come, then," she said.

I did not move.

Her eyes opened fully, green as moss. Slowly she spread her arms, her cloak unfolding like dark wings. Unpinned, it slid off her shoulders and crumpled behind her, revealing the red *stola* girdled under her breasts, the road-grimed white tunic beneath.

I exhaled softly.

Like one in a dream she came toward me. Her fingers were stained with pitch, the nails torn. She embraced my neck.

I seized her wrists and forced her hands down. Aurima resisted with a withy strength I had not expected. Her skin and hair smelled like a fir forest after rain, sharp and sweet.

Excitement sparked in me, the Dark Lord kindling my own desire into wildfire that overran my defenses. Our fingers had married, palms pressed against each other. I had only to push harder to be upon her, and I could take what I had wanted since that day on the battlefield.

Before the temptation could grow too strong, I let her go.

Aurima spat into my face. "Make me beg for mercy," she hissed. "Make me weep at the power of Rome." She spat again, this time onto my cheek when I turned my face aside.

"We must go," I said brusquely, taking a step toward the chariot.

She lunged at me, and our bodies collided. I felt her hand at my waist, scrabbling for my knife sheath.

All at once I understood: the crescent carving was a boat, the Boat of the Dead, carrying her to her gods. The amber at the crossroads would have been a sign to the sky maidens where to find her. But they would come for her only if she died in battle. Only if she died resisting me.

I pulled free. "The goddess Diana does not permit weapons in her grove."

Shock froze her white-rimmed eyes. The corners of her mouth drew down to show her bitten lip, her bloody teeth. She uttered a sound I had never heard a woman make, a roar of deep frenzied rage, and hurled herself upon me.

I fell onto my back in the sodden moss. She landed on top of me, digging into my shoulders and neck with nails like knives. Saliva and hot breath sprayed in my face.

Her sharp teeth grazed my nose, then snapped shut like clashing stones when I clouted her in the jaw. Her fingers tore at my hair and my arms; her knees and elbows pummeled me. Still she roared, a mad bellow that must have come from the womb within her. And I, who had always scoffed at the idea that a maenad could tear a man to pieces, felt my manhood shrink with terror.

At last I managed to immobilize her by throwing myself bodily upon her. When I did, the amber pendant tumbled out of the front of my tunic and swung on its cord into her face.

Her glaring eyes fixed on it. Her breath caught, silencing her awful fury. "The bones told . . . you are to free me," she gasped.

And finally I understood it all: her slave's misery; the icy remoteness that was the self-command of a woman preparing for death.

She closed her eyes. "Then Austro has left me."

I shifted my weight. My hand, streaked with blood, lay flattened on the moss by her shoulder. I was aware of the pulse that fluttered in her exposed throat, of her leg between mine, bared up to the thigh by her twisted skirts. Of the growing hardness in the front of my leather breeches.

With my thumb I brushed back a strand of red hair that saliva had glued to her cheek. There was no change in the inflection of her silver-green eyes. A defeated fighter knocked to the sand, too proud to raise a finger for mercy.

Moments earlier I would have taken her, reveling in my greater strength. But the battle was over, and she had fought too bravely not to be spared.

Inwardly I sighed. I had begged Mithras for discipline, and he had granted it to me. It would be impiety to test it any further.

"Time to leave," I said.

What is it like to return to life when you have prepared yourself to die?

I imagined Publius asleep on the starlit steps, unaware that Father despaired of saving him. Had he lived, he would have become Caligula's trusted adviser, one of the most important young men in Rome. His brush with the ferryman would have made him wiser, warier, a better counselor.

I rubbed the back of my arm across my face. The mares trotted on, content to be nearing their stable. The declining sun flickered in Aurima's tousled hair. She was asleep on her knees, oblivious in her exhaustion as the chariot splashed through sloughs and jolted over ruts.

I did not think she had told Maelo what she planned to do. Rather, the maid was to have informed him of her mistress's disappearance, and when Aurima's body turned up, he would naturally have accused me. As for her father, nothing on the frontier would have been safe from the fury of Ingiomar Ironhand when he heard of her death. It was a monstrously daring plan to free herself from captivity while destroying the truce, dishonoring Rome, and ruining me.

I glanced down at her again. Her weight pressed against my leg as the chariot jarred over stones. It seemed a cruel thing to return her to the city, but she was no innocent captive. Anyway, truces have always been stained with the tears of females traded to an enemy.

The sun was falling behind a bank of cloud when I rolled up to the livery stable where Jason waited. He froze in mid-yawn, eyes widening at my battered appearance. I told him to fetch Aurima's maid from Nina's house and meet us outside a *taberna* near the house of the Marcomanni.

This time Aurima made no protest when I transferred her to a hired litter. Bending to her level, I said, "Remember what I told you. You must say you were with my sister all day."

"Give me my fire-stone," she muttered.

"Later, perhaps. If you do as I ask." I swung up onto my horse and set off with her litter through the dusk.

Never before had I encountered a girl of such courage and strength of will. I thought of her with her hair ablaze beside the shrine to Hecate; of her bravery in goading me to attack her, so that she might kill herself. I wanted to escape with her to some lonely place and teach her to love life again. To love me . . .

"Here you are, your honor." The litter captain planted his staff on the pavement, and the bearers stopped. "Leda's Swan."

A torch in a bracket shed light on the outside wall of the *taberna*, where a crudely painted Leda embraced a swan with a thunderbolt in its beak. The door stood open on a smoky fug with a sour understink of wine and vomit.

I dismounted. "We will wait here for my slave."

The darkling street was busy with tradesmen shuttering their shops, bearers conveying their owners to dinner, customers traipsing upstairs to the brothel, and slaves fetching food from the cookshop next door. I leaned down and drew back the litter's water-stained curtain. Torchlight knifed in across the edge of the thin, patched mattress and greasy pillow. What a squalid conveyance for a maiden of such bravery and resolve!

"Aurima," I said.

She was all darkness within the litter, wrapped tight in her dark cloak. I crouched lower, trying to make out her face.

A troop of toga-clad Praetorians tramped noisily past, coming off Palace duty. When they had gone by, I whispered, "Remove your spell from me."

"Where is my Aurima?" a voice shrilled in Germanic, and I had to step back to let the maid reunite with the mistress she had thought dead.

This infatuation—bewitchery, or whatever it was—must cease. As the son of a Friend of Augustus I was prime breeding stock, as much a pawn in alliance-building as Aurima herself. I had no choice but to marry the daughter of some noble *paterfamilias* and sire little Roman citizens. Now that my promise to the girl was fulfilled, it was time to pick up the reins of duty I had dropped.

She was outside the litter now, gripping her slave's arm with a force that dimpled the woman's flesh. "What place is this?" She eyed the boisterous disorder of Leda's Swan.

"If anyone learns where you were today, it will go ill with you," I warned. Of course, it would go much worse with me.

"Take me to my mother's brother."

"Your house is just past those trees. You are free to go."

She began to turn away, lifting her hood over her hair. I said in a low voice, "Aurima."

She stepped out of my shadow. Firelight gilded her windburned cheeks.

I held her gaze, waiting for her to promise me silence. For a long moment she simply stared, with doubt creasing a V between her brows. "Never has the Goddess shown her will thus," she said at last, and added caustically, "Do you think I want that it is known?"

She stalked down the street with her maid. A few moments later, male voices exclaimed distantly in Germanic. She was safe.

I felt a twinge in my heart. Although I had come within a hair's breadth of disaster today, I would not have hesitated to do it all over again.

Jason demanded, "What happened to you, Marcus?"

"Nothing happened," I growled, aware now of aches where she had clawed and punched me. "Keep your mouth shut."

He followed me as I led my horse to a mounting block. "Did I do something wrong?"

I bit back a retort he had not earned. "You did well, Jason."

His gloomy face was transformed by a grin of contentment. Had no one ever praised him? "Hurry up," I said. "The hour is late." And I must think of some way to explain my condition to my father.

By Fortuna's grace Father was out at dinner, which left only Phormio to confront me. As I trudged in from the stableyard, he appeared from nowhere, his thin face pinched in an accusatory frown.

I came closer to the lamp in his hand. "What . . . ?" he began. He stared at my bruises and stained garments, then told Rufus to bring water to my bedroom.

There I sank down on my bed, legs splayed in weariness. He bent over to unfasten my knife belt. "Fell out of the god-damned chariot, I suppose," he muttered in Greek, the only language he blasphemed in. "Do you think you are still a boy, to take chances . . ." He interrupted himself as the wide neck of my tunic slid off my shoulder, baring the marks of Aurima's teeth.

Another slave, not Rufus, came in with hot water. Phormio pulled the tunic up to hide the bite mark. When the slave was gone, he let my sleeve fall again and stepped back, holding the belt and knife sheath.

My stiff fingers had nearly frozen on the reins. I plunged my right hand into the basin of hot water with a sigh of relief. "It is not what you imagine."

He shook his head. Rufus appeared with a steaming bowl of something savory. Phormio hardly noticed. "Marcus, I have been thinking," he began slowly. "I would like the sea air. To share a bed again with my old shrew . . . and our daughter is there at the villa, too: Phile, your mother's clothes-patcher. I could help with the accounts, the household. . . ."

"And abandon me?" I said, pretending it was a joke.

"I can do no more with you, Marcus Carinna. I am too old for distressing shocks"—he heaved a breath—"like the one you are about to give me."

I hesitated. Phormio plucked a pine twig from my hair. "Confess," he said, as if I were a sticky-fingered child.

I told him everything as I ate. He doctored me, washing the broken flesh with sour wine. Only when I finished describing my return with Aurima did he say, "Tell me again that you did not ravish her. And look me in the eye this time."

"I swear by Mithras that I left her a maiden. Do you doubt me?"

He shook his head. "Ah, Marcus . . ."

"Spare me your advice; I know it already. I am done with her."

"Do you really think this girl will keep quiet? Or that young fool Jason?"

I would have shrugged, but my shoulders hurt too much. I slumped back on my sleeping couch. "Phormio, you would not really leave me, would you?"

He made a face, acknowledging the game; he was the slave, not the master. "Antium is not so far." He drew the covers over me. "You can write whenever you need my counsel—which you will then ignore as usual."

I smiled faintly. Time enough to dissuade him later.

"Marcus."

"Hmm?" I yawned.

"Your father was displeased not to know where you were today."

"He is better off not knowing," I said.

Within the walls of my room, her amber pulsed a deep translucent gold in the lamplight, a small fiercely glowing heart of fire. Austro, I thought. I could not sleep.

CHAPTER 15

SNOW BLIND

That night the weather turned cold. Ice skimmed the atrium pool, and people breathed white clouds in unheated parts of the house. It made a good excuse for long sleeves and a neck scarf to hide the marks of Aurima's frenzy, and also meant that Caligula's return from Pyrgi would be delayed. I told Rufus to go to the stable anyway and have my roan saddled.

Phormio closed the message tablet that had come back from the Palace and clasped it against his middle. "When your father asks where you have gone, what should I say?"

I tried not to wince as I lifted my pinned cloak over my head. I had thought myself in good condition, but had not reckoned with the many aches from her attack or the protest of sinews long unused for driving.

"Marcus?"

I knew what he meant. "I told you I was done with her," I said. "I am going to visit Gemellus." That shut him up.

When I arrived in the yard, the stablemen were squinting up at heavy gray clouds. Jason and Rufus waited by my horse, both of them in short capes of flea-brown wool. I spotted Jason casting hostile glances at the Thracian boy. Such is always the fate of a new slave in the house; Rufus would have to suffer until he made his own place.

Jason stubbed his toe as we emerged into the gloomy street, an ill omen. Rufus seemed unaware of the mishap. His eyes darted every which way over the pot of duck in prune sauce he hugged under the folds of his cape.

I reined in on the Clivus Palatinus. The guesthouse where the Marcomanni were billeted was a spear cast away, just before the street pitched downhill to the Forum. "Off you go," I told Jason.

He gathered the swaddled pot from Rufus. "Any message, Marcus?"

Before I could think better of it, I said, "Tell her there are fine gardens on the crown of the hill where she may walk."

Watching him tramp off, I chewed on my lip. As much as I wished to see Aurima again, I would not have the Marcomanni think I was besotted with her. Besides, besides, *besides,* she was not for me. Why could I not accept that?

The roan stallion, Spider, crabbed in alarm as Rufus darted behind him. "Stop jumping about," I snapped. Had it been my warhorse he tried to creep behind, Boss might have killed him.

"I think I see a man I know, master." He slunk closer, hiding his bright hair under the hood of the cape.

"You are part of our *familia* now, so act like it. Stand straight." I leaned over and yanked his hood down. "And you may not cover your head unless I do."

A column of Praetorians marched past; again it was almost time for the Palace watch to change. I followed them toward the House of Tiberius, making Rufus precede me so I could keep an eye on him. In public our slaves were expected to appear sedate and deferential, as befitted members of the noble family of Licinius Carinna. Seldom were they ever beaten, although I did not want the boy to know that yet.

On the way, I debated my strategy. I meant to make peace with Gemellus if I could, and tell him some truths about the legions' importance that he might not know. Perhaps we might even go out together for a few convivial hours at the baths. In order not to dash salt in his wounded pride, I would leave Rufus outside tending the horse.

White flecks began to swirl through the air, sparsely at first, then in a thickening scrim. My thoughts drifted. Snow, rare in Rome, might make a girl of the North feel less homesick. Could I not think of an excuse—

Oh, stop, Carinna! By Mithras's Dog, put her from your mind.

The snow was dense now, hiding houses and shop fronts. I halted where the street forked at the Palatine Gardens. The Praetorians trooped on, tearing lines of bootprints in the gauzy slush.

Laughter crackled from across the street. Passersby hurrying to shelter had paused before a daub on the red-stained front of the house of the Silii. "Young Carinna," shouted one of them. "I suppose you brought this cursed snow with you from the wilderness."

He was an old comrade from my days in the Roman Youth cavalry, bony then and still as gangly as a beanstalk. "Why, on the Danube we would call this a pleasant day," I said. We clasped hands, and I asked what he was laughing at.

He made a face. "Let a foolish lampoon go around about Romulus and Remus, and now everyone must ridicule the Princeps."

The wall bore a crude drawing of the famous statue of the she-wolf, but instead of suckling peacefully beneath her, the infant brothers were fighting each other. Ignare issued from the mouth of one, while the other was saying Sceleste. Which was the dolt and which the villain was unclear, though perhaps it did not matter.

"Phoenix has much to answer for," I remarked, this time knowing better than to grin. He grunted, and I went on innocently, "Do you know who he is?"

"Phoenix?" He squinted at me. "I rather think it is your old friend Silius."

My guess confirmed, I shrugged. "We have not been friends for years."

"No? They say your finding the lampoon in Gemellus's house was another prank by the two of you." Stamping slush off his large feet, he looked up at me from under his brows. "Personally, I do not believe you would have so embarrassed Caesar's son. After all, he is said to have given you a slave you wanted, in token of his esteem." He glanced pointedly at Jason, who of course was not the slave in question.

"And I have given him a present in token of mine."

"Then you and Silius are still of like mind." His tone cooled. "Here he is. Enjoy yourselves." He tramped away through the falling snow.

A procession was making its way down the street. At the center of the group, surrounded by clients, secretaries, slaves, and guards, strode Silius himself, this time without Pertinax at his elbow. Snow silvered his dark hair, and his nose and ears glowed scarlet with cold.

When he saw me, his eyes brightened. "Come to visit, Carinna? Why wait outside? My household knows you are welcome."

My belly clenched, but again I was caught among witnesses eager for gossip. I tilted my head toward the drawing. "I came to see that."

Silius grimaced. "Scurrilous thing. I will have it painted over on the next good day." He gestured toward his house. "Come in; you have not met my wife."

The house was his own, for both his parents were dead. His father, like mine a friend and comrade in arms of the great Germanicus, had been falsely charged by Tiberius with impropriety in the province he once governed. To avoid the dishonor of a trial, he had killed himself. His wife, in the best Roman tradition, had chosen to die with him.

"I am enjoying the snow," I said. "Walk in the gardens with me."

"You must be joking." Silius eyed with distaste a nearby trio of cinnamon-skinned Egyptians, whooping like children as flakes melted in their hands.

"And leave your mob here. Except for Leander."

He looked at me silently, then without further protest dismissed the others, all but the body slave who was devoted to him. We crossed to the Palatine Gardens. Oleanders at the entrance hunched drably, haggard with cold.

Silius shrugged up his cloak to keep his neck dry. "This is madness," he grumbled, trudging beside me along the snow-stippled walkway.

"Are you still helping Pertinax to win his stripe?" I said. "Or must he wait longer to inherit his family's millions?" It was pure malice. I would have heard if the man had been nominated for the Senate.

Silius sliced a glance at me. "He looks after business here while his father attends to their vineyards in the Province." I was about to make a derisive comment about Gauls and grapes when he went on, "Perhaps you do not know he lost his wife to childbed fever two months ago. The infant, too."

"Bad luck," I said lamely, and concentrated on the path for a few slippery strides. "Nina wrote me of your wedding."

"Oh, I am well fettered now: wife and mistress both." He nodded to a man passing with his entourage, blurs in the snowstorm.

"Yet you have time to write, it seems."

"What?"

"The 'Romulus and Remus' was not bad."

His surprise became amusement. "I am pleased you think me so clever."

"You are Phoenix, are you not? Confess; I will keep your secret."

Silius blinked snowflakes off his lashes. "Not so fast, Carinna. If you believe I am Phoenix, prove it."

His playfulness annoyed me. "Did you intend to infuriate Caligula?"

"Jove's thunderbolts!" He stopped. "Am I slogging through a blizzard just to be rebuked?"

It was an old habit of his to pick a quarrel when he wished to distract me. Being wiser now, I said nothing. The snow fell heavily, whitening the windward side of the yews and mounding on statues' shoulders, turning our footprints into dark stitchery on the paths.

His feigned irritation faded. "Come home with me," he said. "You can congratulate my wife on her excellent marriage. Since you like snow, you may not mind her iciness."

"Not now," I said. I would not be caught in the same trap again.

"Oh, come along. My house is warm, even if the welcome is not."

"Another time."

The snow drifted down between us in a cottony curtain. Our attendants waited, stamping their feet. The horse's reins jingled as he twitched his head.

Silius took a step away, but seemed reluctant to go. "I have forgotten to compliment you on your appointment. Does it please you, rubbing around the ankles of men who can help you become Caligula's lap cat?"

"I hear it is Gemellus's ankles you prefer."

"Ah! Marcus, you are political at last."

"Is it true?"

"I will answer you," he said. "But not here."

The Libraries of Augustus were closing early, since the light was too poor for study. Silius's attendant passed a few coins to the porter and we entered. Slaves aimlessly mopped the polished floor of the atrium as snow falling through the compluvium melted around them.

The Latin library was deserted and silent, distant sounds muffled by hundreds of scrolls closed away in their latticed cabinets. Snow plastered the many panes of the great arched window, making the two-story reading room as dim as vesper.

"Much better." Silius roughed his hair with both hands to shed the wetness.

Coming here with him had been a bad idea. "Speak quickly," I said, slouching into a chair. "I am hungry and tired."

Instead he crossed to a statue of Augustus, kissed his own fingertips, then touched them to the marble toes of the first Princeps. "Glory to you, O divine Augustus! May you be praised for this magnificent place, even though there are not enough good authors to fill it."

"Silius, I am in no mood—"

"Patience, Carinna; I will explain." Twisting his damp cloak out of the way, he hitched himself onto one of the tables. "Suppose you are hunting on the far side of the Danube, as Nina says you were fond of doing. You stray in pursuit of a stag and lose your companions. While looking for them, you come upon a band of barbarians."

"In Mithras's name—"

"Just listen. You discover that they are the advance party of a horde on its way to attack the fortress. What will you do?"

"Ride back and warn the garrison. But—"

"It is ten miles back over mountains and bogs. Since this is a fable of my invention, I can give you one horse or two. Which would you prefer?"

"Two. Naturally."

He said, "Gemellus is the second horse."

I snorted. "The analogy is preposterous."

He sat with his arms braced on the tabletop, swinging his legs like a boy. "Rome was governed for centuries by pairs of leaders."

"That Rome was smaller than any province today."

"All the more reason to share the responsibility between two men."

"Would you split the empire, like Antonius and Augustus?"

"Hush." He touched a finger to his lips. "His statue may topple over and smite us."

I lowered my voice, not for Augustus's sake but because of curious ears out in the hall. "Men of our class once felt it their duty to set Rome's welfare before their own. That day is past. Two men can no longer share power; each will try to seize it from the other."

"But if there is only one man, it is a dictatorship." He stopped swinging his legs. "I want no more fatherly autocrats, no more pernicious tyrants."

"Caligula is no tyrant."

"If you think so, you do not know him."

The derision in his voice rankled me. "Is the grandson of Tiberius Caesar, who caused your parents' deaths, so much better a choice?"

He settled back in satisfaction as if I had finally asked the right question. "Gemellus will serve one term, then step down for consular elections," he said. "The principate will be dissolved."

For an instant I could only stare. Then, outraged to be thought so credulous, I lunged out of the chair and headed for the doorway.

"Where are you going? You wanted to know about Gemellus."

"I already know about him. He thinks he is Alexander reborn, and he is no more likely to give up power than you are to fly to Elysium."

Silius slid to his feet. "He has vowed to restore the Republic."

"Has he?" I said. "Who will kill Caligula for him?"

He gave a voiceless laugh, just an exhalation with a glint of teeth. "Times have changed." The wet hem of his mantle dragged a glossy trail on the marble floor as he came toward me. "Caligula will be banished to some distant isle, where he can debauch the local officials' wives to his heart's content."

I shook my head. A legally empowered Princeps deposed and exiled by a usurper? There would be an uproar in the Senate. Riots in the city. Demands for Caligula's restoration from Julian-party governors. The northern legions, who idolized him, would mutiny. "Disaster," I said hoarsely. "The barbarians will overrun our frontiers. The empire will break apart."

"Marcus, listen to me." His dark eyes were earnest, his voice low and cajoling. "Your father's obsession with Caligula has blinded you. Gemellus knows the failings of the principate—"

I stepped back. "Has that fucking Gaulish wine peddler turned you against Rome? You were not like this."

"Not like what? Like a man whose father stabbed himself because a Princeps wished it?"

"I will not listen to you talk treason."

Silius caught me by the sleeve. "Even though Caligula cost your brother his life?"

But it was I, stupid and heedless, who had truly failed Publius. How could Silius, who had known me for so many years, not realize that? I gripped his wrist with the strength of three years' war-play and shoved it away.

His eyelids twitched with transient pain. "You do not understand, Marcus," he said evenly. "But no matter. I will avenge us both."

——◦— ◦——

It was Silius who left first. I heard him speak to Leander in the atrium; then the bronze doors thudded shut behind them. In my mind our voices still brawled around the twilit chamber.

I had hoped there would be respect and a reserved amity between us, but Publius's death stood in the way. Silius had willingly revealed his beliefs to me, trusting me with his life, or at least his liberty. But my family's honor was bound to Caligula Caesar, so I could not keep his confidence. Duty compelled me to tell my father what I had just learned.

The snow was still falling, swarming like a host of moths in the lamplit atrium. Sunk in unease, I tightened the cloak around my neck and went outside. Beyond the eaves of the portico Silius's and Leander's footprints inscribed the white cascade of the steps, but the two of them were already out of sight.

Tail to the wind, Spider nickered to me from the foot of the steps. Ice crusted his coat and enameled his eyelashes. Rufus, a hooded figure crouched in the horse's lee, rose to his feet.

"I told you to keep walking him," I began angrily, then saw the face under the snowy hood. "What are you doing here?"

It was Jason. "I followed your t-tracks, Marcus." Stiff-lipped with cold, he managed to grin. "They w-were almost covered, but I saw the horse droppings. Then Leander told me you were here."

"Where is Rufus?" I scrubbed ice off the roan's face with my cloak.

"The little savage was p-pissing himself with fright. Said you were being followed." Jason threw a scornful glance around the snowy courtyard. "In this weather—I ask you!"

"Where is he, Jason?" I repeated sharply.

"Uh . . . h-hiding at home, I think."

"You *think*?"

Jason's dark brows met over his ruddy nose. He clamped his jaw.

"What did you say to him? Answer me!"

"I s-said, 'You're not Marcus's outside slave, you foreign fuck-boy.'" He wiped his dripping nose with his palm. "I said, 'Go home. I'm his *servus viator*, I w-will wait for him.'"

I looked around the courtyard as if the Thracian boy might be there, a snow-covered lump on the pavement. Suppressed rage from the quarrel with Silius boiled up behind my teeth.

Jason said defensively, "He was Gemellus's slave. He knows all the hidden ways through the libraries and the temple and the Palace." He pointed to the Greek library wing. "He went through a door over there."

He was probably right: long before we reached home the boy would be there, dry and warm. "I will deal with you later," I said grimly. Melting snow was trickling down my face and neck. I looped the reins over the horse's head and vaulted into the saddle. "Follow me home. As quick as you can."

I booted the stallion into a trot, with Jason jogging after me. I was too angry to care whether he fell behind. Giving orders as if he were me! This was what came of according slaves too much license. Anarchy—just like Silius's new republic.

I was so deep in my ill humor that I paid little heed to a voice shouting behind me. Then a woman shrieked, "Help! Murder!" and I hauled hard on the reins, realizing too late that the shouts I heard had been Jason's.

CHAPTER 16

THE GATES OF HADES

Men wrestled in the snow-covered street behind the libraries. A woman peered down from a balcony, her hands braced on the railing.

The grappling figures lurched across the street and crashed into the wall under the balcony. Snow cascaded on them from a fig tree clinging to the brick.

I jerked the horse to a halt. "Jason," I shouted, unable to make out what was happening. A hoarse cry cut off in a grunt.

A pale face flashed at me. "He's finished. Go," one of the assailants cried. Two shadows fled, slipping and sliding, toward the Clivus Palatinus.

"Stop," I bellowed, kicking my horse. Spider lunged forward and knocked down the nearer man. They both screamed, the man because the stallion was rearing over him, and the horse because he was not trained to kill. I felt him jolt down atop flesh and bone. A curved *sica* flew into the street.

The other man held his ground, brandishing a sword. I reined in, then spotted a dark blotch in the snow under the fig tree. When I turned toward it, the man rushed to his downed accomplice.

I flung myself off the horse. "Give me light," I shouted to the woman on the balcony.

Jason slumped against the tree's twisted trunk, half buried in fallen snow. I slid down on one knee and put my arm under his shoulders. "Easy, boy. I will have you home in a—"

Light bloomed suddenly from a lamp or lantern on the balcony. And as I lifted the young slave, to my horror his head tipped back, and back, and back.

His throat had been cut. The darkness I had seen was his blood, and I was drenched in it.

The censer rattled on its chain as the priest of Palatine Apollo shuffled around me, intoning a prayer. I shivered in a borrowed tunic. My eyes watered from the sweet musty fumes.

When my frightened horse had arrived riderless at home, our people had followed his tracks in the snow. The assailants had vanished into the night, even the one I had ridden down, all traces lost in the trampled slush of the Clivus Palatinus. While our slaves took charge of Jason's body, I went straight to the temple to cleanse myself of violent death. Sluiced three times with holy water, I knelt now before the Sun God's altar and prayed for a chance to avenge my slave.

His mulish scowl swam before me. He had been a grimy-fisted toiler without good looks or cleverness or skill, but he had not deserved to die behind Augustus's libraries under the knife of a nameless brigand.

Had some enemy of mine killed him because they could not get to me? Maelo and a comrade, seeking revenge because I had carried off Aurima? But the attackers had spoken Latin, and neither had been bearded.

A temple acolyte held out a basin of water. I washed and dried my fingers, then rose stiffly to my feet. I had nothing to offer as a sacrifice, but I promised Mithras Light-Bringer a bull calf when the slayers were brought to justice.

Hurried footsteps marched across the marble floor. It was Father, his embroidered *himation* swirling around his legs. "Marcus, are you hurt?"

Ironically, it was the scratches and bruising from Aurima's assault he saw. "I will be all right," I said, and unexpectedly began to tremble. Only by reviving my anger was I able to quell the shakes.

"Come, my litter is waiting," he said. "Where is your cloak?"

"We must send for the Watch commander," I began. "Perhaps—"

"Hush. When we are alone."

As we went toward the entrance, I saw he still wore his gilt-embossed sandals. He had rushed here from someone's house without pausing to put on outdoor shoes. "Father, they said, '*Habet.*' And one of them—"

"Later, Marcus."

The temple doors groaned shut behind us. Father's guards were waiting on the steps. They murmured when we appeared, and even though one of our *familia* had died, they broke into smiles of relief. As the only surviving son of the house, I was the future of them all.

Unable to find my own cloak, I put on someone else's that stank of old sweat. The roan stallion nosed me nervously as I took his reins, and I held his head for a moment against my chest. If I had not ridden ahead, would Jason still be alive?

I glimpsed him again in the light falling through flecks of snow, the ruby slash that opened and kept opening as his head tipped back. . . .

And I, who had prided myself on my cool wits during and after a battle in which scores on both sides were killed or maimed, bent and vomited up my certainty that I could keep my family safe.

"It was too dark to see their faces," I repeated. "One had a shortsword, the other a *sica*."

"Gladiators," Lepidus said with his mouth full of ground meat. He spat out a piece of bay leaf. "Have you any idea who sent them?"

"None." I averted my eyes from our patron's assault on another liver patty. The three couches were set corner to corner in our dining room so we could see one another, and the smell of cooked liver had a stomach-turning likeness to the stench of gore. "Their clothes must be bloody. And the one who was trampled must have broken bones. Why are we not telling the Watch to look for them?"

"In good time." Father tipped more water into his cup of wine. "Let us talk it over first."

"I have told you all I know." I sat up, still cold despite the heavy quilt around my shoulders.

"Listen to your father." Lepidus reached for his napkin. "You are no longer a tribune with troops at your command."

How well I knew it! I said, "I will go out and look for them myself."

"Where?" Father scoffed. "In every *taberna*? In every whore's cubby? They may have left the Palatine. Will you search all the kennels in Rome?"

Lepidus did not look up from wiping his fingers. "Whom have you angered?"

"Livilla," I said.

His hands stilled. He and Father looked at each other.

"Gemellus," I added, on the chance that my gift had not mollified Caligula's adopted son. And then, reluctantly, "Silius." He had left the libraries before me. If he repented of having told me about Gemellus, he could have sent Leander ahead to order a couple of his bodyguards to set up an ambush. They might have chased after me as I was riding away, and Jason—loyal, brave, and foolish—had tried to stop them.

"By Jupiter!" Lepidus raised his thick brows. "For so little time in Rome, you have made serious enemies."

Father sighed and leaned back on his elbow. "This is too delicate a matter for the Watch. I think we must inform Saxa."

I almost said, *He is an enemy, too*, but they would not have appreciated the dark humor.

"Caesar will be back tomorrow afternoon," Lepidus said. "He must be told."

"Why stir the hive now?" Father argued. "Let us wait until there is proof."

"He should know that Gemellus may have tried to murder your son." Lepidus sat up on his couch. "We have been offered a gift, and we must use it."

Father shook his head. "He is barely recovered from the brain fever. We cannot risk unsettling him now."

Lepidus's cheeks burned red above his beard shadow. "You persist in regarding him as a hothouse flower."

"He need not face betrayal yet."

"Confound it, he is a Caesar! He comes of hardy stock: Augustus, Drusus, Germanicus. He will do what must be done."

Father's eyes were dark beneath drawn brows, and the creases beside his nostrils had deepened. "Would you ruin all we have worked for?"

It was as if the earth had turned upside down. He had always been deferential to our family's patron, as a client should be. When had the balance shifted between them?

"Are you with me, Carinna, or not?" Lepidus snapped.

Father said, "It is your loyalty that Caesar may doubt, Marcus Aemilius, if you bring him a tale accusing your rival."

With that, the fog cleared from my eyes. Our patron came from an old and noble family that had intermarried with the Julii. If Gemellus was gotten out of the way, Lepidus would be well placed to become Caligula's successor.

At that moment I decided not to report Gemellus's supposed vow to restore the Republic. With only Silius's word for it, I could not risk allowing the patron to go out on a limb for what might prove to be a lie or a trap.

Father and Lepidus were eyeing each other like a couple of fighters in the arena. I said, "We cannot accuse Gemellus of the attack without proof. What if it was nothing more than two drunken thieves trying to rob a patrician's slave?"

"Caesar will believe whatever you tell him," Lepidus said.

Did he know Caligula had begged me to learn the truth? Or was he just guessing that the Princeps would listen to me because I had saved his life?

Lepidus rose from his couch. "Gemellus will act. The timing is either his or ours." He called for his slaves, then said to Father in a lower voice, "Do as you wish for now, Titus. If Caesar taxes me later with my silence, I will say you did not want to trouble him with speculation."

They embraced as if there were no discord between them. Seeing Lepidus's dark head close to my father's silver-gilt hair, I was reminded that they had been allies during the battle to protect the young Caligula from Tiberius. Now, inevitably, they were at odds between Father's aim to keep him in power and Lepidus's ambition to replace him.

"Marcus." Lepidus opened his arms toward me. I stood up and touched my lips to his stubbly cheek as he clasped me against him.

"You must be more careful, young man," he said, resting his hands on my shoulders. Father made some comment, but Lepidus was not listening. "What is this?" he asked, fishing from my tunic the pendant he had felt.

"A spoil of war." I pulled the drop of amber out of his fingers. It was my talisman now, a trophy from Austro's priestess.

Father accompanied our patron to the atrium while his litter was fetched. I should have gone with them, but the stress of the day had sucked the marrow from my bones. I sank onto the nearest couch.

It was not enough that I had agreed to serve Caligula; now Lepidus wished me to lie to him! By Mithras's Dog, I would not do it. I could not, by my honor as a soldier of the God of Truth.

The curtain in the doorway stirred, and Rufus slipped into the room. The boy was infuriatingly hale, his blue eyes bright, red-gold hair as thick as wheat.

This worthless slave of Gemellus's should have been the one to die, not a *vernus* born and raised in our family. "Get out," I shouted. "And keep out of my sight, you little maggot!"

He fled. I dropped my head into my hands.

"How just is it," panted a voice, "to punish a . . . slave for your own . . . misjudgment?"

"Leave me alone, Phormio," I mumbled.

"If you . . . assure me you . . . are unharmed."

The hitch in his breathing made me uncover my eyes. He was leaning against the doorjamb, one hand resting on the narrow shoulder of Turtle's little grandson. "I have done worse to myself on the racecourse," I said wearily. "Calm yourself, old dear."

"'Calm'!" he shouted, trying to push himself forward. "I hear you have been att-attacked in the street . . . covered in blood. . . . I did not know if . . . you would s-see daylight." Spittle flew from his lips. "And then . . . to look on the face of . . . that wretched b-boy Jason . . . wra-wrapped in . . . your cloak!"

He stopped, pressing a hand to his chest. His face went ashen.

"Phormio," I barked. His mouth opened, gray-lipped, and his eyes goggled at me, swollen with panic. I said, "Astyanax, take him to my room. Quickly."

The frightened boy pulled on Phormio's arm. My *paedagogus* crashed to the floor with a thud that made coals tumble in the brazier.

I leaped up, expecting to find him limp and unseeing. He lay on his back, blinking at the little slave trying to haul him to his feet. He was breathing again. Rosiness flooded into his face.

I crouched beside him, astonished. "What miracle is this?"

"It seems," he panted, "Hades has . . . spat me back."

My old *paedagogus*, who had survived two climbs over the Julian Alps, the crudity of life on the frontier, the rigors of a vexillation on the march, and the terror of ambush by barbarians, had been betrayed at last by his staunch heart.

He lay on his pallet with his eyes squeezed shut, half hidden by the stooping shadows of Lepidus's physician and his assistant. The light of several lamps glowed on the plaque of Mithras in the niche above them, a reminder of the god's promise of deathlessness.

My chest felt trapped in armor that had been too tightly cinched. I asked, "Will he live?"

The physician straightened up. I looked for omens in his pale pebbly eyes and his high brow, scratched with wrinkles. "A difficult question, young

Carinna," he said, fondling his curled mustache and beard into order. "The gods grant us only as much time as they wish."

He was Greek, of course. I said, "In other words, you do not know."

His small mouth pursed. "I do know he has been refusing the tonic I prescribed for him."

Having felt unwell for several days, Phormio had apparently confided in his friend Nicander. Nicander had sent to the patron's physician for a remedy that Phormio then rejected.

I listened with mounting anger to this tale of stubborn pride. Nicander lowered his eyes. "Of course it was not proper to keep this from you, Marcus. But I did not think it would make a difference."

"That was not your decision to make," I said coldly. "No one else knew?"

"Only that redheaded boy of Gemellus's." Father's secretary was so distraught that his white hair ruffled up like a heron's crest. He looked around. "Where is the wretch?"

Without answering I told him to see to preparation of the physician's new potion. Then, alone at last, I looked down at Phormio. His hands were knotted over his breastbone, his teeth bared in a grimace.

Few boys, I had often been told, were fortunate enough to be looked after by a *paedagogus* of such good moral character, education, and judgment. He had been with me since I was named, and I had never known a day without him.

When I squatted beside him, his eyes glinted at me through narrow slits. His face was pale, and sweat glossed his balding forehead. "I am . . . leaving you," he whispered.

Excesses of emotion are unmanly, so I did not weep. But some moments passed before I could swallow the knot in my throat, and a few more before I trusted my voice. "You old mule," I said. "Take your medicine, or I will have them pour it in your other end."

He was snoring beneath piles of covers, drugged with foxglove and poppy juice, when Father came in. I sat cross-legged on the bed scrawling a message to my sister. Nina would hear about the assault and Jason's death soon enough, and I did not want her to worry about me.

"I came to say that I will acquire two guards for you from the school in Capua," he said, "but clearly you are also in need of a secretary." To see what I was writing, I was bent double over the tablet with a lamp in my other hand.

"I would rather have a guard who knows the family," I said.

A small pause. Then he said, "Very well. I will let you have Ollius and—"

"Ollius alone will suit me." *Who they were is a mystery to me*, I wrote. Closing the tablet's leaves, I handed it to the waiting messenger.

Father walked around my bed to look down on Phormio, who did not stir. He turned then to study the plaque of Mithras slaying the Bull of Life. "Have you found a shrine to your god in the city?"

My suspicions prickled: it was unlike him to make small talk. "He has so few worshipers here that I must make do with Apollo."

He sat down on the end of my bed. "Perhaps you are wondering about my difference of opinion with Lepidus. I wish to explain, since it concerns you."

I was spared having to respond by a mutter from Phormio. Leaning over to set the lamp on the bedside table, I saw him fretting with his quilt while he slept. Perhaps the sound of my father's voice had stirred up a dream in him.

"Caligula," Father began, then stopped. "I use this name because it is how I first knew him: as the youngest son, the darling of a large and close family—three boys, three girls, with a mother he adored and a father meant to be Tiberius's heir. He was just learning his letters when Germanicus was poisoned. A great tragedy"—he paused reflectively—"yet his mother held together the family with her ambitions for his brothers. Then Nero died, and after him Drusus and Agrippina herself. Last, of course, was the death of our Publius, whom Caligula held dearer than he did his brothers." His glance flicked away for a moment, then back to me. "Of his once-fortunate family there remain only his three sisters."

"And his uncle Claudius," I interjected.

Father smiled thinly. "Claudius is well aware of the noble blood that runs in his veins, and he means to keep it there."

Movement near the floor caught my eye. A small hand, the size of a fourteen-year-old boy's, slipped out from under my bed to draw the disarranged quilt up under Phormio's chin. Father could not see it from where he sat, so I said nothing.

He went on, "So Caligula has drawn a charmed circle around himself and his sisters. Those within, he trusts absolutely. No one else. Not Lepidus; not even me." He took a deep breath. "When I persuaded him to adopt Gemellus, I thought only of appeasing the Tiberian faction. I did not recognize what it would mean to him."

I said slowly, "You mean he has brought Gemellus inside the circle."

The tightness around his eyes eased. "Do you see, then, how discovering treachery in the boy would distress him?"

I must know if his heart has been turned against me, Caligula had told me in the horse stall. I looked down at my scabbed hands, then up at my father. "Are you asking me to find out if Gemellus is betraying him?"

"Perdition! Of course not." Though he kept his voice low, it had the intensity of a shout. "Keep away from Gemellus. Have nothing more to do with him. I will not force you to return that slaveboy, but I wish you had."

I shook my head in perplexity. "Father, I do not understand you."

"Marcus." He leaned toward me and dropped his voice even more. "A Princeps with a successor only seven years younger than he is? Gemellus must be removed, but for a reason people will accept."

"But if he is truly disloyal, you cannot avoid distressing Caligula."

He drew back. "Lepidus and I hope he will have you to rely on."

"Why should he allow me into this . . . this fortress he has walled with the dead of his family?"

"Because of Publius," Father said simply.

I shook my head again, disbelieving.

"Trust me, Marcus. The time will come when Gemellus is off the stage. I hope it can be done peacefully. Lepidus is less optimistic, and perhaps he is right. In either case, Caesar will need a friend."

"But in the meantime, I am not to accuse Gemellus."

"Say only that the attack is being investigated." He rose. "With your colorful injuries, you should receive a sympathetic hearing."

"I want no part of this, Father."

He heard in my protest that I would not disobey, and his voice gentled. "You would rather be on the frontier, I know, with your days ordered by the trumpet and your decisions set out in black and white. That is for lesser men." His ice-blue eyes assessed me without tenderness. "You are my son."

I sat unmoving for a while after he left. Eventually I stripped off my outer garments and pinched out the light. But sleep was impossible; fragments of the day, mixed with his horrific confidences, whirled and scurried through my mind.

Aurima's pendant rolled against my collarbone. I clasped my fingers around it. *My fire-stone.*

"Are you awake?" I asked softly. Phormio snuffled as if he had heard me, but his stertorous breathing resumed.

The first tiny plashes came from out in the atrium. It was beginning to rain again. The blood and beauty of the snow would soon be gone.

I said into the darkness, "Remember last winter, the night Placidus lost his fur-lined cloak to me? He kept trying to win it back and I had to push him out the door at last. It was well into the second watch. . . ."

The snow had been up to the eaves; the surgeon cursed my luck as he clutched his slave's arm and stumbled down a path dug between snow-banks higher than their heads. "Teuta was drinking too," I went on dream-ily, "and it made her talk. . . . Things her mother had told her about their people . . . how grown men would slide down hillsides on their shields when it snowed, just to amuse themselves . . ." The notion made me smile, as it had when my half-Sicambrian bed girl told of it.

The rain was a steady rustle now. My *paedagogus* moaned to himself, deep in the caverns of sleep. Most likely Rufus too was asleep in his hiding place.

"Just imagine, Phormio, a language that cannot speak of tomorrow, only yesterday and today! They do not build for the future; glory to them is a brave death, and truth has no meaning. . . ."

I rolled onto my back, staring up at the ceiling beams. "We fight for or-der, and they fight for disorder." It was not Ingiomar Ironhand and his men I had in mind, but Aurima: her desolation when I had cut off her escape at the Spartan Baths; her ferocity in Diana's grove when she realized I had cheated her of death.

I turned onto my side again to look down at the drugged man. "My old treasure, I thank Fortuna I was not born a barbarian." I sighed. "And yet . . ."

Phormio did not ask how I would have finished this unthinkable thought. Beneath his knotted brows his eyes were closed, and his sonorous breath wheezed back and forth like the stroking oars of an outbound galley.

I fell deeply asleep at last. And thus I missed Jason's final leave-taking from the house of his birth, attended by the wails of our women, on the way to the public pyre outside the Esquilina gate.

CHAPTER 17

FOUNTAIN OF THE NAIADS

D reaming of a girl whom I wanted to be Aurima, I moaned in pleasure as she stroked the arches of my feet, my soles, my toes.

"Marcus, Marcus . . ." crooned a voice.

It was bald old Turtle, Father's body servant, rubbing my feet. When he saw me open my eyes, the wrinkles in his face drew up on both sides like daintily lifted skirts. With a gap-toothed grin he patted the bulge under my quilt. The heir of the house had not only survived but was ready to carry on the line.

I mustered my wits to growl at him. Waking me was a task reserved for Phormio.

Phormio.

I bolted upright and leaned over the edge of my bed to make sure my *paedagogus* still breathed.

He blinked up at me from his pallet. Someone, perhaps Rufus, had already brought him a bowl of broth.

"Master wishes you to join him in the main reception room," Turtle said.

That meant we had company. "He will have to wait," I retorted testily. "I am not washed, shaved, or dressed. And as you have noticed—"

He straightened up from whispering to his small grandson, who disappeared. "Pardon, Marcus. He said not to delay."

"I will be there when I am ready." I doubted that he wanted me unshaved and grimy, showing the scabs and bruises on my bare arms.

"The commander of the Special Cohort is here, and the district magistrate."

Saxa? Here?

Turtle edged to one side so our junior seamstress could slip in past him. Pink and breathless with haste, she pressed a hand to her heaving bosom. Her eyes grew rounder and her blush deeper as I looked at her.

"As quick as you can," Turtle said, and let the curtain fall shut behind him.

So I was feeling quite the young master when I strode into the reception room, intent on demanding that no effort be spared to capture Jason's killers. But the swagger of my arrival went unnoticed by Father and Saxa, who were talking quietly together. And I had overlooked Turtle's mention of the local magistrate.

Silius rose quickly to his feet, his toga arranging itself into stately folds as lesser mortals' seldom do. He stepped closer to shield us from the others and murmured, "Our conversation yesterday . . ." His gaze flickered toward my father. Meaning: Had I revealed what he had told me in the library?

I said, "Is that why you are here?"

"In part. And partly to see how much damage was done to you last night." A familiar gleam of mockery lightened his voice. He looked me over, but my wounds were well hidden beneath sleeves and a long tunic.

"I am not the one who died."

"It was Jason, your father said." He knew all our household, of course, as I knew his. "But when you dragged me off into the snow, your attendant was a redheaded boy."

"Ah, Marcus," Father interrupted loudly. He paused to wipe his nose. "Commander Saxa says you and he have met."

Leaving Silius's questions unanswered, I turned to Saxa, who came out of his chair like a lion out of an arena gate. He was dressed in drab clothing of good quality: a man who wished not to be noticed but, if noticed, not to be underestimated.

I half expected to be met with scorn, for he had last seen me when I demanded my brother's file. But although he knew the truth had made a fool of me, his mastiff face wore only grave courtesy. He said, "I regret the loss of your slave, young Carinna."

Someone brought in another folding chair, and I sat down. "What have you found out about the men who killed him?"

Sallow light from the doorway marked out two lines between Saxa's heavy brows, running up like wheel tracks to creases across his forehead. "It is not the Special Cohort's duty to investigate crimes against property, you know."

That was all Jason had been: property. A tool that speaks. Before Father could respond, I said, "But we must rule out the possibility that Caesar's quaestor-designate was the target of this attack."

Behind Saxa's shoulder, Father raised his brows. Evidently it surprised him that, after commanding vastly more experienced centurions, I dared speak up to the head of a Praetorian cohort.

Silius said, "I have already sent my bailiffs out looking, and notified my informers. But it would be helpful to have better descriptions."

I shrugged. "It was dusk, with snow falling."

"Did they wear gladiators' armor? Helmets?"

"They hardly needed armor to kill a house slave."

"Tall? Short? Lean? Stocky? Dark-haired? Fair?"

"I cannot say, Silius. Sorry."

Saxa said, "More to the point, Quaestor, what were they after? Did your slave carry your wallet?"

Father sat back, nursing the remains of his grippe, while they continued to question me. Silius was careful with Saxa—and no wonder, for the Special Cohort would be pleased to lay hands on the irreverent lampoonist Phoenix. Servers glided around, replenishing cups from steamy jugs.

Though vexed that the brigands could be burrowing deeper into hiding while we talked, I held fast to my patience. Finally I said, "Why should it be hard to find a man with a hoofprint on his chest and broken bones beneath it?"

Saxa stifled a belch. "Not hard at all, if he acted on his own. If someone else sent him, he has probably been gutted and thrown off a bridge by now."

I exhaled and cast a glance at Father. But the Special Cohort commander was not done. "You say you cannot imagine why anyone would attack you. Does that include the barbarians you brought to Rome?"

Did he know I had visited them and had smuggled Aurima out of the city? Was that fat eunuch his spy? I put a quizzical frown on my face. "The Marcomanni are bearded."

Except for that stripling Odo.

How sure was I of having seen the crescent blade of a *sica*? I had been anxious and confused by the turmoil. Could it have been a bronze knife I saw, like the ones Maelo and his warriors carried?

But Jason had been killed by a slash from a weapon with a honed edge, not a knife thrust. "It was not them," I insisted.

"You hesitated for a moment, Quaestor. Why?"

"Maelo is the brother-in-law of Ingiomar Ironhand. If he attacked me, we could declare the truce broken and the life of Ingiomar's daughter forfeit."

"You know them all, these Marcomanni? You have spoken with them?"

"At various times."

"The girl? The hostage? You have spoken with her, too?"

"Commander, it is impossible to escort a group of people for a month and never speak to them."

"I mean, does she know Latin?"

"I was told her father wanted his sons to learn Latin, and she took part in the lessons. That was before he turned against us, of course." I did not bother to add that I had picked up some Germanic from my bed girl.

"I will send someone to question them."

"They did not kill my slave. I would stake my life on it." In fact, I already had. If Maelo had wanted revenge for my deception with Aurima, he would have cut my throat, not Jason's.

Saxa ruminated for a moment. "It seems unlikely that the motive was robbery. And since you were not assaulted when you went to his aid, I conclude that the attack was not directed at you, but at the Senator." He swung around to my father.

Father seemed unsurprised. "I have considered it. But it is a vile tactic to put a man's only son at risk just to send a message." His eyes drifted to Silius.

Silius's olive skin flushed darker. "I cannot imagine who would send such an infamous message, Senator."

"Thank you, Magistrate. You ease my mind."

Did he mean he was satisfied that Gemellus's supporters were not involved, or that Silius was unaware whether they were? My father's mind was like an onion, sheathed in layer after layer that appeared transparent, belying the opacity at its core.

I stood up, surfeited with gabble and guesswork. "If you are not interested in searching for these killers, Commander, I am. And whatever their purpose was, I will make them pay."

Father and Saxa spoke at once. Father won. "Caesar's quaestor-designate cannot be rampaging through cutthroats' lairs and gladiator barracks."

Saxa nodded. "Exactly right, Senator. Your son should avoid appearing in public until this is settled. I will put out the word among my own informers—who are somewhat more numerous than those of the honorable magistrate."

I glanced at Silius. He was slouched in his chair with a forearm across his chest, his forefinger at his lips as if blocking a secret that sought to emerge.

"Let them know I am offering a reward," Father suggested to Saxa.

"Not just yet, Senator. Let us see what we find without a public uproar."

Silius rose, shrugging his toga higher on his shoulder. "We do not want it thought that a Friend of Augustus would have so unscrupulous an enemy."

There was no disagreement with that. He said, "I will take my leave, then, and see what crumbs my little rats have brought back." He bowed slightly to my father. "Senator, I will do my best to learn who is responsible for the attack."

"I am grateful, Gaius Silius." Father inclined his head in return. Silius exchanged cool farewells with Saxa, and I said I would see him out.

Before the crowd of retainers waiting in the atrium could engulf him, I said, "Phormio was heart-struck last night; come and say a word to him."

Rufus backed away from the sick man's pallet as we pushed into my little bedchamber. I asked, "How well is the boy looking after you, Phormio?"

"As well as . . . can be expected," he wheezed. It hurt my own heart to see him, gray-skinned and shrunken in less than a day's time.

His eyes rolled past me to Silius, who came over and looked down on him. "Will you live, old pepperpot?"

"Longer than . . . you will, you reprobate."

"Possibly." Silius grinned.

He glanced at Rufus. "Here is my redhead," I told him. "No mystery." I looked him in the eye. "Is there?"

He lowered his voice. "Gemellus would not have ordered the attack; I swear it."

"Yet I think he is not fond of me."

His grin glinted again. "He believes you like boys, but it pleases him to know men's weaknesses. And he still hopes you will give him your friendship."

Did the little tick think me so valuable an ally? My comedy performance as a disaffected Julian must have been more successful than I had thought.

Silius was already shouldering his way past the door curtain. As we reemerged into the atrium, I murmured, "What you told me yesterday . . . I had not imagined restoration of the Republic. But I do not see how it could be done."

"We will talk later." He gave me a sidewise look through lowered lashes. For the first time I realized that we were eye to eye; the incurable peacock had built-up soles on his shoes.

I laughed, pulled his head toward me, and kissed his cheek.

Talk and movement around us stopped. "What . . . ?" Silius blurted.

"I would not have my father think we were talking politics," I said.

A fur-swaddled old man chafed his hands together. "Slaves murdered right here on the Palatine, in a public street! Imagine such a thing!" His breath came out in a billow of frost.

"Foreigners," his stout companion muttered. "Thieves, cutthroats, whores, leeches, the dregs of the world. They come here, and we feed them."

The old man tipped his freckled face up to the wads of grimy cloud that hung overhead. "We never had such weather when I was a boy."

"At this rate my tenements near the Circus will flood by the end of the month. Do you suppose I can find more insurance? Not at any price."

Grumbling, they shuffled away past lumps of ice that had once been snow. Ollius snickered. "That dried-out old turbot's had all the sun he needs."

"Brave words, Baldy! Better cover that skull, or your brains will shrink," Cleon jeered. Ollius punched him, a blow that would have knocked down an ordinary man. Cleon only grinned.

"Enough," I growled. Faced with my stubborn demand to scout around on the Palatine, Father had insisted on his own chief guard accompanying me as well as Ollius.

The talk in the streets and shops was all about last night's attack near the Libraries of Augustus. A slave had been killed. A patrician had been killed.

A man and his slave had both been killed. A horse had killed a slave. It was a quaestor's slave; it was a Senator's slave.

Trees and eaves dripped a constant patter. From the Julian Forum came the distant sound of trumpets and a chorus rehearsing for one of the festival events. "My belt buckle's scraping on my backbone," Ollius complained. "Let's get some lunch." He hunched his massive shoulders, humping his cloak up around his ears. "What are you looking at, Marcus?"

I cast a last glance at the silent house of the Marcomanni. The two guards fell in behind me. As we passed a wall posting about the Isis festival, they began to argue about the races. The faraway chorus stopped, started again, stopped.

Hooded at Father's behest, I wandered unrecognized among cutpurses, hucksters, beggars, provincials, and mountebanks swarming the streets, as thick as flies. There might have been fifty or a hundred brigands among them with *sicas* hidden under their cloaks. Worry about Phormio sharpened my frustration, as if finding the killers was the only hope of saving him. I elbowed my way into a hot-drinks shop to ask about customers last evening who had been bloody or crippled.

"Waste of time," Cleon grumbled. "Someone will turn them in." He swiped his cudgel at an overhanging branch, showering ice splinters on Ollius.

I stopped, tossed Ollius a sestertius, and told him to fetch me a drink from the thermopolium I had just left. When he was gone I said, "Cleon."

He grunted, ogling a girl carrying a water jug.

I spun him around and slammed him against the wall. "Start behaving like a Senator's chief bodyguard," I said into his scarred face, "or you will be one no longer."

At first he was too astonished to respond. He had always seemed so dangerous that I had never before dared lay hands on him. Then he blinked, and the surprise in his eyes annealed into something darker. "Just larking around, Marcus. No harm done."

He hated to ask my pardon. I was the boy who made excuses to avoid sword training, who stumbled home late at night and spewed on the atrium floor, whose pranks with a confederate angered and exasperated our *paterfamilias*.

Three years earlier, the glare of this man who had killed a hundred opponents would have wilted me like a boiled asparagus. But I was too angry to be docile. With my hands fisted in his cloak, I rocked him forward, then smacked him harder into the wall. Icicles as thick as thumbs snapped off the eaves and tumbled onto his head and shoulders. "Do you understand?" I said.

Ice-melt ran down his battered nose and across his upper lip. "I understand," he muttered.

Ollius soon abandoned his horseplay without Cleon's lead. They stamped their feet and blew on their hands, hoping I would take the hint to go home, but I lingered over the hot watered wine Ollius had brought. How could no one have seen two cutthroats in bloody clothes, one of whom might be unable to walk?

I was looking at the rain-washed sketch of the quarreling infants on Silius's house wall, wondering if his "little rats" had brought back any useful tidbits yet, when Ollius laughed and pointed across the street toward the Palatine Gardens. "Look at that two-legged haystack! Don't tell me bald ain't better."

I pushed back my hood to see better. Near a copse of pines stood a tall German with long russet hair and a thick beard. It was Maelo of the Marcomanni, and his eyes had just lit on me.

"Tribune, you are alive," Maelo exclaimed.

Three of his warriors were playing a knife game nearby. Where was Aurima? Curse it, had she not come with them?

A man watching the knife play turned toward me, cocking his head. A leather patch covered one eye, and with a small shock I realized who he must be.

"We heard you were killed," he said. He spoke Latin fluently, but with lingering Germanic gutturality. "Or hurt, dying."

"My slave, not me."

"Then gods be praised for sparing Caesar's new quaestor." He lifted a hand piously toward the heavens. Extravagant gilt embroidery flashed on his fine wool cloak, dyed that fashionable reddish black called "dried blood."

I said, "You have the advantage of me."

"Your pardon," he said. "I am Julius Flavus." He was, in fact, the brother of Harman the weasel—Arminius—who had caused the greatest disaster in living memory. From Germanicus's memoirs I knew Flavus had fought against his renegade brother and had lost the eye to an enemy arrow.

Though his tribe and the Marcomanni were related, he and Maelo could not have looked less alike. Unlike Aurima's rough-bearded uncle, big and brawny with a chest like an ox, Flavus had softened like a candle left too near the heat. A fleshy belly pushed over his belt, and the yellow hair that must have given him his name had faded. The eye patch on his bare face was black with age.

He was inspecting me, too. "You look like your noble papa, gods grant him long life." Once comrades in arms, they would of course know each other.

After I found Jason's killers, this would be an acquaintance worth cultivating. "There is much I would learn about the North," I said cautiously. "Perhaps you can help me."

Flavus pressed a palm to his breast. "Come to the *Vetrfest* in seven days! Top men from all the tribes of Rhine and Danube are coming to my villa in Bovillae. We drink like troopers and eat like kings." Looking behind me, he added, "The daughter of Ammisia has leave to come, since *Vetrfest* is a holy thing. 'Winter Feast' you would say in Latin."

"Mars' cock!" Ollius muttered to Cleon behind me. "Is that the girl?"

I turned. And for a moment forgot how to breathe.

Aurima came toward us, talking with her young cousin Odo. The hood of her cloak hid her red hair, except for a lock that had blown across her cheek.

I could not look away. What could I say to her? *Are you resolved to live? Have you forgiven me?*

She looked up, so deliberately that it was obvious she knew I was there. And I saw my answer in her face: pride, defiance, wariness. Not the despair I had seen earlier, the empty gaze that looked through a living man into the next world.

A smile began to burn through my gloom. *Gravitas*, I told myself, and smothered it. "I am pleased to see you, daughter of Ammisia."

The casual effrontery surprised her. I had always before called her by her father's name, not by her mother's as is the Marcomanni custom.

I would have liked to hear her cry, *You are alive*, ideally with more pleasure than Maelo had done, but she did not even smile back. Young Odo glared arrows at me.

"She was gone to see your sister," Maelo said.

"I am happy you approve," I said. And even happier that he did not know she had really gone to Diana's wood with me.

Aurima's eyes moved over me. I saw an alertness come into them, as when a wild creature senses something too subtle for a man. "What is it?" I asked.

She stepped back. Her hand went to her throat for the amber talisman that was no longer there. It lay against my own chest, beneath my tunic. I might have smirked.

She bent down for a stone and hurled it at me. I yelped.

She said, "So you live."

"Of course I live." I rubbed my wrist, scowling. "Did you think I was a ghost?"

"A ghost is with you," Aurima said.

Her gaze was unblinking. Despite myself I glanced to the side, then turned and looked behind me. There was nothing and no one but Ollius and Cleon, staring at me with eyes like goose eggs.

The whisper I had heard on the Via Flaminia swam back into my thoughts, and the voice that had told me to spare Rufus. Speaking more harshly to hide my confusion, I said, "Ridiculous. You said nothing about this when we— when I brought you home from my sister's house."

"He was not with you then," she said. "The spirits who are not at peace, it is death that calls them."

Publius's own death, though his ashes were entombed? The death I had been about to command for Rufus?

Maelo cut in, "Sister's daughter, leave him." He sounded uneasy.

"Wait," I said hastily. "Aurima, I must talk with you."

"The girl is superstitious and ignorant," Flavus said. "Pay no heed to what she says."

Maelo retorted, "Aurima is like her mother a priestess, and she sees true."

Whatever the priestess saw in my face resolved her mind. "Come," she said curtly to me, and added a command in Germanic to the others.

"In Rome this is not done," Flavus sputtered, but they stayed where they were.

I matched her pace on the path to the Fountain of the Naiads, avoiding the many furrows cut by rain and melting snow. "Tell me what you saw." I felt breathless. "Do you still see him?"

"I do not see. Not with eyes."

"Do you feel him, then?"

She looked at me. After a moment she said, "Not now."

Disappointment stabbed me. With all my will I tried to detect my brother's presence. Perhaps there were too many other people walking in the gardens.

She said, "Before, I felt . . . wanting. Pain. Anger, perhaps."

"What does he want?"

"Ask him."

"How?" I said, and was rattled to hear the anguish in my voice.

She stopped and held out her hand. "Give me my fire-stone."

I felt like a man tumbled by violent waves across the bottom of the sea. Had Publius's spirit visited me? Or was all of this, even the whisper beside our family tomb, a hoax perpetrated by a girl who wished to be thought a witch?

I tried to regain my common sense. "Why should I believe you?"

Her eyes in the hood's shadow were as green as a millpond. "Death was near you a little time ago. Not so?"

Jason's. Phormio's, still hovering. Perhaps my own, barely avoided.

She nodded, though I had said nothing, and began walking again. "The spirits are all around us, but you Romans do not honor them. You honor nothing. With streets and walls you kill the living earth."

She touched the trunk of a yew clipped to resemble a fluted column. "The poor trees, no longer free. And look!" She stabbed a finger at a young courier rubbing the well-worn erection of a herm, imported from Greece by some acquisitive benefactor. "Such a thing for all to see!"

I said, "Surely your people pray to make grain swell in the ear, cows get with calf, and women get with child. So do we pray for virility and good fortune."

"A man and a woman, that is holy," she insisted.

"It is life," I said. "To be enjoyed for as long as Fortuna allows."

We reached the fountain. The long-haired naiads rose above us, water soaring high around them. Aurima sat down on the broad curb. "That is what you wished to do in the woods of Diana." As she tipped her face up to mine, the wind caught her hood and blew it back, uncovering the coppery splendor of her hair. "Not so, Tribune?"

O sweet desire! How in Mithras's name had I been able to control myself in Diana's grove? I looked away to keep her from reading too much in my eyes.

Her voice rose, rougher and haughtier: "So why did you not take from me what you wanted?"

"I made a vow," I said.

"A godly Roman!" She made it sound like a freak of nature—a white wolf, or a calf with spots in the shape of a man's hand.

I dared to reach out and lift away a strand of hair that had blown across her brow. It seemed there should have been a spark when my fingers touched her, so charged was I with lust and longing. "If anything had happened to you," I said huskily, "I would have been ruined."

"I wish to go there again."

The breeze ruffled the pool behind her, blowing away the spray in a misty rainbow. I took a deep breath. "One day, perhaps."

"Tomorrow."

"Impossible."

"I swear by the Goddess to tell no one."

"I dare not."

"Because you are afraid I am going to run away?"

"Because my god may not save me twice."

Our eyes met. I saw her wondering what to make of me: a haunted man, driven mad by some wild dart from Cupid's bow.

A merry voice broke in: "Who is this stunning creature, Marcus?"

Two women approached us from the far side of the fountain, skirting the arc of spray-silvered gravel in its lee. The one who had spoken was a plump matron with brown curls peeping past the *palla* that veiled her head: my mother's stepsister Fufilla. And the other: black-haired, sleepy-eyed . . . hmm, liked to bite in bed . . . Milonia? Milicia, that was it.

"Is she new here?" Milicia peered nearsightedly at Aurima, who stood up. "By Juno's girdle, a giantess!"

"And what gorgeous hair—just like new copper!" Fufilla tucked her arm through mine. "But after the hardships of the frontier, dear nephew, surely you want a woman with more to cuddle." She hugged my arm against her breast.

"I told you it must have been someone else who was attacked." Milicia kneaded my other arm. "How hard you are, Marcus."

I disentangled myself. "This is Aurima of the Marcomanni, here to—"

Milicia plucked a strand of Aurima's hair out of its braid. "See how bright it is, Fufilla."

Aurima wrenched herself away. "Milicia, stop," I said sharply. "You are frightening her."

"They do not frighten me," Aurima growled.

Milicia protested, "Tell the girl I mean no harm, Marcus darling. I simply want to buy her hair. I will pay five hundred sestertii."

"A thousand if it was never cut." Fufilla tried to peer at Aurima's back.

"Two thousand if it reaches her waist," Milicia barked.

"Milicia, Fufilla, stop this." I tried to sound commanding, but their farcical obsession made me fight back a smile.

"You are insane," Fufilla cried to her friend. "Your husband will erupt like Ætna."

"Let him," Milicia retorted. "Who else will have a wig that color? Two thousand."

"Three thousand," shouted Fufilla.

Aurima's eyes turned glassy. She bolted.

I started after her, but Fufilla snagged my cloak. "Marcus, tell her it will grow back."

"A few minutes with my hairdresser, and she will be rich," Milicia pleaded. "Two thousand sestertii—"

"Three," Fufilla snarled.

"Aurima is a free woman," I broke in. "If she will not sell her hair, you must make do with what nature has given you." I took Milicia's hand in one of mine and Fufilla's in the other. "Which matches so adorably above and below," I added, and kissed each of them on the cheek.

I had to run to catch up with Aurima, splashing through rills carved through the gravel. "Calm yourself, girl." The condescending term spilled out without thought. "They intended no insult."

"You laugh!" Her face was chalk-white. "If they cut my hair, my spirit is slaved."

"Nonsense," I retorted. Flavus was right about her ignorance. She probably buried her nail parings, too, to keep them from ill-wishers.

"If they try, I kill them!"

Her people were gathering around us. I said, "Stop this foolishness. You are under Caesar's protection, and I will keep you safe."

"Safe! Like my mother?" She spat at my feet. And turning so sharply that her cloak flared around her, she bolted down the path past her uncle.

Her mother?

I was struck dumb. The first rule of warfare is to know your enemy, but I had never before wondered why Ingiomar Ironhand had no wife.

There was no mistaking Maelo's mood now. His eyes were blue flames, and an edge of broken teeth showed above his lower lip. "Keep away from my sister's daughter, Roman." He forked his fingers at me, a shocking thing, and strode away. One after another the other warriors did the same.

Did they sense something, too? I tried again to discern my brother's spirit, but felt only the hopelessness of my own blundering desire.

Cleon and Ollius hung back: the two hulking brutes were frightened of me. "You have nothing to fear," I snapped at them. But as we left the gardens, I could not stop looking for the shadow of a troubled ghost.

I was sitting on the side of my bed when Phormio stirred on his pallet. "Sleep well?" I asked.

"I sleep too much. I dream all the time." Pain deepened the furrows around his mouth. "What are you doing?"

I held out the cup and squinted at it. "Drinking some rather nice Setian." Its sweetness would have benefited from more thinning, but I was tired of heavily watered wine. "Bought for Nina's wedding, I think."

"Are there . . . cobwebs here?"

"What?"

"You reached like this"—he pinched his fingers in the air—"and felt above you."

It is death that calls them. Did Homer know it, when he sang of the trench of blood with which Ulysses had made the thirsty dead speak to him?

"Thought something might be there," I said.

He moved, straw rustling beneath him. "Is there . . . any news?"

I waved the cup. "Nothing. No news from li'l rats. Nobody cares a stupid slave was killed."

"Marcus, how much . . . have you drunk?"

"Not enough to see my brother," I said.

He sighed. "Rufus, bring me the slop jar."

"Lissen, Rufus," I said, forgetting my anger at the Thracian boy. I poured myself more wine, omitting water entirely. "He saved your life. Publius saved your life. Know that?"

"No, master," the boy murmured.

"'Spare him,' he told me. Never said why." I shook my head, paused, and peered at him over the cup. "Got any idea?"

Twin lamp flames glittered in Rufus's eyes. "No, master," he said again.

I chuckled. "'Master,'" I repeated softly, and saw Jason's face again. I grimaced and drank.

Rufus edged past to empty the slops. In the doorway he met Turtle's little grandson, who said that Father wished to see me. I set down my cup and rose, swaying a little. It was about time he had news of Jason's killers.

In the atrium the house steward was handing a steaming cup to a man in a traveler's cloak. The newcomer pushed back his hood to drink, baring a shaven pate. A twinge of familiarity made me pause.

Seeing me, he bobbed his head respectfully. Then his gaze swept past me, and his face slackened in surprise. I was curious enough to turn around, but saw only Rufus returning with the slop jar.

"—On the mend," Father was dictating to Nicander. "With thanks, et cetera." His expression changed to a frown as I ambled in unsteadily.

I met his eyes with a truculent stare. "What is it?"

"Two things. First, Gemellus will personally sacrifice to your god Mithras for protecting you." Father picked up the top tablet from a stack on his desk and handed it to me.

I flipped it open. The message began, *My condolences on the death of your slave, worthless though he was.*

"How dare he pass judgment on our family?" I burst out.

Father twirled his forefinger. I kept reading. Gemellus's letter did not sound as if it had been sent by someone who had meant to have me murdered. In fact, it ended by urging that we dine together soon. Had Silius told him I might be converted to his cause?

I dropped the tablet onto the others. "I will talk to him tomorrow. Resolve this once and for all." I swung around too abruptly and had to fend myself off the statue of Ares.

"Marcus." The sternness in my father's voice made me turn back. He said, "Let the Special Cohort investigate."

"You 'spect them to intergrog— to question Caesar's son?"

"The situation with Gemellus is delicate. You have done enough. No more." He paused, trying to catch my eye. "Do I make myself clear?"

"But Caligula needs—" I began, then caught myself.

All was quiet for a moment. Soft voices came from the atrium, the *thunk* of a bucket on the cistern's lip as someone drew water.

I cursed myself for failing to guard my tongue. Caligula had told me particularly to keep his worry about Gemellus from my father. Haltingly I tried to mend the slip: "He ought to be told . . . I mean, if Gemellus did order it . . ."

Father waited silently. I bit down on my babbling. "You said two things."

Lamplight glinted on the silver in his hair as he looked down at his desk. He set aside Gemellus's letter and picked up another tablet, black-framed like the one that had warned me to keep quiet about the accident at the stables. He said, "You are asked to look at a body taken out of the Tiber this afternoon."

"A body? Whose?"

"That is the point. Saxa's adjutant wishes to know if you recognize him."

"Father, I never saw those men's faces."

"Understandably, Quadratus does not wish to keep the remains longer than necessary," he said, as if he had not heard. "He expects you at the Temple of Tiberinus tomorrow, at the third hour."

I wanted to confront Silius about how the two killers could have managed to disappear down a rabbit hole. Now I would have to put that off until after this pointless journey to Tiber Island. "Waste of time," I grumbled.

Father squared the tablets on his desk. "Do you think flirting with women in the Palatine Gardens is more useful?"

My face was already too warm with wine to show a flush, but I felt the sting of his sarcasm. Before I could do more than gather my breath to answer, he cut me off: "You should have been at the Palace this afternoon, reassuring Caesar you are well and undismayed by this . . . mishap." Cold as ice-melt, his eyes settled on my face. "But since you prefer to drown what you imagine are your sorrows, I will write to him saying that you beg to join him soon. Nicander?"

The secretary opened his note tablet and drew a stylus from its loop. I said, "I can send my own message, Father."

He gestured invitingly toward Nicander.

"In my own time."

"Then go to bed," he said curtly. "You will not want to keep the Special Cohort waiting."

CHAPTER 18

THE BODY IN THE TIBER

Quadratus reminded me of a centurion of the Fifteenth who had once ordered a javelin volley before I was out of range. He had the same nailhead eyes, the same dagger-slash of a mouth. "Boatmen found the body snagged on a dead tree," he shouted over the splashing of the river. "Otherwise he'd be halfway to Sardinia." He tucked his vine staff under his arm. "Ready?"

"I am," I said, the words a puff of vapor in the crisp air. I was not looking forward to this exercise.

A ray of midday sun fingered roof ridges and porch columns of the many temples jammed together on Tiber Island. The Temple of Tiberinus, set on a high podium to escape floods, was squeezed between the Temple of Aesculapius and a shrine to Minerva Medica.

I followed the adjutant down the dark slippery passage, reeking of fish, that ran alongside the river god's temple. The brown Tiber swirled at the temple's back wall. If there was a boat landing, it was underwater now.

Quadratus mounted a couple of steps and rapped with his stick on a slime-mottled gate, which jolted inward on squealing pivots. Three small brown men waited in a courtyard overshadowed by the temple. "Bring our pretty boy out so Caesar's quaestor can get a look," the centurion ordered.

One of the men unlocked a door under the temple, and all three entered. A whiff of rotting flesh drifted from the dimness within. "Egyptians," Quadratus said to me in a voice like grating millstones. "Some clan that deals with the dead." He tapped his vine stick against his leg, no more at ease than I.

The swollen corpse, naked and hairy, lay on a broad plank. The small men carrying it had to tip it on edge to get it through the doorway. They jostled it out into the daylight and laid it on a couple of trestles.

Most bodies hauled out of the Tiber are of old and sickly slaves. This man had been young and muscular. Frost covered his face, smearing his features. Great bloody holes gaped where his eyes had been. "Recognize him?" Quadratus asked.

The man's chest bore no hoof marks, and his ribs looked intact. I shook my head, thankful that the cold kept down the flies. "Where was he found?"

"Just downriver of Potsherd Hill."

The skin was like cheap papyrus, reused and rewashed until it is gray. Where the genitals should have been was a ruin of shredded flesh and wisps of hair: a tasty snack for the Tiber eels. I tried to sound unperturbed: "He looks well marinated for having gone no farther than the refuse dump."

"Because of this." Walking around to the corpse's blackened and toeless feet, the centurion tilted his stick to pick up an empty loop of rope that led from the swollen ankles. "Stone slipped out of the knot. Sure you don't know him?"

"I told you I never had a good look at them."

"See that half-moon scar on his forehead? Looks to me like a *sica* slash."

"A gladiator?" I glanced down again, trying to keep my gullet closed. The man was still unfamiliar. If he had been one of Jason's assailants, I was no closer to knowing who had ordered the attack.

Something gleamed inside the dead man's jaws. I said, "Open his mouth."

Quadratus forced the end of his stick into the half-open mouth and pried while one of the Egyptians held the corpse's head. Teeth crunched and shattered. He applied more force, and the jaw hinges broke with a grinding crack. He withdrew the stick, scattering fragments of blackened teeth. "Take a look."

This desecration unnerved me, but I was determined to be stolid. I leaned over to peer into the mouth, edged with spikes of tooth and bone.

A bulging head shot out at me, gaping jaws jammed with needle teeth, blind eyes glaring. I yelped and jerked away, stumbling backward until I hit the courtyard wall.

"*Merda!*" Quadratus said shakily.

The moray eel slithered back down the corpse's throat. I gagged, but managed to keep from losing my breakfast.

The centurion followed me out of the courtyard. By the time we reached the front of the temple, the horror had receded enough that I could take the reins of my horse from Ollius with a reasonably steady hand.

"Well," said Quadratus, and drew a gusty breath. "If you hear of anyone missing a bruiser like that, let me know." He touched his vine stick to his brow and strode off.

⇒⟨· ·⟩⇐

"An *eel*?" Silius stopped looking around to see whom else he knew and stared at me. "Jove's thunderbolts! I would have pissed myself."

"It has taken away my appetite for fish," I admitted. He had agreed to meet me by the statue of Minerva in the Saepta Julia, where rich Romans go to be separated from their money. As usual, he had been late.

I offered him the cabbage leaf of roasted chestnuts I had bought while watching a cockfight. He waved it away. "Strangely, my appetite has vanished too. Help me find Saturnalia gifts for Crispina and Torquata." Fabia Crispina was his wife. Junia Torquata was not.

I cracked a chestnut in my fingers and flicked off the bits of shell. "And Pertinax?"

"Very amusing." He raised his dark brows as I passed the last nuts to Turtle's grandson, my attendant for the afternoon. "Your *servus viator* grows younger all the time. Next you will have Ollius carrying it in a cradle."

"I left Rufus tending Phormio. The old mule does better, I think."

"May it be so."

"Where do you want to look?" I gestured at the shops under the surrounding portico. "Perfume? Jewelry? Paintings? Slaves?"

The intermittent sunshine had brought crowds into the Saepta. A glimpse of coppery hair made my heart leap, but it was only a Celt with double braids. Someone jostled us, exclaiming to a companion, "The Chaldean was bribed to say she would have a boy! I vow the Tiberians bought that prophecy. Mark me—"

"I vow we did not," Silius murmured.

He headed toward the other end of the portico, skirting a gladiatorial bout in the center of the vast court. Over the spectators' cheers, jeers, and shouted wagers he said, "So you do not think this drowned man was one of the killers?"

I pushed past a couple of well-dressed youths roaring encouragement to the fighters. "I have no idea. They might have been blue-skinned Picts or snake-eyed Silk People, for all I know."

Silius paused to clasp hands with a client, who winked at me. Annoyed, I turned away and found myself next to a tray of silver combs. The one inlaid with tortoiseshell would suit her, I thought; I could wrap it with a clever little tag: *With this gift you may tame your fiery locks, though not the heat you kindle in me. . . .*

"Will you stop mooning over that rubbish? I am speaking to you."

What had gotten into me? I was here to seek information from Silius, not to compose doggerel for an illiterate girl. "Sorry." I stepped away from the vendor's entreaties.

Silius lowered his voice as we moved through what seemed to be half the population of Rome, with our personal slaves and guards following. "There may be a reason why Saxa cannot catch them."

"Because he was behind it? But what reason would he have to kill Jason?"

"I do not say he did it, but he knows who did."

"Then whom would he protect? And why?"

He shrugged, unable—or unwilling—to answer.

Near the fountain a fire-eater was belching a gout of flame as onlookers moaned in awe. A portly man stepped in front of him and raised his hands for attention. "Noble sirs and ladies, this entertainment is provided by Favor of Neapolis. If you wish your beloved to be on fire for you, choose among the finest perfumes in the world from Favor of Neapolis, available here in our shop."

"There you are," I said. "Just do not get the same fragrance for both."

Silius appeared to have forgotten about buying gifts. Casually he asked, "Is your new boy of any use? Did he tell you Gemellus's favorite wines, or whether he prefers roasted doves to dormice?"

"He was Gemellus's *vitellus*, not just a server."

He cocked a dark brow at me. "So?"

I did not answer. I was not about to tell him that Rufus had confessed to joining Livilla in Gemellus's bed.

Yelling boys chased a ball along the edge of the portico. Ollius cut past us and gave the pig's bladder a boot that sent it higher than the fountain spray.

We climbed the steps to the shelter of the portico. A bearded Greek bowed to us. "Special prices to honor the Princeps' recovery, honored sirs."

He swept a hand toward the antiquities spilling out of his shop's interior: a round shield bearing a Spartan lambda, a black-figured *krater* for mixing wine, a *kouros* with staring eyes and an archaic smile, looking as stiff as the stone he was carved from.

I turned away, shaking my head. Time now for Caesar's quaestor to truly become *one who seeks.* "It is not what I thought it would be, returning to Rome."

"Do you miss your benighted little garrison on the Danube?"

"I miss being a man," I said. "Not a game piece for my father."

We threaded our way along the colonnade, avoiding shoppers and merchants. Silius said, "At my parents' funeral, while everyone else wept and lamented, you said I was lucky to be fatherless." He sidestepped a cluster of empty plant pots. "Do you remember?"

He knew I had been bitterly envious of Publius, possessor of all Father's pride as a friend of the great Germanicus's youngest son. I said, "Now he wants a consulship from Caligula, and he has put me in my brother's shoes to gain it."

"Your family owes a great deal to Caligula."

"And he to us. I think the debt is canceled."

Silius paused to study a painting of Achilles fighting Hector. "Many Senators are angry at his treatment of Gemellus. Tiberius had good reason to distrust Caligula, you know. He meant the two of them to share power equally."

"And you think that is possible?"

For a moment I feared I had been too ingenuous, but Silius smiled thinly. "It could be, if Caligula wished it."

He halted again, this time to greet a group of men on their way to the adjacent Spartan Baths. In that time I debated with myself whether to ask if I might aid Gemellus's plans. Could Silius identify my deceptions as easily as I recognized his?

Then I too was accosted by old comrades joking, "Ho, the Terrible Twins are together again."

"Watch out for the big Gaul," one of them warned. "He has never been fond of you."

"What will he do, beat me with his abacus?" I shot back.

Silius frowned as they ambled off, chuckling. Before he could speak I said, "Gaius, old friend."

His mouth relaxed. "What, Marcus?"

"Buy earrings for Crispina."

I went down the portico steps. He pitched his orator's voice to reach me without drawing attention. "I thought you might be of more help."

I looked up at him. "In the new year I will become a glorified clerk. Unless there is some change in the next few weeks, I ought to practice counting money instead of spending it." With a lift of my brows I challenged him to respond.

"If there were a change before then . . ." Silius said slowly.

"'Ifs' are no use to me." *Tell me when Gemellus plans to act.*

A vendor of honey cakes shoved his wares at me. Little Astyanax drove him off with a shrill admonition.

I lingered for another moment, then turned away with a small shrug.

"Carinna," Silius said behind me.

His eyes, dark as chestnuts, were clear and warm in his handsome face. He smiled at me. "Happy New Year," he said, and then I lost him in the crowd.

At the critical moment, I had balked at pressing him about Gemellus' plans. Why? Had I expected to be ridiculed for a clumsy attempt at deceit? Or had I feared that the friend I once loved might answer me, and so prove he was plotting treason?

Nor was I farther ahead in learning who had murdered Jason or why. Apart from the appearance of the moray eel—a memory that still made me feel lightheaded—viewing the body pulled from the Tiber had been useless. Perhaps, at least, I would find Phormio in better health.

There was indeed news at home, but not of a pleasant sort. Rufus had run away.

Breathless with agitation, the house steward puffed, "Some herb was needed . . . for Phormio's potion . . . so Phormio sent him to the market with the sauce girl, who knows the merchants—"

I guessed the rest: "And he disappeared while her back was turned."

"She was talking to a friend of hers, a seller of pot herbs. I will have her thrashed." He looked wretched; our family had never before had a slave run off. "I have had every available man out looking. The master will be furious."

"I will report it to the magistrate." I sank down wearily on an atrium bench to let Turtle unlace my boots. Why had I thought I could make a civilized servant out of a backcountry barbarian? The Thracian boy had had a wild streak that no amount of decent treatment could erase.

"With that red hair, he'll not get far," the steward said vengefully.

If Silius's bailiffs did not find the boy, the slave catchers would. There was no question of what would be done with him next: an iron collar and a fugitive brand, the auction block, and a short, miserable existence while a new owner worked him to death.

"I always thought he was hopeless," Turtle muttered.

I snapped, "No one asked you."

In the bedroom I found Phormio trying to stand, as tottery as a new foal. "Sit down," I ordered, shoving a tablet at him. "Write a message to Silius that the boy is gone."

"Marcus." He slumped onto my couch, looking up at me anxiously. The effort of rising had bleached his face white. "I do not think . . . he ran away. Something . . . happened to him."

"Write," I said, too angry to care.

"Yesterday . . . in the atrium . . . the messenger from Gemellus saw him. The man . . . glared at him, Rufus said."

"And Gemellus has always frightened the piss out of him. So the boy ran away." Now it would be rumored that our family was in difficulties. Scandalmongers would recall that my brother had been charged with *laesa maiestas,* that my mother had left my father's house, and that I myself had refused to return at the end of my year's service as a military tribune.

I cursed the boy. "Spare him," indeed! Far better if Cleon had disposed of him as I had intended.

An errand boy trotted off to notify Silius of Rufus's flight. On impulse I placed a hand on our household altar, but the only sound I heard was the shrieking of the sauce girl being caned in the stableyard.

"*Merda!*" I said, far more viciously than the centurion had said it earlier, and slapped both hands down on the altar. A fine flurry of ash spurted up between my fingers, as if admonishing me.

CHAPTER 19

RUNAWAY

"You should have gotten rid of the boy as I advised," my father said. A crow squawked in the plane tree as he stepped down carefully into the stableyard. The sun had not yet risen over the wall, and the packed earth was slippery with frost. The slaves stopped mucking out to watch, leaning on their forks and spades as if his appearance were not a daily routine.

I stumbled down beside him. He still did not know that Rufus had told me of being abed with Julia Livilla. No excuse for letting the boy live after that would have been acceptable, certainly not my claim to have heard my brother's spirit. The sound of a ghostly mule-bell might be a touch of theater; obeying a dead man's imagined voice was pure weak-mindedness.

Watching him confer with the stablemaster about the well-being of men and beasts, I wondered if Rufus was now stammering out his tale of Livilla to someone who would take it to his ward captain or the head of his guild, who in turn would confide it to a Senator of the Tiberian faction. I had tormented myself half the night imagining the effect such a public disgrace would have on Caligula's dignity and authority. Even if his *maiestas* survived the scandal, he would never forgive Father for allowing it to happen.

The pale crown of the sun slid over the tiled ridge of the wall. I raised my hands and spoke the Parthian sun-salute: "*Nama Mithra.*" Hail Mithras; hail Lord and God, unconquered Sun. . . .

The sorrel stallion, tied to a post while his stall was cleaned, rolled an evil, glittery eye at me. When I finished the prayer and reached to fondle him, he turned away to nibble at his fetlock.

Father turned. "By the way, Marcus, you must make arrangements to sell that beast. He costs a fortune to feed, and you will not need him here."

The big warhorse stamped an arrogant hoof, and at that moment the world seemed to distill into an image as clear and contained as a reflection in a raindrop: the muscular arch of his neck, creases deepening at his throat as he tossed his head. Reminded of a proud and brave barbarian girl, I sighed to myself.

Father signaled me to follow him into the kitchen garden. The old man who had charge of the roses and the fruit trees got up stiffly from his bench. Father spoke with him and with the boy who looked after the herb and vegetable plots, then sent them away. He sat on the bench, gesturing for me to join him.

"I had hopes of that drowned man," he said. "There was nothing to identify him?"

"No clothing, no rings, no tattoos. Quadratus thought him a gladiator. He was not a soldier." There is no mistaking the flat, horny feet of a man accustomed to marching twenty miles a day.

Above our heads, smoke from the hypocaust drifted down from the eaves. Father said, "I spoke of this yesterday with Caesar and Lepidus. We suspect it is part of a Tiberian plot to create popular unrest."

"A plot?"

"A scurrilous lampoon is circulated, deriding the Princeps for adopting Gemellus. Now a slave belonging to the Princeps' chief adviser, one of *my* slaves, is murdered scarcely a stone's throw from the Palace. It is not coincidence."

This was the moment when I should have told him that Gemellus might act before year-end. But there were still two months before the new year. Worming my way further into Silius's confidence might allow me to expose the plot—or, better for Caligula's tranquility, force the conspirators to abandon it. So I said only, "Silius told me the Tiberians had nothing to do with Jason's death."

"Ah, yes." He shot me a skeptical glance. "What about Silius?"

"I am going to see him this morning. To tell him we will offer a reward for Rufus."

A small bird lit on the tortured branches of the espaliered pear tree beside us. Father said, "That is not what I am asking."

When I did not respond, he went on, "I am willing to be thought out of date. Even Caesar tells me pleasure is pleasure, no matter who plays the sword and who the scabbard." He looked up at the bird. "It is not so important between boys. But for a man to play a woman's role . . . to submit to another man . . ."

Our old yellow mouser peered up from under a rosebush. The bird flew into the pale green sky. I said, "You need have no fear of that."

His shoulders relaxed. "I am in negotiations for your future wife, and such things are important to fathers."

Serpent take it! "Who is she?"

"I will not say just yet. But if we can reach agreement, it will be an excellent match." He added cryptically, "She is closely related to the Princeps."

I would ask Nina to find out whom he had in mind. All of Caligula's sisters and female cousins were already married or betrothed, but that is no hindrance when *patresfamiliae* are plotting alliances.

Sudden dread struck me. "Tell me it is not Julia Livilla."

"If I were able to arrange a marriage with one of the Princeps' sisters, Marcus, you would be the most fortunate young man in Rome."

"Father, I beg you—"

"Do not dare beg me for anything! I have not sacrificed so much to see our family brought down by your whims."

It would be no surprise if pairing me with Publius's former *sponsa* was part of his plan to peg me into the hole my brother had left. To him it made no difference that Livilla, whom my brother had loved, now whored her favors to anyone she chose.

I raised my voice. "I will have a say in choosing my wife."

"You will marry whomever I wish," he snapped. "I do not care whether or not you are grateful. My sole concern is to improve our family's position."

The yellow cat was sharpening its claws on the cherry tree. Father said, "In the meantime, meet me tomorrow at noon for the public banquet." He got up with an effort.

I managed to keep my voice even. "In the Julian Forum, as before?"

A curt nod. "Remember that it is a festival. Smile, embrace our clients and friends, and ask what they need. Scat!" He stamped his foot. The cat merely looked at him, forepaws still braced on the tree.

"Very well," I said.

"I will have gifts on hand." He reached down for a stone. At that the cat fled, but the stone struck it so hard that it tumbled over among the cabbages.

"You have made a good beginning, Marcus." He turned back to me, brushing his palms together. "Do not fail me now."

Julia Livilla! To be married to a woman who would flaunt her infidelities to me, whose children—my family's heirs—might be sired by any man in Rome! I almost pursued my father into the house to blurt out Rufus's secret. Even he could not wish a wife upon me who had been to bed with a slave.

Phormio was awake. "Have . . . you found him?" he asked in a groggy whisper.

"Not yet," I said savagely, bending to put on my boots.

"He said . . . it was too bad that . . . his life had no value." He took a slow rasping breath. "Or he would thank you . . . for sparing it."

I wrenched at a bootlace. What concept had a Thracian brat of gratitude? When the little wretch was found, it would be my duty to oversee his punishment.

The bootlace broke. As if it had broken the seal of my lips, I said, "Father plans to espouse me to Julia Livilla."

Phormio was silent while I knotted the lace together and tied up my boots. At last he murmured, "Do you think he does not know . . . of your German girl?"

"What has that to do with it?" Jason, Cleon, and Ollius had all seen her, so I knew my infatuation must be household gossip. "Sabinus told me to make sure she settles well in Rome. I promised him a report."

He made no reply. I snatched my cloak off the peg. It was the lighter one; the other had been ruined when Jason died. I thought of the time he had given me his own patched cloak to keep me warm, and my anger burned higher. "I will have someone bring your medicine," I said to Phormio, and left.

The Special Cohort's Palatine office was located in what had once been someone's house. I stepped around piles of sand and broken brick in the atrium, acrid with lime and echoing with the tap of brick hammers and the squeal of barrow axles.

The duty centurion's adjutant thought he could not reveal anything about the search for Jason's assailants, but I disabused him of that notion. "Sorry, sir," he said, coming off his stool to stand at attention. Like all Praetorians he had an inflated sense of his own importance, and needed an army man to put him in his proper place.

It was much effort for nothing. Tips from informers had proved vain; no man with crushed bones in breast or back had been found. "It strains belief for a search to turn up only a waterlogged corpse," I complained.

"It may be that the man died of his injury and his body has gone to the public pyre," said the adjutant. He sat down again, brushing brick dust off his tunic.

"Tell me about the personal guards of Caesar's family. Are any missing?" I dared not ask particularly about Gemellus's men.

His face stiffened at the implication. "We do not keep records of that, sir. Bodyguards are hired with the Princeps' household funds." He stood up once more. "I regret I cannot be of more help."

"Wait," I said. "There is one more thing. . . ."

The Palace gate was just clanging shut behind us when Silius's personal slave, Leander, darted through the crowd of gawkers and petitioners toward me. His hair stood out in damp spicules, and his face was flushed with exertion. "Marcus Licinius, I have looked everywhere for you. Will you come to my master's house?"

"Of course," I said at once. "Is it about Jason's killers?"

We were hurrying along the Vicus Triumphalis Augusti, dodging puddles and horse droppings. "I am sorry, it is not," Leander wheezed.

I slowed. "About my Thracian slave, then?"

"It concerns the barbarians."

I turned so quickly that he took a step back. "Barbarians?"

I knew all four of them. They were part of Aurima's escort, although neither she nor Maelo was with them. Leaning against the wall and sprawling on benches in Silius's vestibule and atrium, they eyed me as I entered. On the floor lay the smelly split carcass of a cow.

"Here, you brutes! Make way for a patrician of Rome!" The doorkeeper kicked the trousered leg of the nearest man, broken-nosed Cotto, who clapped a hand on his empty knife sheath. Beside him, Segomo pressed down his thick gray beard and spat at my feet.

"Let him pass," a voice called, punctuating the command with a steely rap on the floor. I told Ollius to stay in the vestibule and made my way past the two warriors. A burly man in a studded leather cuirass saluted me with his knob-headed staff. "Long time, young Carinna."

"Not long enough, Durus," I said.

The bailiff's own slaves guarded the two others. Young Odo appeared to have lost a dispute with a paved street. The last, a man called Bodico, sported a mat of bloody hair over one ear. All four Marcomanni eyed me with hostility and defiance.

Durus explained that the four had rifled a butcher shop in a Palatine arcade. They had flung much of the pork, mutton, and other meat into the street, and a brawl had ensued when the butcher tried to keep them from making off with the side of beef. Passing Praetorians had brought them to the Tenth District magistrate, and Silius had decided to consult me.

I asked Segomo where Aurima and Maelo were. His blood-streaked face creased in a truculent sneer. "Maelo goes to find Flavus."

"And Aurima?" I pressed, but he only shrugged.

Silius swept into the atrium, dressed in his toga. A frown tensed the black brows over his bronze-dark eyes and scored the corners of his mouth. "I am glad to see you, Carinna," he said with feeling, and clasped my elbows for a kiss of greeting. Wine and cinnamon scented his breath.

"I need a word with you," I said.

He nodded to the bailiff. "Keep them quiet, Durus."

"As you say, your honor." Durus gave him a grin lacking several teeth. After serving Silius's predecessors, no doubt he found irony in being commanded by a scapegrace he had more than once fished out of trouble.

We went down a corridor away from the atrium. Silius said, "If this is about your redheaded slave, there is no word of him yet."

"Not that," I said. "Let us walk in your peristyle; it is more private."

"I have had enough of freezing my balls when we talk. Come into—Crispina, what are you doing here?"

He had taken me into an anteroom that led to his own chamber. A young woman confronted us with her fists clenched by her skirts. Behind her, a slave ran a dust whisk over a chair with practiced indolence.

"I came in to be sure the cleaning is properly done, husband." She jerked her chin at the slave. "You know they will loaf unless they are supervised."

Silius's mouth tightened, and he looked past her toward his room. She reddened, embarrassed that I had seen she did not have the run of her own house.

"My wife, Fabia Crispina," he told me, though I had met her when she was his *sponsa*. Crispina was a pale-faced girl of perhaps fifteen, no beauty but not ill-favored. When she looked at Silius, I saw the adoration and eagerness to please that her pride tried to keep on a short leash. It is always easy for one votary to recognize another.

I greeted her with polite regrets that I had missed their wedding. Her answer—"You honor our house, Marcus Licinius"—was distinctly chilly.

Silius snorted as she left with the slave. "She is jealous of you," he said. "Of Pertinax, too. Of anyone she thinks I might feel affection for."

I shook my head, not without sympathy.

"Worse yet, I sowed the fields to no avail every other night for months. I fear the poor little bitch is barren." He sighed, slouching into one of the two armchairs. "Which means no career preferment for me as a father."

"Not to mention an end to your family." I sat down too.

"Well, I can marry again." He loosened his toga. "What troubles you, Marcus?"

"It is thought that the 'Romulus and Remus' lampoon and the attack on Jason were both directed by Caligula's enemies. Is that true?"

Silius exhaled slowly. His gaze slipped from my face to the garlands painted high up on the wall, then back to me. "If you think me capable of sanctioning the murder of a slave in your *familia*, I suppose our friendship is truly at an end."

Shame washed over me. If I was to penetrate this conspiracy, it would not be through Silius; I was unable to sustain ill will toward him. I stood up. "Let us return to the barbarians."

He remained in his chair. "Do you fear Saxa will come for me?"

I did not answer, but he smiled. "Then we are even for the fright you gave me when I heard you were dead in the snow." He nodded toward his room. "Go look. It is just as it was."

His father's armor gleamed on a stand in a corner, the breastplate and helmet polished as brightly as if the old general might be back any day to claim them. In another corner, winged-footed Hermes stood transfixed in midstride. Someone had removed the clothing that was usually tossed over the statue's outstretched arm. A latticed cabinet sheltered Silius's collection of Greek and Latin erotica. And innocuous in the dusk stood the broad sleeping couch.

His footsteps sounded behind me. "But here is something new, after all," I said, touching a marble bust of Aristotle.

"A gift from Pertinax." Silius looked down at the bearded philosopher. "He hopes it will remind me to think before I act."

A faint fragrance hung in the air. Not his. Torquata's?

I turned away. "Tell me more about this scuffle at the butcher shop." I made my voice businesslike. "Where is the complainant?"

"He went to have his broken arm attended to." He paused. "The matter merits a fine, at least. He will have to close his shop or hire a meat cutter until the arm heals."

"You have not held a hearing, then?"

"Not yet. See here, Carinna: I am inclined to rule that this case be tried before the Princeps. Do you have any objection?"

"If your decision is already made, why did you send for me?" The memories crowding around were making me uncomfortable.

"I wanted you here as Caesar's witness."

"Then let us get it over with."

My brusqueness rankled him. "Very well. Had I not been waiting for you, I would have thrown the stinking brutes out of my house."

The hum of voices from the atrium suddenly rose to an uproar. I heard several men's voices and a woman's, all shouting in impenetrable Germanic.

"Jove's thunderbolts!" Silius said. "What is that?"

"Trouble," I said.

I saw Aurima before she saw me. Hooded in her cloak, she stabbed a finger toward the side of beef with anger crackling in her voice. Durus and his men stared, astonished and amused, as the four bold warriors shrank to sheepish boys under her scolding. Ollius grinned openly.

She fell silent as Silius entered the atrium. He smiled at her. That meant nothing; he smiled at most women, particularly if they were nubile.

I stepped out from behind him. She had had time to prepare, for she must have recognized Ollius; but still her cheeks flushed scarlet.

I said, "Your honor, this is Aurima, priestess of Austro, daughter of Ingiomar, war chief of the ten tribes of the Marcomanni, and of Ammisia, niece of the great king Marbodo, a hostage entrusted to Caesar for the peace between Ingiomar and Vannius, king of the Marcomanni."

She tried to break in, but I would not let her interrupt the elaborate introduction. When I was done, Silius said with impeccable manners, "I am Gaius Silius, magistrate of the Tenth District of Rome. It is a pleasure to meet you." His dark lashes flickered as he inspected her.

She threw back the hood of her blue cloak with a shake of her head, as though girding for battle. Her coppery hair blazed in the dull light.

He sucked in his breath. "So this is your Amazon," he murmured in Greek.

Aurima said, "I am here to make free my people."

He tore his eyes away from her to glance at me. I said, "We must wait for your uncle Maelo." Fortunately the folds of my tunic hid the evidence of my mindless desire. Serpent take it, her spell was stronger than ever!

Aurima said, "My women weep for their families in the Mark." She looked from one of us to the other. "They refuse their husbands to sleep with them, and the men cannot hunt, so they drink and fight. When they see what they want, they take it because they are warriors."

It could not be pleasant explaining to two Romans why her guard of honor had pillaged a butcher shop and stolen half a cow. My admiration and desire for her grew. I resolved to buy her jewelry, combs, mirrors, fine fabrics from the Saepta Julia. I would take her to the countryside whenever she pleased. And she would say, *Yes, I will be your lover, if you find me an old husband with a shriveled radish between his legs.*

"You understand?" she concluded. "So do not wait. Free them now."

"They assaulted a Roman citizen," Silius explained. "I must judge whether to bind them over for trial."

"You cannot trial my people. We are not Romans."

He frowned. "This is only a preliminary hearing. Please calm yourself."

Aurima's accusing glare shot from him to me. She said, "These are free men. Let them go."

"A law has been broken, and the magistrate must hear what happened." I tried to sound reasonable. "Surely it is the same among your people."

Aurima said something in Germanic to Odo and Bodico. The older man nodded, but Maelo's son scowled. She spoke more harshly, gesturing at Silius, and Odo agreed sullenly. "They are going to tell you what happened," she said.

Silius nodded. "Then we will proceed as soon as your uncle returns."

"I speak for my people, Magistrate. And for my uncle."

"You tell her, Carinna," he muttered.

"Tell her yourself, you lizard."

He sighed. "I cannot proceed without your uncle. You have no standing in law."

Her face colored again. She swung around to the warriors. "Do you hear, my brothers? The daughter of Ammisia and granddaughter of Fridurica has no voice under the law of Rome."

The Marcomanni roared and shook their fists. The bailiff and his men tensed. Ollius braced his staff in both hands.

Silius did not like it either. "Stop them, Carinna, before they begin rampaging through my house."

I said, "As a hostage, Aurima is legally in Caesar's *manus*, not her uncle's. I will take responsibility for her in Caesar's name."

He raised a brow. "You will speak for her?" he said for Aurima's benefit.

Disbelief flashed across her face. I made the mistake of touching the spot between my collarbones to remind her of the amber pendant.

She turned on Durus and tried to wrest his staff from his hands. Bodico hoisted the side of beef and charged the bailiff with it. Odo threw a bench, felling one of the slaves. Segomo and Cotto surged into the fray.

Ollius bulled his way through the brawl to protect me. Silius retreated into an opposite corner, yelling for his slaves. "Stop them," I shouted to Aurima. "If they harm a Roman official, they will die."

Clubs thudded on flesh. Men howled, cursed, shouted in pain. A bronze statuette whacked bone. Blood spattered like scarlet rain.

I bellowed in Germanic, "Stop it *now*."

The command in their own language confused the Marcomanni. They paused, looking around at me. Cotto, who had splashed into the impluvium, retreated as if it were the Styx.

I ordered the bailiff to call off his slaves. The only sound then was panting and the slosh of water chasing itself back and forth in the shallow pool. "Now what?" Silius asked under his breath.

Aurima turned. From her expression I knew she would have liked to set her countrymen on me.

"Justice will be done," I told her, speaking loudly so everyone could hear. "But not today. Let your warriors go home and tend their wounds. Caesar did not realize your people were hungry, and I will see that meat is sent to you. The magistrate will let you know his decision later."

Her brows tilted in puzzlement. "Go," I said again, more softly. "Before it is too late." I raised my voice. "Durus, give them back their weapons."

Moments later the doorkeeper slammed the bar down behind the last of them. He pulled the spy port open to cry, "Get gone, then. Be off to your kennel." A knife tip waggled through the hole at him, then withdrew to raucous laughter. He clapped the panel shut. "The god-cursed savages are pissing on the doorstep."

Silius adjusted his toga's folds. "I see I can no longer presume to give the orders in my own house." He was only half joking. "We need a drink." He motioned me into the reception room.

I was in no mood to be teased about Aurima. "I cannot stay."

"Come, give the barbarians a chance to wander off." He pressed me forward with an arm around my shoulders. "Leander! Where were you, you scoundrel—hiding while my precious skin was at risk? Bring some of my best wine, quickly."

"Silius," I said. "The meat I promised them: I want it seen to now. Beef, fresh and bloody. Not the one they stole. Delivered with my compliments."

"Take care of it," he told Leander. "Have the bill sent to the Quaestor." He turned to me. "Will you stay for dinner? It is just a light meal, Crispina and I." He added casually, "We are having eel."

I opened my mouth to decline, then caught on to the jest. "Ass," I grumbled, sinking into a chair near his own. "What makes you so merry?"

"A brush with danger makes life sweeter. You know that, beloved." His dark eyes gleamed at me.

For a moment neither of us spoke. Leander came in with a server who poured out deep amber wine. Silius lifted his cup to his mouth, then paused. "What did you shout that fixed them in their tracks?"

The wine was hardly watered, and its warmth began at once to loosen the knots of ill humor in me. I said, "I just told them to stop." A quiver of incredulity and relief rose in my throat and threatened to erupt in my voice.

"I should have thought of that." Flinging out an arm, he cried squeakily, "Stop, you great hairy beasts, before I soil myself."

He grinned, and I started to laugh. We were howling helplessly together when a blurry shape rustled into the room. Wiping my eyes, I made out Fabia Crispina standing stiffly by Silius's chair.

"I was quite frightened, husband," she said. "Could you not have sent me word that all was well?"

"Dealing with lawbreakers is a magistrate's business, Crispina! Get back to your spinning or whatever you were doing." As she turned away, he added, "And if you try to serve us poorer wine, I will notice."

She yanked the folding doors shut behind herself. Silius knuckled wetness from his cheek. "May you be spared a parsimonious wife, Marcus."

"Little danger of that," I said. "My brother's *sponsa* is not known for frugality."

His eyes widened. "Livilla?" Then he laughed again. "Why fret? She will be too busy with other men to notice when you take your fire-maiden to bed." We drank fine wine until I smelled the aromas of his dinner and took myself home.

A message had arrived from my mother in Antium.

"I am glad she is well; I mistrust the seaside in winter," I said, untying my boots. Her letter lay on the kitchen bench beside me, sealed in its case.

"Thought we'd never get here." Damulus, one of Mother's guards, wrenched down his pungent leather riding breeches and kicked them aside. "I swear, a slug would have traveled faster." He turned his back to the stove and pulled up his tunic to warm his buttocks. The cook hooted lasciviously, and the sauce girl and scullery boy uttered pleasantly scandalized shrieks. Damulus winked at them.

"Why so slow? Heavy traffic?" I rubbed one of my icy feet to bring back the blood; the walk from Silius's house had been damp and frigid.

"The pen-pusher," Damulus growled. "He got off to walk so many times, I reckoned we'd be on the road till midnight." He scratched his reddened backside vigorously with both hands and heaved a sigh of satisfaction.

"What pen-pusher?" asked Ollius from the doorway.

"Dio is here?" I supposed my parents had some legal dealings that required my mother's secretary to confer with my father's. Made independent by the Law of Three Children, she was able to own and manage property of her own.

Damulus sobered. "Did you hear about the prophecy?"

"That Agrippinilla would have a son? Yes, days ago."

"Turns out that wasn't all the Chaldean foretold." Damulus lowered his voice. "He also said the boy might kill her."

The kitchen slaves gasped. They all made signs against evil.

"Where did you hear that?" I guessed at once that this might be another tactic to shake the stability of Caligula's rule. "What mountebank says so?"

"Babbalus. No, Balbillus. Something like that. Son of the old Princeps' astrologer." Damulus grimaced. "He moved to Antium, to the villa, when they all left Capri."

"Has he been questioned about this horoscope?"

"Hah! No, they found it in his workroom this morning. He got aboard a ship to Alexandria yesterday."

The scullery boy laughed nervously, then clapped a hand over his mouth.

How inconvenient for those who wanted to know if he had been bribed. But sensible, given the nature of the prediction. I said formally, "We will make a gift to Juno Lucina for our cousin Julia Agrippina's good health."

Everyone nodded, although I saw they were still shocked. Death in childbirth is always a possibility, but to voice it as a prediction for Caligula's eldest sister was to doubt *Fortuna Augusta*, the Princeps' talismanic good luck.

The news would horrify Nina. If she was with child, I did not want her to sit alone fretting about it. It was troubling enough that they were the same age. Agrippinilla had never borne children, and twenty-two is old for a first birth.

I got to my feet and reached down for the letter case. Damulus, still planted with his back to the stove, was too preoccupied to make room for me to pass. "Are you warm enough?" I inquired. "Shall I add more wood?"

He was startled, then caught the bantering lightness in my tone. "If you don't mind, young master."

I picked up a stick of firewood. "Bend over, darling. This will hardly hurt at all."

Damulus guffawed at the coarse humor. Ollius began to tell of the Marcomanni brawl at Silius's house, and I left them more cheerily anticipating the next day's feast of thanksgiving for Caligula Caesar, confident that Father and I would keep the family safe from the displeasure of gods.

Every stain, every scratch on the worn leather scroll case was familiar. How many times had I fingered that nick in the edge of the cap while reading my mother's first letter to me in Carnuntum? For a moment I was that desperately homesick young tribune again, colder than I had ever dreamed possible in a place where inside walls ran wet as the night's frost melted from them.

Cross-legged on my bed, I snapped the seal that bound the cords of top and bottom and pulled the case apart. The scroll slid into my hand. "Do you wish to listen?" I said to Phormio. "I will read a little louder."

He had struggled up from his pallet when I came in, lips squeezed together to stifle any sound, and now slouched on a low stool with his back against the wall. A nearly empty cup stood on the floor, but his face was still tense with pain.

When he was settled, I read the letter aloud:

To my son Marcus from his mother, warmest greetings.

Your father has informed me of the attack that left poor Jason dying in your arms. I am sure such an assault would not have happened but for your insistence on going about with the most meager of escorts. For my sake if not your own, please accept the bodyguards your father desires you to have.

He informs me that you are also in need of a private secretary. I have decided to make you a gift of my Dio, who is too intelligent to waste his talents here in the countryside. You know Dio is clever. He is also discreet, and his knowledge of noble families will help you greatly.

Be well, my son, and remember your mother who loves you.

"She has given me Dio," I said, stunned.

I read the letter again to be sure I had not misunderstood. Phormio gave a long sigh. "Forget what I said . . . about the villa. . . ." His tongue was thickening; the opiate at last was taking effect. "I am a coward . . . thinking only of myself." He darted another glance at me from under his brows, then tipped his face down so I could see only the shiny crown of his head, framed in wooly curls.

I nearly spoke, to reassure him that he had already given me all I would take from him, but held my tongue.

"Little I can do now . . . a sick old nuisance." His eyelids drooped. "But, Marcus . . ." He forced them open. "If anything happened to you . . ."

He sighed again. His eyes closed, and he slept.

I eased him back onto his pallet. Covering him with the quilt, I said softly, "And I, too, Phormio, if anything happened to you."

By the time I headed back toward the kitchen to find some supper, night had fallen. There was little chance now of news about Rufus. Hiding? Caught and sold? Dead? Like Jason's two killers, he seemed to have vanished without a trace.

I was musing over political motives for the astrologer's dire prophecy when my mother's gift surprised me. His hair was still wet from the bath, and he was hobbling on the outer edges of his sandals.

"Welcome home, Dio," I said.

He stopped. One might have taken him for a free man of good birth, so fine was the weave of his travel-creased tunic. "Thank you, young master. Is it still permitted to call you 'Marcus' at home?"

"Of course." Why had Mother chosen to inflict this cocklebur on me? Uninterested in women's slaves, I had paid him no mind before I went north. He, I was sure, considered me an ignorant lout. No doubt he bitterly resented the bad luck that had led Father to plant me in my mother's belly and him in a slavewoman's.

We now looked even less alike than before. Dio was pale-skinned and short, not quite fat but far from lean. Though he had not yet reached thirty, his dark hair had already begun to retreat from his brow. Deep lines around his eyes told of hours spent reading and writing in poor light; his mouth was a colorless seam, and his nose as sharp as a goose quill. I saw nothing of Father in him.

He was studying me, too—exceedingly presumptuous behavior for a slave, but I let it pass. "I scribed that letter for your mother," he said, nodding toward the cylinder in my hand.

"So you know she has given you to me."

"Do you intend to keep me?" he asked. His tone was not light enough to hide his anxiety. He wanted me to send him back to Mother. Back to his pleasant life of gossip about neglectful husbands, ungrateful children, the Princeps' sisters and bedmates, the price of someone's new jewelry.

I did not answer immediately. I lacked a personal slave, not a secretary. Dio could not replace Phormio, much less Jason or even Rufus. Still, as a quaestor I would need someone to manage my calendar and correspondence.

Dio was waiting for an answer. "You can accompany me to the festival in the next few days," I said. "I will decide your future later."

CHAPTER 20

PRIESTESS OF AUSTRO

The Marcomanni ponies milled in the shadowy street, huffing out clouds and shying at everything: a knife sharpener chanting his services, a sedan chair passing, a dog slurping from a puddle. The front door of the house stood open, with wet footprints trailing across the pavement.

Odo held the reins of the four restive mounts. Eyeing my approach, he called out, "*Fader*."

The Marcomanni lord sprang down the steps and strode over. Without waiting to be snarled at, I said, "Good day, Maelo."

Actually, it looked like being a gray, indifferent day. I had spent a poor night, disturbed by Phormio's grunts and snores, and had slipped out alone in the foggy half-light while my father was still dressing for the opening ceremonies.

Tiny drops of mist glittered in Maelo's tangle of hair. He mumbled something.

I went on, "Today we begin a festival in honor of Isis, a goddess of Egypt. I came to invite you and your people to the races tomorrow."

Could any man not be interested in racing? Yet suspicion still gleamed in his wild-boar eyes. "Horse races?" he said.

"Chariots," I corrected. "The best teams and drivers in the world."

He glanced at his son and shook his head. "We go to the villa of Flavus for *Vetrfest*. The women are gone by cart already."

He turned and spoke to Aurima, who was coming out of the house cloaked for travel and carrying a bundle. And I, who had meant to apologize for allowing her to be embarrassed by rude women in the gardens and humbled in Silius's house, found my tongue in a knot. I managed to ask, "When will you return?"

Aurima lashed the bundle to her saddle, ignoring me. Maelo shouted, "Segomo! Come." He took his pony's reins from his son, then seemed to remember my question. "Flavus arranges it." He hoisted himself onto his mount.

Gray-bearded Segomo trotted down the steps, gnawing on a pig's foot. Behind the two open doors hovered the dark shape of the big eunuch, no doubt glad to have his troublesome guests out of the way.

Maelo barked a command, and the others mounted their ponies. Aurima pulled her skirts down over her knees, but a length of pale shin still showed above her boot top.

Despite the many times I had seen her with her legs around a horse, the eroticism of it stirred me afresh. I said gruffly, "I have told you, civilized women do not ride like that."

"You Romans think of nothing but fornication," she growled back.

I tugged the hem of her tunic down to hide her calf. "You make it difficult to think of anything else, my honey."

She gave me a shove with her foot that made me stumble back. Odo laughed. Aurima smiled, just a fleeting curve of the lips.

I love her.

Oh, of course not. Professions of love are for randy youths and poets. A man loves only his close friends and some family members—including, with time and good fortune, his wife.

Aurima's smile vanished, and she pulled up the hood of her cloak. In a minute she would be gone. I must think of something to say.

But before inspiration struck me, Maelo nudged his pony closer. "People from many tribes come to the villa of Flavus," he said.

"So I have heard."

"Then Aurima sees the man she marries. So says the Goddess."

His mustache flared in a smile. And I could do nothing but scowl as the little cavalcade trotted down the Clivus Palatinus and out of sight.

I had promised Father to join him and fulfill my duties as his heir. Each of the guilds would have tables at the holiday banquet, as would the wards of the Subura, the lower Aventine, and other districts where we had allies and clients. But there would be enough gaiety, gambling, heaps of food, and fountains of wine in the three forums that I hoped my absence from his side would be unnoticed for a while longer. There was something else I had to do first.

$$\longmapsto \longleftarrow$$

When we were young, Nina and I used to seek each other at the same time without knowing which one needed the other. The instinct that pulled me toward her had not faded, for when I arrived I saw she was greatly distraught.

"O Juno Lucina, protect her," she whispered, fingering her amulet. "Juno Primigenia, grant her a healthy child." Her red-rimmed eyes watered. "If she cannot deliver . . ."

"Fortunetelling is nonsense," I said. "Only a fool would put his faith in stars and planets." Or in tumbled bones that foretold when a girl would see her future husband.

Nina retorted illogically, "You never liked Agrippinilla."

No one with sense would remind her that she had once called Caligula's oldest sister an abacus-eyed bitch. Instead I said, "'Pinilla is healthy. And as tough as a boot sole."

"So was our mother! Yet one of her children was stillborn, and another lived only months." As her voice rose, an albino crow squawked from its perch beside her. "Oh, shut up," she cried to it, and her tears flowed.

I suspected it was not Mother's problems in childbearing, or Agrippinilla's, that disturbed her. "Hush, sister, hush. Be of good heart."

Nina wiped her face with her sleeve. "I am all right," she mumbled, and the crow stopped its hoarse barking.

I moved my chair closer to the brazier, kicking a basket of scrolls out of the way. Once Varro's neatly organized office, the room was now as cluttered as a scribe's cubby.

Sniffling, Nina dug her fingers into a poppy-seed roll on the table between us and shredded it into crumbs. "Marcus . . . has *he* come to you again?"

Did she fear summoning Publius's ghost by naming him? "Perhaps," I said, reminded of Aurima's insistence that she had sensed a spirit in the Palatine Gardens. Then I thought of myself imagining that I had been told to spare Rufus's worthless life, and I added, "But probably not. It is all foolishness, like stargazing." I rescued a roll to fill my empty stomach.

The crow watched greedily as she kneaded the bread crumbs into pellets. "I think he saved you the night poor Jason was killed."

I stopped eating as horrific images rose in my memory. I forced them away. "Perhaps," I said again.

We talked about Phormio. I told her that Rufus had run away, and that Mother had given me Dio. "What in Mithras's name will I do with him?"

She sighed. "I sometimes think our slaves are our children."

That was too extravagant a notion for me, and depressing to boot. To cheer us both I described Gemellus's discovery of the "Romulus and Remus" lampoon, and mimicked for her his sputtering indignation. Laughing, Nina agreed with me that Silius was a shrewd satirist, but a moment later she became somber again. "Poor Caligula! Just twenty-five, and already the vultures circle."

"There is plenty of time for him to remarry and beget an heir of his own," I argued. Augustus and Tiberius had both lived to a very old age. Barring accident or assassination, Caligula Caesar too should have a long life.

"The gods have been cruel to his family. What if his next wife dies in childbirth, like poor Junia?"

Wife reminded me of Livilla. I grimaced. There must be some way to change Father's mind. Or Caligula's.

Nina did not noticed that my thoughts had wandered. "He was so handsome before his illness," she said wistfully. "You should have seen him in the Forum, at the Circus, radiant in the applause. Everyone adored him."

She picked up a pellet of bread and studied it. Poppy seeds speckled the whiteness of her hand like soot flecks on snow. "Young Icarus, when he put on the wings his father had made, soared into the sky. But he wished to outdo his father, even at the cost of offending the gods. He flew higher and higher"—the morsel rose in her hand as the white crow tipped its head to follow—"until the sun's heat melted the wax of his wings."

With a flick of her finger she launched the pellet into the air. The crow glided down and gobbled up the bread when it hit the carpet.

"And so," she murmured, "fell poor Icarus to his death."

The crow cawed. "Clever bird!" she said, and tossed it another pellet.

"But Caligula has not fallen."

"Not yet," she said. She held up another morsel. The crow hopped onto her couch and took it from her hand. "But they are watching, the envious gods."

"Clever!" the crow croaked, and flapped up to its perch.

"Father expects me at the Julian Forum," I said, and stood up. As I pulled my chair out of the way, I glimpsed light glinting on a hair caught in its carved arm. On the point of teasing her about going bald, I did not realize until I plucked the long strand free that it was not brown. It was copper.

Wordlessly I held it up to her. Nina nodded in resignation. "She came to see me. On the day it snowed."

"To see you?" So when Maelo said that Aurima had called on her, it was not just the false visit he meant. "Why?"

"She said . . ." My sister twisted a ring on her finger, then looked up at me. "She said I was with child, and must be careful or I would endanger it." An uncertain smile wobbled at the corners of her mouth.

I had guessed as much from her anxiety about childbirth. But how had Aurima known? "You must have told her."

Nina shook her head. "She knows things."

The crow watched, eyes glittering, as I wound the hair around my ring finger. Aurima had been here the day after I had taken her to Diana's grove. "Did she speak of me?" I asked.

Nina snorted. "Do you think we had nothing better to talk about?"

"You discussed matters of importance, then. Hairstyles? Horoscopes?"

"As it happens, know-all, we talked about magic. I am to tell you to stop sending her food with dream potions mixed in."

"Dream . . . She dreamed of me?"

Nina scowled. "You are besotted because she is beyond your reach."

"You have no idea how I feel about her."

"I saw you looking at her in my garden. Do you think that because my husband is half a world away, I no longer know how it feels to burn with desire?"

I stared blankly at my sister. Instead of her dark-browed beauty and comfortably shawled curves, it was bright-haired Aurima whom I saw, shouting at me for my ignorance about her mother.

"Oh, Nina," I murmured. For Saxa had told me why Ingiomar's daughter hated Rome and would never warm to me.

Nina's voice softened. "What is it, brother?"

I hesitated, then sat again. "We owe blood money for a murder," I said.

Saxa had come to the house while I was at breakfast, brooding over Aurima's departure for the countryside. "I am fortunate to find you at home," he said, bending his head to remove his black-plumed helmet.

Hoping to speed this crow of ill omen on his way, I told him I needed to leave soon, although in truth I was in no hurry to array myself for the festival. My father had already left for the Field of Mars, where the new temple to Isis was being built.

Following me into Father's office, Saxa said, "You will do your utmost, I suppose, to discredit this so-called prophecy about Caesar's sister?"

I told him yes, naturally. He was in full dress uniform, and since a cuirass and skirt of armored strips are not comfortable for sitting, I too remained on my feet. I asked if he had brought news about the men who killed Jason.

"In a way." He studied the statue of Ares, then turned to me. "Why did you deny knowing the man found in the Tiber, when he was here in your atrium a few days ago?"

"Who was he?"

"He was Lucius Scarnus, known as Lunula for the crescent scar on his forehead. The imperial gladiatorial school at Capua trained him as a *hoplomachus*. He retired from the arena two years ago."

"Two years ago? And since then?"

"His patron"—Saxa paused, eyeing me—"has been the Princeps' youngest sister, Julia Livilla."

Livilla? I shook my head in perplexity.

He did sit down then, hitching up his black cloak. "Your doorkeeper confirms that this man accompanied the lady here."

Then the memory came back to me: arriving home from the wine warehouse to find Livilla in the atrium, with a hulking brute trying to pull Rufus out of Phormio's grip. I had not noticed his scars. All bodyguards are scarred.

"A former *sicarius* called Purpureus has also disappeared," Saxa said. "The stone weighing him down may have been tied more securely."

"Livilla had no reason to kill my slave."

"Had he done anything to offend the lady?"

"Jason? Impossible."

"Then you yourself perhaps ended an affair in a way that displeased her."

"Never."

"Could it be that you spurned her advances?"

"Rome would be a necropolis if she killed every man who refused her. Have you asked her about this Lunula?"

"She says she has not seen the man for days."

"Perhaps she loaned him to someone else."

Saxa's eyes slid sideways to the serving tray in a corner of the room, but I was not inclined to offer him refreshment. He said, "The imperial family's bodyguards gather in a guardroom off the courtyard when they are not needed. Anyone can send them anywhere."

"So perhaps it was Uncle Claudius who had my slave killed."

Neither of us smiled at the gibe. I went on, "Is this all you have found? No other trails to follow?"

"It is always possible that they mistook your slave for someone else."

"In short," I said, "you are at a dead end."

Seeing that he did not dispute this, I stood up. "Good day, then."

Saxa did not move. "You asked for information about Ammisia of the Marcomanni, did you not?"

The affray at Silius's house had almost made me forget the request I had made earlier at the Special Cohort office. "I did."

"Perhaps another time, then, since you are rushing to the feast." He hauled himself out of the chair, helmet clasped in one arm.

"Commander, I would like to hear Ammisia's story."

He eyed me for a moment, then set down the helmet and poured himself a drink. "You know her husband, Ingiomar, brought his people to Siscia for three summers to be trained as auxiliary infantry." His mouth twisted. "We generously taught him our way of fighting so he could slaughter us later."

I had never been to Siscia. Its forum is said to be the handsomest in southern Pannonia, although what visitors chiefly want to see are the bloodstains. "Tell me the rest," I said.

"Poor man, he must have been frantic," Nina said. "And of course she would not refuse a legion commander. Did she save his wife?"

"No. I suppose the woman had bled too much." I kicked the basket of scrolls again, this time by accident, and reached down to position it more precisely on the pattern of the floor tiles. "But perhaps Ammisia would have gone, no matter who asked for her. She was a priestess. A healer."

"But a barbarian! And her husband let her go alone into an army fortress at night?" Nina frowned. The cup of spiced wine brought in by a serving girl vapored by her couch, untouched.

"He was out hunting with her brother and sons," I said, as Saxa had told me. "So she took an old man with her." I paused, wondering how to soften the next crude details, and decided not to try. "They found him in the forum at daybreak with his head split open."

She drew in her breath. "And the healer?"

"In the river, dead. Raped, beaten, and stabbed."

Her eyes widened. "Who did it?"

"There were no witnesses." I sipped from my own cup. "But four men from the same cohort were seen at the soldiers' baths the next day with fresh bites and scratches."

I saw her horror subside. "Four men from her husband's auxiliary cohort, you mean?" It is not so shocking for outlanders to murder each other.

"No, *cara*, four Roman legionaries. One of them actually had her silver knife. When they were questioned, they said they had met her in the forum by the Temple of Divine Augustus, where the whores wait. They said they used her, paid her, and left her there. Alive."

Her dark eyes flickered as if she saw Siscia's forum. "I do not suppose Germanic priestesses offer themselves to strangers, like priestesses of Isis."

"Certainly not." I rested the cup on the arm of my chair. "The soldiers said they never saw the old man. Knew nothing about him."

"Were they— Was there a trial?"

"A court martial, yes. The legion commander was on his way to Rome with his wife's ashes, so it was the senior tribune who gave judgment."

Even if complicity in murder could not be proved, the soldiers' injuries would have been strong evidence of rape. I would have sentenced them to thirty strokes of a centurion's stick and cashiered them afterward, since Ammisia had been an allied commander's wife. "He sentenced them to field punishment," I said. "To march for three days on the parade ground with their packs."

Nina gazed at me with a puzzled frown.

"That is the penalty for being drunk and disorderly," I explained. "For breaking benches in a *taberna*. Pissing on a temple wall."

Ingiomar must have thought the tribune had imposed this mild sentence out of arrogance and contempt. That he considered the lives of a priestess and an old man to be worth nothing because they were barbarians. But the truth was worse. Ever since the northern legions had mutinied at Augustus's death, no senior officer dared take their obedience for granted. Seeing the legionaries clamor in support of their accused comrades, the tribune had surely feared they would revolt if his judgment was too severe. The risk to the province, not to mention his own career, would have weighed heavily on him; for with the legion commander gone, the responsibility for these five thousand men rested on his young shoulders.

"The husband cried out for justice," I went on. "The healer's brother, her sons, her daughter all protested. They were removed from the fortress."

Nina sat up so abruptly that she jostled the table by her couch. The tipping winecup was rescued barely in time by the serving girl. "But you said he was a Roman citizen."

"He was." Ingiomar had been granted citizenship years earlier for helping to settle a kingship dispute. Naturally, it was revoked when he attacked my vexillation. "So he went to provincial headquarters and appealed to the governor."

"Sabinus? Was it Sabinus, five years ago?"

I nodded. "Sabinus refused to see him, because he himself was facing a treason charge." Yet even if the governor had not been waiting for Tiberius's judgment, he would have let the verdict stand. He, too, knew the risk of mutiny.

"But this dreadful story happened years before you went to Pannonia. What does it have to do with you?"

"This man I am telling you about, the healer's husband, is Aurima's father. Ingiomar."

"So it was her mother who . . ." Nina's face twisted in a grimace of sympathy. "And she was there when the tribune announced the sentence?"

"Do you remember I told you they call him 'Ironhand'?" I drained my wine. "After the trial, Ingiomar took his people home to the Mark. Then he came back with his oldest son, and they captured the four soldiers, one at a time. With his bare hands Ingiomar tore open each man's belly"—I swiped a thumb across my own hips—"and hauled out his tripes."

The girl refilling my cup thrust out her tongue in a grimace of horror and delight.

Nina's cheeks paled. "But he should not have taken his own revenge. He could have . . . have petitioned the Princeps."

I did not comment on that; we both knew the odds of a Germanic auxiliary commander making a successful appeal to Tiberius Caesar. "He left the bodies at the Temple of Justitia Romana to mock us. To mock our justice."

She said quietly, "So that is how rebellions start."

I nodded. "He would have raised his people against us then, but the old king in exile, Marbodo, asked him to keep the peace. So he did, until Marbodo died early this year."

"Oh, Marcus! To think that you might have died this summer because of an injustice five years ago."

"We should have made restitution. I will advise Caesar to offer compensation—horses, cattle, weapons, armor. Perhaps it is not too late."

Despite these optimistic words, I had doubts. We Romans—the Ninth Legion's commander, who had let his troops slide into indiscipline and brutality, and Sabinus, who had not bestirred himself to aid an ally seeking justice—had turned a friend into a foe. It was another sign of the rot that had spread downward from an old Princeps too treason-obsessed to attend to the frontiers, and outward from governors who feared to discipline their legions. The very legions Caligula would rely on in his campaign.

"And poor Aurima! No wonder she is . . . as she is."

"No wonder," I agreed, remembering her frenzied assault on me in Diana's grove. I heaved myself out of my chair again. "Well, that is nothing to do with you. Come to the races with me tomorrow. We will see if this young Malleus is as good as they say."

"I have been asked already," she said. "But I think I will not brave the crowds. Stop on the way home and tell me who won."

Before I could ask why she would pass up seeing her friends, the front door knocker clacked distantly.

Nina sat up. "Trebia, quick, help me brush off these crumbs."

A man spoke assertively in the vestibule. Probably Galerianus, come to check on his stepmother. I went to greet him.

But it was Lucius Pertinax, Gaulish wine merchant and would-be Senator, his bearish bulk wrapped in a heavy mantle that a slave was presently removing. Seeing me he lifted a hand, and the slave backed away.

"What are you doing here?" I said, not smiling. It was hardly proper for a widower to visit a woman whose husband was in Crete.

"Why, I am just leaving," he said, signaling the confused slave to wrap the mantle around him again. "Congratulations on surviving the dangerous streets of Rome, Carinna. May we meet more pleasantly some other time."

The curls framing his lean face, I saw, had faded from the yellow of raw wood shavings to silver gray. "You have not answered my question."

"Perhaps your sister will tell you," he said. "Good day." The doors shut behind him.

I returned to Nina. "Why is that man calling on you?"

She glared up at me. "You are not entitled to be so rude to a friend of mine." Color burned in her cheeks. "I wrote you that Pertinax often comes here to dine, with Silius and a few others."

"You did not say he also visits you by himself."

"He has been lonely since his wife died," she snapped. "So go away; you do not need to protect my honor." She stood up, turning toward the girl Trebia, who hovered nearby. "I want to rest."

I did not apologize. It is a brother's duty to protect his sister's good name. "Is that why you know how it feels to burn with desire? Because Pertinax is your lover?"

"He is not," she said vehemently. "I know you blame him for turning Silius against you, but he is witty and amusing. I enjoy his conversation."

"I see," I said. In spite of her denial, pain augered into my belly. I stood behind the chair, hands braced on its back.

"And I will avoid the turmoil at the Circus to protect my little bud." She laid a slim-fingered hand on her belly. "So be happy for me, brother."

"Of course I am, Nina." She stood on her toes to kiss my cheek, and I managed a reassuring smile. "May your child be born strong and healthy."

Whose child? I wondered, slipping the coiled strand of hair into the money pocket on my leather cuff.

CHAPTER 21

CIRCUS MAXIMUS

Never have I heard, before or since, anything like the shattering roar with which the crowd in the Circus Maximus greeted Caligula. Its raw power was the sound of adoration: their tribute to Germanicus's son, and perhaps his reward for all he had undergone to become Princeps.

Blinking in the sunlight after the dimness of the passageway, he tucked up his mantle and seated himself in a high-backed chair. Father, Lepidus, and other Friends of Augustus had already taken seats near the front of the imperial enclosure, basking in the spectators' acclaim like actors on a stage. There appeared to be little opportunity for me to cozy up with Caligula, but I was too enraptured to care. Pausing in the aisle opposite the more distant row to which I had been assigned, I took in a view I had craved in my frontier backwater.

All around the elongated loop of the track, the high wooden stands teemed with color and clamor. Every citizen, provincial, foreigner, and slave in Rome seemed to have jammed into this long narrow valley between the Palatine and Aventine hills. Morning sun sparked off the golden orb atop Cleopatra's obelisk on the mid-track *spina*, flinging its shadow toward the gates from which the chariots would emerge. A man on horseback chased dogs off the course, their prints swirling across the raked sand. Above the highest row of seats, a light breeze furled and unfurled streamers of the four racing companies: red, white, blue, and green.

It was a pity that Nina had not wished to come, and that Phormio could not. But even though morose Dio was my only companion, I looked forward to a day of forgetting my troubles and the Caesars' family strife.

A slave asked me to move aside: Drusilla was coming down the steps arm in arm with Gemellus's sister, Julia. "I am sure she puts no credence in that so-called prophecy," Drusilla was saying. "None at all."

"Such a sensible woman." Julia saw me and smiled.

"If Juno Lucina is kind and the baby lives, Caligula will name him Nero for our brother," Drusilla said. By then they were past, so I did not see Julia's reaction to this hint that Caligula would adopt the boy, making her brother's position shakier.

Julia's husband, Blandus, followed them in conversation with her uncle Claudius, who limped down the stairs on a slave's arm. "We should divert the river's course as the Divine Julius proposed. It would pay for itself within twenty years. I have seen the estimates." Blandus was scanning the crowd. "Where is Gemellus? I thought he was already here."

Dio draped my designated seat with my fur-lined cloak, for this was an occasion to be ostentatious. I sat down, wishing Aurima were here beside me to watch the spectacle. Not twelve miles away, meeting the man she would marry.

A long-familiar voice broke into my thoughts. "Guards swarming like weevils in a bread bin! But who can object, if it calms our beloved Princeps?"

Two Praetorians in togas were checking Silius's invitation at the entrance to the enclosure. "Let us pass; you know very well who he is," one of his companions protested.

As they were waved forward, Silius's eye lit on me. "Jove's thunderbolts, it's young Carinna." He led his flock down the steps. "Heard any good lampoons lately, Marcus Licinius?"

Seeking praise for his own cleverness, the preening cockerel! His friends chuckled obsequiously. I said, "Caught my runaway slaveboy yet, Gaius Silius?"

His smile faded. With a cool nod he continued down the steps to a better seat than mine.

Horns cried out from the Tiber end of the Circus, and the crowd burst into cheers. Below the winged Victory high atop the wall-like *oppidum*, the alcoves that sheltered posturing gods, and the elegant columns and pediments, trumpeters in silver armor flanked the processional gateway. Through the arch came a rider on a white steed, followed by two more white horses drawing a triumphal chariot. Men waving leafy branches clustered around its wheels.

The man in the chariot was obviously the junior consul, Rebilus, editor of the races. But who was the rider?

Caligula rose, leaning over the balustrade. The rest of us stood up too. Someone exclaimed, "Gemellus!"

Gemellus made a bold figure on horseback, prancing ahead of the consul and his white-clad attendants. Behind them trailed priests carrying statues of the gods on litters. Clouds of aromatic smoke streamed from censers swinging to chanted hymns. It was a shameless performance by Caligula's adopted son, and to judge by the delighted screaming around us it was a great success.

My neighbor, a Senator of perhaps seventy, decided that because of my military service I would enjoy hearing about his uncle's experiences at the battle of Philippi. My attention drifted as he talked, and veered away entirely when Livilla appeared. She was accompanied by the Praetorian Prefect and his wife, who was rumored to be one of Caligula's mistresses. There is no accounting for tastes, as the saying goes; I saw nothing attractive in the gaunt woman whose pinched, flamboyantly painted face bore up a mound of red-rinsed curls.

Livilla appeared not to notice me, which suited me well, and I was able to study her from my elevated seat. A man might look on her and say, *What a pretty girl*, not knowing she was fully nineteen and slender only because she had never borne children. Laughing and animated, she teased Lepidus and the Prefect. No doubt she had slept with them both.

I imagined myself married to her. It was impossible. The first time I suspected infidelity I would divorce her, Caesar's sister or not.

Gemellus sauntered in, flushed of face, eyes bright with excitement. When the crowd saw the Princeps rise to receive his filial kiss, a bellow of acclaim swelled from every tier of the Circus. Another chair was produced, and he seated himself triumphantly at Caligula's side. Livilla stroked his arm, beaming.

I studied them all from my loftier seat: Claudius, Blandus and Julia, Gemellus, Livilla, even Drusilla and Lepidus and Caligula himself. If the cutthroats who murdered Jason had indeed been imperial bodyguards, which one of the family could have sent them? And why?

During the first race, clouds rose from behind the Janiculum Hill and the sun vanished. More furs appeared, lap robes, and fuming braziers. I left the garrulous Senator to stretch my legs, stopping here and there to speak with people I knew. It was as well that the Marcomanni had not come, for I discovered that they were commonly thought to be my slave's killers. With barbarians, no motive for murder was considered necessary.

The Princeps, his family, and visiting potentates gestured and glittered, chattered and drank. None of the Caesars seemed troubled by star-cast prophecies. Slaves brought around ewers of spiced wine and trays of delicacies. Musicians played; jugglers juggled. Chariots dashed around the track, and small fortunes were made and lost.

I watched the second race with a former consul who had been a legate in Upper Germany, the third with a half-uncle and his fourth wife, and the next with Julia and Blandus. I liked Blandus, who had just returned from governing Africa. But if I was allowed an alternative to Livilla, I would take sweet-tempered Julia from him without an instant's regret.

The sky continued to darken. Slaves hoisted an awning as big as a trireme's sail over the imperial enclosure. On the far side of the Circus the gay banners trailed limply from their poles, but I saw few empty seats. Who would miss the match between Ferox and Malleus, with its million-sestertii prize?

During the final circuit in the fifth race, an icy rain burst from the swollen clouds. The track disappeared from view. Shrieks exploded all around; the stands heaved as people scrambled for the exits. The awning snapped up, then down with a furious clap.

I retreated with the others, annoyed by the tempest's bad timing. But the cross-corridor's sweaty turmoil of pushing and elbowing, babbling, perfumes and piss soon became so unbearable that I returned to the aisle by my seat. Rain still roared the length of the Circus. Overturned chairs by the balustrade spoke of the haste with which Caligula and his family had fled.

Dio appeared, clutching a tablet on which he had been scribbling people's names. "The master has gone home," he said.

"And where have you been?"

"Collecting the winnings." As tenderly as Nina patting her unborn child, he laid a hand on the bulge of the money pouch under his mantle.

The bedraggled flag hanging on the *spina* was red. "What winnings?" I said. "You know I bet on Green."

Dio looked smug. "A small wager of my own."

I glowered at him. "By what right do you shame our family?"

He blinked. "Ollius said it was permitted for me to bet my own savings."

"Did he need to tell you a slave must not wager against his master?"

A flush crept up his neck. "I am new to this. The mistress never gambles."

"The damage is done," I snapped. "Everyone is already chattering about the Carinnas' ill-behaved slaves." I jabbed my forefinger into his chest. "Your winnings are forfeit to me."

The color mounted his cheeks. "So be it, master," he said, tight-jawed.

I stamped down the steps. The problem with Dio was that he hardly considered himself a slave, so permissively had my mother raised him.

At the front of the enclosure I leaned over the railing to study the track, now a slippery morass of hillocks and lakelets. The last race should be postponed. Conditions that tested a driver's skill were all very well, but it was no pleasure to watch great-hearted horses break their legs.

When I bent over farther to look for the track crew, my hand slipped on the wet railing. Caught off balance, I pitched forward over the low balustrade. The expanse of racetrack flashed up at me, twenty feet below.

A fist seized the back of my tunic. I teetered over the drop, rain pelting my head and shoulders. A second fist, another yank, rocked me back onto my feet.

Dio.

The glance I flung at him caught a glint of relief that vanished at once. Blank-faced, lashes lowered, he smoothed out the creases his fingers had clamped into my clothing, then leaned down to pick up the broken tablet at his feet.

People were beginning to return to their seats as the rain lost its fury. They glanced at us curiously, but no one seemed aware of what had happened.

I inhaled deeply to slow the hammering of my heart. The fall would have left me badly injured or dead.

Once I had shrugged my mantle back into place and my breathing eased, I looked at Dio. His face was paler than usual. I tapped his hidden money pouch with my knuckle. "Keep your winnings," I said.

Out on the course, a five-man pyramid of acrobats rode atop two mud-splashed horses. "What are the odds now?" Caligula asked.

"Evens on Malleus," I said. "Ferox at five to four."

"Rebilus will drop the handkerchief early to give Ferox a quick start."

"I say he will not," Lepidus objected. "Two thousand on it."

"Done." Caligula grinned at me. "Your patron is too trusting, Carinna."

As if the calamity in the horse stall had never occurred, we conversed about racers' bloodlines, trainers' regimens, and the tactics of driving on a wet course. Wedged between Lepidus and some Eastern prince, I took care to drink only wine that others had safely swallowed, and avoided sweetmeats entirely. It is less pleasant to be a guest of the Caesars than one might think.

When the track groomers finished their circuit of the course, the sheaves of brush on the logs they dragged were shapeless with mud. With such perilous footing, it would be a heart-stopping race.

"Ferox has no hope." Lepidus scanned his secretary's notes of his wagers.

"Victor told me Malleus will take it," I said. There was a general murmur of acknowledgment; everyone knew the trainer.

Gemellus objected, "It rained on Neptunalia, and Ferox won by ten lengths."

"My granny has cast a curse on his inside horse," Livilla said. "She made the dearest little stallion of clay and bound it with wire, and we buried a curse tablet with it this morning."

I increased my own gamble on Malleus, with side bets that White would lead at the start and only three of the four teams would finish. Caligula took my wager that Malleus would lead in the last two laps.

If Aurima could see me now, joking and trading bets with the Princeps of Rome! And all because he had noticed me standing at the front of his enclosure.

Dio bent down and hissed in my ear, "This is quite a lot of money you are wagering." I waved him away.

Trumpets blew. The noise from the stands quieted. The consul, a small figure in purple, rose in the editor's box on the other side of the Circus and called out something unintelligible. Criers repeated the announcement that because of track conditions, there would be no charioteers' parade before the race.

Gemellus pulled off his blue mantle and brandished it like a flag. "Neptune speed Ferox and his horses," he cried. An answering bellow came from the better seats. Most Senatorial families favor the Blues.

Caligula sprang up beside his adopted son. "Isis, Queen of Heaven, grant your favor to Malleus and his team," he shouted, lofting a green cushion. Another roar from the crowd. The Whites, then the Reds rallied their supporters.

The consul stood up again, a handkerchief in his hand. Thousands of feet pounded the wooden stands in a ragged rhythm: *Bam. Bam. Bam. Bam.* "Now, now," I shouted with the rest.

The four teams burst from their gates, racing for the starting line below the editor's box. The shriek of the crowd must have been audible in Ostia.

The consul dangled his handkerchief over the end of the ribbon stretched across the line. The White driver hurtled headlong toward it. Green and Blue—Malleus and Ferox—followed side by side. The Red charioteer held back. The spectators' screaming rose to a howl: "Drop it!" Unless the handkerchief was released, the race would have to begin again.

The bit of cloth fluttered down. The crowd thundered. And as slaves hauled in the ribbon, White charged across the start with the other chariots close behind. Ha! One bet won.

White drove furiously to stay in the lead. Ferox lay second, his horses' blue plumes already sodden with mud. I could just make out the determined thrust of his beard beneath the leather helmet. Malleus was outside of Red, in last place.

On the first turn, I leaped up shouting when Malleus nearly collided with the Red team. My voice was lost in the crowd's great bellow as Ferox pulled abreast of White. He caught the other chariot's outside wheel with his own and swerved. The linchpin sheared off the axle, and White's wheel flew into the air.

The White chariot slewed into the *spina* and exploded. The four horses panicked, dragging the wreckage and the driver, tethered by the reins tied around his waist.

Malleus swung wide to pass the carnage. The Red driver was too close and had to haul on his reins. When Malleus spurted ahead at last, making an opening, Red tried to veer around the demolished chariot. But as the driverless White horses skidded around the end of the *spina*, the wreckage they towed slid under the front legs of the Red team. Vehicles, horses, and men, White and Red, smashed together in a horrific tangle.

The din grew deafening. Ferox was partway down the Aventine straight, with Malleus gaining behind him. In a few heartbeats they would round the Capena turn and start back toward the pileup.

Mounted men galloped along the track, dragging stretchers and chains. Slaves jumped down from the *spina* to catch the loose horses and haul the two charioteers out of the wreckage. One moved feebly; the other lay limp.

As Ferox and Malleus closed on the accident, the area cleared in the blink of an eye: tow horses hauled off wreckage and dead animals; others dragged the charioteers strapped to jolting sleds. The less injured racehorses, some still yoked together, were ridden away.

There was no time to smooth the track. The last slave leaped to safety on the *spina* a heartbeat before Ferox charged past with Malleus's team close behind. They slewed around the end of the divider, muddy spray spewing from hooves and wheels. I was screaming but could not hear myself, blasted by the crowd's roar like a gale wind.

Two laps left.

Ferox swerved into the path of Malleus's team, blinding them with the slop from his wheels. They faltered, and he shot ahead. Malleus shouted and lashed his outside horse.

My heart leapt into my throat. The young fool meant to pass on the inside. Ferox would crush him against the stone of the *spina*.

Malleus's horses' noses disappeared behind the side rail of Ferox's chariot. Swift Passerinus, Flamma, Admeta, Celer, the green of their harnesses now mackled with mud.

Ferox swung sideways to pinch them off. His wheel hub crowded closer and closer to the legs of Malleus's outside horse. Passerinus, on the inside, was so near the *spina* that the spray he kicked up spattered across its statues.

Malleus pressed on through the torrent of muck. He was sure to crash in a moment, his horses somersaulting head over hooves, his chariot smashing into shards, and he himself, arrogant young idiot, catapulting from glory to become a smashed carcass on a torn-up track.

Ferox jerked suddenly and put up an arm. Malleus lashed out again, and Ferox tried to block the blow. Thrown off stride by the shift in balance, Ferox's inside horse bumped into Celer and shied away. Malleus gave his team their heads. They wedged their way into the gap and pulled ahead. Miraculous beasts!

Ferox whipped his own horses. He came abreast of Malleus again. Almost to the Capena turn now. Less than a lap to the finish.

I strained my eyes to follow Malleus, a crouched blur in the flurrying mud. If he made it through the turn, he had a chance of pulling ahead on the straight.

Then, catastrophe.

Malleus cornered around the mammoth cone of basalt at the *spina*'s end. The mud was badly churned there, but he did not slow his team.

Passerinus fell. I saw his hind legs skid in the mire; he landed on a haunch, then scrambled up again. Malleus had all four horses in hand within moments, but moments were all Ferox needed. He plunged ahead.

They hurtled down the Palatine straight. Ferox was a length ahead, then two, while Malleus tried to coax his team back into their ground-eating gallop. But he was on the muddiest part of the track, and the horses slipped and slid.

Without looking away I shouted, "What of your curse now, Livilla?"

A moment later Ferox's chariot slewed. His outside horse stumbled into its yokemate, and I knew at once that a trace had parted.

The chariot cartwheeled. The shaft snapped. Ferox's horses tripped and collided and fell. They thrashed to their feet again and bolted, dragging the upended chariot through the mud until the harness broke and freed them.

Ferox's body rolled and tumbled with the wreckage. I saw a glint from the knife he had used to cut the reins. Then he moved—the lucky bastard was alive! He lurched up on one knee, saw the other chariot and team coming, and launched himself toward the safety of the *spina*.

The full width of the track lay in front of Malleus. But as Livilla shrieked in glee, he lashed his horses toward Ferox and trampled his rival beneath their hooves.

CHAPTER 22

THE VENUS CURSE

"Livilla fornicated with a slave?" my sister asked. Lamplight glittered in her wide eyes. "Does Caesar know?"

"He will soon," I rasped, still hoarse from yelling. With a smile I did not let her see, I reached for a wedge of fried squash on the table around which the three broad couches clustered.

Nina leaned forward to wrest a cushion from under herself. When Pertinax reached from his couch to help, I had to restrain myself from clubbing his arm away. Visiting her after the races, I had been unsettled to find she had invited Silius, Torquata, and the big Gaul as well.

Junia Torquata said, "Oh, Nina, if you had seen him! The winner's wreath on his brow, and splashes of blood on his arms and his corselet . . ." She sketched it on her own arms and breast. "He looked around at all of us and the guards with the chest of money, and grinned. . . . Juno's crown! He could have had any woman on the spot."

"Any woman who cared to rut with a boy smeared with boar shit," Silius muttered.

Some drivers think boar dung keeps horses from stepping on them, but I have seen too much evidence to the contrary. It had certainly done Ferox no good.

Malleus had just killed a man, and the primitive scent of that violence radiated from him as he stepped into the imperial enclosure. When he glanced around at us, indolent observers of others' peril and pain, I had felt the contempt of the grin on his mud-splashed face. *I am more man than any of you*, that grin had said, and women around me had responded with sighs.

As the many guests in the imperial box surged to congratulate him, it had been easy for me to take him by the arm and hiss into his dirty ear, "Lady

Julia Livilla. Turn left, second right, unmarked gate." He had cast me a wary glance, not recognizing me from before. I tipped my chin toward the corridor archway, then backed off to let someone else slap his back and gush over his fearlessness.

Disquiet creased Nina's pale brow. "You actually saw him with her?"

"Purely by accident," Silius explained blandly. "We took the wrong gate." He left out the minor detail of having distracted the guard while I opened the gate, both of us shouting that this was our way home. "Marcus and I found him slithering out of her litter."

"Just the two of you?" Her face relaxed. "Then it can be kept quiet." She cast her gaze around the dining room, enjoining the four of us to silence.

I said, "Unfortunately, we were not the only witnesses." Other departing racegoers had eddied in behind us, curious about the racket.

"Oh, the stupid girl! What will Gemellus's supporters make of this?" Nina glared at me as if I could have prevented it. But really, I had hardly done anything. Just told Malleus how to find the private corridor where Livilla was accustomed to leave her litter, which I knew from having accompanied Publius when he met her at the Circus. It was Livilla herself who had jumped at the bait.

Pertinax asked, "Who will tell Caesar?" He looked at Silius. "It cannot wait until a mob starts shouting in the Forum."

Silius split a walnut in a nutcracker. "Let one of Caesar's friends give him the news." He flipped a piece of the shell at me.

"What will happen to that charioteer?" Nina asked. "Is he not a slave?"

Pertinax said, "Nina, 'that charioteer' is the toast of Rome." He waggled his oyster spoon at her to emphasize the point. "Caesar will not dare touch him."

"So Livilla alone will be punished? But that is not just."

"It is what she deserves," I said cheerfully, holding out my cup for more *mulsum*. Livilla's outrageous behavior meant I would no longer be pressed to marry her. Even her notorious grandmother Julia had not sunk so low as to publicly dishonor herself with a slave. Caligula's only hope of minimizing popular outrage, which the Tiberians would surely try to stir up, would be to exile her promptly.

"She deserves it? Because she is a woman?"

"Because she may introduce a slave's blood into one of Rome's most distinguished families. That is why you, sister dear, may not amuse yourself with a lover"—I shot an unfriendly glance at Pertinax—"while your husband may have as many bedmates as he wishes." I did not mention her own pregnancy, since she had said nothing about it to the others.

"No lovers!" Torquata clapped a dramatic hand to her cheek.

"Only me, *carissima*," Silius said. He brushed back her blond hair and murmured something in her ear that made her smile.

I was disconcerted to discover her smoky cat-eyes watching me watch him. Torquata had been a brunette when I last saw her, a Senator's pampered wife whose slaves often bore the marks of her bad temper. She was still married, but the Senator was now a proconsul happily enriching himself overseas.

"Luckily my brother will not be called on to judge Livilla," Nina said. "He has already condemned her for a crime that would be no crime, were she a man."

I shook my head at her outlandish notion of equality between the sexes. Torquata aimed her feline gaze at me. "It does seem unfair to condemn her for behavior that is no outrage in yourself."

"What? Next you women will want to dress up as legionaries and fight battles."

"Oh, you are an idiot," Nina snapped.

I said, "It matters to me, if to no one else, that she was Publius's *sponsa* and has disgraced our family as well as hers."

My sister's brows drew together. Before she could speak, Pertinax put his hand on hers. "Let it go, *cara* Nina."

It was so unpleasant a surprise to hear him call her "dear" that I missed some of what he said next. "—A great triumph for the Princeps. They cheered him as if he had won the race himself."

"He beamed like the lighthouse at Alexandria," Silius agreed. But his tone was mocking, as if Caligula were a witling.

I said, "Perhaps he envisioned standing there with Agrippinilla's son in his arms."

"He already has a son," Silius shot back.

"He needs children of his own," Torquata said. "Two years is long enough for him to mourn my cousin, rest her shade."

Pertinax frowned. "Arriving to cheer you, Nina, we bring only gloom." He snatched up the engraved brass racing program beside him and flung it through the doorway. "Begone, cares and woes! I propose a competition for the cleverest poem about the day's events, the winner to be chosen by our hostess."

Being well enough educated to fancy ourselves clever, the rest of us agreed. A slave passed out tablets, and for some time there was no sound except the mouse-scratch of styli and murmurs between Silius and Torquata.

Pertinax led off:

Eighteen ended, a hundred and eight began;
Subtract from the track the number of feet
To see how many also ran.

This epigram was quickly deciphered, with Silius the first to recognize that a four-horse chariot and driver have eighteen feet. We drank to the Gaul.

Next was Torquata. Apologizing prettily beforehand, she recited:

Today was a day of upsets, O Malleus:
You overturned horses and chariots
And, after the race, a governor's wife.

More applause. Another round of drinking.

Silius's turn. He read out his submission baldly:

Who would win the Princeps' prize?
Young Malleus was the favorite,
But who took it home did not matter to Rome
As much as who publicly gave it.

Applause and toasts greeted this sally. A decent impromptu effort by the celebrated Phoenix, I thought. Only Nina, who had not seen the race prize-giving, frowned at him. "I do not think I understand, Gaius." Her face was pink with *mulsum* and the room's heat.

"Ah, well." Silius smiled. "Lepidus reckoned he was to present the million sestertii to Malleus. He got up, all blue-jowled and smug, while the mob cheered him. Then Caligula held up his hand. 'Wait,' he said; 'I want my son to do it.'"

"Lepidus must have been furious," she breathed. Half of Rome would have seen our patron dismissed in favor of a boy scarcely old enough to shave.

"Gemellus took some time adjusting his mantle." Silius mimed the boy's insolent primping. "Then he said, 'Shall I let you embrace me, Lepidus?'"

"And did he?" Allowed to clasp Gemellus's arms and perhaps give him a public kiss of affection, Lepidus would have been able to retreat with dignity.

Silius leaned back on his elbow. "You tell her, Carinna." His eyes glinted wickedly. "You were nearer."

Making me recount Lepidus's mortification was his revenge for being used to uncover Livilla's disgrace. I said, "He told Gemellus, 'You need me.' Gemellus said, 'I think not,' and he patted Lepidus's forearm as he went by."

"The little louse," Nina huffed.

Of course, Gemellus too would be tainted by Livilla's scandalous behavior. His mistress discovered consorting with a slave! And not just any slave, but a boor from the provinces who raced chariots.

Nina smacked me on the shoulder with her tablet. "Are you dreaming, brother? You are last. What have you written?"

"Oh, just drivel," I said lightly, and read it aloud:

Today was a day of exploits at the Circus,
But not all the action was out on the course.
A certain man's sister first did a horse-driver,
And still feeling lustful, she then did the horse.

My sister said, "That is disgusting, Marcus! And cruel."

I shrugged. "So who wins?"

"Not you," Nina said. "You are too sour for my taste." She pulled herself to her feet. "May Venus curse you with love-madness one day, so you know the pain of fever in the blood."

"I was only joking about the horse," I said.

In her absence the conversation dwindled to lazy mutters, none of us eager to brave the cold night. While Pertinax and Silius argued a point of adultery law, I mulled over my success that day with Caligula. He had seemed a likable fellow after all. Perhaps he would readily agree to restitution for the Marcomanni. And later, after my quaestorship was over, would grant me the role I wanted in the northern campaign.

Torquata rose from Silius's side and moved next to me with a perfumed rustle. "Are you in love, Marcus Licinius?" she murmured.

I was startled at first, then intrigued. "Do I appear to be?"

She stroked my knuckles with her fingertips, stirring currents of desire. Perhaps sweet temperament in a wife was overrated. She was certainly a woman a man would enjoy bedding.

"I have no lover," I said huskily. I followed her heavy-lidded gaze down to my signet ring, which she was turning around my finger. "But you do."

Torquata drew a fingernail slowly down the back of my hand. "Is he watching?"

I nodded, and a contented smile curved her lips. So this byplay was just to make him jealous.

Nina came back into the room. Silius glanced away from Torquata and me. "Who has won the competition, most charming judge?"

She wriggled onto her couch. "The judge is unwilling to applaud death and disgraceful behavior," she said. "There is no winner. Instead, I will inflict a new poem of my own on you." She rummaged among rolls of papyrus in a wide-mouthed leather cylinder.

Over approving mutters from the others, I said, "A love poem?"

I had not meant to sound condescending, but she scowled. "So it is, brute: a poem without spite or malice. I know it will seem less witty than yours."

Her erotic poetry had always made me marvel at the imagination of a woman who had known but one lover, and he a staid grandfather thrice her age. But that had apparently changed. I did not care to hear an amorous tribute to the burly Gaulish Senator's son on the opposite couch.

I sat up with an excuse ready. Too late. Flattening a scroll against a cushion, Nina looked around. "It is called 'The Voyage,'" she said. Her voice drifted languorously:

My love and I are voyaging.
Where we embarked is all forgotten,

Where we will land is all unknown.
Once affrighted by not knowing,
Now I laugh and map our course
In the curls upon his chest,
Closing greedy legs around him
As his thrusts propel us farther
Over dark and restless Ocean.
When the storm erupts within,
It shakes us both; he gasps aloud
And grips me as we tumble,
Torn by whirlwind, tossed by waves,
Until the voyage of our making
Hurls us both upon the shore.
"My dearest love," he whispers
As I rise; and from in me
Spills a warm and salty trickle of the sea.

The scroll rustled as she furled it again. "And now, my friends," she said with a sweet smile, "I wish you all a good night."

Pertinax headed toward his home on the Quirinal with a stout escort. Silius's house was not far from ours, so I walked with him beside Torquata's litter, her lantern bearer leading and our slaves trailing behind. Smoke hazed the starless sky, and lights and laughter spilled from celebrations in other houses.

Nina's poem had woken something in me. Would I ever have a dearest love? Or did my attraction to the wrong women doom me to the solitary flight of a bee in a thistle patch?

Absurd. One would think Venus's curse was already at work.

"What now?" Silius asked.

"Tomorrow? The gladiator show; then Father and I dine with the clients."

"I meant tonight." He stopped. "Torquata has taken a fancy to you." He slid a hand under the curls at my nape and stroked the back of my neck with his thumb. Torchlight from a house behind me gilded his long lashes and struck sparks in his dark eyes.

"Come home with us," he urged. "My wife will not disturb us."

It took a moment to find my breath. I said, "Ask Pertinax. Or has Torquata already tired of him?"

Frowning, he withdrew his hand. "Why would I ask Pertinax? The man is as prim as Cato."

"You did not think so four years ago."

The curtains of the litter stirred. "Where are we?" Torquata mumbled. "Why have we stopped?"

I walked on. I would leave them at the next corner, to take my father the report of Caligula's sister's depravity.

Silius fell in beside me. He said, "Four years ago, Marcus, no one took me seriously. I saw Lucius Pertinax was respected for his discipline and steadiness, which I was not; yet he did not have the connections to seek high office, which I did." He shrugged. "I sought his help to advance myself, and compensated him well. It has been a simple arrangement of mutual benefit."

All these years I had thought that Pertinax had stolen his heart, but the Gaul had merely captured his ambition. "You never told me that," I said. My voice grated like a dry wheel.

"I did not like to tell you I had changed, when you had not."

"Have you changed?"

His silence told me that he recognized the incongruity with the invitation he had just offered. "Be content with your mistress," I said.

"Marcus . . ." His voice was reproachful, seductive.

"I am trying not to embarrass my father too greatly, or break my vows to Mithras. I cannot afford reckless behavior."

"Jove's thunderbolts! Which brother am I talking to?"

"The reformed one," I said, and turned up the street toward home.

CHAPTER 23

YOU WILL FEAR ME

When Father and I arrived at the Palace, the night was as black as a raven's crotch and it seemed only the guards were still awake. "My son and I must see the Princeps on an urgent matter," Father said.

I stuffed my hands in my armpits to warm them. My euphoria at having rid myself of Livilla had turned to discomfort. For me to be the one who informed Caligula of his sister's behavior seemed ignoble, but my father would not hear of allowing the news to reach him from his enemies.

Most of all I wished I were in bed asleep. The convivial dinner parties had ended; trees and houses hunched beneath a hissing wind that felt like the breath of an ice-clad Alp. The air had a feel of impending rain or even snow.

Recognizing Father, the guards admitted us at once. Sleepy servants emerged as we were brought into what I now knew to be the public atrium. It was deserted and chilly, with only a few torches reflected in the shivering pool. "Wake him if necessary," Father ordered the Princeps' moon-faced chamberlain.

I murmured, "What will you do if Caligula . . . becomes distraught?"

"That will be for you to worry about, Marcus," he said grimly. He showed no impatience or discomfort during the lengthy wait until another freedman came to lead us into the private side of the house.

Through an incense-scented haze I saw a shabby little dining room, less impressive than either of our own. The frescoes of scantily clad Hesperides in the garden of golden apples were nearly colorless with age. Stains and scars marred the mosaic floor.

Acrobats were dancing to the trill of a double flute. Gold dust glittered on a dancer's oiled skin as he launched himself from the shoulders of another, flipped in midair, did a handspring off the bent back of a third, and landed on the floor like a cat, palms outstretched as if such agility and grace were no effort at all. The flute music ended with a flourish.

"Senator Carinna," the freedman intoned. "Quaestor-Designate Carinna."

Heads turned. "Come in," Caligula said testily, rolling away from the half-clad woman beside him. "What is it now? Crocodiles in the Cloaca Maxima?"

Lepidus slid off his couch and came to greet us. I heard a fragment of his murmur—"damned prophecy"—before Father took his elbow and began to whisper into his ear. I advanced uncertainly into the room.

Drusilla glanced up at me from the couch her husband had left, her chestnut hair frizzed out of its pins and ribbons. Her uncle Claudius lay somnolent nearby while a reader mumbled from a scroll. There was no sign of Livilla or Gemellus.

"Well?" Caligula snarled. "Say something amusing. Dance a jig. Anything to liven up this dismal company." The disheveled woman curled an arm around his neck and tried to kiss his ear, but he shrugged her off. I recognized her then as the wife of the Senate Leader, rouged, bare-bosomed, and probably old enough to be his mother.

Father took a step away from Lepidus. "This news may be better kept in the family, Caesar." He glanced at the woman without showing that he knew her.

"Off with you, Claudia." Caligula swatted her on the rump, like a farmer driving away a cow.

"But, Gaius—"

"Now!" he barked, and without another word she gathered her clothes and departed.

When she had gone, Father continued, "A regrettable incident occurred after the races today."

Caligula's fingers tightened on a cushion until the knuckles showed bone-white. "What?" He tried for the same savage tone, but I heard a minute hesitation. Hard to believe that no one had told him yet. Most likely no one had dared.

"My son witnessed it. He will tell you."

Face to face with Caligula, I felt my mouth go dry. If Malleus realized that the man who had steered him toward Livilla was the same man who had slain his horse, he was unlikely to keep quiet. And then she might not be the only one exiled.

I cleared my throat, at which point their uncle woke up.

Silius once said that if someone fell on top of a wax model of Augustus, the result would be Claudius. Strands of gray hair framed a squat, creased face finished off with ears outthrust like amphora handles. He squinted at me. "Have they ca-ca-caught the villains who waylaid you, young Carinna?"

I had stopped correcting people who thought I had been assaulted, since it made an excuse for the wounds Aurima had inflicted on me. "It seems they may have been disposed of after attacking me by mistake, Tiberius Claudius."

I turned back to Caligula. There was no way to sweeten the truth, so I said flatly, "After the last race, Caesar, the charioteer Malleus was seen leaving Julia Livilla's litter."

For a moment I was not sure he had heard. Then he said through stiff lips, "Seen . . . by whom?"

"A friend and me, and five or six others I did not know. We were—"

I stopped, for he had leaped up and was striding through the doorway, shouting Livilla's name.

Unfortunate man! To confront a monstrous scandal involving his youngest sister so soon after the astrologer's prophecy about Agrippinilla's death.

Lepidus sat beside his wife and muttered to her. Drusilla nodded with eyes downcast. Claudius sighed, belched, shuffled his feet into sandals, and limped out on a slave's arm. Father had disappeared.

Suddenly there was an outburst of shouting. Caligula thrust Livilla, tottering, into the room. Her unpinned hair cascaded over her shoulders in disheveled billows, and her unpainted eyes were puffy with sleep.

"Is it true?" he said viciously, as she brushed at the wrinkles in her pink night-tunic. "Did Carinna really see Malleus crawl from your litter?"

"What?" Her eyes went wide. Then she saw me, and her spurious consternation became hostility. "He lies! He tried to rape me in Gemellus's dining room. Gemellus surprised him, or he would have done it."

"That is not true," I said hotly.

"Ask Gemellus, brother! He will tell you."

"Answer me," Caligula snapped. "Did you let that slave fuck you?"

"I am not a child to be held to account," Livilla shrilled at him.

"I am the head of this family, Julia Livilla, and you will do as I say!"

Servers shrank out of her path as she flounced toward the doorway. Caligula caught her arm. Brother and sister shouted obscenities at each other. He slapped her face. She struck back at him.

Before the blow landed, he caught and twisted her wrist. "A charioteer! In Isis' name, what next? A goat? A dog?"

She shrieked, "Let me go!"

"You beg me to let you stay in Rome: 'One last chance, brother dear.' Now this!" He pushed her away. "Start packing. You will wait for the Etesian winds on Pandateria."

"Where Uncle sent Mother? You would send me away like Mother, to be forgotten and starve?" Her face was a rictus of fury. "I will not go. You cannot make me go."

Caligula struck her again, so hard this time that she fell back against a couch. Before she could gather herself, he clawed his fingers into her hair and dragged her onto her knees. "Bring me a slave." Raw rage coarsened his voice. "The acrobat. He will do."

Livilla pounded him with her fists, screeching. He pulled her head back against his thigh. "Love me you may not—but by Isis, you will fear me!"

"Caligula, stop," Drusilla cried. She would have rushed to him if Lepidus had not held her back. "Please, brother, let her go."

Two servants hauled in the acrobat. He was a brown-skinned youth, slim but well muscled, his dark eyes sheened with belladonna.

Livilla wept, her head trapped against her brother's leg. He snapped his fingers at a server. "Give me that knife."

It was a sharp, thin blade for deboning fish. Livilla shrieked at the sight of it and flattened herself on the floor, protecting her face with her arms.

Caligula let go of her hair. "Hold him," he said to the servants. He slashed the ties of the small leather apron the acrobat wore, baring his private parts. The youth screamed and struggled, and kept screaming while Lepidus and I stared in a ragged frieze of horror. Drusilla covered her eyes.

"Look," Caligula said, yanking on Livilla's hair to tip her face upward. "Look at what you so prize." In his other hand he held the boy's bloody testicles.

Lepidus gasped and took a wobbly step backward. His legs folded, and his head hit the floor with a *whack* like a dropped log. Drusilla uttered a wifely cry and fell to her knees over him.

Guards dragged away the acrobat, as gory as a gutted deer. Caligula released Livilla. She fell forward, her palms skidding on the floor. "Swear you will obey me," he rasped.

She sat up and began to scrub her hands frenziedly against the front of her tunic, blazoning the rose-pink wool with crimson smears.

He let his trophies drop. In a softer voice he said, "Lilla, you know I did this for your own good."

He touched her dark curls, but she jerked her head away. "Castrate them all! Who cares?" She lurched to her feet. "You will be surrounded by eunuchs." Her wild laugh was half a scream. "Eunuchs in the Senate, eunuchs in the law court, eunuchs in the Praetorian—"

"Be still!"

"What will you do, brother dear? You cannot castrate *me.*" She tried to laugh again, but her voice broke.

I was helping my groggy patron onto a couch when she went by. But she was sobbing in dry breathless heaves, and I doubt she saw me.

Caligula's eyes went to the scarlet scrawls on the mosaic floor where the acrobat had lain. His face was freckled with blood. "She . . . Shuh-Shuh-She . . ." He ground the heels of his hands into his eyes. "Gods, I m-m-must not . . ."

Just twenty-five and already the vultures circle.

Without looking at me he said, "G-Go. Leave me."

I was ready to go. Although I considered myself no stranger to butchery, my stomach was trying to climb into my throat. It was a flash of fancy that stopped me: the sound of an inner voice much like my brother's.

Look at what you have done, it said. *This was my friend. That was my* sponsa.

I reached to the table for someone's cup and took a gulp of wine. Caligula's blood-brindled eyes sprang open as I pushed the cup into his cramped fingers. "Drink this," I said. "And come with me."

⤙⤚

Smoke hung thick in the cavelike *taberna*, below street level in a passage off the Vicus Apollinis. The door stood open for ventilation, and water puddling on the sill from the drizzle outside spilled down the uneven steps and meandered across the earthen floor.

The *tabernarius* lit a tallow candle from the guttering stub of the old one and jammed the one on top of the other. I thanked him and pinched it out. He had frowned at Caligula earlier and hissed to me, "Who is that?" I told him who it was and said that the guards, secretaries, clerks, slaves, and Senators would be along directly. He winked. It is no bad thing to have a reputation for japery.

"She will not see reason," Caligula muttered into the gloom. He sat stiffly beside me, his back spear-straight as if the half-log bench were a throne. "But sweet Isis, to exile my own sister . . ."

I thought of suggesting that he send her to one of those far-off islets where the lunatics of noble families live, but it is never a good idea to offer advice about a man's sister.

Caligula's eyes were sunk deep in wells of shadow. "And Agrippinilla . . . That prophecy, have you heard? I could not bear to lose her. . . ." His head rocked slowly, wearily back and forth. "I could not bear it. . . ."

"Look here," I said. "A good fuck will relax you." I gestured at the bosomy serving girl ladling wine out of a jar set in the counter. She smiled back, apparently recovered from the surprise of Ollius rousting other drinkers out of the place. "She is quite energetic, as I recall."

"I need not pay for a barmaid. I can have any woman I want."

"Then make your choice and marry again."

He grimaced. "Still commerce. Merely paid in trouble instead of coin."

My thoughts drifted to a girl with hair like copper, and then to all the obstacles between us: birth, language, customs, history, injustice, enmity. "The greatest good fortune," I murmured, "is to love someone who wants nothing but yourself." Then, embarrassed to be thought sentimental, I called out to the *tabernarius*, "Harpocras, we perish of thirst."

"Water's almost hot," he called back.

I was about to start my appeal for reparations to Aurima and her people when Caligula inhaled deeply, shoulders tight and neck rigid. "Talk to me about Gemellus, then. What have you learned?" He stared at the water glittering down the steps as if it were an executioner's sword.

The serving girl brought each of us wine with a pitcher of hot water. Mixing my drink, I sought to muster the right answer. "There is a conspiracy against you," I began, low-voiced. "They say Gemellus has promised to restore the Republic, but I do not know of my own witnessing that he is with them. He likes to talk of what he would do as princeps, and they may have taken that for complicity."

A long moment later he said, "You seek to give me comfort."

"I will not call it truth if I do not know it to be true."

"Find me the truth."

"Saxa—"

In a hard voice he interrupted, "You, Marcus. For the sake of the love we shared for your brother." Who, by committing *laesa maiestas* in his presence, had put him at risk of Tiberius's retaliation.

I hesitated, surprised by his use of my first name. "Then I must," I said. No other argument would have made me disobey my father's command.

Caligula tipped hot water into his cup and held it, but did not drink. "Why did you bring me here?"

"I thought it would please you to stop being Livilla's brother for a while."

Another silence. A board laid on the muddy floor slewed as the barmaid brought us a dish of olives. She padded away without a word.

"How the child defies me!" His ring began to tick against the side of his cup. "No one knows how I restrain myself."

The memory of newly severed gonads clenched in his fist soured the wine in my mouth. "Better control would serve you well, cousin."

"You cannot know what presses on me!"

I rummaged among the olives with my finger. "There is a game the Parthian cavalry play to make themselves more agile in battle." Finding a fruit that might be unbruised, I held it up to what little light there was. "They divide into two teams, decapitate a captive, and bat his head around from horseback until one team hits it over the other's goal line." I let the olive fall and flicked it at him.

The tapping stopped. He said, "It is dangerous to take my trust for granted."

"Do you trust me? Why, I suppose you must, since I was able to entice you here with none of your guards knowing." I rolled another olive around with my finger.

"Then now is your chance to tell me the price of your love. Speak."

"My price?"

"You have not yet said what you want of me. What is it?"

My anger flared at the insult. "Did you ask Publius what he wanted, too?"

"You really wish to atone for him? What an honorable man you are, young Marcus." He touched his cup to my chest in an ironic salute. A slop of wine soaked into my tunic. "But I forgave him long ago."

"I must forgive myself, then." I put the olive in my mouth.

"For what?"

I shook my head again, spat out the pit, and reached for the pitcher to replenish my drink. He leaned closer. The wet hair molded to his skull made him seem younger and more innocent. "Why does your brother's memory haunt you?"

I drew away. "Let me tell you a story that happened in Siscia, in Pannonia, five years ago."

"Fuck Pannonia." His hand clamped over mine on the pitcher's handle. "Answer me."

Before either of us could speak further, light flooded into the *taberna*. Ollius, who had been guarding the door, clumped down the steps backward with his hands raised. Two Praetorians stood on the threshold, one holding a bared sword, the other lifting a lantern to peer into the wineshop. Rain streamed down their helmets and plastered their cloaks to their shoulders.

I stood up beside Caligula, taking care to keep my hands in sight. One of the soldiers whistled to unseen comrades. A slender man in a wet cloak slipped past and picked his way down the steps: the Princeps' Alexandrian freedman.

Before he could begin his exclamations and reproaches, I bent over Caligula. "No doubt you will have a lecture from Saxa about this night's escape. I regret bringing it on you."

"I will commend him on an effective search," he said grimly.

As a centurion tramped down into the *taberna* and the steamy breath of horses filled the doorway, he rose to go toward them. Partway there, he turned. "You are right," he said, his expression indistinct in the lantern shadow. "But a man is fortunate to have even one friend who wants nothing else but him."

The scandal broke the next morning like a hailstorm. When I took my horses out for exercise, I had to skirt a throng outside the Palace demanding that

Caesar punish Livilla. Walls bore new scribbles in charcoal: EXILE LIVILLA and PALATINE WHORE, with obscene drawings of her and the charioteer.

On the way home I paused to rest the horses across from the house of the Marcomanni. It stood silent, doors shut against the raucous traffic of the Clivus Palatinus.

Flavus had said the Winter Feast would start tomorrow. Twelve miles to Bovillae, more or less, on the Via Appia: an easy morning's ride.

Foolish whim. What would I do amid a horde of unfriendly barbarians? I eyed the clearing sky to gauge the hour and continued home to the anthill frenzy of cooking, cleaning, and garland-hanging as our household prepared to feast the most valued clients.

When they and we had all gathered on our couches, Father made a little speech asking the gods to preserve the bonds of loyalty and friendship that had held fast over the years but would continue to be tested, presumably by me.

As the heir of the house, I was expected to offer a few words of my own. So when we had spilled a libation, I rose to my feet and said to the seven guests, who were waiting impatiently for their dinner, "I cannot equal my father's eloquence"—he smiled frostily at this—"but I share his pride in the strength of our family. Rome has need of men with courage and honor, men who will uphold justice for every free person in our dominion. If we stand together for truth and order, then may we hope for the favor of *Fortuna Romana* and of Mithras, Lord of Creation, who will judge us all."

A short silence greeted this. Then someone said, "Bravely spoken," and they applauded politely.

As the evening passed, there was much speculation about Caligula's future. His silence on the matter of Livilla's infamous behavior had caused him to be defamed in public. Rumor had it that the Tiberians hoped to use the scandal to prevent him from adopting Agrippinilla's boy-child, should it live. We drank to a long life for him, then to *Fortuna Augusta*, the gods, our family's ancestors, my father, Lepidus, each other, me, and so on.

After the guests had gone, clutching gifts and leaning on their slaves in various degrees of inebriation, my father put his arm around my shoulders. I yawned, longing for bed. Phormio, who had inched along on a walking stick today, was no doubt already snoring in exhaustion.

The many toasts had caused Father to drink more than usual; he had some difficulty focusing on me. "Marcus," he said in a hoarse whisper. "This"—he moved his free hand, searching for a word—"this passion for Mithras. I did not believe you could worship him, so unrelenting a god. And I thought less of you, I admit, for believing in gods and not in the ideal of reason."

I took off my crown of flowers and cast it into the atrium pool at our feet. It floated amid transparent panes of ice, the serpentine ribbons reminding me of Rufus drowning in the horse trough.

"Listen, I will tell you a secret. Pay attention." He leaned closer, breathing spiced wine on my cheek. "There will be a family dinner party in a few days, on Agrippinilla's birthday. Caesar plans to invite you."

"Me? Why?"

"Because he is grateful to you. 'Tis not what I would have done, taking him to a hole-in-the-wall drink shop, but you did well, my son. My fine son."

I was afraid he would kiss me, which I could not have borne. "But, Marcus"—he leaned closer again—"one more thing. You must get over your itch for this Germanic hostage, the rebel's daughter."

I said nothing.

"I understand perfectly," he said. "I do. When we captured Arminius's wife, big as she was with the renegade's child, I was afire to get under her skirts." He snorted reminiscently. "Like every other officer and man in Germanicus's army."

Petals drifted like snowflakes in the pool. I said, "It is not revenge I want."

"Of course it is. This girl was taken in battle—so she is brave, I expect. A virgin, eh? Also, I hear, she is bold in manner and appearance." He nodded, convincing himself. "Naturally you want to master her. Penetrate her. Possess her. That you are not free to act merely inflames your desires more."

After a moment I said, "And the solution?"

"The solution?" He massaged a back tooth with his tongue. "The solution is this: Caesar desires you to have charge of Julia Livilla."

"What?" I lost my balance, and would have reeled into a column if his arm had not restrained me.

"He is willing to entrust you with his sister. A very great privilege."

"I will have to marry her?" I croaked.

"No, you ninny. Simply keep her out of trouble until April. Until the sailing season."

"Will she go into exile then?"

"To Ephesus. To join her husband."

I shook my head. Was this my reward for befriending Caligula the previous night?

"Marcus." He rocked me from side to side with his arm as if chiding a young boy. "Caesar is far too busy to attend to her. We cannot let the Tiberians think she may further dishonor his *maiestas*."

"Let him send her to a desert island."

"Living in Asia will be exile enough." He tried to peer into my eyes, but I was staring at the garland. "Just a few months. That is all he asks."

"Here in our house? Will Gemellus come, too? And that witch she calls her granny?"

"She is forbidden to see Gemellus except at family gatherings. You will have a husband's authority, and she must obey you in all things."

"A husband's authority! I would not touch her to save my life."

He stiffened. "I told you, this is Caesar's request."

My cheeks went hot. "So I must obey, because years ago my brother wronged him? Let the Vestals guard her until she can be sent away."

"Perdition! Have you lost your taste for women, now that Silius is making eyes at you again?"

I stepped back, out of his grip. "Perhaps you should ask your bed girl, Father."

My father seized the front of my *chiton* and pulled me toward him with such force that the delicate fabric tore. "Perhaps I should take a new wife," he said in a hiss, "so I may sire better sons."

Fending himself off the corridor wall, he stalked away into the interior of the house.

I, who had led cohorts and stopped a rebellion, now a whore's doorkeeper!

Except for Phormio's slow breathing the small room was silent, the darkness broken only by a lamp's tiny flicker. I stared at the ceiling, burning with humiliation and anger. Father was willing to tarnish my personal honor and make me the laughingstock of the city, simply because Caligula desired it.

It had already been decided. Livilla would come here in three days. And I would be her guardian until the god-cursed winds blew fair for travel to the East.

I opened a box on the bedside table and took Aurima's amber in my hand. It was cold, the swirling silver wires like rills of ice binding a frozen flame.

I felt inside the box for the fine copper thread of her hair, but my fingers were too clumsy from drink. I gave up and rolled onto my back, dangling the pendant above me. The drop of amber winked gold in the lamplight.

O Mithras, make me dutiful. Only with duty can there be strength. Only with strength can there be order. Only with order can there be light.

But I could not stop thinking of the gathering at Flavus's villa. She had already been there for two days.

And Aurima sees the man she marries.

CHAPTER 24

THE WINTER FEAST

Flavus's villa hunched on a small rise, its whitewashed walls splayed on either side of a pillared entrance. In the damp chill of the afternoon, smoke behind the villa climbed straight into a soiled-wool sky. I heard distant shouts, dogs barking, laughter.

My escort drew in around me, Ollius and Dio wincing after nearly three hours of bumping on muleback. Even the groom, Thalus, looked tired. We were all mud-spattered from fording streams that had overflowed banks and culverts. Our mounts' coats prickled, sodden and spiky.

Too late, I regretted my impulse to join the barbarous festivities with which Flavus and his guests would celebrate the beginning of winter. As I rode toward the villa, my heart was beating hard. "Mithras protect me," I muttered, but was not sure what I feared.

The woman who glided toward me was as pallid as a ghost: gray-blond hair in a braided coronet, an ash-gray *stola*, pale blue eyes empty of emotion. Taking her for Flavus's wife, I reckoned she must be weary of her husband's guests.

More shouting rang out. Behind me Dio caught his breath as a bearded giant holding a drinking horn stumbled into the atrium and rocked to a halt. The woman ignored him, and he blundered out again.

"Welcome, Marcus Licinius Carinna," she said. "You honor our house." Her accent was very like Aurima's, and desire stirred in me like a tame fish that rises at a familiar footfall.

"I wished to sacrifice at a temple not far from here," I said shamelessly, "and recalling Flavus's invitation, thought I might stop to meet some of his guests. If it does not inconvenience you too greatly." While I spoke this blather to Flavus's lady, my eyes drifted past her. Other people were roaming the house, but I did not see Aurima.

"Flavus will be glad." Light glinted on a silver bracelet as she gestured to a reception room. "You must be thirsty. I will bring you something to drink."

"I need nothing right now. Perhaps you can tell me where to find your husband?"

Surprise transformed her face, like a mask shattering. She said something I did not catch. I bent closer, and she repeated, "He is not my husband, but my husband's brother."

After a moment I said, "You . . . were Harman's wife?"

Hearing his Germanic name startled her more. After a moment she inclined her head. "I am Thusnelda." Her eyes met mine. "I remember your father, the Tribune Carinna. He gave me food in the camp of Germanicus. He said his wife, too, was with child."

"My sister and I were born that fall," I said.

So this was the Great Traitor's widow. Germanicus had described her in his memoirs as a loyal Cherusci leader's daughter, snatched away by Arminius and ever after his willing helpmeet. *When given up to the mercy of Caesar by her father,* the general had written, *she neither wept nor cried out in despair, but in proud silence was conveyed with her unborn child to Italy, leaving behind her husband, her family, and her native land.*

An extraordinary sensation came over me: I was at the same time my father gazing at the young Thusnelda, myself viewing her as she was now, and my former self seeing Aurima as she came into Carnuntum to begin her own exile. Ingiomar Ironhand's daughter had looked just the same, betraying none of the anguish and fear within her.

Flavus ambled into the atrium. "Welcome, young Carinna," he cried. "Rome must not be in such turmoil as they say, if you have found time to visit."

He embraced me as if we were old drinking companions. His eye patch was gone; gray tendrils straggled damply around his flushed face, and sweat glinted in his chest hair where he had loosened the laces of his crimson tunic. More barbaric yet, he wore striped woolen breeches and soft leather shoes tied with thongs. In a gust of ale-soured breath he said, "I see you have met my dear Thusnelda."

"He stops a while to meet your guests, brother-in-law."

"You must go no farther today, by Thunraz! A storm is coming. Stay the night with us. Thusnelda, have a room made ready for him."

I protested, but not too much. I had left word of a sudden desire to visit my mother in Antium, so Father would not expect me back for a day or two. Mithras forgive me the untruths I told so readily.

Thusnelda said, "He must meet Heriberhto. They are of an age."

Flavus leaned close enough for me to see a white seam of scar tissue that ran like a tear track from his empty eye socket. "You have never been to a Winter Feast, I expect?"

"Never," I said.

He belched. "You will not forget it."

⟞⟝ ⟞⟝

A boy led me along a colonnade, one of a pair enclosing a terrace thronged with Germans. Having expected something rough and outlandish in the room he indicated, I was disappointed to find an ordinary sleeping couch and other furniture.

I washed off the road grime, hearing arguments and admonitions, shouts and guffaws, childish shrieks, yapping dogs. A mongrel trotted in through the terrace doors as Dio was shaking wrinkles out of a tunic. He yelled and stamped his feet, and the beast scuttled out.

Early dusk was falling when I came upon Flavus surveying his domain. Smells of roasting meat and wood smoke thickened the air. I thanked him for stabling my mounts and feeding Ollius and Thalus, who would bed with them.

"Some people are asking, 'Why is a Roman here?'" He tilted his head. "You will not mock, eh? *Vetrfest*, Winter Feast, is a holy time for us."

A rosy maiden offered us twisted cow horns full of ale. Men diced on a cowhide. Yelling boys chased each other with dogs running alongside. A girl on a bench braided another girl's hair. Women dandling infants eyed my bare legs as if they had never before seen a civilized man. One of them muttered what I took to be "These Roman girls are not so pretty," and there was a roar of laughter. It was a gaudy crowd, clad in a jumble of colors and patterns with enameled brooches in violent hues.

Flavus knocked his drinking horn convivially against mine. The barley ale was as robust and bitter as the brew sold in ramshackle taverns in Carnuntum's shadow.

"Ha!" He wiped his mouth. "Is it true Caesar's youngest sister lay with a charioteer after the races? I hear men are shouting, 'Shame' and 'Down with Caligula' in the Forum." He twisted his neck to aim his one eye at me.

"The Forum was quiet this morning," I countered. Chiefly because the troublemakers had been caused to disappear.

From where we stood between the villa's two wings, steps curved down to a lower terrace. This in turn gave onto a long pool and statues, pale as pearls, set amid shrubbery. Beyond the pool, dark figures frolicked around a bonfire.

Agile despite his tipsiness, Flavus trotted down the terrace steps onto a walkway beside the pool. Puddles scattered in our path glittered gold, and the water burned with firelight. Dancers frisked around the blaze, hair streaming and skirts flying as Pan-pipes howled. Flavus said, "Ah, the young. So much vigor! Will you dance with them, Carinna?"

As if any man of good birth prances around in public! I did not let myself be baited. "Where are these people from?"

"Everywhere. Cherusci, Bastarnae, Chatti, Chauci, Marcomanni, Quadi, Batavi, others. You did not know, perhaps, that there are so many of us in Rome? It is like slaves; if you knew how many, it would frighten you, eh?"

Someone splashing in the shallow pool shouted to him. While he paused to respond, I gave my empty horn to a server and kept on toward the bonfire.

The deep-throated piping was manic. Women capered with men as others on the outskirts drank, laughed, shouted. Sparks whirled into the darkening sky. It reminded me of a spring festival on our farm near Volsinii that ended with the dancers pairing off in the fields and orchards, giddy with music and drink.

But where was Aurima? Not wanting to betray myself by asking, I looked everywhere.

Then I saw her. Her cheeks were pink, her eyes bright, her mouth open in a breathless laugh. Hand in hand with other dancers, she skipped sideways toward me, breasts bouncing, the long braid leaping around her shoulders, feet flying under her billowing skirts.

I had never seen her so merry. This girl whose mother had been brutally murdered, who had charged into battle to avenge her, and who herself had nearly died from the shock of uprooting to Rome, was carousing blithely. . . .

With a man. A young man with dark-blond hair who held fast to her hand, watching her as they danced. He wore a tunic blotched with sweat, ankle-tied trousers, and soft leather shoes dyed with madder.

Jealousy swept over me. In vain did I tell myself this was to be expected. After being treated for so long as a trophy of war, here she could enjoy the attentions her youth and beauty merited.

Her companion pulled her out of the ring of dancers. It seemed he was well known; many of the others spoke to him or slapped his shoulder. Someone passed him a swollen goatskin. When Aurima shook her head, he lifted the hairy bag and squirted drink expertly into his own mouth. He stood half a hand higher than she did, which meant he was taller than I. When he stripped off his tunic and draped it around his neck, I saw he was also thicker through the chest.

"A handsome couple, eh?" Flavus said beside me.

Aurima saw me, and her smile vanished. The young man caught her hand again and tugged her into the spinning circle. She danced edgewise toward us. Hair that had escaped her braid flew around her face, so I could not see her eyes. Her companion, lolloping along behind her, saluted Flavus with a grin and a nod.

"Who is he?" I said.

Flavus beamed. "My nephew, Heriberhto."

My mouth nearly fell open. Harman's son?

After the first shock I realized that Aurima could not possibly marry him. He was the tallest tree in a dry forest, and she was a bolt of lightning that could set off a wildfire. With malicious satisfaction I said, "It appears the omens were wrong," and Flavus gave me a half smile, not understanding.

Dio had been supposed to join me after salving his saddle sores. When he had not appeared by nightfall, I went back to the room and surprised him writing by lamplight. He dropped the stylus and leaped up, hiding my view of the tablet.

"What is that?" I asked.

"A few notes," he said nervously. "I wanted to record what is happening. It is very unusual, this festival of barbarians."

"Of which you so far know nothing." I held out a hand. "Let me see."

"I am sorry, Marcus." He hesitated. "I was ordered not to tell you."

"Tell me what? That you are informing on me to my mother?"

I recognized the flicker of apprehension in his eyes. "My father?" I said. Disbelief flared into fury. "You are spying on me for my father?"

"The master ordered it," he mumbled, looking at the floor.

I struck him with my open hand. He fell back against the table and would have overturned it had I not caught the front of his tunic. Our shadows sprang wildly around the room as the lamp joggled back into place.

"I am your master," I shouted into his pale long-nosed face. "My mother gave you to me, you fucking little papyrus beetle. You owe your loyalty to me, not to him. Understand?"

His cheek began to redden. "I beg you to be reasonable. Everything you possess, your father owns. I cannot disobey him."

It enraged me all the more to hear a slave talk back to me like a god-cursed law teacher. "You are not a woman's secretary any more, Dio. This is the arena, and you cannot side with both fighters." I gave a last wrench to the fabric bunched in my fist and released him. "Did you ever think about why you were sent to me? Not because I enjoy fawning on Caligula Caesar. Because it is up to me to expiate what Publius did. And I have no one else to trust."

I stopped, breathless. The words had burst out of me, words I had never even said to myself. With an effort I concluded more evenly, "I see I have asked too much of a slave. When we return home, I will send you back to Antium."

Dio bowed his head, whether in acquiescence or shame no longer mattered. "Come along," I said. "While we are here, I want to learn these people's names and customs. Bring your note tablet."

He followed at my heels as I started down the steps from the upper terrace. Still fuming, I was slow to notice dark shapes at the foot of the stair. They mounted toward me: Maelo, his unpleasant son Odo, and Cotto with the flattened nose. Lit from behind by blazing torches, they hulked around me like bears.

When I made to pass them, Maelo blocked the way. He said, "I think Caesar does not know you took Aurima to the woods of Diana." Enough light caught his face to show the cold gleam of his eyes. "A fine trick you play on me, eh?" He drew his knife from its sheath.

I was pinned against the balustrade, my own longknife out of reach. No hope of aid from useless Dio, who stood paralyzed several steps above me.

With as much boldness as I could muster I said, "Does she accuse me of insult?"

His mouth was a fanged snarl in his bristling beard. "What do you think?"

"I think she is strong and brave. And has good reason to hate injustice."

We stared at each other. Odo wrenched his own weapon out of its sheath, jabbering something in Germanic. Probably "Just stab him, Father."

Maelo waved him back without looking away from me. Silver glinted in his long ruddy hair, tied back at the crown. "Five summers ago, I with Ingiomar and Friduric his son killed the murderers of my sister."

I had not known he took part in the disemboweling. My own entrails knotted in apprehension. "Put away your knife. I have no quarrel with you."

Cotto muttered something. Maelo grunted, and the point of his blade dipped to within an inch of my belly. "How long do you have courage when you see your guts burst to the ground?"

"For what offense?" I retorted. "For letting your sister's daughter pray to her goddess?"

Maelo lowered his head. His beard bushed out on his chest like the mane of a bull aurochs about to charge. "Aurima marries who I choose, or I tell to Caesar about the woods of Diana."

"And I will tell Caesar that I did nothing but stop her from killing herself. Otherwise you would be on your way home with her ashes."

His eyes bulged. "Now let me pass," I said, and pushed between him and his two companions.

I walked on toward the fire at a pace that I hoped was slow and deliberate enough to hide the quivering in my limbs. Dio followed wordlessly, his sandals crunching over gravel on the pavement. I was glad the knife tip had not actually touched my stomach; a slave should not see his master wet himself.

When I regained my composure, I looked in vain for Aurima among the fire shadows. Nor, more worrisome yet, could I spot her dancing partner with the strange name.

But he found me. Looming out of the fireglow, he held out the goatskin to me. "All this smoke, I guessed you might be thirsty," he said in fluent Latin.

He had dangerous eyes, their glare darkened by flat frowning brows. His dark-blond hair was brushed straight back so it winged behind his ears, barely short enough to be civilized. He also kept his jaw shaved, a nod to Roman convention that exposed a small mouth drawn thin in challenge.

I did not trust him enough to accept the offering. His brows tightened. More stiffly he said, "I am Heriberhto. Flavus is my father's brother."

"Your father was Harman."

A curt nod. His amber eyes stared unblinkingly at me.

Did he expect me to embrace him and share his drink? In his veins ran the blood of the man who had murdered fifteen thousand Romans. He should have been strangled at birth.

I said, "I am Marcus Licinius Carinna, son of Titus who fought your father."

I was aware of Dio nearby, shivering with his arms tucked inside his mantle. Silent lightning flickered far to the west, behind the smoke of the bonfire.

"Why are you alive?" I said bluntly.

Heriberhto's face did not change. "The old king Marbodo asked Tiberius Caesar to spare my mother and me. We lived with him in Ravenna, where you Romans keep all your unwanted barbarians."

"And now that Tiberius and Marbodo are dead, you are here."

"Why not? I am a friend of Rome. My uncle is a Roman citizen and a friend of Caligula Caesar. Like you."

"Why have you sought me out?"

I was prepared for him to say he wanted Aurima. Instead he shifted his weight, turning a shoulder to Dio to make our talk more private. "Your father was in the last war. You will be in the next one." My surprise must have shown, for a corner of his mouth twisted up. "Oh, the campaign is no secret."

I kept quiet, not knowing what response to make.

"Afterward you will need trustworthy men to keep the peace." He puffed out his chest. "My mother's father was chieftain of my people, as my mother's brother is now. I myself am much loved by the Cherusci."

"And who better than Harman's son to persuade them that the *Pax Romana* is not so dreadful?"

"My father did not raise me," he said, goaded into anger. "Marbodo did. He was a great king and an ally valued by Rome."

"So that is what you want, to be king?"

"One day. For now, I want you not to be my enemy."

Lightning fluttered again on the horizon. It was late in the year for a thunderstorm. A bad omen, the augurs might say.

Heriberhto scuffed a foot like a restless horse. "I will try to keep an open mind," I said. "However . . ."

His eyes widened expectantly.

"I will advise my cousin Caligula Caesar that you are an unsuitable husband for Aurima of the Marcomanni."

"You are Caesar's cousin?"

He looked into the distance, perhaps reviewing the attractions of Ingiomar's daughter, then back at me. "She is too contrary to be a good wife, anyway." He gulped from the goatskin and held it out to me again.

I lifted it and sucked down ale. He wiped his mouth with the back of his hand. "Are you coming to the feast?"

"I will join you later," I said. I did not want Flavus's other guests to suppose we were comrades. He tossed me the now-flaccid goatskin and went toward the villa.

I wanted to laugh. "Too contrary"? Harman's son was too tame for the intemperate wench!

Content to have frustrated his and Maelo's designs, I drank ale and watched the late-night revelry. A few girls danced on their own by the waning fire, but Aurima was not among them. Tired children were carried away. A dogfight drew a horde of yelling boys. Deciding I could not miss an opportunity to make myself known among the northern tribes, I went in search of the warriors' feast.

Candles flared, as straight as wheat shoots, on trestle tables set in a courtyard. The banqueters massed around them, gabbling, gobbling, guzzling. Above their shaggy heads, swags of fir garlanded the courtyard columns, adding a sweet forest tang to the fug of hot grease, ale, and smoke.

I was puzzled not to see Heriberhto. But there was Maelo, telling a story with wide drunken gestures to an old man from another tribe. As I was about to announce myself, Flavus bellowed from his seat, "Over here."

Voices stilled. Heads lifted. A fat man in a fur vest lost his balance and fell backward off his bench. His tablemates brayed laughter as his kicking jolted bread, bones, and drinking horns into their laps.

Flavus elbowed the stocky young man next to him. "Make room." The fellow mopped meat juice with a crust and stuffed it into his mouth, mumbling something. Flavus clouted him lightly on the back of the head. "Stop eating, you pig! This is the son of Senator Carinna, Caesar's adviser." To me he said, "My son, Italicus."

Italicus moved over on the bench. He wore his brown hair longer than his father did, perhaps as a warning that he was less domesticated. "Welcome to the Winter Feast," he said in almost accentless Latin. He showed broken teeth in a perfunctory smile before returning to his food.

"He speaks well, eh?" Flavus leaned aside so I could fork myself in between the two of them. "The best tutors. Grammar, history, rhetoric, law. And he led a cavalry wing. Two years at Vetera with the Fifth."

"Well done." I was more impressed by the experience of this hard-living princeling than that of his cousin Heriberhto, who no doubt had learned slipperier lessons from the wily old Marcomanni king Marbodo. I signaled for a drink.

Flavus twisted on his seat. "I have an Alban you may like."

I shook my head. "You have revived my taste for ale." He grinned approvingly when I drained my drinking horn and handed it back for refilling. Once Livilla moved into our house, I would not dare consume anything unless it had been tasted for me.

Determined to quash a possible alliance between the Marcomanni and the Cherusci, I said, "Flavus, it is impossible for Aurima to marry your nephew."

He took a joint of beef from a heaped platter. "Why?"

"You know why. Harman's son may not marry Ingiomar's daughter." I drew my knife and sawed meat off the carcass as others were doing. It tasted of nothing: no sauce or spice, not even salt.

Italicus swigged ale. "So you have met our Thumelicus, have you?"

That was why the name "Heriberhto" was unfamiliar: the renegade's son had been called Thumelicus. Italicus saw my confusion. "Changed his name to 'Bright Warrior' when the old king died," he explained. "'Thumelicus' was not distinguished enough for him."

Flavus scowled at his son. "Heriberhto has kingly blood from both his grandfathers." He wiped grease off his face with the back of his hand. "I raised him to be what his father was not: a man whose nobility is . . . what is the word for hardening a sword?"

Italicus spat out gristle. "Tempering."

"Whose nobility is tempered by loyalty to Rome." Flavus turned more fully to fix his eye on me. "Useless to resist the might of Rome. Cherusci"—he swept his beef bone in an arc around the tables—"and Bastarnae and Marcomanni and Batavi and . . . and all the others here, they know it."

Something furry brushed my shins under the table. Italicus kicked it away. I drank more ale. Two men were throwing knives at a roast goose crammed like a greasy hat over a statue of Mercury. Where was Heriberhto? Was he with Aurima? What was happening out in the darkness?

Flavus tore into the meat again, chewed, swallowed. "She is a firebrand, true. But Heriberhto will tame her. As his wife, she will cause no uprisings." He passed wind noisily.

Away from the brightness of the bonfire, there were secluded spots among the greenery where a man might take a girl. Where a maiden who had lost her freedom might willingly give her last treasure to the Great Traitor's son.

By Mithras's Dog, I was not her father! If anyone should guard her virtue, it was her uncle Maelo, now shouting over his ale at the next table.

I cursed. Whether it was duty or obsession, I could not let her surrender her virginity. I pushed down on the shoulders of father and son to hoist myself off the crowded bench. Stepping back, I stumbled on another dog that had settled unnoticed behind me.

Laughter as raucous as ravens' honks rose over the clamor. "Strong ale, eh?" Flavus chortled. "I brew it myself."

Something made me look up just then, perhaps a nudge in the ribs from Fortuna. Aurima was striding into the courtyard.

CHAPTER 25

STORM

At first she was ignored in the hubbub. Flavus yelled drunkenly at a fellow who had slipped in a puddle and soaked his breeches. Some men farther away were bellowing out a song, pounding their knife hilts on the table.

Italicus was still sober enough to notice. "Why is the priestess here?"

She stalked toward us with long masculine strides that whipped her skirts around her ankles. A few of the men hailed her, but the anger in her bearing silenced them. When she halted, they gaped at her.

Not I. It was desire that darkened my thoughts, not fear.

She was so close that when she fisted her hands on her hips, I saw the gooseflesh on her bare arms. Her coppery hair bristled in the damp like frazzled rope, its thousand tiny ends lit with fireglow.

Flavus remembered he was her host. "Daughter of Ammisia," he said in a blurred voice. "What is wrong?" With an attempt at jocularity he added, "If you cannot deal with it, I am not sure what we men can do."

"'Men'?" Aurima's glare savaged them. "I see cattle. Cattle who let themselves be driven wherever Rome wishes." She jerked her chin at me. "He says come here, go there, do this, do that—and you obey!" Her voice dropped. "I, the sister's daughter's daughter of the great king Marbodo, call you cowards. I call you slaves, who sell the freedom of your children to Rome!"

Flavus spoke to her in Germanic. Aurima retorted, "It is you I insult, you gelded ox! And I speak Latin so those from the far lands will understand what I say." She glowered around at them, from Bastarnae of the upper Danube to Batavi from the Rhine mouth. "The gods weep to see you in such a place."

She seized the evergreen boughs spiraling around the nearest column. They cascaded down into her hair, onto her dark-green *stola*, and around her feet. Strewn with sprays of fir, firelight glittering on her contorted face, she stretched her hands to the swollen sky. "Hear me, Austro, She who brings life, and mighty Tiwaz, Father and giver of law! I have fought for my people's freedom. Am I not as brave as these around me? Or am I braver than they? For I would sooner die than deliver my brother's wife to be banished, or my sister's daughter to be sold!"

Though she spoke now in the harsh sibilance of her own language, I somehow understood. Dazzled, I could hardly breathe for the violence of my lust.

"Maelo," someone croaked.

Maelo said nothing. He would not stop her.

Her hands settled upon her head and began to rend her hair, tearing it from its plait until it seethed around her face in a chaotic mane. In a cracking voice she cried, "From this day, Tiwaz the Just, do I curse all those who have betrayed me." She took a deep breath to pronounce the oath.

"No," I shouted. I leaped up onto the bench and then upon the table. Drinking horns and cups reeled around my feet. "In Caesar's name, I forbid it."

There was a dumbfounded stillness.

I glared down at her. Her curse on my vexillation had cost me my scouts and nearly a hundred good soldiers. I would not allow her to damn these men who might be needed in the northern campaign. "I forbid it," I said again.

In a voice as low as thunder she said, "Then I put my curse on you, Marcus Carinna."

A worm of unease squirmed inside me, but I gazed back into her face. I was a soldier of Mithras, not to be cowed by a barbarian spell. I even smiled at her. Oh, I was to pay dearly for that smile.

Flavus at last found his wits. "I cannot believe . . . Will someone fetch Thusnelda? . . . Of course Aurima does not . . ." He got up, stumbled over someone's foot, and pitched against a table. Steadying himself, he spluttered, "Foolish girl . . . needs a firm hand . . . Thusnelda! . . . Italicus, fetch your aunt."

Italicus rose, shaking his head, and shambled out of the courtyard. Then the others got up with a grinding of benches and table legs and departed, group by group. Last to leave were Maelo and the Marcomanni, muttering in consternation. Aurima pursued them with her mad glare, until all were gone but Flavus.

I jumped down and straightened my disheveled clothing. My back was to her, but I saw Dio's fear as he looked past me. "Superstitious idiot," I growled. And as Thusnelda came in with her hair all undone, I went out of the courtyard too, leaving Aurima alone with Harman's widow and Harman's brother.

The rain came first in noisy splats against the colonnade outside, then settled into a loud drumming on the roof tiles. I turned over, hoping its steady mutter would help me fall asleep. It seemed I had lain awake for hours, yet every time I looked at the night lamp, its wick was no shorter than before.

My heart was pounding. Instead of calming as I tried to drowse, it seemed to grow fiercer, like a fever pulse. I ached, imagining I could feel Aurima's heat through the many walls between us. Was it the amber pendant that kindled this fire? I took it off, but felt no better. Within me, Priapus could not understand why I did not simply get out of my bed and go to hers.

The doors onto the terrace rattled and flew open in a gust of wind. Curled in a quilt on the floor, Dio did not stir. I envied his sound sleep so bitterly that I almost woke him to close them.

In the end I got up myself. I was standing in the doorway when a streak of lightning lit up the darkness. The pillars of the colonnade sprang out like black bars against a pale expanse of garden, and the wet paving of the terrace flashed like polished steel. I flinched at an ear-piercing crack of thunder.

Dio sat upright, round-eyed. "Stay here," I said over the roar of rushing rain, and stepped out into the colonnade.

The terrace was deserted now; no light peeped past the doors in the other wing. I padded on slippery tiles to the semicircular *exedra* at the colonnade's end.

The storm rampaged over the countryside. Cypresses whipped sideways like the spars of a heeling ship. Spray lashed through the air, bouncing off the pillars and floor of the *exedra*. A wind-swayed curtain of rain poured off the roof. A cushion tumbled end over end down the steps and disappeared into the pool.

I leaned into one of the columns, pressing my cheek and groin against its cold stucco curve. This was absurd. All I needed to cure my misery was a bed girl, which any Roman host would have offered out of courtesy. On the next market day I would go to the slave auction near the Temple of Castor—

A blaze of light cracked open the black sky. The fracture lengthened until it reached a grove in the distance, and with a deafening boom a tree exploded.

Again I saw Aurima tearing down the wreaths, cursing the docility of her countrymen, raging at them for trading away her life as they had Thusnelda's. Longing as sharp as a knife twisted inside me. She would marry some trousered clod, a man she met here if the omens spoke true. And I, if I survived nursemaiding Livilla, must wed some high-born little pickle. . . .

With a growl I unstuck myself from the pillar. My tunic was soaked down one side, but I was too tormented to care. Thalus would be trying to calm my horse, who feared thunder. I might as well spend the rest of the night in the stable.

As I turned back toward my room, a patch of darkness seemed to move across the doorway. I blamed the shock of looking at lightning; everyone knows mortals should not witness the gods' anger.

Thunder bellowed again when I went in. Dio still perched on his mat, owl-eyed. At the edge of my sight, a figure slid out from behind the open door.

No time for thought. I slammed him against the wall, grabbing his wrist. Mithras grant the man was not left-handed.

Dio cried a warning, and I froze. The man was not a man.

She held still in my grip, quivering with the force of her heartbeat like a snared rabbit. It was her dark-green *stola* I had spotted in the doorway. The tunic beneath had been girded up so its white hem did not show.

Thinking I understood, I pushed her away. "This is the wrong room, *cara*. I cannot say where Heriberhto sleeps, but it is not here."

Her eyes went past me to Dio. Some wordless message passed between them, and he shot out into the storm. She closed the doors behind him and swung the latch to lock them. "Do it," she said to me.

⚔ ⚔

She did not want tenderness. No kisses, no teasing, no gentle introduction to the mystery. She turned her head from mine, shoved away my exploring hands. When I knelt on the bed above her, she spread her knees like a harlot. "Do it," she said again. Her body was as cold as snow.

I was on fire. I broke into her like a man breaking down a door.

Words tore in her teeth, but the storm swallowed them. "Stop," she cried once. "Stop, it is done."

Too late for her. Too soon for me.

She tried to free herself, and I fell off the bed with her in a tangle of covers. A thunderbolt struck nearby with a crash that shook the villa. Obviously her gods meant to strike me dead as soon as they found the range.

The tumble to the floor had parted us, but the frenzy was fully on me now. I seized her and forced myself into her again.

All this time Priapus howled and fought for release. The battle only excited him more, for he is soulless in his own dark way.

At last I could restrain him no longer. Then the lightning found its mark, and blasted me from root to crown.

⚔ ⚔

She hardly breathed after I released her, lying on the floor amid the clothes and covers. The storm moved on, flailing toward Rome. The wrath of Thunraz had become a grumpy scolding, and I was not dead yet.

Aurima reached for her clothing with a sob of finality. I pushed myself up on my elbow and put a hand on her arm. Her skin was still icy. "I am sorry to have hurt you," I said. "Come back to bed, and I will please you better."

A sharp scent of fir clung to the light-gilded hair that trailed across her shoulders. She sat up. "It is done, what I came for."

Still I did not understand. "Stay," I coaxed. "Give me this night to love you as you should be loved." I tugged her down beside me, flinging a corner of the bedcover over us both.

Her hair cascaded onto my neck and shoulders as she struggled to pull away. "What more do you want?" she said. Her breath was harsh in her throat.

I guided her hand to my cheek. In silence I brushed her fingertips over my eyes, my eyebrows, my nose, my mouth, my jaw. Then I pushed the hair back from her face, skimmed the tear tracks from her cheeks, traced her lips with my forefinger. "We were made for each other," I said over the rustle of rain. "I knew it when I first saw you."

I tried to tip her mouth up to mine, but she refused. "Be my concubine," I pleaded recklessly. "You will be the mistress of my household; I will acknowledge your children."

She sat up again, fumbling among the garments tangled on the floor. "It is an honorable estate. I am a Senator's son, not a peasant."

Aurima's chin lifted in that familiar prideful jut. "I," she said, "am the daughter and granddaughter of chiefs and priestesses."

I reached for my rain-damp tunic. When I began to wipe the wetness from her thighs, she uttered a choked sound and tried to jerk free. Seizing her nearer leg by the ankle, I lifted it and ducked under it. As she tipped over onto her back, I came down on all fours over her.

"Well, my dear," I said to her wide glistening eyes, "I am descended from the triumvir Marcus Antonius, who gave up everything for a foreign woman."

Her fingernails sank into my shoulder. Her jaw clenched tight, and her back stiffened to iron.

Coldness trickled through me. I said, "Why did you come here?"

Aurima said, "Because Heriberhto would not take me."

A fist squeezed my chest, forcing out all the breath. I sat back on my heels. Mutely I watched her scramble to her feet, saw the pale blur of her tunic rise and spill down over her shoulders.

"Now you do not have a virgin to sell," she said, her voice trembling despite its venom. She pulled the dark *stola* over her head. "This is my curse upon you." Unbolting the doors, she disappeared into the night.

The rim of the cup rattled against Dio's teeth. The wine from the bedside jug must have been icy, but I did not think to send for hot water.

The jumbled bedclothes on the floor looked like snowy foothills. I picked up my tunic and stared at the smudge on it.

Maiden's blood. Her blood.

I wanted to put my head in my hands and groan aloud. Even if I swore it by everything holy, who would believe that a virgin hostage who hated Rome had willingly given herself to a Roman?

She had seen that the brave chiefs and warriors at Flavus's feast all bowed their heads to Rome. In Thusnelda, a hostage like herself, she saw the desolation left by rage burning in too small a space, like fire confined to a chamber of stone.

What irony: Heriberhto had unwittingly given her to me. "He turned her away." I meant to laugh, but it came out as a hoarse chuckle. "He would not risk a kingdom for her."

The heat of exertion had gone; I was cold now. "Bring me a tunic," I said. Dio set down the cup and went over to a chest by the wall.

I said, "For my soul's sake I held back my desire." The lamp flame was huge, blinding. "And now I have forsworn myself."

Dio's voice was unsteady: "Is she a witch?"

It was a while before I heard him. "The spell is broken," I said.

⋯

Thusnelda looked at Flavus. He rubbed his unshaven jaw. "If she will not come," I said, "then I will go to her. I must speak with her before I leave."

The mosaic floor glittered, still wet where slaves had mopped up the puddles. The impluvium reflected a rosy dawn, dappled with leaves blown in during the storm. My servants waited with our mounts in the villa's forecourt while I stood in the chilly atrium, cloaked and booted, being rude to my host.

Had it not been suicidal to set out across the flooded countryside on a rainy, ink-dark night, I would have tried to return to Rome at once to escape being gutted by Maelo or torn apart by a horde of Germans. Instead I had blundered to the stables and sat outside Spider's stall until daybreak with a sword across my knees. Ollius and Thalus had waited with me, knowing only that I had had a deadly dispute with another of Flavus's guests.

Now I saw in Flavus's sore-headed grumpiness and his sister-in-law's cold courtesy that they had no idea what had happened. For reasons I could not fathom, Aurima must have told no one. Not so far, at any rate.

"Bring her," Flavus grunted to Thusnelda. "Quickly. She has already caused enough trouble."

While we waited, he invited me into his reception room and sent a slave for hot drinks. He said something about Italicus and the northern campaign, but I paid little heed. Within days I might be packing for some dreary backwater, where I would molder in disgrace until it pleased Caligula Caesar to pardon me. If ever.

Flavus yawned, putting his fist against his mouth to keep out spirits. "You wish to talk to Aurima about her behavior last night, I suppose."

His single beady eye glanced inquiringly at me. I did not reply.

"She is willful, and speaks without thinking. Unmarried girls of her age are too full of excitement." He sipped a hot brew that reddened his lips. "Married to a sensible fellow— But here she is now."

I set down my untouched drink. Flanked by her sour-faced serving woman and gray Thusnelda, Aurima stood in the doorway.

With both hands she clasped a wolf fur around her shoulders. The dark-green *stola*, seamed with wrinkles, had been thrown over her long grimy-skirted tunic, and her feet were bare. Her coppery mane bristled behind her in a long tail bound by a crisscrossed ribbon. When I saw her face, I felt an instant's pang; for with her pallor and puffy eyes, she looked so much like the way I felt that I thought Flavus must surely notice the resemblance.

Aurima glanced from one of us to the other. Flavus said, "Our noble guest Carinna wishes to talk with you about your shameful outburst at the feast."

"In private," I said.

Thusnelda made an objection. Flavus snapped, "Stupid woman, she cursed him! Of course he may speak privately with her."

Aurima said stonily, "I have nothing to say."

Flavus scolded her in Germanic. She retorted in Latin, "I am here because of him, old man."

His face flushed as red as his berry-stained lips. He was about to snap back at her when I interrupted, "Enough! Leave us, all of you."

Thusnelda murmured to Aurima's maid to remain. I said, "I am expected back in Rome. And I will not be late just because you do not understand what 'private' means. Out!"

I closed the folding doors of the room behind them. Aurima stood where I had left her. Her gaze was withdrawn, her lips tightly compressed.

Fatigue parched my eyes. "What do you want?" I said.

She hugged the fur tighter and looked down at her toes. Color began to brighten her cheeks, but she did not speak.

"For your silence," I prompted impatiently. "What do you want?"

The blush ebbed out of her face, and freckles on her cheeks bloomed again like tiny sun-kisses. Under one ear I saw the faint blue smudge of a bruise, a thumb mark I had left in our rough lovemaking.

My heart twisted. I had been tested by the Dark Lord, and had failed. I was no holy warrior, no Parthian adept, but I would have kept my oath had she not tempted me.

Yet how could it have been otherwise? I had broken rules and done as I pleased all my life. Why should a year as a follower of the God of Truth have changed me?

Then I marked the minute swelling at the corners of her mouth, the thickening of her lower eyelids. She was gloating. She knew she had me at her mercy, and she was gloating.

Still she had not answered. I barked, "Well?"

"Caesar has never greeted me," she said. "I am a royal hostage trusted to him by Vannius, king of the ten tribes of the Marcomanni. He must give me respect and honor."

I pictured her ranting at Caligula that he had failed to protect her chastity. Added to the taint of Livilla's scandal, this news would antagonize his staunchest supporters. Word would sweep from Numidia to Thule that a Princeps who planned an ambitious military operation in the North had been cursed by a ravished northern priestess.

"Not 'in private,'" Aurima went on, echoing my phrase scornfully. "My mother's brother must be honored as the sister's son of Marbodo. There must be many gifts."

Maelo too? Even better. Perhaps the ceremony was meant to end with the disemboweling of Caligula Caesar in revenge for the death of her mother. "That is what you want? To be received by Caesar?"

"It is a part," she said. "A part of what I want."

It would not be difficult to arrange. I had been sure she would demand to name her own husband, or even to return to the Mark. "I will think about it."

"While you think," she said, "I will tell my mother's brother what you have done."

I had expected this threat. "You did not ask what I want."

The notches of smugness deepened at her mouth's corners. "I think you want not to have your belly slit."

"I want you to keep quiet about what happened."

She would have uttered an explosive laugh had I not put my hand over her mouth. Thusnelda and Flavus might be near.

I took my hand away. "Listen to me, Aurima. If you stay silent, I will arrange for Caesar to receive you." I leaned closer. "But if you speak to anyone, here is what will happen."

Her almost-sneer was gone. She stared defiantly into my face.

"First of all, Caesar will believe me, not you, because I am his kinsman. Next, the treaty for which you are hostage will be annulled. Do you understand? Troops will be sent to seize your father and bring him back to be put to death."

She opened her mouth. I overrode her. "As for you, you will not wed Harman's son and stir up trouble in the North. I will persuade Caesar to give you to a black man or a yellow one who will take you to the other side of the world."

This was a monstrous threat to a clannish German. Her face went white. "No. No. I tell my mother's brother to kill you."

"Then I will go to your mother's brother now and show him this"—I reached inside my tunic and drew out the golden drop of amber on its cord—"and tell him you came to me last night."

Aurima stared at the amber pendant. Only when I tucked it out of sight did she blink and look at me. I saw her trying to assess what I had said.

"Shall I do that? Or do you agree to keep silent about what happened?"

She looked back at the small lump the stone made inside my tunic. It seemed to be hard for her to breathe; her nostrils widened, and her lips parted. "You—" Her throat went dry, and she had to suck up saliva. "You snake."

"Does that mean you agree?"

"You crawling louse! You dung beetle!"

One might guess she had learned her Latin in an Army camp. I nodded. "So we understand each other."

I reached for the folding door, then turned back. She glared at me, the very hairs of the wolf fur vibrating with fury. I seized her by the waist and kissed her so hard our teeth clicked together. Then, crossing the atrium to the entry doors, I fixed my eyes on the trees that marked the road to Rome and did not look back.

ICARUS FALLEN

I had ample time on the return journey to envisage the wrecking of my life. No matter what I said, it would be assumed that I had assaulted a hostage entrusted to us by an allied king—a crime that meant unimaginable dishonor for our family. And I was the second of my father's sons to disgrace our name. Men less proud than Titus Carinna had committed suicide sooner than live with such shame.

Yet how could I rely on Aurima to stay silent? Having already dared rape and death, she might care little about my threats.

I told myself I should have silenced her before she could betray me. Strangled or smothered her, left Flavus's villa in the night, and dropped her body in a swollen river rushing to the sea.

We were just then crossing a bridge over a roiling stream that had burst its banks. I twitched my head away in a shudder and the horse shied, thinking I had seen something to fear.

Dio trotted alongside and asked to speak to me. He had been quiet so far, in contrast to Ollius and Thalus who were hooting to each other about barbarian behavior. I nodded tiredly. It was no use trying to swear him to silence. As he had reminded me, he was Father's property, not mine.

"I will vouch for you," he said quietly. "If you wish me to."

Was this a trick? I said, "He will not believe you either."

"She cursed you. You had no choice."

"It will not matter to him."

I was watching men wrestle a sheep out of a mudhole when he said, "I may have forgotten to include it in my notes."

I turned to stare at his sharp profile. "Why?"

"My reasons are not suitable for a slave to tell his master." Dio's gaze was fixed on the tuft of mane between his mule's ears. "But if you must explain to the master, of course I will make my account correspond with yours."

A moment later I said, "She may keep it to herself, to have a hold on me."

He nodded, or perhaps his head simply bobbed with his mount's gait.

"Otherwise I will be disgraced. And they will make her disappear."

"I understand."

So I resolved to say nothing to my father. It was a desperate gamble. As the first tombs of Rome came into sight, I recalled the whispered *Your turn, little brother* that might have been Publius's warning, and wondered if it meant I would become as infamous as he had.

When I entered the house, leaving the others attending to the animals, the doorkeeper boomed, "Welcome, Marcus. I hope the mistress is well?"

I had forgotten that everyone thought I had gone to Antium. Without answering I said, "How is Phormio?"

"Better, thank the gods and spirits."

The atrium was full of chests, boxes, and furniture. I kicked an empty birdcage out of my path. Not so empty; its inhabitant lay limp-feathered inside. "What in Hades is all this?"

The house steward appeared. "These are some of the Lady Julia Livilla's furnishings." Noticing the dead bird, he clicked his tongue in vexation. "Dolts! They should have covered the cage; it is too cold here in the atrium."

The matter with Aurima had driven all thought of Livilla out of my mind. No doubt that was why I had heard a Forum crowd roaring agreement with an angry speaker as I rode up the Clivus Victoriae. They were reviling Caligula's shameless whore of a sister, who would move here in two days.

The doorkeeper's boy brought the saddlebags into my room. When he was gone I drew from one of them a crumpled tunic, which fell open to show a stiff dark smear of blood.

I ought to burn it. If Aurima accused me, this was all the proof anyone would need. But I brought it to my face, though it held no scent of her. Was she resigned to what she had done? Or had she charged me with rape after all, rousing her countrymen to a fury that would soon break upon the Palace?

Hearing an approaching shuffle of feet, I stuffed the tunic back into the saddlebag and flung my bed quilt over it. The curtain rings jinked. In the doorway Phormio, gaunt and wan, clung to his walking stick.

"Are you trying to bring on another seizure?" I demanded.

"Must . . . walk," he gasped. "Costive . . . as a clam." He pressed his fist to his breastbone. "You are back . . . sooner than I . . . expected."

My breath hissed out between my teeth. Could the man not bear me to be gone for a day, but must confront me as soon as I came through the door?

He backed out through the curtain. I said, "Phormio, wait."

"Later," he puffed from the atrium. "I see you . . . are weary."

I exhaled and went after him. Phormio protested, but let himself be helped into my room. No wonder Hades had spat him back; he had become as dry and meatless as an old gamecock.

I lowered him onto my couch. "Any word of Rufus?"

He shook his head. "Your father is . . . meeting with the Tiberians." He paused to catch his breath. "The Senate Leader warns . . . riots about Livilla. . . ."

Gemellus's supporters could not know that even better ammunition might await: the scandal of Caligula's quaestor-designate violating a hostage. Gingerly contemplating this prospect, I did not at first notice Phormio's fingers probing the lump beside him. He pulled the coverlet back. "What is this?"

Alarm shot through me. "Nothing important."

He pulled one of the saddlebag flaps open and sniffed. "Your clothes need airing."

Before he could pluck a garment from the open pouch, I yanked the saddlebags out of his hands. "Leave my affairs alone!"

I hurled the bags at the wall. They hit with a leathery *whump* and fell onto the clothes chest. In the silence that followed, I heard the echo of my own anger.

Phormio sighed. "Knew . . . you would grow . . . too old for me," he mumbled. "Hoped for . . . more dignity in it." He struggled to rise.

"You were right. I am weary, and I need to bathe," I said, not looking at him. "We will talk later. Astyanax, come fetch him!" Phormio was like a cat at a rat hole; he would be after the saddlebags again if I was not careful. I waited until they had both gone before pulling out the bloodstained tunic. I buried it deep among other clothes in the chest, and went off to my bath.

A dry leaf floated in the hand basin, curled fore and aft like a tiny ship. Slumped against the wall with sweat trickling down my face, I watched it through the steam suffusing the tiny sudatorium.

I lifted the ladle out of the basin and splashed cool water onto myself. When I dropped the ladle back in, the little boat sank in a turbulent vortex.

I let out my breath slowly and tipped my head against the wall. The mosaic tiles were slippery with oil; the sheen of it glistened on my chest and legs.

I raised my arm to look at the red gouges below the point of my shoulder. She had marked me more vividly than I had her.

Sexual pleasure is no occasion for shame. But by yielding to my natural passions, I had violated the Mithraic precepts of duty and order. If I truly honored my god, I would flee like a beetle from the light of the sun.

A noise came out of my throat, midway between growl and groan, and I slammed the edge of my fist against the wall.

When Father came in with Cleon behind him, I was on my belly being scraped. At his signal, the bath slave put down the strigil and left.

I began to push myself up, but the big bodyguard set a calloused hand on my shoulder. "Rest easy, Marcus." He used the towel that had covered my buttocks to wipe grimy oil off the strigil's edge, and walked around the massage table. I tried to pretend it meant nothing to have a killer behind me wielding a sickle-shaped tool capable of scooping out a kidney.

Father leaned against the wall and crossed his arms. "I understand you went to a feast at Flavus's villa, not to your mother's."

It was a relief to detect no anger in his voice. "Much gorging, swilling, and belching," I said. "Thusnelda remembers you."

"Does she? Was her boy there too—Thumelicus?"

"Her 'boy' is my age, Father. He calls himself Heriberhto now."

"How has he turned out?"

"With proper respect for Rome. Which he hopes will win him a kingship."

"Interesting." He studied me thoughtfully.

Unease clutched my belly. Had Dio betrayed me after all? Was this a trap to see if I would volunteer what had happened with Aurima? I said, "I also met Italicus, Flavus's son. Another kingly candidate. Cleon, leave off toying with that strigil behind my back."

Father unfolded his arms. "It must have been quite a house party, to set you chattering like a magpie." He nodded at his bodyguard to come out from behind me. "Agrippinilla has arrived in Rome for her birthday celebration, the day after the Nones."

"The day Livilla will come here?"

"Yes. Speaking of Livilla, I expect you to make everything ready for her."

I had had enough of disobedient and scheming women. "Father, is there no way to avoid this?"

My father looked at me for a long moment. His nostrils were white with the effort to hold himself in check. At last he said, "Shall I emancipate you?"

This question astonished me as deeply as his threat to marry again. "Of course not," I said. If he emancipated me, I would cease to be a member of the family. And he would have no heir.

"Then do as you are told," he said. He went out, his sandals squeaking on the damp tiles.

Cleon slid the blunt-nosed strigil between my thighs and tugged. I gasped. "My, my," he muttered. "Something down there after all."

The Marcomanni had not yet returned to Rome by midafternoon, when I was admitted to a small audience chamber where the Princeps was hearing petitions. Waiting for a private interview, I prepared myself to acknowledge his charge to watch over Livilla, a tactful reminder that he was in my debt. Then, after telling him about the murder of Aurima's mother, I meant to encourage him to send the girl home as part of the reparations her family was owed. With the promise of freedom, I ought to be able to assure her continued silence. And the northern tribes would be impressed with Caligula's *clementia* and *justitia*, which would bode well for the coming campaign.

Time passed as I watched Caligula and his secretaries answer requests for tax relief from a flooded town, a post for a provincial magistrate's son, and a pension for a poor widow. The Princeps was snappish and at times barely listened. Told that a hamlet sought honors for a resident who had sired hordes of grandchildren and great-grandchildren, he snorted, "Honors! Surely the poor wretch would rather be sent to the Libyan desert for some peace."

He stood up abruptly. "No more for today. I am tired."

After he left, I spoke to the round-faced Alexandrian Greek who was his chamberlain. "Indeed, he has not slept well lately," said Helicon, with candor earned by a large bribe from my race winnings. "But you will be high on his appointment list at the next opportunity, your honor."

My state of mind was not greatly improved when I left the House of Augustus. The complement of Praetorian guards appeared to have doubled, so it was through a rank of white togas that I glimpsed chests and baskets being carried into the House of the Augusta across the courtyard.

Of course: Father had told me of Agrippinilla's return. Dio prodded me to send in greetings to her, since she was a cousin whom I had not seen for years. I argued with him out of bad temper before yielding to my own curiosity. How well was Caligula's oldest sister coping with the latest gloomy prophecy?

Somewhat to my surprise, the expectant mother agreed to see me. I found her stiffly posed on a window seat, her belly as round as a wasp's nest. As the slave who had brought me upstairs glided into the background, she said, "I was horrified to hear of the attack on you, Marcus Licinius. Thank the gods you escaped with only scabs and bruises."

She wore her blond hair in side waves that tucked behind her ears, a mannish style that had been out of favor for years. It was the same way her mother wore her hair in a cameo portrait I had often seen.

I acknowledged her courtesy with a nod. She, at least, could not have sent cutthroats against me. "You are as thoughtful as you are lovely, cousin."

"And I am more intelligent than I am gullible, so kindly dispense with the flattery." She shifted and laid a hand on her swollen womb. "Open the shutters, please. I am in need of fresh air."

Leaning past her, I lifted the latch and pushed the shutters wide. The action made me think of unlatching the doors of my room at Flavus's villa. Here, though, the view was not a tempest but a tidy peristyle guarded by a chestnut tree.

In the brighter light I saw that Agrippinilla's narrow face was heavily made up and that her fair hair had thinned. She looked more than ever like her own mother. "Has Ahenobarbus come with you?" I asked.

A brief smile showed the double tooth on one side that she had always insisted meant good luck. "He is not among Caesar's friends." That was an understatement; Tiberius had given her a husband who was a haughty, lying swine.

"May Fortuna smile on you and on the child to be born," I began.

"Oh, stop boring me. May we simply talk as one Roman to another?"

I had to smile. "You have always intimidated me, Agrippinilla."

Her grunt might have been a chuckle. "Sit here beside me."

I sat. There was obviously no need to ask if she was troubled by the prediction that she might die in childbirth. "So what do you have to say to me, as one Roman to another?"

"I want your promise to support my son if anything happens." Her sky-blue eyes met mine. "Gods willing, he will be the next Princeps."

"Agrippinilla—"

"Agrippina. I am no longer a girl who must be distinguished from her mother."

"Julia Agrippina, you know that in such a situation my first loyalty must be to Lepidus."

"I have considered naming Lepidus his guardian," she countered. "Ahenobarbus is not well enough to protect him."

Or perhaps her husband prized his own skin too much to risk it. In any case, guardianship of the child would bolster Lepidus's claim to Caligula's powers, and might be the only way for the boy to survive. If there was a boy.

I got to my feet. "You honor me in asking for my support. But I cannot give you an answer now."

"Has Livilla already persuaded you to champion Gemellus? Take care: that witch she calls 'Granny' can make your cock break out in burning sores."

"What makes you think your sister will have access to it?"

"Is she not moving to your house in two days? Surely I need say no more."

Agrippina smiled at the darkness she must have seen come into my face. "Caligula would never send her into exile, not after what Tiberius did to Mother." She picked a hair off her *stola* and flicked it away. "At least you need not fear any by-blows. Livilla has had too many abortions; by now she must be sterile."

I took my leave as civilly as I could. Her voice followed me down the stairs: "Let us talk again at my birthday dinner, Marcus Licinius."

A soft rain had begun to fall, and paving stones and gate grilles glistened in the light of Ollius's torch. I walked bareheaded, with him ahead and Dio trudging behind. Here was where Jason had stopped to look at his reflection in the puddle. *Could you not bring a slave who is more comely?* Under this tree, I had dragged a name from my new redheaded slaveboy. And not far away was the guest house that Aurima had left.

Perhaps her silence was already broken. She might have roused the many barbarian lords at Flavus's who would soon rampage into the city, burning and looting. Or perhaps Maelo would reckon that Rome had broken the truce and, after waiting his chance to eviscerate me, would take his people back to the Mark. After which, Ingiomar Ironhand—

"Marcus," Dio said. I had passed the turning for our house.

"I will see if the Marcomanni have returned," I said, and walked on.

The house on the Clivus Palatinus still stood dark and quiet. Gazing at it from the shelter of an arcade, for the first time I let my mind vault over the repercussions of what I had done to relive the doing of it. Stroking Aurima's small breasts and long thighs, pale and clammy as if she were a Nereid newly dragged from the sea. Plunging deeper and deeper inside her until I was set ablaze like a candle. And when I was done, and undone, the sharp scent of forests in the hair that trailed across my arm. Medusa's hair . . .

I remembered then that Medusa had been a maiden sacred to Athena. Only after her rape by Poseidon did the affronted goddess transform her into a snake-haired monster whose glare turned men to stone.

I was sworn to uphold truth and order. I must not look back at battles lost or won, only to those that lay ahead. Yet the mist and smoke of the wet evening leached my will to keep fighting.

"Dio," I said, hardly trusting my voice, "go home. Ollius and I will follow later."

⚬

I looked into the ruby depths of my cup. "I suppose Torquata no longer fancies me," I said. "Since I turned down your offer earlier."

"I would not say so." A faint smile hovered in his voice.

I glanced up.

Silius's smile broadened, warm and familiar. "She is here now," he said. He sighed again, happily. "I was wondering what to give her for Saturnalia." He laid his hand on mine, then drew it away as he sat back and picked up his cup.

⚬

Heat vapored from me in the cold night as I followed Leander from the house baths, mouth dry as sand. Torquata's maid, asleep on a mat in the anteroom, did not stir when I padded past.

Two lamps burned in the bedchamber. One was set by the display of armor, its reflection shining like a little sun in the breastplate's silvered landscape. The other, on the bedside table, showed me Silius rising from the couch where Torquata reclined. The rich lamp-glow turned their pale tunics into buttercream.

He crossed the room. To greet me, I thought—but he said nothing, nor did she. He went past me and pivoted the bust of Aristotle to face the wall.

His dark eyes, as long-lashed as a girl's, were black with desire. The small scar by the corner of his mouth, made by my ring in a forgotten brawl, vanished in the crease of his gambler's grin. I clasped his head in my hands and kissed him, his hair cool and silky between my fingers.

Oh, I did love him. Or perhaps I loved what he allowed me to be.

It was a long kiss and a hard one, with nearly four years of estrangement to redress. All the pain thawed in me, leaving only wildness and heat.

"What about me?" asked a plaintive voice from across the room.

I let out my breath in a gust of anticipation. But Silius's fingers were still on my back, holding us together. He pressed his cheek against mine. "Forgive me, best beloved."

I did not want apologies. I looked at Torquata, whose hand was curled between her golden thighs. She liked watching us together. Well, I had guessed she would.

Her smoky eyes narrowed as I came toward her, and her lips curved in a feline smile. "I am told," she said, "that you will do anything." She stretched out her bare leg and stroked the inside of my thigh with her toe.

"Try me," I said.

CHAPTER 27

THE SPARTAN BATHS

In the dream, Publius and I were cantering along the bluff above the Danube. With a grin I told him, "I knew you could not be dead."

He reined in his horse, looking down through the trees at the river. The foxy amusement in his face faded into somberness. Scores of little boats, from here no bigger than a fingernail paring, had set out from the far bank.

"The barbarians are coming," he said.

My horse reared. The jolt of its hooves thumping down became a hand rocking my shoulder. Apprehension from the dream flared into alarm.

I sat up. Dio said, "The master wishes to see you."

"At this hour?" I swung my feet onto the icy floor.

Perhaps it was not as early as I thought. The sky had begun to gray when I came home, vaguely aware of Ollius cursing as he stepped into unseen puddles.

As I washed my face, Dio said, "Will I accompany you to the Palace?"

My visit to the House of Augustus seemed long ago; I needed a moment to recall that I must tell Caligula about Aurima's mother. "Of course," I said, taking a towel from him. Having grown up in this house, he would have guessed where I had been last night, but his face was blandly submissive.

I passed slaves mopping around the atrium pool. It was still raining, or raining again, and lamps were already lit to dispel the gloom. My thoughts drifted to Silius's promise that we would resume this coming night; to Torquata's parting kiss, as deep and slippy as a lily's throat. I wanted to smile, but swallowed the impulse. The threat of Aurima's return to Rome still hung over me.

Father sat sharpening a quill with his penknife. I steeled myself. I had not demanded discretion of Ollius, who in any case could not have maintained it if Father questioned him.

But it seemed my night's adventures were not the issue. Without preamble he said, "You are invited to dine with the Caesars tomorrow. It is the private dinner I told you about, to celebrate Agrippina's birthday. You will accompany Julia Livilla."

I had guessed that would be the price of my invitation. "As you wish, Father."

"It is as Caesar wishes," he corrected sharply.

He moved the lamp on his desk to see me better, and I realized that his own face was drawn with fatigue, his eyes bloodshot. He went on, "Tomorrow morning he and Agrippina will sacrifice to Jupiter and Juno on the Capitoline, and will then progress through the Forum to the Palatine in company with the Senate and other officials."

"A public procession? Is that wise?"

"It is as Caesar wishes," he repeated. "Of course the way will be guarded by Praetorians. I want you to take part, but on horseback, wearing your armor. Not your toga."

Perhaps Caligula was bold enough after all to display himself to the people, reminding them of their love for him and his oldest sister's matronly modesty, but it seemed an unnecessary risk in a city teeming with discontent and conspiracy. He said, "Can I still count on you?"

"Why do you need to ask, Father?"

His reply was a stare, knowing and disillusioned.

I said defiantly, "We did not talk politics."

Father scrubbed a hand over his jaw. "Then I will tell you something you may not know. Caesar has informed his family that he will marry by year-end."

By Mithras's Dog! Had I inspired this with my casual remark in the wineshop? "Marry whom?"

"He has not yet decided. But it means that by next fall he could have a son of his own."

"So Gemellus is being backed into a corner."

"And that young man now counts among his supporters, besides his faction in the Senate and their *clientelae*, two Praetorian cohort commanders, at least three governors, and the assistant prefect of the naval base at Misenum."

He pushed himself out of his chair. "The next two days may see the first spark of a great fire. If you value our family's future, you will help me douse it."

Later that morning, the Senate convened in emergency session to discuss unrest in the city. The official announcement that Livilla would be held under house arrest until spring had not placated the Tiberians, or the morally outraged in Caligula's own party.

I learned of many worrisome signs. A praetor had declaimed in the Forum that the "Romulus and Remus" lampoon mocked the Princeps' lenience with his wayward family. There was nostalgic talk about the Republic, even though scarcely a man now living had known its alleged golden years. The most disturbing news came from one of the poorer city wards, where idlers were being recruited for an unknown purpose, with a bonus for former soldiers.

In the end, Father told me, the Senate Leader prevailed with his counsel to avoid inflammatory decisions. It was agreed to recommend that a new copper *as* honoring the Princeps' father, Germanicus, be struck with *Senatus consultum* stamped on the reverse, to remind people of Caligula's distinguished lineage and the legitimacy of his rule.

That typically meek resolution would be of no use in quelling public disorder. I resolved to inspect our household armory as soon as possible. If riots ignited, the Palatine was an inviting target. The unworthy thought crossed my mind that if Aurima was set on bringing her grievance to Caligula, he would hardly give her a hearing amid eruptions of violence.

The Marcomanni had still not returned by midday, which was good. But imperial audiences had been suspended until the danger lessened, which was not. I needed to see Caligula face to face; a written plea for reparations would only be passed from functionary to functionary.

While I was examining the rusty swords, dented shields, and dull-edged spears in our strong room, weapons no doubt last used during the civil wars, Silius sent me a message to meet him at the baths. There are scores of bathhouses in Rome, but to both of us this meant the Baths of Agrippa, which people call the Spartan Baths because men exercise naked, or nearly so, in the *palaestra*.

No one would be running or throwing javelins or playing handball today in the rain that still lashed down. After ducking into the main entrance hall, I moved out of the stream of comings and goings while the slave I had brought consigned our wet cloaks to the porter.

On sunny days, light burns through translucent stone panes of tall mullioned windows, bejeweling frescoes on the vaults of the sixty-foot ceiling. Shards of light, reflected from jets of perfumed water, dance on the walls of polished russet and yellow and black marble. Today, however, the great hall was gloomy and cold, and there were fewer visitors than one would have expected. Passing the polychrome columns that supported an overhead gallery, I heard bits of somber conversation: "At Carmentis' shrine, blood splashed on his tunic"; "fields flooded from Vitinia to Ostia."

I did not see Silius anywhere. Vexing, but not unusual. I was waiting by the shops under the gallery, our meeting place in years past, when a pretty *meretrix* turned up to ask if she might pleasure me. Roused from a satisfying daydream, I smiled and shook my head. "Find me later, chick, if my friend does not appear." I gave her bottom a pat.

Then a familiar face caught my eye: that of Nina's stepson, Varro Galerianus. Since he performed the daily sacrifices at her house in his father's absence, he might have news of her. I called out to him, but had taken only a few steps in his direction when the babble of voices near the entrance grew louder.

Cries of "Hail, Gemellus" and "Good luck to the son of Caesar" heralded the arrival of that pale young man, surrounded by friends, guards, and slaves. He lifted one hand in a languid wave, and a chorus of voices greeted him by name. Then a burst of more excited shouts erupted behind him, subsiding into a rhythmic bellow: "Mal-le-us, Mal-le-us, Mal-le-us."

The young champion sauntered in with his own hangers-on. People flooded around him. He made Gemellus an impudent obeisance, chin tipped down but eyes boldly raised. Gemellus saluted him with a lifted hand, as if the nervy little charioteer had not debauched Livilla.

Varro Galerianus had disappeared into the throng, as had the girl. I stayed where I was, watching the two princes' progress through the entrance hall. Despite his dislike of being touched, Gemellus submitted gamely to handclasps, embraces, and whispered exchanges.

He veered toward me. The loathsome amulet he had worn to counteract poison was nowhere in sight, although his perfume had a tinge of something medicinal. "Marcus, my friend," he said. "I am sorry about your bad luck with slaves."

I could not object to the taunt about Rufus's disappearance. "And I hope you are having better luck with glassware."

He stepped back from the formal embrace. "Have you met the fearless Malleus?" he said, with a flourish of his hand.

It was too late to slide into the crowd. I faced the driver, who gave me a meaningless broken-toothed grin. Then his eyes slitted. "I know you."

I smiled easily, ready to deny that I had directed him to Livilla's litter.

"You're the bastard who killed my Fulgor."

"To protect Caesar," Gemellus reminded him. "An odd mishap, eh, Carinna? For a horse to mistake a man for a mare." Some reckless souls in the crowd obliged him with lewd laughter.

Malleus squared himself, the breadth of his shoulders emphasized by a tightly cinched belt. "I'd find a different sport to follow, if I was you," he growled. "Racing can be hard on the health."

I said, "Yes, that is why there are no old charioteers." Turning away, I told Gemellus, "I hear we may dine together tomorrow."

His pale eyebrows lifted. "At the banquet for Agrippinilla? Livilla will be amused to hear it." He turned toward someone else's greeting, and the entire party drifted down the hall toward the baths. Still there was no sign of Silius.

It struck me then that I, once second in command of a legion, was waiting at the pleasure of an ambitious man because he reminded me of my youthful folly; and that for his sake I was neglecting my duties to my father, to Caligula Caesar, and to the Marcomanni truce for which loyal soldiers had died.

I sprang away from the column I was leaning on and told the startled slave to fetch my cloak and my bodyguard. I was standing on the entrance steps in the lightening drizzle, looking for my own conveyance in the thicket of litters, sedan chairs, and slaves in the forecourt, when Ollius's gruff voice rang out behind me: "Hold on, girl."

The pretty harlot was scampering down the steps, skirts flying and bracelets jingling. "Cupid's prong, I almost missed you." She pulled up her thin mantle to keep her curls dry. "A gentleman wants to see you, sir."

Reckoning it was Silius at last, I followed her back inside to one of the curtained alcoves used for private encounters. *I cannot stay, Silius; pleasure will have to wait.* Not stern enough. *I must, for my family's honor . . .* O gods, give up both Torquata and the friend who knew me better than any other?

It surprised me not to recognize the bearded slave who stood outside the alcove. He gave a coin to the girl and told her to go.

"One moment," I said as he drew the curtain aside. My narrow escape the other night had given me new respect for hidden traps. "Who wants to see me?"

"No one who wishes you harm, young Carinna," called a voice I knew. Telling Ollius to wait outside, I ducked beneath the drapery and found myself face to face with Nina's stepson, Quintus Visellius Varro Galerianus.

Slightly built, high of brow with receding hair, he looked exactly like what he was: a state official charged with overseeing accounts of the public treasury. "Please join me in a cup of wine," he said, gesturing to a table set between two angled couches. "I was sorry to hear of your slave's death the other night. But you seem to have survived with little harm, thank the gods."

The gods were certainly reaping praise today, earned or not. "I was fortunate," I said as he poured the wine. I chose one of the cups and sat down.

Varro Galerianus took the other couch. "To your health," he said.

"And yours."

I pretended to sip and set down my cup. "Look, my dear nephew, why the mystery? Is it about my sister?" I did not think so, for he had made sure we were alone with no slaves to overhear.

"Not really, uncle," said my step-nephew, who was a decade older than I. "Although she does seem bored and bad-tempered of late. Do you think a dwarf or a hunchbacked boy would amuse her?"

My scant patience ran out. "Why am I here, Galerianus?"

His air of chattiness dropped away at once, and he fixed his dry, intelligent gaze on me. "It is time for influential men to take sides."

I managed a small laugh. "You are blunt enough."

"The Princeps is not well. Look how he has winked at Livilla's infamous behavior! Even his supporters fear his mind is unbalanced."

"Rot," I said robustly.

He leaned closer. "What did happen in that horse stall, Carinna?"

"An accident. The horse panicked."

"Fortunately, you were not afraid to act before it could do more harm."

I did not speak. What was there to say?

Galerianus drew back with a deep inhalation. "You are a man who chafes under his father's thumb, true? How long will it take you to achieve the authority and influence you want? Fifteen years? Twenty, thirty?" He paused, studying my face. "Yet it could be yours in a day."

"How so?" I asked warily.

"Caesar trusts you."

My fingers curled on my thigh. I understood what he meant, but did not want to believe it.

Galerianus went on, "Tell me what you want. Is there a woman your father will not allow you to marry? Would you be Roads Commissioner, or Prefect of the Grain Supply? Very lucrative positions, both of them. Or if it is a matter of pleasure, there is a charming villa in Baiae, with a view of Vesuvius and a sandy cove for bathing. I have been there myself."

Once, in Caieta, I had been in an earthquake. I felt the same now: stunned, fearful, groping for sense in a violently deranged world. This was Varro Galerianus, after all, the heir of my sister's husband.

"Come," he urged, "you have been in battle. You are not afraid to use that ferocious *pugio* sheathed at your back."

He could not see my longknife. Nor did Gemellus know about it, for I had not worn it on the day I visited him.

But Silius had seen it.

The drone of voices from the great hall seeped past the curtain. A guffaw, coughing, the chime of strigils and an oil flask on a slave's belt. "Are you suggesting I use it on a man who trusts me?" I hardly recognized my own rasp.

"Are you afraid?"

"I have no desire to commit suicide."

"We will arrange for the guards' commander to be a sympathizer. You will be in no danger."

"How soon?"

"The time is not set. Between now and the new year."

He sat back and sipped from his cup as though we were discussing some minor matter of my sister's household. "Your father's life will be spared; I have seen to that. He will be free to leave Italy for any place of his choosing, except

Egypt. This will avert dishonor for your family—and mine, too. My father is fond of your sister, and I would not want him to have to divorce her."

I was not too stupefied to realize that this was nonsense. A man who murdered the Princeps would be executed as publicly as possible, and his family would be ostracized. I cleared my throat. "I have sworn an oath to protect and obey Caligula Caesar."

There was another silence between us.

"I much prefer this weather to the snow we had," Galerianus said, looking up at a fresco on the ceiling. "Walking in the gardens must have been unpleasant."

I was reminded that the one time I had played him at Twelve Lines, he had soundly beaten me. "Silius knows where my loyalty lies."

"It lies now with him, if I am not mistaken."

He meant what had happened the previous night. He could not mean anything else. Which implied that Silius knew what I was being asked to do . . . because he, with his spurious invitation to the baths, had arranged it.

A great anger ignited deep within me. I fixed my eyes on my cup, willing myself to end this with dignity.

"But if you cannot bring yourself to act—" he began.

I broke in. "Galerianus, do you expect me to keep quiet about this because we are related?"

His thin scholarly face puckered as if he had eaten a sour grape. After a moment he said, "I think you will keep quiet because I am your sister's guardian, and you do not want her to miscarry again."

I doubted my ears at first. Then I threw myself on him, upsetting table and cups between us. Galerianus let out a yell. I shoved him down on the couch and dug my thumbs into his throat. He clutched my wrists, choking noisily, his feet flailing against the cushions. His face turned the hue of a ripe pomegranate.

I bent down until my nose nearly touched his. "Cause her harm, and you are a dead man."

His tear-flooded eyes bulged in terror. "Do you believe me?" I hissed.

He nodded frantically. I let him go and slid back onto my feet.

The noise had brought our slaves and Ollius rushing in. They stared at Galerianus, gasping and wheezing with his hand to his throat. None of them knew what to do. Senators' sons do not usually come to blows with praetors.

My head throbbed with the fury that had rushed through me. To let my breathing calm, I took my time straightening the garments he had disarranged.

"You . . . will regret . . . this," Galerianus croaked.

"Not as much as you will," I said.

I looked hard at my sister's stepson. But judging by the fury in his blood-shot glare, we had no more to say to each other.

Father listened gravely to the account. "Why did they think you would murder Caesar?" he asked. His fingers, reaching for the little bronze horse, seemed to move as slowly as in a dream.

I could no longer claim to have done only what Caligula had requested. "For the same reason you asked, Father, if you could still count on me."

He made a noise in his throat like a purr. "Year-end," he mused, fingering the scroll-weight. "Saxa has already instructed the Praetorians to confiscate all weapons in Caesar's presence."

"A weapon is unnecessary. You can crush a man's windpipe with your forearm, or crack his head open on a marble step."

He sighed. "I will let Saxa know. If only it were not Galerianus." Family is family, no matter what.

"Tell Saxa it was a man I did not recognize," I said. "I will take care of Galerianus."

At dawn word came that there had been another attack on a public official. The victim this time was my nephew-in-law, the Treasury quaestor. "What happened?" I exclaimed, squinting in the smoky daylight.

"He was beaten on the way home from dinner last night," Turtle said, pouring *mulsum*. "His bodyguards were overcome, and his bearers ran away."

Phormio uttered an exclamation. I said, "He is not dead, I hope?"

"It seems not." Turtle handed me the cup.

"What I heard—" Turtle's grandson began.

The old slave interrupted, "Astyanax, you must not spread tales about the Lady Nina's stepson."

I drank thirstily and cleared my throat. "Let me hear it. Speak up, boy."

"I heard they didn't just beat him," Astyanax said importantly. "They bent him over the seat in a *forica* and raped him."

I raised my brows. "Gods save us!"

Turtle smacked the child's bottom. "You are too young to speak of such things. Be off and make yourself useful in the kitchen."

"Does Galerianus know who they were?" I asked.

He shook his head. "As soon as they dragged him from his litter, they threw something over him."

"A manure basket," Astyanax cried from the doorway, and ran off chortling.

"Terrible," Phormio muttered. "The news will be . . . all over the city."

"How unfortunate for Galerianus," I said. "But perhaps it will cool his ardor for Gemellus's cause."

No one spoke for a moment. Then Turtle's eyes glinted in his wrinkled face. "I did wonder why Cleon and Astivus were hard to rouse this morning. And why Ollius and Iacer are still asleep."

"I gave them leave to do a little roistering last night," I explained. "Since they have been under such a strain lately, guarding Father and me."

Dio pushed into the room. "The Lady Julia Livilla is on her way here, Marcus. Your father wishes you to attend her when she arrives."

"Well, to work," I said, clapping Turtle on his bowed back. "Is my armor ready, Phormio? Today Rome will gawk at the Princeps and his brave and gravid sister Agrippina." To myself I added, *Let Silius beware, for we are enemies now.*

CHAPTER 28

RAINBOW

The newly arrived litter, bearers, and servants crowded the atrium. As the litter curtains stirred, I said, "Good morning, Livilla."

Heavily wrapped and veiled, she descended stiffly. When she raised the veil, I saw that her eyes were watery and her nose was red. "I have caught the perishing grippe," she mumbled.

"I am sorry to hear it," I said. "Shall I ask Lepidus's physician to attend you? He has not killed many people lately."

"I do not want your help. Leave me alone."

Father welcomed her formally to our house, and I took her to my mother's rooms at the back of the peristyle. Without a glance at the stylish old furnishings, she said, "Send me my singer, the Chian boy. And my lyre player. I will rest."

"You were to bring only female slaves with you," I said. "The others have been sent back to the Palace."

Her dark blue eyes blinked dully at me. In silence she went into the suite of rooms where her women waited for her.

A pity her illness could not last until the start of the sailing season. But at least it would make her a quiet partner at the Caesars' family dinner later today.

I told Phormio to see that she was made comfortable, and reminded him that no male slave was to be alone with her. He nodded somberly. Perhaps he was not an ideal Cerberus, having only one head and a maimed heart; but knowing of her adventure with the charioteer, he did not lack for vigilance.

A voice droned in Livilla's room: "Handsome Glaucus stepped from his chariot to greet the queen. . . ." The reader stopped when I pushed on the door.

Livilla lay under a mound of covers. She opened her eyes when I sat on the edge of the bed, facing her with a knee crooked before me. Her dark curls were damp and tangled; her cheeks were flushed, and she smelled of wine. Drink is one way to get through a bout of the grippe.

"'Handsome Glaucus': that is something to dream of," I said. "I dreamed that my brother had hidden from Tiberius all these years, and was not really dead."

"What do you want?" Her voice was as harsh as a heron's.

"Tell me about that *hoplomachus* of yours, Lunula."

"Is he the one who drowned in the river? They all drink too much. Stupid oaf probably fell off a bridge."

"After tying a stone to his feet?"

Her women's faces turned toward me, as pale as mushrooms in the gloaming. Livilla had already made the room her own. All trace of my mother's lily perfume was gone, banished by the strange and potent scent of roses. Roses bearing thorns.

"Did you set him and his partner on me?" I demanded.

"You have lost your mind. Go away." She yanked the quilt over her head.

I snatched it down again. "They murdered my home-born slave. And they might have killed me. How did I wrong you, to merit that?"

"I have no idea what you mean. Let me alone. I am ill." She turned away.

I pulled her back. "Livilla, I believe those men were waiting for me."

"I do not give a fig for what you believe." She turned over again.

"Did you have them killed when they returned from attacking Jason?"

"I did," she said into the bedclothes.

"You did?"

"I took one swipe with my sword and lopped off their heads. Are you satisfied?"

I took a different approach. "Yesterday, a friend of Gemellus's tried to bribe m— someone I know to harm your brother. What is going on?"

She rolled over toward me. Her face was more haggard than before. "Marcus dear, Gemellus's only concern is avoiding the grippe. If you know a better potion than the one he is taking, he will crouch on all fours and frisk like a puppy for you."

I stood up, admitting defeat. "Go to sleep, then. You will not wish to doze off at the banquet this afternoon."

"The banquet? You are joking."

"You mean you will not celebrate your sister's birthday?"

Her eyes glistened spitefully at me. "I am too ill to attend. Since you are my escort, neither will you."

"That is a pity," Father murmured when I told him. "But at least you mended bridges the other day with Julia Agrippina. That may be more important."

I did not care whether Agrippina was happy with my possible support for a possible boy who might not survive and might not become Lepidus's ward. What mattered more was catching Caligula in a benevolent mood so that I could ask reparations for the Marcomanni. "Pardon me," I said brusquely. "I need to get ready for the parade."

"Ah! I forgot to tell you, Caesar and Agrippina will sacrifice at the Temple of Palatine Apollo. The procession from the Capitoline has been canceled."

"Canceled? Is the people's mood so dangerous, then?"

Father turned the scroll-weight over in his fingers. "Yesterday, after Caesar dedicated a ewe to Carmentis for Agrippina's safety, he found blood on his toga."

"You should counsel him not to believe in omens, Father. How is a bloodstain different from an astrologer's prediction?"

He set down the scroll-weight with a click. "Also, the Forum has a foul odor because the sewer is rising. So I advised against the procession. However, you should be at Apollo's temple at noon in case you are needed. Is that clear?"

To me, it seemed perfectly clear that after his indulgence toward Livilla, Caligula lacked the courage to face the Roman people. I grunted ill-humoredly and left to put on my armor.

Water raced down the street to the drains, carrying away straw and leaves, pine sprills and twigs, furling around mounds of manure like a miniature Tiber flinging itself around its island. The rain had stopped, but everything was bedraggled: the last leaves drooped on plane trees, eaves dribbled, and sodden clothing sagged and clung like plaster.

I felt my helmet's rain-soaked crest wobble heavily as Boss, my sorrel war-horse, pushed through a noisy throng that clogged the wet street. He was aptly named for the shield boss that legionaries use to force back the enemy, and the excitement around us heightened his restless energy. It took all my strength to keep him in hand.

Praetorians waved me into the forecourt of the Temple of Palatine Apollo, filled to the garlanded pillars of its surrounding portico with a seething mob. Beneath Apollo driving his chariot across the temple's brightly colored pediment, the *pronaos* was bare. No officials. No Caesars.

Toga-clad Senators milled under a sagging canopy in front of the temple steps. A line of Praetorian guards, also in togas and not visibly armed, shielded them from the crowd. They were First Cohort men, taller and brawnier than average, which told me someone must be expecting trouble.

Above the mob's babble, a man bellowed, "Bring out the whore!"

"The whore!" others shouted. "Exile the whore!"

An egg splatted on the temple steps. A frost-blackened cabbage hit a Praetorian in the chest. A clot of dung flew between the guards and struck a Senator's shoulder. Rotten apples smashed into guards, onto the steps, against the high podium to one side of the steps. The Senators huddled together, drawing their togas over their heads.

With Livilla's heedlessness still fresh in my mind, I was content to watch from Boss's back while the mob vented its anger against her. Spoiled fruit harmed no one.

"Exile her!" a woman screamed. Someone roared, "Bury her alive," the punishment for an unchaste Vestal, and others in the crowd took it up: "Bury her! Death to the whore!" Rocks began to fly toward the Senators.

That was a different matter. A centurion's whistle squalled above the yammer. Armed soldiers began issuing from the Greek and Latin libraries, which flank the temple on either side. By then Boss had shoved through the mob to the most belligerent group of men.

I shouldered the stallion in among them, relying on his size to intimidate them. I did not want to draw my sword against Roman citizens. "Break it up!"

Boss was as tall at the withers as some men, with hooves the size of cobblestones. Most of the troublemakers dropped their missiles and retreated, but one of them had already hauled his arm back. The rock he hurled toward the temple hit a companion's shoulder, rebounded, and struck the horse on the nose.

Boss flung up his head. Had I not ducked, he would have knocked me out of the saddle. As it was, I lost one of the reins in a hasty grab at a saddle horn. It made no difference to a horse trained for close-order combat. He rose on his hind legs, flung himself forward, and flattened the three nearest rabblerousers before I could bring him under control.

People screamed and shrank back around us. He savaged another man's forearm. "Stand," I shouted, the command to desist.

A detachment of armored Praetorians forced their way through the mob, thrusting people aside with their shields. The officer called for me to back my horse away so they could attend to the rogues.

I aimed the stallion toward the clear space in front of the guards in togas. Beneath his red-gold coat, his neck muscles shivered with excitement. "Enjoyed yourself, did you?" I muttered. His ears swiveled toward me, and the bit jingled as he bobbed his head.

The armed soldiers filed behind their toga-clad comrades, where they were hardly visible. This was to correspond with the quaint belief, dating back to the Divine Augustus's day, that a Princeps needs no protection from the Roman people. Guards wearing the togas of citizens are a subterfuge that everyone winks at. A display of armored guards with swords and shields, on the other hand, would clearly give the lie to Augustus's notion.

I halted Boss by the end of the line of togas, facing out at the crowd as they did. Again we waited.

And waited. People began to grumble and stir. Children wailed. The clouds darkened, threatening more rain.

A voice behind me said, "Quaestor? Quaestor Carinna?"

It was Caligula's goat-bearded freedman, Kallistos, with an underling. They stopped a healthy distance away, evidently uneasy about my vicious warhorse. Patting Boss on the neck, I told them it was safe to approach.

"Zeus, you are a sight to frighten any barbarian," Kallistos observed.

It was extraordinary familiarity for a former slave to use with a patrician. "Have you a message for me?" I asked coldly.

His charcoal eyes shifted past me to scan the restless throng. "Caesar wishes your opinion."

"On . . ?" I prompted, when he paused.

"On . . . whether it is too risky for him to appear."

If Caligula was nervous, why would he invite my view and not that of the commander of his guards? Or was it Agrippina who sought my opinion, in order to induce her fearful brother to show himself?

"I think," I said deliberately, "that Caesar's people need to see him. To be reminded that he is *praelectus*, the chosen one." Let him find his backbone, or grow one.

Kallistos inclined his head, not quite a bow. He and his companion turned.

"And say that I regret I cannot join him for dinner," I added impulsively. "His sister Livilla is unwell."

Kallistos' subordinate frowned anxiously at him. "It will be bad luck to have only seven for dinner." Flouting the tradition of "nine to dine" is unwise on important occasions.

"We must see if Rubellius Blandus can join his wife."

"And Tiberius Claudius might bring Aelia Paetina."

Kallistos grimaced and shook his head. He glanced up at me again. "You may still be welcome at dinner, Quaestor. Despite the Lady Livilla's absence."

I was skeptical. "Why would that be?"

"Let us see how your advice is received," he answered, and the two of them melted away toward a side entrance into the temple.

When trumpeters on the temple podium sounded a fanfare, the crowd lunged forward. Boss pricked his ears and pawed the ground, reckoning the blare meant a parade. Both rows of Praetorians came to attention.

Moments later Caligula and Agrippina appeared, arm in arm, between the columns of the *pronaos*. I saw the little jerk with which Agrippina tugged her taller brother forward. They stood together, fair-haired children of Germanicus, facing the throng above steps littered with smashed fruit, ordure, and stones.

At that very moment the sun broke through and smote them with molten gold. The cries of the crowd swelled into a shriek of delight at this sign of the gods' favor. Their impatience, their disgruntlement, their anger at Caligula's pampering of Livilla might never have existed. He was still their darling, a hero's son. They will forgive him anything, I thought in amazement.

Caligula's frozen grimace widened into a grin of elation. Beaming, he offered himself to their cheers with both arms flung wide. Agrippina smiled serenely at his side. Beneath the snug wrapping of her *palla*, her free arm cradled her gravid belly. Who could be blamed for imagining that her fertility meant good fortune for Rome?

The turmoil increased. The Praetorians linked arms to hold back the mob. Despite the frantic efforts of attendants, sedan chairs overturned and canopied litters crumpled as people climbed atop them for a better view of the Princeps and his sister. Others clambered into the plane trees, boughs sagging beneath them.

As I rode back and forth, helping to hold off the throng with my big horse, there was a sudden upturning of faces. Arms shot upward, fingers pointing, as a rainbow began to shimmer against the purple clouds. The crowd yelled with joy at this new manifestation of divine grace. Not until brother and sister had retreated into Apollo's temple did I recall that in Homeric legend, an appearance of the rainbow goddess Iris does not signal the end of a storm. It presages one.

On our return, Father and I found the household in disarray. Livilla's servants were demanding exotic fruits and basins of mountain snow for her. The house steward had delayed obeying these unusual orders, and the cook was so unnerved by tales of her sinister "granny" that he had drunk himself into a stupor. While I was trying to restore order, a message arrived from Kallistos confirming that I was still expected for dinner. On top of Caligula's triumph at the temple, this news further improved Father's mood. He told me to make my preparations for the banquet; he would put all to rights in the house.

Turtle shaved me. Rufus had surely been captured by the Tiberians, he confided. After drinking his blood, they had used his body parts to conjure spells against Caesar.

"I doubt the little worm has met so useful an end." I wiped my face. "I told you I wanted the blue *chiton*, not the rose one. And hurry; I do not wish to arrive late at the House of Augustus."

"Dio will send word," the old slave grumbled. "I do not believe your mother ever complained that he caused her to leave home for a banquet too late.

Or too early." He wrapped a rag around the razor. "Besides, you are dining at the House of Tiberius, not the House of Augustus."

At Gemellus's house? Should I bring Father's food taster? But I had once already showed my lack of trust in Caligula; to do so again would be unforgivable. Besides, the Caesars surely had tasters of their own.

A boy held up a salver of mint leaves. The sharp taste took my thoughts to Phormio, who often demanded to inspect my breath, teeth, ears, and fingers before an important engagement. He dozed in my bedroom now, exhausted from guarding Livilla.

The poor man's wits had begun to wander. Earlier in the day he had asked how I was hurt in Bovillae. I reminded him that Jason's murder had taken place here in Rome, and reassured him that I was unharmed. This troubling sign of debility made me wonder if he would see out the year.

And where would I be? Disgraced and in exile, if Aurima betrayed what had happened. I would gladly let her remain in Bovillae until the end of the world, as long as she kept quiet.

"Are you no longer in haste, Marcus?" Turtle poked the jewel casket under my nose.

I rubbed the drop of amber on its cord. He frowned. "You do not mean to wear that, do you?"

"Mind your tongue, old man! I will wear what I please."

His wrinkled face cleared. "Pardon me. I forgot that amber turns color in the presence of treachery." He handed the casket back to the *exornator.* "Or does it draw poison from food?"

"It clouds the mind with thoughts of its giver," said my father from the doorway.

Did he guess that the amber was Aurima's? But there was no irony in his eyes when he held out a golden ellipse that glinted in the lamplight. "Wear this instead." He laid his torc into my hands.

I was awkward in my thanks. He seemed indisposed to linger, but on the threshold he paused. I looked up, still holding the renowned gift of Germanicus.

"Take care at the Palace, my son," he said.

CHAPTER 29

PROMULSIS

"Gemellus, you are a greedy little shoat," said Agrippina. "Why should you be my brother's heir? You have never held an elected office; the people do not know if you can even keep the streets clean." She stooped, awkwardly because of her bulk, to adjust her jeweled tiara by her reflection in the polished buttock of a silver Venus.

Gemellus halted amid the extraordinary clutter of his large reception room. "If Drusilla inherits, she will give everything to Lepidus. Your little infant will be tossed onto the midden with me."

"Not exactly, my dear. When you are too old to rule an empire, he will be in his prime."

"If he lives that long."

Agrippina cocked her head. Her tiered eardrops snicked like a drawn knife. "What do you mean by that?"

"Smile, Aunt 'Pinilla; suspicion gives you wrinkles." Gemellus rattled aside some dry papyrus fronds to see Julia and her husband, who had risen from a couch. "Welcome, sister! How elegant you look. And Blandus, I am glad you will dine with us after all." I, too, was glad the former governor of Africa was there. He seemed a man of sense.

Gemellus's good cheer vanished when I appeared from behind a large urn. "Carinna? But I thought Livilla was ill." He looked around for her.

"Forgive me, Gemellus dear. I forgot to tell you that Caligula wished him to join us nonetheless," Agrippina said with her panther smile.

"Oh? Well, that is fine." His own smile unfurled. "Welcome, Marcus Licinius."

"The pleasure is mine," I said, fancying I saw a malicious gleam in his twilight-colored eyes.

Lepidus arrived, his wife's hand tucked under his arm. Drusilla freed herself to give Gemellus an affectionate embrace. "Caligula comes directly; he was meeting with the augurs about a wedding date."

Gemellus wiped the cheek she had kissed with an edge of his mantle. "How can they fix an auspicious date if they do not know who the woman is?" With an edge of irritation he added, "He is only catering to the mob."

I put down a stuffed baby crocodile with emerald eyes. "Do you find fault with that, after leading the parade at the Circus?"

"And seducing my little sister." Agrippina flicked a contemptuous glance toward the atrium. "Who could not be bothered to master her sneezes for a few hours, to honor me."

"I am not the one who would steal her from her husband," Gemellus muttered, narrowing his eyes at me.

"For shame," Lepidus broke in. "Young Carinna deeply respects the sanctity of the marriage bed. As you do, I am sure."

This preposterous untruth silenced everyone for a moment. Then Agrippina said, "Drusilla, how I envy you a husband with a sense of humor." Her bracelets flashed as she beckoned to the other women. "Come, sister, Julia: let us wait for Caligula and Uncle Claudius in the dining room."

"Patience," Gemellus said. "We must enter together."

"Why?" Lepidus asked, an instant before I would have.

He smiled broadly. "It is a surprise for Cousin Agrippina's birthday."

The twisted cables of the torc seemed to tighten around my throat. Was our surprise to be slaughtered as we walked in?

"Drusilla," Caligula rasped from outside. "Drusilla, my barge is ruined." He swept in, trailing a mantle of Tyrian purple that caught on the elk-antler legs of a small table. His uncle Claudius, limping in behind him, collided with a slave hastening to untangle it. "The supports washed out, and the keel fell over. They say it has twisted like a wood shaving."

"Washed out?" Lepidus echoed. "The shipyard is flooded?"

"The Tuh-Tuh-Tiber rose four feet today," Claudius said. "Near Ostia, duh-docks are underwater."

"I fear the drains will back up tomorrow," Blandus said.

"Disgraceful." Gemellus snorted. "For the greatest city in the world to flood like some lowland hamlet."

Caligula's eyes brightened. "Gods send me a vast flood. A flood to make everyone forget all others."

"Brother dear—" Agrippina began.

"The year I was born, Father Tiber raged through the city," he told Gemellus. "It was a calamity, men and buildings swept away. Not so, Lepidus?"

Lepidus nodded. "The Cloaca Maxima was inundated, the drains backed up, and the lower city flooded. I remember taking a boat to the Capitoline with my father to sacrifice to almighty Jupiter."

Caligula bent over a hollow elephant's foot that held a faded banner and a Germanic battle knife. He pulled out the seax, whose cutting edge was stained dark with rust. "It was unfair. Augustus already had Varus's disaster to mark his reign." He sliced the blade back and forth through the air.

"Stop, Caligula, you are frightening us," Agrippina said. "Is no one else hungry? Gemellus, now that we are all here, will you escort me to your surprise? I am a bit unsteady, you know." She slipped her arm through his. A clever woman—and brave. Since she was the guest of honor, he would have to lead the way. If there was a trap, he would meet it first.

Caligula shoved the seax back into its grotesque receptacle. "Gemellus, you should have seen the mob cheering me today! It was extraordinary, was it not, 'Pinilla?" His eye was caught by a model ship made of seashells. He picked it up. Murmuring wistfully, "My beautiful barge," he tipped it back and forth as if it sailed in rough seas. "Oh, dear." He let it drop. "Shipwrecked."

Gemellus whirled at the crash. Caligula put on a face of mock lamentation. "All for nothing."

Drusilla tucked the trailing end of his purple mantle into the crook of his arm. "Never mind, dear. There is time for you to build another."

"That was a gift from the king of India," Gemellus said hotly. He cleared his throat and managed a lighter tone. "Come along, everyone."

Caligula crunched through the brittle shells. "Why do you keep these moldering relics of your grandfather's rule?"

"They remind me of what he achieved," Gemellus said stiffly. Perhaps his devotion kept Tiberius's malign spirit lingering in this house of the old Princeps' birth, bringing ill luck to those who passed through its doors.

Agrippina led him from the room; Caligula and Drusilla followed. I reached down for the battle knife. Lepidus seized my arm and shook his head.

Why would he not wish me to arm myself? Did he want us to die undefended?

Blandus said in a low voice, "Carinna, what do you fear?"

"The fool thinks he will save us from Gemellus," Lepidus muttered.

The former governor glanced at me, and back to Lepidus. Even more quietly, he said, "Let him take it." Julia, behind him, drew in her breath.

Beads of sweat stood on my patron's upper lip. "A naked weapon in Caesar's presence? The blame will be mine."

Claudius spoke up suddenly: "Look at this." The rest of us might fear being massacred in moments, but the old pedant had found some oddity to amuse himself with.

Gemellus cried from the atrium, "Lepidus, where are you?" I heard Caligula's voice add something unintelligible.

"We are just coming," Lepidus called back. His glare was fierce. "Marcus, leave the knife."

My family's patron, my father's friend. How much could I trust him?

"Young C-Carinna," Claudius said in a more urgent tone. What he held was an ancient bone. It might have been from a chicken's wing, if chickens were the size of elephants. "The bone of a giant from Nubia. It was guh-given to Augustus." He thrust it at me. "See for yourself." His gaze was intent.

Discolored and pitted, the artifact was as heavy as marble. Whatever it was, it would make a useful club. He suggested, "Perhaps you muh-muh-might examine it over dinner."

"Perhaps I will." I let my hand hang by my side, so the bone-thing was concealed by the folds of my mantle.

Lepidus pressed me forward. "Blandus, I will be next after you," he said. "Julia, stay back with Claudius."

The day had darkened, and lamps burned in niches. The air was heavy with unshed rain. Gemellus's slaves bowed as we followed the others to the curtained doorway of the dining room where I had grappled with Livilla. Odors barraged us: grilled fish, beets, roast meat, sour pickle, wine, ginger, fennel, garlic. Sharp voices and the bang and rattle of pans and utensils came from nearby: the familiar sounds of preparation for a dinner party.

Gemellus said, "You must enter with your eyes covered. I will tell you when to look."

Agrippina said, "Really, Gemellus, is that necessary?"

"It is part of the surprise. You will be pleased, I promise."

She looked at Caligula. So did everyone else. "Sweet Isis," he growled. "Lead on with your blasted surprise, or we will have no dinner."

I said, "Agrippina, allow me to enter before you. After our cousin Gemellus, of course."

No one protested. Drusilla must have sensed the general disquiet, for she tried to put us at ease: "Gemellus, do I smell mussels?"

"You do, sweet Drusilla; with leeks and cumin, just as you like them. Line up, everyone, and cover the eyes of the person ahead of you."

Agrippina's hands shut off my sight. I felt Gemellus step in front of me. He said, "Put a hand on my shoulder, Carinna, and follow me. Is everyone ready? Do not look before I give the word."

Clutching the huge bone in my hidden right hand, I gripped his shoulder with the other. If he had an ambush waiting for us, his would be the first death. *You can crush a man's windpipe with your forearm.* Or with a giant's bone.

The curtain rings rattled. He started into the room, towing me behind him. I heard the others shuffling after me like a chain gang of slaves. If we were cut down as we entered, one by one, what would the historians make of our docility?

I twitched my head to dislodge Agrippina's grip, but her thumbs were tight against my temples. My heart beat so thunderously I could not hear my own footfalls. The air became warmer, with smells of hot beeswax and perfume.

"Now you may look," Gemellus cried. "Uncover your eyes."

Agrippina's hands fell from my face. The room was utterly black.

One of the women shrieked. Someone bumped into me. A man exclaimed. Rustles and thumps near the doorway. Fingernails dug into my arm, dislodging my hold on Gemellus. "Protect me," Agrippina gasped. Sandals slithered; a body thudded to the floor.

Blandus bellowed, "Where is Caesar?"

"Someone pushed me down." Caligula's muffled voice was shaky.

"I thought we were in danger," Lepidus said. "Carinna, where are you?"

"Is everyone all right?" I tightened my grasp on the giant's bone.

"Be still, all of you," Gemellus shouted.

The shapes of my fellow diners coalesced from the darkness. A gabble of exclamations and nervous laughter sprang up when it was apparent we were not under attack. Agrippina's claws unclenched. Lepidus helped Caligula to his feet. "Quiet," Gemellus shouted again. "You are spoiling it."

"Listen," Julia exclaimed. A nightingale sang in a corner of the room.

A tiny flame flickered high up, then another and another. Little lights burst into life on the other walls until a constellation of them surrounded us. "Stars," Drusilla cried.

This effect brought murmurs of surprise. Its cause was soon apparent: a score of black slaves standing on scaffolds had opened the doors of dark lanterns.

The night bird's fluting ceased. One by one the slaves snuffed out their candles. When all was dark again, they climbed off their perch, dismantled it noiselessly, and disappeared behind a screen on the far side of the room.

A diffused brightness grew there while flutes played the chirps and trills of birds at daybreak. The screen sank down to reveal a framework shaped like the face of the sun, studded with blazing tapers. The glowing circle crept upward, its light shining on walls festooned with garlands and cages in which real birds pecked and preened.

Agrippina clapped her hands. "You clever boy, you have given me the sun for my birthday."

Had I been the only guest, my blunder would have rankled less. But I was a distant relative of this family, a makeweight thrown in to avoid bad luck. I myself had precipitated the panic among them, having insisted to Lepidus and Blandus on the need to arm myself. By Mithras's Dog, I had almost borne a naked blade into the dining room!

I saw the same sheepish expression on the faces of others that must have been on my own. Tucking the giant's bone under my arm, I joined in the applause for Gemellus's dramatic feat.

His eyes were hard, his smile bitter. "Be welcome," he said, and gestured us to our couches.

⊸⊹⊹⊱

The wine spilled in his libation was as red as heart's blood. It left its spattered repose before him and trickled across the floor, meandering through tiny channels in the worn mosaic, to the broad couch I shared with Blandus and Julia.

Pipes, lyre, and silvery cymbals struck up a tune behind the screen, and slaves came around to pour *mulsum* for us. I had watched them dip the wine, this one pale as flax, from a wide-mouthed jar in a tripod. They mixed it with honey in a spouted bowl, and poured it into a silver ewer. And now, into our nine cups.

Gemellus's cup was the last to be filled. The many lights of the artificial sun danced on it as he held it high. "May the gods smile on Julia Agrippina," he said. "Let us drink to her health, and to a bright future for the child she carries."

Julia lifted her cup. "Wait," muttered Blandus.

The torc pressed into my neck as I reclined, a reminder that I had promised myself to consume nothing unless it passed Gemellus's lips. I too raised my cup, but did not drink.

Across from us, Lepidus examined one of Drusilla's rings. On the head couch, Claudius's cup quivered in his palsied hand as he tried to blot a wine stain on his tunic. Beside him Agrippina leaned over to whisper to Caligula.

Gemellus looked around at the eight of us. A muscle worked in his jaw. "Even now you mistrust me," he said. "Very well. Long life to the babe; may he be better loved than I." He gulped the contents of his cup so abruptly that wine welled onto his lower lip and chin. "Enjoy your dinner." He thrust himself off the couch.

There was a moment of shocked silence. Then passionate protest came from Drusilla and Julia; apologetic reassurance from Agrippina. Claudius burbled a remonstration. Lepidus looked pained; Blandus, worried.

Caligula rolled to his feet. He had been given the place of honor at right angles to the host, so he and Gemellus stood together between their two couches. He glared around at us. "I have been patient, but my patience is at an end."

He lifted his cup and drank. "I trust my son!" He hurled the cup to the floor. Bile-yellow runnels crept out from beneath the couch to vein the blood-red libation, like the effusion from a belly wound. To the youth's lowered face he said, "Be not offended. Such rumors have poisoned us as would make a man doubt his own mother."

Gemellus looked away, wiping his chin with his sleeve. Caligula turned him to face us. "This is my son. If you do not love him, it means you do not love me." His piercing gaze traveled around. I stifled an urge to make sure the giant's bone could not be seen beneath my couch cushion.

Gemellus said, "Your . . ." He stopped to rasp huskiness from his throat. "Your esteem, Father, means more to me than a Triumph."

The couches creaked as they reclined once more. The music resumed.

Doubly shamed now, I sipped *mulsum* and made a semblance of studying the Trojan War scenes embossed on my silver cup. Blandus must think me lacking in nerve and judgment. What hope had I now of persuading Caligula to listen to me and grant compensation to a barbarian?

A stout *nomenclator* read out the dishes to be served for the *promulsis*: salad with lavender, truffled eggs in vinegar sauce, casserole of roses and lamb brains, mussel and shellfish salad, pickled peaches, and dormice stuffed with pork, pepper, and pine nuts. Much praise for Gemellus, who had commanded such delicacies to whet our appetites.

A slave displayed the first appetizer: chopped greens arrayed with split olives and curls of lavender. Gemellus waved him over, stirred the salad with a spoon, and scooped a sample of it into his mouth.

Caligula interrupted his murmured conversation with Agrippina. "Gemellus, you know food tasting is unnecessary among ourselves."

The youth chewed and swallowed. "It pleases me to make my family feel safe." He signaled the slave to serve the rest of us.

Though he spoke derisively, his tasting of the food improved the atmosphere. The level of conversation rose as two servers made their way around with the salad. Julia and Drusilla began to speculate about whom Caligula might marry. Still abashed, I ate salad and avoided Lepidus's eye.

Agrippina's voice cut through the others': "Except for Tiberius's bed books, you have little knowledge of literature. As for philosophy, my dear, how can you rule educated men when you do not know Socrates from Sophocles?"

"I will not waste my time in a *stoa* listening to dotards debate the nature of the universe," Gemellus retorted.

"Your grandfather did." She picked an olive from her plate, muttered, "Not that it improved his disposition," and popped it into her mouth.

"Leave off, aunt; I am not about to quit Rome. Much as you wish it."

Drusilla regarded a leaf from her salad. "This lettuce is wonderfully tender, Gemellus. Really, isn't it amazing what can be done in hothouses?"

"Really, do you know how imbecilic you sound?" Agrippina snapped. "Juno save me—one sister who pretends that rotten fish smells like roses, and the other who might as well lift her skirts in the middle of the Forum."

"'Pinilla!" Caligula sat up and scowled at her. "Sweeten your temper at once, or I will send you back to Pyrgi tomorrow."

She was not intimidated. "Brother, I merely see things as they are. You would be well served to do the same."

Drusilla's eyes had filled with tears. Laying a hand over hers, Lepidus said to Agrippina, "Dear sister-in-law, we are here to celebrate a happy occasion. Let us be civil, at least for the evening."

Blandus added his deep voice to the appeal. "We old men, it takes so little to upset our digestion. Eh, Claudius?"

Claudius blinked like a boy woken by a teacher's prodding. "I make a puh-point of not interfering among my buh-buh-brother's children." He paused to knuckle saliva from his lips. "But I should be sorry to miss the tr-tr-truh . . ." His tongue bogged down like a cart in mud.

"Truffles?" Gemellus said.

"Truffles!" Blandus trumpeted. He turned to me. "I wager you had no such delicacies in Pannonia, young Carinna?"

"Alas, no," I said, welcoming the less tindery topic. "All stewed nettles, porridge, and *posca*."

"'*Posca*'?" Julia frowned in attractive incomprehension.

"The soldiers' drink. Watered-down wine vinegar."

She shuddered and sipped her sweet *mulsum*. Rinsing my fingers in the bowl a server proffered, I went on, "It is very refreshing. And does not cloud the senses like wine, which is important when men must be ready for battle."

"Were I to go into battle, I should certainly want as much wine as I could hold," Agrippina declared. When the laughter ebbed, she added, "And afterward, too."

More laughter. The dinner party seemed on the verge of conviviality. Emboldened, I put my head next to Julia's and reminded her of the time we had hidden from a summer shower in her grandmother Antonia's garden temple.

Her smile touched her sad eyes for a moment. Blandus warned me in a good-humored rumble not to lead his wife astray. It was fortunate, Lepidus joked, that I had been away in the North while Blandus was away in the South.

I was aware of the chief server presenting the next appetizer, of Gemellus tasting the dish—"Ambrosia! I do love truffles"—and taking another spoonful while Agrippina made fun of his greediness. But my senses were chiefly engaged with Julia. Perhaps I could make pleasure chase the melancholy from her face.

She looked away from me to a dish in front of her. "What is this? Oh, the truffled eggs. Give me some. Perhaps this vinegar sauce is the noblest use for your *posca*, Marcus Licinius?"

"I do not doubt it," I agreed. As the server finished spooning chopped eggs in a dark sauce onto Julia's plate, I decided to put aside my usual inhibition about mushrooms. Besides, Gemellus himself had sampled the dish, not once but twice.

The server's tunicked waist moved into my field of vision. With a careless nod in his direction, I said to Julia, "People taste like what they eat, you know."

"Then we will all be quite delicious by the end of the evening, will we not?" She pointed past me with her spoon. "Did you want some, too? Because the server has ignored you."

"What?" I saw the slave's hands taking the pan of eggs away from me, then his back as he pivoted to return to the kitchen. "Boy, are you blind? Bring that back here."

I turned to Julia. "I fear your brother's servers are not the equal of his cooks. How are the eggs?"

"One moment, and I will tell you." She bent her head over her plate, chasing a slippery chunk of egg with her spoon.

The slave stood in front of me again, waiting. "Just serve me," I said impatiently.

He gripped the pan with one hand. But instead of taking up the spoon to scoop out a serving, he placed his other hand across the open face of the dish.

Without pausing for thought, I struck Julia's plate from her fingers. It clattered to the floor. "What—?" she gasped.

I looked up. The server's hand rose to his head and snatched off a woman's flaxen wig. Bright blue eyes stared back at me beneath shorn red-gold hair.

"Rufus," I said, thunderstruck.

CHAPTER 30

LAESA MAIESTAS

"How did you get loose?" Gemellus blurted.

Rufus began to back away. I grabbed his tunic. "Where have you been?"

He tried to pull free, still holding the pan. His face was thinner and pale as snow, and fear stared from his eyes.

"Seize him!" Gemellus screamed.

One of the black slaves hurried from behind the screen. When he caught Rufus's arm, Gemellus sank down on his elbow again. "That boy has been a problem." He dragged in a breath. "Get him out of here."

"Not so fast," I said. The question of where he had been could wait. "Rufus, is something amiss with the eggs?"

The Thracian boy nodded emphatically.

Spoons clattered down on plates. "Great Mother, save us," someone said.

"Take him away," Gemellus snapped. "He's a liar, a troublemaker. Slaves!"

Two more of the Nubians rushed into the dining room. Lepidus tried to rise, but Drusilla clung to him. Blandus seized Claudius's plate. Agrippina pushed herself off the couch, thrust a spoon into her mouth, and retched.

I vaulted onto my feet. Which of the Caesars or their in-laws had interfered with the food? As much as I distrusted Gemellus, he had not hesitated to eat it. "Rufus, who is responsible? Do you know?"

He tried to turn, perhaps to point someone out, but his captors gripped him too firmly. "Just tell me," I said. "Who is it?"

"Stay out of this!" Gemellus too was on his feet, barricaded behind his couch. "You slaves, take him away at once."

Rufus cried out in wordless protest. Dropping the pan, he opened his mouth wide. And in the instant before the slaves hauled him off his feet, I saw a black stub where his tongue should have been.

In the voice I had used to carry across a parade ground, I shouted, "Take your hands off this boy."

"Remove him now, or I will lash your hides raw," Gemellus shrieked.

"I am Marcus Licinius Carinna, son of a Senator, and I command you to obey me."

From the opposite couch a familiar voice said, "I am Marcus Aemilius Lepidus, Senator and pontifex, and I too order that the boy be released."

The Nubians let Rufus go. I said to him, "The eggs are poisoned?"

He nodded, pointing to the pan at his feet.

"Is anything else?"

He shook his head. So the salad and the *mulsum*, at least, had been safe.

Rufus turned and pointed at Gemellus. Or rather at Gemellus's place, for I saw only the tail of our host's *himation* as he dashed behind the screen.

"Bring him back," I shouted to the Nubians, who had edged away to follow their master.

"Let him go." Lepidus sat on the end of his couch, sliding his feet into his sandals. "Where can he hide?"

"Carinna, you are mad. And you too, Lepidus." Caligula's voice cracked, then strengthened. "Did you not see him eat the eggs himself?"

Rufus went into a frantic pantomime. He feigned mixing and drinking something. Then he spooned up some of the truffled eggs and mimed eating them. He rose again, dropping the spoon, smacked his lips, and rubbed his belly.

Blandus understood at once. "That potion he takes to ward off the grippe."

Lepidus's voice was harsher. "Yes, that infernal potion he swigs every day. Made up for him by that witch Locusta!"

"All this time . . . he has been making . . . himself immune to poison," Agrippina gasped, "and none of you noticed?" She gagged again.

Drusilla giggled, a sound that startled everyone into looking at her. She pointed at her sister, then covered her own mouth as if realizing amusement was unseemly. But the giggles turned to chuckles, and then to waves of laughter.

Gemellus's cause was not yet lost. He would flee to his supporters, who doubtless needed only a signal to launch a massacre of Caligula's adherents. "Carinna, where are you going?" Lepidus demanded.

"To stop him," I said, and added, "You had better attend to Caesar."

Caligula sat upright between his sisters, one hysterical and the other vomiting. His face was so white that his staring eyes seemed as dark as cinders.

As I ducked behind the screen, Blandus said in a tone of horror and disbelief, "My dear Julia. Your brother would have poisoned every one of us!"

There were no servers or musicians behind the screen. Hearing what happened, they had fled.

Sandals pattered behind me. I tensed, but it was Rufus. I said, "Help me. We must catch him."

Pots and pans steamed on the kitchen stove. A plank on trestles held the next dishes to be served, with final ingredients waiting. A pot of peppercorns had overturned, and the precious seasoning was scattered across the floor. There was no human presence, not even a sauce girl.

Under the roofed portico enclosing the garden was another ghost cookery: braziers with spitted meats still smoking over the flames, a roasted kid partly stuffed with speckled cheese, figpeckers newly plucked for the oven.

In my haste I slid across wet tiles into a portico column. A little tumulus of figpecker heads toppled off the chopping board. They rolled across the pavement at my feet, pebble eyes blankly staring. Like Caligula's.

There was no sign of Gemellus, and no one to ask. The rush of rain drowned any telltale voices or hurried footsteps. He was not dressed for the weather, but it was possible to cross much of the Palatine Hill under cover of arcades and passages. "Where will he go?" I demanded of Rufus.

He shrugged his uncertainty. I cursed. Time was too valuable to waste looking in the wrong places. "Take me to the guards' courtyard. Quickly."

A score of Praetorians huddled under the overhang of the stable roof, watching a dogfight by the light of a swaying lantern. They howled and shouted bets at each other as blood sprayed through the silver rain. I splashed across the courtyard, calling out to their commander, "I must find Tiberius Gemellus."

"Eh?" He gave me a brief glance. One of the dogs ripped open the other's throat. "*Habet!*" he yelled, pumping his fist in the air.

"There has been an attempt on Caesar's life," I shouted above the tumult. "Alert the Special Cohort officer of the watch."

Startled, he stared at my dinner clothes and the gold torc around my neck, then jerked his head for me to follow him.

The guardroom at the end of the stable block was empty except for Saxa, who dozed in a chair tipped against the wall. The rain masked our approach, so it was not until the Praetorian officer's boots thudded across the threshold that he woke, snapping forward and rising to his feet in a single movement.

The officer saluted. "Sir, this man says—"

"What is it, Carinna?" Saxa demanded.

The troops who had gone out to watch the dogfight started to crowd in noisily and were ordered out again. As I told the tale, Saxa's eyes shifted between me and Rufus. "Was Caesar poisoned?"

"No, but he is too stunned to command you." In truth I was not sure whether Caligula had eaten the truffled eggs, but uncertainty could lead to chaos.

Saxa did not respond. I was about to shout at him to move when I realized he was deciding whether to believe me. If Caligula should be dead or dying, who was likelier to seize power: Gemellus or Lepidus?

"The odds are two to one against Gemellus," I said. "If you arrest him, Caesar or Lepidus will reward you."

He pulled his black cloak off a peg. "Which way did he go?"

"Give me four men," I said. "My slave may know where to find him."

Rufus led me and the Praetorians to Gemellus's private rooms. Scented silk hangings, as soft as clouds, swept down on either side of small erotic paintings. Fastened into the wall next to a gilded sleeping couch was an iron ring from which dangled a bar of handcuffs.

The boy untied one of the colorful ribbons around his wrists. The skin beneath was ringed with chafes and bruises, and the side of his hand was cruelly lacerated. The answer, obviously, to Gemellus's exclamation, *How did you get loose?*

Trumpets outside brayed a call to arms. A wardrobe attendant said that Gemellus had gathered up a cloak and a casket of jewelry before fleeing with a few companions.

The trail vanished near another garden in an unused part of the house. With rain still lashing out of the darkness, it was impossible to find any sign of where he had gone.

Saxa was talking with Praetorian officers and imperial freedmen in Gemellus's reception room. The clutter of Tiberian memorabilia had been shoved back against the walls. On the couch where Julia and Blandus had waited before dinner, Lepidus sat hunched with elbows on his knees and hands over his eyes. Behind him, Dio gave a cry of relief. "Marcus, you are not poisoned?"

"By good fortune, I am not," I said. "Nor you, Marcus Aemilius?"

Lepidus looked up. "I was about to take the first bite when you knocked Julia's plate out of her hand." Seeing his fingers tremble, he closed his hands into fists. "I stopped Drusilla from eating. But she has lost her reason. She is curled up sobbing like a child."

"And Caesar?"

"Only Agrippina and Claudius tasted the dish before you raised the alarm. They are both undergoing a physicking." With a sigh, he pushed himself to his feet. "Jupiter! I am shaking like a jelly."

"Livilla must have known," I said. "She pretended illness in order to avoid the dinner." Her haggardness might have meant she regretted the imminent death of her entire family, but I could not pity her for that.

He sighed again. "Blandus has taken Julia home. Come with me to see how Caesar fares."

"I would rather search for Gemellus," I said. I had no desire to witness the demise of Caligula's trust in his adopted son.

"I will accompany you, Lepidus," said Saxa, joining us. "Carinna, you would do better to return home. I will send guards with you to make sure the Lady Livilla goes nowhere until we are ready to deal with her."

"Have you sealed the city gates?"

"Yes, and my men are combing the Palatine. I will have the houses of his supporters searched when more troops arrive from the Camp."

"What about the wharves?" Lepidus said. "He may try to make for Ostia."

"If he embarks in the darkness, Father Tiber will take care of him." Saxa's teeth showed. "The river has risen to the last step of the embankment."

"Go home, Marcus," Lepidus said. "Inform your father. And let Julia Livilla know her 'granny's' handiwork will not go to waste."

With reluctance I said, "Very well." It would be fitting for Livilla to take her own life with the poison she had meant to use on us.

His gaze traveled from me to Rufus. "I admit, I did not think you crafty enough to put a spy in Gemellus's household." He clapped a heavy hand on my shoulder and left with Saxa.

⚬━⚬ ⚬━⚬

As I was about to depart with Dio and Rufus, the boy collapsed. It was exhaustion, too much effort after his brutal maiming. I hoisted him onto a couch and sent Dio to find a donkey or a mule to carry him home.

In the meantime, men and women continued to gather around us in the atrium. Their livery, like Rufus's, bore the imperial household's red stripe at the hem. Soldiers came and went, bringing more of them.

Rufus struggled to rise, but I pushed him down again. As he sagged into the cushions, I said, "So you did not run away?"

He shook his head listlessly. His bone-white face was glossed with sweat, his red hair as wet as seaweed.

"Gemellus's men captured you in the spice market."

He nodded.

"And because I had refused to give you back to him, he did that to you?" I gestured toward his mouth.

His eyelids drooped shut. He lay motionless for so long that I thought he had fainted, but finally I saw the almost imperceptible wag of his head.

"That was not why he did it?" When he failed to respond, I prompted, "Why, then?" As soon as the question was out of my mouth, I wondered how I expected a boy with no tongue to answer.

Rufus lifted a hand and cupped his ear, then tipped his head in the direction of the dining room.

"You heard . . ." I puzzled over what he could have heard, and then knew. "You heard him plan to poison Caesar."

The boy looked up at me. I saw the answer in his pain-filled eyes.

When I had asked days earlier if Gemellus intended to kill Caligula, he said he did not know. There was no excuse for such a monstrous untruth, but I asked anyway, "Why did you not tell me?"

Rufus made his hands quiver to show fear.

"What you said— What you showed me about Gemellus making himself immune to the poison, was that true?"

He croaked out a word. But even from his mangled mouth I understood it: "*Verum.*" It is true.

Dio appeared in a sodden cloak. "All is well at home," he said, pushing his hood back. "Your father has put the family on guard. Your litter and escort are waiting for you in the courtyard here."

"What of Livilla?"

"Julia Livilla tried to flee soon after you left for the Palace, but the master stopped her." He drew a bundle from under the cloak and set it on the table. "I have brought you dry clothes."

Rufus slid onto the floor and slumped on his knees. Dio eyed him curiously. "Did you really send him out as bait for Gemellus?"

"Do you think I am that crafty?" I said.

The boy's confession lay heavily on my heart. If I honored my vow to the God of Truth, deceit was an offense I could not condone.

In silence I exchanged my wet clothes for two thick tunics. By the time my boots were laced, I had reached a decision. "Rufus, I am going to pronounce judgment on you. Stand up."

He wavered to his feet, eyes downcast. I said, "Look at me."

Blinking hard, he obeyed. In a flat, formal voice I said, "You lied to me, your master, endangering the Princeps and his family. For that, the penalty must be death."

Dio looked shocked. Rufus's expression did not change.

"Yet you escaped your bonds and saved our lives at the risk of your own." I lifted my eyes and my hands heavenward. "Witness all the gods, the spirits of my ancestors, and Dio, a *vernus* of our house, that I, Marcus Carinna, rescind your punishment to reward your loyalty."

Rufus's eyes flickered in confusion.

I was suddenly weary of dreadful choices. "Dio will explain it to you. In the meantime, since we are not needed in the hunt for Gemellus, let us go home and find something to eat. Can you walk?" I swung my cloak around my shoulders. "These Caesars keep a damned poor larder."

⊰⊹⊱

But before leaving I stopped in the reception room, where Saxa's adjutant Quadratus was briefing his men. "The Trigemina, Flumentana, and Carmentalis gates have been reinforced, and we are putting guards on the embankment to stop any boat traffic." His stubby forefinger traced the western quadrant of the city wall on a map. The table beneath teetered on its antler legs.

He lifted his nailhead eyes. "The Seventh Cohort will be on its way at first light to shut down the docks in Ostia." He bent over the map again.

A man who dared to boat down the fast-flowing river could be in Ostia hours before troops arrived at the seaport. If Gemellus reached the sea, he could bribe a fisherman to smuggle him to Gaul. He had friends in Massilia with men and money—and more powerful friends farther north with legions.

A courier rushed in with news that Gemellus had been sighted near the Temple of Janus in the Forum. With a bark of triumph Quadratus ordered a cavalry squadron to encircle and search the area. Some of the officers jostled out, talking excitedly.

I was ready to leap on a horse and pursue Gemellus myself, forgetting my weariness and hunger. But the chase was up to the Special Cohort, who were trained for it.

I had just said, "Good hunting," to Quadratus, hoping my envy did not show, when raised voices erupted suddenly in the atrium. Caligula's freedman Kallistos hurried in as Lepidus shouted behind him, "We will have a confession."

"Most illustrious Senator, I regret it, believe me." The Greek raised both hands to command attention. "Hark, all of you: the pursuit of Tiberius Gemellus must stop. All troops must return to the Praetorian Camp, except those on regular Palace duty."

Dumbfounded faces looked back at him. "By whose order?" Quadratus rapped out.

It was Lepidus who answered, "By order of the Princeps." His glare singled me out. "Caesar does not believe . . ." Anger strangled his voice. "Caesar does not believe there was an assassination attempt."

Kallistos nodded confirmation. "Thank you, Senator," he said, and left in a swish of robes.

Incredulous at first, I became incensed. "Then I charge Gemellus with stealing and mutilating this Thracian slave, my property." I pointed to Rufus. "I demand that you continue pursuing him and arrest him."

Saxa said, "We are not police." He glanced meaningfully at Quadratus. "But it may take a while to pull back all our men."

"I will try to convince Caesar of the truth before then," I told him.

As I pushed through the crowded atrium toward the private part of the House of Augustus, Rufus tugged at my sleeve. He was staring at a bald-headed slave with a piggish face, the same man I had seen on my earlier visit and had taken for Gemellus's house steward.

The brute spotted him. "Lost your tongue, little redbird?" He grinned malevolently. "Too bad you can't pleasure the master so well without it."

Rufus's eyes beseeched me to retaliate, but I had no authority to order the punishment of another man's slave. "Not yet," I said.

"Why would he not flee? First you suspect him, completely without foundation, of attacking us. Then you accuse him of poisoning our dinner!" Caligula paced the audience chamber. Attendants moved nervously out of his way. "And you dared command his own slaves to lay hands on him!"

He threw himself into his high-backed chair so violently that the long claws of the leopard skin covering it rattled together. "No one is harmed. My sister and my uncle have been made miserable for nothing."

Perhaps he would have been less enraged in Lepidus's presence, but my patron had been drawn into urgent conference elsewhere about the flooding of the city. I said, "You promised me an hour."

"Then stop wasting it!" He reached for the sandglass beside him and flipped it upside down.

To my relief Saxa said, "We can begin now, Caesar." He came toward the Princeps' chair with the bald slave I had encountered in the atrium.

"One moment, my lord," the slave said to Caligula. "If I don't die, could I ask for a little gift . . ." He licked his lips. "Say, a thousand sestertii?"

Saxa grabbed a fistful of the man's tunic. But Caligula snapped, "Agreed."

"Thank you, my lord." The slave grinned like a dog that has eaten another dog's puke. "I just want to buy me a boy to keep me warm in my old age."

"Rufus," I said. "Serve him."

Rufus left Dio's side and held up the pan of truffled eggs to the man who had maimed him.

The slave scraped the spoon around in the serving dish. His head, shaved as bald as a ballista stone, met his muscular shoulders with only a crease to separate them. "The young master said not to kill the boy, just make sure he never talked again. So I put my knife in the fire before I cut off his tongue. Kept him from bleeding to death. Didn't I, redbird?"

"Stop yammering, Hanno, and eat," Saxa said. "Or I will shove that food down your throat."

The slave leered at Rufus. "Know what I did with your tongue? I cooked it. And ate it." He opened his mouth wide and shoved in the spoonful of egg.

Caligula sat up. The slave displayed the empty spoon. "Two bites, the same as Gemellus," I said, and watched to make sure he swallowed. Only after he downed the second mouthful did I notice Kallistos whispering into Caligula's ear. The Princeps nodded, and the Greek padded from the room.

The sands were running swiftly in the hourglass. I cleared my throat. "How is the egg?"

The slave grinned again, but with less bravado. "Cold, sir. Could use a little fish-sauce, too."

My father strode hurriedly into the room, his muddy boots marking the polished floor. "Well timed, Titus Licinius," Caligula said. "Your son has accused mine of trying to murder me, and we are about to see which one is the liar."

Father's pace slowed, and he looked at me. I kept my eyes fixed on the slave.

Saxa scratched his cheek. "While we wait, Hanno, tell us about Lunula and Purpureus."

The slave did not notice my surprise. "That pair! I got more sense in my bunghole than either of them two hollow-heads."

"They told you they finished off the boy, correct?"

Hanno snorted. "Except it was the wrong boy."

"It was supposed to be him." Saxa gestured at Rufus.

The slave nodded. "Young master blew up when he found out, but too late. I'd already taken the two of 'em fishing." He grinned at the macabre joke.

They had meant from the outset to murder Rufus, not me. And would have succeeded, had Jason not taken it on himself to send Rufus home.

"Why did your master want the boy dead?" Saxa asked.

A shrug. "I just do as I'm told."

"So you killed them both: Lunula and Purpureus."

The slave shivered. Perhaps deciding he had said enough, he went over to a pedestal on which stood a gold and ivory statue of Isis in her cow-horned headdress. "Guard me, Fortuna Servatrix!" he said, rubbing the goddess's breasts.

"Why else would Gemellus have gone to such lengths, first to retrieve Rufus and then to silence him?" I insisted. "The boy knew he was giving himself small doses of poison so it would not affect—"

"Enough," Caligula exploded, slamming his hand on the armrest of his chair. "There is nothing wrong with this man. Marcus Carinna, you have tried to turn me against Gemellus from the day you returned to Rome. Now you have driven him away from me." Fury darkened his thin face.

Father said quickly, "Caesar, if my son is mistaken, it is only because of his zeal to protect you." He tried to catch Caligula's eye, but the Princeps' glare was fastened on me. "Do not condemn him for his loyalty."

"His loyalty! He sleeps with that rabble-rouser Silius and the Senate Leader's niece. Gemellus gave him a slave, and look how your son has repaid his generosity."

"Gaius Julius," Father said more softly, "try as I may, I cannot make him more like Publius. But he would never betray you, never."

Caligula stared straight ahead. Father went on, "I raised both my sons on tales of your illustrious father. Many times I reminded them that you were destined for greatness yourself." His voice grew caressing. "Just as I told you the world would someday be yours."

"Gemellus has done nothing," Caligula said stubbornly, but his rage was ebbing. "He loves me."

"But he fears you, as his grandfather did. Tiberius would not have kept you on such a short leash, like a young lion, had he not been terrified of you."

"Yes, he was." Caligula's eyes flashed, but he was looking at something within himself. Father had managed, seemingly without effort, to bring him pleasure while diverting his anger. "Still, Gemellus—"

There was an almighty crash. We had forgotten the slave Hanno.

CHAPTER 31

FLOOD

I sis broke into pieces. The hand with the *sistrum* skidded across the floor; the carved bells of the instrument struck my leg. The goddess's head, with its ivory horns enclosing the gold Sun disk, spun to the foot of Caligula's chair. The rest of the statue lay where it had fallen.

The slave reeled drunkenly toward us. His face was crimson, and when he stretched out a hand, I saw a red rash growing on the inside of his arm. He tried to speak, but nothing came out except a jackdaw croak.

Caligula sat rigid with horror as the appalling creature staggered up to him. He tried to ward it off with feeble brushing motions of his hand, but it clutched his wrist. "Get away," he shrieked.

Saxa seized the slave. "Tincture of Atropos. Do you see his eyes, Caesar?"

Hanno swayed, clutching his throat. The centers of his eyes were as big and black as Spanish olives. His breathing had become a horrible voiceless rasp.

Caligula edged out of his chair, staring at the poisoned man with eyes that bulged in horror. He stumbled over Isis' crown, and the chair arm caught the swag of his mantle. With a wild cry he dragged the chair with him until it released his clothing. He fled, pursued by my father and scurrying servants.

Saxa let the slave topple to the floor. "By Dis, I feared he would never start to show the poison."

I backed away as the frantic brute groped for my ankle. Saxa looked down at him. "I am told it makes people see visions, or the gods lift them up to soar through the skies." He shrugged. "Of course, it is hard to know for sure since they cannot talk." He prodded the slave with his boot. "Much like having no tongue, eh, Hanno?"

The man reached out a trembling hand. Saxa went on, "They gasp for breath as if a weight grew heavier upon them by the hour. The old Princeps' son, may his spirit be at peace, took a day and a half to die."

This would have been me. And Caligula, Lepidus, all the others.

"I must return to the hunt," the Special Cohort commander said. "You, boy, bring that pan of—" He broke off. The serving dish containing the last of the truffled eggs was no longer on the floor by Rufus's feet.

Dio was tipping it over a brazier several paces away. The tainted food slid into the hot coals, sizzled and spat, blackened, and burned.

The slave Hanno fouled himself. His eyes were pits of terror in his inflamed face. Saxa grimaced at the stink and strode from the room.

I followed him. The slave did not deserve mercy. Let him die slowly, twitching like a crushed cockroach.

But after a couple of paces I paused and turned. "Rufus," I said, "hold his head."

The boy crouched and seized his torturer's ears. When Hanno arched his neck, trying to free himself, I stamped on his throat.

For the few minutes it took him to choke to death, I let Rufus watch. It is an important lesson for a slave, that his master will reward loyalty. When I glanced up at him, the little ruffian was smiling.

Then Truth, which had pursued Caligula as he ran, overtook him at last. He wailed from the heart of the House of Augustus, and the last of the sand slipped through the hourglass.

⟞⟀ ⟀⟝

Gemellus had not been seen since his reported appearance near the Temple of Janus. But the city swarmed with soldiers searching places where he might seek refuge, so his capture was thought to be imminent.

I went home with my little retinue. The doors were double-barred, our slaves armed, the Praetorians guarding Julia Livilla's quarters awake and vigilant. Phormio still slept, unaware of the drama.

Dio had burned his hands destroying the poisoned food. I scolded him for wishing to escape his duties as my secretary. "For a while I did think . . ." he began wryly. But I did not hear the rest, for I lay down and at once fell asleep.

A light bobbed in the atrium. Sandals squeaked past the curtained doorway: a watchman making his rounds. Dogs were barking all over the city, which must mean the hunt continued.

I did not recall hearing Father return from the Palace. He might still be trying to reconcile Caligula to his adopted son's betrayal. No doubt I would be told that I should have been there too, but it was revenge on Gemellus I craved, not solacing Caligula.

A whimper came from the floor beside me. Rufus was shouting in his sleep, or perhaps sobbing. His limbs moved convulsively under his quilt.

I shut my eyes, but my thoughts kept chasing Gemellus. Had he sought refuge with the Chief Vestal, the Senate Leader's sister? Was he disguising himself as a slave or a woman to slip out when the gates opened at dawn? Could he escape through an inspection shaft into the Cloaca Maxima?

This last possibility fastened like a thorn in my mind. Despite the turbulence of the storm water, he might be able to ride one of the small inspection skiffs through the sewer outlet into the Tiber, and then bribe his way aboard a larger boat to Ostia. It would take nerve and foresight, but Gemellus had both.

I rose and reached for my clothes without disturbing Rufus. I longed for a pursuit, a battle, a fight to the finish: retribution for what had nearly happened to me at the Palace. Although there might be nothing else I could do, it would not take long to see if the sewer mouth was still open.

The stars overhead had faded, but the Clivus Victoriae was still sunk in darkness. Shutters and doors were closed tight; there was no early-morning smell of new bread from the bakeries, and slaves venturing out to fetch water were guarded by others. Letting Spider make his way carefully down the frosty slope, I heard the river's roar grow louder and more savage.

At the Romana gate near the foot of the hill, a silent throng carrying small children, cooking pots, bedding, and other bundles waited to climb to the higher ground of the Palatine. As I passed, a voice called out, "Why are the Praetorians deploying, your honor? Is our Caligula safe?"

"Caligula is perfectly safe," I said loudly. "The soldiers are to provide security because of the flooding."

Bless him, they cried. *Gods save him. Gods grant him long life.*

Torchlight glittered in spreading pools on the grounds of the Forum Boarium, and water snaked around temples and shrines beside the ramp to the Aemilian Bridge. Slaves carried heavy baskets down the steps of the Temple of Portunus to waiting wagons.

A mounted patrol splashed up to me, demanding the watchword. It was a new one, "Fortuna Augusta," changed after Gemellus's disappearance. They thrust a torch toward my face, decided I was not him, and trotted off.

Anyone hearing Quadratus's comment about guarding the city gates would have thought Rome as securely walled as a fortress. But here, where the high fortified bank of the river served as the city wall, warehouses had accreted like oysters on a quayside. One would hardly know the walls were there.

I rode onto the Aemilian Bridge, joining onlookers who crowded both railings. And the unlikelihood of Gemellus's escape by water at once became obvious.

Upstream, the Tiber raged around its narrow island, hurling spray onto the bridges that impeded it on each side. Trees and bushes swirled down the river amid dirty-yellow foam, along with a fat piling from some disintegrated dock and a body that at first looked human but was a pig's.

The piling headed like a battering ram for one of the piers of the Sublician Bridge. I turned the roan stallion around. Frantic wagers were made among the spectators. When the piling slammed into the bridge, tearing away facing-stones and some of the brick beneath, the crowd cheered.

I sat watching for a while longer to see if the Sublician would collapse. My grandfather had watched it being washed away when he was a boy. When I became a Senator, I would not vote to rebuild it unless the old superstition against using iron was abandoned.

When I became a Senator . . . what conceit! My election to the Senate would never happen while Caligula blamed me for exposing Gemellus's treachery.

On the far side of the river, a shrine on the Janiculum Hill glowed with luminous purity. Nearly sunrise. Enough gawking; I would be needed at home to prepare for flooded-out clients seeking shelter. There was also Livilla to be returned to the Palace. I did not want her doing away with herself in my house.

I turned the horse back toward the embankment. The usual agglomeration of small boats and ferries moored along the river wall was gone, showing the mouth of the Cloaca Maxima all but submerged in the surging Tiber.

So Gemellus was probably still in the city. At least until the gates opened at dawn, when he might be smuggled out.

I rode off the bridge and down to the Trigemina gate, which another mounted patrol was just entering. When I asked if they had noticed anything suspicious, one of the two Praetorians yawned. "Not a cursed thing."

I jerked my chin toward the gate, now closed again behind them. "I saw people gathering on the road."

The other trooper wiped a drip from his nose. "That was Malleus."

"The charioteer?" My heart thumped harder.

"Out for a pipe-opener on the road to Vitinia, he said."

I frowned at him. "You must be mistaken."

"Nothing wrong with my eyes, laddie. It's him."

A drawback of the old Servian Walls is that one cannot go from the Flaminian district of the Field of Mars, where the racing stables are, to any of the southern roads without entering the city precincts through the Carmentalis gate, traversing the Forum Boarium, and leaving the city again through another gate. It would have been simpler for Malleus to have crossed the Tiber by the Agrippan Bridge to exercise his horses in the fields on the Vatican side of the river. Instead, he had brought his team through two closed city gates and across a flooding plaza in order to drive them on the Vitinia road.

Which happened also to be the road to Ostia.

Malleus was not alone. Once outside the Trigemina gate, I made out two figures in the predawn murk standing higher than people clustered around them. Each was aboard a two-horse traveling chariot, like the one I had taken to Diana's grove with Aurima.

Both teams pulled onto the road as I approached, one behind the other. I hurried the stallion into a faster trot, and was closing on them when the driver in the lead turned his helmeted head toward the river embankment.

Two dark figures darted out between the sheds and storehouses, splashing through water ponded beside the road. One swung into the first chariot, the other into the second. Whips snapped, and both teams lunged ahead.

The crowd that had swarmed around Malleus was slow to disperse. By the time I cut through them, the two chariots had disappeared around the curve of the Aventine Hill. On its far side, the road would combine with two others to become the Via Ostiensis, running beside the Tiber to the sea.

The thunder of Spider's hooves racketed from the city wall. He jumped a streamlet flowing across the road and landed in a splatter left by the two chariots' wheels.

To the right, upwelling water had islanded the great warehouses by the river. On the left, I passed the junction with the road from the Lavernalis gate. The triangular side of Cestius's tomb spiked up ahead, marking the second road from the Raudusculana gate. Malleus was out of sight. Should I keep trying to overtake him, or turn back to seek help at the Raudusculana?

Time would be lost in informing the gate guards. And even troopers on fast horses could not overtake Malleus if he had too great a lead.

The decision was made for me when I spotted a mob of laden carts, foot traffic, riders, and carriages waiting to enter the closed gate. Galloping past Cestius's pyramid, I followed the two charioteers and their passengers onto the turf track beside the Ostia road.

CHAPTER 32

THE RIVER GOD

Malleus had crowded an oncoming mule litter off the road. Attendants were running toward the litter, on its side in the ditch with one mule trapped beneath it and the other struggling in the shafts. Amid the beasts' braying and screams from the litter, a young man turned his horse and chased after me. "Halt!" he cried furiously, grabbing at my reins. "Do you and your friends think other people have no right to this road?"

I struck his hand away. "Ride to the gate. Tell them Gemellus is headed to Ostia."

"What? Gemellus . . . ?"

"Tell the gate commander to send cavalry. Say, 'Fortuna Augusta.' Go now!"

He fell back. Over my shoulder I saw him dismount to help an elderly woman crawling out of the litter. With a grimace I settled back into the saddle. It seemed I would need Spider's great stamina.

Once the taverns and liveries, monuments and mausolea fell behind, there were only pines and leafless poplars beside the road, with the occasional track leading to a villa or farm. The river serpentined on the right, swinging closer, then away. Pools and lakelets flashed in the dark fields, reflecting the glassy sky.

Foot travelers and carters gaped from the dry pavement as the two teams flashed by, spinning up great rooster-tails of mud and grass from the soft turf beside the road. Whenever I drew close I had to fall back, for the spray blinded me to the dangerous gouges that wheels and hooves had made.

Malleus soon realized he was being pursued. Heads turned to inspect me. Both chariots stopped.

Could it be that he and his colleague were merely taking two racing-club investors for a jaunt? I cantered closer, but still could not see the passengers' faces. "Give yourself up, Gemellus, or you will be stopped in Ostia," I called out.

Malleus's passenger exclaimed. For a moment I saw his profile, and mixed satisfaction and anger shot through me. It was indeed Tiberius Caesar Gemellus, who had nearly poisoned me and for whose sake I had been humiliated by Caligula.

I drew my longknife, shouting, "Surrender." My horse leaped forward.

Malleus bared his broken teeth in a grin. "Go," Gemellus cried. When the chariot lurched into motion, he would have fallen out had Malleus not seized him.

I was so intent on them that I hardly noticed the other chariot moving. Then its passenger turned to face me, pulling a sword from under his cloak. I had not expected a bodyguard.

He whipped the blade back and forth, shouting insults. But since he was facing backward, the driver obstructed his sword arm.

I swung Spider to the left. The bodyguard warned the driver, and the chariot swerved to cut me off.

I shifted the knife into my other hand. The guard yelled, "Wrong-fisted," and the driver swung right, slewing across a rut in the track.

I swapped the knife back into my right hand and brought my horse up on the left of the chariot. The guard swung backhanded at me but missed. His elbow hit the driver, who flinched toward me. I slashed his arm. His whip jerked and struck his near horse on the neck, and the stung beast veered into its teammate. A wheel tipped into a rut, and the linchpin broke. The wheel wobbled and spun off, the axle end spiked into the dirt, and the chariot slewed, spilling its occupants. One down!

I rammed my knife back into its scabbard to have both hands free. The roan stallion flicked his ears back, huffing strongly, nostrils distended. "Go, you brute," I urged, my eyes streaming with wind-tears as I leaned close to the bristle of his mane. "Go like the horses of Mithras!"

On the far side of a rise, the field between the road and the river was flooded. A line of trees stood marooned in a sea of brown water, marking where the Tiber had burst its banks. The only vehicle in sight was Malleus's chariot.

I prayed aloud to the Lord of Light, imploring him to grant my horse endurance and guard him from mishap, to help me stop these men who would bring chaos upon Rome. The pale oval of Gemellus's face turned as if he had heard. Malleus cracked his whip for more speed.

A milestone flashed by, too quickly to be readable. Foam flecked the stallion's black cheek. We were gaining on the chariot.

Vitinia must be nearby. There might be a stable with a fresh horse I could borrow. Perhaps other mounted men to join the pursuit.

Now I could make out fear on Gemellus's face. Clutching the craven's bar, he shook his head at something Malleus said. Malleus yanked Gemellus's cloak over his head and threw it into the air.

Spider's head jerked up as the great dark shape soared back toward us. He was not trained for such shocks, but I managed to steady him. Once past the fallen cloak, he let himself be coaxed into a faster gallop.

If he put a foot wrong, I would break my neck. But a sort of battle joy had seized me; nothing mattered but stopping Gemellus.

The line of flooded trees crept closer to the road. The river, having swallowed the field, now sucked at the road embankment. It was a muddy immensity, not raging as it did between the city bridges, but rolling and swirling as if some great creature swam beneath its disheveled surface. Vultures soared above the floating carcasses of sheep.

Then Fortuna, who so far had withheld her favor, seemed to smile on me. A line of ox-drawn wagons trudged toward us, taking up the width of the road. To the right, the embankment plunged steeply into the flood; to the left it dropped into a stubbled hayfield. Malleus would have to slow in order to squeeze past.

The lead drover yelled, waving his goad. The wagons were laden with blocks of marble packed in straw, far too heavy a load for evasive maneuvers.

Gemellus cried, "Ease up! You will kill us." He screamed as Malleus swerved down the causeway bank into the hayfield.

Then I saw that Fortuna's smile had been an illusion, for neither horses, chariot, nor men were disabled by the plunge. Indeed, Malleus had found a path along the edge of the field. Somehow Gemellus still gripped the rail.

I launched my stallion down the bank. He skidded down in front of the chariot, hooves spewing clods of dirt and grass. "Surrender," I shouted again, grabbing for my knife, but the scabbard had slid out of reach on my belt.

"Run him down," Gemellus yelled. Malleus lashed his team, and they charged me.

The collision rocked Spider backward off the path. Before he could take me down with him, I flung myself onto Malleus's near horse, a big brown mare.

The mare crow-hopped to throw me off. I clung with both hands to the yoke that humped across both horses' withers. Impossible to bestride her without being bludgeoned by the chariot shaft.

Malleus brought the team back under control. Between the mare's ears I glimpsed what he was heading for: a grassy ramp that ran back up to the road. "Stay out of this," I shouted. "Let me have Gemellus."

The weighted end of his lash struck my arm like an ax blow. I roared with pain. Another crack. My cheek burned, and hot blood ran into my ear.

I clutched the wooden yoke one-handed, splayed across the mare's back as she blundered over the rutted path. With the other hand I groped for my knife, buried somewhere beneath my twisted cloak.

I felt the scabbard. Digging my nails into its leather covering, I tried to tug it close enough to reach the hilt.

The whip bit into the nape of my neck. I yelled.

The mare's back was so sweat-slick that my thighs had little purchase. I clung to the yoke, my right hand straining behind my back to find—

There! My fingertips grazed the pommel of the knife.

The mare and her teammate lunged up the bank. The lurch swung me sideways, and my fingers slipped. Abandoning the knife, I clawed at the yoke to save myself.

The team leveled out at the top of the embankment. "Stop here, and you can get rid of him," Gemellus shrilled.

"Not yet," Malleus shouted. "Let's have some sport."

I tried to haul myself up on the mare's neck. My fingers skidded on the bloody yoke.

The wagons had passed, but people were scattered here and there on the road. A bent-backed old man turned from looking into the floodwaters, and his toothless mouth fell open at the sight of the horses churning toward him. "Run!" someone cried, but he had nowhere to go.

Just before the team would have trampled him, Malleus swung them away. An iron wheel-rim squealed against stone; then the wheel mounted the curb with a jounce. There was no thump of impact, just a thin cry and a splash.

"Take care! We might have gone in with him," Gemellus shouted.

Malleus laughed. "Your horse-killer friend sticks like a burr. Maybe this will rub him off."

He swerved toward a woman who fled down the road, dragging a child with such force that its bare feet flew off the ground. Her skirts tripped her, and both of them fell. With a shriek she threw herself on top of the child.

The horses jumped over her. As the chariot wheels lurched across her body, I lost my hold on the slimy yoke and sprawled head down across the mare, an arm's length from a maelstrom of flailing hooves.

"A quicker death than you merit," Gemellus crowed. "Farewell, Carinna."

I managed to crook an arm over the yoke and fumbled again for my knife. Somehow the twisting and wrenching had brought the scabbard closer. I tugged the blade free.

Kill the mare? But with the other horse at a gallop, her collapse would crash the chariot. I would probably die. Gemellus might survive.

"He has a knife," Gemellus shouted as I pulled my hand from under the wildly flapping cloak. "Malleus, do something!"

I slid the blade under the mare's chest strap, one of the two harnessing her to the yoke, and sliced through it. The two halves of the strap flapped free. The frightened mare tried to rear, but was dragged onward by her yokemate.

Gemellus yelped. Malleus cursed.

Half adrift, the yoke sawed forward and back beneath me. Again I had to hang on with both hands, nearly cutting my own cheek with the clenched knife. I twisted my head away and glimpsed, far behind, the woman being lifted to her feet by a man. Then something large and dark blocked my tear-blurred view: a horse. By Mithras's Dog, my stallion was chasing us! I shouted, "Spider, to me."

The team pounded on. The yoke ground back and forth. Cramp lanced my arms, so agonizingly that I thought they must part from my shoulders.

Ahead stood a monument marking the dedication of a humpbacked bridge that carried the road across a branch of the Tiber. The twin towers of the bridgehead flanked the roadway, as tall as pines.

"Call him again," Malleus yelled. "I admire a well-trained horse."

He meant to crush Spider against the stonework of the bridge. He had done it scores of times to rivals on the track.

"This is not the Circus," Gemellus cried. "I cannot rule if I am dead."

"I know what I am about," Malleus shouted.

I managed to pull myself up on the mare's neck and reached down to cut the girth strap. The whip shot past my ear like a striking snake, and the weighted end struck my hand. I screamed. It could not have hurt more if my fingers were crushed in a nutcracker.

And the knife was gone.

Spider was overtaking us. The reins flew loose around his sweat-rimed shoulders. I nearly wept in despair; I had no command to make him keep back.

The bridge monument flashed by. Malleus's fanged grin broadened.

Suddenly Gemellus leaned out of the chariot. Grasping Spider's rein, he thrust his foot up on the rail and tried to throw himself onto the stallion's back. Spider veered away in alarm, and Gemellus fell into the road. He rose onto hands and knees, then collapsed. I croaked out a laugh.

Malleus cursed again, his cutthroat playfulness gone. With a flick of the whip he aimed his team at the outer bridge tower. He would sheer away at the last moment, flinging me under the horses' hooves or down the steep embankment into the river.

"He . . . tried to poison . . . his family," I gasped. The words jolted out as the team thundered on, faster and faster. "Why are you . . . helping him?"

"Amusement," Malleus said.

A likeness of the river god scowled down from the bridge tower. His voice swelled louder, from a grumble into a deep-throated gobble.

I clutched the mare's neck, scrabbling with my free hand at her belly harness. With every hoofbeat another last dram of strength ebbed away.

"But this," Malleus said savagely, "is for my Fulgor."

His lash snapped to send the team into a lethal swerve. With a final desperate yank I hauled the girth strap out of its buckle and kicked the mare's flank. As I rode her out of the harness, her yokemate shied away from the flying straps and buckles.

And ran head-on into the bridge tower.

The chariot sheared off its axle and tore apart like paper. Malleus should have been flung headlong into the stonework. But by the time I had the trembling mare in hand, he had cut himself free of the reins and was hauling himself out of the wreckage. Crimson smeared his upper lip as he wiped his nose.

To walk away from that ruinous crash with only a nosebleed! He was Fortuna's favorite, and no mistake.

He glared up at me. And then something happened.

The Tiber gushing into its offshoot stream must have undercut the bank, although some might say the river god simply reached up for him. Whatever the reason, the wreckage shifted under Malleus's feet. He looked around in surprise as a wheel that had somehow stayed upright rolled down into the flood. I saw him bend to pick up something that might have been Gemellus's jewel casket. Then his feet went out from under him as the chariot debris slid farther down the muddy embankment.

He started to crawl up to the road, hugging the casket under one arm. Beside him, the axle and a shattered corner of the carriagework slipped down into the river. He grabbed at the shaft to pull himself up, but must have felt it start to give way.

He looked up at me again. "Help me," he said.

A moment later the rest of the wreckage slid down the slippery bank: the dead horse still harnessed to the shaft, the caved-in breastwork, the sharded floor of the chariot. And when the brown water had swallowed it all, he too was gone.

"Amuse yourself," I said.

I waited to see if he would surface, but only a few pieces of wood floated up. Some fragments whirled under the bridge. A smashed wheel spun off toward Ostia. But the broken curve of breastwork stayed where it was, bobbing in the flood, until I tired of watching it and turned the mare away to capture Spider and retrieve Gemellus.

CHAPTER 33

A GOOD DEATH

Gemellus killed himself that night, at the hour when the passage to death is shortest.

"Opened his veins," Blandus said, his deep voice hoarse with fatigue. "A few tears when he said farewell to his sister, but then he became calm." He looked around at those of us gathered in Lepidus's reception room. "A good death," he said, and sat down.

A few of the men gave heavy sighs. Lepidus's eyes closed for a moment. "And Caesar's response?"

"We do not know," Blandus said. "Titus Carinna says the Princeps is receiving no one." His gaze rested on the bloody marks, black now in the lamplight, that Malleus's whip had made on my forearm. He had not seen me since I rushed from the dining room in pursuit of Gemellus.

I rose stiffly. Every bone and muscle ached.

"Marcus Licinius, it is not yet daybreak," Lepidus said. "Stay until the streets are safe."

With a glance I acknowledged being addressed as a man of worth. "Thank you, Marcus Aemilius. But I must see to my family."

A piercing shriek burst from the back of the house. Word of Gemellus's death must have reached Livilla, sent here into Drusilla's keeping. Her fate had yet to be decided by her brother. Privately I thought the decision should be given to Agrippina and Claudius, who had managed to survive not just the poison but the treatment for it.

When I appeared in the atrium, Dio woke from his sitting doze on a bench. "Marcus," he began, then drew back as Lepidus came out of the room behind me.

"You understand, Marcus, why it must be so?" our patron said softly.

My silence forced him to go on: "Public confidence has been shaken. It is better for people to believe Gemellus was arrested before he could flee the city."

There were few witnesses to the contrary, just the Praetorian cavalry squadron that had trotted up while Gemellus still lay unconscious from his fall. Following my orders, the Praetorians had bundled him over a saddle to take him to Saxa. I saw them glance at the brown mare rolling loose in a hayfield and the country-folk gathering at the bridgehead down the road, but they were too excited by the importance of their captive to investigate.

"And you know Malleus's immense popularity," Lepidus continued. His eyelids flickered. Perhaps it was because of my stolid stare, or perhaps only tiredness. "What good would it do to give out that he was aiding Gemellus? Our task now is to bind the people together, not divide them further."

Gemellus's companions in the second chariot were probably not eager to talk. When the cavalry passed their capsized chariot on the road, both men and horses had disappeared. "Better for his death to be known as an accident," Lepidus said. "The harness broke while he was exercising his team near Vitinia. It could happen to anyone."

No doubt a few stable slaves would pay for their purported negligence. Gemellus's kitchen staff had already been put to death, as the poisoner Locusta would be when she was found.

I remembered the easy confidence with which Malleus had asked for my help just before the river took him. "Yes," I said, "it could happen to anyone."

"Though you will receive no public recognition of your valor, you have my gratitude." Lepidus held out his hand. "I am in your debt."

I hesitated, then drew back my sleeve to extend my own bandaged hand.

When my father entered from the street a few minutes later, so large was the crowd of attendants waiting for their masters that he did not notice Dio cloaking me. Father had been one of the witnesses to Gemellus's death, and when Lepidus drew closer and murmured to him, I heard him sigh. "At least he found enough honor in himself to spare us a trial."

Something drew his gaze to me. "Marcus, I thought you were at home," he said, as if I had crept out over the rooftops.

Without waiting for a response, he tucked his hand into the crook of Lepidus's arm as our patron told him, "Junius Silanus will not leave the city. He says he is innocent of any crime. . . ."

The Senate Leader, who had headed Gemellus's Senate faction, was to be charged with extortion in his former governorship. It was the same accusation laid against Silius's father thirteen years earlier. Why change a stratagem that worked?

Out in the street the fountain splashed merrily, spilling yet more water into a drain that was backing up elsewhere. Someone had brought me my other horse, but I was in no state to ride. Fortunately Father had arrived in our litter.

Dio said in a whisper, "Imagine what it will mean to have the patron indebted to you."

"Later, Dio," I said. "I am tired to death. Let us go home."

On the way I changed my mind. Dismissing the litter, I limped down the grassy lane behind the Temple of Victory, alone except for Dio. Ages earlier I had walked this path with Jason, arguing with myself about whether or not to leave Aurima to her troubles.

I stopped by the old well and sat on its rim. A great stillness lay over Rome. In the dark pasture before me, even the insects were silent. Moonlight glistened on water standing in the low parts of the city. Caligula might not be granted his wish for a record-breaking flood, but it hardly mattered; the first winter of his reign would be memorable enough for the historians. His own cousin, his adopted son, had tried to murder him. And had paid for it.

My chest felt tight and swollen; a giant hand squeezed my throat. I wanted to weep but could not.

A good death.

Publius had worn a chalk-white tunic. He looked at me several times during the sacrifice, and his calmness had quieted my rebellious fury. It was impossible to believe he intended to die.

Until he did.

He doubled over the knife and fell to his knees. Father cried out and dropped down beside him. He clutched Publius tightly to his breast and rocked from one knee to the other, his face hidden in my brother's dark hair.

I was told Mother had fainted, but did not remember it. I had no recollection of the mourning or the funeral. It was as if the scribe who wrote my life upon my heart had simply stopped recording.

I limped a little way down the hill, distancing myself from the past. There was no link between the two deaths . . . except, perhaps, Caligula.

He had not raged or reviled Gemellus when his adopted son was brought to him. He merely said, "Be dead by sunrise," and had the youth taken away.

I looked up into the night sky, to the Great and Little Bears guarding the North. How I longed to be there, out of this den of wolves. On the frontier, truth was clear, order well defined: friend or foe, commander or commanded, triumph or defeat. As Caesar's quaestor enmeshed in accounting for the imperial *fiscus*, what hope had I of claiming the honor denied me for thwarting Gemellus's grab for power?

Thinking of the North, I thought of Aurima. I had sent for her. And hoped she would come to me.

As she stepped out of the shadow of the peristyle the next afternoon, the bright copper crown of her head brushed the *tintinnabulum*. She checked herself at the chime of the little bells.

Mouth ajar, young Odo sidled past the dangling Priapus figure. His hand was curled around the hilt of his knife, but the rounding of his eyes as he glanced about him told me he saw no need to draw it. He did not know.

Aurima had kept to herself what had happened the night of the storm.

Amid vast relief I felt a twinge of curiosity. "Daughter of Ammisia," I said without rising. "You are welcome. Be comfortable." I gestured at a chair placed on the flagstones.

Sunlight bathed the sheltered corner of the garden where my couch stood. I reclined with an arm draped over the headrest, a pose that was painful but expressed composure.

Aurima looked around as her cousin was doing, taking in the statue of Narcissus gazing at his reflection, the tall papyrus in a water garden at the far end of the peristyle, the now-leafless almond trees that shaded the back of the house in summer. Her spine stiffened when she spied Ollius taking position by a nearby column, his staff planted on the floor.

"My mother's brother waits for me with Cotto and Segomo," she said bluntly, tilting her head toward the entrance of the house.

"Good," I told her. "That which is desirable should be protected."

She blinked. I did not give her time to respond. "Please, sit down. Wine? *Mulsum?* Something to eat?" I gestured at the plate of pear wedges and cheese slivers on the table between us.

Gathering her cloak around her, she sat. "Paris says that Gemellus wished to kill Caesar and his family, and you saved them. Is that true?"

Pleased by her knowledge, I shrugged as if the deed meant nothing. "Your Latin is improving, I see."

I might as well not have spoken. She went on, "Then Caesar must agree to receive me, if you ask it."

I had not really expected her to hoist me on a pedestal for saving the Princeps, but it was disagreeable to be tripped and pushed into the gutter. No doubt my face showed as much.

Aurima picked up my hand, no longer bandaged, and inspected the scrapes and nicks from Malleus's lash. A current ran through me, as violent as the river surging through its narrow race.

She spoke some Germanic, meaningless to me. "Plants to heal you," she explained, letting my hand go. "I do not know the names in Latin."

"Send him for them." I gestured at Odo, who rose warily from the edge of Narcissus's basin.

"He does not know them! It is not a man's thing."

"Use another excuse, then. I don't care. Just get rid of him."

Her face grew still, her eyes suspicious. I said, "Rufus, fetch my *pugio.*"

When the Thracian boy brought my knife belt, I drew the longknife from its sheath and laid it on the low table with the hilt toward Aurima. She looked at it, then at me.

"Odo," she said, "go and wait with your father."

And we were alone. I did not know, or at the moment care, where my own father was. The only sounds were those of slaves: scuffing their feet as they waited for my bidding, sweeping up leaves under the trees, talking indistinctly as they cleaned my mother's empty rooms.

Except for a new string of blue glass beads around her neck, Aurima was dressed much as usual: blue cloak, faded red *stola*, stained boots. But her face was less angular than before, the whites of her eyes snowy, her hair gleaming like polished copper.

"You look very fine. Is that a new necklace?"

She touched it. "A gift. From Heriberhto." A flush rose into her neck.

My mood chilled. Would she demand to be married to Harman's son? Was that the bargain she wished to strike for her silence?

Her gaze became a glower. How beautiful she was: the pride and temper of a leopard, and no more likely to be tamed. "You sent for me," she announced belligerently. "What do you want?"

I want you. But pride would not let me speak past the memory that she had offered herself to Heriberhto before she came to my room.

"About Caesar," she reminded me. "With so great a—an owing, is it not a small thing to ask him to receive me?"

"Not now," I said. "He is busy rooting out Gemellus's supporters."

"'Rooting out'?"

"Bringing to justice."

"This means they must . . . hmm, make vows to him?"

"Giving their oath is not enough. Many of them will die or be sent away."

"Why?"

"Because they cannot be trusted. Men do not always honor their oaths."

I reached for a pear wedge. She said, "Do you always honor your oath?"

I tossed the fruit back onto the plate. "I try to. And I rely on you honoring yours, priestess of Austro."

She lifted her chin. "Do not bother to say your big threats again."

"Big threats?"

"About killing my father. About a husband with skin like a dead man. Or no cattle."

"Any man would steal cattle for you, Aurima."

"Are you insulting me?"

"That is not an insult. 'Crawling louse' is an insult."

"You are a louse. A worm."

"Oh, be fair. You called me a snake before. Surely that is more accurate?"

She blushed at my smile. "What you did is not for laughing."

"Kiss me," I said. "I will make you laugh."

"What?"

"You do not know what *Basia me* means? You, whose cow has been stolen?"

"It is not for laughing!" she snapped.

I imagined her neatly plaited hair loosed and flowing over me, and an ache between my legs joined the many others. "The day grows cool. Shall I send for hot wine?"

"Is that why I have come from Bovillae? For you to make fun?"

"No," I said. "Aurima, I did not know of your mother's death. Though it is too late for justice under the law, the Roman people owe you a blood debt. I will ask Caesar to pay it."

Surprise and suspicion chased each other in her eyes. "Why do you say this now?"

"I have just learned it. And I want you to know that I will not tolerate it."

Aurima sprang to her feet and strode away. She stopped by the basin and stared down into the water.

It would be folly to talk to her of freedom, for Caligula might refuse. But if he did allow her to return to the Mark, it must not be as Rome's enemy.

I sat up, stifling a hiss of pain. "Aurima . . . Caesar plans to take fifty legions with him to campaign in the North. The Divine Julius subdued Gaul and the Rhineland with only ten."

She turned her head sharply. Freckles blazed across her pale cheeks like a spray of embers.

"You and your father must choose. If he rebels again, our army will crush your people utterly. Every man, woman, and child will be killed or sold into slavery."

Still no response. I went on, "Or you may make peace with us and remain free. This is what I desire, as I hope you do."

"For now, I go back to Bovillae," she said. She strode toward the entrance to the peristyle.

I raised my voice. "Wait. Will you honor your oath?"

She paused. "I threw the bones for you," she said. "Many times."

I sighed, impatient with tales of fortunes cast.

Her gaze fell to a gap between the flagstones where a straggly dog violet still bloomed. "I saw water that runs. And behind it, darkness."

That jolted me. I, who had disparaged prophecies to everyone else, wondered if she had seen that I might die in pursuing Gemellus. No, of course not. The flooding Tiber must simply have suggested the image to her.

Her dark-gold lashes lifted, and she looked at me. "Then I saw a spirit that stood before the darkness, and would not let you pass."

With this revelation, she stalked out. I recovered my wits in time to have Ollius follow her. Even though her own men accompanied her, he might be useful if they encountered hostility in the flooded city. And I wanted to know if she really did leave for Bovillae.

A spirit stood before the darkness.

Had my brother's spirit protected me from falling under the hooves of Malleus's team?

It defied reason. Moreover, if spirits could indeed return to this world, it must not be easy or there would be millions of them around. Why would Publius have made such an effort to rescue his feckless little brother?

Ridiculous. I was making far too much of a superstitious girl's imaginings.

"Marcus," said Dio's voice. "I did not wish to interrupt you, but . . ."

I opened my eyes. His arms were full of message tablets and scrolls. "Your sister worries," he said, depositing them on Aurima's chair.

Nina had already congratulated me on my discovery of Gemellus's plot. Now, having belatedly heard of my bloody return, she wanted to know if enraged supporters of Gemellus's had waylaid me.

Poor Nina: distressed first by Jason's death, then by the attack on her stepson Galerianus, and now by injuries to her meddlesome brother. "Tell her I had a riding accident," I said to Dio.

"Are you sure?" he asked. We both knew she did not like to be deceived.

"Just do as I say."

He tucked his hands against his waist and bowed. "It will be so, master."

"And leave off the sarcasm," I said. He had been unnerved by my strained relations with Caligula, until hearing Lepidus declare himself indebted to me. I liked him better for his anxiety, which said he had truly cast his lot with mine.

After he went off, I looked at what he had brought. Small gifts and messages: more offerings of gratitude for saving the Princeps' life. Nothing from Silius. That was good. I wanted my wrath at his betrayal to grow unhindered.

Stabs of pain made me wince as I went through the missives. I wished I had Aurima's salve or potion, whatever it was.

Lying back on the couch, I echoed our conversation to myself. Had she believed me about the blood debt Rome would finally pay? Would she dismiss my attempt to moderate her hatred of us? O Mithras, would she keep quiet about her deflowering until I could persuade Caligula to release her from hostageship?

Rufus came into the peristyle and drew a small pot sealed with pine gum from his bloused tunic. I said, "Where did you get that?"

He drew an imaginary braid on himself and made a summoning gesture. "So you went with her?"

He nodded. "Are you bewitched too?" I asked wearily.

He tapped the pot and pointed to his scabbed wrist, then to his open mouth. I hoped the salve was effective. He could not yet eat solid food.

He looked expectantly at me. "Later," I said. "Is Phormio still asleep?"

Another nod. I sat for a while longer, summoning my strength. How sweet it would be to forget about death and betrayal, to tease and pleasure someone I loved. Deluded about spirits Aurima might be, but I wished she had not left.

When Father returned, I was upstairs tallying the weapons that had been replaced in the armory. Leaning over the railing, I watched him enter the lamplit atrium with his usual escort. Our eyes met.

He shed his heavy mantle into Turtle's hands. "Still falling," he said heartily to the house steward. "The river is down two feet since yesterday."

"Praise the gods," Dio muttered beside me, casting his eyes to the rafters.

I shook my head. "Flooding keeps down mobs." Father went into his office. Slaves scurried around to stoke the brazier, to bring food and drink and a warmed lap robe, while his retinue went their several ways. "See what news there is," I said, and turned back to inspect the sharpened swords.

Dio found me later in Publius's old bedroom, where a couple of servants were carrying out my brother's bed. "We have had enough of sentiment," I said to the reproach in his face. "From now on, this will be my office. You can find me suitable furniture tomorrow." I sat on the clothes chest. "What did you learn?"

He took a deep breath. "The Palatine is closed to all who do not live or have business here. The Princeps has not been seen in public for two days, nor in private since yesterday." He blinked tiredly. "Crowds are shouting in the Forum, and soldiers stand guard in front of the Senate House."

I said, "Caligula must show himself. People must know he is in charge."

"So the master wished to advise him. But Caesar will speak to no one."

"Not even his sisters?" That was strange. If he was sorrowing over Gemellus's treachery, why not let it be seen? No one would fault him for it.

"People are greatly troubled. Astivus heard men in a wineshop saying, 'How did we so anger the gods?' And 'What will become of us?' Some wanted the Senate to consult the Sibylline Books."

"As serious as that?"

He continued, "The funeral has been set for the day after tomorrow. That seems wise, does it not, to keep passions from building?"

It was an indecently short period of mourning for someone of Gemellus's rank, but perhaps not for a failed parricide. "The sooner, the better," I agreed.

"I hear the Greens will spend seven million on it."

"Will they?" My response was quick, but there must have been enough of a hesitation to be noticed by my sharp-witted secretary.

"And Gemellus's funeral will be a day later," he said smoothly. Had he been Phormio, we might have joked about the misunderstanding, but I doubted I would ever be so easy with my father's by-blow. He went on about the funeral arrangements, and I had to tell him I did not care.

A vast procession flowed from the Circus Maximus toward the pyre in the Field of Mars. Empty chariots splashed through puddles behind Malleus's racehorses, their bridles sprigged with cypress. Flanked by his green-tunicked teammates, the charioteer's body was a veiled shape on his bier, strewn with flowers and tokens thrown by the grieving crowd. I did not know how they had retrieved him, but the story of a fatal accident had apparently been accepted. Few knew he had died helping Gemellus to flee.

"I felt sure Caesar would come forth to honor him," said one of the men who had gathered with Father and me to watch from a Palatine terrace. "At the last races, he said he had never seen a finer charioteer."

With his eyes on the funeral parade Father said, "The Princeps is thinking of the people. He did not want their love for him to color their grief for Malleus."

This was the purest fable. The truth was that Caligula had closeted himself in the House of Augustus and refused to emerge. Meanwhile, charges had been levied against a score of officials and private citizens, besides the Senate Leader. Galerianus was implicated. I did not know about Silius.

In the street below, wild-haired women bloodied their cheeks, screaming like maenads. Men wept and groaned aloud. The agonized howls might have been from souls condemned to eternal darkness. "You could not pay professional mourners to keen so fervently," someone murmured.

"I doubt it will be bettered tomorrow morning," said a stout Senator. He added pointedly to Father, "Will we see Caesar then?"

"I do not know who will accompany Gemellus's bier," Father said.

The others grew somber. To die unmourned by friends, colleagues, relatives, and clients is not to have lived.

The shrieks and wails grew more distant as we walked home. Father half closed his eyes against the morning sun. "The greatest service Caesar's friends can do him now is to show they can be trusted." He stopped. "You above all. He needs to know you will not abandon him."

I said, "Father, I will not promise that."

"You must try, Marcus. Or you will become the man who destroyed his trust in Gemellus, and he will hate you."

Had I not done enough? Caligula had accused me of bad faith, of turning him against the adopted son he himself had doubted. How could I now hope to become his faithful friend . . . his Publius?

Father said, "Rescue him." Not a command this time, but a plea.

The cries of the mourners were as faint now as the shrieking of crows in a faraway field. Jaw set, I left his side and crossed the street to the House of Tiberius.

Cypress hung on the double portals of the house, black in the dull morning light. Fragrant smoke swirled around the atrium. Wet-eyed women backed away as I approached the bier where Gemellus lay, feet toward the door.

Death had not disfigured him. Except for the bruise that marked his fall from the chariot, his calm young face was as white as the purest Luna marble.

Farewell, Carinna, he had cried as I clung by my fingernails to a galloping horse.

Where was his soul now? How had Mithras judged him for attempting to poison all his kin, and goading Malleus to kill me?

I touched his cheek with a battered finger. "Farewell, Gemellus," I said.

Agrippina was having the baskets and parcels repacked that had been so recently unloaded. "He told me I would be safer here," she said from her armchair, as maids and manservants rushed about. "I would rather eat sardines and black bread in Pyrgi than banquet in Rome on larks' tongues and poison."

"Caesar did not want to see the danger," I said quietly. The strum of a lyre hid our conversation from her attendants.

"Indeed." Her smile thinned. "If you had announced the taint in our food a few minutes sooner, it would have spared me much wretchedness."

"It has cured Claudius of gluttony, I hope."

Her light-blue eyes narrowed. Then she smiled again, stroking the pearls that cascaded to the cleft between her heavy breasts. "Have you thought over my appeal to protect my son?"

"Naturally I favor Lepidus's succession as Princeps," I said. "With your son as his heir, perhaps."

"Will you endorse Lepidus as regent until my son comes of age?"

"This is not some sand-blown little princedom, Agrippina. You cannot give Rome to an infant like an ivory rattle."

"We shall see." She lifted a hand to call over her steward.

I interrupted the gesture by closing my fingers around hers. "Do you fear your brother will not be granted a long life?"

She gave me a look of such bland innocence that I knew I was right to be suspicious. "Do you, Marcus Licinius?"

"When I tried to see him just now, his chamberlain said it was impossible. And I noticed a cubicle full of undelivered messages."

Agrippina beckoned to the steward. "I will have Gemellus's jewels for my husband," she told him.

"I fear they have been lost," I said. "Will you take me to see Caesar?"

She dismissed the man. A moment later she said, "He talks to the dead."

My fears were realized: Caligula was at Hades' gate himself. Now I would have to do all I could to help Lepidus succeed him.

Agrippina laid her hands, one atop the other, over her cumbersome belly. "What do you want of him?"

I was silent, unwilling for her to weave my desires into her own web. Her finely drawn brows rose. "Why so shy?" she prodded. "Are we not allies now?"

"I mean him no harm," I said.

"I would suppose no differently," she said. Allowing me to lift her clumsily to her feet, she led me to Caligula's lair.

CHAPTER 34

PATHS OF REVENGE

Caligula's moon-faced chamberlain tried to bar the way. Agrippina snapped, "Stand back, Helicon; this is not Thermopylae. Brother," she called through the door panels, "young Carinna wishes to ask you a favor."

There was no response. She pushed the door open.

Shutters had been closed over the window and cushions stuffed against them. By the light from the open door I saw a rat's nest of covers on a couch and a table littered with plates. The room stank of an unemptied chamber pot.

"Caligula?" Agrippina sounded less sure of herself. She took a step forward. "Where are you?"

"Go away," croaked a disembodied voice.

"Close the door, Carinna. Quickly," she said. "Then unlatch the shutters."

A muffled howl came from the covers. I shut out the curious stares of those outside and made my way in darkness to the window. As cushion after cushion tumbled away, letting daylight leak through the shutters, the voice shrieked, "Stop."

I unfastened the shutters and pushed them wide. Cold air flooded in, and sallow winter light.

He cursed at his sister when she pulled off his covers. "Go away!" He was naked, reeking of urine, his hair matted and face furred like a beast's. "Douse the light! Leave me!"

"Caligula," she said sharply, and struck his cheek with her open hand.

He froze, mouth agape.

"I am here, darling." Agrippina sat beside him, took his face in her palms, and kissed his forehead.

340

His breath caught, and a tear rolled down the side of his nose. "I tried," he whispered. "I tried to be brave. . . ."

She cradled his head against her gravid belly and caressed his fair hair. "Poor boy, I know."

"Don't tell Papa."

"Hush, hush. I will not tell him."

He sobbed into her lap, a muffled retching of deep despair. Agrippina unfastened the pin at her shoulder, pulled down her gown, and turned his face to her breast. When he began to suckle her, something flashed into her eyes too quickly to be read. Then her face smoothed, and she murmured, "Make them fear you, my love. Then no one will hurt you ever again."

Shock and fascination had kept me rooted where I stood, but my twitch of surprise jostled the table. An overturned cup rolled amid spilled wine, stale bread, congealed stew, an untouched lobster shriveled in its cloven shell. And the forequarters of a mouse, guts gleaming in a pool of blood.

Pink saliva trailed from the corner of Caligula's mouth to Agrippina's nipple. His eyes were pale and blurred, as if made of flawed glass.

"Sleep now," she said, kissing his drowsy face. "Sleep, my dear." And as his eyes closed, she whispered, "When your father is long forgotten, you will be remembered."

He did not wake while slaves carried him from the room, sponged him clean, and laid him in a bed of scented linens and thick quilts. Only then did Agrippina relax her vigilance and sink down upon a chair. His physicians came rushing in, and other functionaries I did not know.

My message brought Lepidus hurrying to the Palace. He glanced past me at the attendants buzzing in whispers around Caligula's bed. "Did he say nothing of his will? Of an heir?"

"He said nothing sensible." I was still dazed with horror and revulsion. Discovering treachery had done more than unnerve Caligula; it had driven him mad. "I must inform my father."

"Stay, Marcus, while I speak with Agrippina."

I leaned on the rail of a balcony above a garden, breathing deeply to dispel the remembered stench of the upper room. Had I really thought to assure this lunatic of my loyalty? I would have better luck talking to my horse.

Agrippina spoke inside the room, her words inaudible. Lepidus must have been nearer the balcony door, for his response was distinct: "Dear Agrippina, his senses have deserted him. I must inform the Senate." She spoke again, and he said, "If he does not appear at Gemellus's funeral tomorrow, they will think he is dying or dead."

I moved farther from the doorway, having no appetite for their intrigues. When Lepidus became Princeps, I wanted to be able to respect him.

The physicians suggested bathing Caligula in cold water, making him breathe spirits of brimstone, or suffusing him in smoke from the burned heart of a sacrificial calf. Agrippina silenced them. "Let him sleep."

Drusilla's voice rang inside the room, shrill with worry. A few moments later Lepidus joined me on the balcony. He said, "Will you stand watch on him?"

"Ask my father to do it." Everyone knew Father had nothing to gain if Caligula died, and much to lose.

"The fewer who know of this, the better," Lepidus said. Meaning he did not plan to inform my father, his own ally. He turned away from the light so no one could read the words his lips shaped. "Look after my interests," he murmured.

My knuckles tightened on the railing. "What do you mean?"

"You know what I mean." He did not pretend to be shocked. "I must know by daybreak whether he recovers. Do you understand?"

If Caligula was still out of his mind, a hastily convened Senate could transfer his powers to Lepidus. I said, "If he has not stirred by cockcrow, I will wake him."

He was pleased by my decisiveness. "Have a slave do it, in case there is a malign spirit in him."

Lepidus took Drusilla with him when he left. Without her wails the room quieted. The doctors stood impotently around Caligula's bedside, arguing with each other in muttered Greek. Agrippina dismissed everyone else and settled heavily in her chair.

I looked at the Princeps of Rome, heir to greatness. It was intolerable that a man for whose sake so many had suffered was made of such pitiful stuff. He had never merited the principate. Those who granted it to him had wrought a calamity that could destroy peace in the world.

How easy it would be to take a pillow and smother him in his sleep. *Look after my interests.* Was that what Lepidus expected, despite his denial?

⇥⇤

Julia Livilla raised her eyes from her brother's face. "Every man has a price. What is yours?"

There was no trace of the grippe in her voice. In the lamp glow that lit the hushed room, her eyes were clear and her nostrils as delicately pink as rose petals. I said, "Go back to your room, Livilla. Your treachery is still unpunished."

"I think you should ask Lepidus to adopt you as his heir." She picked up a cushion and pressed it experimentally against her breast. "To inherit the imperium and great wealth together: that would be a just reward for having eased his path to the principate."

"Be still," I hissed, glancing around. Agrippina had disappeared, but the three doctors conferring by the balcony door were looking at us curiously.

"Do not pretend you have not thought of it. I can see it in your eyes."

"Get out," I said.

"I am his sister, and I will stay with him if I wish." Livilla spied the dice Dio and I had been tossing on a folded cloak. "Are you gambling on his survival? Did your brother bet for or against it, Dio?"

Dio's expression of deference froze. I said sharply, "Do not call me his brother. I am his master."

"You are both whelps of a mad dog." Sweeping her skirts out of the way, she perched on the stool where Dio had sat. "Gamble with me, Marcus." She clawed up the bone dice.

"Leave at once, Julia Livilla, or I will have you removed by force." My voice was too loud. Caligula gave a muffled groan, then subsided into sleep again.

"If you try," she said in a vicious whisper, "I will say I overheard you talk about smothering him."

I glared at her. She stared back, her eyes as blue as night descending.

I sat down. Livilla smirked. The bitter creases around her mouth accorded ill with the girlish style of her dark hair, swagged low on her brow from a middle part and crimped on either side into a drawn-back tumble of curls. Against the pallor of her neck I saw a familiar sway of gold, green, and russet.

She jiggled the dice. "What shall we play for?"

"Your earrings," I said.

With her free hand she touched one of the earrings Publius had given her. "I will not venture them."

I said, "The earrings or nothing."

She hurled the dice at me. They bounced off my chest and fell to the carpet.

Caligula muttered, and his eyes moved restlessly under the shells of his lids. One of his hands emerged, gripping the edge of the covers. Augustus's phoenix ring clung to his forefinger, the great seal outlined in dark dirty threads.

"He will wake soon," Livilla breathed. "Blessed be the Great Mother."

"Why so grateful? You meant Gemellus to murder him."

"I would have become a Princeps' wife," she said, as if I were a lackwit.

The shutters thumped in a rising wind. Outside the aura of the bedside lamp, darkness hung in corners of the room.

"Hark," Livilla said. "I will put up the earrings." She unhooked one of the glittering pendants and laid it on the table.

"Against what?"

"If I win, you will come to my bed."

I snorted.

"You are afraid."

"I am uninterested." I rose and went to Caligula's side. His brows were clenched, and the skin around his closed eyes had pinched into creases. Was Publius's spirit with him? Did he face Mithras now, or Osiris, or whatever judge would weigh his soul?

"Uninterested? Why?" Livilla's voice hardened. "Are you spent from frolicking with Torquata and Silius?"

Caligula mumbled again. I was glad of the distraction. "Listen: he talks to frogs."

Livilla thrust the earring at me. "Help me with this." She tipped her head sideways, drawing the curls away from her ear. It was an exquisite little ear, its arcs and whorls gilded with lamplight. Touching her lightly, I slipped the hook through the small piercing in her earlobe—a task I had performed for other women, often a spur to sexual excitement.

She jerked her head away so that the tiny pearls flew around the emerald and carnelian trefoil. "'*Rana*' was his private name for your brother. Did you have your head in a wine jar all the time you were growing up?"

There was much I could have accused her of in return, but a fuss would have drawn the physicians' attention. I picked up a poker and stirred the nearest brazier until the embers glowed a sullen gold.

"Ah, my Publius . . ." Her voice sank until only I could hear it. "I desired him to madness. I wrote love ditties about his dark-whiskered thighs, his stalwart shaft." She sighed. "He would kiss my forehead and say, 'In good time, dearest.'"

I snorted again. She said defensively, "He did not want to anger Uncle."

How I had envied my brother, betrothed to such a pretty and lighthearted girl. Pretentious literary readings made her yawn, but she was always first to relay a new satire or mordant graffito. She knew racing odds better than I did, and would stop her litter bearers in the street to bet on two dogs fighting.

The shutters rattled again. Cold air darted through the cracks, fluttering the lamp flames. I gave her a hard stare. "But you could not save him, either."

Livilla rolled the three dice over so that sixes were uppermost. The Venus throw. "When I heard he was accused of treason, I begged Uncle to forgive him. I sobbed and wailed. The old vulture said, 'I will find you a better husband, child.'"

I tipped my head toward Caligula. "And what did he do?"

"Him?" Contempt soured her voice. "He cowered out of Uncle's sight." She stacked the dice carefully, one atop another. "'Pinilla tried to help me slip off the island—I had friends in Baiae who could help me get to Rome to see him. But Uncle's guards took me from the boat."

This touched me unexpectedly, but I was too bitter to admit it. "And when you heard he had killed himself, whose bed did you jump into?"

She shifted each of the dice so the stack was off-center, then looked up with a smile I did not understand. "Do you really want to know?"

"Never mind." I sat down and reached for the dice.

She brushed my hand away. Without either of us touching them, they fell and scattered across the cloak. A single tiny circle showed on the first die; the same on the second; two pips on the third.

345

Livilla tipped over the last one to make Dogs, the lowest throw. "When I heard," she said softly to the dice, "I ran to the place where he used to sit with my brother, and stood wanting to leap out over the sea. . . ."

"But you did not."

"I did not." Her head lifted. "After I came back from the cliffs, I mourned so meekly that Uncle praised my fortitude." Her dark-blue eyes looked into mine. "And that night I went to Caligula's room."

I jerked back. "Very well," I said after a moment. "I insulted you; you mock me. Let us stop there."

Her eyes widened. "But I am not mocking you. I got into his bed and told him I needed to be consoled. . . . Truly, I did. And I will tell you a secret." She leaned closer and whispered, "I still do it, whenever he becomes too prideful." Her breath stirred the hair in front of my ear. "Because he likes it. And then he hates himself."

Struck dumb, I glanced at Caligula. He slept with his head to one side, his long scrawny neck as graceless as a plucked fowl's.

Livilla's melancholy expression transformed into a lioness's grin. "A woman has few paths of revenge open to her, Marcus." She drew back. "Now it is your turn. Tell me a secret."

Hers was so savage a vengeance that I could hardly stomach it. "Is that why . . ."

"Why I grant a husband's rights to anyone I like? Only fitting, is it not, since I could not give them to the man I loved?"

"Who do you intend to spite? Tiberius is dead."

She tipped her chin toward Caligula. "But he is not. Nor you."

"Then you did well," I said, very low. Time after time, news of her behavior had caused me helpless anger and humiliation.

"So do not judge me—you who shamed your family, drinking and gambling and whoring while your brother faced death."

I felt the skin tighten across my cheekbones. She had wrenched on an arrow whose barb festered deep in my flesh. Livilla nodded, pleased with the effect of her words.

"He slept," a splintery voice said.

The physicians perked up and rushed forward, babbling. Livilla leaped to her feet, commanding them to be quiet.

Caligula's mouth unsealed, hinged with dried spittle. "After waiting in vain for a pardon from Capri, the noble Senator Carinna came home before daylight to find his younger son asleep." His crusted eyes cracked open. "His brother's last night above the earth. And he slept."

Livilla said to me, "You left him alone on his last night?"

I had no answer. I had never had an answer, only excuses.

Caligula's gray reptilian tongue slid out to lick his lips. "Lilla, I am thirsty."

She drew a deep breath, calming herself. "I rejoice to see you back from the dead, brother."

His slave hastened to him with a cup. He gulped from it, then pushed it away. "Where is everyone?" He threw back the covers and struggled to sit. "Carinna, help me up."

He let me pull him to his feet, almost a dead weight, then clenched his hand on my forearm. "Has Lepidus deposed me?" His terrible breath was like a fist in my face. "Am I a prisoner?"

"You have been unwell," I said hoarsely. "But you are Princeps still."

"Open the shutters." He shambled toward them, thin-shanked as a colt beneath the droop of his wrinkled tunic.

I unlatched the tall shutters and pushed them apart. As he went onto the balcony, the wind caught his tunic. Unbelted, it billowed and flapped around him.

Someone yelled down in the garden. And all at once there was tumult: screams of surprise and ecstasy, shouts of thanksgiving and praise. Hands lifted like white flowers in a field of darkness, summoning the gods' blessings on him.

"I am back from the underworld," Caligula said. "I am back because I cannot die." He gave me a smile of great sweetness, then lifted his tunic and pissed on the pale faces below.

It seemed a long time since I had watched Malleus's funeral procession that morning. I hoped the sharp night air would relieve the tumult in my head, but on the way home I could not stop thinking of the creature Agrippina and I had found kenneled in the dark. If some vengeful spirit or evil force had possessed him then, how could he have been so astonishingly lucid when I left?

Rufus's light shone on a group striding toward us: a torch carrier, guards, and bearers transporting a closed litter. Ollius recognized the attendants. "Well met! Marcus, it's Lady Nina."

Nina thrust her head out between the curtains. "Gods be thanked!" Her litter halted beside me. "How is Caligula?"

"Better than ever," I said. "He has declared himself immortal."

"That is an exceedingly impious joke, brother."

"It is no joke, but you are welcome to laugh at the absurdity of it. Were you looking for me at home?"

"I went to visit Phormio. What does this mean, Marcus? Are we to sacrifice to him? Will he build a shrine to himself?"

Her voice rang in the narrow street. "Not so loud," I cautioned. "Agrippina may persuade him to keep it to himself."

Nina sank back against the cushions of her litter. "'Pinilla is always sensible. She will make him see reason."

I grimaced, remembering Agrippina's advice—*Make them fear you*—and Livilla's incestuous revenge upon her brother. With those two hovering over him, Caligula had no need of Furies.

Nina did not notice. "He still loves you, does he not? Ask him to drop the charge against my stepson. Tell him Galerianus acted foolishly, without malice."

Remembering very well how Galerianus had acted, I changed the subject. "Are you well? I hear you are bored and temperamental."

"Only because I must avoid excitement to protect my husband's child." She spread her hand tenderly over her belly.

The simplicity with which she said this lifted a weight off me. It was Varro's child. Not Pertinax's.

Unfortunately, my twin recognized what I was thinking. "Marcus, I told you I was chaste!" I stepped back warily, but the only weapons within her reach were the litter's cushions. "While you, you faithless lout, think it perfectly fine to go tomcatting hither and yon." She fixed me with a glinting eye. "Junia Torquata is boasting all over Rome about her two lovers. She calls them Castor and Pollux, but any nitwit can guess who they are."

"That is finished," I said.

"Good. What will you give me not to tell Father?"

I stared at her. She looked back, her dark eyes guileless.

"I will try to save Galerianus," I said at last.

"Thank you, brother dear." Nina gave me a contented smile. "Come and see me soon—before Caligula moves into the Capitoline temple with Jupiter."

Father gargled long and loud like a badly plumbed drain, then spat into a basin. He wiped his mouth with a towel. "I discussed that with him some time ago. A claim of godhood can be a political device to awe enemies and provincials. So if word escapes, it will do no harm." He peered into a mirror, contorting his mouth into grotesque shapes. "And it is a clever way . . . to set himself above his rivals."

I said, "This was not a political device. I saw him lying in filth; he hid from the light like a maggot. He suckled from his sister as if she were his mother."

Father filled his lungs and enunciated a nonsense rhyme full of fricatives and plosives and other speech sounds.

I was almost too tired to stand. "You told him, did you not, that you found me asleep in the atrium on the morning Publius died?"

He paused for a moment. Then a slave held up a splinter of wood with its tip afire and he sucked in his breath, his chest expanding slowly, until the bright spark of flame died in a tiny swirl of smoke. "Do you practice your voice exercises daily, Marcus?" he said in a slow, controlled exhalation.

"If you wanted me to become his friend, why tell him something that shames me?" I feared that Caligula had welcomed me precisely because I had stupefied myself with drink that night. Because I seemed as craven as himself.

"Start training your lungs now, and they will not fail you in public later. There is nothing more ludicrous than when a man rises to speak on some important issue, a man whose opinion should be weighed, and from his lips comes the squeak of a mouse or the honk of a goose."

He began to project his voice, speaking first in a normal tone, then with greater resonance until he could be heard throughout the house. I shifted my weight, trying to ignore the allure of the bed against the wall. "You refuse to answer me?"

He paused and sighed. "Listen, then. After Germanicus died, Vipsania Agrippina was sure one or the other of the two older boys would succeed Tiberius. She had no time to spare for Caligula."

I nodded. It was a story I had grown up with.

"Although I offered to raise him with my own sons, she sent him to his great-grandmother, the Augusta. Move; you are in the light." He bent toward the tray with its assortment of nostrums. "I saw his room once. He was then, I think, about nine years old." He chose a blue glass bottle. Turtle bowed and backed away with the tray to mix the concoction. "In the floor, under loose tiles, he kept an earring of his mother's, a lock of her hair, and a little phial of her perfume."

A pathetic hoard. "He showed it to you?"

"His *paedagogus* did. The man had told your brother's personal slave that when Caligula misbehaved, the Augusta punished him by putting him down the furnace hole for a day or two at a time."

I had once gone down the furnace hole in this house with Jason, who fed the fire in winter. It was early summer so the maw of the hypocaust was dark and silent, but it had been all I could do to hide my unease as I crawled after him through the smoke-blackened maze of stumpy columns that held up the floor. I laughed afterward, to seem as indifferent as he was, but I never went down there again.

Father said, "Of course I had him taken back to his mother at once."

"What has this to do with Caligula now?"

"Use your head, Marcus. A boy may become a man without outgrowing what he has learned." Taking a cup from Turtle, he inhaled its vapor deeply, then tossed back the contents in a gulp. He belched and uttered a noisy "Aahh."

The pitch-dark room. The fear and isolation. The loss of control. "He was punishing himself. For what? For the death of Gemellus, who tried to kill him?"

"Go away and think about it." He snapped his fingers. A girl came in: one of the cook's daughters, docile as a cow. She took off her tunic and got onto the bed on her hands and knees.

"But still . . . you let him think I was indifferent to Publius dying." I was distracted by the girl's breasts, hanging full and ripe.

He gave me a look of irritation. "Good night," he said, and climbed up behind her.

CHAPTER 35

A DREAM OF EAGLES

Not long after Gemellus's death, the Senate Leader, Junius Silanus, killed himself. Shivering in dread, many of those who had backed the Tiberian cause against Germanicus's sons besought Father, and me too, to save them from a Special Cohort officer's knock upon the door.

Father spoke calmly to them. There was nothing to fear, he said. The Senate Leader, knowing he had failed to quell seditious talk within his party, had simply chosen not to live with dishonor. Still, more than a few of the frightened men found excuses to leave Rome for a villa at Tibur or farm in Campania. Father told me privately to keep away from Caligula until the pain of Gemellus's betrayal eased, a reversal of his earlier advice that suited me well. In the meantime I refused to bear witness against Galerianus, so he went unscathed. Of Silius I said nothing.

The rains ceased and the river continued to fall, but the nauseating stench of backed-up sewers permeated the whole city. The lowest part of the Forum was a lakelet of filth. An army of public slaves toiled around its shores, scrubbing the bases of monuments, buildings, and arches. Flies buzzed and crawled everywhere. As if that were not affliction enough, smoke from household charcoal fires condensed into a malodorous winter fog that shrank visibility to a couple of horse-lengths. We became a city of wraiths groping from one landmark to another, noses muffled in clothing or rags, avoiding collisions by listening for other people coughing. I was glad Aurima breathed the cleaner air of Bovillae.

These conditions did not stop the Plebeian Games, which are given during the first half of November. The mob packed the amphitheater, seeking gladiators' blood as a distraction from muck and murder. Drusilla, leaning frailly upon her brother's arm, accompanied him in public. Julia Livilla was seen nowhere. Nor was there any talk of immortality, so Agrippina must have prevailed.

When I recovered from the racking Malleus had given me, I spent some days in the company of Caligula's finance secretary, who supervised the currency and the mints, the collection of taxes and duties, and the management of imperial property. It was this freedman to whom, as Caesar's quaestor, I would represent the Princeps' interests.

On the afternoon of the third day of this, I asked to speak privately with my father. He was in his office, talking with his chief secretary while a scribe took notes.

Father signaled them to leave. "I am writing to Calvisius Sabinus about the death of Gemellus," he explained, "urging him to have sacrifices of thanksgiving performed in all the temples of Pannonia."

How ironic that the governor had been so desperate to affirm his loyalty to Tiberius that he had denied justice to Ingiomar. Now, five years later, it was his allegiance to Caligula that was thought lacking.

I sat down. "I think it soft not to decree *damnatio memoriae*."

"Caesar asks only for nothing new to be done in memory of Gemellus."

I shook my head. In his place I would have ordered my traitorous son's face obliterated from paintings, his head struck off statues, and his name erased from public monuments and coins. But with luck, Caligula's weak-mindedness would soon be of little concern to me. I cleared my throat. "Father, I need your advice on a matter of importance to our family."

His gaze sharpened.

I had prepared the opening with care. "I know Publius wished to bring greater honor to our family and to you. Instead, he imperiled the last of Germanicus's sons." I heaved a breath. "Even though he paid with his own death, it diminished the luster you and our ancestors have brought to our name."

An almost unnoticeable nod invited me to continue.

I swallowed. "I want to restore what we have lost, and more. To accomplish a task that will gladden the Senate and the people, inspire the legions, and bring glory to Rome. And to Caesar," I added belatedly.

Father said, "You want to find the lost Eagle."

Had I been so transparent? I said, "I propose to finish the coming year of my quaestorship. Then I want to ride north to seek the Eagle. I will bring it home before the campaign begins. It will become our talisman of victory. Of vengeance."

I sprang up, unable to sit still any longer. "It is just what Caligula wants: a way to prove he is as clever and lucky as his father. He will begin his great campaign with the Senate, the people, and the legions acclaiming him as the avenger of our honor."

"When would you leave?" My father's voice was noncommittal.

"In spring, as soon as the Alpine passes are open. I know how to plan the mission. Men, animals, supplies, routes. It will be a small group, to travel faster and avoid upsetting the locals. I know tribespeople who will guide me."

I paused, but he did not speak. "Father, now is the time to bring back the Eagle. For Caligula, for Rome. For the family." I shot my last arrow: "If I do this, surely your name will advance on the list of consular candidates."

"You forget two things," he said. "You may not succeed. Even if you do, there can be only one triumphant hero in Rome. And his name is not Carinna."

"Will I not be known as Caesar's quaestor? If he sends me north, all the honor and glory will be his."

My father made a sound in his throat. His eyes went far away. Hoping I had said enough, I dropped into my chair again.

At last he sighed. "If I had not held you in my hands when you were newborn, wrinkled and red and wet behind the ears"—he shook his head—"I would have thought you foaled by one of Diomedes' man-eating mares."

He did not smile, but it was not exactly anger. I grew hopeful.

He went on, "Did you know that while you were on your journey home, I was ill with an inflammation of the lungs? Very ill."

The slaves had spoken of his sickness, but I—being young and healthy—had made little of it. "I thought it was only the grippe," I said weakly.

"When I began to recover, I asked your mother not to tell you about it."

So that was why she had been in Rome. Not to greet me after all.

"While I lay in my fever, with every cough a dagger in my chest, I thought, *Marcus will be home soon. Our family will not be without a head.* Over and over I said it to myself, and it gave me peace."

It shocked me that he had thought himself so near death. My eyes smarted.

"The point is, Marcus, that I am fifty-one years old. If you are lost in the wilds of Germania, what will become of the family?" He gestured toward the unseen atrium. To the altar where we sacrificed every day to our gods and our grandsires; to the death masks, the portrait busts, the relics of our family's valor.

It was a blow I ought to have foreseen, one perhaps fatal to my plans. No divine judgment is severe enough for a man who willfully brings his family to an end. I floundered: "But, Father, men of your age may have decades before them. Tiberius was seventy-eight. And Augustus lived to seventy-five, did he not?"

"Nearly seventy-seven, and ill most of his life. He would have been glad to die sooner, he said, had the gods spared just one of his heirs."

"Next year," I faltered, "perhaps . . ."

"Perhaps you will marry? My boy, you are widely known to be fearless and headstrong; few fathers of daughters will trust you until you have proved disciplined and dutiful as well."

Until I had made greater progress on my civic career, in other words. "A year of searching is all I ask," I blurted out. "I will return then, whether or not the Eagle is found."

"A year longer," he responded dourly, "before I may have a grandson."

I dreaded a question about the Marcomanni truce or about Aurima. It seemed increasingly certain that she would not betray me, yet she had never made a promise. But he said next, "Caesar must approve such a quest."

"Shall I ask to see him? Has he forgiven me?" I had not forgotten the need to seek redress for Ammisia's murder.

There was a tap at the doorpost. "One moment," Father called out. He lowered his voice. "If this needed deciding at once, you know my answer would be no. And no it may later be. Say nothing to Caesar now, and we will see how matters stand in a sixmonth." He called toward the door, "What is it?"

I was in turmoil, barely attending. Would it be no, or yes, or maybe? Was he holding an apple before my nose that would be whisked away in half a year?

"Master, a messenger brings word from the mistress."

It was Damulus, who had brought Dio to Rome earlier. Mother would arrive from Antium by nightfall, he said. She would stay with Nina. "Did you send for her?" I asked my father when Damulus had gone.

"Your mother does as she wishes," he said briefly, and added as I was on my way out, "like you."

While Mother went to Nina's house, several of her women arrived unexpectedly at ours. Before I knew anything about it, Phormio was being removed from my room. "What are you doing?" I demanded as two of the chair bearers carried away my bundled-up *paedagogus* on his mat.

Plump Flora, Mother's wardrobe woman, looked up at me. She was his wife, a union that was of course not legal but was recognized within our family. "It is not fitting for him to be in your room, young master. Not when . . ." Her voice caught in her throat.

"I want him there." But when had I last paid heed to him? Day after day I had left him drugged and sleeping, with Rufus to tend him.

"He will not eat or drink." Tears slid down her cheeks, still ruddy from the cold day's travel. "Gods protect him, I fear he no longer cares to live."

I trailed the little procession like a dog. "Where are you taking him?"

"Sosander said we may use an empty stall."

"That is no place for him! It will be cold, and—far from me."

"Marcus." Flora paused, wiping her face. "He knows you love him. But it is not right for you to sleep with a dying man beside your bed." She held up a chapped hand to stop me from following. "Let me settle him, and then you may come and see him if you wish. I will make him comfortable, never fear."

I stared after them, my thoughts frozen like fountain spray in a sleet storm. I had reckoned he was getting better.

With a vague notion of needing warmer clothes to visit the stable, I turned and collided with another of my mother's women. Quilts spilled out of her arms, and she exclaimed in vexation. I recalled the question I had forgotten to ask Flora. "Why has my mother come back, Helena? Is my sister well?"

Her sharp tongue was tamed at once. "Pardon, young master, I did not see you. She has come to help Lady Nina in the early days of her childing."

Flinging the end of a heavier mantle over my shoulder, I ran down the steps into the stableyard. The horses nickered from their stalls. I ignored them, crossing the puddled yard to the open door of the loose-box where house slaves and stablemen had gathered. They fell silent and parted to let me through.

Phormio's pallet was cushioned by heaps of straw. On the other side of the large stall, separated from him by frayed netting, was the old half-blind donkey used for carrying heavy loads. I opened my mouth to protest, then saw the practicality of it: the beast helped warm the space. It was no colder here than in my own bedroom.

Flora squatted over Phormio, tucking around him the quilts Helena had brought. She rose and moved out of my way.

I took in my breath. My *paedagogus*, once robust in color and strong of feature, lay gray-cheeked on his pallet. His eyes had sunk into their sockets, and his nose beaked sharply above a shrunken mouth.

He was not recovering. He would not recover.

"Leave him with me," I said. "Flora, go feed and warm yourself; you have had a long journey. You too, Helena."

The onlookers melted away. I sat down in the prickly straw and took Phormio's hand, as dry and weightless as a dead leaf. "Can you hear me, my dear?" I said in Greek.

His face turned slightly, but he did not speak or open his eyes.

When had I last spoken with him? "I have been occupied," I said lamely. "I did not know."

No change in his shallow wheezing. I took a long breath. "Phormio, I will remember you and honor your spirit with those of our ancestors."

A brief hitch; then the rasping resumed.

"And I will have a tomb marker made, so my children and my children's children will know you. 'Phormio,' it will say, 'age forty-seven, faithful servant of Marcus Licinius Carinna. He took a boy and made a man of him.'"

A hint of shadow in his cheek. A smile? Or had I imagined it?

"You should have lived to teach my first son." My voice shrank to a ragged whisper. I cleared my throat. "Is there anything you would ask of me?"

The creases deepened around Phormio's eyes, but still he did not respond. The donkey snuffled curiously, its breath wet on my neck.

I sat brooding for a time, watching his face while noises of the stable welled up in the growing darkness. Straw rustled; the donkey's belly gurgled; one of the horses pissed; a stablehand bolted stall doors.

Father's fear of abandoning our family echoed in my mind. Was my *paedagogus* distressed about what might become of me, whom he had been charged with raising? Could he but live to see me return with the lost Eagle, he would know his life had been well spent. My triumph would be his.

I tucked my mantle around myself more securely and lay down full length beside him. "Imagine this, Phormio," I said quietly. "People line the

Via Flaminia, applauding as we ride by. Men hold up their children to see history made. The Eagle that was lost is shrouded on her standard, but everyone knows what she is, that she is coming home. Do you see it?"

His eyelids flickered.

"At the steps of the temple I dismount and make a little speech: 'For the greater glory of Jupiter Best and Greatest, et cetera, I have the honor of restoring the Eagle of the Eighteenth Legion to the Senate and the people of Rome.' I lay the standard in the hands of Marcus Aemilius Lepidus. He climbs the steps. At the very top he uncovers the Eagle, bright and gleaming, and presents it to Caesar."

I sighed, lost in my own vision. "The people cheer wildly, a huge noise that frightens birds out of the trees. Caesar announces that we march to push back the northern frontiers, and the cheering rises all the way to Olympus. 'At last,' says Mars, and rubs his hands together. 'My little city-state has been so peaceable, I almost regret seducing that girl who said she was a princess. . . .'"

A line of wetness crept onto Phormio's lashes, and his breathing became labored. My flight of fancy vanished. "Do not worry, my dear," I said more matter-of-factly. "All is well. I will restore our family's greatness."

He rolled his head on the rag-stuffed pillow. In a dusty flurry of straw I got to my knees and laid my hand on his bald brow. "Go with honor," I said. "You have done all that was asked of you." I leaned over and kissed away the salty trickle on his gaunt, stubbly cheek. My heart was as sore and swollen as if it might split.

With frightening suddenness his fingers clenched on my free hand. I exclaimed and recoiled as if a dead man had stirred.

His tear-edged eyelids cracked open. Soundlessly he said, *Marcus.*

I regained control of myself. "I am here."

He pointed shakily at his head. Pain sliced across his face with the effort. His arm fell like a sawn-off bough, and he began to gasp. I heard him try to push out a word, scarcely more than a hiss of air.

Burn, he was saying. *Burn.*

Tartarus and the torments of the damned rushed to my mind. Then I realized he must simply be asking for cremation. We had long ago agreed that if the soul survives death, burning must free it sooner from its mortal husk. Gruffly I said, "I will light your pyre with my own hands."

Phormio's arm twitched in a spasm, and the wheezing worsened. I knew he did not want me to watch him suffer, nor could I bear to see it.

My guardian, my tutor, my friend. With him would die my youth and my young manhood, my ignorance of the great untruths in the world.

I clambered to my feet. Flora waited outside with Rufus, a pot of soup steaming in his toweled grip. Before they entered, I turned back for a last look at Phormio. His bony fingers were bent, as if he still gripped the hand I had withdrawn.

CHAPTER 36

BETRAYAL

When Rufus woke me the next morning, I pushed my legs out of bed and paused, staring at the empty space where Phormio had lain. "How is he?"

The boy nodded and shrugged, managing not to drop his tray of bread and olives. "What does that mean?" I demanded.

The curtain swished, and Dio came in. "He took soup last night from Flora." He set a cup on my bedside table and filled it from a pitcher.

I drank off the watered wine somberly, thinking of the Phormio who had been robust enough a few days earlier to restrain Caligula's treacherous sister.

Dio replenished the cup. "Perhaps he wishes to see the new year."

"Do you think men can choose the day of their death?"

"Are you asking for my opinion, Marcus?"

"I am, curse you." I bit into a piece of salt-crusted bread.

A wrinkle creased Dio's high forehead. "I read about a commander of hoplites at Marathon who was mortally wounded by a Persian archer. When the battle was over, his comrades were astounded to find him still alive. He asked who had won. And when they told him victory was theirs, he smiled and died."

"Perhaps the gods prolonged his life to reward his valor."

He ran an ink-stained finger along the pitcher's handle. Without looking up he said, "Then it is much the same thing, is it not?"

⸎

Father had left for some guild event when the doorkeeper's boy appeared in Publius's bedroom, now my office. "Gaius Silius desires to see you, young master."

My gaze froze on the panoply of arms and armor I had mounted on a stand in the corner. I could not believe Silius dared show himself after betraying me. Finally I said, "Admit him, then."

Dio, who was tired and cross, seized on the excuse to stop reading me a report of last year's revenue from Judaea. "I will have the servers bring out the best wine for the magistrate."

"Serve him nothing," I said. "He will not be here long."

I entered the reception room carrying my sheathed sword, its belt doubled and dangling. Silius's eyes widened. He straightened in his chair, nearly upsetting the cup of wine that, despite my prohibition, he had been served.

"What is that for?" he asked, with a smile that was almost natural.

I set the scabbard down on the servers' table and drew out the sword with a businesslike rasp. "I brought it," I said, swinging it to test the weight, "for you to use on me, since you missed your opportunity at Gemellus's banquet." I reversed the sword and held it out to him hilt first.

The smile disappeared. "Don't be ridiculous."

I tossed it in front of him. He flung himself backward as the weapon clattered at his feet. The chairback smacked into the plastered wall, and the contents of his cup splashed across his chest.

He recovered quickly. "So your red-haired 'runaway' was a spy in Gemellus's bosom all along." He flicked a bold glance at Rufus, who had ghosted in behind me. "I would not have guessed it of you, Carinna."

"There is much I would not have guessed of you, Silius."

An ashy pallor beneath his eyes made them darker, like glittering jet. "You should have come back for a second night. You could have learned even more."

My anger exploded. "Curse you, you knew what he meant to do!"

He blotted his tunic with his mantle. "You were not supposed to be there."

"What of his sister, Julia? Poor old Claudius? Drusilla, who would not harm a fly? You were not troubled, thinking of them?"

"You saved them. Well done. Are you as pleased to have saved Caligula, whose reward was to call you a liar and a traitor?"

I snatched up the sword again, nearly blind with fury. "Stand up."

He called out from his chair, "Leander!"

"Stand up!"

His body slave slipped in past the curtain and at once wedged himself between us to shield his master. What foresight to have had the point of the blade sharpened! I might be able to spike them both with a single thrust.

"Carinna, put down the sword." Silius's voice had the tiniest of tremors. "I did not know you would dine with them. I swear it on my father's ashes."

"And you told Galerianus to bribe me."

"Can you blame me for that? I thought—"

"You thought you had won me over? So I reckoned at first." I sidestepped to see him better. His slave pivoted, still blocking my blade. "But you know me. You knew I would tell my father that Caligula was to be attacked by sword or knife by year-end." I gulped, panting in my rage. "When the plan was to poison him the next day."

He dodged the accusation. "How can you defend that weakling—a man who had too little honor to stand by your brother?"

"I will not break my oath to him."

"Or what?" Silius sprang to his feet, thrusting Leander aside. "What will happen? Your Parthian god in the liberty cap will throw you out of his holy army? Your father will disinherit you? What could possibly be worse than that crackbrained runt of Germanicus's litter ruling Rome?" He stopped for breath. Foam had crept into a corner of his mouth.

He took a great risk confronting me barehanded. We had once been alike, Silius and I, in our contempt for death. I had come to respect it more after it took my brother in an eye-blink.

But his temper cooled mine. I lowered the sword. "Pack up your wife and your bust of Aristotle, and go to your villa in Herculaneum."

He took a deep breath. "At this time of year? Too unfashionable." He flashed his old grin, rascally and beguiling. "Besides, Crispina does not care for the seaside."

"I am warning you, Silius."

"Very well, I am warned." He brushed bits of plaster off his shoulders. "I came to tell you that Pertinax is returning to the Province. His mother is dying."

"Too bad. Get out of my house."

He took a pace or two toward the doorway, then stopped. "Do you remember the first time I kissed you?"

After a footrace at the Spartan Baths, in May of my ninth year. I kept my eyes on the sword I was sliding into its scabbard and said nothing.

"What a scrawny young cockerel you were. So nervous you trembled." I heard the huff of breath as he let out a voiceless laugh. "You did, and you blushed as red as a beetroot. As soon as Phormio saw you, he knew what had happened."

I was trembling now in the aftermath of rage. The carrying rings chinked as I shoved the sword hilt against the throat of the scabbard.

Silius touched me, sliding his hand from my elbow up inside my sleeve. I knocked his arm away. "Save yourself," I said harshly. "Tell Caligula you support him. Dio can write a letter for you with all the proper flourishes."

"Why? So you can show it to your father? *Look, Papa, I have forced Gaius Silius to eat his pride. See how he grovels to Caesar! Are you not proud of me?*" His voice rose. "You will never take your brother's place in his heart, not if you bring all Caligula's foes to heel and save the misbegotten wretch a hundred times."

Heat rushed into my face.

He said, "Thank you for the advice. But I will not cower or flee, nor will I ask you to use your credit with Caesar on my behalf." He beckoned to Leander. "I think you will find you have too little to spare."

I needed a drink. Several drinks. And not at home, where everyone in the family was agog at the clash I had provoked.

On the western end of the Palatine, partway down the Steps of Cacus that lead toward the Circus Maximus and the river, was a *taberna* that Ollius favored, where the stink of the recent flood was half smothered in the sharp, smoky reek of wet ashes. Slaves with billhooks were pulling down the remains of a charred apartment building near the foot of the steps. Tenants escaping the flood had left a lit candle to deceive looters, Ollius said.

He shouted to the black-bearded *tabernarius*, a man I did not know, who was dipping from an amphora set lip-deep in the counter. "Bestia! Welcome my patron Marcus Carinna, lately senior tribune of the Fifteenth."

"Pleasure, Tribune," the barkeeper said. "Bavius Bestia, centurion, Sixteenth Gallica." He straightened up, wiping his hands on his greasy apron, and nodded toward a niche in the wall. A little shrine had been made there with a crude portrait of Malleus, a few dried blossoms, and two long black hairs, all arranged with reverence on a clean cloth. "Them flowers are from his last winner's garland, friends," he said. "And the hairs come from the tail of his mare Flamma."

"Let us all drink to his victory," I said, sourly amused.

The other customers let out happy shouts. "Ummia!" the barman bawled. "Lend a hand, you lazy cow."

A couple of workmen vacated a table for me. The barmaid thumped down a jug of water. When she returned with a wooden cup of wine, Rufus reached to taste it for me. "No need," I said. I added a splash of water and drained the cup.

"Gods rest you, Malleus; you won me twenty sestertii." Someone splatted a libation on the pavement outside.

"Thank 'ee, Tribune. Your good health, sir."

"Good health and long life, your honor."

Bestia looked as if he might have something sociable to say, but my scowl told him I was in no mood for chatter. Rufus refilled my cup.

Talk slowly resumed. "Might be it was Gemellus's shade pulled Caligula into the underworld."

"And Germanicus, gods rest him, sent him back." A belch. "He'll have told him, 'My sonny boy, it ain't your time yet.'"

I gulped more wine and watched over the serving counter as the rubble wall of the *insula* broke apart. But my anger at Silius, instead of dissipating amid these distractions, rose up more strongly.

The provocations swirled around my heart like flames in a fire pot. His claim of being uninvolved in the poison plot; then his insistence that he had not known I would dine with the Caesars; his double-edged attempt to suborn me into joining Gemellus or trick me into passing along a lie about the threat to Caligula; his deriding of my honor, my manhood, my surrender to his guile . . . and . . .

I did not want to look into the fire's heart. Instead I stoked my fury with the other insults, searing myself first with one, then another.

When I sat down I had scattered a handful of coins to pay for the drink, and as I tormented myself, I rolled a brass sestertius between my fingers and

363

drummed it edgewise on the scarred tabletop. Finally I held it up and stared at the noble and aloof profile of Caligula Caesar. Whom I had saved from trampling, from poisoning—

You will never take your brother's place in his heart—

I slammed my hand on the table. The coins jumped. Conversation stopped.

I should have cut Silius down. Even if I stood trial for murder, the satisfaction would have been worth it.

Wrong. It would have been cast as a lovers' quarrel between two grown men of noble birth—shaming my father, embarrassing Caligula, who had named me his quaestor, destroying any hope of pursuing and finding the lost Eagle.

I could not even tell Saxa of Silius's role in the conspiracy without confessing how I had been used. Curse it, was there no way to revenge myself?

And then Fortuna, with fine timing, brought an opportunity to the door.

The mutter of drinkers outside the serving counter, permeated by the breathless huff of passersby climbing the steps, was suddenly interrupted by a *clunk*, a cry from the barmaid, and the slosh of water. "Teach you to keep that bucket out of the way, girl," puffed a familiar voice.

My view of the half-demolished tenement was blocked by the head and meaty shoulders of Aulus Vitellius, a Senator's son the same age as I, and once as avid a charioteer. He glanced into the *taberna*. "Ho! Who tastes your truffled eggs here, Carinna?"

He limped in with a companion I did not know. Bestia brushed two other customers off a bench and dragged it over to my table. The newcomers flung themselves down on it, still breathing hard.

The barmaid hurried over. "Cup of best," ordered Vitellius's companion, pawing through my dish of olives.

Vitellius's snaggle-toothed grin showed a black incisor, like a mouse turd in a spill of wheat. "Packed on a little weight, Marcus? No more racing for you." He tried to pinch my upper arm, but the muscle did not yield.

I moved my cup out of his reach. "Hark to the Great Ocean calling a piss-puddle wet! It would take a team of oxen to drag you around the track, Aulus."

"Since you mention pissing, I hear Caligula lets you hold his cock for him. How does he like the new satire?"

I shook my head uncomprehendingly.

"Ctesippus's bookshop sent me a copy," Vitellius boasted. "He knows I want to be the first to hear a new 'Phoenix.'"

"I admire your love of social commentary. What is it, then?"

He helped himself to the pitcher, swigged a mouthful of wine, and declaimed so lustily that everyone else in the *taberna* was silenced:

Night burned at the edges with daylight,
A morning mist clouded the lake;
In coverts and dells, in valleys and glens,
The dryads and fauns came awake.
But one of the fauns still lay sleeping
Alone in the dew-jeweled morn,
He was fair, large of hoof, and long-legged,
With a butterfly perched on one horn.

"A pastoral idyll?" I jeered. "Where is the satire in that?"

His companion spat out an olive pit. "Keep listening."

Vitellius resumed:

Three dryads ran over to wake him,
But he moaned as he stirred, and cried, "Odd:
Metamorphosis seems to have gripped me.
I think I'm becoming . . .

He paused. I supplied the ending: "'A god.'" It was a gentle jab at Caligula's claim to immortality. But how had the satirist learned about that?

Vitellius shook his head. "'A goat'!" he announced, and he and his friend guffawed.

"They'll have the tricky bastard chopping rocks in a stone quarry for that," the companion chortled.

Had I thought it gentle? It was a vicious insinuation that Caligula was becoming as sinister as Tiberius, known to all who loathed him as the Old Goat.

"That's fucking infamous!" Bestia whacked the counter with the poker he used for the fire beneath the hot drinks. "After all our Caligula has been through."

"They ought to crucify the bastard that wrote it," someone else shouted.

Vitellius pushed back his end of the bench. "I can see why you like it here," he sneered, "among your own people." He and his comrade stumped out.

I did not mind. As I sat there finishing my wine, I began to smile.

At home I went to my office, wrote down the satire from memory, and sent a message. While waiting for a response I looked in on Phormio. He slept, moaning in dreams, with Rufus curled against him for warmth. He had taken more soup, Flora said, but refused the nostrum that eased his pain.

I told her not to chafe. A man should face his death clear-eyed, not sodden with poppy juice. Phormio's ancestors had been citizen-soldiers of Achaea; it was bad luck, not lack of courage, that had caused him to be born into slavery.

Back in my office, I settled in a chair and read some of the messages requesting favors. Would I ask Caesar to restore a stolen inheritance, rule on a bid for Via Aurelia repairs, name the sender as procurator of Hispania Baetica?

I got up and paced across the room. A narrow stripe of color was worn away where the bed had bucked against the wall as Publius tumbled his bed girl. His virility had brought him and the family no luck; he had died unmarried, without an heir.

The front doors opened. Heavy boots tramped up the vestibule steps. Two or three guards, an aide, perhaps a clerk. A boy ran in to announce my visitor.

I questioned myself again, as I had before giving judgment at tribunals. Had the misdeed really earned so harsh a penalty? But I had only to remember what I had done for love, and rage and humiliation rushed hotly into my face.

So be it. After an appropriate interval I entered the reception room. Saxa lounged at his ease near a glowing brazier, alone. He wore his fringed black cloak over a shortened tunic. No armor, no helmet.

"This is very welcome," he said, saluting me with a cup of hot wine as I sat down. Having extended this olive branch, he went on without further niceties, "You say there is something I should know."

I took a deep breath. "I am not a man to complain about humor and high spirits." I met Saxa's lusterless eyes. "But this morning I heard a satire that is new in the bookshops."

"And?"

"I was at the Palace when Caesar awoke from his . . . sleep." I saw that he understood. "I believe the satire I heard should be suppressed."

He uncoiled out of his slouch. "Do you have a copy?"

"I made my own." He reached for it, but I shook my head. "You must hear it spoken aloud."

I recited the lines to him. He was silent for a moment, then stretched out a hand. I let him take the tablet.

Studying my scrawl in the dark wax, he said almost carelessly, "The work of Phoenix, would you say?"

"I am hardly qualified to offer an opinion."

"Only Phoenix dares publish such scurrilous work."

I did not want to seem too eager for the poet to be punished. "It is the satire I would silence, not the satirist."

"This is not satire. It is *laesa maiestas.*"

I frowned. Saxa heaved an impatient sigh. "Let us stop sparring." He scratched his cheek with the corner of the tablet. "After Gemellus's betrayal, there must be no question that Caesar is in complete command. We cannot allow his *maiestas* to be ridiculed with impunity."

"You speak as if you plan to put Phoenix on trial."

"What should I do, Quaestor? Award him a laurel wreath?"

"Perhaps he needs only a scare." I looked down at the wine swirling in my cup. "Perhaps he has made light of his friends' warnings."

His response was as swift as a lion's leap: "Who is he?"

So he did not know. I set down my cup. "Commander, I do not agree with beating dogs because they bark."

"Then you have wasted my time." He tossed back the last of his wine. "I am busy ridding Rome of Gemellus's conspirators. At the moment I am investigating the role of the Tenth District magistrate. He has hidden his tracks carefully, but I am sure he was involved."

"And?" I prodded, just as he had said it. Was this an unrelated threat to squeeze the satirist's identity out of me? Or did he already suspect Silius was Phoenix?

"The disposition of his case could go either way."

"You must do as you think best." I uncrossed my legs as if to rise. "By the way, could a man on a mission in the North expect support from local agents of the Special Cohort?"

The creases deepened in Saxa's brow. "That would depend on the man. And the mission."

"Let us suppose it is a man of some birth and experience. And that after counting silver and gold for Caesar, he seeks a prize of bronze worth far more."

The server edged forward with his ewer. Now I would see if I had interested Saxa. Would he take more wine, or get up and leave?

"The Eagle of the Eighteenth," he said. He let the server fill his cup.

I sank back. "Would your agents help him?"

He grunted. "Failure would reflect badly on Caesar. On Rome."

"Your support might make the difference, Commander."

"And your father?" He corrected himself sardonically: "This man's father?"

"Would be grateful to have the odds of success improved."

His escorts mumbled in the distant vestibule. Someone coughed hoarsely. At last he said, "And in return?"

I let out a breath I was not aware of holding. "I will give you Phoenix."

"Done," he said.

"You promise me the information I ask for, use of the imperial post, connections to allies and informers. Whatever I need to bring back the Eagle."

"Agreed."

I took a deep breath. "Gaius Silius is Phoenix."

His jaw twisted: tonguing a back tooth, or hiding a grin. "Your proof?"

I had no proof. "It is I who say it."

His eyes flickered over me. I imagined his thoughts: *Grew up together, then no longer friends . . . now sharing the Senate Leader's niece . . . perhaps betraying Silius in order to have her to himself.*

I stood up. "For now, keep this theoretical example to yourself."

"Understood." This time Saxa did grin, baring large crooked teeth. "We all have our secrets, young Carinna."

I had expected to feel triumphant in my vengeance. Instead my belly began to roil as I watched the Special Cohort commander depart, and I had to hasten to a corner of the garden to avoid vomiting in front of the house slaves. I lingered there, breathing the cold evening, until my composure returned. Bad wine at Bestia's, I told myself.

Lamplight poured from the reception room where Father was examining the damaged wall. He turned to me, hand on hip. I had forgotten my sword, which still lay in its scabbard on the servers' table.

"I could not persuade Silius to take his oath to Caligula." I attempted a smile.

He had been in council at someone's house. "There is a new satire about," he said. "Something about metamorphosis; I have not heard it."

"I heard it in the city. I told Saxa about it." Better to forestall questions; he would already know from the doorkeeper that the man had been here.

"You have had a busy day," he said dryly. "Come and tell me the satire while I dress for dinner with Lepidus." He grimaced. "He refuses to believe that Caesar is fully recovered and able to govern."

I realized that I had not returned the gold torc to him after Gemellus's banquet. When I offered to fetch it for him, he considered for a moment. "Keep it safe," he said. "I will ask for it when I want it."

It was very cold in the thickening dusk. My horse's tail bannered sideways in a sharp wind that tried to carry away my cloak. All was tranquil as I went past Silius's house. A flaring torch by the front doors lit the gilded oak wreath carved into the lintel, a symbol of the honorary Triumph awarded to his father. The graffito of the she-wolf was gone.

I envisioned the pounding on his door, the Special Cohort soldiers in his atrium, the fright on his wife's face, his own consternation and fear. And before long, he would know that it was I who had informed on him.

I turned the horse's head and rode homeward.

A most peculiar event occurred on the way. The wind had scoured away the city's blanketing smoke, and the night sky was so bright with stars that thin shadows marked every seam of the road. As I reached the summit of the Clivus Palatinus, a shooting star plummeted across the sky. I was staring after it when another, even brighter, flashed down in its wake. Then there were three more, five, ten, twenty. The night rained stars, and my hair stood on end.

I had seen star showers in the North, said to result from stars losing their grip in the deep cold. But clear skies on winter nights are so rare in Rome that the sight of a plunging star is thought to foretell some great event, often a catastrophe. If that was true, what might such a massive star-fall portend?

The wind was dying. The remaining stars began to twinkle as I watched, and then to disappear. I knew they were only hidden by the gathering haze, but it seemed the heavens were being denuded.

A deep murmur rose up all around. The street was full of people gazing upward. All but one of them: Aurima, on her doorstep, was looking at me.

Occupied with my own frustrations and believing her safely tucked away in Bovillae, I had stopped watching for her return. Now I gazed back at her, surprised and disturbed by her stare.

Then I did a foolish thing. I reached up, plucked an imaginary star from the sky, and offered it to her on the palm of my hand.

Aurima glanced upward as if to see evidence of my theft. A moment later she vanished inside the house, and the door thumped shut.

"Sad news, young master," the doorkeeper said as I entered the vestibule.

I was so weary and preoccupied that his words did not penetrate at once. "What?"

The slaves in the atrium glanced at one another to see who would speak. It was Dio who told me Phormio had died.

I paused to assess the shock, but felt only relief that my old companion had been released from his suffering. "May he be at peace."

"They found him in the kitchen," Dio said.

I stopped with my cloak half stripped off. "In the kitchen?"

"He must have felt better and sought some food. And the gods took him."

"He would have wanted it thus," said Nicander, his friend. There was a general murmur of agreement.

A message had delayed Father's departure for dinner, so he had been at home when it happened. Of course he had ordered the body taken outside, so death would not pollute the house. I felt no desire to see it. I had already said goodbye.

"Phormio was an esteemed member of our family, and will be honored in death as befits his worthy conduct in life," I said. "Wash his body and anoint it. Let a pyre be prepared for him near our family's tomb, and a place for his ashes made ready in the columbarium. Dio will know my wishes for the inscription."

They nodded, satisfied. This was what they all wanted for themselves, the acknowledgment of their years of loyalty and toil.

I embraced Flora, who sobbed her remorse that she had not been with him at the end, and at last gained my bedroom. Someone had lit the lamp, probably Dio, for an unfurled scroll suggested he had been reading there.

He followed me in. "There is something else, Marcus. . . ."

"The starfall?" I unlaced a boot and kicked it off. "It means nothing."

Dio shook his head. "The master was in a fearsome temper before he left, though I do not know why." He furled the scroll.

I did not give a rotten nut for my father's state of mind. Sorrow for Phormio was crumbling beneath the weight of exhaustion from the troubled night before. Yet once in bed, I felt a prickly restlessness as if scores of gnats were biting at my brain. I turned and sighed and tried to quiet myself, but the unease persisted. The last thing I was aware of was Aurima's voice saying to me, *The spirits who are not at peace, it is death that calls them.*

It seemed only minutes later that I woke in a heap of bedding on the floor, with booted feet inches from my nose. "Master wants you, Marcus," Cleon said.

I stumbled to Father's office, seething with confusion and outrage. He stood by the statue of Ares, his expression as darkly savage as the war god's. Laid out on his desk was a tunic, craggy with wrinkles and stiff with dried blood.

Maiden's blood.

CHAPTER 37

BURN

He shook the tunic at me. "Is this your blood?"

I had buried it in my clothes chest. Who could have found it and given it to him? Dio? Rufus? Turtle?

"Is it?" he roared, thrusting the bloody fabric under my nose.

"It is a woman's."

"What woman's?"

I thought of naming some other female of childbearing age with whom I had been intimate. Some men do not like to bed a woman during her monthly flow, but I doubted Father knew my propensities.

He did not wait for my answer. "Did you take the virginity of that Marcomanni hostage?"

I braced myself. "I did."

It wrong-footed him, as if he had not expected honesty. "By force?"

"She came to me."

"She was to marry a high-ranking ally. Do you expect me to believe she gave herself to you?"

"It is the truth."

"Who else knows?"

"No one. How did—"

"Hold your tongue unless you are answering me! I suppose it is too much to hope you took precautions. Might she be with child?"

"Not likely," I said, my anger mounting to match his.

"Praise heaven for that! What is your question?"

"Who gave you the tunic?"

"It was in your *paedagogus*'s hand when he fell."

Phormio must have found the tunic among my clothes and taken it. *Burn it,* he had tried to tell me, being too weak by then to do it himself. I groaned at my own stupidity. He had even gestured toward the pillow where he had hidden it!

When I told him my grandiose plans for finding the Eagle, he realized the bloody thing could be my ruin. He had not gone to the kitchen feeling better but, in an extremity of devotion, to cast the tunic into the fire.

I turned my head away. Father said, "Are you about to weep? I could not bear to have a son who bawls like a girl."

I struggled back from the shock. "She will not talk. So she can still be wed—"

"You fool!" He wiped spittle from his lips. "In a few miserable weeks, you have destroyed what I have worked for years to build. Do you suppose I will ever be nominated for a consulship when this is known?"

"No one—"

"Listen to me. You will have no further contact with this girl. Woman. None. Do you understand?"

"But she is—"

"Shut up while I am speaking. Nod to me if you understand."

I sighed in frustration. He slapped me lightly on the cheek, a promise of violence. "If this scandal can be managed, we will proceed at once with your betrothal to Claudia Antonia."

"Claudius's daughter? She is a child!"

He slapped me again. "You will marry in three years, when she is thirteen. And you will have no more to do with Gaius Silius."

"I already—"

"He is about to be charged with treason. Do you know he wept when he learned you were going to Gemellus's dinner party?" He almost spat the next words: "Before any of us knew about the poison."

The blows were coming too fast. I felt like an archer's target swung from a gallows, jolting and spinning as the arrows struck. My humiliation was so great that I could not speak.

Such was Father's rage that he, who relished histrionic stances and gestures, had barely moved in all this time. Now he went behind his desk and faced me, flattening his hands on its top.

"If there were gods, I would implore them for mercy. To give me the joy of a loyal, dutiful son, only to force mine to be the hand that sacrificed him!

And now, to crush so brutally my hopes that you would take his place." He lifted the bloody tunic and flung it down again.

There was no sound but his harsh breathing. Finally he said, "What obligations do you have today?"

I tried to order my mind. "Only for my *paedagogus*. To sacrifice for him. And to execute his will."

"In the rest of the time, reflect on what you have done to those who relied on you." His voice roughened. "Get out of my sight."

The night-dimmed atrium was deserted except for young Rufus, sitting against the wall with his arms around his knees. Cleon stood out of earshot by the doorkeeper's cubby and pretended not to notice when I left Father's office.

Phormio's body had been placed in an open cart in the stableyard. Drawing back the oiled cloth protecting it from the elements, and the winding-sheet beneath, I held a lamp high and looked upon the face of my oldest and dearest friend.

Lightless now were the eyes that had warmed with affection and glinted in anger; stilled forever, the tongue that had counseled, instructed, chastised. Hidden were the ropy arms that had lifted me to see processions, the knotted hands that had helped me shape my letters, the sturdy legs that tramped wherever I went.

Was there a heaven where he would be welcomed? Would a divine justice reward him for dying in a service of loyalty to my welfare, which had been his responsibility for so long? Was there even a Mithras who led men in their duty, or only the delusion of such a god?

Rufus padded up beside me. He looked at Phormio's body, and his shoulders sagged. "His time had come," I said. It sounded callous, something one might say of any worn-out old slave.

I covered the corpse again. At the end I had been a disappointment even to him, who had tried to shape me as a man of duty and honor. "Leave me, Rufus," I said. "I need to be alone."

With the family gathered in the chilly atrium, Father prayed for Phormio's safe journey to the world of spirits. Struggling to maintain the calm and dignity that the house's heir should display, I read out the will that shared his meager belongings among his wife and friends. He had bequeathed me his copy of Aristotle's *Eudaimian Ethics*, given him by Lepidus to assist in my education.

When Father went out near midday, he handed me the bloodstained tunic. I laid it on coals atop the stove and watched it burn. The wind swirled flaming fragments of cloth and ash around the kitchen and up the smoke hole, much as it would finger and strew the mortal remains of my *paedagogus* in the morning, and I was undone by grief that outweighed all my other sorrows.

Dio came to me not long afterward. I had wandered out to the peristyle and was sitting on the bench by the fountain, staring at nothing. "May I have a word, young master?" he asked formally.

I was surprised he had sought me out. Most of the household were silent and bewildered, knowing my disgrace had something to do with Phormio's death.

He crouched in front of me, an uncharacteristic pose for one so conscious of his dignity. "Rufus told me what the master said," he muttered.

I was sure the only reason the Thracian boy had been allowed to overhear was that Cleon knew he could not tell anyone. "He did?"

Dio flipped his fingers impatiently. "I can understand him well enough." He shifted awkwardly from one haunch to the other. "The master thinks you forced the girl. The hostage. You must let me tell him the truth."

"I forbid it," I said.

He was so startled that he had to brace himself to keep from falling over. "You do? But . . ."

"It does not matter, Dio."

His lips shaped another "but" that he did not voice. There are limits to what a slave—even a privileged one—can expect to be told. And I would not admit to anyone that I feared the truth would make no difference to my father.

"I forbid it," I repeated.

Dio lurched upright, ungainly in his long skirts. "As you wish, young master," he murmured with eyes downcast, and went away.

Some time later, while I was reviewing preparations the women had taken with Phormio's body, the doorkeeper's boy ran out to announce that Lucius Pertinax wished to see me. "I am not at home," I said, and turned back to Flora.

"Excuse me, young master, but he said it was very important."

My gaze lit on the silver obols on Phormio's closed eyes, Athenian owls that he himself had saved for this day. After a moment I said, "Let him enter."

Pertinax loomed up in the doorway of my small office. It was beginning to rain, and his graying curls had unfurled into wet strands. "What can I do for you?" I said curtly.

The big Gaul had a farmer's squint, his eyes showing only in slits between the lids. "We have had a misunderstanding," he said.

"Have we?"

"I think you need to know that I have tried only to guide Silius. Steady him. He is a magistrate now, and one of the best young orators in Rome. There is talk of a seat in the Senate as soon as he is old enough."

"And for that you credit yourself?"

His cheeks reddened. "I do not care for credit." His tone was even. "I have neither his birth nor his advantages. It is enough to see him become the man I cannot be."

Had he no inkling of Silius's role in the conspiracy? I looked more carefully. Though a broad-shouldered man he had a lean face, with vertical seams below the cheekbones and a wide mouth that ought to have been curtained by a drooping Gaulish mustache.

He did not like being stared at. "May I be seated?"

"If you wish. But I do not see why you are here."

"He has been charged with treason. Imagine, Saxa thinks he is the satirist Phoenix!" Although he had just asked to sit, he took a couple of restless paces to the far wall where my plaque of Mithras stood.

I cleared my throat. "Did Silius admit it?"

Pertinax turned. "Of course he did. 'I am Phoenix,' he said. 'I wrote "Metamorphosis."'"

I had nothing to say. My revenge was tasteless in my mouth.

Wicker squeaked as he lowered his bulk into a chair. He leaned toward me. "Caesar is furious about the satire, and Saxa needs a success to atone for failing to uncover Gemellus's plot. He will make sure Silius is stripped of citizenship and property and is sent into exile."

"What a pity," I said. "With every gift the gods can bestow—beauty, charm, wit, wealth—he cannot stop risking them all, time and again."

Pertinax regarded me oddly. "I would speak up," he went on, "but my father needs me at home without delay. You must do it."

"Ask Saxa to drop the charge? On what grounds?"

"By telling him you are Phoenix."

"What?"

"You are Caligula's favorite; he will never allow Saxa to prosecute you. You can say that while you were on the Danube, you sent new lampoons to Silius; he merely circulated them for you." His face was tense with resolve. "I have thought it all out, Carinna. It will work."

"Why should I do that?"

"By Hercules! You are her brother."

I stared, not understanding.

"Very well." He stood up. "Try to keep her quiet. I will look for another answer."

"Wait," I said. "I cannot . . ." And then, in disbelief: "Nina?"

He sat down again. "Have you not guessed?"

"You mean . . . she is Phoenix?" I tried to laugh. "Are you serious?"

He pulled open the neck of his outer tunic and reached into the pocket it made blousing over his belt. "She gave me this yesterday." He drew out a curl of inked papyrus. "Sometimes Silius gets them first."

I unrolled the paper. While my eyes ran over the words "Night burned at the edges with sunrise" in my sister's neat cursive writing, I heard him say, "We have our scribes make more copies, and leave them anonymously where they will be appreciated: in a clothes niche at the baths, or in a bookshop in the Velabrum."

I thrust the papyrus into the brazier. One end lit, and then fire raced the length of it. "Silius knows?" I asked unthinkingly.

"Of course he does. He would not take the blame otherwise."

I leaned on an elbow and covered my eyes with my hand. Nina was Phoenix! My sister a biting satirist, when I had imagined her penning innocuous love poems!

It was a catastrophe. Never would she allow Silius to be punished for her sake. She would insist on accepting responsibility for the lampoons. Those who believed her would be scandalized; many who did not would say she must be his mistress, taking the blame in the hope of saving him. Either way, the loss of her good name would compel Varro to divorce her.

But perhaps she had not yet heard that Silius was charged with treason. There might be time to stifle her protest.

"You are the only one who can persuade her to keep still," Pertinax said. "Tell her you will insist you are Phoenix, whether she likes it or not."

He mistook my anguish for reluctance. "No one but you has a hope of escaping a charge of *laesa maiestas.* You must see that."

"Go home," I said. "I will take care of it."

He paused before leaving. "Someone will pay for this." His face darkened. "I swear that when I find out who denounced Silius, I will rip off his balls and force them down his throat."

I did not doubt that he, Silius, and Nina herself had all amused themselves in keeping Phoenix's identity from me. "We will see about that later," I said. "A horse, Rufus. Now."

━✛ ✛━

Too late.

I heard Nina's voice as soon as I set foot in her house. "I will not hide behind him!"

Mother said, "Nina, I told you: we will discuss it when your father—"

"If you will not let me write to Silius, I will go to his house myself."

I saw my sister on her feet, shouting orders to have her litter readied. Mother demanded that she return to her couch. Nina's old nurse wept; the white crow screeched.

"Marcus." The fury in Nina's face dissolved into relief. She sat down on her couch. "You must take a message for me to Silius. He is accused of—"

"I know what he is accused of." I raised my voice over the crow's raucous cries. "Someone remove that bird."

Mother's eyes glittered under her thin brows. "You were aware of what your sister was doing?"

"I am now." I tossed my cloak over a chair.

"Then I expect you to resolve this disgraceful state of affairs." She swept from the room, rigid with anger. A slave followed, carrying the crow on its stand.

Nina looked up at me meekly, but I saw a sly smile in her eyes. "When did you find out?"

"Did you think it was comical to keep this from me? Saxa is salivating to hang Phoenix on his cuirass like a medal."

"All the more reason for Silius not to bear the blame."

"My dear sister." I sat down, trying to control my dismay. "What were you thinking? Did you not care how it would affect your husband? Or that if he divorced you, he would take the child you are carrying?"

"You sound like Mother! What I wrote had to be said, and no one else would say it."

"So you took it on yourself to write those cruel satires? That . . . vile insult of a 'Metamorphosis'? You adore Caligula."

Her eyes narrowed. "Not after he accused you of lying about Gemellus. How could you keep such a thing from me? As for the others, scribbles on any wall in the Subura are ten times worse." She stopped and pressed a hand to her lower belly. "A man will never understand what it is like to have no voice. As Phoenix, I am heard. People talk about what I say."

"Women have a voice through their husbands."

"And where is mine? Serving the State a thousand miles away, until it pleases the Princeps to let him come home."

"If he hears you have been writing treasonous lampoons, you will not have much longer to lament being neglected!"

Her lips tightened. "I expected more understanding from you, brother. You think it admirable that Aurima leads men."

All I could manage to say was "You are not Aurima."

She winced again. "Hand me that . . . tablet and stylus behind you. I must write to Silius."

"Indeed you must not," I said. "Listen to—"

"Shall I write to Caligula instead?"

"You will write to no one."

"I will not allow Gaius Silius to be accused in my place!"

"Nina, be quiet! He will not be accused." When I had her attention, I said, "I will say I sent the satires to him. So it will be obvious he was not involved with the worst of them—the 'Romulus and Remus' and 'Metamorphosis.'"

"'Worst of them'? Thank you kindly! You could not write anything half so good if you tried for the rest of your life. Which you may end up doing, to pass the time in exile." She pushed a damp strand of hair off her face. "I will not let you ruin yourself. Caligula will never forgive you if he thinks you mocked him."

"I am not asking permission. I am telling you this is how it will be."

The color heightened in her flushed cheeks. "You are worse than Father. Move out of the way." She slid off her couch again. "I am going to see Drusilla. She will help me."

I stood up. "You mule-headed woman, you are in no condition to go anywhere!"

She tried to edge past, but I stepped in front of her. Tears of rage and frustration boiled up in her eyes. She cried, "Let me pass."

"Get back to bed, or I will have you locked in the storeroom."

"Please, Marcus." She lifted her sleeve to wipe her upper lip. "Ask Silius to come here. I cannot bear that he thinks I will cower behind him."

"I will not have Saxa's informers led to you."

Nina let out a yowl. I stepped back, thinking she meant to strike me, but realized in the next instant that it was pain in her cry, not fury. I caught her as she bent over.

"Not now," she wailed, clutching the front of my tunic as I tried to raise her to her feet.

Mother hurried in. And though she could not know it, her cry of accusation found its mark with dreadful force: "Marcus, what have you done?"

CHAPTER 38

THE BARBARIANS ARE COMING

The dying glow of Phormio's pyre fluttered on pine trees and the pilasters of the tomb. Some of the logs glowed incandescent. Others thrust black and gaunt from a bed of fiery coals.

I kept vigil in a dark-dyed toga unworn since my brother's death. Heat seared my parched eyes and cheeks. In the gloom among the trees, the guards argued about something.

It was a slow journey back to the Palatine, everyone somber and tired, the rumble of the handcart that bore the smoking urn drowning out the pace count of my chair bearers. Passing through the darkened Forum, I looked up at torches lighting Jupiter's temple.

How often I had imagined being here when my fellow officers jabbered about "Rome wants this" and "We heard from Rome yesterday." Now I, so recently a minor hero for ending a barbarian rebellion, would become known as the infamous poet who had satirized Roman pretensions. Father would not find Caligula so willing to betroth his uncle Claudius's little daughter to me.

The house of the Marcomanni came into sight. Out in the street, Maelo's son was trading insults with a youth who held three waiting horses. My bearers were still some way off when the front doors opened. Light spilled onto the pavement, and the two boys sprang alert like hounds.

Flavus came out. As he took hold of one of the horses, Maelo stepped down after him. Then Heriberhto emerged onto the doorstep, fastening his cloak pin. He called over his shoulder in Germanic, and Aurima responded from inside the house—"Good night" or "Farewell" or perhaps "Until our wedding day."

After the calamity of Nina's miscarriage, I thought I had no desires left. I was darkness in the sky where a star had been. But my heart began thudding within me, loud and fast. I wanted to do violence to Harman's duplicitous leech of a son. How could she even look at him? *Mine,* said my blood-pulse. *Mine, mine, mine.*

I made myself look away and let the bearers carry me on.

A painter had been in to repair the fresco damaged by Silius's chair. It did not seem a good job; the red was far too bright.

"Cinnabar is difficult to handle," Father said behind me. "He says it will never completely match the rest."

"I am sorry for that," I said. The words came out flat and formal, as if pressed with a hot iron.

"Come to see me when you have changed your clothes." He turned away.

"Father," I began, and then caught myself.

He studied me with a sort of weary indifference. "What is it?"

I straightened, acting as if I still had pride. "What will be done about Aurima?" Brave Aurima, whose chastity I had stolen, and to whom I could give only a spirit-star in requital.

His face tightened. "A man I know spoke with Julius Flavus, who says his nephew is greatly taken with her. It may be possible to arrange a quick marriage and send them off to live with his tribe."

Heriberhto. I swallowed. "If she were to . . . make a fuss, would it not be better if she were farther away from her homeland?"

"She is very strong-willed, according to Flavus. The best way to keep her from making a fuss may be to give her the man she wants."

I began to point out the risk of allying rebel families from two Germanic nations, but his departure cut me off in midsentence. I winced, as I was meant to.

He was reading a scroll by the light of the three-tongued lamp when I entered his office, having changed from my mourning clothes. Without looking up he gestured at a tablet on the side of his desk. "A message from your mother."

I picked up the tablet, whose seal was already broken, and read her words:

The child is lost, but Nina lives. If the gods in their mercy restore her strength, I will take her to Antium to attempt the healing of her heart. You may resolve this Phoenix affair as you please. The damage has been done.

I shut my eyes to hide my misery. When Saxa revealed that I was Silius's betrayer, this burden too would be laid upon our family.

Father laid down his scroll and placed weights to hold it open. "I am told you plan to insist you are Phoenix."

How else could I atone? "I will not let Nina take the blame," I said. "And Silius is innocent."

"Not innocent of conspiracy against Caesar, it appears."

"I would not spare him anything he has earned. But he did not earn this."

His breath hissed out. After a moment he said, "This stain must not be allowed to attach to our family. Neither to your heedless sister or yourself."

"So you would let Silius bear it, for love of Nina?"

"Silius is the son of a brave and honorable man. Unfortunately, he too is a fool." He moved a scroll-weight an inch to one side. "This fellow from the Province, Pertinax: what does he most desire?"

"Noble birth. Failing that, a Senator's stripe."

"Perhaps I will support his election to the Senate when his father dies."

"Why?"

"*Perhaps*, I said. If he obliges me by claiming he is Phoenix." He shifted the little weight again. "Do you see any problem with that?"

"He will not be here. He is leaving Rome on a family matter."

"Excellent. If he absents himself for a year or so, Caesar's anger may abate."

If Pertinax accepted responsibility for the lampoons, the burden would be taken from me. Relief overwhelmed me, then disgust at my eagerness to be bought out of trouble. "And Silius?"

"He may be able to avoid prosecution by going into voluntary exile. Does he still own his father's estate near Mount Ætna?"

I did not know. He tightened his jaw. "Very well, I will make the arrangements. Go." I had not reached the doorway when he added in a tone of leathery hardness, "If there were no other choice, I would let disgrace fall on your sister before allowing you to take it upon yourself."

My spirit was at too low an ebb for argument. I bowed my head and left.

So Silius might save his wealth and citizenship by retiring to Sicily. I had no doubt that he would accept the offer and be glad of it. It was better than he deserved, due solely to the old friendship between my father and his.

Nor would Pertinax suffer. He would gain a powerful ally when he was eligible to stand for the Senate, and in the meantime would dine out all over Narbo on the strength of being the notorious Phoenix.

But Nina, my sweet, clever sister, who had so wanted a child . . . How could I face her again? If only I had not been so blind and stupid, never imagining the sharp-tongued poet might be a woman. . . .

There was a fellow in Carnuntum when I was there who had trained a bear to engage with him in mock combat. They were a popular attraction in the forum until, one market day, the bear knocked him down and clawed his face off. Everyone said how docile the animal had always appeared to be. But that was no solace to the man who had made the wrong assumption.

So the dream began just as before: Publius and I rode on the bluff along the Danube while barbarians on the other side embarked in boats to attack the province. I had just turned to say we must warn the fortress when I saw, far below, an enemy aiming a spear at us. "Look out," I shouted, trying to protect my brother. But he had put his arm out to shield me, and the spear pierced his side.

On the ground I cradled him, weeping as his blood ran over my fingers. Selfishly I pleaded that I could not bear him to die so soon after Phormio, so soon after what I had done to Nina. Yet the brush of breath on my cheek ceased, and he gave up his spirit.

The shock of it wrenched me from sleep with tears sticky on my face. At first I was in both places, in my bed and on the bluff, lying on my side with an arm outstretched to cushion his head. Then, as the dusty grass of the Danube track faded away, his absence transformed slowly into a presence.

I stopped breathing, all my senses tensed, like a child sensing some midnight apparition near his cot. The presence became an embrace without touch. It was familiar and comforting, not fearsome or cold.

The forgotten fragrance of his orris-root scent came to me. I caught my breath in an elated gasp.

Know the truth, he said into my ear.

"What truth?"

Know the truth. Honor me.

"How? What truth?"

He was waning. "Stay with me," I cried.

The darkness became only darkness; the scent became only lamp oil and woolen bedding and my own sweat. I rolled up on my elbow, staring around wild-eyed. Rufus, huddled against the wall, gaped back at me.

"Come back," I called, but there was no response. Perhaps his spirit could not stay in this world for long, even if drawn by death.

I lay down again. I was short of breath, my heart beating hard. All my doubts and denials, the consequence of inflexible logic, had dissolved at last. I believed now that Aurima too had sensed him, and that his had been the whispers I had heard.

Had his spirit returned to help me? By telling me to spare Rufus, he had saved my life.

Then I realized I was wrong. He had acted to save Caligula, not me. Rufus's survival meant that Caligula was not poisoned. My pursuit of Gemellus meant that Caligula was not overthrown in a civil war. Even in death, my brother remained true to the duty for which Father had bred him.

Know the truth. Honor me.

I had learned the truth behind Caligula's fears, the truth of Father's conflict with Lepidus, the truths of Gemellus's ambition and Silius's treachery and Nina's audacity. Rome swarmed with truths. I had no appetite for learning more of them.

And I already knew the truth of Publius's own treason, which had nearly dragged the last prince of Augustus's line down with him.

Did I not?

I sat up and thrust back the covers. "Rufus, light the lamp. And wake Dio. I must speak with him."

"I do not remember, Marcus." Dio shivered, kneading his hands. He wore only a long sleeping tunic, and his feet were bare on the tiles.

"Think, Dio. Were they here when Publius died?"

"You cannot expect me to recall. So much distress and upheaval . . ." He combed back his thin dark hair with his fingers, leaving it more disheveled than before. His gaze lurched back from the past to my face in the lamplit bedroom. "No one imagined, of course, that the pardon would not come. . . ."

"Yes, I know. Think. His body slave, Apolophanes? Phryne, his bed girl? His accountant . . ."

"Phoebus, yes." Dio's eyelids shuttered as he looked down at his hands, now entwined at his waist.

Slowly he shook his head. "None of them were here," he whispered, raising his eyes to mine.

I exhaled softly. Between thumb and forefinger I clasped my brother's ring on the little finger of my other hand.

Know the truth.

Dio crossed his arms for warmth. Rufus, cross-legged on the floor, wriggled deeper into his quilt.

I put the signet to my lips and let its icy kiss linger. I could dismiss them both back to bed, struggle on in dutiful service to Father and Caligula, and pray for the Eagle quest as a reward. . . .

But would his spirit let me sleep?

I remembered something Caligula had said when we first met beside the seething Tiber: *Is it not enough that I am driven into the streets to escape him?*

I said, "Dio, I wish you to scribe me a letter. And I will have it delivered immediately."

Caligula's response came within the hour. He was not asleep, either.

The stir within the atrium woke my father. "A summons to the Palace," I explained, not adding that I had prompted it.

"A problem?" he wanted to know.

"We will see," I said, following my escort down the vestibule steps.

Ollius paused outside the door, peering up and down the street. "Black as Hades' navel." His breath puffed into the cold night. "Get that torch lit, fleabait."

The uneven paving stones jutted hugely in the light of Rufus's torch, like broken ice in a river. A thick pall of smoke and mist smothered the sound of our footsteps; even Dio's sneeze was muffled. No one spoke. Our shadows darted in and out of doorways.

Had it really been only a few hours since my return from Phormio's funeral? I ought to have been weary, but aches and exhaustion no longer mattered. Someone else looked through my eyes at the refuse-littered pavement, the nail-studded doors, the shuttered shops.

Honor me, my steps echoed.

I waited in a candlelit anteroom amid yawning Palace servants. Bits of conversation escaped from the next room with the opening and closing of the door. Caligula was talking about patrician women: Domitia Lepida, Plautia Urgulanilla, my onetime lover Junia Torquata. Too old, this one; a strain of epilepsy in the family of that one; a tendency in the sisters of a third to bear girls.

He was discussing brides. Brides for a Princeps who needed an heir.

"None of them is worthy of me," he snapped at last. "Find me a woman of strong blood, Kallistos, a Hera to my Zeus. One who will not tangle me in the feuds and ambitions of her damned family."

The Pan-bearded freedman emerged with a tablet under one arm and frustration on his face. I slipped in before the door closed.

Caligula straightened up from a scroll-covered table. "Carinna?" His cheeks were hollow, his eyes shadowed. The smells of snuffed candles, stale wine, and charcoal smoke embalmed the stuffy room, yet he was heavily dressed in long tunics under a sleeveless fur-lined robe.

The man beside him had been deformed by age or disease into an upended hook. He wore a close-fitting leather cap cut to expose big ears with bejeweled lobes, and a gown embroidered with odd symbols.

Caligula put down a hand to stop the top scroll from furling. "I did not ask you to come now."

"I am sorry to interrupt," I said. "I have been troubled of late."

He mistook the reason: "Your sister." The harshness went out of his voice. "How does Nina fare?"

"We dare to hope she will recover." I saw the letter I had sent earlier lying unrolled on a couch behind him, the scribed message distinctive in its brevity. "Caesar—"

He spoke at the same time: "I have just removed her name from the list. I dare not take a wife who cannot bear healthy children." Now I could see the scroll under his hand, with its orbs and arcs and signs like those on the astrologer's robe. A horoscope.

I did not care that he refused to marry my sister. "Caesar, my letter."

"If this is about your friend Silius, he has forfeited my clemency with his insults. I will have him deported so far away that Latin is an unknown tongue."

"I am not here about Silius."

"Then come back another time. Do you not see that I am occupied?"

"It must be now," I said.

"How dare you—" he began hotly. Then his gaze met mine and his eyes widened, as if I had turned into a crouching wolf.

He scooped the scrolls together and thrust them into the Chaldean's arms. "I must talk with my quaestor," he said without looking away from me. The astrologer huffed through his nostrils and shuffled away.

I waited. "Your letter," Caligula said. He gave me a thin smile, but his pale eyes were uneasy. He picked it up and glanced at it. "What does this mean: you want to know the truth? The truth about what? Do you think I am an oracle?"

"I think you know what it means. The truth about why Publius's slaves disappeared when he returned to Rome. And why my father says he sacrificed him."

"Those questions would be better asked of him. I am not privy to his thoughts." He spun the piece of papyrus toward me. It landed at my feet.

"Clavus," a voice said.

The voice must have been mine. But why would I call him a boot nail?

Caligula wet his lips. "Rana," he whispered. "Rana, for pity's sake."

Rana was his private name for your brother, Livilla had said. Had "Clavus" been Publius's nickname for him?

"I am not my brother," I said.

"Then how did you know . . ." Still staring he dropped down on the couch, clumsy with stupefaction.

"He sent me here," I said. "To learn the truth."

His shoulders bowed. He put his face in his hands.

"Tell me." I tried to harden my voice. In the unforgiving light of a hanging lamp, the crown of his head showed pink through his thinning hair. He wore a wreath in public, always.

I had already learned so many secrets that one more should not have unmanned me, but my belly churned with fear. Unable to look at him any longer, I turned away to study the opposite wall, on which was copied the famous fresco of Alexander the Great routing Darius at Gaugamela.

"He will not let me sleep." Caligula's voice was thick and unsteady. "He speaks, but I cannot make sense of what he says."

I stared at Alexander on his great stallion, grimly pursuing Darius's chariot through the thick of the battle. I felt cold.

"Is that what he wants? Is that why he will not rest?"

I made myself face him. "I do not know."

He lurched up. "Rana, is that it?" he called out to the four walls. "Is that what you want?" Silver glittered on his lashes.

There was silence.

"Will you rest then, best beloved?" His voice rose to a cry of anguish. "Will you leave me in peace?"

An icy sweat prickled on my back and arms. "What is the truth?"

Caligula stilled himself. Half his face was dark, the other half firelit. One bloodshot eye glittered at me. "Meet me tonight at moonset."

I tried to move my lips. Finally I managed to ask, "Where?"

"In the farther courtyard of the House of Tiberius, there is a fishpond." He paused to catch his breath. "Come alone, and the past will speak to you."

As I backed away, my glance was caught by the painted face of the fleeing Persian king. His eyes were haunted, his head turned back toward Nemesis closing on him. "I will come," I said.

CHAPTER 39

THE FISHPOND

Nothing broke the stillness of the fishpond: no floating leaves, no bubbles, no spreading rings from a fish rising. It had a foul smell, as though something large had drowned in its depths long ago.

I sat muffled in my cloak on the pond's curb, yawning with nerves. Rufus squatted by my feet. I had been there long enough to begin doubting that Caligula would meet me. If he had decided my questions were dangerous, I would be an easy target, for I had left Ollius at the guard post.

Pearlshine glossed the sky behind racing clouds. When I looked up, it seemed the clouds were fixed and I was being hurled forward at an impossible speed. I dragged my eyes away and touched the gold torc at my neck for luck.

A cock crowed somewhere near. Rufus leaped up.

Footsteps shuffled through dead leaves in a grape arbor beside the house. A low voice said, "Now summon up your courage, for you will need it."

I knew the voice. And the words: they are the Sibyl's to Aeneas, when she conducts him to the underworld.

"Are you still willing?" Caligula stepped out of the arbor, wrapped in a cloak. "This journey cannot be undone."

I rose to my feet. "Where must I go?"

"Follow me." He threw me an unlit torch. "Here is your golden bough."

I told Rufus to wait. But when I started after the Princeps' hooded figure, he seized my arm, shaking his head.

I pulled myself free. "If I do not return by daybreak, go home," I said, and followed Caligula.

He waded through an orchard sodden with rotted apples to a wooden gate in its far wall. The bar lifted without difficulty, but grass had grown so high that it took both of us to drag the gate wide enough for a man to pass.

I squeezed into the opening after him. The moonless sky disappeared, and my groping hand struck another door directly opposite. I was in a tiny chamber roofed and hidden between two stone walls, invisible from the outside. A stairway led down to a glow in the earth.

Caligula was nearly at the bottom of the steps. When he turned, the light behind him made his shadow lunge up at me. "Bring the torch," he commanded.

My unease grew. As a boy I had explored the Palatine heights as thoroughly as any surveyor. I knew where Romulus had built his hut, where the cornel tree grew that had sprung from his spear, where the cave gaped in which he and his twin had suckled from the she-wolf. But I had never known of this opening in the earth.

"I need more light," Caligula barked. Iron struck iron: a key in his hand, prodding at a hidden door.

Fixing my eyes on the fireglow, I made my way after him. Thirteen, fourteen, fifteen steps. Cold sweat leaked down my cheek.

The light came from a cresset behind a latticed iron gate. I poked the torch through the grille and lit it. Caligula twisted the key, and a bolt groaned out of its socket. He shoved the gate open. Shadows fled back into a crevice beyond, barely wider than my shoulders.

I could hardly believe we were still in the mortal world. This cleft in the hill might be a *mundus*, leading to the realm from which the living never return.

Caligula looked at me. His face too was slicked with sweat. "Do you seek this journey?" he asked again, as if hoping I would refuse.

My feet seemed rooted where I stood. Must I do this to bring peace to Publius's spirit? "Guard me, brother," I said aloud. I tried to sense him nearby, but felt only the damp chill of the earth.

"Lead," Caligula said. "You have the light."

I swallowed, made the Sun sign to shield myself, and lunged apprehensively into the sewer reek of the crevice, holding the torch at arm's length. My boot soles skidded on slime. Beetles fled up the rock walls, and something scuttled over my toes. I stopped with a grunt of revulsion.

"Go on." Caligula's voice was shrill. The cleft pressed close on either side, and he blocked it behind me.

An incantation against the gods of the underworld came back to me, forgotten since childhood. I muttered it as I edged forward.

Then the passage widened, flinging up a scene beyond the torch flame that made me gasp. For Caligula had taken me to that part of Hades' kingdom where the wicked and impious are tormented forever.

This Tartarus was cramped and murky, the air thick with smoke and the stink of excrement. A fire flickered atop three goatish legs. Crouching shapes wavered behind a grove of barren, stick-straight trees. Seeing us, they cried out in a cacophony of fear and desperation.

Panic shot through me. I would have bolted like a thunderstruck horse had I not heard a whisper amid the shrieking.

Courage.

I clutched at the admonition. "Help me, brother."

And he was there, calm and confident. I even turned, expecting to find him beside me, the secret amusement that usually warmed his eyes transformed into gravity. But there was only smoke.

Caligula had pinched his hood around his lower face. He seemed unaware of Publius's spirit, and unawed by this hell pit. He had been here before.

He nodded toward the trees, which before my eyes turned into the bars of cages. Had he brought me here to imprison me, too? Or was I meant to recognize someone?

Summoning up my brother's bravery, I covered my nose with my cloak and advanced across a mat of moldy straw. A rat fled the light of my torch.

The howling and jabbering stopped. Three creatures with matted beards and ropy hair gaped at me from their cages. They were not vaporous ghosts, but living men.

A hand shot out from between the bars. I flinched. "Nasty!" cried a voice behind me. A stick cracked down, and the prisoner squealed.

The bare-skulled dungeon keeper was so begrimed, skin and clothes, that he had been indiscernible in the smoke. He showed rotted teeth in a grin. "Here to buy a charm, are you, my lords? Best place in town, the Fishpond." His cudgel pointed at areas of my body. "Hearts, livers, cocks, balls. Hands, that's best. If every corpse had four hands, I'd be a rich man." He spat into the tripod brazier.

Caligula stepped closer, looking from one prisoner to the next.

"But this ain't a *popina* with takeout service. Off with you." The keeper pointed his stick at the mouth of the cleft. "Leave your order at the Temple of Latinus."

"I seek a man who has been here for three years," Caligula said, muffled in his cloak.

Into the spirit that had heartened me came a kind of tension. Pain or anger? Grief?

The dungeon keeper shook his head irritably. "Can't kill one of 'em for you, no matter how much you pay. I have to keep 'em alive."

I coughed on the smoke. "Which of these men has been here for three years?"

"He is deaf." Caligula flicked his eyes at the captives. "Ask them."

"Ask what? If they have kept track of the years?"

"Ask if they came from Capri."

Before the nearest wretch could let go of the bars, I clamped a hand on his fingers. "Were you on Capri? Were you with Tiberius Caesar?"

He struggled, mewling. "Have pity, sir! Pity!"

I tried to glare at him, but my eyes watered in the foul air. "Are you from Capri?"

"From Ancona, sir. Tell my father." Tears and mucus leaked into his beard. "He will pay anything."

"Scum," muttered the keeper. "Raped a priestess of Vesta."

I let the Anconan go and shouted to the next prisoner, "Did you come from Capri?"

"Didoo com fom Capri?" The man scratched his armpit.

I coughed again, appalled by the filth behind him. "Jove's Villa on Capri. Were you there?"

"Knows something he shouldn't," the keeper said. "Or used to. Daft as a mercury miner now."

Beaming toothlessly, the prisoner offered me a turd.

My head felt as if it would split. Caligula was as mad as any of these miserable captives. Why did I not drag him into the open air and force out of him whatever secret was buried in this ghastly place?

The third prisoner was warming his fingers by the torch flame. "And you?" I demanded. "Did you come from Capri?"

"From Belgica, your honor," he croaked.

None of the three was from that accursed island. I turned to confront Caligula, but he was already standing at my elbow. "Do you remember me?" he said, and let the sides of the hood fall open.

Fear flooded into the Celt's inflamed eyes. He retreated deeper into his cage and squatted down, hiding his face in his arms.

"Speak," Caligula said. "Who am I?"

The Celt mumbled into his knees, "You are the young Caesar."

"And you are the man who betrayed my friend and me."

"Impossible," I blurted out. "That man died under questioning."

Caligula glanced at me, with a look in his eyes that was both sorrowful and smug. And the truth rushed toward me, gaining speed like a ballista stone falling from the peak of its arc.

Saxa's report had been false.

I sensed, or heard, a sigh beside me. Publius's presence began to fade. "No," I cried, but it was gone.

The Celt hugged his knees tighter. "Be merciful, Caesar. I have paid."

"Tell this man the truth. What did you say to the Special Cohort?"

The Celt rocked on his haunches, moaning, shaking his head.

Caligula thrust his face next to the bars of the cage. "If you want to ever see the sun again, tell him! Did his brother say those words?"

The head-shaking became more violent. The Celt dared not obey.

No. He was shaking his head because it was not Publius who had made the treasonous joke.

I tried to catch my breath, but it was like inhaling fire. "It was you?" I said to Caligula.

"He died for love of me," said my brother's dearest companion. His eyes were starbursts in the flare of my torch.

Horror swelled in my throat. I groaned.

"For his sake I have made you my friend." His hoarse voice coaxed me to understand. "For his sake, I will do you honor."

I must tell Father, I thought. *Tell him Caligula lied to him—*

"Your father did not want you to know," he said. "But I can bear it no longer."

I took a step back, slithering in the straw. His hand clamped on my wrist. "Free me, Marcus. Free me from your brother's ghost."

Shouts and howls pummeled me. My head rang with an endless shriek, until crushing blackness robbed me of my senses.

The next I knew, I was groping empty-handed past the grilled gate to the stairway. I struggled upward, bruised and panting. My legs trembled as if I had run for miles. Reaching the secret walled chamber at the top, I caught my toe on the last step and sprawled headfirst.

Rufus wriggled past the half-open gate. With him pulling on me, I crawled and stumbled into the orchard. He let me down into grass that crackled with frost.

Sounds came from the depths: the crash of an iron grate, the rattle of a key. Rufus stood up. Morning mist curled around his bare legs as he edged back through the narrow gap.

Not mist. Smoke.

Pale lines of smoke began to rise from the mouth of a dancing Pan, the lotus-shaped crest of a dry fountain, the rim of the fishpond. I pulled myself up and reeled toward the pond. Smoke spouted from gaps hidden behind a decorative coping. I heard screams, or so I thought.

Caligula burst gasping through the orchard gate, his fair head bent next to Rufus's red hair. Behind them, a chittering horde of rats poured out into the grass.

The sky was like new silver, bright and pale. I tried to call my brother's spirit back, but the words seared my throat and I could only cough.

CHAPTER 40

FEVER

Even in the Grove of Diana beneath pine trees laden with snow, I could smell the Fishpond. When I was done retching, we would trudge farther, sometimes coming across our own half-melted tracks.

Without any memory of leaving the House of Tiberius, I had found myself in a *taberna* with Rufus. My head was filled with dazzle, and I had no voice. When the floor trembled and cups began to rattle, someone cried, "Earthquake!" and I swayed outside with the others.

From the direction of the Palace a great column of smoke plumed into the sky. Someone brought the news that a chasm had opened in a courtyard where an old fishpond had been. Spirits from the underworld were flying out in a cloud of noxious vapor.

I went back into the *taberna* and refilled my cup. Ollius and Dio found me there, abandoned in the general panic. Dio asked if the world was ending.

I laughed. Suddenly the dreadful reek filled my nostrils and he became the dungeon keeper, holding out a severed hand to me.

I vomited the wine. Take me to the Temple of Apollo Latiaris, I said.

Ollius and Dio argued in mutters that swirled around the high conical roof where the pigeons nested. "Tiberius buried a curse tablet there," Ollius insisted. "That's what made all Caligula's bad luck."

Dio said, "It was a cistern collapse. I saw it, caved in like a rotten squash."

I pushed furs away and clambered to my feet. Ollius turned toward me, ruddy-cheeked. Dio paused, holding a cup in a hand wrapped in rags. Rufus looked up from braiding grass into a snare. They wanted me to say, "Fetch the horse and the mules. I am ready to go back to Rome."

Instead I set out again with Rufus and Ollius when the sun rose over the hill. The day warmed; diamonds dripped from the pines. I followed our own frozen footprints peppered in the snowy track. Here was where I had stopped the team. Here, the fallen tree where I had deposited Aurima. From there the prints wandered uselessly. The snow made everything different.

But this day Fortuna relented, and I found it. I ran my fingers over the upturned crescent, the crude skirted figure.

She had expected to die here. By preventing it I had earned her vengeance, vengeance that still tortured me with jealousy and grief.

I had lost her. I had lost them all. Father, mother, sister, brother. Phormio. Silius.

I knelt in the snow, leaning my head against the trunk of the old pine, and burned with heartache. I wanted to weep but could not.

Father would have told Publius it was his duty to save Rome from civil war. If Caligula was executed for treason, there would be no able-bodied male of Augustus's family to succeed Tiberius. So they had deceived the old Princeps, suppressing the only witness, falsifying the records. *Let us not tell Marcus the truth,* Father must have said to the others. *He will not understand. He will not be able to keep the secret.*

On my brother's last night, I had berated him for not defending himself from the treason charge. He had known there was no hope. No escape from the knife he would take from Father's hand.

Snowmelt trailed down my neck like icy fingers. I hoisted myself, wiping bark-scoured hands on my tunic. Ollius was gone, and Rufus faced the mouth of the clearing. Between the dark pines stood a tall red-haired girl in a cloak.

I thought I must be dreaming. There was no reason for her to be here. No way she could have known.

"You are wounded," she said.

Confusion and shame overwhelmed me. No longer was I the proud son of a respected Senator of Rome, confident in my honor. I lowered my eyes and turned away from Ingiomar's daughter.

Day faded. A fire sprang up beyond the temple, its light glittering in the waters of the holy spring. Fat popped and spat from small carcasses on a spit. Dio, Rufus, Ollius, and the youth Odo squinted at me across the flames. Aurima did not look up from stirring a pot at the fire's edge.

My head churned with fog and lightning. I saw rats pouring through the orchard gate. Triumphant pride gleaming in Caligula's eyes. *He died for love of me.* Father slapping the bloody tunic down on his desk. *Mine to be the hand that sacrificed him.*

"You have been to the world below," Aurima said. "You saw what is not to be seen."

I pressed against my horse, who stood under the trees with the shaggy German ponies and my men's mules. Spider pushed his black nose against my tunic, and his dark eye met mine. The reproachful gaze of the dappled horse I had killed flashed at me.

"Go away," I croaked. "Let me be."

But in truth I did not know what I would do or where I would go. Even Diana's sacred grove reeked of smoke, shit, and madness.

Aurima's nostrils flared. Perhaps she could smell the Fishpond too, witch that she was. She gripped my upper arm through my cloak. "Look at me."

The fire behind her limned every wild wisp of her hair. As I stared, the wisps themselves shot sparks and turned to flame. Her face dissolved, and there was only fire.

Then it ignited inside me. My heart raged, and a lust for violence roared through my veins. I wrenched myself from her grasp. . . .

And it died away. My chest heaved, but there was nothing to bring up. I staggered like a poleaxed sacrifice.

She caught her breath. "You are cursed."

I grinned. "And who . . . cursed me?"

Shadows leaped and shrank. *Make them fear you*, a voice whispered. A half-eaten mouse materialized where I was about to tread, and I lurched aside. Jason lay in rags of snow beneath a barren tree, his blood flowing as black as the Styx. *Marcus, what have you done?*

A cup steamed in Aurima's hand. "Drink this," she said.

"Where . . . is my brother?" My voice grated with smoke and disuse.

Her face hardened. She pushed the cup against my chest.

I coughed. "Need to tell him . . . I understand. Now I understand."

"Drink," she repeated.

I looked down at it. Had she come to complete the curse?

She thrust the cup at me, silent and stern.

With my eyes on hers I took it and raised it to my mouth. The bitter liquid was nauseating, but I drank every drop. If it was poison, what would I feel first? Numbness and lack of breath, like the slave Hanno?

I sank onto the temple steps. Stars crowded between the dark borders of pine, more than on the clearest night in Rome. In places the sky was white with them. How was it possible for so many to have fallen the other night without leaving gaps?

I shrugged my cloak back to cool myself. Sitting here just as I was now, Publius had seen the Milk Road spanning the sky, a bridge to the upper world. How consoling, he had told the old priest, to believe souls were eternal.

He was at peace now. And I was the one tortured by truth.

A rill of perspiration trailed down my backbone. I shifted uncomfortably on the stone step.

Aurima sat by the blaze, close to Dio and Rufus. The boy gestured with his hands like an actor. Light flickered on Ollius's face as he sharpened his knife. Odo yawned, hunched against the *stela* marking the sanctity of the spring.

I fingered my cloak away from my neck. A drop of sweat trickled out of my hair and down my jaw. On this raw winter night, I was sweltering.

"What have you done?" I whispered to the priestess, who stood beside me.

She tugged on my forearm. I stumbled to my feet and followed her to the priest's hut beside the temple. But when she pulled aside the hide hanging in the low doorway, I balked.

"Go in," she told me. Yet her gaze seemed to waver.

Reflexively I reached for the knife behind my back. It was not there.

"Ollius," she said.

My bodyguard loomed up beside her. "Help me," I said. "I am unwell."

"I know, young master." He slung an arm around my shoulders. "Let Lady Aurima try to help you." He propelled me into the hut.

My head hit a rafter. Straw thatch bucked up with a noisy rustle, and a rush of snow fell onto my neck. I was reeling in a crouch toward the entrance when Aurima caught me. Too dazed to push back, I fell onto pine boughs that crunched under my weight.

I struggled to rise. "Hot." My scalp itched with sweat. I wanted to throw myself into the spring.

She knelt and unfastened the pin of my cloak. The heavy folds fell away, and I was cooler. But not for long.

Fever scorched my cheeks and nostrils. With fumbling hands I ripped off my tunics, my loincloth, even my boots. Still I sweated, and stank of the Fishpond.

I tried again to get up. I must go to Apollo's temple. Only the Sun God could save me.

Aurima threw everything through the doorway. "Odo," she cried.

Fitful shadows broke the fireglow. I was burning up. I was locked in a cell under the Fishpond with fire spreading from the fallen torch.

"Free me," I cried as the flames grew. "Cousin, the key! Let me out!"

Someone tied a fat bandage on my bare chest. Was I wounded? But instead of pain I felt two heartbeats: mine, thudding hard, and a second, fainter and more rapid. Tiny talons scrabbled against my skin. Something inside was trying to dig free.

I shouted in fright. I could not move my arms to claw it away. My father was holding me down.

I thrashed desperately. "Father, let me go."

Scum, he said. *Raped a priestess of Vesta.*

"I cannot help it. I love her."

I would burn to death. He would marry again and beget better sons. Better than me. Better than Publius.

That complacent smile. Father's. Caligula's. *He died for love of me.*

"You gave his life for C-C-Cah—" The stutter burst into a roar. With a heave I launched myself toward him, my fingers arched into claws.

Hands restrained me. I shrieked and wept, afire in gold-seamed darkness. Voices hummed and warbled.

After a long time, a gush of cold water slapped my face. It drenched my shoulders, my chest, my genitals, my legs. I felt myself rise up and away from the fire at last.

Outside the hut, my nostrils pinched tight and my balls shrank. I swayed on bare feet in the bitter cold. Someone heaved branches onto the fire. A scrap of white caught my eye, then vanished in smoke pluming from the green wood.

Aurima's hair was torn from its braid, her clothing wet and disheveled. "Let him stand," she said, and whoever was holding me backed away.

401

In a great shout she invoked her goddess. Her breath streamed like a flag in the frosty dawn. She brushed me with a pine bough, called out again, and touched the branch to the bandage on my chest.

I stared crazily. If I shut my eyes, I would collapse.

With the butt of the branch, she made a circle on the ground. Odo untied the binding around me. She took a bundle from the binding, placed it in the circle, unwrapped it. Inside lay the limp body of a young hare.

She touched it with the evergreen bough. "Rise in the name of Austro, Goddess of Light."

Useless. The animal was dead; my fevered raving had killed it.

No one spoke. The fire smoked and snapped. Resin flared bright.

Then the hare's hind leg twitched. A shiver swept over me, and the men nearby drew in their breath. Panting, the creature staggered up and shook itself.

"The Goddess bids you, go!" Aurima pointed her wand toward the trees, and the hare streaked off into the night.

Her firelit face relaxed. In my daze I thought her supernatural, a wood nymph whose beauty would lure any mortal man into sacrilege.

"The curse is gone," she said to me.

The stars whirled. I let my eyes close, and my knees gave way.

I slept. And slept. Once or twice I stumbled out into daylight to relieve myself, then burrowed into the furs and quilts again. There were no dreams.

When I fully woke, it was night. Firelight trickled in through gaps in the wattle. The others had crawled into the hut and wedged themselves around me, rolled in their cloaks. I smelled the homely fug of unwashed bodies and lived-in clothes. Someone was snoring.

I turned my face into the resiny tang and warm-animal scent of my bedding, then lifted my hand to my nose and inhaled the tang of purifying smoke. The clean tunic Rufus had pulled over me smelled of leather saddlebags. The stink of the Fishpond was gone.

I hauled myself to my feet, forgetting to crouch. My head hit the thatch again, and debris showered down.

"Need me, Marcus?" Ollius rumbled.

"Enjoy your beauty sleep." I dragged up the fur that had covered me and groped toward the doorway.

The clouds and storms were gone that had blurred my mind. I knew now what I must do.

The fire was a glowing mesh of gold. Aurima had burned all my clothing, even my cloak; only boots and belt, still musky with smoke, had been spared. As I knelt to suck spring water from my hands, Spider nickered from across the clearing. One of the mules brayed, jolted from sleep, and the two Marcomanni ponies thrashed to their feet. So did Aurima and Odo, who had been curled in cloaks beside their mounts.

She spoke to her cousin in Germanic. I did not try to guess her meaning. She had seen me weak, naked, incoherent, weeping like a child. What proud woman could respect such a man?

Shivering, for my single tunic was scant protection from the cold, I laced up the boots and buckled the belt. Last, I flung the wolf pelt around my shoulders.

When I looked up, she was standing in the frost-spangled track that led past Apollo's temple. An ice-blue moon rising over the hill crest cast her cloaked shadow toward me.

Meet me at moonset.

Pure silver slid down my bare arm. Every hair on my body, already bristling with cold, shot sparks.

I crunched across the frozen grass and climbed the temple steps. In moments I heard her booted feet behind me.

She halted a few steps down. Moonlight grayed her hair; I might have been seeing her in old age. Quietly she said, "Are you free of the darkness, Marcus Carinna?"

"Why are you here?" I said. The words scraped in my throat, seared from screaming.

I half expected that her magic had told her to come, but she answered, "Flavus said your father worries. He looks everywhere for you."

I mounted the last of the steps without looking at her. "So you rode here to find me, just you and Odo?"

"I am not a girl of your people, soft as a mushroom."

I pushed open one of the doors and went inside.

Cold night filled the temple. The portal's creak woke doves who rustled overhead, half seen in the darkness, as if the roof itself were shredding and blowing away.

Great Apollo rose toward the circle of starlight, reaching over his shoulder for an arrow. A small drift of snow glittered on leaves and pine needles blown against his plinth. To shield my madness Dio had sent the priest away, so there was no one now to sweep the floor clean.

I stood at the altar, a hip-high block of worn marble, and laid my hands on the sacrificial dish at its crown, silky with ashes from the last sacrifice. To the tall figure of the Sun God I prayed aloud, "Mithras, Lord of Light, unconquered Sun, who died and rose again: I give you thanks for delivering me from my soul's darkness."

"Austro delivered you," Aurima interrupted. "Not that thing of stone."

"Go back to bed, priestess," I said, my eyes still on Apollo. "I will be away at first light."

Almost soundlessly, as if fearing the Furies might hear, she said, "To kill your father?"

So she had understood my fevered ranting. I let out my breath slowly. As if Mithras did not already know the truth, I said into the well of silence that surrounded the god's image, "He made my brother take the blame when Caligula spoke against the old Princeps. Made him kill himself, so the golden prince might be spared Tiberius's wrath."

The words came faster. Spittle flew from my lips. "He hid the truth from everyone, so my brother's name was blackened. Then he told me I must redeem the honor of our house with poor Caligula, so recklessly endangered by his best friend's treason."

A faint echo of my forceful whisper murmured from the walls like rippling water. My hands on the altar had clenched into fists.

Aurima said, low-voiced, "Caesar allowed this?"

"He boasted to me that my brother—" My throat went dry. "That my brother died for love of him."

I looked up at Apollo again, trying to regain my calm. "Now go, so I may finish my prayer." Belatedly I added, "I am grateful to you."

She did not move. "Among my people, a kinsman or a friend fights a king without honor. And kills him, if Tiwaz wills it."

"I cannot fight the Princeps. I swore an oath to protect him."

She circled around the altar to face me, eyes agleam in the starlight. "When you tell the free men of Rome what he did, they are not going to let him be Princeps. You can kill him then."

Knowing what must be done when I returned to the city, I had no desire to argue. Between us lay the full breadth of civilization.

"Are you afraid?" she flared. "You told me, 'I do not surrender. When I want something, I fight until I get it.'"

I had thought myself numb, but her scorn lacerated me. I looked from her accusing glare to the bold bones of her face, the curve of an ear peeping through a swag of hair, the pale shaft of her throat half sheathed in darkness.

"Saddle your horse," I said, making for the door. "We will leave as soon as my men are ready." The moonlight was strong enough to mark the way back to the Via Appia.

Behind me she said more roughly, "When I came to you, I thought that you"—she snatched a breath—"at least would not shame me in—in taking my maiden-gift."

I swung around so quickly that she stepped back against the wall. "Did you want a man who would break a sacred oath?"

"Of course I did not!"

With both hands I fished beneath her cloak for the clasp of the necklace Heriberhto had given her. We stood very close, her hands flattened against my chest, my fingers probing beneath the damp mass of her braided hair. She did not blink.

I had no patience with the fastening. I ripped the necklace apart. Beads rolled down inside her clothes and pattered on the floor.

I cupped the base of her skull in my palms, my thumbs just touching the silken skin in front of her ears. We were pressed together now, her body taut against the force of my wanting. Her heart bounded.

"*Basia me*," I said, and touched my mouth to hers.

It was as though the hand of a god lifted me off the earth and threw me into a headlong plunge. I had not even time to be amazed, so dizzying was the rush of her desire.

We clung together against the wall, her fingers clenched in my hair. My heart thundered. I kissed the corner of her mouth, her ear, her throat, and slid a glance around the little temple. Cold walls, hard floor. Not here.

Aurima's hands clasped my cheeks. "I did not tell you the truth."

"I don't care," I said.

"On Winter Night, I did not go to Heriberhto."

"Good," I said. I slid an arm around her and drew her outside.

It was dark under the tree. Arms and legs in all the wrong places. Clothes that tangled and snared. Pine needles prickling. Our hands searched, found each other's face. A deeper kiss.

"There is a stone under—"

One leg was bare. Then another.

"I cannot unwind this—"

She gasped softly.

I felt her mouth with my fingers. A smile.

Mina hertan, she called me. My heart.

CHAPTER 41

THE RECKONING

I saw Saxa first, rising from his couch. His dinner clothes were plain, but lamplight gleamed on gold at his wrists.

Lepidus reclined on another couch, holding a small plate. His grip went slack, and empty snail shells fell chittering onto the floor. Last fell the spoon, with a silvery chime.

Caligula's eyes met mine, then slid away. "Enter Orestes," he rasped, and popped a piece of seed-roll into his mouth.

I looked past him at the last diner. Father had raised himself on his couch, pale but unruffled. "Leave us," he told the lyrist, whose plectrum had stilled on the strings. The woman laid down her instrument and slipped from the room.

"You others, out," I said. The various attendants glanced at their masters and were dismissed.

So here they were: the four conspirators gathered together in my family's own dining room. I kicked Saxa's couch aside and took two strides toward Caligula. The coldness of the journey came out of my clothes, and the heat of the dining room shrank away.

"Caesar," I said, "I can serve you best by recovering the lost Eagle of the Eighteenth Legion. This is my desire and my intention. Surely you will give me your approval to leave as soon as possible."

He tilted his head to look at me. I saw shock in his deep-set gray eyes.

Lepidus said, "Sit down, Marcus. We can resolve this. Titus, let us have another couch brought in."

Father's greeting was harsher: "We must know whom you have told."

I did not look away from Caligula. I needed his consent to requisition men, horses, and supplies, to review official records about the Eagle search, and to arrange for assistance from the Germanic chieftains to whom Flavus could introduce me. "Further, I wish the Marcomanni hostage, Aurima, to come with me as guide and interpreter."

Saxa squared himself, prepared to stop me if I attacked the Princeps. "Answer your father's question."

I ignored him. "If you refuse, I will publicly withdraw as your quaestor-designate and let the reason be known."

Father smacked his hand on the table. "Whom have you told?" he shouted as the table toppled, spilling cups and wine.

I looked from Caligula to Lepidus. "Who knew?"

They glanced at each other. Finally Lepidus said, "The four of us. No one else."

"Because you silenced Publius's slaves, who might have guessed the truth."

The house steward appeared, drawn by the crash of the table. Father sent him away.

"Answer your father," Saxa repeated.

I pulled my borrowed cloak over my head and tossed it onto the empty couch, showing the longknife sheathed within reach of my right hand. "I have told no one who is not loyal to me."

"Name those who know," he barked.

"Suck me," I said rudely.

He went white with anger. Lepidus warned, "If it becomes public, I will make it known that the exile of your dear friend Silius has unbalanced you." His stare beneath the dark brows was like granite. "The common people will delight in the scandal—and in the pitiful lie you dreamed up to retaliate against Caesar."

Saxa edged closer to my knife hand. I stepped behind his couch, and he halted. "Caesar, what is your will?" he asked, still eyeing me.

Caligula coughed rustily and spat on the floor; he had swallowed more Fishpond smoke than I. "I will have my council's advice," he croaked.

"I am cold and hungry." I turned away. "Tell me when you are done."

"Marcus Carinna, you are still my quaestor-designate. Stay where you are." He coughed again. "Saxa?"

The Special Cohort commander's slitted eyes roved over me. "Young Carinna has persistence, boldness, and a noble name. His search for the Eagle may be more successful than ours."

He had no reason to uphold the pact I had made with him, so I wondered briefly at his support before I understood. He did not trust me and preferred to have me out of the way. With so many agents at his command, it would be easy to make a troublesome Roman disappear in the wilderness.

"I cannot agree," Lepidus said. "I have known him since his birth; his *paedagogus* was a gift from me. He is a loyal son of a loyal family, and cannot be frightened or bribed. You need such men here in Rome, Caesar. I will vouch for his silence on the matter of his brother's death." He turned to me. "I promise, Marcus, we will find you some great reward to equal the Eagle's recovery."

This was no surprise. Our family's patron, brother-in-law of the Princeps, did not want me far from hand if an occasion should arise to seize power.

Caligula leaned back on his elbow. "And you, Titus Licinius?"

I turned away from my father. On the dining room wall, Hippolyta gazed at me from beneath her tipped-back helmet. When we were children playing mythological heroes, Nina was always the Amazon queen. I was Theseus.

Father cleared his throat. "He is right to be angry. We should not have hidden it from him."

What a triumph: he acknowledged a mistake. A small error of judgment, quite apart from the larger matter of sentencing his own son to death.

It was my mistake to have expected more of him. As Silius had once said, *Fatherhood is a shudder and a sigh; all the rest is money.*

Lepidus's couch squeaked as he shifted impatiently. Caligula growled, "What do you advise, Titus?"

Father said quietly, "I will abide by your decision, Caesar." Perhaps he thought withholding his opinion would soften me toward him.

I turned to Caligula. To honey-coat the ultimatum, for he would resist being coerced in his counselors' presence, I said, "Rome needs her Eagle back. I ask again for your approval to seek it, Caesar."

Head down, he was drawing a pattern with his forefinger on the cushion. "I have heard rumors," he said, tracing the small box over and over. "But I would not credit them. You, I thought, would not leave me. You would not betray me."

"There is no place for me here," I said.

For a long moment he did not look up. Then, abruptly, he pushed himself off the couch. "Carinna, Saxa—one of you, summon my slaves." Kicking his sandals into place, he tried to slide his feet into them.

I stood in his path. "Will you give me your permission to go north?"

"I will think about it. Give way!"

His attendants jostled in from the atrium. One squatted to hold his sandals so he might step into them; another slid the sleeve of a fur-lined robe over his outthrust arm.

I tried not to shout. "I must know now."

"See me tomorrow," he snapped.

I moved forward. Saxa blocked the way, growling, "Don't be a fool."

Teeth gritted, I stepped aside as the Princeps' servants bustled him into the atrium. I heard the gruff voices of his guards, the shuffle of feet as bearers brought his litter into the house.

Saxa paused beside me. "If he authorizes your expedition, you will have the Special Cohort's full assistance."

I would need the aid of his agents and informers even if the trip was not sanctioned. "That was not our bargain."

He shrugged. "Silius was not Phoenix." A grim smile notched his cheek. "But we will try to recover your bones, at least."

The dining room still seemed crowded when he left. Our slaves were cleaning up the mess from the fallen table, and a few of Lepidus's attendants had come in to wait for instructions. Our patron put his arm around my father's shoulders and murmured to him.

Father said bitterly, "He could have been a governor's quaestor, learning something useful." He looked at me, not caring that I overheard. "Another year or two, and Caesar would have been more at ease with his power."

I had had enough. I forced my way through the throng in the atrium. Dio, Rufus, and Ollius were in the kitchen, gorging themselves like starvelings. The cook beamed at me; the kitchen maids gave kisses and smoothed down my hair. It was well, they said, that I had gone to the Temple of Apollo Latiaris after the *mundus* opened at the House of Tiberius. My sacrifices had evidently pleased the god, for the underworld spirits had flown away and the hole was being filled.

I kept on into the garden, where the evergreens huddled pinched and melancholy under a shroud of smoky sky. Sandals scuffed behind me. Father's voice said, "I warned him to keep silent. Again and again."

"He could not help himself." I studied the almond trees. "It ate its way out of him."

There was no birdsong on this darkening afternoon, no fountain splashing, not even the chime of a *tintinnabulum*. From out in the street came indistinct shouts and cries as the three guests and their retinues made their departure.

"For your mother's sake, I ask you not to tell her. Or Nina."

"I do not intend to."

He came around me. "You may continue living in this house, provided you will speak respectfully to me and of me."

I looked away from him. It was not a promise I could make.

He broke a sprig off the hedge and rolled it between his thumb and forefinger. "Phormio, may his spirit rest, risked himself to spare you my anger."

A sudden weariness washed over me. It seemed a long time since my *paedagogus*'s death. I would have given anything to have him here, with the constancy of his prickly affection.

"You understand he chose to die for love of you. But you cannot see that your brother made the same choice."

I looked straight at him, letting the contempt show. The light was still full enough to betray every crease and scar in his face. "What do you know of love? Your craving for Caligula's favor has cost you your older son and the devotion of your wife."

He flicked the sprig away. "Very well. If Caesar agrees, you will be sent to find the lost Eagle as you wish."

I stared at him, hardly believing I had heard right.

"If you return with the Eagle, I will welcome you and all will be as it was. If you cannot recover it"—he let his cold gaze impress upon me—"do not come back."

"Father," I said, aghast.

"I will marry again, as I warned you I would, and you will no longer be my heir. You may go and live with your beloved barbarians."

"That is not what I wish—"

"Clearly nothing but your wishes matters to you." His anger was more contained now, as if, having delivered my sentence, he had tightened his self-control.

He closed his eyes for a heartbeat, then regarded me more temperately. "You cannot conceive of the agony of that decision. It was not just Publius I had to sacrifice, but the honor of our family."

I held his eyes.

"I looked to you to restore it," he said very softly. I watched him walk across the garden, the hem of his mantle brushing over withered leaves on the path, until he disappeared in the dark portico on the other side.

And I remembered.

It was the last night of August, the night before my brother was to be tried for treason. Moths with burned wings twitched among the patterns of the mosaic floor, and trees and bushes painted on the walls flickered in the lamp glow.

"Go away," he said. "There is no use your haranguing me." His dark curls were stringy with sweat.

"Tiberius will back down," I insisted. I was mortally afraid that Father would not.

"Marcus, you are too drunk to understand. Go to bed." To the slave waiting in the shadows he said, "Fetch Euhemerus. I must write a few more letters." Letters of farewell, he meant.

I leaned closer. My tunic pulled tight, stuck to my back. "Trust Caligula. Your friend. He will persuade Tiberrus . . . Tiberius to pardon you. I know it." I tried to speak with confidence, but the words slurred off my tongue. "Say you are ill. Make them postpone the . . . the trial."

Publius huffed a sigh through his nose, abrupt and impatient.

"Let the Senate decide, then. Ten to one, they will quit . . . acquit you."

"So you keep telling me," he said. His gaze shifted like the wavering frescoes.

His secretary shuffled in, red-eyed. A thread of mucus glittered in his trim beard. Publius told him to sit down.

"Bacchus's belly, it was only a joke! A stupid, god-cursed joke!" I whacked my cup down on the arm of my chair. Wine splashed, blood-warm, on my bare knee. "Our family honor will survive it. Your honor will survive it."

He ignored me. "A letter to Julia Livilla." He spread his elbows on the chair arms, fingertips touching. "To my dearest Livilla from her loving *sponsus*." He toyed with his signet ring. The secretary's stylus paused over the tablet in the crook of his arm. "Her loyal *sponsus*. Perdition! Leave it at 'loving.'"

My cup hit the floor. I bolted out of my seat and grabbed him by the shoulders. "This is between Father and Tiberius. Save yourself!"

He pulled back, but not before I felt the vibration running through him like the seethe of a fever. He glared at me. A dark arrowhead of sweat had soaked through the breast of his tunic.

Then his anger dissolved. In its place I was dumbfounded to see humor emerge, the brow-quirked amusement that always gave him the look of a clever monkey. He said, "I can see that when your turn comes, Dis will have to drag you down to Hades by your heels."

Tears sprang into my eyes. His grin faded. "I have made my choice, little brother," he said gently, as if I were nine and not nineteen.

"I will not allow it," I shouted. "I will not let you do it."

I kept ranting until he shoved me out and shut the door. My head ached. I wanted to obliterate myself until the next day was over and I could be sure the Senate had acquitted him. It was too late to appeal to the old Princeps myself; not even a courier pigeon could have reached Capri in time.

Gods above, Father could not let his first son die, his treasured heir! Any moment now he would come through the doors, admitting that he had given in and begged Tiberius for a pardon.

I resolved to sit up and wait for him. But as I turned, the atrium swayed around me. My hand flew out to steady myself.

In the frozen moment before I was able to back away, I stared at my fingers splayed on top of our household altar, its bone-white marble stained from decades of burnt offerings. The fly-curtains beside me hung gauzy and straight from the eaves over the pool, and with the murmur of weeping that filled the house, the atrium seemed to be full of rain.

CHAPTER 42

FRIEND OF CAESAR

A contented household has a certain music. The level of voices is pleasant, sandals patter as people go about their tasks, pots and pans clang, someone may hum or sing, someone else may laugh at a joke.

The music had gone from our household. The slaves who had so happily welcomed my return from the countryside now eyed me with apprehension and resentment. Even though Dio and Ollius would have told them I could not speak of what had happened to me, they knew I had turned their world upside down.

I did not care. If it had been possible to leave immediately, I would have saddled my horses, gathered up Aurima, and started north. But the Alpine passes would be snow-blocked for months more, and I needed the time to plan, enlist an escort, and organize supplies—all of which would be immensely simpler with Caligula's approval.

In the meantime, I did not intend to be parted from her. I told Dio to call on the ward captains who were our clients and find me a small apartment with a garden.

He did not move. After a minute or two I looked up from the letter I was writing to Nina. "What is it?"

"When you leave to find the captured Eagle . . ." He paused, then went on in a nervous burst, "You will need records kept, dispatches written, and so forth."

Rufus had just lit a lamp. The light picked out creases of diffidence on Dio's high forehead and gave his pointed nose a shadow like the gnomon of a sundial. He asked, "Do you intend to take me with you?"

I said, "We will be mounted." And he was the worst rider I had ever seen.

"You will need a baggage cart. I can drive it."

As far as I knew, he had never driven a vehicle in his life. "You are better off with my mother, Dio. I may never come home."

He took a deep breath. "With all respect for your lady mother, I would rather not die a woman's secretary."

I turned back to the letter. It took a moment to master my voice, and then I told him I would give it thought.

When I left the house with Rufus, the street was already smutty with dusk. I walked quickly in case she had already arrived, but no one waited in the shelter of the great beech tree. On a bench in its shade, Silius and I had hatched many of our best schemes—like gumming old Capito's false teeth around the shin of a statue of Marcus Antonius, whom he had despised.

The branches were bare now, and soggy leaves littered the bench. I swiped it clean with my cloak and sat.

My father's ultimatum lay heavily on my heart. If it took more than a year to find the Eagle, or if he wrongly heard I had died, he would divorce my mother and marry a woman with a grown, or nearly grown, son he could adopt. And I, returning home after being given up for dead, might find a usurper in charge of my family's destiny.

Darkness thickened in the narrow street. A stray dog padded to the fountain where water splashed from a god's mouth. It lapped briefly, then scuttled away. Shop shutters banged down. Our doorkeeper emerged onto the step and fixed a flaming torch into its bracket.

I stood up and paced, breath punching into the cold air. Where was she?

I was about to head for the house of the Marcomanni when Rufus rose from his crouch, peering toward the corner. And here she came, alone, striding in her dark cloak with her boots making the merest lapping on the pavement.

I stepped out from under the tree to be more easily seen. Her steps quickened. I opened my arms and embraced her as she rushed to me. O gods and goddesses, it felt as though my heart leaped right out and melted into her.

"Beloved . . ." I cradled her head for a kiss, my fingers woven into her thick hair.

"*Mina druda*," she breathed against my cheek. Then her clasp loosened and she pulled away. "Go! Go, before he comes."

I released her. "What is the matter?"

More footsteps. To my puzzlement it was Odo, whom I did not think a serious threat. He was too much in awe of Aurima to act on his loathing for me.

But when he came into the light from our distant doorstep, I stepped back warily. Wisps of the hair straggling to his shoulders hung in his face, half hiding a black eye and blood crusted around his nostrils. He walked like an old man.

His father came behind him, followed by the four other warriors. Maelo breathed in harsh snorts, like a boar about to charge. Indeed, with his bristling hair and beard and the fur vest belted to his girth, he looked more beast than man.

I put myself in front of Aurima. "Get the guards," I told Rufus, and he ran. Maelo halted. His men spread out behind him.

"What is your custom?" I said. "Do we fight with knives? If you kill me, you will be crucified or die in the arena. Or would you rather live, and hear what I have to say?"

Under my cloak, my hand closed on the hilt of my longknife. I could not possibly fight them all. Let our guards be at hand, and let them understand what Rufus said. By Mithras's Dog, even an errand boy and a horse handler would do!

"Aurima was promised to the son of our king's brother," Maelo growled. "Then you said she is to be the wife of a foreign king or a king's son." He thrust his bearded chin toward Aurima. "Who wants her now, no longer a maiden?"

"I belong to Austro," Aurima broke in. "You have been too much among the Romans, my mother's brother: you think women are to buy and sell like silver coins. You do not own my maiden-gift, and Rome does not. It is Austro's. And she has chosen."

Her uncle launched into Germanic. Hearing "Flavus" and "Heriberhto," I gathered that Harman's brother had told him she would marry Harman's son. "I am Aurima's man," I interposed, remembering to add, "by the grace of her goddess. In the spring I will return to the North, and she will come with me."

"What?" Maelo looked from me to Aurima, who looked as astonished as he must have felt. "You lie, *kveda hunda*. You Romans are liars, all of you."

I knew what he must be thinking of. "I will see you are paid for the death of your sister."

He had had enough of negotiating. "Five winters I wait for Rome to pay. Long enough! Soon I talk to Caesar himself. Flavus makes it happen." His teeth clenched, luminous in the torchlight. "And you, sister's daughter: I tell Caesar he must to a husband send you. Come with me."

"I have chosen," Aurima said firmly.

Maelo seized her by the arms. I pulled my knife from its sheath. He shoved her toward his son—"Hold her, you useless *goukh*!"—and drew his own blade. Our roars of anger were interrupted by yelling and the slap of running feet from down the street. My shadow slewed wildly across him as someone grabbed the torch from its socket by our door.

"Hurry," I called to them, starting toward Aurima. But at a bellow from Maelo, one of the warriors lifted her and flung her screaming across his shoulder. The others lunged forward, protecting his retreat. Everyone was shouting. Blades glinted and blurred in the lurching light. I skidded on wet leaves a spit's distance from their knives, and cursed in helpless rage as they bore her off into the dark.

The rescuers pounded up to me. "You are safe, Marcus?" panted Ollius.

I stared mutely after the Marcomanni. If I had been determined before to compel Caligula's approval of my journey, now my resolve was incandescent.

⊷ ⊶

A breach had been ripped in the orchard wall. Rubble choked the stairway that descended into the earth. A stream of slaves shouldering heavy baskets trudged across the courtyard and dumped rocks and dirt into a broad depression where the fishpond had been.

"The underworld is closed for the year," a voice called. "Come back in August."

Julia Livilla looked down on me from a balcony of the house. I had not thought at all of her, my brother's *sponsa*. She had a right to know the reason

SHERRY CHRISTIE

for his death, but it was Caligula's place to tell her, not mine. I said, "Have you finished packing for exile?"

"Oh, Caligula and I have made peace with each other." She brushed back her dark curls to show a glittery earbob. "I am willing to do the same with you."

"But I am less quick to trust," I said, and her coy smile became a scowl.

Someone blew on a cow horn. Work stopped. The laborers retreated through churned mud where the orchard had been.

When I glanced up again, Livilla was gone. In her place other women had spread out on the balcony, chattering like starlings. "Here he comes," someone shouted, and they leaned eagerly over the railing.

An unearthly screech split the air, like legion trumpets sounding the attack mingled with a hundred iron spade heads scraping stone. A monster lumbered into the courtyard, great head bobbing, trunk swaying, ears flapping. Each huge foot was the size of a gladiator's shield. Rufus moaned and edged behind me.

"An elephant," I told him, as if they were as common as cattle.

The creature's rider directed it down a ramp into the pit, where it trampled the new fill. I tried to study the beast, knowing the Parthians use war elephants against our infantry, but my attention kept straying to the argument I would make to Caligula about a triumphant beginning for his campaign. Let him but nod to me, and I would have Aurima out of her uncle's hands within the hour.

Something sank under one of the elephant's feet. It squealed and reared back. The crowd gasped, then cheered when the rider brought the beast under control.

"Your honor, your honor," an imperial slave shouted over the din, "Caesar's chamberlain bids you come now."

I cast a silver denarius into the depths. It fell among the stones and earth, and was buried when the elephant trod on it. "Be at peace," I told the dungeon's spirits, if they lingered here, and followed the slave to my audience with Caligula.

⊶ ⊷

"Your honor is generous," Helicon purred. He summoned an underling with a tablet. "The delegation from Syracuse will leave soon. Then the next group . . . hmm, a special audience. I will try to make time for you afterward."

"I would rather see him when the Syracusans leave."

He shook his head, which I took to mean that the special audience had been

bought with a heftier inducement than mine. "But the new group will not take

long. I have told them no more than a quarter of an hour."

Aware of the power wielded by the round-faced chamberlain, I made an effort to thank him. The evening before, I had wanted to arm every able-bodied man of our household and free Aurima by force, but common sense returned as my blood settled. This was the right course of action. Maelo would have no choice but to hand her over when I told him it was Caligula's will.

In this unfinished addition to the House of Augustus, light flooded in from windows high on both sides, paned with translucent *petra specularis*. Partly completed frescoes of the Olympian gods surrounded the windows and covered the arched ceiling; marble of many hues gleamed on the floor and lower walls. Polished columns separated the central hall from side galleries where secretaries, clerks, scribes, and petitioners transacted business.

Despite the drone from the galleries, I could hear the Syracusans with perfect clarity. Dignified men with long beards, they sought funds to rebuild walls and temples that, as they forbore from pointing out in their flowery Greek, had been damaged in our sack of the city many years before.

Caligula had descended from his high-backed *solium* to look at the plans unrolled on a long table. Coughing occasionally, he asked about the agora and temples now in use.

Syracuse too had once had an empire. A small one, to be sure. But here they were a century or so later, begging help from the people who had conquered them. In another hundred years, would we be petitioning a power greater than Rome for funds to restore our temples and monuments?

I thought not. I hoped not. I looked at Gaius Julius Caesar Augustus Germanicus, assuring this delegation in his own fluent Greek that we would rebuild their beautiful and historic city, and something twisted deep in me at the thought of leaving Rome.

"Quaestor." Helicon was at my elbow. "The group for the special audience has not arrived. I will present you next."

The Syracusans trailed off to one side, where they were enveloped by their entourage. Caligula took a cup from a slave and drank from it as he conferred with his chamberlain. Helicon must have mentioned my name, for he looked up at me. His expression stiffened.

I was ready. If he really wished me to make my appeal here, so be it. He would find it hard to turn down a public request to bring back the lost Eagle.

Suddenly there was shouting. Heads lifted in the galleries; other wait-ing groups turned. The great doors of gold and ivory crashed open. Guards scuffled in backward, trying to bar an onrushing throng. In their lead, roan beard bristling over his bare chest, was Maelo.

He stopped, gawking at the splendor of the place. Guards crowded around to herd him and the others out. Helicon halted them, bending defer-entially to a swarthy man in flowing silks.

This must be the audience that Maelo had threatened the day before. Yet he could not have arranged it so quickly by himself. Somehow he had bought the help of that dandy Julius Agrippa, an Eastern parasite I had met years earlier.

Aurima came around her uncle. Her coppery hair was braided down her back and bound in silver at her brow. She wore her long dark-green *stola* with a white tunic beneath. No cloak.

How could I ever have thought her too strong-tempered for beauty? The fearlessness of her bearing, her slender strength, the proud jut of her chin, her cool gray-green eyes: this was no barbarian, but a princess of the Mark.

And there was Flavus in his gaudy finest, proudly wearing the eye patch that testified to his sacrifice for Rome. He spoke to Maelo, who left off gaping at the inlaid floors and porphyry columns. The rest of the Marcomanni, men and women both, swaggered in and clustered at the end of the hall. From their throats came a sound whose terrible familiarity raised the hair on my nape: a shrill war-yammer like the howl of ravening wolves.

As it died away, Julius Agrippa bowed to Caligula. He had grown up as a guest in my great-great-aunt Antonia's vast household, a claimant to one of the tokens of *hospitium* her father, Antonius, had strewn around the East. They embraced, the dark Jew a head shorter than the thin fair Roman. Agrippa spoke, gesturing to Flavus, then to Maelo. Caligula gave a resigned, unsmiling nod.

This was what Aurima had craved, her presentation to Caesar, and that epicene camel-fornicator had managed it. Did he lust for her? Was she the bribe Maelo had offered him?

The Jew moved aside, and Flavus stepped forward. He was nervous and spoke too fast. *Peace in the Danube lands,* I heard. *Respect and affection for Rome.* While he rattled on, functionaries straggled from one of the galleries to stand behind the *solium.* Slaves brought in strongboxes on carrying poles.

I kept watching Aurima, wanting her to look at me, but her eyes were fixed on Caligula. Maelo caught sight of Rufus's bright hair and searched until he spotted me at the side of the hall. I met his glare impassively.

"That brute should be dodging beasts in the arena," someone said nearby.

"Oh, we must not annoy the barbarians," someone else muttered. "They might help themselves to a province or two."

Caligula's eyes roamed the throng. Some of these warriors, or their sires, might have fought his father; now they, like the Syracusans, had to acknowledge the greater power of Rome. It was not really a victory, of course. With uncivilized tribes, peace is never achieved; it must constantly be earned.

He cut off Flavus's oration with a wave. Aurima straightened herself, but Flavus beckoned to her uncle instead.

Maelo took a deep breath that lifted a medallion on his hairy chest. A bearskin cloak flapped against striped breeches as he strode forth, and his long mane fluttered with the briskness of his step. Breaking protocol, he spoke first. "It is good to meet you, Princeps. I met one time your father, Germanicus."

"Forgive me if I cannot pronounce your name," Caligula said frostily, a chastisement for his discourtesy. Then he relented—how easily I recognized my father's mannerisms!—and rose to embrace him.

Gestures in the gallery caught my eye. Livilla held a hand to her cheek in mock horror. Her companion, a cousin of mine recently returned from some lethargic southern province, mimed a shambling warrior shaking a spear.

Maelo presented Aurima. People around me murmured at her striking looks and her confident bearing. Possessive pride and tenderness nearly stopped my breath.

Caligula himself seemed to forget her uncle. "You are the hostage of whom I have heard." He studied her. "Beautiful as well as brave."

Aurima said, "On behalf of . . . of my people, I am proud to meet the Princeps of Rome." From the slight falter I knew his greeting had startled her.

"Turn around, please."

"Turn?"

He spun his finger in a circle. Aurima pivoted on one foot. When her back was to him, he picked up her braid and brushed it against his cheek. "Like spun copper, yet soft as silk." He laid the plait down, his thumb running the length of it down her spine. His gaze fell to her haunches. "You will bear some lucky man many sons, I expect."

My dark jealousy turned to alarm. *Be rude to him, Aurima. Belch and pick your nose and forget your Latin.*

"The Goddess gave my mother five children," she told him. "Four still live."

He coughed and nodded, examining her like a mare he was thinking of buying. Aurima went on, "Princeps, there is a matter of justice about my mother. Her brother asks for your judgment." She gestured to Maelo.

"And you are fluent in Latin!" Caligula spread his arms to display her to everyone. "This young woman embodies my vision to bring the peoples of the world together. We will have not a Roman empire but a universal one, so knit together by marriage and guest-friendship that cousin will no longer war against cousin, or friend quarrel with friend."

Applause spattered around the chamber. The Marcomanni looked puzzled.

Aurima would not be cheated of her purpose. "Your empire must have justice. From far away we come to seek it from you."

"Then I shall hear you." Caligula coughed again. "But justice is dispensed only on certain days. Your uncle must make an appointment with my chamberlain. In the meantime, I have gifts to show the Roman people's esteem for him and our other friends from the North." He glanced at her breasts. "I regret I have nothing fine enough to compliment your beauty."

Aurima smiled. "The pleasure to meet you, Princeps, is the only gift I wish."

Had I not heard this with my own ears, I would not have believed it. Did she think flirting with him was likelier to win her the reparations she was owed?

Pledges of amity between the Marcomanni and the Roman people were renewed, and presents were offered. Maelo held his gift high for all to see: a handsome saddle, inset with red leather and trimmed in silver. It was completely unsuitable for his runty pony, much like putting a pillared portico on a mud hut.

More gifts were distributed: cloaks, belts, mirrors, wristlets, pairs of scissors. In the noisy pushing and shoving that followed, I lost sight of Aurima among her countrymen. "Rufus, get her for me," I said. "She must come alone." I nodded toward the side door leading to the Augusta's gardens. "I will be outside."

The midday sun was dull, as if here too it was filtered through stone. Just around a turn in the path was the secluded terrace that overlooked the Capitoline Hill. The sounds of vendors calling their wares, shouts, barking dogs, and banging doors drifted up from the streets.

I paced among the oleanders and scabby-barked pines. Could she evade Maelo in the turmoil? Mithras witness me, he would not take her from me again!

At last I glimpsed her coming along the garden path with Rufus, and desire that had burned within me for two days and a night flared into exultation. This time I did not embrace her, for this place was public enough to make a display of affection ignoble, but I took both her hands in mine. Her gray-green eyes were clear, the beautiful curves of her cheek and throat unmarked. "You are all right, *amanda mea*? He did not hurt you?"

"My mother's brother? Of course not." She cast a quick glance back the way she had come. "I did not expect you to be here."

"I came to seek Caesar's approval of our journey." Unable to keep from caressing her, I stroked my thumbs across her palms.

"It is true then, what you said? You are going to take me back to the Mark?"

"I will explain later." There was no time to spare; her uncle would not be distracted for long by his trinkets. "Come with me, before Maelo realizes you are gone." I tugged her gently by the wrists.

"I have waited for justice from Caesar," she protested, pulling back toward the audience chamber doors.

"I will see to it for you. Come; you will stay with me until we leave. You can send for—"

"What do you mean? I cannot leave my people."

I groped for an alternative. "Then listen, beloved. You must tell Maelo and Flavus you want to return to Bovillae at once."

She jerked out of my grasp. "To Bovillae?" Her voice was almost hostile. "Why?"

Because I have said so, a man's natural response, would have no effect on her. "Because I fear Caligula knows I love you. And that means you are not safe."

"You are—what is the word? You do not like that he desires me."

Her stubbornness was maddening. "I have told you the kind of man he is."

"But if he is lovestruck, will he not want to please me?"

"Lovestruck?"

"Is that not a word? To be desiring someone?" She smiled coyly.

She meant to ignore my warning, so passionately did she want redress of the wrongs done in Siscia. My anger gave way to entreaty. "*Carissima*, promise you will stay in Bovillae until I come for you."

"I must help Maelo speak to Caesar about my mother. His Latin is not good." She would not meet my eyes.

"I will deal with Caesar." I gripped her shoulders, forcing her to look at me. "Say you will go to Flavus's villa. Swear me an oath."

The shine in her eyes became a glitter. I adored her for her courage—a woman bent on demanding in person that the Princeps atone for her mother's murder!—but my fear for her made me ruthless. "Aurima, you must agree."

She blinked. Her hand went up to the cord at her neck, to the gift I had given her in place of Heriberhto's necklace. She pulled the pendant out from under her tunic. "By Austro I swear I will go to Flavus's villa," she mumbled, and kissed the golden amber. Without another word she twisted away and hurried back toward the House of Augustus.

I ran after her. She heard me and turned and we collided, almost falling into an oleander bush. I gathered the mass of her fir-scented hair in both hands and kissed her, tasting ale and honey. "I must go," she said, but her hands slid inside my sleeves to pull me closer.

Footsteps crunched on gravel nearby. Aurima wrenched herself away. Her cheeks were glazed, and her loosened hair made a frayed halo around her head.

"I will come for you in Bovillae," I promised her.

She reached inside the arm-slit of her *stola* where it bloused over her belt, and drew out my father's torc. I closed my fingers over the gold circlet, voluptuously warm from her body. I had worn it to the Fishpond, and had not thought of it since.

"My love," she said. "My heart." She held my face lightly in both hands, gazing at me with an intensity that was almost desperation. "Your honor is mine."

She disappeared behind an ivy-covered pergola. "I am yours entire," I said after her, dazed by how utterly she had vanquished my conceit.

"Oh dear, we are intruding," cried a gay voice. Livilla appeared from behind the pergola, arm in arm with my oafish cousin. "Were you victorious over the barbarian, Marcus? Or did we interrupt too soon?"

"Poor Carinna looks quite dashed," my cousin said.

"Oh, he does not suffer for lack of love," Livilla retorted, but the amusement in her voice had an edge like broken glass.

The audiences were finished for the day, Helicon said. Before departing for a rehearsal of *The Trojan Women*, the Princeps had left a message that if I wished to return the following afternoon, he would have an answer for me.

Curse him, he hoped delays would weaken my will! I had a reckless impulse to chase after him, but tangling with his guards would be pointless and humiliating.

At least Aurima had escaped. Watching the other Marcomanni showing off their gifts to her as they jostled out of the audience chamber, I told myself that she had sworn by her goddess to leave Rome, and so she would be safe.

CHAPTER 43

THE GIRL WITH RED HAIR

Sleet rattled against closed shutters. By the time I was summoned, the premature darkness had become true night, and I was angry and impatient.

I had arrived at the Palace promptly at midday, after making sure the Marcomanni had left for the country. Whatever the excuse, Aurima had managed to persuade her uncle to return to Flavus's villa. She might be vexed with me, but I was glad she trusted my judgment about Caligula.

It would be best for her to stay in Bovillae for a few weeks or even a month. He had vowed to marry before year-end, which should keep him occupied for a while. We might be able to leave Rome as early as the end of March and find the Alpine passes open.

Then second thoughts crept in. Since he too had had a murdered mother, perhaps she would have had no problem with him. He might have granted her freedom and anything else she asked for. And my sending her to Bovillae might have drastic consequences. What if Maelo and Flavus seized the opportunity to wed her forcibly to Heriberhto? The risk of Rome's displeasure might seem minor compared with the benefit of quashing her affair with me.

I waited in room after room for hours, pacing and muttering, while people around me came and went. Again and again I cursed myself for not having compelled Caligula to give his consent earlier, when I had had him cornered.

At last the Princeps' chamberlain appeared. "I regret the delay, Quaestor," he said, his smooth round face bland and remote in the lamplight. "Bid your slave to wait here." He nodded to a lamp bearer who led the way past richly decorated private rooms, empty but for servants waiting to be needed.

When he started up a narrow stair, I hesitated, remembering the half-mad creature Agrippina and I had discovered in that upper room after Gemellus's suicide. Helicon glanced back, frowning. "Lead on," I told him.

It was colder at the top of the stairs. Sleet rustled on roof tiles. The chamberlain scratched with a fingernail on the closed door. "I bring Marcus Carinna, Lord Caesar."

Caligula said from within, "Let him enter alone."

Helicon and the slave drew aside. I opened the door on blackness.

"Enter and shut the door," his voice said.

"Why is there no light?"

"There will be."

"Who else is here?"

"No one."

I stepped warily inside. My body blocked most of the glow from the slave's lamp, but I glimpsed the furniture where it had been before: the couch where Caligula had burrowed under his covers, the table that had borne the bitten remains of a mouse. Then the door closed behind me and the room vanished.

Straining my senses, I heard the *plip!* of water dripping into water. Drapery rustled, and the firefly gleam of a low-burning lamp swam into the darkness. A hand set it down, rummaged on the table, and drew up the wick with tweezers. Light swelled slowly.

At first it seemed his head had turned to ice. He wore a silver helmet whose visor was a mask. A silver wreath crowned silver ears and silver locks of hair; only the eyeholes showed the face beneath.

"What does this mean?" I said. "You will not answer me man to man?"

"Caesar will answer you." His voice was hollow and distorted.

He was hiding, as when we had met on the Tiber quay. Very well, I would play the game. "Will Caesar consent for his quaestor to pursue the lost Eagle?"

"You need not go so far to escape your father." Gray eyes blinked in the passionless silver face. "With all the wealth of Caesar's purse, would you not rather ask for a fine house? Slaves? A country estate?"

Weariness overcame me: too many nights with little sleep, and disbelief that he still evaded my will. I sat on the couch without being invited. "Caesar has already been generous," I said, groping for silken words. "I would recover the Eagle to honor him, and to make an auspicious start to his war in the North."

"Caesar desires his quaestor to remain here," the mask said.

Anger tightened my throat. "I will accomplish more for Rome by finding the standard of the Eighteenth Legion."

"And if you fail like all the others, what will that accomplish?"

"I do not expect to fail. I will represent a new Princeps, new policies, new alliances. And I have connections among the natives."

The roof leak was loud in the silence, spattering into a basin lined with gold leaf. He said, "The woman with red hair: you are fond of her."

"The hostage?" I tried for a derisive snort.

"You were seen in the gardens together."

Livilla, gods curse her! I opened my mouth, then closed it.

"A handsome woman," he murmured. "But that is not correct, is it? She is a girl still. A maiden."

"A barbarian," I reminded him, to make her seem less attractive.

"But perhaps a noble family could be persuaded to adopt her. She might become a Caecilia, a Sempronia, a Valeria, a Munatia."

If she was adopted into a Roman family, I could take her to wife. Our children would be citizens. When we returned with the Eagle, we might live in a country villa, perhaps a gift from the Princeps—

Caligula pulled on the fastening of his mask's visor and lifted it. His long thin face glimmered in the lamplight, sheened with sweat. "Germans breed well, do they not?" He pulled off the helmet and set it on the table. "If she bears me a healthy son, I will adopt it. A symbol of my universal empire for all to see."

It caught me completely unaware. When I could finally speak, my voice was a growl. "You know that is nonsense." Rome would never accept a half-breed as heir to Augustus's bloodline.

"Is it? Who will tell me no?"

"What has this to do with my search for the Eagle?"

"I want to know what means more to you than the Eagle." For the first time his voice sounded strained.

I lunged to my feet. "I will resign as your quaestor-designate."

"I do not want your resignation."

"Then what do you want? Is it a matter of desire? Fine, there is no need of promises or threats." I began to unwrap my mantle. "I will lie with you."

He seized my wrist. "You think it cost me nothing to let him die for me."

I said, "I think you are paying for it every day."

The leak was worse. Water dripped faster—*plup! plup!*—into the bowl.

He released me. His haunted eyes drifted away. "A year ago I groveled to stay alive. I crawled; I licked Tiberius's hand. Rana was to have been the one I could lean on, the one I could trust in everything." His lower lids glittered. "I was not supposed to be left with nobody!" He slapped both hands on the table. The silver helmet jounced. Its visor fell shut with a *clack* that held a quiver of music.

"But you would rather die in the wilderness," he said to his hands.

I said nothing. It was true.

"Go, then!"

Such explosive relief possessed me that I was almost to the door when I heard him say softly, "I will have her in my bed tomorrow."

He looked up and gave me his razor-edged smile. "Perhaps you will advise me. Being a barbarian, will she want me to be rough?"

Sleet pattered overhead. "She has no part in this," I said. My tongue felt like cracked leather.

"But what an honor to be fucked by the Princeps of Rome." He said it like an endearment. "Again. And again."

I grabbed his mantle in both hands and hauled him to me. "Leave her out of this!"

His smile vanished. His eyes went black as onyx. The scent of irises and rage-sweat smoldered in the heat of his throat.

I came to my senses. What was the penalty for manhandling the Princeps? Exile? Death? I let go and backed away.

"Tell me she is mine," he hissed. "Then we will see about your Eagle."

"Caesar." I heard my voice break to a lower register. "Yes, there is something else I want. I ask you . . . I beg you, leave her alone. Let me take her north with me."

His face darkened. "How gratifying not to be the only one begging." He opened the door. "Go home and ask your father about the nature of loyalty." Through the doorway I heard him descend the stairs with the slave, his cough fading into the rustle of the sleet.

I could have gone after him, capitulated, apologized. But I would not stoop to his yoke as Father had bent to Tiberius's.

It would be easy for him to learn where Aurima was and to send men after her. I must keep her safe—but how?

I picked up the lamp to light my way downstairs. The basin was full to the brim, glowing in its golden depths like a magic bowl. A rivulet spilled onto the table and rolled across the polished wood to circle the helmet. I took the lamp away, leaving the silver face in darkness.

Sleet was still falling; the litter lurched and dipped as my bearers slid on the paving stones. At the Palace courtyard gate I heard my name, then Ollius's deep voice. A moment later he pulled the litter curtain aside. "It's a messenger from that one-eyed German. Wants to speak to you."

This news gave my nerves another twist. I peered out into a night lit by sputtering torches as a man in an ice-streaked cloak limped closer. "Quaestor Carinna?" He nudged back his hood to show a face, scarlet with cold, that I recognized from the Winter Feast. "My master Julius Flavus asks with respect why the Marcomanni hostage and her escort must remain at his villa."

"Surely he did not turn them away?" I said, horrified.

"Certainly not, sir." Sleet pelted against his cheeks and dripped from his chin. "Can you give me an answer for my master?"

So Aurima's excuse had been that I had willed it. "The priestess cannot worship her goddess here in Rome," I improvised, "so I permitted her to return to the country. Tell your master I thank him for his hospitality, in Caesar's name."

"I will, sir." He drew the hood up.

"Wait. Let him know also that this has been done as a particular courtesy to her, despite the law. So it will be . . . greatly appreciated if he tells no one."

"Most kind, sir. I will inform him at once." He took a step back.

"At once?" He could hardly rush back to the villa in pitch darkness and pelting sleet. "What do you mean?"

"My master is at his city house, sir." He nodded southward. "Off the Vicus Armilustri."

"Take me there," I said.

Flavus's city house was a narrow building on several levels, wedged among others on the unfashionable side of the Aventine Hill. In an eerie repetition of his greeting at the Winter Feast, he was flushed with drink, eye patch gone and breeches mottled with stains. The place stank of ale. "Welcome, Carinna," he cried. "Come in and warm yourself, if you dare. Heriberhto is here."

That was small consolation now. "I must speak with you at once," I said as Heriberhto swayed into the atrium. "Aurima is in danger."

Heriberhto bellowed incoherently and lunged at me.

Flavus shouted for his son. The two of them managed to pin Heriberhto against a wall before I had to use the knife I had drawn. "Heri, calm down," Flavus urged. "Save your quarrel for later. He says there is danger for Aurima."

"From him," roared Heriberhto, red-eyed with rage.

"Does it bother you that she prefers a bull to an ox?" I shot back, and would have come to blows with him if Flavus and Italicus had not separated us.

Harman's son subsided into sullen fury as Italicus towed him into a room. Following them, I went on more temperately, "Caesar desires Aurima."

Flavus guffawed. "I told you, Heri: he could not keep his hands off her." With a flourish of his ewer, he topped off a cup of ale and handed it to me.

Heriberhto did not appreciate the humor. His amber eyes watched me over the rim of his own cup.

"He will take her for himself," I said. "By force, if necessary."

Flavus stopped in the midst of pouring. "That I do not believe."

Heriberhto sprang up. "This is a trick."

Italicus, who had been silent so far, held up a hand. "Maybe so, maybe no. Let him finish, Thumelicus. Then we will decide."

Heriberhto sat down, glowering. "The Princeps of Rome would not do such a thing. Steal a woman like some . . . bandit chief of a Langobard dunghill."

"Who will tell him no?" I retorted, echoing Caligula's words.

"It is how the Lord Augustus took a wife, after all," Flavus mused.

"Wife?" Italicus seized on this. "Would he marry her?"

I was appalled by the turn the conversation was taking. "Listen to me! You must hide her until I can take her away."

Heriberhto snorted. "You would have us antagonize the Princeps?"

"He will rape her and cast her aside."

They all spoke at once. First to me, then to each other in loud Germanic. I got up and poured myself more ale. My icy clothes clung to my skin.

Finally Flavus shouted for silence. "Here is what we will do," he announced. "I will go to Caesar." His nod urged the two younger men to agree. "I will thank him for the gifts to Maelo and for . . . for his praise of Aurima. If he says nothing"—he waved his cup, spilling ale—"then all is well, eh? Carinna is wrong."

I snapped, "And if he says, 'Deliver her to me,' what will you do then?"

"If he wishes to marry her . . ." he began. His head turned to Heriberhto.

Italicus said to me, "That cannot be done under the law, can it?"

His father interrupted, "Caesar is the law, as Carinna says. If he chooses to take a Marcomanni wife, who will say he cannot?"

Italicus too looked at Heriberhto, who bristled. "What does this mean?"

"After Caesar took the wife of Scaurus as his mistress, he gave Scaurus a priesthood and land in Aemilia." Flavus scratched his chest. "If we say you are Aurima's *sponsus*, what would he give you?"

Heriberhto's belligerence faded. He drank from his cup, eyes distant.

"And if she bears him a son," Flavus said, "Italicus, Heri, think of it: a child of Wodun could rule Rome!"

I had heard enough. "Have you no honor?" I knocked the cup out of Heriberhto's hand. "You spineless excuses for free men! I should have let her curse you, who would deliver up your women for crumbs from Caesar's table!" I grabbed my wet cloak from Rufus and slammed out of the house.

By then it was very late, and the streets were deserted in the chittering sleet. Ollius sprang up from his seat on a mounting block. "Home, Marcus?" He wiped his nose with the edge of his hood.

"The house of Lepidus," I said curtly, and flung myself into the sodden litter.

He leaned closer. "The boys are frozen, master. And sore and bloody from falling on this fornicating ice."

"No matter. Get them moving."

As the bearers slipped and skidded toward the Circus Maximus, I cursed Flavus and his two lickspittle whelps. The miserable turd-eating hirelings would sell her for their own profit!

A front corner of the litter dropped suddenly. A thud, a cry, an oath.

Moments later it was level again. Ollius pulled aside the ice-crusted curtain. "His leg is broken, Marcus," he said. "Can I send Rufus to fetch help for him? The others will shift around to get you home."

There was no shelter in the icy street, and I was too impatient to wake some householder to look after the injured man. "Put him in the litter," I said. "I will walk. Let us take the Steps of Cacus; it will save time."

Head bent against the sleet, I climbed the slippery steps on foot with the remaining bearers heaving the litter up behind me. We passed the *taberna* where I had first heard the "Metamorphosis" lampoon. Even then Nina had recognized Caligula's monstrous conceit.

Wet ice piled on my shoulders. Again I thought of Jason handing me his own cloak with a mutter of "Curse it all, here." No more manners than a swineherd, but as fierce as a hawk in my defense. "Rest well, Jason of the Licinii Carinnae," I said aloud to his spirit.

Ollius gave the password at the top of the steps. As we trudged through the gate, I heard the guard ask where we had been on such a foul night. But no one answered. We were all staring.

The Palatine Hill was covered in ice. The sleet had stopped during our ascent, leaving every blade of grass, every twig, every clot in the street swollen and sealed. Trees sagged like battered warriors. Icicles poured in frozen streams from the caps of walls. The reflection of a torch at the Temple of Apollo seemed to ripple for miles in the glassy surface of the street.

With a sharp crack, a tree somewhere shattered beneath the weight of its ice-laden limbs. Then I moved, breaking the spell, and we went on.

Lepidus's guard dog began to bark even before Ollius slammed down the knocker. I called the other men away from the Nereid fountain, where they were trying to slake their thirst. Its flow had shrunk to a trickle amid mounds of ice, and the bronze ladle was frozen to its side.

I brought them into the atrium with me, litter and all. Goggling at us, the dog handler dragged away his bellowing beast. Someone ran to inform Lepidus—who, unless he slept like a dead man, must already have awakened.

I shook ice off my cloak and looked around, rubbing my hands together. We were a ragtag group, noses and knees crimson with cold, hair plastered flat, legs scraped and bloody from falling on streets and curbs and stairs.

"Almighty Jupiter! What has happened?"

Lepidus stared from a doorway, bundling a robe around himself. I said, "May I beg hot drinks for my men?" He signaled to a slave, who vanished toward the kitchen. I thanked him and moved closer so the others could not hear.

"What is it?" he repeated. His lashes were flecked with sleep-sand, his jaw dark with stubble.

"Marcus Aemilius, you told me you were in my debt," I said. "I have come to collect."

Drusilla peeped in once, her eyes anxious. Lepidus rose. "Nothing to lose sleep over, *cara*." He kissed her. "Just a woman problem. You know our Marcus."

When I finished my tale, he let out a sigh. "What is it you think I can do?"

I hooked a leg of the brazier with my toe and dragged it closer. "Will you try to calm Caesar? Persuade him it is not a betrayal for me to seek the Eagle."

He pursed his lips. Behind his head, the tags on the rack of scrolls danced in the rising heat like a flock of butterflies.

I continued, "If he is still intent on possessing Aurima, you must remind him of the outrage it would stir up. The people do not like departure from tradition."

"And there are many still living for whom 'German' is a curse word," Lepidus observed. He sipped from his cup. "What of her own people?"

"If she is hurt or dies, I would not give a rotten nut for the truce." I leaned forward. "Marcus Aemilius, he will listen to you. Make him see that my decision is right for Rome and not deserving of reprisal."

He grunted again. "Indeed, that is the question."

I waited. The brazier mumbled over its lumps of charcoal.

My patron set down his cup and leaned back in his armchair. "Considering that no one saw you for three years, you have made strides in gaining credit with the Senate and the people." He rubbed his lower lip with fingers naked of rings. "For those of us who know your role in stopping Gemellus, of course, the brightness of your future has never been in doubt."

I sensed what was coming. My jaw began to tense.

"If you leave Rome now, you will be forgotten. Other young men will take the posts that should be yours."

"Who will forget the man who finds the lost Eagle?"

Lepidus reached for his cup again. "Who will remember the man who cannot find it?"

I had no answer for that. He added without malice, "More experienced men than you have sought it for almost thirty years."

I pulled my feet beneath me, about to rise. Lepidus held up his hand. "Wait. Listen to my proposal." He put down the cup once more and bent toward me. "Lay your plans. Send your scouts north. Do your best to locate the Eagle, if it still exists. You can fetch it when Caesar heads out on campaign, and the glory of finding it will still be yours." Seeing me about to speak, he raised his hand again. "I will make an arrangement with Saxa. If his agents uncover the Eagle in the meantime, they will keep it hidden so you can claim it for the Roman people."

"That is not what I want."

"Not what you want?" Incredulity echoed in his voice. "Honor, glory, and the gratitude of the Senate and people of Rome?"

I got up. Running my fingers around the golden disk of his water clock, stilled for the night, I said, "I will pay my own way to find it."

"Marcus." His chair scraped the floor as he came to his feet. "By all that is holy, do not flout Caesar's wishes! You will harm yourself, your family, and me."

He stopped halfway to me. "Sacrifice is sometimes necessary," he said, in a voice as cold and heavy as the ice that felled trees.

"I will not be sacrificed for Caligula Caesar." I snatched open the curtain over the doorway. "Nor will I allow Aurima to be."

Lepidus said, "May you break your damned neck before you leave the gates of Rome."

I looked back. The mask of reason and good humor had slipped from his face, revealing an ugly snarl.

I swallowed hard and stepped into the atrium. "Ollius, time to go." There was one last hope: the man who had endorsed my trip north.

⊨⊧

Wiping his freshly shaved cheeks with a towel, Saxa ambled into the clerk's office where I slouched. "Sorry to keep you waiting," he said. "I make it a rule to let nothing distract a barber with a razor at my throat."

I took my feet off the table and sat up. Although it was still before cock-crow, Saxa looked alert and rested. He leaned against the wall, crossing his arms. "You had a dispute with the Princeps, I hear."

"He is reluctant to let me leave Rome. Help me change his mind."

Saxa bent forward with his towel and wiped the table where my boot heels had rested. A trace still remained of the ashes with which the icy Palace courtyard was strewn. "I cannot side with you against Caesar," he said.

"Surely we can come to some agreement."

He shook his head. "Not on this."

My eyes ached with fatigue. "He has threatened—"

"It makes no difference. I follow his orders. As you should." He loosened his belt and began to polish the bronze buckle with the towel.

I could not believe that in this shabby little room smelling of old papyrus, mildewed leather, and damp charcoal, I was being lectured by a man who had falsified records to deceive Tiberius Caesar. But this time I held back my temper. "You will not like having me against you, Commander."

Approaching footsteps overrode the echo of soldiers' voices in the corridor. His adjutant loomed in the doorway, squinting into the lamplight.

The Special Cohort commander threw down the towel and tightened his belt again. "My advice, Carinna, is to go home and write a letter regretting that you angered him. Tell your most trusted slave to give it only into his hands." On his way out of the room, he paused to add, "Perhaps then he will forgive you."

CHAPTER 44

NEMESIS

In the unripe daylight that grayed the sky, I could see Thalus was distracted by the stablemaster saddling my roan. I slapped his shoulder. "Repeat what you will tell her."

He pulled down a rucked-up sleeve. "I will say she must take to her bed at once and give out that she is unwell."

Spider nuzzled my cheek, blowing wet vapor down the neck of my tunic. "What else?" I prompted.

"She must seem too ill to leave the villa." The stable lad's eager gaze strayed back to the horse.

"Tell her to stay there until I send word." I unhitched Boss from the post he was irritably gnawing.

"I will, Marcus. And fear not, I will take care until the ice melts."

"No. Go as fast as you can. If one horse falls, take the other."

He eyed me wonderingly. "Go now," I said.

He mounted Spider, and I handed him Boss's long rein. As he rode across the icy yard with the other horse following, someone swung open the gate. Icicles fell and shattered. Spider shied, and his hooves slipped.

"Watch him, you oaf," the stablemaster snapped. Spider regained his footing, and Thalus guided him into the street with Boss in tow.

Was this folly? If he was injured on the hazardous roads, my message would never reach Aurima. I had not dared to wait until the ice thawed, for fear that Caligula's emissaries would have left earlier and would find her in Bovillae, ignorant of her danger. Thalus was lighter than I was and could ride faster.

Day was brightening beyond the clipped limbs of the plane tree. Somewhere in the city other believers would be raising their open palms to Mithras, Lord of the Morning. As I climbed the slippery steps to the house, a crack came from the direction of the kitchen garden: a tree splintering beneath the weight of ice. It sounded uncannily like the snap of a horse's leg.

Sounds came from Father's bedroom. The cook's daughter emerged in her shift, saw me, and scampered off.

I could not rest yet. There would be no help from Lepidus or Saxa, and little hope of Heriberhto coming to his senses.

Father came out of his room. As he looked me over, the corners of his mouth turned down. Normally he would have inquired what I was about so early, but he knew I would not answer.

I had considered asking him to intervene for me with Caligula. But even if I could master myself enough to make the request, his response would be the same as Lepidus's: Obey. Do your duty. Sacrifice what you most love.

Protecting Aurima was the essential. I would send her north at once with Maelo and two other warriors. The remaining men could escort the women and wagons later. I would then prepare for my own journey and meet her next spring at the head of the Adriatic. I did not fear Caligula's spite. Other than strip me of my quaestorship, what could he do? Possibly he would even change his mind and give me his approval, although that was nothing to count on.

"Dio," I said, "if one wished to send four people as far as Aquileia as quickly as possible, how much money would it take?"

Late in the afternoon, a message came from Nina. I read it for myself, peering to make out her marks in the wax amid the smear of many erasures:

> Marcus, I do not really know how to answer your letter. My wits have vanished in smoke, like the poor little being I so foolishly cherished.

A tremor of pity flickered in my ironbound heart. But weeping for an unnamed child was a woman's due; how much more it would hurt to learn that Publius's death had been Father's doing—which I would never tell her.

I know it was you who gave Silius up to the Special Cohort. He believes you did not act out of malice, but truly supposed he was Phoenix.

So Silius had not told her that I gave Saxa his name because he would have let Gemellus poison me. Perhaps he, too, wished to spare her.

In April he will have to leave for Sicily. Pertinax departs even sooner for the Province, wearing my guilt like an actor's wig. O Juno help me, I am bereft of solace.

Why did you never suspect I was Phoenix? Curse it, Marcus, you have no inkling what women are capable of! We are not frail witlings, or beasts to be bred to anyone whose cock will stand up.

By the time you read this, I will be on my way to Antium with Mother. Farewell.

I snapped the panels of my sister's letter together. Her words stung, and with reason. I had underestimated her cleverness and audacity. I should have learned from Aurima, who had dared to spit in Rome's face by giving a Roman her maidenhood.

At the reminder of her peril, fury and dread boiled up in me again. I reached for the ivory plaque of Mithras slaying the bull that I had brought from my bedroom. "Lord, keep me strong," I muttered, and kissed it.

It would be dark within the hour. I made myself sit and began dictating to Dio a letter for the Marcomanni to carry north with them.

A child's running footsteps slapped across the atrium. Little Astyanax, whom I had put on watch in the stableyard, burst through the doorway to say that Thalus had returned.

The stablemaster was unsaddling the sorrel stallion when I strode into the yard. Both horses' heads drooped with tiredness. When Thalus pulled off Spider's bridle, the roan shambled to the water trough like an old nag.

"Did you speak with Aurima?" I demanded.

Thalus gulped a double handful of water. "She was gone," he mumbled, wiping his face with a grimy hand.

"What? Did someone come for her?"

He shook his head. "They say she just took a horse and left."

Where in Mithras's name would she go? "Could you have passed her on the road?"

"It was yesterday she left, Marcus. Just a few hours after they arrived."

"Yesterday!" I was more confounded than ever. If she had simply gone to a nearby woods to talk to her goddess, she would have returned to Flavus's villa by nightfall.

"Her uncle was acting like a horsefly bit him in the balls. He said his son went with her." Thalus hefted the saddle in his arms. "I gave him the message for her. Was that all right?"

He trudged off to the tack room. I stood staring after him.

Perhaps she had ridden all the way to Diana's grove, and had been forced by the sleet storm to shelter overnight in the temple. But why would she not be back at the villa by now? An injury, perhaps? A slip on the ice, a broken bone, or worse if her pony had fallen on her? Yet Odo would have returned to get help.

Fear lodged like a lead sling bullet at the base of my throat. "Rufus, fetch my cloak and boots," I said. "And come with me."

Paris told me that Aurima and her young cousin had returned to the house late the previous afternoon, soaked by rain that had not yet turned to sleet. "She said she forgot something needed for her priestessing."

"Is she here? Let me see her."

My relief was short-lived. After spending the night, she had left the house on foot around midday and had not returned. Odo was still out searching for her, the eunuch said, though it was by now fully dark.

She would not be at Nina's house, since my sister had left for Antium. "See if the slaves know anything," I ordered.

For all its complement of servants, the house seemed deserted without the rowdy Marcomanni. The calf's head had disappeared from the altar. Caligula's bust presided alone, his bronze face shining boyish and guileless in the lamplight.

Paris waddled back an eternity later. "All I can learn, your honor, is that she took a green silk *peplos* with her." He saw my surprise. "It was a gift from Julius Flavus for her presentation at the Palace, but she refused to wear it."

I frowned, bewildered. Where would she have gone with a silk gown?

Then a possibility struck me with such force that I lurched back a step. The eunuch's brow wrinkled. "Are you all right, sir?"

If my guess was right, she had never intended to return to the house. I ran down the vestibule steps. Perhaps it was not too late to stop her.

"The Princeps' chamberlain will attend you soon," a Palace freedman promised. His eyelids drooped as he studied me discreetly. My face was hot with exertion, my hair windblown.

I said, "Tell him it is urgent. Extremely urgent."

"I did give him your message, sir."

"If he does not come at once, you wooden-headed slipperlick, you will regret it."

He bowed impassively and departed. Straining my ears, I heard only distant music and a slave somewhere crying the hour. Two toga-clad Praetorians guarding the private part of the house eyed me stonily, an unwelcome level of security since Gemellus's death.

Nerves and lack of sleep kept me moving around the cold atrium. If Helicon had not appeared by the time I took fifty paces, I would create a clamor to wake the entire Palace.

Looking for the cursed chamberlain, I realized Rufus had vanished. But I had no time to seek him, for Livilla was gliding toward me, wrapped in a crimson *palla*.

She looked me up and down. "You are brave to show yourself after offending Caligula," she jeered. Her scent, that costly rose perfume of Capua, bloomed over me.

"I need to see him. Where is he?"

She shrugged, fingering the emerald tiers of her necklace. "Retired for the night, I suppose. Why?"

"Is someone with him?"

"Someone usually is." She smiled nastily. "Did he ask you to make a third?"

"Who is it?"

"Why? Have you lost someone? Your barbarian lover, perhaps?"

"Have you seen her?"

Livilla swept her skirts beneath her and perched on a bench. She looked up at me with sapphire eyes as innocent as a young girl's. "What is it worth to you?"

I had neither time nor patience to spare. I grabbed her arms and yanked her to her feet. "Tell me, blast you!"

She tipped up her chin, sneering. I slapped her, and she jerked back. An instant's remorse pricked me, for the deception about Publius had warped her, but my fear for Aurima overpowered all else.

Tears leaked from one of her eyes, veining her reddened cheek with kohl. The other eye glared at me, furious and triumphant. "The slut is in his bed! Listen—can you hear her now, moaning with pleasure?"

Rage fogged my mind. My hand folded itself into a fist.

Livilla's shrill laugh was a Harpy's cackle. "She came to him herself. You poor fool, she used you to get to him." Over her shoulder she called, "Keep listening. Perhaps he will make her scream," and laughed again as she went away.

I lurched blindly toward Caligula's private apartments. "Wait," a voice whispered. A hand shot out and caught my wrist.

Rufus. Brows drawn, blue eyes earnest.

I ripped my arm free. "Wait," he repeated, the word distorted in his tongueless mouth. "I go." He had found and donned an imperial household tunic that would let him pass through the Palace unhindered.

"Find her," I rasped. He nodded and disappeared behind a swag of drapery. "Stop her," I shouted after him.

The Praetorians drew themselves up more stiffly, leery of trouble brewing. Helicon strode across the atrium, the hem of his embroidered tunic whisking around his ankles. "You asked—"

A shriek of anguish cut him off. I ran toward the cry, into Caligula's rooms, before the stupefied guards could stop me.

CHAPTER 45

GNOTHI SAUTON

Crimson splotched the pillows and rumpled bedcovers. It thrilled the eye, like a blazon in the snow marking the end of a hunt. But I saw no sign of Caligula, or of Aurima.

"I am dying! Fetch Drusilla. . . ."

He was sprawled on the floor at the far side of the bed. I crouched beside him, shoving aside his old body slave. Caligula's chest and stomach were dark with blood. It striped across a thigh, painted his genitals, stained the carpet beneath him. Horror dizzied me. What had she done?

He batted at me frantically. "Get away! Help, guards!"

I feared she had eviscerated him as her father had her mother's murderers. But when I wiped away the blood, I saw that the gash from navel to hip was too shallow to spill his guts. Another slash, perhaps meant to cut his throat, had opened his upper chest and shoulder.

"Get away! I want Drusilla!"

Servants and guards were pouring into the room. "You are not dying," I snapped. "Where is Aurima?"

"I am not?" The panic went out of his face. "Are you sure?" He groped at his scrotum.

Rage misted my vision again. "What did you do to her?"

"She had a knife, a curved knife, hidden in her hair—"

Rough hands hauled me backward. The two Praetorians slammed me against a wall and searched for weapons.

The voices around Caligula rose to a hysterical gabble. Had she been found? Cursing, I fought against the soldiers' grip. "Let me go, you whoresons!"

Caligula was helped to his feet. The top of his head rose in the crowd, then sank. Voices chorused in fear and dismay.

Two walls of the room were curtained. One probably hid a balcony door, the other a servants' entry. No one yet had raised a cry about finding a girl under the bed, and I began to hope she had escaped.

Saxa strode in, pushing servants out of the way. Curse the man, how had he arrived so quickly? As he took in the bloodstained bed, an aide behind him blew a whistle. The clamor died down.

"What happened?" bellowed the Special Cohort commander. Several people spoke at once. Scowling, he pointed at me. "You. What happened?"

"I heard the Princeps cry out," I said. Let him work to learn more. It would give her time to disappear.

"Show me your hands."

Caligula's blood seamed my fingers, though I had wiped them on the bedcover. "Take him out," Saxa told the Praetorians. "Guard him until I can question him."

I did not want to leave in case she was still in the room. "Wait," I shouted as he plunged into the crowd around Caligula. "I only tried to see—"

Moments later I was pushed into a dark cloakroom off the atrium. The two guards took position outside the doorway, deaf to my demands and threats.

If she had already fled the bedchamber, Rufus might find her. His service with Gemellus would have made him familiar with the Palace's many passages, its shortcuts and hiding places. With his help she might escape.

If she did not, if they caught her, she would die for what she had done.

A massive chest and wardrobe made the cubicle too small for pacing. Cloaks on pegs snatched at me; bootstraps entangled my feet. My heart was so anguished with fear for her that I thought she must sense it, wherever she was.

Your honor is mine.

That was why she had played the flirt with Caligula. Why she had come back to Rome after carrying out her promise to go to Bovillae. I had told her, who was dearer to me than all else, that I could not take vengeance on Caligula myself, so she had resolved to do it for me. Had Nina not just told me, *You have no inkling what women are capable of?*

I punched my fist through the latticed front of the wardrobe. The guards spun around at the crash.

Frightened people rushed back and forth through the lamplit atrium. The Praetorians ignored me when I demanded to send word to Lepidus, then shouted for Saxa.

It began to rain, a cold downpour that thrashed the surface of the atrium pool. I found my own cloak and wrapped up in it, but was still cold.

My father came, alerted by some Palace informer. "This is my son," he told the guards. "Let me see him."

"Sorry, Senator. Orders from Commander Saxa."

"Perdition! Where is he?"

If they gestured I did not see it, for I had turned my back. "Marcus," he called from outside the doorway. "Tell me what this is all about." I said nothing, and eventually he left.

There had to be a way out of this trap, but I could not think of one. Whether Caligula lived or died, the Senate and people would demand retribution. If Aurima was found, she would be executed. If she escaped, the most convenient surrogate would be me, her presumed accomplice.

Footsteps hurried across the atrium. "Caught her in the garden," someone crowed, and ran on.

"Aurima," I shouted. Horrors stormed my imagination: a gang of vengeful soldiers kicking her, beating her, raping her. I shoved my way out between the guards.

One of the Praetorians grabbed my outflung arm. I hit him in the face. His nose sprayed blood, and he folded like an unpegged tent.

"Halt," Saxa shouted.

I had taken only a few more steps when the second guard seized the back of my cloak. The knife in his other hand pressed against my throat.

I stopped and spread my hands in surrender.

"Useless to run," Saxa said behind me. "She has been caught."

I said, "I was running to her."

Father stood with Saxa at the end of the atrium, looking hard at me. Behind him was Dio, whom he had probably compelled to reveal everything about my plans.

Saxa told the Praetorian to release me. "In there," he ordered, pointing to another doorway. A slave scurried ahead with a lamp.

I listened for voices that might be hers or her captors'. All I heard was rushing rain and the noise of a crowd outside, attracted by calamity.

"I want to see Aurima," I said, not moving.

"They will bring her. Do as I say."

It was a clerk's room: a crowded shelf behind a table, a storage chest heaped with tablets and scrolls. Saxa cleared the top of the chest with a swipe. "Sit," he said. "Not you, slave. Out."

Dio retreated to the atrium. Saxa hitched himself halfway onto the table, keeping one foot on the floor. He crossed his arms. "I am listening."

"How does Caesar fare?" I tilted my head toward the bedroom.

It was Father who answered, "He will recover, gods willing."

I smiled. "Not so sure of his immortality, was he?"

Saxa said, "Why are you here?"

"I need no excuse to visit my cousin's house."

His eyes narrowed. "You will talk, young Carinna. Why make it difficult?"

Father looked at the hand I had smashed into the cabinet, scraped and bloody, the knuckles purpling. "Did Lepidus put you up to this?"

He drew in his breath, affronted, when Saxa held up a finger to quiet him. The Special Cohort commander shouted, "Guards!"

When they trooped in, he asked them about me. The one who could talk said that I had been with them in the atrium until they heard the Princeps yell.

Father put a hand across his eyes, and stiffness went out of his shoulders. By Mithras's Dog, he had thought it was I who attacked Caligula!

The injured guard mumbled into the neck scarf held to his nose. The other one relayed, "He spoke to the Lady Livilla, sir. And hit her."

Still no sound of guards bringing a captive. My mind supplied terrible reasons.

"Carinna!" Saxa snapped his fingers in my face. "Answer me. Why did you strike her?"

I recoiled, snatched out of a murderous fury. "It was personal. A personal matter."

"Did you come here with the girl?"

"I did not know where she was," I said. And heard, finally, the scuffle in the atrium I was expecting.

The guards braced to stop me. "Let him pass," Saxa said.

The two Praetorians in the lead held a woman by the arms. Her sandaled feet scuffed along under a green silk *peplos*. A scarf twisted around her head showed the brightness of red hair above her brow. Her face was tipped down in defeat.

But something was wrong. She was not tall enough, not proud enough.

She was not Aurima.

Saxa must have seen my expression change. He lunged forward and dragged the scarf off the captive's head. "*Merda!*"

He grabbed Rufus by the neck of the *peplos*. "Where is she?"

"The boy cannot talk," I reminded him.

"Dis take you!" He shoved Rufus away and bawled to the stricken soldiers, "Search the Palace, every inch of it. Quickly, you buggering idiots!"

Rufus untied a girdle around his chest and shook balled-up rags to the floor. I let out my breath in a muffled laugh. Hugging him with one arm, I whispered into his ear, "Did she get away?"

He nodded, and I kissed his hair. The boy was a lionheart.

Father shrugged his mantle up onto his shoulders. "We leave you to your hunt, then," he said to Saxa.

"Not so fast. Your son goes nowhere until we catch the girl."

"You have no reason to detain him." Father's tone was cold. "Your own men said he was here before and during the attack."

The Special Cohort commander gestured at Rufus in the silk gown. "This slave of his was part of it."

"You are sure? Has no one here ever desired a boy to dress as a girl?"

"He is hiding something, Senator, and you know it."

"He is obviously not hiding a murderess. Nor am I. Call on me tomorrow if you wish to talk to him." He stalked on. I followed, Dio and Rufus trailing.

"Senator, I must insist—"

Father rounded on him. "You may not insist! Your guards allowed a woman with a knife to attack the Princeps in his own bedchamber and flee unscathed. My son happens to be nearby, pursuing a private quarrel with Julia Livilla, and you assert, with absolutely no evidence, that he is implicated." He was red-faced with wrath. "It will not do, Commander. Find someone else to blame for your negligence."

It was a superior display of righteous indignation, as good as anything I had ever seen when he prosecuted or defended in a court of law. Jaw tight, Saxa nodded for the guards to let us depart.

My thoughts began to churn before we had even left the atrium. Aurima would head for Odo and the house she knew. I must find somewhere to hide her overnight, then spirit her back to Bovillae and, when the frenzy died down, try to bargain for her freedom—

"Senator!" Saxa barked triumphantly.

Kallistos, Caligula's Pan-bearded factotum, stood beside him. Saxa said, "Caesar wishes to see you both."

Father muttered to me, "You must tell him where to find her."

I shot him a stony glare. His mouth thinned, and he gave me a tiny emphatic nod.

The room we entered was the one to which Agrippina and I had brought Caligula from his filthy lair. It was lit now by a score of small lamps, spotted throughout the darkness like the watchfires of an encampment.

Light glinted from the gilded frame of the couch on which Caligula lay, and on the silk stripes of pillows that propped him up. Swathed in furs from the waist down, he looked like an image of a god to be borne in a procession, but there was a bandage instead of a *chlamys* draped over his bare shoulder. Drusilla and Livilla hovered above his couch, aiming baleful stares at me.

Father warmed his voice. "Caesar, your bodily strength is as remarkable as your strength of will."

"I am . . . sorely hurt," Caligula wheezed. His fair hair was dark and stiff with sweat, his eyes rimmed in red. "Does that please you, Marcus? You meant for her to kill me."

Drusilla bent over him with a murmur of distress. He sipped from the cup she held to his lips.

Livilla glared at me. "You knew she was with him. You told me so."

"I would have stopped her, had I known what she intended."

Father interposed, "My son is loyal to the Princeps, of course." He moved forward, blocking Caligula's view of me. "This is all a misunderstanding. It shames me to admit it, Caesar, but my son is besotted with the girl. He would have had nothing to do with her entering your bed."

"Why would she act on her own?" Livilla snapped, before her brother could speak.

"Her mother was killed by Romans," Father said, as Dio must have told him. "She shares her rebel father's thirst for retribution."

"Why was I not warned?" Caligula whined.

I said, "She did not seek revenge for herself."

It took a moment for the three of them—Caligula, Father, and Saxa—to grasp the truth. In the stillness Drusilla asked, unaware, "For whom, then?"

"For Publius," I said, just as Caligula cried, "Saxa, shut him up."

"We are all distraught," Father interjected. "Let us withdraw, Caesar, so you may rest. It will end soon, once the commander's men capture the girl."

"Let us end it now," I said. Something flashed in Caligula's eyes, and I added, "Or do you lack the courage?"

"Sisters, leave me," he said hoarsely. "All of you, go."

The two women protested. "Out!" he insisted. "I am safe with my counselor and my watchdog."

As they left, accompanied by the slaves, Saxa glanced uneasily at the doorway. Clearly he wanted to summon guards, but the secret we all knew was too dangerous.

Caligula paid no attention. His bloodshot eyes were fixed on me.

"I did warn you," I said. "I begged you."

He managed a sneer. "She only proved I cannot die."

"I ask you to pardon her."

"Pardon a madwoman who tried to kill me?"

"Who thought you did not deserve the life you took."

His gaze leaped to Father and Saxa.

I said, "Swear you will let her return unharmed to her homeland."

"I, swear to you? You insult my *maiestas*." His laugh became a cough.

"If you do, I will keep to myself what I learned beneath the Fishpond."

Father said quickly, "Caesar, my son has twice saved you from harm. For the sake of that service, forgive his discourtesy."

Caligula did not seem to hear. "I will have her palms burned with hot irons"—his voice rose—"and send her into the arena with weapons she cannot hold. And you, my quaestor, will sit beside me and watch wolves tear her apart."

Dread fought with rage inside me. I said, "Do you think that would silence me?"

His fist with the imperial ring clenched on the covers. "You forget I have other ways to silence you."

Saxa shifted from one booted foot to the other, the fringe on his black cloak swaying. He was unarmed, as we all were, but this reminder of his presence was menace enough.

I made my tone more conciliatory. "Be merciful. Let her return to the North."

Caligula said, "You beg for mercy, who have none for others?"

I saw then the trap that my willfulness had laid for me. He would not pardon her unless I agreed to stay in Rome. To give up my hope of freedom from my father, my yearning to fight for Mithras and achieve distinction on my own terms. Despair lodged in my gullet.

It was not supposed to end this way. I ought to have the upper hand. Caligula was in the wrong, who had let an innocent man die in order to save his own life.

He coughed again, clasping his belly beneath the furs. Some frenzy drove him; any other man would have been faint with wound shock.

Father clutched my upper arm. "Have you forgotten your duty?" he whispered. "Help bring her to justice, and it will count for you." He searched my face. "You know where she is, do you not? Or you can guess."

Of course I could guess. Or hope, at least, that she had reunited with Odo. But I did not think the empty house would feel safe to her. Until the two of them could flee to Bovillae at first light, she would hide somewhere. But where?

In a woods. Or the closest likeness to a woods she knew: the Palatine Gardens. Even if Saxa's men thought to search there, they were unlikely to find her in the dark.

Father read his answer in my eyes. "Your pigheadedness will cost us everything, Marcus! Tell him!"

"Perhaps the alternative is not clear enough," Saxa broke in. "If you do not deliver her to me, I will charge you with dereliction of duty for failing to punish mutinous troops."

I looked at Caligula. "I have explained—"

"You will be tried by a Senatorial court," Saxa went on. "Men who lived through the panic after the Lord Augustus's death, when the Pannonian and German legions mutinied. They are unlikely to acquit you. Am I wrong, Senator?"

Father's eyes glazed with horror. The public accusation alone would mean immense shame for our family. If found guilty, I faced censure by the Senate, with the expectation that I would commit suicide; or else loss of citizenship and exile.

Caligula breathed heavily. "Nothing to say?"

I blinked against the candles' spangles of light, too stupefied to reply.

"Saxa, we both heard . . . his confession." He coughed again, grimacing at the pain. "Prepare the charge . . . and inform the Senate."

"Yes, Caesar. And I will find the German bitch," the Special Cohort commander promised.

The interview was at an end. Saxa turned to escort us toward the doorway.

I said, "Caesar." My voice sounded as rough as a slide of gravel. "I will swear by Mithras to obey your wishes in all things, if you let her return to the Mark."

His face changed, but I could not fathom his expression.

The silence stretched. He wanted to hear me plead. And so I did: "Will you accept my oath upon it?"

He said, "Show me you will obey. Come and kiss my ring."

It was an outrageous demand. I was his kinsman, not a conquered enemy. I glanced at Father, but he was staring at the Princeps.

"Hands where I can see them," Saxa warned.

I stepped forward carefully, as if on a precipice that might crumble beneath me. Caligula's eyes were furious and frantic, the whites brambled with tiny veins. A stain like an early rose had budded on the bandage around his chest.

His couch stood on a platform draped with the striped hides of zebras, so that his hand, half hidden beneath a white fur coverlet, was at the level of my hips. He did not trouble to disentangle it.

Instead of bowing deeply to kiss the ring on his forefinger, I put my palm under his and raised his hand to my lips. It was not so different from the time he had held my own knife to my throat.

His fingers gripped mine. "You will no longer seek to leave Rome?"

"I will not," I said.

Augustus's phoenix ring bit into the side of my hand. "You will tell no one else . . . what you know of your brother's death?"

"I will not."

He gave an odd smile that canted up at the corners like an arrowhead. "Then we are agreed," he said, and released my hand.

My father sighed. At one stroke I had saved the family from disaster and given him what he most desired: my obedience to his beloved Caligula and the end of an unthinkable affair with a barbarian.

I straightened and stepped back, relieved that I had won Aurima's freedom. I would not contemplate the cost of it. Not now.

Caligula's gaze roved over me with possessive triumph. "You say you . . . will obey me in all things." His breath was shortening.

How many times would he humiliate me? "I will," I said.

"So you will not object . . . when I send the German woman to the arena."

"No! You gave me your word!"

"I once told you, Marcus Licinius, that . . . I would not take you unwilling. Your surrender . . . is worthless to me."

"What of your honor, Gaius Julius? Is it worthless, too?" The fury I had long withheld burst out from between my teeth. "The great Germanicus must be proud of his last son, who let his best friend die because of his own cowardice."

Caligula began to speak, but smoke from the Fishpond caught in his throat. He coughed so hard his eyes watered.

Choke on it! Seize him, you Furies, and tear loose his heart in his chest.

Time seemed to stop. In an interval as he gulped a drink, the Praetorians' voices came distinctly from the atrium. "A fornicating *boy*!" one of them hooted.

Caligula found his voice. "Marcus Carinna, I charge you with *laesa maiestas* . . . for attempted murder and . . . threats to my sovereign power." His brow gleamed with sweat. "You are judged guilty, and the sentence is death."

I goggled at him. I was too stunned to be afraid.

"My dear, you are fevered. You need your sisters' care, and healing sleep." Father brushed past me and put a hand on Caligula's arm. "Let us address this at another—"

"Shut up!" Caligula struck off his hand with such force that Father flinched. "I weary of my debt to you."

"A great man should be ruled by reason and logic, as your father Germanicus was." The trained voice was still mellifluous, but more urgent. "Not by destructive emotions."

Caligula said, "Did you hear me, Saxa?"

Saxa rumbled behind me, "I am not sure I understand, Caesar."

"Young Carinna has vowed . . . to obey me in all things. So I am ordering him to take his own life. Bring him a weapon."

"What?" I said, disbelieving.

"As you command." Saxa's nailed boots rasped, *scrud, scrud, scrud,* on the marble floor as he went out. He would find Lepidus or someone else to remind Caligula that a Senator's son could not be condemned without a Senate trial.

"Gaius, I entreat you, do not say such things while pain has disturbed the balance of your humors," Father coaxed. "My son had nothing to do with the attempt on your life, and he has sworn himself to you. This is unreasonable."

"I will decide . . . what is reasonable." Caligula's breath came harder. He pressed a hand against the red spot on his bandage.

Father turned. "Apologize, you idiot boy! It was not Caesar's fault." He glared at me. "I had to choose between them. Don't you understand? I had to choose."

Still speechless, I could only stare at him.

Saxa returned. He stopped in front of me and held out, hilt first, the sheathed longknife I had surrendered on entering the Palace. On the guard of this knife, my father's army knife that he had carried through Germanicus's wars, that had pierced my brother's heart, that had protected me on the northern frontier and in the streets of Rome, ROMA looked up at me.

Your turn, little brother.

I felt an acid trickle of terror. How courageous I had thought myself, leading cavalry to flank Ingiomar's ambush, then facing down Maelo, when in truth I had merely been outraged that anyone would challenge my superiority as a Roman. No one could have brought this absolute fear upon me, this weakness in the legs, this slackening of the bowels, except a man to whom I owed obedience.

I pushed the knife away with my bruised hand. "Is this the reward of devotion to Caesar and Rome?" I said, hating the faint tremor in my voice.

"You speak of cowardice . . . who are less brave than your brother," Caligula jeered.

"My brother thought you were worth dying for."

Publius's courage had sprung from faith in the value of his sacrifice, a sacrifice wasted on this lunatic. Why did I allow him to tyrannize me? "I will not kill myself for you," I said. "If you wish to be rid of me, I will leave Rome."

As I turned toward the door, the Special Cohort commander stepped into my path. "Caesar's judgment has already been given," he said pleasantly.

Caligula struggled to sit up. The rosebud on his bandage began to flower. "Saxa, you will do it. Execute him now."

Incredible as it seemed, I was meant to die. "Father, do you accept this?"

"Gaius, please compose yourself." Something had happened to my father's magnificent voice. It was as thin and reedy as an old woman's. "Have I not taught you to act with a clear and calm mind?"

Caligula's face went blood-red. "Who dares teach me?" he shrieked, so frenziedly that spittle flew from his lips.

Father dropped down on his heels beside the couch, his hand curved on the pillow as if to stroke the cheek of a fevered child. "Not both of them," he said in a rough whisper. "I gave you Publius. Please, not both of them."

I almost pitied him. Never before had he sounded so helpless.

"Saxa." The Princeps coughed violently. "Finish it. Now."

I heard the whisper as my longknife was unsheathed, and managed not to wince at the *crack* of the scabbard hitting the floor. Father gasped and rose, but Caligula snatched at his sleeve. "Watch," he said harshly. "Watch him die."

"Kneel down." Saxa stepped behind me.

"No," I said. A Roman should face death on his feet. Mithras grant my body would not betray me.

"Down." He rammed the pommel of the knife into my shoulder.

I went down on one knee on the cold floor, then the other.

"And take off the torc."

Slowly I forced apart the ends of the gold collar and pulled it off. I would have held it out to my father, but my grip had become shaky. To hide the tremor I hooked the torc in my belt and folded my fingers over it.

Father's hands knotted together under the swag of his mantle. Shock crossed his face as he stared at me, then became stark grief. Perhaps he had just realized he would have no heir.

But after all, he could sire more sons.

Saxa pulled my cloak and tunics down to bare my neck. I fixed my gaze on Caligula Caesar. I would rather have died a thousand times in battle or on the racetrack than this. Yet I was a Carinna; he must not see me afraid.

Flat scowling brows darkened his eyes, and his comely Julian lips contorted in a snarl. "You had to know."

"He was my brother." This time I managed to keep my voice steady. "What else could I do?"

Saxa's calloused palms squeaked on the hilt as he reversed the knife. I heard his intake of breath as he raised it in both hands. At least it would be quick.

I tried to prepare for Mithras, whose judgment awaited me, but it was Publius I thought of. Where was his spirit, with my death so near?

A gleam of gold caught my eye. Father wept, his tears flashing in the lamplight.

"Caesar?" Saxa muttered. One last chance for reprieve.

"Do it," Caligula screeched.

Father moved suddenly, his hand slipping out from under his mantle. In it was the small blade he always carried. "No," he said, and struck.

After an instant's shock, Saxa roared, "Guards!" He hurtled past, knocking me down.

I heard the muffled thump of bodies colliding and a furious rustle of clothing. "Father," I shouted, heaving myself up on hands and knees.

"Sorry," my father was saying breathlessly as he jabbed the thrashing bundle of robes and furs that was his foster son, his great accomplishment. "So sorry, Germanicus. . . ."

Guards were pounding in, but Saxa reached him first. I saw the tip of the longknife touch the blue tunic on Father's back, exposed by his slipping mantle. The blade sank, and blood spurted over Saxa's hand.

I cried out.

Saxa wrenched him away from Caligula so violently that my father flew backward on top of me, slamming us both to the floor.

He was still alive. His eyes, wet with tears, rolled to see me. Something molten gurgled in his throat.

"Papa," I whispered. The sinews of my arms and shoulders quivered as I held him up off the knife embedded in his back. Its haft jabbed into my belly, joining us like a lethal birth cord.

"Too late," he mumbled. A dark trickle escaped his clamped lips and drooled down his jaw.

There was much I should have said. That I understood, that I forgave him, that I did love him; but I was too choked with horror to give him any parting gift except a swift death.

I kissed his brow and breathed a farewell against it. Then I laid him down as gently as I could.

As his weight came onto the knife, a gout of blood surged from his open mouth. Cradling his head, I let him sink until the blade would go no deeper. His eyes dulled, and the soul left him.

Scrabbling onto my knees I hugged him to me, his head and shoulders against my breast. The core of strength within me collapsed, leaving a hollow filled with agony. I had lost him, I had lost him, I had lost him. I clutched my father tightly to my heart and rocked from one knee to the other, my face hidden in his silver hair.

CHAPTER 46

THE SMELL OF INCENSE

H ad Caligula died, Rome's future might have been greatly different. The
Senate would probably have granted his powers to Lepidus, cutting off
the line of succession that was to lead us in a few decades to chaos. Or perhaps
they would have restored the Republic, as Silius hoped.

But the tears my father wept for his dreams had blinded him. Clothes,
bandages, pillows, and coverlets absorbed most of his blows; Caligula survived
with slashes across his arm and hand.

Lepidus came to see me two days later. He arrived after dark with his personal slave, hurrying in by the back door to avoid the mob pelting the front
with stones and filth. "There is a dead dog on your doorstep," he told me,
unlacing his hooded cloak.

I thanked him for coming and took him to the atrium. Shouts of "Traitor!"
and "Parricide!" still penetrated from the street, but it had begun to snow.
Even the diehards must soon disperse.

Father lay on his bier, wearing his Senatorial toga. His hands were crossed
on his stomach, the right one uppermost to show his signet ring. I had put
Germanicus's torc around his neck.

Lepidus studied him. Snow fell through the compluvium, dappling the
pool. Our breath wisped in the lamplight.

He turned to me. "When is the funeral?"

"As soon as my mother arrives."

He grunted. "You should have cremated him yesterday and fled."

Perhaps he was here to warn me of imminent arrest. It was only because
of the pandemonium following the assault that I had escaped through an
obscure service passageway with Dio, Rufus, and Father's body.

Our family was gathering, eyes red, faces swollen. For privacy I took the patron into Father's office, where I had been reviewing household accounts. He turned as I shut the door behind us. "A funeral procession is forbidden," he said. "No clients or friends. And you may not hire mourners."

I said nothing. It was what I had expected.

He sat. "I have talked with Saxa about the girl."

I paused with the pitcher in my hand, then poured wine and splashed in hot water.

"We want the whole thing erased. That way there need be no official notice, no trial, no complications with our northern allies."

"Erased?" My voice was raspy. "How so?"

He took the cup. "I will leave that to Saxa when he finds her." In other words, she would meet with an accident.

I frowned. Lepidus shrugged: a would-be assassin could expect no better.

"As for you, your family will be allowed the usual nine days of mourning, starting from your father's death." A muscle bunched in his dark-stubbled jaw. "Then everything he owned will be confiscated."

Silence fell, except for the hiss of the brazier. "I did not expect . . ." I said gruffly, and had to clear my throat. "Marcus Aemilius, buy our slaves. I will give the Treasury the money instead."

"I will not," he said. "I cannot be seen to do your family any favors."

His blunt refusal staggered me. All of our slaves, most of them born in the family, would become ciphers in the tally of ten thousand imperial servants, sent to any corner of empire where a quaestor needed a clerk or a praetor's wife a clothes-patcher. . . .

I mastered myself. "What of my mother?"

"The life interest in Antonia's villa is hers by inheritance. The State has no claim on it, or on her property."

In the midst of catastrophe, the realization that she and Nina were safe unmanned me. I sat down heavily. "And our clients? Am I to abandon them?"

"I will take them on. Those who wish it."

Thus casually was our family stripped of its public and private influence, our duty to our freedmen, the city ward, the guild, and the town in Etruria of which we were patrons. All for the sake of a man who could not bear not to be loved.

I realized Lepidus had spoken. He repeated, "What will you do if the gods grant you your life?"

"Does Caligula not want it?"

He exhaled slowly. "I cannot guess." He polished the silver rim of his cup with thumb and forefinger. "He veers from rage to panic. Last night he woke screaming, tearing at the dressings on his wounds."

"What has he to fear?" I said bitterly. "He is immortal."

"This morning he set a bloody handprint on his sisters' foreheads." His lips twisted. "So they will be immortal too." He drained his cup.

I said, "I will leave the city on the ninth day. I will take the two slaves given to me, and the personal goods I brought from Carnuntum."

Lepidus seemed relieved. "Very well. Tell the appraisers not to include them."

The appraisers. Enumerating and valuing members of my *familia* along with the dishes and chairs, the books and statues, the dining couches, the bed I had been born in. I felt sick with grief.

I pushed myself up. "If there is nothing more, I bid you farewell."

"Where will I find you?"

"After someone else has rid Rome of Caligula? Fear not; Saxa will know."

Lepidus flicked a warning finger against his lips. "Perhaps we will meet in better times," he said. I stepped back to avoid an embrace.

In the atrium, he gazed again at the body on the bier. "Titus, I will miss you," he murmured, and took his cloak from his slave. The man muttered to him.

"Oh, this is for you." He nodded to a cylindrical case the slave pulled from a pouch. "Seeing your house was besieged, the messenger came to mine."

The wax seal was imprinted with a bunch of grapes and a harvesting knife, the signet my mother used. When I looked up from it, Lepidus had disappeared toward the back door, behind the crowd of servants.

I felt their eyes on me, and my heart quailed. How was I to tell them of this ultimate shame that had befallen us?

I put my hand over my father's, cold as marble. "Give me courage," I implored him. But I had no sense of his spirit near, nor of Publius's, which had so comforted me earlier. They were, perhaps, tormenting Caligula.

The weight upon me grew heavier. As *paterfamilias*, if only for a heart-breakingly few more days, I could not put off my duty to the household. I told Dio to assemble everyone in the atrium and retreated to my office with the letter case. At least Mother would be here soon. She would understand what I felt, and her strength would revive me.

I could not recall what I had scribbled to her after my dazed return from the Palace. When I unfurled the scroll I saw I need not try to remember, for she had sent it back to me.

To my mother, Antonia Terentia, from her son Marcus:
Father is dead. He was slain in an attempt to kill the Princeps.

When he struck, I heard him apologize to Germanicus. Not, I believe, for attacking Germanicus's son, but for what he had made of the boy Germanicus entrusted to him.

I, whom he died to save, survive. Come as soon as you can.

At the end of the letter Mother had written *I will not return.* She had slashed a line across my message, so fiercely that she must have destroyed the nib of the pen.

Nothing more.

I rolled up the papyrus and pressed it to my chest. Rufus watched, owl-eyed. Absently I rumpled his already-disheveled hair to hearten him, and brushed my knuckles over his jaw. He was too young to grow a mourning beard.

"They are all gathered," Dio said from the doorway. He spied Mother's letter, and a spark of animation came into his voice. "When will the mistress be here to manage the household?"

"Listen," I said. "What I will tell the others does not apply to the two of you. You are coming with me."

"Where?" Rufus mouthed.

"What about the others?" Dio asked. But he spoke to my back, for I was already walking out into the atrium.

The whispers and muttering stopped. No noises came from the street now. It was still snowing, fine flakes that gusted over my father's body. No one had had the presence of mind to hang weather curtains around the pool.

I stood by the altar, counting heads, as they shifted to see me. Cleon had vanished after we brought Father home. But he, like Ollius, was a free man and could find work guarding someone else.

The household quieted still more. Sosander, the house steward, cleared his throat nervously, his head bobbling. In just two days, he had aged decades.

In the silence I began, "Nothing was more dear to my father, the father of this family, than the peace and prosperity of the Roman people." I steadied my voice. "He died as he lived, with a devotion to Rome worthy of the great men of old."

I looked around at them: at old Turtle grasping little Astyanax's hand, white-haired Nicander and Father's other secretaries, the stablemen, cook and kitchen help, servers, housemaids and seamstresses, litter bearers and runners, bodyguards, and others. My family. Emotion had overcome them as I spoke; some wept openly.

I went on, "When we honor him at his funeral tomorrow"—there was a stir at the suddenness of this announcement—"we will pray for him to watch over us as he did in life."

I halted again, this time to nerve myself. "Three years ago, we endured . . ." My throat caught. ". . . Endured the pain of my brother's death."

"Gods rest his shade," they murmured. "Gods grant him peace."

"Now I ask you for bravery, for we must suffer again."

The crowd swayed, friend clutching friend, parents their children, lovers each other.

A swirl of wind blew snow across my face. "I must leave the city. My mother, your mistress, is safe in Antium with Nina, and will not return to Rome." I fixed my eyes on broad-shouldered Ollius. "You who are free may become clients of Marcus Lepidus, or go where you will."

Melting snow ran down my cheek like cold tears. In front of me the old gardener clasped to his heart the hand of his only child, a kitchen maid.

I cleared my throat. "The rest of you will become property of the State."

The outburst of wailing and sobbing, the shouts and groans, struck me like blows to the body. They besieged me with pleas to accompany me, to join Mother, not to be parted from one another, not to be forced from our home. "Stop," I said several times, and finally shouted, "Quiet!"

Their quiet was like an undulating sea, all sighs and moans. I put a hand on our family altar. "Father Jupiter and you other gods of Rome! I call on you, and the *di manēs* of this house, to witness the vow I, Marcus Licinius Carinna, make to my family."

Again I looked around at them, although this time my sight was less keen. "I will come back one day and find you all, every one, no matter where you are. I will retrieve our sacred things from the Vestals' keeping, and we will be together again."

I held out a hand to Dio. "Give me your knife." Apprehension flared in his sunken eyes, but he passed me the small blade he used for sharpening quills.

"In token of this vow, I give my own blood." With the razor edge of the knife I carved a crude *R* into the back of my left wrist. I held it up for all to see the wound, and let the dripping blood splash upon the altar. "*R* for *Roma*, and for my return. If I prove false, may Father Jupiter and the other gods of Rome, and the *di manēs* of this house, cause my blood to be spilled in the wilderness and there cause me to die."

There was utter silence in the atrium. I wrapped a fold of my mantle around the cut and walked around my father's bier into the room I had made my office. The light was dim and fluttery. No one had refilled the lamp.

I ran my fingertips across the chafe mark on the wall from Publius's bed, and laid my palm on the fresco of Hercules as if I could take into myself what the demigod had seen. When I picked up the plaque I had brought home from Carnuntum, the God of Truth looked gravely at me as he slew the bull and brought change to the world.

I flung it down. The ivory shattered into flecks that pricked my feet, like snowflakes made of stone.

⟞⟝ ⟞⟝

"Gods curse the whoreson!" a voice screeched. As I leaned forward to light the torch from a fire pot, a clot of dung hit my shoulder. Someone roared, Ollius perhaps, chasing the thrower. Useless to pursue them; they would only scuttle back again like rats.

A cold night fog swirled around the tomb, wreathed the pyre, dripped from the pine trees. Resin mingled with the smell of incense, strong and fragrant. "May the spirits of our family welcome you, Father," I said, and flung the torch onto his shrouded body, drenched in spices and aromatic oils.

An edge of yellow flame made its way along the shroud. Groans and wails rose from the servants around me.

"Dis take his rotted corpse!" someone shrieked from the roadside. Another howled, "Go to Tartarus, murderer!"

"Clear the road!" It was a different voice, harsh with authority. "Make way for the magistrate." Staves thudded on flesh. Screams and grunts echoed in the darkness.

Silius appeared out of the fog. He too wore a black mourning toga. Mist jeweled his dark hair.

His arrival caught me off guard. With the bitterness between us, he was the last person I would have expected to keep me company here. "So he is gone," he said. "At last you are as fortunate as I."

"You are bold to come," I said. "Saxa's spies are keeping watch."

"So? I am already banished."

I looked back at the tracery of fire rippling over the shroud. The wood beneath was smoking. Learning who would be cremated here, the undertaker's men had simply dumped it in the wet snow.

"Caligula asks if you have killed yourself yet."

"I told Lepidus that I will leave Rome in six more days."

"They may wait another day or two for you to entomb your father's ashes," Silius said. "If you wait six days, you will be dead."

"How can I leave my family helpless against the vultures of the State?"

"I will stay with your family. They know me."

"The appraisers—"

"I will deal with the appraisers. Better than you, I expect. They will not dare trifle with a magistrate."

The wood was still smoldering. Would it never ignite?

"If I asked you to come with me to Sicily, would you agree?"

I grimaced quickly. Shook my head.

"Then I am giving you a letter of credit—"

"Silius, I do not want—"

He overrode me: "—that you can draw on anywhere."

Father's body was fully aflame. I thought fleetingly of his pride in his voice, of his exhorting me to train myself, as he did, to speak like a man whose opinion should be weighed.

"My father's name is still respected," Silius said. He tilted his chin at the pyre. "As his will be, after Caligula is dead."

With a loud crack the fiery length of the body tipped down, feet first, as if Father had raised himself to look back at the city. Then it fell through to the heart of the pyre, the outer timbers collapsing upon it in a cascade of sparks.

I turned to thank my friend of times past. But he was already gone, into the mist.

⟞⟞ ⟝⟝

The horses sensed the somberness of the occasion. They stood with necks bowed while farewells were said, tears cried, embraces shared. Only the brightest of stars gleamed through the smoky haze. It was a few hours before daybreak, a time chosen to draw little attention from watchers.

I mounted Boss at last, with Spider on a long rein. Dio, on muleback, and Rufus, on foot, led pack mules. We set off, following Ollius's torch down the snow-edged street.

My own tears spilled in the darkness. Images of the people I was leaving ran through my mind; things I had forgotten to tell Silius; items I should have given him for safekeeping. The streets of the Palatine, the house of the Marcomanni, the monuments and temples of the lower Forum passed unseen.

When I roused from the churning of my thoughts, the torchlight struck a glint ahead: the Golden Milestone, the marker at which all roads begin. On the right began our road, which would become the Via Flaminia; on the left, the road that climbed to the Capitoline's summit.

I straightened in the saddle. "*Reveniam*," I called up to the Temple of Jupiter. And to the Palatine I shouted it more savagely: "I will return."

⟞⟞ ⟝⟝

When we reached the mausoleum we could see the remains of the pyre, still wisping smoke, in the frostbitten grass. I dismounted, unlocked the door, and took the urn with Father's ashes from Dio.

The interior of the tomb smelled of musty stone and cold earth. I groped to the table in the middle and set the urn on it. Rufus brought in the torch, Dio the bread and wine. The circular wall sprang into view, banded high up with frescoes and notched everywhere else with recesses and smaller niches.

From a recess I took the canister engraved *P. Licinius Carinna*, and crouched for another marked simply *Phormio*. My old companion would have to wait for the tomb marker I had promised him.

There is a formula for such things, full of prayer and eulogy. Bowing my head, I promised the three spirits that I and my family would honor them as long as we lived. To each I offered bread and a splash of wine, and asked them to keep us safe on our journey.

Leaving the door open, we broke our own fast outside with the remaining food and drink. It was a poor funeral feast, with only the four of us and a few crows as mourners. Still, when I relocked the door of the tomb, another door seemed to close on the deepest of my grief.

We moved on. Roosters were calling all over the city, from garden villas on the Esquiline to the Jewish quarter across the river. Perhaps they had been crowing for a while, for the sky was pale above the Sabine Hills. The Tiber drew away from the road, beginning the loop around fields and orchards that would soon bring it across our path.

A whoop came from Ollius. Cleon was jogging after us with staff in hand, a pack and scabbard bouncing on his back. "Thought you'd leave without me?" he panted.

I hugged the sweaty lout, my heart lightened by his arrival. Ollius punched his shoulder, and Rufus beamed. Even Dio looked less grim.

We neared the Milvian Bridge. With what joy I had greeted it a few weeks earlier: the first bridge of Rome! Now it was the last; and knowing the cold mountains and dark forests that lay ahead, I let out a tense sigh.

Mistaking the reason for it, Dio glanced over his shoulder and shook his head reassuringly. We were not being pursued.

Foot travelers looked up at the clatter of hooves as Boss charged onto the bridge, towing Spider past Cleon and Ollius. A flock of sheep was jostling toward the far end of the span.

I reined in. The water seemed to suck at my will. I longed to reach the other side, but was loath to cross this final frontier of my past.

The swollen river slid through its glutted arches. Half-submerged trees and bushes stretched early-morning shadows downstream. I saw myself on the flood, elongated, inching across the shadow of the parapet with horses' heads in front and behind.

The sheep spilled down the far ramp in a final bleating scurry. My heart was galloping. I could hardly breathe.

Aurima waited beyond the end of the bridge.

Pent-up breath burst out of me. On the night of my father's death Rufus had found her in the Palatine Gardens, as I expected. Dio and Ollius had smuggled her and Odo off the Palatine Hill by a little-known route, and Ollius had accompanied them back to Bovillae.

She sat astride her pony, Maelo beside her, the others fanned out around them. Her women peered from their wagon on the roadside. In thumb and forefinger she clasped her amber pendant. Her face was stoic and guarded, as I had so often seen it. Perhaps she thought she had failed me by merely wounding Caligula.

I felt for him the blackest loathing, yet he had been almost right: a man who would be great must have both the "Roma" and the "Amor." But he must be able to balance them: duty to what is eternal with love of what is mortal and flawed. A balance my father had found at the last, and that I must find in myself.

My family would soon be scattered to the four winds. I no longer had a home, a patron, or clients. But I was the son of a man I honored, and the lover of a woman who owned my heart. The rest I would earn back—if need be, in my own blood.

We want the whole thing erased.

First you must catch us, Saxa.

I dismounted in front of her. "We have a long journey ahead," I said, and brought Spider forward. "I would see you better mounted."

She stared at me, unsure if I knew what it meant for a man to offer a horse to an unmarried girl.

"Well?" I asked, rough-voiced.

She looked down at my hands: one still bruised from fighting to escape, the other scabbed with a vow to return. A light came into her eyes.

"Well, Roman," she said. "Now you are free."

GLOSSARY

A

Achates: in *The Aeneid*, the close companion of Aeneas; hence any faithful friend

aedile: one of the municipal officials responsible for clean streets, brothels, honest weights, etc.

amanda: beloved (fem.)

amor: love

as: the lowest-denomination coin, of copper; subsidized price of a loaf of bread

atrium: a house's central reception area, open to the sky

Atropos: in Greek mythology, one of the three Fates (Clotho spins the life thread, Lachesis measures it, and Atropos cuts it)

augur: a municipal official responsible for finding and interpreting omens

aureus: the highest-denomination Roman coin, made of gold

aurochs: shaggy wild ox (now extinct)

auxilia: native troops, part of the Roman army

B

basia me: kiss me

bestiarii: wild-animal fighters in the arena

C

caesti: brass knuckles with spikes

caldarium: the "hot room" at the baths

cara, carissima: dear, dearest

caupona: a bar and grill (the owner/manager is a **caupo**)

cella: the holy central space in a temple

centurion: noncommissioned army officer, head of an eighty-man "century"

chiton: a light Greek garment like a tunic

chlamys: a Greek mantle

clavus: boot nail

clementia: mercy

clientela: group of people who depend on and support a man of higher status

compluvium: the open space in the atrium roof

consul: one of the two most senior elected officials, junior only to the Princeps

convivium: a dinner party (as opposed to **cena**, a more sedate dinner)
cymbala: small cymbals with a chiming note

D
damnatio memoriae: obliteration of a person's name and image from public record
decurion: officer of a small cavalry unit
denarius: a silver coin worth four **asses**; there are twenty-five denarii in an **aureus**
dignitas: merit, worthiness, distinction
di manēs: spirits of the departed
Dis: an old name for the god of the underworld
domina (dominus): mistress (master), terms used by slaves
domus: mansion
druda (Old Germanic): lover

E
Erinys: any of the three Furies, deities of vengeance
exedra: a sheltered, semicircular recess in the wall of a garden or building
exornator: servant in charge of jewelry

F
fader (Old Germanic): father
Falernian: type of wine
familia: all those for whom a *paterfamilias* is responsible, including slaves
Flamen Dialis: high priest of Jupiter
forica: public latrine
Fortuna Augusta: the personified good luck of the Princeps
Fortuna Romana: the personified good luck of Rome
frigidarium: the "cold room" at the baths

G
genius: a man's inner spirit
gladius: legionary shortsword
gnôthi sauton (Greek): know yourself
goukh (Old Germanic): bastard
gravitas: dignity, gravity, authority

H

habet: he's had it (the crowd's cry when a gladiator is clearly defeated)

haruspex: an augur who reads omens in the entrails of sacrificed animals

herm: a bust of Hermes on a squared pillar, sometimes including male genitals

hertan (Old Germanic): heart

himation: multipurpose Greek garment worn like a toga or cloak

hospitium: mutual aid relationship between a Roman and someone outside Rome

hunda (Old Germanic): dog

hypocaust: furnace

I

imperator: supreme commander

imperium: power, dominion

impluvium: pool under the atrium's roof opening that catches rainwater

insula: an apartment building

J

juno: a woman's inner spirit

justitia: justice

K

kantharos: a drinking cup with high handles

kouros (Greek): a youth, or an archaic statue of a youth

krater: big bowl in which wine and water are mixed

kveda (Old Germanic): filthy

kyrios (Greek): master

L

laconicum: sweat-bath

laesa maiestas: "injured majesty"—treason

Lar (plural **Lares**): a family's protective deity

latrinarius: a slave responsible for a water closet

legatus: a general or legion commander

lemur: spirit of an unburied person

M

maiestas: grandeur, dignity, sovereignty

malleus: hammer

manus: legal power over a dependent

manēs: spirits of the dead

merda!: shit!

meretrix: prostitute

mina hertan (Old Germanic): my heart

mulsum: wine mixed with honey

mundus: an opening to the underworld

myrmillo: type of armored gladiator

N

nama Mithra (Parthian): hail Mithras

nomen: a Roman's family name

nomenclator: a servant whose duty is to remember and/or announce names

P

paedagogus: an educated child-minder assigned to a young boy of good birth

palaestra: outdoor gymnasium

palla: woman's garment used as a mantle

Pannonia: Roman province between the Julian Alps and the Danube River

paterfamilias: head of a family, including its slaves and freedmen

Pax Romana: the Roman peace over its dominions

peplos: a chemise-like garment for women, bloused at the waist

peristyle: a columned walkway around an area (usually a garden)

petra specularis: translucent stone

pietas: duty to respect, honor, and obey the gods, one's parents, etc.

pontifex: priest

popina: restaurant with food available for takeout

posca: wine vinegar drunk by soldiers

praenomen: a man's given name, used only with family and close friends

praetor: high-level official with judicial authority

Priapus: god of fertility

Princeps: leader of the Roman State (literally, "first chosen")

principia: legionary headquarters

promulsis: appetizer course at dinner

pronaos: the columned "porch" of a temple, entrance to the *cella*

pugio: soldier's longknife

pulvinar: the imperial enclosure at the amphitheater or circus

Q

quadriga: four-horse chariot

quaestor: lowest public official, usually given financial responsibilities

R

rana: frog

regnum: kingdom

retiarius: type of gladiator armed with net, trident, and dagger

reveniam: I will return

S

salutatio: morning call made by clients on their patron

salve: hello (literally, "be well")

servus viator: personal slave accompanying his master or mistress outside the house

sestertius: brass coin; average cost of a liter of cheap wine

Setian: type of wine

sextarius: a liquid measure, about $3/4$ of a liter

sica: curved sword used by Thracian-style gladiators

signifer: military standard-bearer

sistrum: a musical instrument with bells, used in the worship of Isis

solium: high-backed chair

spatha: long cavalry sword

spina: the long central island in the middle of a racetrack

sponsa (sponsus): betrothed wife (husband)

stela: an inscribed stone slab or pillar

stoa: a covered walkway where Greek philosophers often held lessons

stola: long tunic worn by women

strigil: a scoop-shaped implement for scraping oil, sweat, and dirt off the skin

sudatorium: sweat-bath (similar to **laconicum**)

T
tablinum: reception room
taberna: tavern (the barkeeper is a **tabernarius**)
te amo: I love you
thermopolium: shop selling hot drinks
tintinnabulum: wind chime
toga virilis: a man's toga, conferred at the age of seventeen or eighteen
tonsor: barber
triclinium: dining room
trigon: three-man handball game

U
unguentarius: servant in charge of perfumes and scented oils
ustrinum: crematory altar

V
vale: farewell
vernus: slave born in his master's house
vestispica: servant responsible for her master's or mistress's wardrobe
Vetrfest (Old Germanic): Winter Feast
vexillation: army detachment sent on a mission
vincit: he conquers
virtus: manly valor, an important Roman virtue
vitellus: bed boy (literally, "little calf")

AUTHOR'S NOTES

ARMINIUS, THE GREAT TRAITOR.

The instigator of the infamous massacre of Varus's three legions was known to Romans as Arminius. Although no one is sure of the man's original German name, it seems likely that "Arminius" is the Latinized form of "Harman." German folklore refers to him as "Herman," but if that were so, I think Tacitus and other historians would have called him "Erminius." Also, just as Arminius's brother Flavus was named for a personal characteristic ("Yellow Hair"), I like the idea of the renegade having been called "Weasel" by his own people.

CALIGULA'S AFFLICTION.

We don't really know what struck down Caligula in October of 37 AD, just six months into his principate, but his life was despaired of. Some scholars speculate that he had a breakdown under the burden of expectations placed on him. I think this is very likely. After more than two decades of rule by gloomy old Tiberius, Romans had welcomed him to the throne amid wild acclaim. He was young, handsome, the son and grandson of military heroes, and the great-grandson of Augustus. To his credit, Caligula tried to live up to what was expected of him; but struggling for years under the thumb of a paranoid great-uncle, with the constant threat of being murdered like his brothers and parents, was bound to have affected his mental stability.

"Gaius" or "Caligula"?

Reportedly, Gaius Caesar banned the use of his childhood nickname of "Caligula" ("Little Army Boot") once he was an adult. As Princeps, he would naturally want to be addressed in a more dignified way. However, it's likely that he had fond memories of being a child in his father Germanicus's military camps, where he felt safe and loved and where he was given his nickname, so he may have made an exception for people who had known him and his family when he was young. Thus, the Carinnas call him "Caligula" (except for Titus Licinius, who thinks his formal name of "Gaius Julius Caesar" is more appropriate). It's likely that in the first year of his principate, many Romans still called him "Caligula" out of habit, irony, or malice, at least behind his back.

The Germanic language.

For snippets of Ancient German, I'm indebted to the 1909 *Wörterbuch der Indogermanischen Sprachen, dritte Teil: Wortschatz der Germanischen Spracheinheit*, by August Fick, Hjalmar Falk, and Alf Torp, published in digital form by the University of Pennsylvania Department of Linguistics. All mistakes are my own. And yes, Ancient German apparently had no future tense, only past and present. To the Romans, who had six tenses in Latin, this must have made the Germans seem truly uncivilized.

Mithras.

Known as the Lord of Light and identified with the sun, this Eastern god's role was to assist mankind in the world battle between good and evil. Only men were admitted to the fraternity of his followers. Mithraism was eventually adopted throughout the legions, starting in the first century AD. I've posited that Mithras worship reached the Fifteenth Legion early in this period through transfers from a legion that had served in Parthia. One of the cave-like Mithraea in which worshipers gathered to share a sacrificial feast has been found near the Carnuntum fortress.

PLACE NAMES.

I've used Roman names for towns and provinces, with a few exceptions: the more familiar "Greece," "Egypt," and "Gaul" rather than Achaea, Aegyptus, and Gallia. When referring to landmarks, for clarity's sake I've usually translated the Latin into English: Field of Mars, Golden Milestone, Caelian Hill, Capena gate. Just to keep some Latin in the mix, you'll see "Via Flaminia" and "Villa Publica."

POETRY.

As far as I know, the Romans didn't go in for rhyming verse. However, well-educated aristocrats in the early Empire did enjoy writing poetry (Augustus himself is said to have composed erotic poems), and clever satires were much admired. I've added rhymes to some of the verses in ROMA AMOR to help make up for my own deficiencies as a poet.

GAIUS SILIUS.

Silius was a real historical figure who was to get into serious trouble during Claudius's principate. I've taken the liberty of imagining what he might have been like 15 or 20 years earlier. His wife in ROMA AMOR, Fabia Crispina, is fictitious. Using authorial license, I've premised that she was his first wife, whom he later divorced in order to marry his mistress, Junia Lepida Silana (who really was Silius's wife later in his political career). To avoid confusion with other characters, I've called her Junia Torquata, a cognomen from another branch of her family.

WEEKS AND MONTHS.

For civil and religious purposes, the Romans reckoned days of the month by counting backwards from three markers: the Kalends, which were always the first of the month; the Ides, which fell on the 15th of March, May, July, and October (originally the only 31-day months), and on the 13th of other months; and the Nones, eight days before the Ides. In everyday life, the week was used to measure from one market day to the next. Each of the (eventually) seven days of the week was named for one of the major gods: Sun's Day, Moon's Day, Mars' Day, Mercury's Day, Jove's Day, Venus's Day, and Saturn's Day. Festivals were another way for ordinary folks to keep track of time throughout the year, a practice that has out-lived the Romans (St. Crispin's Day, St. Patrick's Day, etc.).

ACKNOWLEDGMENTS

Any author whose opus has taken as long to see daylight as ROMA AMOR has is bound to owe thanks to many, many, many people. If you encouraged or critiqued or advised or booted me in the rear and are not mentioned below, it's due to memory flaws, not a lack of gratitude. Please forgive me.

CREATIVE MENTORS.

It was my incredible good luck to take a college course in creative writing from **John Williams**, author of the National Book Award-winning *Augustus*. At that age, unfortunately, I was more interested in storytelling than craft. It took me a stupidly long time to realize that storytelling without craft is schlock. I so wish for a do-over with the brilliant Mr. Williams.

A funny, finicky creative director, **Duane G. Abram** struggled for years to teach me how to pull the most important bits out of a gargantuan mass of information. Like Dewey himself, I still tend to write long. But if not for his patient coaching, the copy of ROMA you are holding would have had to be delivered by forklift.

In all the revisions this story has undergone, no one's opinion has been more valuable to me than that of **Ruth Cash-Smith**. Ruth, a novelist herself and co-author of *The Graphic Designer's Guide to Better Business Writing*, is blessed with 20/20 insight into what works and what doesn't in both the creative and practical realms. Her constant encouragement lifted me out of doldrums and propelled me faster along the salt flats of manuscript revision. I can't thank you enough, Ruth.

Dennis Lehane, who co-led a Popular Fiction workshop during the Stonecoast Writers' Conference, was the first honest-to-God author I'd met whose books I already loved. He was in the process of finishing *Mystic River,* the breakthrough novel that would expand his readership far beyond the mystery genre. From Dennis I learned that writers need to keep tackling new challenges that scare them. Even with an established career, they never quite get over the fear of having to go back to driving a cab.

The other leader of this amazing workshop was **Sarah Smith**, an iron editorial fist in an elegant velvet glove. Sarah's historical novel *The Vanished Child* was a *New York Times* Notable Book, closely followed by *The Knowledge of Water* and *A Citizen of the Country.* Sarah, thank you for urging me to launch my story quickly with a minimum of characters, not to end in hopeless gloom, and to write authentically. I was unable to determine and mimic the rhythms of first-century spoken Latin, but I did explore a field commander's attitude toward his troops.

"I would be very suspicious of any novel that can be summarized in one sentence," **Michael Lowenthal** told a group of us at a Maine Writers and Publishers Alliance workshop he was leading. Hooray for complexity! At the end of a terrific discussion of suspense and structure, Michael (author of *Avoidance* and later the historical novel *Charity Girl*) told me my writing was of publishable caliber. I believe my feet never touched the ground on the way home from this conference.

At workshops in her farmhouse, **Cynthia Thayer** helped me organize a sprawly story into one with a more coherent controlling idea and better pacing. Cynthia, who has published three novels including the acclaimed *Strong for Potatoes*, dedicates untold hours to helping our creative community thrive. And she lives only a county away from me! In rural Maine, that's like being a next-door neighbor.

John Fanning and **Kerry Eielson** run La Muse Writers' and Artists' Retreat in a 16th-century manor house perched on a remote hillside in Languedoc, France. John and Kerry are muses themselves, providing space and stimulation that draws writers, artists, photographers, musicians, and other creatives from around the world. I've been on eight blissful retreats there, immersing myself in writing without everyday distractions. I couldn't have pulled this off without you, *mes amis.*

OTHER LITERARY GODPARENTS.

Special thanks go to the friends, fans, and fellow professionals who helped bring ROMA AMOR to the printed (and electronic) page. Among them, I would like to name:

Kristin Adolfson of StillPoint Press Design Studio, a genius at simplifying complex maps and family trees.

Deborah Bailey of Barnstormer Design Group, my brilliant Web designer.

Carey Christie, fellow novelist (*I, Mordred*), who gave me life-sustaining feedback on a previous draft.

Colleen Cunningham (now Colleen Groezinger), who with amazing patience typed and retyped and *re*-retyped an even earlier version of ROMA AMOR.

Le Herron, mentor and friend, who really knows how to keep the pressure on. ("I'm 94 this year, Sherry! How much longer do you expect me to wait?")

Olivia Mellan, my longtime pal and work partner on five money psychology books, as well as a gazillion columns and feature articles.

Laurel Robinson of Laurel Robinson Editorial Services, my excellent copy editor. Any mistakes you find in the book are mine, not hers.

Last, and totally out of alphabetical order, **my husband Harry**, who didn't realize all those years ago that he was also marrying an unfinished historical novel. Thank you, my dear, for never once doubting that I could do it.

ABOUT THE AUTHOR

At an early age, Sherry Christie became fascinated by things the Romans built that have lasted over 2,000 years: roads, aqueducts, temples, theaters. What if something had happened in the early years of Empire to destabilize this civilization, preventing it from maintaining peace and prosperity in most of the known world? Something like . . . having a well-intentioned but unbalanced emperor? It did happen: Caligula. His potential to tip the Roman world into chaos failed because of a few principled men like Marcus Carinna, who makes his debut as a young, self-doubting ex-tribune in ROMA AMOR.

Sherry's career as a writer began on a New York magazine, progressed into advertising, and eventually led to her own financial writing business. In addition to client work, her reconnection with "money therapist" Olivia Mellan at a college reunion has resulted in more than 200 magazine articles and five books about money psychology, including *Money Harmony: A Road Map for Individuals and Couples* and *Overcoming Overspending: A Winning Plan for Spenders and Their Partners.* Sherry also assisted retired CEO Le Herron with *Making Your Company Human: Inspiring Others to Reach Their Potential.*

She is now working on Book 2 of ROMA AMOR from her office in a barn in a coastal Maine village, surrounded by Rome-related artifacts and pictures. She can be reached through www.roma-amor.com.

If you liked the story, please post a review.